After dinner they walked slowly along Fifth Avenue. The night was sharply cool; the windows of the famous stores were as bright and curious as peacocks.

"A nightcap?" he asked.

"All right, but just a quiet drink."

"My place?"

"All right." His heart vaulted over the Plaza Hotel.

Later in his living room, with music and a drink, she said, "I love this room." Then she kissed him.

He held her as though she were porcelain.

"Do you always make love with your clothes on?" she asked.

Green Monday

MICHAEL M. THOMAS

FAWCETT CREST • NEW YORK

GREEN MONDAY

The principal characters and episodes and many of the
places in this book are imaginary.

Published by Fawcett Crest Books, a unit of CBS
Publications, the Consumer Publishing Division of CBS
Inc., by arrangement with Wyndham Books, a Simon &
Schuster Division of Gulf & Western Corporation

ISBN: 0-449-24400-8

The author is grateful for permission to use the following:

Excerpt from *Four Quartets*, "East Coker," by T. S. Eliot.
Used by permission of Harcourt Brace Jovanovich, Inc.
Copyright © 1943 by T. S. Eliot, 1971 by Esmé Valerie
Eliot.

Lines from *Mirabelle* by James Merrill used by permission
of Atheneum Publishers. Copyright © 1978 by James
Merrill.

Lyrics from *Solitaire* © Copyright 1972 & 1975 Kiddio
Music/ Top Pop Music/ Welbeck Music. Used by
permission. All rights reserved.

Lyrics from *The Very Thought of You* © 1934, Campbell
Connelly & Co., Ltd. © Renewed and assigned to Warner
Bros., Inc. All rights reserved.

Excerpt from *The World According to Garp* © Copyright
1978 by John Irving. Used by permission of E. P. Dutton.

Excerpt from *The Year 2025* by Kris Kristofferson, © Resaca
Music Publishing Company, 1975. Used by permission.

Dual Selection of the Playboy Book Club

Printed in the United States of America

First Fawcett Crest printing: June 1981

10 9 8 7 6 5 4 3 2 1

For Mom, and Pop, and Poppi, and my children:
contributors all

The Prophet has said,
"There is a calamity for every people,
and the calamity for my people is wealth."

—Ka'b ibn 'Iyad,
in *Submission: Sayings of the Prophet Mohammed,*
Shems Friedlander, ed., New York, 1977

I

MONEY

1 In the burning haze of late afternoon, the cluster of buildings which housed the ministries and chanceries of the Kingdom seemed to fuse into a single ice-white mass; from a distance, the capital appeared to rise from the rolling desert like a glacier from the sea.

In the tallest buildings, which backed onto a public square over which helicopters of the Royal Air Arm dipped and swooped, the Minister sat in his second-floor office, bent over his paperwork, trying unsuccessfully to seal his mind against the clamor overhead and the horror which would soon take place outside. The windows of his office, like those of the rest of the city, were lidded against the blinding glare of the sun.

He tried, distractedly, to study the reports and cables arranged in piles on his glass and marble desk. Each sheet reported bad news. The situation in Iran continued to vacillate between the inconclusive and the monstrous. His agents reported a secret meeting in Dar-es-Salaam between the Libyans and Nigerians; their agenda contemplated a further bilateral increase in the price of crude oil. On the café terraces in Monte Carlo, the expatriate Lebanese and Kuwaiti oil traders were exulting over a prospective increase in the spot price of Gulf light crude from $55 to $70 a barrel.

It was all disastrous, he thought. The United States *must* act soon. A ten dollar bill scarcely bought half a grapefruit in a decent hotel in London or Geneva or a leg of lamb in Chicago; the price of industrial goods and services, FOB Houston or Milwaukee, was more obscene. The Kingdom, for which the Minister held the portfolios of Energy and External Finance, now possessed dollar reserves which came to nearly $125 billion. Yet, their real value was depreciating at 20 percent a year.

That, however, was only money. The worst news was that the American people could be pushed no further; nearly a decade of inflation and crisis was bringing them to a political activism which four Presidents had tried unsuccessfully to create. His man in Washington had relayed gossip from Capitol Hill which suggested highest-level consideration of political intervention and subversion in the Middle East. There were reports that the CIA and the State Department were sufficiently desperate to launch a bold para-military adventure.

From time to time the Minister rose from his papers and carried his worries to the window, which looked down on the square, an ancient bazaar, pounded flat by generations of camel-stabling, into a small, rectangular plain of compressed gravel and dung. Looking down at the still-empty space, the Minister seemed shrunken in the heavy grip of his thoughts. After a moment's reflection, he breathed a capitulatory sigh and returned to his desk, poring over the reports quickly, distractedly, looking less for information than for auguries of some course of action that might change the trend toward disaster. But he found nothing except additional debits, erosions and declinations.

When he looked at his watch again, it was nearly five o'clock. Time. He gathered his robes around him and crossed the room, hating the destiny which placed him there at this moment but knowing that there was nowhere else he could be. He half separated the curtains and opened the double windows, admitting the blaze and stench of the day.

The square had been cordoned off since early morning. Although knots of people, imploring their right to watch, pushed against the barricades which blocked the connecting lanes and passages, the militiamen were implacable. Public punishments—floggings, dismemberments, beheadings—were

(8)

the only popular entertainments permitted by the priests who adjudicated the secular life of the people, but it was apparent that this time they were to be denied their circus.

At low altitude, the helicopters circled, manned by militiamen with automatic weapons, who searched the surrounding rooftops. They wiped sweating faces with their burnooses as the choppers continued their circling. Below, small figures started to trickle into the square.

Only about a dozen men had been passed through the barricades: imams and holy men, with black-fringed robes and special credentials. They clustered in a far corner, under what little shade was given by the overhanging terrace of the British Embassy, the small space they occupied filling with prayers and incantations, a rising babble of invocations to Allah.

Among the bobbing heads was one whose prayers were muffled by hands steepled in front of his face. The words he muttered were Arabic, learned in the course of taking a doctorate at Oxford. His accent had been perfected by ten years in and around the Persian Gulf, first for British Intelligence and most recently on special assignment to the Américas. He had also picked up a substantial bit of change sharing his discoveries with a contact at Anglo, the consortium which purchased and marketed 60 percent of the Kingdom's production of crude oil. He liked to think that he was a principal reason for the complaints of the liberal British and American newspapers that Anglo knew more about the Middle East than Whitehall or the White House.

He had changed to look the part of a holy man. Contact lenses took care of transforming his irises from blue to black. A special dye had turned his normally tan skin desert-olive. His robes were right: color and fit carefully provided by his local drop, who had furnished the pass that got him through the barricades.

There was method in his pious noises and gesticulations. His cupped hands concealed a tiny camera, about the size of a cigarette pack.

He had whistled appreciatively when the camera had been delivered to him two days earlier at the Dumar Hilton. Dumar was the Kingdom's port city, about three hundred miles to the west of where he stood.

"Jesus," he'd said to his control officer, "where do they think up this stuff?"

"Harry, this is the best yet." Control was an owlish-looking Arkansan, about thirty years old, who notionally functioned at Anglo as a staff engineer. "This little sonuvabitch was designed by Dr. Land personally. Thirty frames a second. It will give you a clear and sharp image at eighty meters—we develop it in Phenidone with next to nothing for light. Just point and shoot, like they say on TV."

"What's the deal, anyway?" Harry wanted to know. Forty-eight hours earlier, on a day's notice, he'd been whistled out of Jordan, which was the one Arab country where you could really still have some fun. It was springtime; the girls taking the early sun on the beaches at Aqaba had absorbed his energies.

"Harry, we got a beep out of Washington. Nothing specific in the way of action. But they're gonna cut a royal up the road and you know how Langley likes to keep their little collection of eight-by-ten glossies and X-rateds up to date. You don't get many chop shots these days. And you never know who might be there. So keep your eyes open and get it all."

Hip talk, thought Harry. The young guys were all that way now, as if the work were a kind of jiving. He was nearly fifty, well paid for this sort of thing, and though it was clandestine and treacherous, it could be tiresome and exhausting.

"I'll see you later," he said, slipping the camera in the breast pocket of his seersucker jacket. Thirty-six hours later he surfaced up the road as a Sunni priest.

One side of the square was dominated by the British Embassy. This was still the governmental capital of the Kingdom, although the main commercial activity was now centered in Dumar. The Embassy was a big, ugly building, a block of London council flats plunked down in the middle of the desert.

"Disgusting," said the ambassador's wife, peering intently through the steel blinds which shielded the sitting room from the heat and glare of the afternoon.

"Disgusting," she repeated, crossing the room to her armchair and taking up her sewing basket. "Barbaric." She stabbed ferociously at her needlepoint.

"Quite so, m'dear," said her husband. He was sitting there in his armchair reading the *Times.* It was three weeks old, but things moved slowly in the nineteenth-century recesses of the ambassador's mind. He was a portly man, shirtsleeved; ruddy from ten thousand afternoons of gin and lemon squash, a glass of which sat at his hand. He kept his gin in the Embassy safe. This was a funny country. No drinking.

"After all, m'dear, it *is* their country and their rules." He was used to placating his wife. They had dwelt together among the heathens for nearly forty years. "And it is a better way, you must admit, than that stoning business they go in for over the mountains."

"Well, I think it's awful. I think I shall hardly be able to watch."

"As you wish, m'dear." His wife was a woman of infinite opinions. He returned to his *Times*. It was a day for relaxing. This business had effectively shut the capital down, he thought, thankfully.

A little later he hardly heard his wife cross to the window. And he was insensible to the subtle, ominous change in the sounds from the square below.

The mullahs were working themselves up into a fit, Harry thought. All the best for him.

He went about his work, a good cameraman working without a script. He panned the four sides of the square, working from the British Embassy on to the Royal Prison, the Chancery, a couple of small office buildings, and finishing up with the Energy Ministry to his left. He was safely covered to his rear; the porch which shaded the knot of priests was part of the nearly completed Royal Mosque.

He swept the square again, noting that all the buildings were shut down and sealed. Except for a double window which stood half opened above him to his left. He worked his prayer movements until the nictating lens of the camera washed the double window. He thought he could make out a dim figure, but he wasn't sure. No matter. The film was better than his eyes had ever been. It was focused sonically: accurate within millimeters. Point and shoot.

He stopped praying. So did the others.

A door set in the wall of the Royal Prison, across the square, opened, and a small group came out into the sunlight.

There were four of them, Harry noted, closing in with the camera. First came what he took to be a guard, then a hawk-like man, probably a priest-magistrate, carrying a scroll, then the prisoner, and, last, a stolid middle-aged man bearing a sheathed sword on his right shoulder.

Harry squinted for a close look at the prisoner. He was still a kid; no more than thirty, thirty-two, Harry guessed. A nice-looking boy. Sallow and scared. Dressed in a white shirt open at the throat and tan pants. The poor bastard had pissed his pants. The dark splotch at the boy's crotch added a demeaning nuance to the spectacle.

Probably would have shit in his pants, too, thought Harry, but he can't have any left. Jesus, this was awful. But Harry kept the camera running. Self-reversing, it was good for an hour's filming.

The little procession halted in the middle of the square. The young prisoner looked around desperately. He could have been a stylish sort once, Harry said to himself. His thoughts were interrupted by the hawklike man, who had unfurled his scroll and was reading what Harry made out to be a bill of indictment. Mortal offenses against the laws of Allah and the directives of the Prophet. Adultery. Disgrace of a family.

"The Prophet decrees the work of Allah," concluded the priest, nodding a signal.

Harry saw then that the guard had gotten around behind the prisoner and that the man with the sword had unsheathed it. What happened next was almost faster than he could follow, but he kept the camera running.

The guard kicked the prisoner's legs from under him. The young man fell face-first in the dirt. His hands were tied behind him with a rope that had been looped once around his chest, so the guard could yank him to his knees. The boy scrunched his shoulders, trying to hide his neck. The executioner moved in, the bared, curved sword sparkling in the late sun. He was trying for an angle.

The guard picked up a stick. Harry hadn't noticed it before. It was about a yard long and the guard used it like a snake's tongue, jabbing and darting, searching out sensitive spots. He found one. The boy's arms tightened, baring his neck for an instant. The executioner had anticipated this moment and was in position, sword poised, raised in both hands. He struck with a sudden, slanting blow.

The boy's head rolled in the sand. For an instant, the body remained on its knees, blood emptying from the open arteries of the headless neck. Then it twitched and fell, twitched again, and lay there, a foot or so from the sightless eyes of the prisoner's head.

As the body fell, the mullahs started to chant again, praising Allah and his justice. Harry thought he was going to be sick but he picked up the chant. "Praise Allah," he muttered, drowning out the closing whirr of the last few centimeters of film.

Upstairs, in the Embassy, the ambassador's wife drew back from her window in revulsion, hand to her throat.

"Horace," she hissed melodramatically. "You would not have believed it!"

But he was asleep and dreaming of green lawns and county cricket, and so he did not hear her words. Nor her rush from the room to be sick.

She wasn't the only one.

The shadowy figure which Harry had seen remained half visible at the French windows in the Energy Ministry.

The Minister was a tall, aristocratic man with a habitual, ascetic tranquillity. An El Greco sort, the British papers were wont to say. He stayed at the window, seeming frozen, despite the pleading of his aides.

"Please, Excellency, come away. Please, it will do no good."

He gestured them away and lingered. Earlier, he had moved into the light, as if to leap down into the square and stay the executioner's sword arm.

When his brother's head fell into the dirt and camel droppings, his insides twisted as if he had been jammed with a poker. He felt his own excrement flow out, dribble on his legs.

"Please, Excellency." A helpful aide placed a tentative hand on his sleeve. Like a blind man, he permitted himself to be guided back into the room. Behind him another aide drew the shutters and closed the room against the day and the scene in the square.

Two days later, Harry was back in his room at the Dumar Hilton, talking with his contact.

"What in Christ's name was the point of going up there?" he asked as he handed over the camera. "I mean, I got it all, I think, if that goddamn thing works. But what's the point? I mean, I've been to a bunch of these things; just for kicks, mostly, I admit. So why all the hush-hush? And the pictures?"

"Ours not to reason why, old sod," said the contact, who'd been reading English spy novels. "We just stand and wait. Why? Who knows?"

It was a simple declarative statement. "After all," the contact added, "in our line of work, you never can tell."

2 "Oh, shit," said the smiling, tired-looking man to no one in particular. He was sitting about halfway back in the packed grand ballroom of the Century Plaza Hotel. His tone of voice was at least an octave louder than discretion normally allowed. He turned an irritatingly sunny countenance upon the circle of disapproving faces which had swiveled to reproach his blasphemy.

"For Christ's sake, David, keep it down," muttered the man in the next seat. "I have to do business with these assholes."

Onstage, the pinched-faced speaker behind the podium was gravely intoning, "It is our Mission and our Responsibility to bring Economic Stability to our Brethren in the Third World." He had a flat, parsony voice which suited his priggish, sanctimonious face.

"Apeshit," whispered David Harrison, to needle his companion. Then, as it often did, his impatient, energetic mind went racketing off on a tangent, an excremental alphabet which satisfied him with his own cleverness: apeshit, bullshit, catshit, and so on, the variants becoming zoologically more abstruse or amusing until he ran up against "X." There he hesitated for a moment, until memory rang up "Xiphias," a swordfish dancing on needlepoint wave tops on a rug in his nursery. "Xiphishit," he said to himself, recalling a sunlit yellow room with no worries; the flight back to his childhood made him grin broadly; the happiness of recollection shut out the heavy, pontifical words from the stage, where the speaker was winding up. "Certainly the mantle of Action must be placed on the broad Shoulders of our own Great Financial Institutions. We at Certified will wear ours with Pride."

The orator was Leslie Merriman, by inheritance chairman and chief executive officer of Certified Borough and Guaranty Bank. Certified was the largest bank in New York, the second largest in the United States, and the eighth largest in the world. Merriman spoke in a practiced, oracular manner which he felt suited the leader of such a Great Institution, inflecting his phrases so that certain words seemed to be capitalized; the vocal equivalent of the typefaces of the old moral tracts with which his ancestors had papered the li-

(14)

braries of the Ivy League. The auditorium collapsed in applause.

"I'll bet you will," said Harrison in the *sub voce* tone schoolboys use to drive their teachers apoplectic. He was a medium-sized man with shortish sandy hair and a perpetual half smile. He was beginning to feel himself thicken with age; the folding seat seemed especially uncomfortable. He was forty-one years old. "A very precocious antique," he would say of himself, "or a relatively aged infant."

The moderator was back at the podium, echoing the audience's dutiful applause and beaming rays of deferential approbation at Merriman.

"We're now open for questions. And, of course, we're grateful indeed for Mr. Merriman's lucid remarks on matters much on the minds of everyone here. Are there questions?"

"Mr. Green." The moderator pointed to a man who had risen in a front row. Harrison recognized him as a stockbroker who sucked up tag ends of business from the big institutions like Certified. The question Green would ask would probably be a plant from Certified's unsleeping public relations machine.

"Mr. Merriman, in the course of your very penetrating analysis," said Green, tugging his forelock, "you have alluded to certain present-day alarmists who have publicly asserted that the U.S. banking system is *de facto* bankrupt; they claim that a run by OPEC on its overnight deposits, combined with a series of defaults on outstanding loans to lesser developed countries such as Zaire and Jamaica, would wipe out the capital and surplus of our major banks."

Merriman's obfuscating answer took ten minutes and made no sense, as Harrison heard it. He thought that facts *were* that the banks had gotten in over their heads, not with the OPEC depositors—the Federal Reserve would freeze *those* deposits if *they* tried a run on Certified or another big bank, the Iranians had learned that; the trouble lay with highly optimistic lending to the barely governable copper and cocoa satrapies.

Merriman's words were accompanied by a series of charts, unreadable from more than five feet, which were produced on signal by a bean-thin young man with a complexion like a battlefield.

"These charts," Merriman was concluding, "and the Figures which I have adduced, demonstrate the unshakable Solidity of the Banking System. Of which, I'm happy to be able to say, Certified Bank considers itself a Cornerstone, Morally, Ethically, and Financially."

"The Beatitudes as written by Young and Rubicam," whispered Harrison to Barney Morgan in the next chair.

"With music from the Messiah and arranged by Barry Manilow," said Barney.

Onstage, the moderator and the panelists and speakers were bobbing and bowing like supplicants at a Japanese cocktail party. The session, which wrapped up the annual Investment Fundamental Outlook Conforium, was adjourned; the real purpose of the shebang could now unfold. Harrison turned to Barney.

"Barney, after having to listen to this, we have to get a drink. Right now. A free drink. Perhaps many free drinks."

"No problem, David. There are about a thousand hospitality suites. Where would you like to start?"

"Let's begin with Freiman. They always have the largest asshole quotient. You need to be reasonably drunk to cope and take advantage and, if worse comes to worse, we can live off their all-beef cocktail sausages."

About three years before, Freiman Partners had been merged with Stuyvesant and Jonkleer, a marriage joining one of the country's oldest Jewish investment houses with an old WASP firm which had in 1637 traded beaver pelts at the bottom of Manhattan. A series of ill-advised bond-trading positions had all but wiped out the capital of Stuyvesant, forcing its partners to seek a merger before their wives sued to protect their capital.

The marriage had been briefly happy, very briefly. After six months, Lazarus Freiman, whose principal private benevolence was his work as chairman of the Holocaust Committee of the Federation of Jewish Philanthropies, had initiated the systematic liquidation of the Stuyvesant partners, a process which was variously celebrated in the demeaning mythography of Wall Street as "the night of broken Steuben," or less elaborately, as "the Jews versus the Genteels." Either way, as Harrison saw it, and said, it was a perfect example of two plus two equaling one.

Still, Freiman was known to serve decent whisky and there was one hell of a good-looking girl working in their Yankee bond department. Harrison was pretty sure she'd show up. Christ, every self-proclaimed expert in international finance was at IFOC. Including me, he thought, half in amusement, half in rue.

Barney agreed. Barney Morgan was Harrison's best friend still in the business. They had known each other for nearly twenty years, when Harrison left his Melville and Hawthorne scholarship and the faculty infighting at Princeton to take up old Clare Verger's invitation "to join the real world, come down the Street."

Barney was fifty and funny. For nine months of the year, he was also fat. Then, urged on by some very stiff wagers with a bunch of clerks who didn't know what determination was, he would lose fifty pounds—at a thousand bucks a pound. It was a handsome, supplementary, and undeclared income. He was a man who had prospered almost entirely as a byproduct of being pleasant and obliging, no matter how cretinous the client. Harrison never begrudged Barney his success; these days, nice was a hell of a lot harder to be than smart.

Even so, Barney was considered a degenerate by the pursed-mouthed dinnertable types who would have sold their wives and children to get in on Barney's legendary financial and erotic action. For a living he peddled stocks and bonds to oilmen and other entrepreneurs who'd made it and who, like Barney, liked to swing. Of course you had to be practical sometimes; which is why Barney had cut Harrison off in the ballroom.

"Be obstreperous only in small groups, where you know everyone," Barney would prescribe. "Be careful what you say in strange bars." He knew his friend David had a rambunctious intellect and a too-ready tongue. Nights when they would sit up together, stoned and flying on some delicacy from Barney's apparently infinite pharmacopoeia, the two of them could get into *shticks* that would convulse a stadium. But there was a time and a place.

They got out of the elevator on the fifth floor and headed for the Freiman suite.

"Will you look at that, for Christ's sake," said Harrison. He pointed. Ahead in the hall, just turning into the Freiman suite, was old Lucius Barrow, ex-Commerce, ex-Treasury, ex-State, bumping along like a great diplomatic blimp and trailing acolytes like scarf ends. Barrow was getting $250,000 a year to provide geopolitical insights to Freiman's clients. He advised Freiman's clients in a vocabulary suitable to a restaurant critic: meaty prospects, tasty alliances, saucy treaties

(17)

were the stuff of Barrow's gastronomically phrased position papers. Barrow believed that the key to world stability lay in finding a Patagonian solution. He had served once as Ambassador to Chile and had never recovered from the self-importance of the post.

"You know," said Harrison, "that old fart is just dying to get back to Washington. Worst case of Potomac fever I've ever seen. He's a big scruples man: sanctity of alliances, that sort of stuff. Shit, he quit the Eisenhower Treasury to help Jack Kennedy against Nixon and then, so help me God, when *that* crook got in the soup, he was right on the shuttle to help Jaworski. Meaty, my ass!"

Barney led the way into the Freiman suite, which was rapidly filling up with parched types from downstairs. Harrison had often observed that Leslie Merriman's oratory had that effect on people: dried up their palates and their minds.

"Well," said Barney, casing the room, "look here. There's Tom Rollins. He ought to have a 'Get Me Laid' button on his lapel. In neon!"

Tom Rollins was the head trader for a $3 billion mutual fund complex in Chicago. He was well known for dishing out his business in return for favors of the flesh.

Rollins sidled up to Barney and Harrison, trying to look subtle. He had a big, jowly face on the body of a dwarf. He was *cap à pié* in bright green polyester, which made him look like an unripe toadstool. He radiated the assertiveness which made most short men unattractive.

"How's things, Barney? Got anything good?"

Barney considered the matter. He had spent ten years in the institutional business and had provided more than his share of uppers and downers for Rollins's fat throat.

Harrison broke in. "Hi, I'm Dave Harrison. That's quite a suit you've got there. Triple-knit?"

Rollins's face darkened.

"Who is this smart ass, Barney?" Rollins clearly figured Harrison as some trading-room palooka for whom he could make very big trouble.

"Forget it, Tom," said Barney. He scrambled in his pocket with his right hand and extracted a couple of paper twists. "Give these a try."

Rollins smirked like a hog with a carrot, wiped it off for an instant to give Harrison an I'm-not-forgetting-you-buddy glare, and turned for the bar.

"What in God's name was that?" said Harrison.

"Just a little light blotter acid," replied Barney. "He ought to stop tingling sometime next week. Nothing too good for our boy Tom!"

They made for the bar themselves. A small crowd had formed around Lucius Barrow.

"Do you suppose those B-school types really work for that old bastard, or does he just rent them for public appearances? Take a look."

Barney looked. "By God, you're right. Just like the Dirty Dozen. One black. One yellow. One white. I'll bet the Chink is called O'Brien."

There was a stir at the door. Leslie Merriman. And cadets.

"Well, well," said Barney. "Look at that expression. Like he smells shit and can't quite locate it! Who's Verdun-face, two steps left and three steps back?"

"That's Arthur Mismer. Around the bank he's known as 'the valet.' They say he takes Merriman's dick out when he wants to piss. You know, Barney, I can't stand the fucking Merrimans of this world. Bunch of sanctimonious pricks who've sold us down the toilet. I'd like to blow the fuckers up!"

There was something almost fanatical in Harrison's tone. His vehemence surprised his friend.

"I know you would, Dave," Barney said, in the consoling tone one uses to a friend who's been diagnosed as cancerous. He was familiar with Harrison's opinion of the financial establishment and the trouble it had caused him.

Merriman advanced on Barrow, Mismer stalking behind, looking as though he ought to spray the room with disinfectant. Merriman and Barrow. Two countries calling on each other, Harrison thought.

"You know, Barney, Shakespeare had a great phrase to describe Mismer's line of work. He called it 'spanieling at heels.' Shit, Mismer should have a fan, and a turban, and blackface."

Barney nodded but he wasn't listening. He was looking toward the door at a girl who had just come in. She was dressed to the nines, a regular Wall Street Walker; she radiated a kind of pretty self-importance.

Harrison followed Barney's gaze and saw his friend's eyes light up. The game was on.

"Oh yes, the demon Yankee bond expert. Mary Stebbins. All yours, dear Barney, decency and geography must prevail. But only for tonight."

(19)

This could be a rare opportunity for Barney, to which Harrison would defer as a matter of principle—and distance. Barney had a wife he liked very, very much back in Manhattan. So he'd made a rule: no screwing around within a thousand miles of the big city. It excluded a lot of unpromising territory, looked good on his inner moral scorepad, and left him free to roam in the really fertile zones: Los Angeles, Dallas, Miami.

Within the free territory, however, Barney went after it with a constancy and determination that Harrison found exhausting just to observe.

"Doesn't this endless pussy chasing wear you out?" he once asked.

"Absolutely," Barney had grinned. "That's the beauty of it. It saves me from overcommitting. At my age, just getting off takes my breath away—and a girl can hardly expect a lasting commitment from a guy who's hyperventilating! By the time I get my wind back, they're usually either asleep or getting dressed!"

Harrison was Barney's best audience; he collapsed with laughter.

Harrison and Barney looked at each other.

"Good guy—bad guy? Just like a cop movie?"

"Right on, bunky!"

Barney moved off to intercept Ms. Stebbins on her way to the bar.

Harrison let him prospect for fifteen minutes, then joined the two of them. They chatted for a half hour. The room had filled up and was too noisy.

"How about dinner?" Barney asked.

"Well, OK," she said, "but early."

"Mind if I come and sit with you for a drink," asked Harrison. "I'm on the redeye back to the Big Apple."

"Sure, Dave." Barney sounded all class and magnanimity. He looked at Mary Stebbins. "What's your pleasure: Chasen's or Ma Maison?"

As they left for Chasen's, Harrison looked back into the humming room. Merriman and Barrow were deep in a chin-scratching conversation, their hangers-on straining to catch every modulation of the two great thinkers' deliberations.

At Chasen's, Harrison drank two Scotches while Mary Stebbins and Barney ordered Caesar Salad, Hobo Steaks, and a bottle of Stag's Leap Sauvignon. Quite deliberately, he said

(20)

a number of offensively macho things, and gave the appearance of being mildly and vulgarly intoxicated; as planned, these combined to produce the desired antipathy in Miss Stebbins.

She turned her attention to Barney, who was by contrast witty, erudite, cultured, and very, very respectful. He had the comforting geniality of overweight men. Miss Stebbins, like most girls on Wall Street, conceived of her work as fundamental as nursing and as abstruse as molecular biology. Harrison had to hand it to Barney; he looked deeply impressed as Ms. Stebbins, with all the gravity of a Nobel laureate, described her efforts on a recent $15 million Finnish bond syndicate. Christ, Harrison thought, Barney's customers did more commission business than that on a bad day. He and Barney kept her glass full.

At nine o'clock David got up and said goodbye.

Ms. Stebbins watched him out the door. "Such an aggressive man," she said, turning a sloppily affectionate eye on Barney. "Not gentle like you..."

"David is a very complicated man. He..." Barney tried to continue but she interrupted.

"I also think he's completely obnoxious!"

Obnoxious. It was, Barney recognized, the ultimate pejorative in the vocabulary of liberated young ladies.

"He's just complex," he repeated. And mixed up, he thought, and wise some days and an idiot the next, and beating himself to death with self-recrimination and that goddamn imagination which took things and went to work on them, stretching, building them up, fantasizing, any word Barney could think of. Every day was like a jigsaw puzzle to Harrison, he knew; a hundred times Barney'd seen him cut his life into a thousand small pieces and try to fit them together in a new way. If Harrison hadn't at the bottom of his being thought that everything was nonsense, especially in this half-assed business, Barney would have expected his friend to deep-six it out the window one day. But Harrison just kept going, living a life two-thirds flying high and laughs and the balance black, cynical moods, making mischief for others—and himself.

Barney saw no point in trying to explain this to an overeducated receptacle of received ideas like Mary Stebbins. Anyway, she was off on her own wavelength.

"*When,* Bernard," she purred, using Barney's rarely employed Christian name, "when are you men on Wall Street going to accept women for the capable human beings we are? And not as another gender?" Jesus, thought Barney, she sounds like Shylock in drag. Have I not eyes? But his eye was fixed on the main chance.

"Well, some of us already do," he said, shyly, and poured her another glass of wine. "How about a stinger with your coffee?" he suggested.

That should just about top it off, he thought, noting with pleasure that her eyes were beginning to unfocus, thanks to the big, heady Cabernet he'd ordered. He saw approvingly that the top button of her cream silk shirt had come undone, intimating delicious little lady's breasts which he was sure would be pearl-pale with nipples like does' eyes.

He lit a cigarette. It was time to get down to cases.

"Forget Dave, Mary. Let's talk about you. Where'd you get that great mind, anyway?"

Harrison took a cab back to the Wilcrest Towers, where he always stayed, even after they tacked that ugly, looming addition on the back. His bags had been brought down earlier. He asked the parking guy to bring up his rented car.

He had five minutes to waste so he went inside to the bar. The Conquistador Room had once been a dark, oaken place with rich leather seats and an air of intimacy. The best bar in the world, Harrison had thought; it was ninety percent of his reason for staying at the Wilcrest rather than up at the Beverly Hills with the rock moguls and management consultants. Three years ago, however, the bar had been redone. The lustrous, scarred paneling had been pulled down and sold for firewood and replaced with the rough stucco and garish tiles which were every bad decorator's idea of Mexican-American. The whole was dominated by an equestrian portrait of the hotel's owner, an Armenian promoter from Harrisburg, sitting uncomfortably on a palomino and wearing Spanish armor. He looked for all the world like a man peering nervously out of a tin can.

He had a drink at the bar. Looking around, he saw Leslie Merriman sitting with a couple of his aides-de-camp at a corner table. Everyone looked very earnest. Primly intense.

For a moment he thought he might play drunk, stagger over to Merriman's table, say something revolting, pee in Merriman's glass of buttermilk. No, he thought, the time will come. Someday. He finished his drink and left for the airport.

* * *

Harrison found his seat on the 747 and settled back. He declined the stewardess' offer of a cocktail; he never drank on airplanes.

Over what he guessed would be Colorado, he looked at his watch. Almost midnight exactly. The action would be getting started at Barney's bungalow at the Beverly Hills Hotel.

He rather wished he could be there to watch, but no worry, Barney would tell him all. Probably telephone him in New York.

But still he *would* like to be a fly on the wall tomorrow, say about six in the morning, when Ms. Stebbins awoke, every orifice sore and mind and memory bleary from alcohol and whatever hallucinogen Barney might have selected to bring the evening to its appropriate conclusion. She'd shake herself awake, see her Guccis and Puccis and V-buckled shoes jumbled on the floor of a strange hotel room; her impressive executive lady's Rolex on the nighttable; and then, beside her, the plump, hairy, insensible shape of Barney, buck naked and snoring like a rhinoceros. He laughed to himself. There would be more to come; Barney liked to finish strong the morning after.

It would doubtless be one of the more memorable wakings in Mary Stebbins's brief but shining Wall Street career. It amused Harrison to think she might be married and would have to explain the evening to a young, sincere husband who had been telephoning desperately all night.

Harrison smiled in the dark, and fell asleep as the plane beat on through the night toward New York City.

3 It was a perfect warm spring day—which made it all the worse that Harrison had to go down to Wall Street.

Ordinarily, he would have hoarded such a rare morning for himself and taken a walk in Central Park, which would be spangled with laughing children. Instead, he was rattling downtown in an unsprung Checker driven by a relentless bigot. The sparkle of the East River did little to mitigate the jarring discomfort of the ride and the venom of the driver.

The cab turned into South Street and lurched the last few blocks, the driver outwitting, successively, a nigger, a spic, and a kike. He pulled up in front of the dun stone building which housed Verger & Co., Harrison's investment banking alma mater and the venue of this morning's appointment.

"Everything OK in Auschwitz, Mr. Gardelli?" Harrison remarked as he paid the driver. "Give my regards to the Führer."

The taxi grated off toward Wall Street, swallowing the cabbie's profanity in the racket of the city.

Harrison looked up at the Verger building. It was one of the few remnants of architectural distinctiveness left in the pre-fab facelessness of the financial district. It occupied an eccentric trapezoidal plot edging on Hanover Square, a crenellated pile from which gargoyles and dragons glowered quietly at the messy, bustling scene below. One Hanover Square. It was a distinguished address. It suited the Verger history, even though the firm itself had been gravely diminished in style and standing by the last ten years of non-Verger management.

Ironical, Harrison thought, to be coming back here as a paid hand, even as a free-lance.

Verger had been one of two stops on the Street for Harrison. He had spent ten years downtown, the outer movements of his structured career, flanking six years in private banking in Paris, before he'd sickened of the endless infighting, and the noisy tummlers and Sammy Glicks who cascaded into the Street in the sixties and took it over.

Harrison now made his living doing financial odd jobs for big clients: corporations looking for offbeat money sources; businesses and loans in trouble; foreigners looking to put their cheap dollars in capitalism's New Jerusalem.

"What do I do?" he would reply to the inevitable question. "I'm a high-class street person." It was a living made basically by putting pieces and people together: a combination of financial architecture and diplomacy.

He had gotten into it by accident.

David Harrison came from a conventional, well-off family. After a childhood in Manhattan, the family moved to Greenwich, where people dressed up in pink and green linen on Saturday nights, and addressed themselves principally to parties, golf, tennis, and well catered, uninquisitive trips abroad. His father, a bluff and truculent man who was a great deal cleverer than he permitted himself to appear or to act, did something "on the Street." His mother, a gentle, confused lady with nervous eyes, kept his father pacified, generally by placing a glass at his elbow.

David still thought of himself in full flight from the vacant alcoholic life in which so many of his childhood friends now seemed to spend their time, reeling drunkenly around hotel ballrooms at charity parties or sitting stupefied at men's club dinners.

Harrison had been a shining student wherever he went. The best teachers passed him on to each other like a gift. He was intellectual and curious but he kept his sense of humor. There was something funny in everything, he thought. It was a point of view that inevitably got him in trouble as he grew older and had to deal with professionally serious types.

One weekend, in the spring of his junior year at Princeton, he had gone off to Yale to visit a prep school classmate. Late Saturday afternoon, when the light was fading from the Green, Harrison and his friend had tired of the caracole at Fence Club, its scuppers awash with the booze and vomit of the richest, most dissolute undergraduates north of Washington and Lee, and had gone off to eat.

They were crossing in front of the Sterling Library when Harrison's friend stopped. "You're a big literary man, Dave. There's a good story about the library over there."

His friend pointed to the carved inscriptions accenting the facade of the building. "Most of the carved stuff is heavy: Plato, Aristotle, Shakespeare, and, as expected at Yale, Samuel Johnson LLD, our household god. But there's one inscription—you see, up above the left-hand door—which goes: 'He was born with the gift of laughter and the sense that the world was mad.'"

Harrison didn't recognize the quotation.

"Well, when they dedicated the library, Sterling and Harkness and all the other big deals came up for the occasion, along with the local giants in the earth, Tinker, Johnny Berdan. Then someone noticed that inscription. Well, none of 'em could come up with the source. Until someone of less exalted taste remembered that it was the opening line of *Scaramouche,* a swashbuckler by Sabatini, who was kind of the Irving Wallace of the twenties. It would be like doing the damn thing today and sticking some gem from Mario Puzo up there with Shakespeare and Henry James. Anyway, they say that when the explanation came out, old Sterling damn near shit his pants. Here he's anted up for a fifteen-mil-or-so library and he's got a line from the equivalent of *The Godfather* chiseled on the goddamn west portal!"

It was a good enough story, Harrison had thought, but the

line made a *great* motto. He appropriated it for himself and, when once he had knocked off a hip fee, had it engraved on a pair of silver tankards which now guarded his New York mantel.

It was a mad world; indeed it was. What it needed in his opinion was something to shake it loose from its paralyzing mediocrity.

He crossed under the wrought-iron V-E-R-G-E-R traced over the lintel. It had been nearly twenty years earlier when he had first walked into Verger & Co. with nothing on his mind more pressing than the discharge of a formality.

He had been a senior at Princeton. It had been a Thursday morning in May, a good, clear day like this. His career at Princeton had been capped two weeks before when the English Department had awarded a Verger Fellowship to his honors thesis, *"Call Me Isaiah: Prefigurations in Melville"*; it provided $5,000 for a year of graduate study and travel.

It was good money in those days. After all, the New York banks were only offering around six thousand to his class' social eminences and the publishing houses and advertising agencies a little bit less for the Phi Beta Kappas. The announcement of the fellowship had caused no little stir at Holly, Harrison's eating club, where his quick wit in his cups had made him a star of the club's long-running late, late show.

"I guess this explains where our boy Dave hides out when we can't find him," toasted the club's president. "Let's hoist a few in his honor!"

He was right. Harrison had a degree of intellectual curiosity he couldn't, wouldn't entirely drink under the table. Every two weeks or so, he would pack it in at Holly and head for his cramped library stall: puzzling out literary patterns and relationships; taking notes; reading, reading, reading. He personally liked two kinds of fiction: the comically descriptive and the apocalyptic. His shelves held Dickens and Waugh next to Melville and Dostoevski. It was an odd mix, but then no one, then or later, ever took David Harrison for a simple, uncomplicated sort.

Verger's signature was on the fellowship check, and part of the tradition was that the annual winner made the dangerous overland journey to Manhattan to take lunch with Clarence Verger.

The first impression on a visitor to Verger & Co. was made by the uniformed black man who manned the long mahogany table in the reception area. All the better firms had them. Were they chosen for the sepulchral darkness of their skin and voice? Harrison wondered. Was there a secret stud farm operated on a pooled basis by the big Wall Street firms to supply them with ebony-voiced receptionists?

He gave the name of the man he'd come to see. Then it had been Clarence Verger himself; now it was MacClintock Lipton, one of the new breed.

The receptionist took his name with a deference unbecoming in this liberated age. He might have been farming squash on a small tenancy in Alabama. Harrison swore he even tugged his crinkly forelock.

The receptionist put the phone down. He had a Caribbean accent as rich as breadfruit. "Misser Lipton would see you shortly, sir. Please do have a seat."

Harrison's first visit to Verger had been, he recalled, very pleasant. Verger had shown him some nice old books, inquired politely about Harrison's father, with whom he had some brief acquaintance, and ushered Harrison upstairs to lunch.

The lunch had been excellent, served by frightened Balkan waiters. Harrison and Verger had been joined by one of Verger's partners, another Princeton man, whose principal conversational efforts, while touching reminiscently on Old Nassau, seemed to Harrison to be mainly directed at impressing Clarence Verger with his own industry and dedication.

Verger's conversation had been wider ranging. He was blessed with that ease of manner which makes some men accessible to their younger contemporaries without seeming familiar or condescending. He seemed to know a fair amount about Harrison's work.

In the course of lunch, Clarence Verger, or Clare, as he was later to be called by Harrison, had said two things that influenced Harrison's life.

First: "The Street is changing, David, and, as they said when Ty Cobb retired from baseball, not for the better either. Most of these fellows are working overtime to kill the goose that's laying those nice gold omelets. The boys on the Exchange are making money as if there's no tomorrow—and that includes certifiable retards, who are lucky to have enough money to buy a seat. The stuff that's being offered to the public is speculative and unseasoned. There are awful people coming into the business: shoe salesmen disguised as brokers. Every day is Christmas or Rosh Hashana down here. But it just isn't going to continue.

"You've studied enough literature, David, to have a feel for life's little anomalies. Well, let me try this one on you. On the one hand, you've got the president of the Exchange, who's a paid flack for something they call 'the people's capitalism,' running around America making speeches which all end with the slogan: 'Own Your Share of America!'

"And, on the other, the inside motto of the smart boys on the floor and the wolves in the board rooms is: 'The public is *always* wrong.'

"Try to make those fit together. There's something skewed in all this. The golden eggs being laid will also hatch a hell of a lot of birds who'll come home to roost."

Harrison, then, knew nothing of the technical side of Wall Street and stock and bond trading and the rest. But, as Verger had sensed, he had a good feeling for metaphor.

Then, as lunch was ending, Verger had said:

"This is still an interesting business, David. Literature may pall on you, God knows I hope it doesn't, since books keep a man sane—along with pictures, women, and decent wine—but you may get sick as hell of Academe. All that infighting for so little money. If life's got to be unpleasant, you ought to get paid for it. Keep us in mind. Just give me a call if and when."

Verger had been right. Six months of watching prospective colleagues, stewards of literature and keepers of the flame, conspire against and villify each other had left him disenchanted. He *had* called Clarence Verger and within a fortnight had found himself behind a desk at One Hanover.

The black receptionist snipped the string of recollections. "Misser Lipton will see you now, sir, Misser Harrison. Ninth floor, please. Through the glass doors."

He got off at nine and was met by a well dressed secretary with a snippy English accent. Very much the current fashion, he thought. Mr. Lipton would be with him momentarily.

He didn't really know Lipton. Lipton was a younger man who'd arrived at Verger out of the B-School eight or nine months before Harrison left. Harrison knew who he *was*, of course; it was his business to keep track of the comets, the young luminaries. It was easy these days, of course; they all gave interviews.

It was a real change in style from what he had first learned on the Street. The client's confidence and prominence came first; the role of the go-between was just that, to bring the parties at interest together with skill and discretion, cards brushing the vest buttons. Money and the client's satisfaction were sole and sufficient compensation for the job. For the last ten years, however, other standards seemed to have prevailed. Young men talking a lean, hungry, and tough argot gave endless interviews about deals, clients, and triumphs in which the actor most frequently mentioned was the first-person-singular. Harrison wondered, sometimes, whether all this braying about investment banking alchemies did any good, attracted other suckers. In the end, he concluded, uncertainly, that it did not, but his conclusion was not firm enough to sleep on with much comfort.

A man came in.

"David Harrison? I'm Mac Lipton."

Both Harrison and Lipton were built thicker than ideal, but Lipton had a soggy quality to him, although he was easily a half-dozen years Harrison's junior. Lipton was overweight but the puffy planes and roundnesses of his face were edged with the gray, desiccated tinge that belied a determined jogger. He was dressed in a variation of what Harrison had long ago designated "Wall Street Important Chic." Shoes both tasseled *and* buckled; a dark suit with side vents that seemed to come up to Lipton's armpits; a Hermes tie wide enough to sleep in. Suspenders needlepointed by the little woman. By contrast, Harrison had dressed the same way for fifteen years: black laced-up shoes, quiet suits, and club ties. "My suits," he was fond of remarking, "represent the best of British tailoring. They look as though they were made twenty years ago for someone else."

Harrison was uneasily conscious of Lipton's sizing him up. His out-of-date appearance, blondish-brown hair, cut middle short, good skin, no gray around the ears, no glasses, gave him what he liked to think of as an unbalancingly youthful look. That, and the clothes, and his elegant, sometimes overcomplicated use of words, spiced with the odd longshoreman's curse, was very off-putting to heavy-minded young men like Lipton who craved to give an impression of tightly wound, alert seriousness.

Lipton led the way back through the forest of open-plan spaces into which Verger's banking department had been converted since Harrison's day. "We are bankers, not brokers," Clarence Verger used to say, although the firm never lent a dime, only acted as go-between between the money and the need.

Lipton noticed him staring around. "You were here yourself?" he asked.

"Oh yes, indeed," said Harrison. "The glory days. Nineteen sixty to sixty-six. Sixty-five hundred and all you could eat. I understand that the B-School graduates are up to twenty-two five. That seems a high price for total ignorance, but then, as Lady Bracknell says in *The Importance of Being Earnest,* ignorance is like a delicate exotic fruit. One *does* pay up for scarcity."

The seeds of Lipton's grasping ambition had been planted as a child in Winnetka, and neither his economics major at Cornell nor his two years on the Charles River at the B-School had given him time for Oscar Wilde. He smiled with the uneasiness typical of the educated illiterate, a tight, wintry rictus.

Harrison followed Lipton into a glass-walled corner office: one of about a dozen that ringed the perimeter of the Floor. From the window, the East River glistened at the end of a corridor of skyscrapers.

The office was as Harrison expected. Piles and jumbles of the detritus of investment banking: placement memos, red-herring prospectuses, bound volumes celebrating this and that deal. Diplomas and road-running certificates in gold frames. A plastic model of a drilling rig: Models and toys; ships, airplanes, industrial apparatus, were badges of eminence in the investment banking world. *Economist* diary on the Sloane desk. Little lucite cubes with underwriting advertisements reproduced in miniature. A silver-framed, colored photograph of toothy children and smiling high-school-sweetheart wife: probably having it off with the local carpenter at this very moment, thought Harrison. He'd bet the Liptons owned the definitive collection of green ceramic frogs in Montclair.

Lipton settled heavily in a leather Eames chair and picked up the phone. "No calls, please, Miss Manchester."

He looked weightily at Harrison. "Dick Spackman tells me you're reliable." Spackman was a great friend of Harrison's who ran the New York office at First Ohio Downtown Bank.

Harrison made palms-up wings of his hands. "I do my best."

"Well," said Lipton, "let me tell you a little bit about the man who's coming to lunch. He has a problem you could help with, for which we would be *most* grateful." Lipton was an entirely quantitative person. Harrison could see; he could calculate and measure gratitude, or love, or passion to the nearest scintilla, and it thrilled Lipton. Harrison wondered idly whether Lipton got an erection at the mention of a large sum of money; what would be his tumescence/value quotient? Fifty million? A hundred? Did Mrs. Lipton gasp the weekly M1 and M2 figures in Lipton's ear as they rocked passionately on their designer sheets?

He was often distracted like this, he thought, refocusing on Lipton's words. It was not a good habit.

"The man who's coming to lunch is named Aristheos Stavrapos. You've probably heard of him."

Harrison had. He nodded.

"Mr. Stavrapos has made a great deal of money in the shipping business. A very great deal."

Harrison knew that also. The arrangements which had filled the Stavrapos coffers were rumored to have brought about the recent disgrace and impending execution of half of the Indonesian cabinet.

"As you may know," which Harrison did not, "we are also fiscal advisors to the Djakarta government and to INOC, *I*ndonesian *N*ational *O*il *C*ompany. Moreover, we handle, in our *A*sset *S*upervision *S*ection, ASS, Mr. Stavrapos's considerable dollar portfolio.

"Stavrapos," continued Lipton, demoting his subject by dropping the "Mr.," "has got himself in a bit of a jam." No Christian names on Wall Street for men in difficulties.

"Do you know the refinery outside of Galveston that Gulf Coast Energy built to handle 25,000 barrels a day of methylene for Allied Petrex?" Lipton asked.

Harrison did. Gulf Coast Energy had been the fastest growing of the Texas oil and gas combines put together in the last twenty years. Gulf Coast's chairman, Wendell Bigler, was well on his way to becoming a Texas legend. He was a gambler and he'd made his biggest bet in the form of a small Galveston refinery, which had cost $137 million, most of it borrowed, and which was hand-tailored to deliver methylene feedstocks to Allied Petrex's big chemical complex on the Houston Ship Channel. But Bigler, his intelligence wearied by long nights in Saint-Moritz and Monte Carlo catering to the apparently bottomless social ambition of his wife, had bet too heavily this time. He'd gambled on the availability of sufficient cheap crude in the spot market to fill his fixed-price contract with Petrex at a profit. But he couldn't get it: not enough, and not cheap enough, not even for cash. He made good for a while on his contract with Petrex, losing $60,000 a day, and then finally shut the refinery down, advising Petrex to sue and his own lawyers to prepare to take Gulf Coast Energy into bankruptcy. Then Stavrapos had stepped in and taken the refinery and contract off Bigler's hands. Gulf Coast had written off its $35 million equity and issued Allied Petrex $8 million in notes and preferred stock to stop its litigations and go away.

"I know the story," Harrison said to Lipton. What he didn't add was that it was a typical American deal: the stockholders lost around $300 million of market value as the Street marked down Gulf Coast Energy stock; four law firms, two Houston, two New York, split close to $4 million in fees; three investment banking houses ate up another two million five for "advice"; and Wendell Bigler had been reelected chairman of Gulf Coast at the most recent annual meeting by an 87 percent plurality and had an annual raise of $90,000 pressed on him by a grateful board.

It was really quite a world, thought Harrison. That morning the *Daily News*'s ace gossipist had breathlessly carried an account of a ball the Biglers had thrown at Rambouillet for the Duke and Duchess of Keingeld and a thousand of their closest friends. There had been a photograph of the Biglers boarding the Concorde at JFK. Alma Bigler wore her Halston traveling suit with the same bouncy insouciance with which she sported the orange "hot pants" she'd been wearing when Bigler discovered her working a Harlingen-Dallas flight. Harrison thought Wendell Bigler himself looked very relieved, even with the prospect of three days and thirty thousand devoted to the entertainment of the Eurotrash.

Lipton continued with the story.

"Stavrapos figured that he could feed Galveston with his Indonesian crude. So he took over the bank debt and secured it with his Liberian ships and went back and redid the contract with Petrex. Now the Indonesian thing's shot to hell, Petrex is screaming for its methylene, the banks are talking about foreclosing on the ships, and Stavrapos is sweating. We don't want to lose his investment business; we don't want the refinery refinancing to go to Lehman or First Boston; but we can't be seen to help Stavrapos or the new government in Djakarta, to whom we are fiscal consultants, will cut our nuts off. So you come in."

It figured, Harrison thought. First Ohio was probably in the refinery credit for $10 to $12 million; his old friend Spackman was probably assigned to the loan on a work-out basis, and had proposed Harrison to Lipton.

"Now you know, and I know," continued Lipton, professional to professional now, "that situations like this don't get cured quickly. The solutions come with time. Guys like Stavrapos are used to trouble and they generally come out OK, but they need *time* to work out of it. You can help him buy time..."

"By creating the impression of action." Harrison finished Lipton's sentence for him.

"Exactly."

"But how would you explain my involvement? You know as well as I do that firms like Verger don't use an outsider on a big piece of business even if they can get Meyer Rothschild—or Adam Smith! What are you going to tell this guy?"

"We've done our homework on that, Dave. Stavrapos is going to be informed that we keep you on retainer specifically for situations where senior-level experience is required to work full time on delicate matters that require deinstitutionalization, context-wise."

"And how much do *you* propose to retain me for?"

"We're thinking five K a month. It shouldn't take more than a couple of months. Three maybe." Harrison hated that B-School substitute of "K" for "thousand."

"Plus expenses?" There could be some travel time on this.

"Plus expenses. Plus, of course, whatever you can get from Stavrapos. That could be three, four hundred K. Maybe half a big one."

"Well..." Harrison paused, "...make it $7500 a month." Why not, he thought; a little equinoctial variety never hurt.

"Deal." Lipton extended his hand and they shook.

Lipton looked at his watch, an especially ugly and large digital model. Harrison wore a stainless-steel Rolex: the cheapest watch they made, bought in the good old pre-OPEC days for a hundred bucks at the Geneva airport.

"He's due here in ten minutes. Want to wash up?"

"Sure. Give you some time to catch up."

"I'd appreciate that. We're doing some pretty important stuff at the moment, basic industry restructuring, you understand, and my people are spread pretty thin. Every second counts."

Lipton wasn't a bad guy, but he could have written the field manual on conscious self-importance. Some guys could be pompous taking a crap.

"Unless you've shifted the plumbing around here, I can find it," Harrison said, gesturing Lipton to sit down.

As he went out of the office, he heard Lipton hit the phone. "Miss Manchester, get me Mr. Erstler."

Erstler was Verger's current senior partner—Harrison guessed that it would still be several months until the local Corsicans got him in a dark alley. Erstler would welcome Lipton's report. A classic example of investment banking at its best: touching all the bases and keeping out of harm's way for enormous fees. What a great business.

Not the way Clare Verger ran it in the old days, thought Harrison, zipping up. But of course all *that* ended the day that Harrison heard a noise in the street below and looked across Hanover Square to the steps of Benny's where Clare Verger went every day for a cheering martini before coming back to face the lunchtime solemnities of his partners. He remembered the scene vividly; he didn't need to be told what the crowd was gathered around, didn't have to run out to have a last look at Clare Verger dead on the pavement.

The funeral was barely over when the civil war started, the firm against itself. Since Harrison was known to have been personally close to Clare Verger—they often lunched together on Saturdays and went to look at books—the contending generalissimos each tried to enlist him. But he hated office politics just as much as he had hated faculty politics, so he stayed out of it. When the sounds of battle had died down and the field cleared of bodies, Harrison saw no future for himself.

So he went. It was a way he had. He could only go to war for large causes and the banners of the heart.

When he got back to Lipton's office there was a slender tan man sitting on the sofa.

Lipton bowed and scraped. "Mr. Stavrapos, I should like to introduce our special associate, David Harrison. I have spoken of him to you, as has our mutual friend, Mr. Richard Spackman of the First Ohio."

Lipton spoke very deliberately, as if addressing an Amazon pygmy. It was a parochial habit Harrison had often

(34)

noted in his countrymen; that they addressed all foreigners in English as if to three-year-olds.

Stavrapos acknowledged the introduction. He spoke himself in a curious clenched, hissing fashion, as if trying to get his words out around a tongue clamped permanently between his teeth. It was a way of speaking which was fashionable among the rich Greeks, a style established by the richest Greek of all, who probably gave elocution lessons, Harrison thought, in order to turn some extra change. The trouble was, it was pretty close to unintelligible.

"Shall we go upstairs? I think you will find our food quite acceptable."

Lunch was a desultory affair. The food was good, although fancier than Harrison remembered it, somehow redolent of those pretentious Hollywood restaurants where the menu was recited aloud by young men named Bruce in smocks and everything was stuffed with pine nuts. Most of the old-time Albanian waiters were gone.

Following accepted investment banking practice, Lipton kept the conversation away from the matter at hand. He dilated on the monetary situation and the investment outlook and offered a series of received political ideas suitably tailored to fit Stavrapos's presumably reactionary point of view. He spoke with the condescending benevolence which comes from complete self-satisfaction.

Twice, however, he was called to the phone. Miss Manchester was doubtless cueing the stagehands.

During Lipton's first absence, Harrison said, "Mr. Lipton has outlined the main elements of the problem. There's probably a solution. It will take some thinking over."

Stavrapos smiled enigmatically and hissed out something which Harrison couldn't understand, even though he smiled and nodded in comprehension.

The second time, Harrison said, "It would be best if we could discuss the situation privately, at a time and place convenient to you."

This time Harrison was able to translate Stavrapos's hissings into a time and an apartment number in the Waldorf Towers.

After coffee, Lipton and Harrison escorted the Greek downstairs to his limousine. Harrison declined what he assumed to be an invitation to a ride uptown, pleading the need for a few minutes' further discussion with Lipton.

They watched the Cadillac out of sight from the steps of the Verger building.

"This ain't going to be easy, Mac."

"We do our best." Lipton smiled. "Good luck."

They shook hands.

Precisely at seven that evening, Harrison, who was always scrupulously punctual, even if it meant arriving early and walking around the block—which he had in fact done—rang the bell at apartment 28E in the Waldorf Towers.

A white-jacketed Filipino opened the door.

He ushered Harrison into a decent-sized sitting room. Harrison knew these layouts well. He had been in on enough major deals and highest level executive adulteries transacted in the Towers to walk through a suite like this blindfolded.

Stavrapos had evidently been reading on the long sofa which dominated one wall of the room. As Harrison entered the room, he rose and put his book down.

"Good evening, Mr. Harrison. It's nice to see you again. Please have a seat." Cut-glass diction worthy of John Gielgud.

Few things stopped Harrison in his tracks, but this did.

"You surprise me, sir. I'd even thought of trying to speak with you in my bad demotic Greek, but I feared that just saying good evening would use up a good 30 percent of my working vocabulary."

"My dear Harrison, think nothing of it and have a drink. I've been reading Waugh. *Scoop,* do you know it?"

"I do indeed. It's my favorite."

"I find it very apposite to our times. I never knew Waugh, of course. He was at Oxford considerably before me. But of course no one seems to have understood better a world in which perceptions count more than facts. What do you think?"

"I agree. I think Waugh would have enjoyed having a go at our young friend Lipton."

"Lipton is a complete ass. He would be disappointed if I didn't make myself sound like Stavros Niarchos. Like all your Harvard Business School types, he comes to the grownup world fully supplied with preconceptions. Anyway, Mr. Harrison, your countrymen seem to value the unintelligible. If it is enigmatic, if it can't be immediately grasped, they think it must be something important or profound. What would you like to drink? Scotch? Vodka? Some wine?"

The Filipino brought Harrison a Stolichnaya on ice. The two men sat facing each other.

"Don't worry about these paintings, Mr. Harrison. They are perfectly awful, but they suit my 'American' image. I have some first-rate things in London. You must come to Eaton Square and see them. These are nothing but bad pictures by great names; poor Monet would commit murder to get that still life out of circulation."

Harrison sipped his drink and looked around the room. Everything was just wrong. This stool was too fancy; that desk was really quite ugly. Too many tassels; too much velvet. It was a nicely conceived and managed effect of expensive tastelessness.

"Over dinner, let me tell you what I think is going on, Mr. Harrison. We can compare notes, and I shall describe to you what the answers may be, what is needed, when and where, and perhaps you'll give me the best of your own thinking."

"Please, sir." Harrison was suitably deferential.

"Shall we dine?"

It had all the artifice of a good dinner, but was absolutely awful. Still part of the artifices of mediocrity with which Stavrapos fortressed himself, Harrison found himself wondering, or were the Greek's many small deficiencies of taste genuine? Real bad taste—or an affectation? It was hard to figure.

Stavrapos made small talk over the Beef Wellington. It was a dish Harrison particularly hated, pretentious and overblown, and he was grateful to be able to give some concentration to the business of scattering the shards of the entree around his plate. The wine was a Lafite, of a bad year, doubtless promoted by an opportunistic salesman in some swank Madison Avenue liquor store. It was sour as quince.

Over a brick-hard Brie, Stavrapos got down to cases.

"I don't know how much Lipton has told you, so let me risk repeating some things which you may already know.

"You are obviously aware of the situation involving the Gulf Coast Energy refinery and Allied Petrex? And of course Lipton has informed you that I recently bought it from Gulf Coast; I'm afraid that Wendell Bigler's many nights at Maxim's have affected his judgment.

"I put down no cash. The refinery was built principally with $103 million borrowed from a group of banks, led by First Ohio—which has been behind Bigler all the way. The banks have written the face amount of their loans down to $77 million and taken the balance, say $25 million, in preferred stock of a new Delaware corporation of mine. All of the common stock of *that* corporation is owned by a Panama corporation owned by me, or, to be strictly correct, owned in its turn by a Liberian corporation which is owned by me through a Lichtenstein depository.

"In return for reducing the principal amount and the interest rate of their loan, the banks required that I secure the new loan not only with the refinery assets but with the shares of a U.S. corporation which I set up just after World War II which holds a number of rather decrepit ships *and,* through a Luxembourg subsidiary, certain very valuable New York real estate, *of which the banks are generally unaware,* since those assets are on the books for less than $50,000. Since they seem to regard the shipping assets as satisfactory security, I have not enlightened them further. It is a difference in perceptions, Mr. Harrison. Ships I can buy tomorrow, for pennies a deadweight ton, but you must agree that it would be difficult to put together again two solid blocks between Fifth and Madison avenues? The banks are happy with the shipping tonnage as their collateral; is it my obligation to go into detail about the real estate?"

This *was* interesting. The way Harrison figured it, doing some quick horseback multiplication, the banks had nearly an extra $70 million of liquid New York real estate behind their loans, if they only knew it. Plus the ships. Plus the refinery. Plenty of cover.

"I can see what you are thinking, Mr. Harrison. Or may I call you David? We Greeks are not a formal people." Stavrapos smiled paternally.

"Well now, your Mr. Mencken once remarked that no one ever went bankrupt underestimating the intelligence of the American people; it's regrettable he didn't live long enough to meet the executives of your great banks. It would have gratified him to see his judgment so richly vindicated at so high a level of responsibility. But then, of course, I suppose a visit to the White House today would give him equal satisfaction."

Harrison had to laugh. Stavrapos was as rich in surprises as he appeared to be in money.

"Anyway, to return to the business at hand, it has taken me somewhat longer than I had expected to get just the right crude supply contract. The refinery cost next to nothing by current standards: less than $3,000 a barrel of daily capacity compared to the $6,000 Shell is said to be paying for its new facility in Louisiana. With the proper crude supply contract, and with the Petrex contract in hand, the refinery should return a cash profit of $45 million a year, which you would agree is an ample yield for an equity investment of net zero."

Harrison nodded, adding, "It really *was* unfortunate to have had the Indonesian situation change so radically against you. And so quickly!"

"Don't give it a thought. I never intended to run Sumatran crude through Galveston. It would be too expensive to transport around the Horn—the Canal can't handle the big tonnages—and, besides, I have learned in this business that it is imprudent to trust or depend on anyone of another color for more than a year or two. No, Mr. Harrison, I have always expected to get my crude for any major U.S. expansion from South America or the Middle East. Unfortunately, a promising but ultimately false trail in Caracas consumed a great deal of time.

"This has made the banks restive. They hear rumors, especially in Houston, which is a veritable bazaar of inaccurate oil and gas gossip, that my Galveston venture is in jeopardy. I suspect that some of these rumors come from Petrex. Banks no longer have confidence in their judgment of people. They believe gossip more avidly than your wife's bridge circle hangs on a juicy tale of adultery; you *are* married, Mr. Harrison? No? Well, in any case, you know what I mean.

"I am close to working out the necessary arrangements on the Gulf. There is crude available in one of the Emirates, but certain special arrangements of an informal nature must first be concluded."

Stavrapos made the last remark somewhat smugly. Harrison floated a trial balloon.

"The son of the emir's proctologist?" It was a bit of London gossip picked up last December at the bar of Bratt's Club. The wags claimed the good doctor had both the ass and the ear of the old emir.

Stavrapos smiled.

"You surprise me, David. Exactly so. With the help of one other person, who is even more important and well placed. Ah. Some champagne?"

The Dom Pérignon was iced within an inch of its death. It hurt Harrison's teeth to drink it.

Stavrapos continued. "It will take another month or two

to put things in place. Normally I would acquaint the banks, or at least the First Ohio, with the exact state of my negotiations in the Emirates. But that would make them privy to a type of dealing very much frowned on by your Congress and your Securities and Exchange Commission. And neither the banks nor I would wish a transaction of this importance, with this much money involved, to excite the scrutiny of that awful Mr. Simon."

Harrison agreed. Sidney Simon was the chief of the SEC's Transaction Section and the self-appointed *Gauleiter* of American Business Morality. He was a quarrelsome, ambitious bureaucrat who used the weight of the law to feed a Freudian, poor-boy need to push important men around, damn the expense and the consequences.

Not that Harrison would have come down squarely on the side of industry. In fact, he often said Simon's noisy pursuit of some corporate transgressor perfectly illustrated Oscar Wilde's description of fox hunting: the unspeakable chasing the uneatable.

The coffee was announced, and the two men moved back into the living room. Harrison expected a sweet syrup, but to his surprise, if equal distaste, he was served a thin, nasty brew. The brandy was good, served in a crystal snifter the size of a fishbowl.

When they were settled, Stavrapos picked up the thread.

"What I need now, therefore, is distraction and action, which will buy time, the two months, perhaps three at most, which I will need to lock everything up in the Emirates. I do not want the banks looking too closely at what they have got as collateral. They might be disposed to move to protect themselves. Once the first barrel of crude reaches Galveston, they will sigh, cross themselves, and all will be as in Paradise. But until then, I need a smokescreen. And I am told, David, not only by Lipton, but by friends in Paris and Lausanne far smarter and experienced than he, that you can do that kind of job as well as anyone in America."

"But may I ask *you*, sir, wouldn't you get something more if you used a large firm, one with institutional clout?" It was an old technique of Harrison's, learned at Clare Verger's knee: always suggest an alternative, especially if you know it's one that won't suit the particular bill.

"David, I have been doing business in this country for over thirty years. Wall Street helped me buy my first Liberty ship in 1945. I have worked with 'firms' most of that time. I have raised money on Wall Street. Some part of my personal affairs is handled there: by Verger, among others.

"When I first started working with those firms, David, I dealt with people who could close deals and who could keep their mouths shut. In my part of the world, discretion is as much valued in business dealings as in romance.

"This was the way that business was done by Clarence Verger, Gus Levy, Andre Meyer, Joe Thomas, or the other men who dominated investment banking in those days. But no longer, alas. Today, the partners in firms fight with each other and boast and publicize their 'conquests' like motion picture starlets displaying their underpants. This is a delicate matter. A great sum of money is involved. It cannot be exposed to the possibility—no, the probability, I would now say—of some fool discussing it out in the office hallway or drunkenly talking at his club or to his lady friend. Everything gets back."

It was the answer Harrison expected. It was one reason that he had quit the Street.

Stavrapos was still speaking. "I know something about you, David; really a good deal. When you were younger, I'm told, you made a great many mistakes. Too many late nights and too much high living. My friends tell me that those days seem to be behind you. That you will supply what I need: brains, experience, and discretion. That you are a cynic, which is an attribute I would think necessary in your line of work. It is frustrating to have to deal with highly paid fools. To outwit them is frequently the best reward."

Stavrapos smiled and sat back. The two men were wordless for a minute or so. Harrison turned the situation over in his mind. There appeared to be plenty of room to maneuver, to keep his nose clean, if things got dicey. Stavrapos had read him correctly. But he had been a big-time boy genius; he had left that behind. He was also past the self-centered insecurity of his youth, when every slight misstep seemed a catastrophe.

He looked pleasantly at Stavrapos. "The job interests me, sir. But I must have your assurance on one thing. I must be kept current as to your progress with respect to the crude supply, what the English call the state of play. My reputation for dealing straight is one of my few remaining bankable assets. If things should not work out *and* the banks should feel that we have been less than candid with them, matters will become very unpleasant for us both very quickly.

"And, of course," he added, "we have to agree on an appropriate level of compensation."

Stavrapos looked surprised. Thirty years of negotiating with investment bankers and other financial go-betweens had educated him that the issue of fee, which represented at least nine-tenths of any investment banker's preoccupation, was as difficult and, apparently, as painful to dig down to as an abscessed tooth. But he had his answer ready.

"I will pay you a retainer of $50,000 a month, against a final fee, when the first barrel of crude is offloaded in Galveston, of $350,000. That sum will be deposited in any currency in any location you may designate. It will be paid on any schedule you prefer. We will review the arrangement after four months."

"That will be acceptable."

Stavrapos spent the next half hour filling in Harrison on all the critical points, giving him names and telephone and telex numbers for contacts. Harrison was pleased to see that Stavrapos used a Houston law firm in which Harrison had good friends and a number of due bills. He knew seven out of the eight banks in the lending group. He hadn't talked to anyone at Allied Petrex in three or four years, but it seemed to him that he knew a couple of people on the board there. He could check that tomorrow. In any case, one of Harrison's specialties was getting to the right guys in the right places. On balance, it looked possible.

He smiled at Stavrapos. "I'll talk to Houston tomorrow. I look forward to working on it."

Stavrapos grinned and extended his hand. "As do I, David. We shall keep each other informed."

Stavrapos got Harrison's coat for him and went with him to the door of the apartment. As Harrison reached for the knob, Stavrapos put a staying hand on his arm.

"One thing, David. You should know that I have been very favorably impressed with your manner this evening. I submitted you to a little test. You did not sneer at the meal, as a Frenchman would have, nor did you praise it volubly, out of hypocrisy, as an Englishman would have, nor out of ignorance, which is normally the case with your countrymen. You did not pocket the silver, like a Swiss. I said to you earlier that your own people, types like Lipton, expect to find me vulgar and ostentatious. My chef is Vietnamese and has been with me for thirty years. He has cooked for kings. Henri Soule tried to steal him many years ago. It nearly broke his heart to prepare that disgusting beef: to ruin a good piece of meat and some excellent *foie gras*. I sent my chauffeur out to buy the wine. He is a young boy just weeks out of the Peloponnesus. He came back with what I expected. We put the champagne on ice at teatime.

"I owe you a good meal, David. We shall have it when this business is over. I am leaving for Switzerland tomorrow. I will telex you any news from there, and from the Gulf next week. Good luck!"

Harrison went out. As he waited for the elevator, he thought to himself: Stavrapos is right. The people he deals with around this country hear "Greek" and prejudge the man. They want to open the door and find Anthony Quinn snapping his fingers and dancing like Zorba. How wrong they were!

It was a clear night, as good as the day had been. There was a wisp of scented warmth in the air. Spring shading toward summer. As he made his way up Madison Avenue, Harrison tried to guess which two blocks Stavrapos owned, but it was a futile effort.

4 In London it had also been an early April day so fine that it demanded to be worshipped. It had begun unpromisingly, with an unseasonal thunderstorm shortly after dawn. The thunder bursts seemed loudest and most threatening over Clapton Common, and nearly drowned out the terrible explosion in Arch Street when a bomb, planted in the night, blew to pieces a bright blue Mini Cooper and its owner, Frederic Markwell, M.P.

The police were still scouring the area when the telephone rang back in Clapton Station and an Etonian voice proclaimed the assassination a triumph for the CAD, *C*ancel *A*rab *D*omination, a radical old-boy fringe group which preached a cooperative Western invasion of the oil states as an end to inflation.

The evening newspapers were full of the Markwell murder. The dead man had been a moderate, ethically unimpeachable politician at a time when such qualities were rare in the world's corridors of government. "Jude" Markwell, the press had nicknamed him, for his constant espousal of hopeless if decent causes.

He was a good friend of ours, thought the Minister sadly,

staring into the mirror as he dressed for dinner. The Kingdom had few such friends these days. They could ill afford to lose even one.

The Minister himself had been in the papers. The mirror only confirmed what the photograph in that morning's *Mail* had suggested: he *was* getting fat. Even his beard, once the dagger-point goatee of a dueling master, looked now more like a Chaplinesque splotch across his thickening chin.

The photograph had shown him arriving in Downing Street, over a headline which screamed: SHEIKH VISITS PM/MORE OIL BLACKMAIL?

He finished knotting his tie. In private, away from the Kingdom, he wore Western dress. He was an elegant man, careful of his appearance, and fond of his stylish clothes. These were tended by the head valet at Claridges. They had been dispatched the day before to his friend Khafiq's fine Regency house in Chesham Crescent, which is where the Minister preferred to stay whenever he was in London. Although the Kingdom's ambassador found this preference exasperating, the Minister could not stand the clamor of the Embassy. The halls were full of supplicants. His people were not yet really fit to travel in the outside world. But they had the money and it was unfair to quarantine them in the Kingdom. So they came to London, got into endless difficulties about their papers and shoplifting, disgraced themselves by urinating in the lobbies of fine hotels, hung their washing on Adam balconies in Wilton Place, and made themselves so generally unappealing that the vast sums of money they spent were cold comfort to the English. The Minister was no populist himself. He thought the spectacle sordid and, aside from required ceremonial appearances, kept his distance from his countrymen.

His visit that afternoon with the British prime minister had gone well enough. As always for state appointments, he had worn his robes, omitting the dagger at his waist, which the British press liked to fasten on as a symbol; he had had his fill of headlines screaming: ONCE AGAIN THE KNIFE AT OUR THROAT. If distant, the lady was extremely well mannered and highly practical. Unfortunately, she had given him little to hope for by way of an improvement in the now tattered relationships between the two kingdoms.

"I am afraid, sir," she told him, "that things are going very badly at present. There is talk in the back benches of making major reductions in military and technical assistance and putting on severe import restrictions against other countries which might seek to take up the slack. Some of my more extreme members have mentioned the possibility of currency and banking sanctions.

"In any case, I am afraid we shall be obliged to run flat out in the North Sea and take our chances that the next decade will either bring a material alteration in the current pricing picture or will offer new forms and sources of energy."

"I'm sorry to hear about the reaction in Parliament, Prime Minister," he had told her. "Our countries have been so close for so long. My father and uncle were educated by English tutors. I myself attended Harrow and the London School of Economics, as did my brother. Our nations have soldiered together and prospered together. It is difficult and perplexing for us to see you, our oldest friends, whom we have done much to enrich, turn against us. Merely because we have sought a fair price for what is ours."

It was difficult for the Minister not to smile at the last bit. Standard OPEC propaganda. The oil was in the ground, put there by the sovereign good fortune of whoever held the territory at the time.

The prime minister *did* smile. But hardly warmly.

The interview ended as irresolutely as it had begun. They paused for the photographers on the steps of Number Ten.

"Never thought I'd see 'em both wearin' skirts!" one photographer muttered behind his Nikon to a colleague. It was a spectacle unparalleled in Downing Street's glorious history.

The Minister had nothing to say to the press. Yes, there had been a constructive exchange of views. That was all. He climbed into the beige Rolls. As it pulled away, he caught a glimpse of his ambassador fuming unnoticed on the curb.

He had taken one substantive thought away with him, he recalled, as he lay his head wearily against the buttery leather. When the prime minister had risen to signal the end of the interview, she had looked at him sharply.

"Do try to go slowly, Minister. I think the Americans are about at the end of their patience. We understand that they may have initiated private conversations with New Delhi."

It was an ominous notion, like the cold edge of a knife running across the Minister's skin. The best-concealed secret in the Kingdom was its inner paranoia about the Indians: the great, hungry subcontinent barely fifteen hundred miles away. It would be a simple enough matter to embark an invasion force at Kutch, traverse the neck of the Indian

Ocean, and seize the desert oilfields, separated from the principal cities of the Kingdom by eight hundred miles of bad roads. The Americans and India making common, insane cause. It was a terrible thought.

He went downstairs.

A chill had come on with the evening; a fire had been lit in the high marble hearth. Khafiq rose as his butler showed his houseguest into the great drawing room. They made an odd pair.

Khafiq was a dapper little man. A man of small, precise movements; small, fine features set off by gold pince-nez; careful accessories; careful words. The Minister positively towered by comparison. What they had in common were bright, dark eyes, lit by the glow of intelligence and humor, although this last was hard to come by these days.

The two men had been intellectually and emotionally inseparable for close to thirty years, the Minister thought as he took his old friend's hand.

"A drink, Excellency." Long acquaintance was no excuse for abridging the appropriate formalities.

Khafiq knew his place. Make no mistake about that; it was one of the reasons for his extraordinary rise and influence. He had been born a nonroyal shortly after the al-Misaz family, of which the present King's grandfather and his own had been first cousins, had seized control of the Kingdom. The guns—and British troops who briefly patrolled the streets of Qu'nesh, the provincial capital—had been paid for with London sterling drawn from the accounts of Anglo Amalgamated Petroleum and Transport. Anglo stretched from Teheran, then a rustic watering place chiefly celebrated by boys' book writers, to Tampico, where the greatest oil wells since Spindletop would plume and die.

Anglo was an anachronism for its time. The ruddy men who made its shaping decisions believed in talent as much as in money. The first big well at Raf Tanar, spouting and flaming for eighty-three days before being choked under control, had been brought in when Khafiq was a little boy scrabbling in the dirt paths of Qu'nesh. His father, a tribal notary, had been enlisted as an accountant at Anglo. He brought his small son to the office, where the child's quiet attentiveness caught the observant eye of the local manager.

The English understood local talent. Khafiq was taken into the Anglo compound school, where dour Scots tutors drilled English and Latin into the children of the engineers and roughnecks who had come out from Houston and Lancaster to drill and develop the oilfields.

It was a difficult, transforming experience for young Khafiq. He was cleverer and quicker than his English classmates, who hated the long, hot days and ruined their lessons with grousing and pranks. Whether Khafiq had known then that his small hand was touching the edge of the curtain which would be drawn back to disclose the modern world to the Kingdom he couldn't say, even now. In those days, the alternatives to school were dirt streets and servanting the Anglo wallahs. He kept to his studies. In time, he was taken from his family and brought to England.

He spent five years there. The habits of his mind were transformed.

It amazed his superiors. "He doesn't think like an Arab," one teacher wrote. "He can make up his mind—*quickly*." It was a capacity entirely unexpected in a descendant of a race in which endless meditation and delay were a matter of course in any decision, however small.

When he returned to Qu'nesh in 1939, barely thirty, he was as English as the most lisping Etonian. He'd acquired other tastes as well, in London.

Days were spent in a routine of precise method and calculation; nights in the dissolute, squirmy beds of backstreet Soho flats. There had been unpleasant episodes: smarmy doings with guardsmen and male dancers. But then, as ever, Anglo had been prepared to overlook. "Do realize," said Anglo's London accounts manager to an exercised police inspector, "that we need these people. Buggery's common enough on this sceptered isle. Oil is not."

When the war ended, Khafiq was a senior supervisor. The powers housed in the huge Anglo headquarters building in Dumar, now a thriving, messy port, felt he had a future. His loyalty was guaranteed by a fat dossier in Cheapside detailing a rich history of "indiscretions." He was due for an important posting: Djakarta.

Khafiq's transfer documents were in the process of being put in final form when a momentous meeting took place at the Garrick Club.

"We need a good man, a local, to work with the wogs," said Sir James Squires to Lord Montnorth, the chairman of Anglo. It was 1951.

Sir James was head of the Wellington Bank. He was a clever, fat Etonian who had parlayed an old Sandhurst friendship with the al-Misaz family's military advisor into a highly lucrative investment advisorship to the Kingdom. While the bulk of the clan's fortune, even then a matter of $97 million, was handled by stone-eyed Swiss bankers, Sir James had carved out a slice of the business sufficient to stock his Leicestershire estate with grouse and pheasant. Lord Montnorth liked the shooting there.

"You know, Eddie," said Sir James, "these wogs won't let you oil pashas keep on this way forever. Better to get a hand on the money too. Or the blasted Yanks will get that."

"Quite so," said Montnorth. He was a man of few words, reluctant to give up the appearance of laconic befuddlement which had earned him a fortune and a peerage.

"You've got a good man out there now in this Ali Khafiq," pressed Sir James. He knew. Khafiq's private dossier, abstracted from the Anglo file room by friendly hands, had been on his desk for a week. "Send him to Indonesia and you're wasting someone valuable. Why not let us have him for a while?"

He added temptingly, "Why not come down to Bourne next Friday? The birds are going especially well." He signaled and let the matter drop; an ancient waiter tottered up with the port.

And so Khafiq came to Wellington. His work was unexceptionable. He soon grasped that the investment business was a sheep's game. He did nothing different from the Swiss, nor from the sweating American bankers who thrice yearly journeyed to the Kingdom to report on the New York portfolios. But he did it in a burnoose and robes. The royal family came to trust him. Although tale-bearers carried back gossip of nasty incidents in London, or in Beirut, where Khafiq went for a time when England got too hot, he was plausible and performed well enough.

"I follow certain simple rules," he told the Minister, long after they had become friends. "I pay for no one's ideas. I engage no advisors. I simply listen for the hoofbeats of the herd." The royal portfolios flourished.

He grew rich. When he departed for Beirut, he sold the pleasant house in St. John's Wood and bought, for a song, it now seemed, a handsome row house in Chesham Crescent. He returned there every summer, adding good furniture bought in Pimlico Road. His agents kept watch for silver and pictures. When the Duke of Dorcester died, and his only son went to jail, Khafiq hired the Duke's famous butler. He was preparing a setting for himself. He knew he would be back.

One bright day in 1970, when the next block in the Rue Maltroit was pulverized by Falange gunners, Khafiq left Beirut for good. He gave his companion 10,000 piastres in an envelope, along with the key to his flat. The companion was grateful. He had been a penniless singer in the Aftallah Club when Khafiq had taken him up. As the Britannia turboprop lifted into the air over the Mediterranean, Beirut, the smooth young men, all the delicious nights at the beach, sank into forgetfulness. Behind him, the early evening light and the even glitter of the lights of the center of the city and the beach cafés faded, along with the flickering bonfires which were stores and houses burning in the Christian quarter. Khafiq knew in his soul he was going home.

Sipping his drink, with the spectacular capacity of the mind to compress lifetimes into a matter of moments, the Minister had recalled Khafiq's life story.

They looked at each other.

"Terrible, this Markwell killing," said Khafiq. "You knew him well?"

The Minister nodded. "Almost from the time I first met you, dear Ali. We were at Harrow together."

Harrow. The Minister's mind turned backward again. Khafiq saw this, kept silent.

The Minister seemed to shake himself. No time for reminiscence now.

"We really must do something," he said.

"I think we must."

"Did you see this?" Khafiq handed him a magazine. It was the current *Economist.* The Minister had seen it. The lead article had featured a full-page photograph of the President of the United States, Fulger Baxter, and Mr. Begin, the Israeli prime minister meeting in Washington. *"What must seem the endless and perplexing patience of the United States,"* the article read, *"may now be seen to be approaching its end. The recent articles of accord between Washington and Tel Aviv suggest, at the very least, the possibility that the tangible arrangements between America and its oldest and best-beloved client state can now contemplate something beyond a protective umbrella. The ribs of that umbrella, symbolized by the three squadrons of F-5 strike fighter-bombers and C-123 tactical troop transport which will be placed on Israeli soil over the next three years, will cast a long shadow even across the Per-*

sian Gulf, serving notice to Qu'nesh and its neighboring capitals that America, to date so tolerant of the depletion of its industrial well-being by the economic voracity of the producing nations, is positioned now to act with extreme tactical rapidity if its self-interest should so indicate."

"Yes, Ali, I've read it." The Minister knew, as did Khafiq, that the journal had a pipeline into the heart of the U.S. State Department, which accounted for its uncanny divination of American foreign policy.

"You know, Ali, I thought it would all be so simple. So logical and therefore so manageable. When I went to the King six years ago and urged him to raise the price of oil, it seemed only just. And everyone I consulted agreed: not only our people, but Caracas and Lagos and our late ally the Shah. We were giving the oil away.

"I remember once, during that year I spent in the States, dining with the parents of a classmate at Stanford. The father, they were rich Danes, said something I couldn't forget."

Indeed. It had been in San Francisco, at the Top of the Mark. The Bay was spread below them like a basket of diamonds. After a good dinner, and much good California wine, the older man had looked thoughtfully out at the splendid panorama.

"A great country," he said, "but confusing. So much taken for granted. No difficulties. The perfect life. But think about it.

"Your country," he said pointedly, age speaking to youth, disregarding the princely rank of his audience, "sells America oil which nature took millions of years to put in the ground. And you sell it to them for pennies. They ship it thousands of miles in tankers which cost hundreds of thousands of dollars to build and operate, and then run it through refineries which cost millions. And then they sell the gasoline on the streets for less than I pay for a kilo of herring in Copenhagen. Very strange."

Unnatural, thought the young prince at the time. His host's offhand observation stayed with him; one of those accidents of conversation which transforms idle speculation into obsession.

Shortly after that, the young man met Khafiq. To both of them, it seemed like yesterday.

By then, Khafiq's house had become a central meeting point in London for all young Arabs of high birth and influence, which tended to come to the same thing. In those days, they were a shabby lot, the young sheikhs, looked down on by the Greeks, French, and English who shared the exclusive classrooms in Gstaad and Windsor. Poor savages whose waterholes happened by chance to sit upon the source of the rest of the world's wealth. Kaffirs. Their fathers, tutored and marched by a generation of British officers, sent them to England, little recognizing that in their zeal to replicate English manners they were exposing their children, the heirs to the Kingdom, to the inimitable, cruel bad manners and insensitivity of the English upper classes, as well as to the vision of luxury.

Khafiq's house, so perfectly English in all superficial aspects, came to represent a small oasis of consolation in a world so entirely, ungratefully unfriendly. Not that anything seemed to have changed so much now, the Minister thought. When we gave them everything, they snubbed us; now that we have taken something back, they seem to hate us.

Khafiq interrupted his woolgathering. "I see no hope for the dollar, Your Excellency. Certainly not with the present leadership in Washington. And the pound looks worse. The lady in Downing Street and her government espouse admirable principles, but matters have gone too far."

There was no need for Khafiq to recapitulate further.

They were called to dinner. Later, the butler was to make known his disappointment that two such eminent and important men should have so little of value to offer to his eavesdropping ears. He had built a nice little sum with his broker in Threadneedle Street by speculating on overheard bits and pieces of Khafiq's table talk. If ever an evening had promised the possibility of a nice turn, this was it. But nothing. Even worse, the two had barely picked at a meal he'd taken great pains to plan.

"Not that it's all a loss. At least they left the wine alone," he said, sharing a bedtime glass of 1964 Haut-Brion with the Minister's driver.

Upstairs, with the coffee cleared and a reflective glass of brandy before them, the two men tried to sort out the economic cancer with which they had to deal.

The facts were simple. The Kingdom's holdings of dollars and sterling, which accounted for over three-quarters of its reserves, had depreciated nearly 15 percent in the last year: this came to slightly less than $20 billion in purchasing power. Inflation in the West had jacked up the price of everything they bought—turbines from Houston, computers from Manchester; telephones from Rome—by at least as much. The army of auditors and consultants they employed seemed helpless to keep prices fair, bids unpadded.

The political situation looked desperate.

"I fear we are very much alone," said the Minister. "If we are moderate, our few allies hate us. This business with Egypt and Israel is an insult; it makes us appear superfluous in the part of the world we are expected to dominate. The situation in Iran is bad; the old man will not rest until his Shiite priests rule Qu'nesh. And, of course, the Americans, who should be our umbrella, are drawing away."

He paused. None of this was news to Khafiq.

"You know, of course, dear Ali, that the American Defense Secretary was in Qu'nesh shortly after President Baxter revived the Egyptian discussions with the Israelis. We discussed the possibility of an American defense system then—an umbrella with its shaft planted in our soil. The price the Americans asked was that we double our production. Double it! It was, of course, a stupid, politically self-serving proposal. Just the sort of thing we've come to expect from President Baxter and his associates. I must say the Defense Secretary, who has always impressed us as a realistic, intelligent man, seemed quite embarrassed to be obliged to put forward so idiotic a notion!

"Naturally," the Minister added, "with the condition our fields are in at present, it would be impossible for us to increase our production by 10 percent, let alone double it!" He went on to relate that an engineering survey had advised that essential rework and maintenance of the Kingdom's producing wells would necessitate a *reduction* of 10 percent in production runs within the next five years.

"I know," said Khafiq. "Benjamin Masters sent me the article in the *Washington Post*. Have you seen it? I'll have it put by your bedside."

"I'd be interested. It's undoubtedly buried in some pile of papers in Qu'nesh. I doubt that we can sustain this aloofness in military matters much longer. But it is equally unlikely that we can make any substantial progress in Washington. Not with this administration.

"Finally," he finished, "I must tell you that my discussions this afternoon have given me to believe that an effort may be under way to involve New Delhi in some kind of adventure."

Khafiq looked up. "You're sure?"

"That is what the prime minister said. She is a devious lady—but no liar!"

The Minister had always looked to Khafiq for the ultimate Socratic answer in times of difficulty. The old man was brilliant, capable of sorting out the most difficult political or financial equations. Now he looked puzzled.

"It has all gone too far down the road, Excellency. We knew it would. I remember what you told our allies in Nigeria and Kuwait: that our friendship with the Americans might be priced out of existence. Of course, they don't listen. They must have their yachts, and airplanes and fancy uniforms!" The older man was exasperated.

"What then would you propose? Short of I, myself, becoming President of the United States?" It was a bitter chuckle.

Khafiq put up a patient hand. "There must be an answer. There will be an answer. It will take time and reflection, and will be unusual, but it will come. Allah will see to that."

It was an unsatisfactory answer. Khafiq excused himself. They shook hands and said goodnight. Khafiq was tired and old, the Minister thought; not what he once was. He remained downstairs for a time, slumped heavily in the red leather chesterfield, staring expectantly into the dying fire as if some genie or djinn might rise from the flames to give him the answer. The fire was dying; the Kingdom was dying.

At length he went to bed. The *Post* article was on the pillow. Khafiq was a man of infinite small courtesies, he thought.

He picked up the article. It was a long, perceptive piece: *"The action limiting a price increase is now seen as having been a friendly gesture to a new administration....No such friendly gestures are likely today; in the present circumstances, it will require positive action by the Kingdom, not just maintenance of the status quo, to allay danger to the economies of the West and America,...which is unlikely because leaders in the Kingdom believe that President Baxter lacks the will to express a preference for the Arab side in the Middle East."*

He read on to the end. An excellent analysis, he thought, but one which hardly made for a reposed state of mind.

The dawn was probing the clouds when the Minister at last found sleep.

5 From the first day he set up on his own, it seemed to Harrison that he never stopped traveling, spending his life in one awful, inconvenient airport after another. New York was no longer the center of things, not for American business, no matter what the city's publicists claimed. So, for the Stavrapos deal, it was back on the airlines.

He started at First Ohio Bank's Cleveland headquarters. It was a clear day when he flew in; you could see the sky. In the onion domes of the Balkan churches which lined the edge of the parkway, the city had an offbeat, exotic touch for Middle America. But then, thought Harrison, who had a bent for historical reflection, Middle America was really new Prague, new Vltava, Riga, Köpenick. Or new Gabon and Congo, to give another side of Cleveland its due.

Dick Spackman was with him. He was a graying, fast-talking, gum-chewing boy—why did Harrison still think of his contemporaries as "boys"? Christ, they were all edging up on fifty! Spackman had been at Verger when Harrison arrived. He was the sort of man who caused the knives to be drawn. "Not really Verger material," was how one of the princes of the cloth put it.

Temperamentally and intellectually, Spackman didn't seem to fit with popular notions of midwestern banking. Too hip and New York stylish. But the job had been there when Spackman needed one, and he had proven surprisingly good at it. He wasn't ever going to be president of First Ohio Bank, any more than he would have been elected a partner at Verger. But he was great at mopping up the messes that the lending officers in Cleveland were lured into.

"Jesus," he said to Harrison at one of their monthly breakfasts at Harrison's club, "it's amazing what a good dinner and a good professional blow job can do to shape a lousy credit decision."

So Spackman had come to be a one-man workout department, cleaning up spills and buying into situations which other banks had abandoned. Spackman liked what he was doing. He was making good money; it was rumored in the bank that he had a 10 percent piece of any recoveries on written-off loans, and *that* really pissed off the pipe-smoking, vested vice presidents in Cleveland.

"Every time we have one of those godawful officers' get-togethers," Spackman had said, "I make sure that those Shaker Heights hausfraus get the word that I cleared a hundred fifty grand last year."

What Spackman didn't add—but Harrison knew, through another friend at First Ohio—was that Spackman had an amazing record of sexual conquest at those hoedowns. An anomaly of modern civilization, thought Harrison: the way those pressed, permanented country-club types, with their circle pins and cashmere twinsets bought on the cheap in Saint Croix, would drop their drawers in a hotel room for a New York Jew who smelled of cheap cigars.

He must introduce Spackman to Mary Stebbins, he thought, as they boarded the Cleveland flight at LaGuardia. Barney's report had been entirely favorable, hinting darkly at interesting if ambiguous sodomistic possibilities.

The taxi turned off the parkway. The old First Ohio building seemed hunched in the shadow of its incongruous forty-story glass annex.

He turned to Spackman. "One more time. How'd you guys get in with Gulf Coast Energy in the first place?"

"Wendell Bigler, the head of Gulf, and Bev Scroddin, the vice chairman of the bank, both come from Tomball, Texas. Tomball! Can you believe it? So they're asshole buddies: high school, Texas A & M. Then, I don't know, the army together, I guess. After the war, Scroddin goes to Ohio State and gets an M.B.A. and ends up here and Bigler starts Gulf Coast in Houston; and, naturally, he needs money to make it grow, so he calls Bev.

"Well, Scroddin was doing well at the bank. But everyone was shitting through their hats because First of Chicago was the only midwestern bank doing any real business in Texas, and there was a ton of business to be done. Scroddin knew about six people in Texas, which made him our expert, so when Bigler called him, they went apeshit and sent Scroddin to Houston. He and Bigler went out and got drunk and shacked up for a weekend with a couple of stewardesses, one of whom is now Mrs. Wendell Bigler. Scroddin came back to Cleveland and got the bank to put up a mil to let Bigler buy a couple of tank trucks which scrounge around picking up oil from wells too small to deserve a pipeline; then five more mil for a pipeline, etcetera, etcetera, and here we are today. We once had $10 million with Gulf Coast Energy. We now have $30 million—and that, Dave, is flatass up against the bank's loan limit—most of it in a refinery which is owned by a Greek we don't know, who's using God knows what for oil to fulfill his contracts."

Bigler had come a long way from Tomball, thought Harrison. Was it worth it, he wondered, to get up in the morning knowing that the day's big event was to kiss the ass of Prince Rainier? And how about having to look at and listen to Mrs. Bigler? Harrison thought there were probably a lot of days when the one dusty street of Tomball still looked pretty good to Wendell Bigler.

"One other thing, Dave." Spackman's tone was cautionary. "Certified is doing some screwing around with this deal. We're the agent for the bank group, and what we say is supposed to be a binding recommendation; Certified's got only $3 million in the refinery deal, three out of a total of seventy, plus the accrued interest, and they only inherited that from a bank they bought in Elmira which has done a bunch of little deals with us.

"Now, I don't want to say anything—or suggest anything. But you know that Merriman is on the Allied Petrex board, and Petrex is a huge Certified customer. No one yet understands why Petrex let Bigler in the middle on this methylene supply deal in the first place. Now, Stavrapos's got deposits with every bank in the group; that's part of the loan agreement. He's playing ball. But he's close to default, and you know in this business it takes a unanimous vote to say not guilty, but only one to convict. Let's say he defaults technically and Certified seizes those deposits to offset them against its loan, the way those assholes at Fiduciary and Guaranty did with American Stores, although *there* they were just being chickenshit while *this* smells of a Petrex-Certified deal. When that happens, Dave, your client is down the rathole. I will guarantee that then Petrex will turn up with enough Certified financing to buy out the other banks and wash out the equity and own that refinery themselves for peanuts!"

Ouch, thought Harrison. Business lesson number one: You haven't got a chance if your biggest customer or creditor wants to buy you out. He'll suborn your defenses: bankers, lawyers, investment bankers, other customers. They're all whores, anyway.

Harrison had seen that at first hand. A dozen years before he'd put together a financing for a fine, small, off-road vehicle company near Canton. Run by a brilliant engineer, it was a small outfit and it subcontracted out a lot of components business. Unfortunately, it bought its chassis assemblies from Consolidated Industrial, which was looking at the time for a cheap, finished-product diversification into a nonaircraft market. First, Consolidated pulled its credit line. Then it delayed delivery on the chassis. Other suppliers and customers held back. The banks pulled the plug. The engineer went home one hot summer night, with the crickets fiddling in the trees along the Tuscarawas River, and blew his brains out. American business at work and play. Consolidated bought the business out of bankruptcy; they'd sold ten thousand of the ORVs since, and were well into the second design generation. Harrison wondered if the crickets were still chirping by the Tuscarawas.

Spackman paid the taxi. Riding up in the elevator, Harrison mused on banks. Bastions of the capitalist system and fortresses of financial privacy and probity. Except when it profited them to act otherwise. He could imagine some vice president at Certified being summoned to Leslie Merriman's fifty-second-floor office, where Mismer guarded the door like Cerberus, to get his marching orders on Stavrapos. It was a grand office; Harrison had been there once, on a state visit with Clare Verger. The walls were lined with glass-fronted cabinets encasing Merriman's famous collection of rare toys. There was a nice Pissarro on the one free wall. In his mind's ear, Harrison could hear Merriman: "Now, on this Gulf Energy business, be absolutely certain that the Stavrapos commitments are letter perfect. Default, even if only technical, is unacceptable to this bank. If it occurs, we will immediately offset and consider certain alternatives at hand." Translation: Push Stavrapos against the wall and blow the whistle; we've got a customer for the refinery. Banks!

Bev Scroddin was a bluff, professionally affable type. "So you've been brought on board to work out this Stavrapos thing," he said to Harrison. "Not a moment too soon. But it can be worked out. Of course, certain of our friends..." He cast a questioning glance at Spackman, who signaled back that Harrison had been briefed on the Certified aspect.

"Now let me bring you up to speed. I just got through upstairs with Tergass." Tergass was First Ohio's chairman. "We have some new developments which are not exactly pleasing. Tergass got a call this morning from Bill Grimsley; you know, the head guy over at Heartland Illuminating Company? Tergass's on his board. Well, Grimsley's on the board down at Petrex, along with Leslie Merriman, and he tells me he's just being a good citizen and he's calling Terg to say he hears—*hears,* get that!—that there's a problem with the loan on that Galveston refinery and that maybe—*maybe,* my ass!—he knows someone who could buy out our position." Scroddin's hands were making rapid circular movements in the air, a physical metaphor of the gathering momentum of high-level phone calls. "Of course, the Illuminating Company buys $160 million a year of natural gas from Petrex."

Harrison observed that Scroddin's face had lost its initial bland geniality. This guy, he thought, is angry. Scroddin kept talking.

"Now, I rejiggered the structure on our refinery loan so that Wen Bigler, who is an old friend and a *very* good customer of this bank, could make a deal with Stavrapos to get out from under. We got a nice loan fee and we have got a good loan. Plenty of collateral. Good collateral: Madison Avenue between Sixty-ninth and Seventy-first streets is a nice cushion, although *that's* a bit of comfort I'm keeping to myself for the moment. Don't look surprised, Mr. Harrison; Mr. Stavrapos is our client, too, but it behooves us to know everything. Don't worry; I'm not about to see his good deal screwed up by those dumbbells at Certified."

The world is indeed filled with surprises, thought Harrison. Verger had told him: "There are about six intelligent men working in the whole universe of commercial banking. You may never meet one. If you do, and he's working the same side of the street, you are riding a very fast horse, David, very fast indeed." Scroddin was starting to look like Seattle Slew.

The three men talked through lunch. They agreed the key was to buy time for Stavrapos to make his deal in the Emirates to get a crude source for the refinery. Scroddin would call a bank meeting—in Los Angeles, in order to make sure that the bankers would get good and boozed up and thoroughly distracted. Harrison would make a presentation. Then there would be a three-week period during which Harrison would prepare a refinancing memorandum; this could be stretched out to six weeks, during which Harrison would flood the lending banks with phone calls, interim progress reports, situation memoranda: all the paraphernalia suggestive of a high rate of constructive activity.

"A key aspect of investment banking," Verger had told Harrison once, "is the ability to sell motion as progress."

"I'll try to keep Certified quiet," said Scroddin. "I'm not

quite sure how. I wish I had a photograph of that sanctimonious prick Merriman with his nose in some callgirl's muff,
but failing that, I'm sure we can come up with something.
But *quiet* is maybe the *best* I can do. One tip. Watch out for
Petrex. Those guys are grade-A sonsabitches. They would sell
their mothers below the bid price. And two. Don't talk to
anyone *here* except Dick and me. No one. I have a lot of good
friends in this world, but not enough in this building. OK?"

"Deal."

Spackman was staying over for a few hours on other business so Harrison left alone. He found a cab outside the bank
and told the driver to take him to the Cleveland Museum.
They drove through black, dangerous slums into the park.

It was still about the best museum in the country, Harrison
thought, strolling among the cases which held the medieval
perfections of the Guelph Treasure. In a place like this, disturbed only by the haste and confusion of touring school-
children, the whole messy world was pushed fifty trillion
miles away. A good-looking girl was making the rounds about
three vitrines ahead of Harrison. He trailed her, speculating
where in God's name you could take someone for an afternoon
quickie in Cleveland. He should have asked Spackman. He
was always up for this game but he never got any closer than
speculation. He couldn't pick them up out of the blue. "I fly
fifty to a hundred thousand miles a year and I have never,
never, had a date with a stewardess," he would remark, often
with the special pride that goes with an utterly dubious distinction. Of course, there had been that Pan Am stewardess
in Rome; they'd gotten really drunk together and ended up
in the Pinciana where she masturbated him as if she was
beating pizza dough, until his cries of pain blended with her
relentless *"fammi venire; fammi venire;* make me come!" in
a chorus which would have done credit to Caligula.

He was composing his opening lines—culture was the
greatest aphrodisiac going—when the girl ahead turned a
corner and vanished into the ladies' room.

Foiled, he finished his tour. His mind was only half on the
pictures and objects now. He was composing his plan of attack
on the Stavrapos business. He felt better. He had good allies,
which was something he'd come to value as the illusory lone-
eagle omnipotence of youth had slipped from him. Clear, discrete, the impressions of the works of art mixed in his mind
with the Stavrapos problem to form a surrealistic pattern.
That was the way his mind characteristically worked. Pre-

hensile. Seizing the bits and pieces of a dozen puzzles and recutting them to fit with each other.

He got back to New York about seven. Nothing was on the books, so he had the evening to himself. It was fine with him, although he was beginning to notice that he dealt less easily with solitude than he had, say, a year or two earlier.

"I live alone," he found himself telling Barney, "and now I work alone. That may be too much alone." Living alone had produced a nacreous selfishness, a carapace of self-interest that really looked better than it felt.

At least he liked where he lived. His apartment was in an old building off upper Park Avenue. It was tucked away like a concealed aerie in the upper back reaches of the building. It was a hideaway; the man who built number 87 before the Depression wiped him out wanted his mistress in the same place as wife and family and had built her the hideaway where Harrison now lived.

That evening Harrison typed out an outline of his plan for Stavrapos. He had always done his own rough work, even in the three firms for which he'd worked before, where, with advancing seniority and importance, he might have commanded platoons of M.B.A.s with yellow legal pads and holstered calculators. He liked to delegate responsibility, not dogwork.

His living room, where he spent most of his time, was his treasure. He basked in it. It was a man's room. "Jesus," Barney had said when Harrison moved in, "this room is a real pants-dropper. When those ladies get a look at this, you're going to need a spare dick." A lot of ladies had been there, for a night or two, but none had stayed. As he grew older and became more set, he began seriously to doubt that he could cope with the psychological regaitings which would be essential in a two-sided relationship.

The room was square and high ceilinged, lacquered a dark burgundy. The furniture was fat, overstuffed wool and leather. The walls were bookshelves, floor to ceiling. There were good books in those shelves—and junk. Books proliferated around Harrison. They were his principal company, along with women. He was a reader: three or four books going at once. Piles and stacks of books sprouted everywhere: never to be read, waiting to be read. There was always something. He had an odd capacity for detail: dates, places, quotations. Long lines of meandering philosophical inquiry made him restless. He jumped around. "For goodness' sake, David," his mother had said to him, "let me finish a sentence! I start something; you assume you know where it's going, and you just drop out; it's as if you had got up and left the room. On to the next thing, you say. It's just not nice."

If a man's home was his castle, this apartment was Fortress Harrison, he thought. He got up from the typewriter and went to the window. The street below was quiet: a couple arm in arm, a man walking a dog. The trees were just beginning to come out. It was elegiac, matching the Haydn quartet on the stereo. Very peaceful. Very lonely.

For a moment or two he played with the idea of making a call, getting someone to come over, share the evening and the night. Harrison was successful with women, once he'd been introduced and a mutual context established. His brains and wit were his prime attractions. You needed to work that in; he couldn't just walk up to some model at a singles bar, fling his mind over her like a fishnet, and drag her away to his cave, his aerie. The mind, the culture, were tradeoffs with the girls he went out with. There I go again, he thought, *girls*. Women. It was a rueful correction. They were trading off, he knew, if you were honest with yourself. He took them to concerts and plays, cooked for them, gave them books which were flattering in their presumption of the recipient's taste and cultivation; in return, they gave back their admiration and affection and their bodies. And you got to share your desperation with each other, a moment's relief from the mosaic of utterly random intersectings, street and cocktail party collisions, that demarcated so much New York life.

He decided against making a call. Lord knows, they were available: perched like sparrows out there in their own high, lonely nests. And the mornings after were so hypocritical. You rolled over and screwed in a bad-breathed, steamy way, maybe had breakfast, and then what? You couldn't really come right out with it: thanks for coming over; we got our rocks off; it wasn't good and wasn't bad. And thanks for giving me the gift of my supposed manhood for one more day. See you.

He finished typing the outline. He was due in Houston tomorrow.

Even though it was early April, Houston was tropical. He rented a car and drove the twenty miles to town. It was amazing, he thought, how all of industrial America had come to resemble northern New Jersey.

He left his car in the hands of the Galleria's doorman, who was drenched with sweat under the weight of an improbable beefeater's costume.

Upstairs in his room he called a lawyer friend who could be counted on to fill him in on the Gulf Coast-Petrex situation. They made a date for noon, the Texas lunching hour, at the Pizarro Club.

As always, Harrison was a little early. The place was already filling up. The usual group was assembled around the corner table in the bar. Harrison knew them all: most of them were in the oil business; all of them rich, the differences only of degree; there was Bob Marklett, a jolly ex-professor who was now with Allied Petrex; hunched and glowering over what would be his third glass of white wine was Dan Cashworthy, one of the big Houston movers and shakers. Cashworthy was a senior partner of the largest local accounting firm. He spent the tax dollars of the five or ten richest families in town. Cashworthy was the first stop for every promoter with an oil, real estate, or cattle deal. He was smart and made money for his clients, and this let him be evenhandedly unpleasant to everyone with whom he dealt.

"Hello, shithead," he greeted Harrison, "how's the poverty racket? Down here looking for a handout?"

This was old hat to Harrison. "Hello, Dan, always a pleasure to see you. You look well. That yellow skin tone's very becoming. Very chic." Harrison had known Dan Cashworthy for ten years and had liked him all that time, even from the moment of being introduced, when Cashworthy had drenched him with a shower of insults on learning he was associated with Verger. His irascibility suited Cashworthy; it set him apart in the back-slapping openness of Houston as much as the heavy tweeds he persisted in wearing right through the most miserable summers, when sweat was like a second suit.

Harrison ordered a Perrier. He drank as much as the next man, but he never drank at lunch and never in the air. Cashworthy motioned for another white wine. That's a lot of acid to load into an already acid psyche, thought Harrison.

The conversation at the table was easy and unfocused. Harrison was an expert listener. He was also adept at turning conversations to bring out whatever dope he might be after.

"How's the refinery business, Bob?" he said to Marklett.

Marklett had a master's degree from MIT and had spent a year in Cambridge doing basic physics at the Cavendish

Laboratory, but he affected the down-and-dirty accents of a tool pusher in Decker Prairie.

"Sure do look like we've cut a fat hog."

"I assume you're referring to your close friend Mr. Beauderon," Cashworthy interpolated. "I hear you're all going to the ranch together for a little shooting." Cashworthy hated Beauderon for his success and he envied Marklett the perks, not the least of which was the 10,000-acre hunting and fishing spread which Petrex had bought in Wyoming. It was a corporate asset no ordinary Petrex stockholder would ever be invited to enjoy.

"Now, now, Dan," said Marklett, who would get nasty only when he was drunk, which Harrison knew he limited to three or four times a week. "No point in gettin' riled. 'Sides, we got this feller Stavapoose or somethin' to deal with right now. A Greek. Niggers'd be easier to talk to. But I b'lieve we just goin' to eat his lunch for him!" There was a lot of confidence in the last statement. A great deal of certainty. Harrison was apprehensive.

"Don't tell me the old man wants to beat up on the Greek," said Cashworthy. Beauderon, the Petrex chairman, a man of grand designs, was known around Houston for brooking no interference with his schemes of conquest. Cashworthy may be a real prick, Harrison thought, but we do have one small thing in common: he hates this big-deal corporate thinking as much as I do.

"Jes' tickle him some," said Marklett. "Got to keep 'Merica for the 'Mericans." He looked up. "Hey, Sam, how y'all doin'?" Harrison's friend had come up to the table.

Cashworthy glared. "Must be lunch break for the ambulances." Another white wine was ordered. The talk turned, as it always seemed to these days, to Washington.

"I hear Oilco paid $42 spot for sweet crude last week."

"B'lieve I heard that myself."

"Piss all that money away to a bunch of fuckin' Ayrabs. Like to kill a man."

It was an old, tired litany. A couple of drinks more, and insurrection and invasion would be prescribed. But Washington was in the hands of the President's advisors. The President was a Cajun pig farmer from the canal country who'd sold the United States a simplistic agrarian vision which the war-weary nation had bought without kicking the tires. Knowing nothing about the sophistries of geopolitics and

(63)

megabusiness, he relied on a coterie of good old boys and high-priced, famous experts which accomplished nothing.

"Ought to kick them coonasses out. Shit!" Marklett managed to stretch the expletive into five syllables.

"Well you just figure out how, Bob," said Cashworthy. "And let me know. Unless something happens, we aren't going to have a probusiness administration again in our lifetime. Never." He returned to the frowning contemplation of his wineglass.

Harrison and his friend excused themselves. Over lunch, Harrison pumped him. Yes, the rumors had it that Petrex wanted the refinery cheap, would have bought it in the first place except that the Petrex chairman was goddamned if he was going to bail Wendell Bigler out. His wife hated Mrs. Bigler. Gulf Coast Energy was said to be dickering for the Niarchos yacht, which would dwarf anything Petrex had. That would be the last straw!

No, the loan wasn't really in default but it was right on the edge. Harrison's friend's firm represented one of the two Houston banks in the deal and they would sit tight. But Petrex could push pretty hard on Certified. Marklett was spending or rolling $150 million a week in money-market bank paper at the bank. Certified was the agent bank in the Petrex revolving credit, $630 million; Merriman was on the Petrex board and Beauderon was on Certified's blue-ribbon Trust Committee. So everyone in the group was looking at Certified.

The scenario would probably unfold this way: Certified would grab its Stavrapos deposits, forcing the other banks to foreclose themselves to perfect their security. Petrex would come skating in with an offer of fifty cents on the dollar for the banks' position *and* leave them with their collateral. This would get the banks out 100 percent when they sold off Stavrapos's other assets. Harrison's friend had heard that the ships were worth $40 to $50 million at salvage value. Any other assets? Not that he'd heard of.

Harrison thought: First Ohio is keeping its information on the New York real estate to itself. That was the advantage of being the agent bank; you got first look at everything.

After lunch Harrison went back to the hotel. He put in a call to Lausanne.

Stavrapos came through clearly. "Hello, David. You have news?"

"Good and bad, I'm afraid. I'm in Houston. I was in Cleveland Tuesday. They'll stick with us and so will the other banks. But the loan triggers in two weeks; it's keyed to your having a crude contract in hand. While the other banks will extend until you get it, everyone here feels that Certified may pull the plug on you. They may be in bed with Petrex."

"Certified, you say? And Petrex. Very interesting. And that's the main problem? Intelligence is so much more valuable than money."

"The plan is to call an all-hands bank meeting in Los Angeles in two or three weeks. Unless we can get a waiver or extension on the crude supply contract by telegram, which Certified probably won't go along with, we'll try to go into a stalling routine."

"It may not be necessary. Certified?" Stavrapos was thinking out loud across five thousand miles; more, if the distance to the satellite were calculated.

"When will you be back in New York, David? Tomorrow night? Excellent. I'll try to call you then. If not, leave word where you'll be over the weekend. Certified, you say? I'll be back to you. And thank you, David."

Harrison hung up and thought for a minute. Then he called Cleveland. Scroddin answered his own line.

"It's David Harrison here, Bev. On the Stavrapos thing. Listen, the talk down here is definitely that Certified and Petrex are in this thing together. My client showed me the loan agreement. The way I read it, the banks can jump on the collateral if the refinery doesn't have an ironclad contract, or commitment, for a crude supply by April 20. Is that right?"

"Essentially, unless we agree beforehand to extend. Which you don't think Certified will do, I take it. It makes no sense for them not to."

"Maybe yes, maybe no. Listen, the bank meeting is a week from tomorrow, right? OK, I don't think you may have to have that meeting. I don't want to say. I just have a feeling. But just to be sure, go ahead and reconfirm it. I'm working on a plan B, just in case. One more thing, is Certified the only bank looking queasy or do we have other woodpile inhabitants to worry about?"

Scroddin didn't think so. The loan was at five points over First Ohio's prime rate. And even if they didn't know it, the lending banks were up to their collective asses in hard collateral.

"Just Certified," said Scroddin. "That prick Merriman. He's dangerous when he gets into business. It was better

(65)

when he was trying to run Certified like a branch of the goddamn State Department. Expensive for his stockholders, but better for the banking community. Take care of yourself. Keep in touch."

There was something that bothered Harrison. Scroddin must have known that Certified and Petrex would be all over each other. So he was back dealing with the old game. Pretty much as he had figured. First Ohio, for all Scroddin's big talk, was still going to want to be asshole buddies with the Certified. The big banks scratched each other's backs. Buzz Tergass wasn't going to blow the whistle and ruin First Ohio's relationship with Certified just to save one of Scroddin's pet clients. It wasn't for First Ohio therefore to be the bad guy where Certified was concerned; Stavrapos might try to muscle the Certified, and if it was traced back to First Ohio . . . well, First Ohio might find itself like a poor kid at Christmas, outside in the snow, nose pressed against the glass, watching hungrily while, warm and prospering, Santa Certified passed out the prestige goodies: participations in the big international corporate syndications. If Stavrapos went down the tube, what the hell; the banks would still get 100 cents on the dollar.

So they needed someone to carry the news; an independent hired hand, a tale-bearer too small for someone like Certified to lean on, who could get the story to Stavrapos or out into the open. Otherwise, Stavrapos wouldn't hear until it was too late. It was like a guy whose wife was screwing around. Nobody'd tell him, least of all his closest friends. The high politics of banking.

Harrison smiled. This deal was done, one way or the other, whatever his role in it. Either Certified/Petrex was going to cream Stavrapos or the Greek would pull a rabbit out of his hat. That was it: no more; no less. He'd been hired as a conduit for information. But that's the way these deals got done. To save Stavrapos, no matter how, was worth $425,000, which Harrison was going to have earned, whether his work took ten minutes to do, or ten years. It really was an idiotic business.

The whole Stavrapos exercise merely confirmed what Verger had said to him years ago one morning while they were stuck in traffic on the East River Drive. "Investment banking isn't sorcery, David, and it isn't nuclear physics. A lot of people down here like to palm themselves off as a combination of Harry Houdini and Isaac Newton. That's a lot of bunk.

Sure, there's some technique in the business, like deciding between a stock and a bond or figuring out what the market's saying the pricing of a given deal should be. Once in a while someone employs a little imagination, but only once in a very great while. Ninety percent of the time, deals get done because one of two things happens: either someone knows someone else and that gets the skids greased, or someone just plain comes up with the most money. The best banker I ever knew did his biggest deals on the back of an envelope. The worst, which is to say the stupidest, never went anywhere without six M.B.A.s flunkying after him and a lot of fancy brochures; I think he closed two deals in thirty years on the Street. An ulcer killed him. I guess he got it worrying that the world might find out."

Nothing Harrison had seen since had dented the strength of Clare Verger's opinions.

He picked up the phone. There was kind of a cute girl who worked over at one of the drilling companies.

By eight o'clock, in a row house out near Memorial, he had her clothes off, and by eight-fifteen he was having the time of his life. Dinner would be somewhat postponed. These Texas girls might talk funny, he thought as he buried himself in her, but like catfish, they sure did make good eating.

At three in the morning, the telephone rang in Leslie Merriman's twenty-three-room apartment on Fifth Avenue. There was no instrument in Leslie Merriman's bedroom; he hardly expected to be awakened by anyone, *anyone,* in the middle of the night. So he was snuffling and rooting in his pillows when his wife's hand shook him awake. He was startled. She hadn't been in his bedroom in three years; he hadn't seen her undressed in nearly ten. That he slept alone would have surprised certain cynics within the Certified who maintained that Arthur Mismer occupied a straw mat on the floor at the foot of Merriman's bed.

"Leslie, it's the telephone. For you. Someone in Paris. They say it is absolutely urgent." Staring up at her through the mists of sleepiness, she looked like a large white prune, looming over him in her long-sleeved, ankle-length nightdress.

He got out of bed and made his stiff, heavy way to his study down the hall. He hadn't been summoned like this for a long time: not since his brother Frank had died under embarrassing circumstances in a Hong Kong massage parlor.

"Yes." He was peremptory, angry.

A French voice asked him not to quit the phone. The connection was surprisingly good. Probably a direct line. Then another voice. "Mr. Merriman? Please to hold for His Excellency."

The Minister came on the wire. "My dear Merriman, how are you?" It was as if they had just met strolling in the Luxembourg, not three a.m. on the transatlantic phone.

Merriman was instantly on his mettle. You couldn't sputter at the Minister.

"It's good to hear your voice, sir. What can I do for you? It's quite late here, so it will probably be morning before appropriate action on anything could be taken."

"Quite so. Well look, Merriman, something has come to our attention which I felt might best be brought to yours."

"Yes sir." There weren't six people in the world to whom Merriman said "sir"; Merrimans didn't call people "sir."

"There is a project outside Galveston, it used to be the Gulf Energy refinery, in which the Kingdom is greatly interested. Greatly interested." The Minister had the voice of an upperclass Englishman, only faintly perfumed with the unidentifiable cadences of his race.

"Yes sir. I believe I know the project."

"Well, we felt that Certified, as our principal American bank, should be aware of our enthusiasm for this venture in its present form, with M. Stavrapos as principal. We know we can count on you to share our opinion."

Merriman thought he was going to wet his pants. Only that morning he'd talked to the Petrex chairman. The deal was all set.

"Indeed you can, Your Excellency. Of course you realize that we do have existing relationships and obligations which we must look into; you would not wish us to contravene those? You would understand that?"

Merriman was supplicating. The Minister held out no comfort.

"That may well be. Of course we must each keep our own counsel. Decide which relationships to keep, which to discard. I look forward to seeing you soon." His meaning was as obvious as a bullwhip.

Merriman tried to pick up the thread of failing hope, but the line had gone dead at the other end. He fumbled in the drawer of the telephone stand for a Certified directory. There wasn't any. He dialed the only inside number he knew by heart.

"Arthur, it's the chairman. Please get the financial and money-desk people together and come over here. Yes. No, right now. Thank you, Arthur."

He put down the phone and stalked back to his bedroom, past his wife, whose staring hatred he failed to notice. He grumbled his way into his clothes.

In Paris, the Minister waited several minutes after replacing the receiver. Then he asked for a London number.

When Khafiq answered, the Minister said, "I have just spoken with Merriman. I waited until it was the middle of the night in New York—to impress him with the gravity of the matter. I think he grasps it."

"You are too generous, Excellency."

"I am pleased to do it for you, Ali. I owe you much. Of course, one can only do this sort of thing once in a very, very great while. This is a private matter of your own. It is no business of the Kingdom's."

He rang off. It was on to ten o'clock. He went to the broad windows which overlooked the Avenue Montaigne. Although he liked Paris best in October, it was foolish to quarrel with April. The shops below were unshuttering. It was a fine day.

He went back inside. The girl from Madame Blaise was still asleep in the big bed. He woke her gently. She was very pretty. He chatted with her while she dressed, took her home telephone number, and, when she was ready to leave, gave her a thousand-franc note.

Like Harrison, the Minister took care of his own details.

Merriman's dawn meeting lasted until midmorning. He hated dealing with his finance and money people. He had no head for figures. The money people knew it and treated him with the undisguised condescension which indispensable servants reserve for their masters.

The position was clear. Certified held $1,876,423,000 in deposits and other moneys from the Kingdom. Five hundred million overnight; the balance in certificates of deposit expiring in sixty to 180 days. The overnight deposits had been with the bank for three-and-a-half years. When the oil price had been raised in 1973, and the Kingdom became calculably wealthy, Merriman had gathered Mismer and some other staff people and headed for Dumar. The Certified's Yale-blue Gulfstream was practically the first of what became an armada bearing the captains of finance and industry, East and

West, all trying to get their hands on the Kingdom's new prosperity.

Merriman and the Minister hadn't really hit it off. The young Minister thought the banker stuffy and posturing. Merriman, whose colonial ideas came from Kipling, thought the young man, Minister or no, insufficiently respectful of his age, standing, and experience. Their conversation was a stilted exchange of pomposities and formalities. The money had to go either to London or New York. Frankfurt and Tokyo were closed to transfers of this size; the sheer amount would have inundated Zurich. Hong Kong wasn't ready yet. And Merriman's publicity machine had been skillful and energetic in disseminating an image of the Certified's chairman as the greatest banker in the world.

Which explained why, as the anxious little group caucused in Merriman's living room while the first sunlight touched Central Park, the Certified, ranked behind the U.S. Treasury, the Bank of England, and the Deutsche Bank, as the Kingdom's largest external depositary among roughly three hundred banks and thirty national treasuries.

"So what happens to us if they pull out the money?" Merriman asked his treasurer.

"They break us. So they won't. And Uncle Sam wouldn't let them. That sort of crap only happens in novels. Look at the Iranians." The treasurer was a tough Irishman who had been hired over from Gotham Bank to take the Certified out of the abacus era.

"Forget a run on the bank. If they close up the overnights, we can go to the window at the Fed. Never worry about depositors closing a bank, Mr. Merriman, worry about borrowers." It was a nasty allusion to Merriman's cherished Third World loans: the Uganda taconite syndication; the Fiji railroad debt; a hundred others, all as deep under water as Atlantis.

"But what they *can* do, Mr. Merriman, is drop us to number three!"

It was the unutterable, the unthinkable. Certified had long since been passed by the Bank of America, with its billions in savings accounts, as the largest bank in America. But it was still in second place, scant millions in deposits and capital ahead of Gotham Bank. Merriman loathed Rupert Ward, the articulate, outspoken man who ran Gotham. Ward stayed close to home. While Merriman was off globe-trotting, Ward honed a team of smart, presentable young men, armed them with lending authority, and sent them out across the countryside to steal Certified's customers. Ten years earlier, Certified had been the lead bank for nearly a quarter of the *Fortune* "500." Now they were down to 65 companies on that list; Gotham had *140*. A major shift in deposits to Gotham would put Ward's bank in the number two slot.

Ward never let up on Merriman. The same day that Merriman's picture was on the front page of the *Times*'s financial section, signing on a loan with some black colonel who would be dead of syphilis within a year, Ward's was on the front page, with Vernon Jordan, committing Gotham Bank to a billion-dollar tri-city ghetto redevelopment. "We lend to America and to Americans," was the Gotham Bank's slogan. The sight of their ad gave Merriman a rash on his left buttock.

Slipping back to number three ranking among U.S. banks. Every man in the room knew it was coming, someday. Soon. Why not accept it. But Merriman ran the bank; he owned the controlling stock interest.

"Well," said Merriman, "we simply cannot have that happen."

Rosmer Esmire Beauderon, "Rebo" to his friends and "His Imperial Majesty" to certain Houston wits who viewed his pharaonic style with some asperity, was the chairman of Allied Petrex. He was a wide, satisfied man with a blunt, studied country way of talking. A common Cajun birthright and an old friendship made him an intimate of the President of the United States. Although Beauderon looked and sounded like he should be tending a crossroads gas pump in Terrebonne Parish, he was important and influential and about as dumb as J. Paul Getty.

On this Monday morning, he sat under a forty-foot cathedral ceiling, staring out across the Houston basin, thinking himself master of all he could see from his sixty-eighth-floor office in the Petrex Tower. A block to the west, the hum of activity and the mantislike dance of the cranes and hoists celebrated the impending completion of Two Petrex Place. The I.M. Pei people were due in next week with the preliminary renderings for Number Three.

The buzzer on his desk sounded. "It's Mr. Merriman. From New York."

Merriman heard the Petrex chairman come heartily on the line. "Mornin', Les. How you?"

"Good morning, Rosmer. How's everything down there?"

"Real good. First quarter looks strong as dirt."

"Rosmer, we've been reviewing this refinery matter, you know, the Galveston refinery that you and I have been discussing in private. Well, my people think that since the other banks are inclined to be patient, we should go along."

There was silence on the other end. When he spoke again, there was an edge to the chairman's voice.

"You funnin' me, Les? Are you tellin' me that we have a problem? Are you tellin' me what I think you're tellin' me?"

"I'm afraid so, Rosmer. My people..."

"Your people, horseshit! Ain't nobody in that bank tells you what to do! I know you, Les; ain't nothin' scares you 'cept not gettin' your picture in the paper. We've spent half a million with Vinson, Elkins gettin' geared up to take over that refinery. We've canceled some other supply deals. And you're talkin' about 'your people'? My ass!"

Merriman winced at the outburst. He disliked profanity. "Rosmer, do be understanding. We go back a long ways together."

"Just up until about three minutes ago, Les. You have left me between the rock and the hard place. That's the trouble with you big international bankers. Some nigger in Bongo-Bongo tells you to jump and you ask, 'How high?' Well, as my pappy useta say, don't get mad, get even. I'll look for your resignation from my board in the mail. So long, Les."

"Listen, Rosmer..." Silence. Merriman's secretary came on. "I'm sorry, Mr. Merriman, the connection's been broken. Shall we try to get him back?"

"Don't bother, Miss Merit." Then he buzzed her back. "Oh, Miss Merit, I think you might destroy your record of my conversation with Mr. Beauderon."

Three hours later, Merriman took a call from the executive vice president who ran the World Corporations Division.

"Les, the goddamnedest thing has happened. We just got a call from Houston. Petrex is dumping us as the agent on the revolver; they're giving it to First Houston City."

Merriman was relieved. At least it wasn't Gotham.

"Any reason?"

"None given. What's your guess?"

Merriman could think pretty fast when his self-esteem was on the line. "It must be that new financial officer. He has other loyalties. Of course, I will certainly resign from the Petrex board in view of this. I've too many boards as it is; I believe I've missed the last three Petrex meetings."

(72)

Miss Merit, listening in and taking it down, could have added: But not the Petrex junket to Persepolis or the shooting trip to Inverurie.

Merriman closed the conversation. "Of course, it's bad publicity for the bank. Who's the officer on the account? Oh yes? Well, he's promising. Normally, losing an account like this would be grounds for dismissal, but let's make an exception here. Transfer him to Kampala."

Leslie Merriman was, if anything, a forgiving man.

6 The morning brought plenty of good news to Harrison.

There was a letter from Hellenic Equities N.V. enclosing a check for $175,000. Harrison sent it on to his accountant with a hand-written note to put it in a money-market fund; that would take care of Uncle Sam. There was a letter from Lausanne, headed SocFinHellas A.G., confirming transfer of SF 428,375 to Harrison's account (31076) at Banque Commerçante, Geneva. There was a cable from his old friend Marc-Antoine Marteau, who ran the Commerçante's investment side: VAST SUM ARRIVED. DO YOU WISH IT INVESTED OR SHALL I PUT IT AGAINST YOUR ACCOUNT MADAME BLAISE PARIS? REPLY EARLIEST. There had been a phone call from Stavrapos, who was effusive: the first tanker from the Emirates was due to offload 100,000 tons of crude oil at New Orleans in the morning; it would be swapped with Amerada-Hess for a like amount to be delivered in Galveston; there was much to talk about; could Harrison join him and friends for a cruise to Hydra and Mykonos for Greek Easter?

Harrison had said yes. He never liked to leave New York for long, but he wasn't in love at the moment and there was money in the bank, so why not? He would meet Stavrapos et al. the following week in the resort town of Vouliagmeni, outside Athens.

After he finished with Stavrapos, he dialed Geneva. It would be four in the afternoon there. The odds were good that Marc-Antoine would be back from lunch, which was generally the most important and absorbing business of his day. Marc-Antoine lived high off the Commerçante hog. It wasn't strictly necessary; his mother had been a heavy-machinery princess from Zug. "That man," a client had once observed to Harrison while watching Marc-Antoine luxuriate in a six-inch Partagas and a private reserve pear brandy, "is to expense accounts what Horowitz is to piano playing."

The son of a French father of authentic, if blemished, pedigree, Marc-Antoine's few scruples were strongly held. That was his best point, Harrison thought. And his father had given him the greatest gift French fathers can bestow: an easy charm which made an obsession with women fruitful.

Harrison and Marc-Antoine went back twenty years. When Harrison left Verger, he had plenty of offers from other investment banking firms. He wanted a change of pace and style, however, so he took up an offer to go to Paris for Mitchener, Suydam, the last of the big American private banks.

There wasn't much to do in the way of a day's work at The Mitch, as the bank was known to its irreverent younger employees. The business consisted principally of taking in interest-free deposits from widows and fiduciaries reassured by the ironlike solidity of the firm and its partners. "Solid" was the measure of all virtue around The Mitch. If a man was "solid," and he could learn to speak as if his mouth was full of oatmeal, and he had thirty years' staying power, chances were that he would make partner.

It was considered vulgar to discuss business at The Mitch. Conversation around the twenty-foot George III table in the partners' dining room tended to devolve upon salmon fishing on the Restigouche, lengthy recapitulations of rounds of golf, and the chances of Princeton against Yale.

At the head of the table sat Carstairs Mitchener, to whose ancestor Sir Bromwell Mitchener an indebted Charles II had conveyed half of what was now Westchester County. Carstairs Mitchener, *primus inter pares,* was a professional curmudgeon whose misogyny was fueled by a burning hatred of Franklin D. Roosevelt, alive or dead. He humphed and garrumphed his way along the firm's corridors, glaring at everyone he encountered. "It's really a contradiction in terms," Harrison once told one of his colleagues, "for a personal service business like ours to be run by a misanthrope." But the partners were rich—enviably so.

"What we do," Harrison had explained one night to a girl at Giovanni's, "is a terrific racket. We take in these deposits and put them into tax-exempt bonds which pay interest. That's what the partners pocket. It works out to about $150,000 a man on average; all tax-free."

"Now, come on, David," the girl had said, "there must be someone there who does something. I know *you* don't."

He chose to overlook her sarcasm. "Actually," he said conspiratorially, "you're right. Down in the basement, in a locked room, there are five or six elderly gentlemen, naked except for green eyeshades and sleeve garters, who keep the records and pick out the choice bonds. They're fed three times a week on scraps from the partners' table." It might have been true.

The Mitch's Paris office was located in a suite of rooms overlooking the Place Vendôme. Although for years it had existed principally to supply the bank's clients and partners with whatever they required, from cashed checks to all-male *partouses*, when Harrison got there the fun and games of the mid-sixties Eurobond explosion were just beginning, and The Mitch had jumped in with both Peal-clad feet. That was when he met Marc-Antoine. The game consisted of peddling the bonds of American corporations to European holders of dollars who wanted in on the big action in New York.

Harrison had been in Paris about six weeks. He'd been lucky enough to take over the key to a small flat high up on the Île St. Louis. In the mornings he looked back up the Seine to the sun spreading across the Louvre, over the tops of the trees which bordered the riverside. It took him fifteen minutes to walk to the office, although he shared the use of a beaten-up Citroën for weekend excursions to Fontainebleau or Vincennes. He loved to walk in the mornings through the awakening liveliness of the city, to come home at dusk with the lights coming up in the ornate iron streetlamps. A helpful friend had given him the name of a handsome blonde girl from Philadelphia who worked in the Guaranty office in the Rue de Rivoli. They were soon spending long hours in bed, practicing acrobatics of a kind which he found surprising for a Quaker lady. Best of all, in those days, unlike every other large city he knew, Paris smelled wonderful: fresh bread, flowers, the perfume of pretty girls in thin dresses, paint, old sandstone. Beaujolais was two dollars a bottle. The world was his oyster.

The Paris manager was a battle-weary Mitchener cousin who spent most of his day with his head under the Riesener table, which served him as a desk, carrying on muttered, apologetic conversations with his tiresome mistress in Neuilly. One morning he signaled Harrison to come into his office.

There was a man sitting across from the manager who rose and turned as Harrison came in. He looked something like an Afghan hound: long, narrow, drooping features, everything turned down; a highstrung, highbred mournfulness accentuated by a Gauloise which drooped so low from his lips that it threatened to spill ash on his necktie. Harrison judged him to be in his late forties, almost ten years older than himself.

"David," said the manager, "this is Marc-Antoine Marteau, managing director of the Banque Commerçante, in Geneva." The two men shook hands. Harrison sat down in the empty armchair; the pair were said to have belonged at one time to Talleyrand and later to Sarah Bernhardt.

Marteau, explained the manager, had proposed a reciprocal arrangement whereby his bank would take The Mitch's Eurobond participations off its hands, for a 60 percent piece of the underwriting commissions.

"After all," said the manager, "we can't sell the goddamn things. New York keeps going in these deals to suck up to Morgan and Lehman but we get stuck with the bonds to place. This way, we keep a piece of the action, the bonds get placed, and New York gets off my rear end."

"Where do *you* place the bonds?" Harrison had asked Marc-Antoine.

"Why, we place them in our discretionary accounts, of course. They never notice."

"I see." Later, Harrison was to hear the same investment philosophy expressed more succinctly by a famous New York money manager: "You see this new issue, Dave. That's the sort of speculative shit I buy only for widows and orphans."

The manager spoke up. "Anyway, David, you've had investment banking experience, so I'm putting this in your lap. You can work out the details with Marc-Antoine. Leave me to deal with the lost Pekingese of our clients and the infected peckers of our partners." The manager's phone buzzed. It was his private line to his mistress. He shooed the other men out of his office. As he picked up the receiver, the expression on his face suggested what Job might have felt on being informed that there were some tribulations waiting in the anteroom.

"How about some lunch?" said Marc-Antoine. Like most Frenchmen of a certain class, he dressed like an English milord off for a day's racing. His suit was London-cut of a flannel heavy enough to stop a bullet. He carried a rolled umbrella with which he emphasized his gestures. Without waiting for Harrison to answer, he made for the door, saying over his shoulder, "Ask your girl to telephone Maxim's and book a table in my name."

Outside, it was cold and January-damp. The morning's rainy snow had stopped, but there were still traces of gray slush in the gutters. It was a drab time of year, especially in Paris. The air was heavy with mist, almost a drizzle, the skies a shade darker gray than the pavement; Marc-Antoine's eternal cigarette left sullen little twists of smoke skulking in the air as the two men strolled along the Rue Royale.

Then, and over lunch, they had discovered they had much in common. Marc-Antoine had been at Harvard. He knew a great many people at Verger; he had worked there one summer. He knew about books, he knew about paintings, and by God he knew about food. And wine.

Lunch was a production. Everyone at Maxim's knew Marc-Antoine. Coats and umbrellas were borne away unctuously; heels clicked like castanets. They were ushered to a good table in the first room. Marc-Antoine called for nonbubbling *champagne nature* and Belon oysters. Then lamb grilled with rosemary, thin green beans drenched in butter, and, to drink, a '55 Cos d'Estournel that God Himself might have made. Next, hard little goat cheeses. Sherbet. Coffee. A trembling pile of boxes of Havana cigars—Punch, Larranaga, Upmann, Romeo y Julieta—was brought to the table. Marc-Antoine chose one imperiously.

Over a glorious old cognac, he had looked at his new, younger friend with a dead seriousness of purpose. "Now," he declared, "Girls. Right?" The question was purely rhetorical.

Harrison's was not. "Girls? Who?"

"From Blaise, of course." Marc-Antoine's sophisticated dismissal of Harrison's naïveté was awesome.

"Blaise?"

"My dear young David. If you are going to be involved in the Eurobond market, as it seems you are, an acquaintance with Madame Blaise and her girls is more essential than a Harvard or Wharton M.B.A."

"Here," he had said, taking out a Hermes datebook, "put down this number. BALzac 2945. It is more indispensable in this business than a knowledge of interest rates."

Marc-Antoine had explained that Madame Blaise was indisputably the free world's classiest provider of paid female companionship. She counted the richest Greeks, Arabs, Japanese, and Texans among her clients. She had a soft spot—

not as to price; after all, she *was* French—for professional men: lawyers, bankers, investment types. She got valuable free advice from them. She was without peer. "You can always tell a girl from Blaise," Mark-Antoine had said to Harrison, "she'll be better looking, better dressed, better educated, and have better manners and conversation than any so-called lady in the room."

It was a bold statement, but it wore. Harrison had tested it extensively and expensively over the fifteen years which followed that first lunch at Maxim's, and Marc-Antoine had been proven right. The funny thing was, he often thought, that sex with a Blaise girl was the least satisfactory part of the deal. As ever, Marc-Antoine had an answer.

"My dear boy, after Blaise has taught a girl about hair, clothes, conversation, posture, she's too exhausted to learn much about screwing. So it's always the same: mechanical blow job, turn you over, a great deal of writhing and moaning, and, four minutes precisely into the act, if you can last that long or haven't passed out, a lot of breathless *'tu me fais jouillir, tu me fais jouillir....'* My dear David, the point of Blaise is to make us conscious that women can be intelligent, well mannered, *and* good looking. All at once. After that, who needs sex?"

So, after draining the dregs of the *fine,* Harrison had found himself in an apartment on the far side of the Etoile, on the Avenue Foch, playing bedroom poker with Marc-Antoine and two of the most stylish, attractive girls he'd ever seen. Later, when a bottle of Roederer Cristal had been produced from the refrigerator, the four of them sat around in the living room, stark naked, laughing and chatting in the friendliest, most amiable fashion.

"I had a Greek last night. I'm so sore," said Janine, patting her rear. "And an Arab the night before that. They smell so pffft...and they don't tip," said Laurence.

"What do you expect," said Marc-Antoine, "they don't have any money. The Greeks make more carrying the oil than the Arabs do selling it. I feel sorry for those Arab kids. They always look poor. They have to save their allowances to call Blaise."

And that was the beginning of a real friendship between the two men. It turned out that they spent a lot of time together in those early days. The Eurodollar market was exploding. There were $90 billion held overseas; ten years later, the figure would be $400 billion to $600 billion, Washington guessed. *Guessed?* No wonder the dollar would sink like a stone, if the guys that ran the mint, which theoretically printed the money, couldn't come within $200 billion—$200 *billion*—of the amount of money in circulation. The fact was, the big New York and London banks and their satellites and affiliates were printing their own money. "Just like southern towns in the Civil War," Harrison was to say, "or like those hundred-lira notes you give at the tolls in Italy."

All that money sloshing around had attracted flies. Harrison and Marc-Antoine would sit in the bar at the Richemond in Geneva, or at the Vier Jahreszeiten in Munich, or Savini's in Milan, watching the search-and-destroy squads of the big American investment banking houses whirl into town, promoting paper which became more questionable in quality with each passing month. It was fat city. Champagne flowed like water. Caviar went down like hamburger. The whole deal was summarized perfectly one evening in Zurich, when Harrison and Marc-Antoine were dining at the Kronehalle. With an annunciatory cry of relief and recognition, they were joined by a London merchant banker they knew and liked. He was making a bond-selling tour in tandem with a self-advertised "dynamic" young partner of a big Wall Street house.

"My God, I can't take much more of this," he had said, mopping a florid, exhausted brow. "This man is incredible. This will be the first corporate offering where the proceeds"—it was a $30 million bond issue—"will be used *in toto* to defray the expenses of the managing underwriter. D'you know. He's just gone to arrange for three—*three*—girls from Madame Blaise to meet us tomorrow in Turin. I may die!" It was a happy lament.

All of this was reminiscence. The phone stopped crackling and popping. A musical voice answered and put him through to Marc-Antoine.

"Hello. David?" There was a pause. Harrison knew what had happened. Marc-Antoine had gotten his cigarette tangled with the cord. "Hello, hello?"

The familiar voice came on the line again. *"Bonjour, mon petit. Comment vas-tu?"* The usual pleasantries. Repeated formalities. Europeans expected it.

"I got your cable. How is Blaise?"

"I really can't say. I heard that Giscard tried to close her up, but the Chamber of Deputies put a stop to that. You saw that one of her girls, you remember Claudine, is now a duchess?"

"I sure did. I read about it in *Time*. Do you think she still works on the side? It'd be amusing to bang her under all those ducal Gainsboroughs. I hear he's the most awful shit."

"But absolutely. Are you coming this way soon? With all this money, you don't have to fly Laker. What do you want me to do with it? My brother and I have an interesting possibility in Basel: an office building. It could be something nice in a tax sense."

Harrison hesitated. Friendship with the French, even Marc-Antoine, had its price. Theirs.

"Marc-Antoine, for the moment I think I'll stay liquid. These are uncertain times, but I may have something brewing. Stick it in one of your foreign exchange baskets." Nothing was brewing, but Harrison and Marc-Antoine, like adolescents, liked to tease each other with hints of big nonexistent coups. It was one of the peculiar traits of their transatlantic friendship, this business of trying to unsettle rather than comfort a friend.

"Look," Harrison continued, "I have to go to Greece next week. After that, I may be able to get your way. You going to be around?"

To get even, Marc-Antoine riposted, "Well, I may have to go to Kuwait." That was standard. "Going to Kuwait" was the banking equivalent of "having tea with the Queen."

"Let's play it by ear, then. I'll call and see what your plans are. *Ciao*." Harrison hung up. He knew, with some satisfaction, that the arrival in his account of a quarter of a million dollars had ruined Marc-Antoine's day. It gave him an unexplainable satisfaction. But maybe, these days, that was what friends were for.

He dialed TWA and booked a flight on the following Friday for Athens.

As the plane wheeled for its final approach into Athens Airport, Harrison rubbed the sleep from his eyes. He was a lucky traveler. He slept on airplanes more soundly than in his own bed; Boeing was a more dependable soporific than Nembutal.

Outside, it was a brilliant day. Harrison had never been in the deep, subequatorial tropics, but it had always seemed to him that the sun burned brightest and clearest on the Ionian Sea. Out the window, Mount Olympus baked peacefully: the Parthenon and the Erechtheum dominated the landscape, which slid smoothly through the cluster of Athens and the Piraeus to the sea. Only from the air, he thought, did you get a real sense of the grandeur of great cities. On the ground you were confronted with honking traffic and harrowing, bumping crowds of people. Up here, whether Athens, or Washington, with the geometry of L'Enfant's city laid out plain, or coming into London, with Windsor Castle lording it over the checkered landscape and then the Thames and its bridges and then Saint Paul's, you got a sense of the great scheme of things. No cripples or trucks or crowds.

He got through Customs quickly. Outside, in the main hall, he saw a shirtsleeved man with a cardboard sign: M. HARSON. He identified himself. His luggage was fetched and he was led outside to a black Mercedes station wagon. On the back seat was a bucket with an ice-cooled bottle of Dom Pérignon and an envelope. The note inside said: *"Dear David. You will want some sleep. A room has been reserved for you at the Astir Palace. We have gone on a picnic to Aegina. We will meet tonight in the bar at eight. Welcome."* It was signed "Theo."

With a great deal of horn-blowing, the station wagon took Harrison to Vouliagmeni. It was a resort about ten miles south of the airport, on the coast. Harrison had been there before. It was the holiday gathering place of the second-class rich Greeks; the biggest hitters had their own islands.

The Astir Palace dominated the cup of the bay. It was an anonymous modern hotel; its replicas could be found in Tulsa, Tripoli, or Bogotá. The stepped hills which encircled the hotel were crammed with bungalows which would have disgraced the meanest Bulgarian railroad hostel; they rented for $500 a day.

He dozed and read most of the day. When he awoke at seven-thirty, the ancient clay hills on the far side of the now quiet harbor glowed dull red in the sunset. It was a color that suggested antiquity beyond experience and imagining. The color of Greek vases. For a moment he stood on the balcony. It was really quite beautiful. The air was cool. The strings of lights on the yachts parked below reminded him of Park Avenue at Christmas.

Showered and changed, he went downstairs. He took his vodka and tonic to a table near a window. He had no time for nature. The daily evening parade of the wives of the sojourning Argonauts to the hotel safe was in full swing.

Freshly bedecked with jewels, the ladies positioned themselves at tables, awaiting their bustling husbands. These, Harrison knew, were doubtless busy sending telexes. Or telephoning shipping agents in Piraeus. The Greeks rose late and worked late.

"David. So nice to have you here."

It was Stavrapos. He was at the head of a small phalanx of people. "David, this is our party. Mr. Harrison, Mlle. duTronc; my cousin, Miss Aleta Pounonis; M. Khafiq." Hands were shaken; they settled themselves at the table and ordered drinks.

Harrison sorted them out mentally. Miss duTronc looked to be a Blaise girl; he could determine that later; he knew that there *was* a Mme. Stavrapos somewhere, but he assumed her to be exiled for the duration. Mlle. duTronc was wearing a raw pearl pendant the size of an egg. Harrison guessed she was *with* Stavrapos. Which meant that Miss Pounonis was for him. She was a slender, dark girl with serious, shy eyes. Stavrapos's cousin. Stavrapos was matchmaking. As for Khafiq, that was a name he knew. It was Harrison's business, in his line of work, to know who the real movers and shakers were. So this epicene, sallow little man, uncomfortable in his snappy resort clothes, was the famous Khafiq. What was it his friend who covered the Middle East for Bache had said: "When they shit out there, Khafiq chooses the color."

They dined under fishnets at a popular restaurant up the road. Small, fried fish; barbecued lamb; retsina to drown in. It was a noisy place. Periodically, one table or another rose and smashed plates on the stone floor. He tried small talk with Miss Pounonis. It was difficult, with all the noise, but he ascertained that she had gone to Smith and had some kind of job at the National Museum. She would be coming to New York that fall with a big touring exhibition of classical sculpture. They danced. She pushed herself diligently against him but he was too tired and noise-deadened to respond.

When they returned to the table for dessert, there was a man standing on Harrison's plate of baklava. Harrison looked questioningly at Stavrapos. The Greek leaned across and whispered: "Don't mind him. He's a younger son. Here they count for nothing. He lives in London and writes a stupid gossip column. He comes back here every Easter and tries to embarrass his father." Stavrapos reached up and tugged at the dancing legs. *"Hola,* Mati, do you mind?"

It was three in the morning when they returned to the

hotel. In the lobby, the small group paused while Stavrapos gave directions for the next morning. "The launch will be at the dock at ten to take you out to the *Zephiros*. Then we sail. Costa will take care of your luggage." He grabbed Mlle. duTronc possessively and headed for the elevators. The rest followed.

In the corridor, Harrison said goodnight to Miss Pounonis. She looked sorrowful.

Before turning in, Harrison stood on the balcony. The lights on the yachts were mostly turned off, except where a launch carried a late party of revelers to bed. He looked straight down, where the hotel lobby opened onto terraced gardens. A small figure was standing there, smoking a cigarette. Khafiq. Then, from the shadows, another figure materialized: lissome, in a striped sailor's shirt. The two figures spoke briefly, then vanished into the dark together, down the walkway which led to the small beach.

Very interesting, thought Harrison.

He got into bed and turned off the light. He fell asleep immediately, into a deep sleep, untroubled by dreams. So deep that he never heard Miss Pounonis's gentle, uncertain knocking at the door which connected their rooms.

7   Harrison would always remember it as a very pleasant interlude. Stavrapos's yacht, the *Zephiros*, was designed for comfort and administered entirely for the well-being of its passengers. It chugged along, smooth, slow, and easy. "I leave speed to my cousins," said Stavrapos, "who go to Sardinia and try to match knots with the Aga Khan." The staterooms were large and the beds comfortable. The showers and toilets functioned flawlessly. The chef, freed from the constraints of Stavrapos's "American" persona, worked daily miracles with fresh fish and lamb and eggplant.

The boat took a wide wallowing arc through the Aegean, calling first at Hydra, where the ship's company dined in the port to bouzouki music under a starlit sky that Harrison thought was the clearest he'd ever seen. They shopped for silver and shawls. This early in the year, the things were reasonable. The Swedes and Germans would be along later to run the prices up. They sat in cafés, drinking raki and great gulps of sweet coffee. The days were long, sunny, and idle. It was the best time of the year for Greece. Later the *Meltemi*, the Greek version of the despondent winds which seem to plague sea-bordered countries, would sweep down from the north and the east.

It was cinematically, irresistibly romantic. On the third night out, randy with *ouzo* and bouzouki music, Harrison knocked at Miss Pounonis's stateroom. She took him gladly. Although she was enthusiastic, she made love in a clumsy, diligent way, but she had a thick, mossy growth between her legs, nice bosoms, and she groaned and murmured with a volume that the creaking rocking of the anchored yacht barely drowned. Harrison enjoyed her noisy raptures. "After all," he had been advised by his late father, who was something of a philosopher in matters of the flesh, "fucking isn't polite dinner table conversation. One has to get down and get after it!"

And there were other dividends of a sexual sort. One afternoon, when Stavrapos and his cousin had gone ashore to pay a courtesy call on a relative in the hills above the port, Harrison, returning to his stateroom for a book, encountered Mlle. duTronc in the passageway. The yacht was quiet. He was very hung over from a late tavern night. She was wearing a short tennis skirt; her legs seemed endless. It was a boiling day and there had been a long, liquid lunch. A look sufficed. He got her up against the bulkhead and pulled down her shorts. He was rockhard and she was soaking wet. He entered her easily. She came the instant he was in; thirty seconds later, she came again, this time in response to him. He had never before been so precisely poised on the pinpoint where pain and pleasure meet. Sweat poured from him. Afterward, she pulled up her shorts, kissed him softly on the cheek, and continued to the stateroom she shared with Stavrapos. He was shaking. He never touched her again, or saw her after the cruise.

Khafiq was an enigma. He stayed distanced from the group; odd man out. Conversation was, anyway, nonchalant and superficial. The men discussed the state of the world, as men will. Nothing profound surfaced. There was always so much to drink and eat and then another excursion, shopping trip, picnic, to be planned and done. In the evenings, after dinner, on Hydra and then on Mykonos, Khafiq vanished into the backstreets of the port. The launch, hitched to the *Zephiros* like a ponycart, idled through the night in the harbors, awaiting Khafiq's dawn return to the quai. He was always there at breakfast. It was as if the yacht contained two separate solar systems: Khafiq's and the rest. They touched only tangentially.

They celebrated Greek Easter in Mykonos. Whitewashed city; like a whited sepulcher, thought Harrison. The Orthodox service in the sailors' church was tremendously moving. The women, veiled and dressed in black, and the men stiff and uncomfortable in Sunday suits, rough material on suntough skin, praying while the plainsong filled the apse. *"O, ces voix d'enfants chantent dans la coupole,"* quoted Harrison to himself, trying to follow the ceremony. Afterward, the chief priest, all dignity in his high black hat and robes, joined them for a feast-day lunch and got sweetly drunk on the endless flow of retsina and raki which Stavrapos commanded. "You see," he told Harrison, "I have no family island, unlike the Goulandrises, for example, who all come from Andros. So I have adopted Mykonos." He turned and toasted the priest.

In the afternoon, they went down to Butterfly Beach for a swim and a lie in the sun. A few early-vacationing blondes were there; Lufthansa and SAS stewardesses, Stavrapos speculated. They paraded up and down, displaying bare, high breasts over monokinis fringed with peekings of blonde pubic hair. It was more than Harrison could stand. Suggesting a swim, he followed Miss Pounonis into the water. She had the same thoughts; when they were shoulder deep, away from shore, he took off the bottom of her bikini; she wrapped her legs around him and they made love below the surface, trying above the surface to maintain an attitude of unconnected, if intimate, conversation.

The *Zephiros* turned north again after ten days. Stavrapos ordered a diversion to Spetsai; he had amusing friends near there, in Porto Heli across the channel, and Spetsai was the last decent shopping port before Athens.

On a hot afternoon, Stavrapos took the ladies off on a shopping expedition. Neither Harrison nor Khafiq could face one more perspiring teatime waiting out the plunder of another island's shops, so they found themselves together on the stern of the *Zephiros* under the awning, sipping iced tea. It was the first time they had been alone together.

A pleasant breeze off the water mitigated the heat; on the far western horizon, the old Niarchos yacht *Creole* could be seen beating toward Coronis under a cloudless sky.

Khafiq had been favorably impressed with Harrison.

Quite apart from Stavrapos's adulatory recitation of the Petrex affair, he liked what he had heard over the tables of port cafés from Hydra to Mykonos. The conversations had generally been meandering and inconclusive. But the younger man had displayed a mordant asperity which struck a sympathetic chord in Khafiq. They shared a common sense that their talents, so obvious to them, had been compromised or circumscribed by the fatuousness or envy of the men in the big offices. Harrison in particular seemed to divide his dislike almost equally between the doddering Eastern praetorians who claimed to have inherited the right to govern America and the incompetent, unlettered bumpkins to whom an exhausted, unhappy electorate had most recently conveyed that right.

Sipping his tea as he looked over to the wooded escarpments of the small isle of Spetsopoúla, Harrison remarked, "It's very nice to be here, away from the miserable world we work in."

"Ah, but even that must have its moments," said Khafiq. "My friend Theo tells me you were most helpful to him in the Galveston matter. It was an affair in which I too had an interest and was happily able to have been of some small service."

So, thought Harrison, this was Stavrapos's "one other," the shadowy figure who delivered the crude contract with the Emirates. Small service indeed.

"You're very kind," he said to Khafiq, "and so is Theo. I don't want to claim too much credit; you know these kinds of transactions. Generally, all that's needed is a push here and a suggestion there, a touch of pressure to correct some unfortunate perceptions. Frankly, I didn't even do that. What I did do was to carry the news from Aix to Ghent. Greater powers than mine took over from there."

He hoped he sounded realistic about his role in things. In business, he knew, realism was usually equated with modesty, and modesty was much esteemed by the men who had the really big business to give out. He knew enough about Khafiq to put him in that class.

"Well, my young friend—may I call you David?—I'm afraid we're living in a world where perceptions have come to count more than facts and self-indulgence has utterly taken over. Nowhere more so that in the States, I fear."

Khafiq's language and diction were surgically precise. He measured each word as if he were counting beads. It was another aspect of a general punctiliousness that Harrison had recognized as distinguishing Khafiq. The man was all of a piece: finely groomed and equally finely tuned. In all the week they had been together, Khafiq had never been less than meticulously turned out. It was true of him in every aspect, Harrison now saw. Yet, somehow, there was nothing about Khafiq that seemed rarefied or epicene. He was a lapidary presence, cut and polished from matter as shiny and obdurate as a gemstone.

"Regretfully, I'd have to agree with you. But the disease seems to be sweeping the world."

"I'm afraid so. Even in my country, where we have always taken a longer view of things. Probably as the result of living in the desert, where the tracks and contours change with the wind, but one must always find his way back to the oasis. One learns very early to rely on fixed things: a star; an old tree; a stone too heavy to be shifted by the wind."

"I can imagine how confusing the general aimlessness must be to your people. We've done a first-rate job of infecting the world with it. And, of course, we've had the leadership to get the job done right. Look at the sequence of some of our most recent presidents: a con man, a crook, a boob, and a yokel." He made no effort to disguise either his sarcasm or his bitterness.

"David, I can sympathize. After all, look at what has happened to us. We hold more dollars than any single entity, political or otherwise, in the world. For a hundred years we have been hectored by our English and European teachers that a strong currency is the cornerstone of a free society. We would decimate our population rather than let the piaster fall a fraction of a percent in the exchange markets. But your government fuddles around, and it has cost us over $20 billion in the value of our holdings. Think of that, David—$20 billion! One could found a new nation with such a sum."

"How well do you know America, Mr. Khafiq?"

"Not well at all, I must confess. I've been to New York several times, but that's certainly not the same thing as America. Even my New Yorker friends will admit it; they always have, although today they do it with shame, while a dozen years ago they'd have made the same statement with pride. No, David, I'm afraid that most of what I know of your country comes through the eyes of one of my countrymen. Don't misconstrue me, however. It's a pair of eyes I trust absolutely."

He was referring to the Minister. As the Minister had noted when they had last dined together in London, it was almost thirty years since he and Khafiq had first met.

He recalled being summoned into the chairman's office at Wellington.

"Look here, Khafiq," said Sir James, "how long've you been with us? Five years? Good. Time for you to try your hand with the younger generation."

A quarter of an hour later, he had left the chairman's office, with its oak furniture and silver-framed photographs and the tall, glaring Raeburn portrait of the bank's founder, charged with providing the better part of a weekend's entertainment for two young princes from the Kingdom, brothers, who would be driven down from Harrow on the Saturday noon.

"Difficult business, this sort of entertainment," rumbled Sir James in parting. His own weekends were devoted to killing things. "But do your best. They say the older boy's quite bright. Gather the younger's a perfect little rat."

Surmising that his normal diversions would hardly suit his young guests, despite what was said to go on in the dark corners of the great public schools, Khafiq had emptied his house of his usual crowd.

"Be a good boy, Johnny," he had said, handing a ten-pound note to his current favorite. "Go and have a good time in Wardour Street. I shall be frightfully jealous, but there it is. I'll see you Sunday." Khafiq had taught himself to speak like a Guards officer. It was fitting; he spent a good deal of time among the enlisted men.

"Not very gentlemanly," Sir James had remarked in the bar at Bratt's, "the way my man Khafiq *will* insist on having it off with other ranks."

He had been waiting on the porch, under a watercolor March sky, when the Embassy Rover pulled up in St. John's Wood and the two young princes got out. They were both very tentative; nervous and uncomfortably out of place in their stiff school collars. Khafiq had some idea of what they were going through. Wherever they went, the Arabs stood at the bottom of the list, snubbed at a level below patronization. The cruelty to each other of boys in schools is terrifying, Khafiq had thought at the time. But then he had thought: They're probably better off at Harrow, being beaten and buggered and cold-showered without prejudice than trying to hold up their shabby end at Rosey or some other fancy Swiss school where wealth and its display counted so much. The young men who "came out" from the Kingdom in those days, royal family or not, didn't have the pocket money to throw around. Not like the Greeks, for example, with their huge gold Rolexes flopping from buzzard-thin adolescent wrists; or the young Africans, who dressed like pimps and flashed teeth embedded with gold and diamonds.

It was ironical, he thought now, that all that Greek money came from carrying Arab oil. It paid for this, he reflected, looking from the stern of the *Zephiros* across the sparkling afternoon water to the pleasant town of Spetsai. There were three other yachts, smaller and sleeker, moored in the channel.

The weekend long ago had proved more pleasant than he had expected. True, the younger boy, who was fourteen, had gotten into the Port after Sunday lunch and had been sick all over the better guest bedroom. He was a scamp, all charm and bright eyes, so that even his most devastating misbehavior seemed forgivable. Khafiq had marked him as someone who would be in trouble or mischief all his life, which might not be a long one.

The older boy had been a different matter, however. He was extremely self-contained, with instinctive good manners and consideration, the rarest of natural blessings and unheard of in the Middle East. He was thoughtful, a quality also virtually unknown among younger Arabs. He described his days at Harrow without rancor, whereas his younger brother braggingly swore vengeance of a painful and obscene sort on the older boys who fagged him.

"This boy will amount to something important," Khafiq had reported to Sir James the following Monday. "He behaves like a true prince. He is not merely a bedouin with some money. We should keep an eye on him and be helpful to him. He will matter some day."

Sir James had written the princes' father, who was a nephew of the old King, and arranged for the boy to spend the summer at Wellington, learning something of finance. Khafiq took him under his wing socially. There was no sexual interplay between the two; their relationship was unbitched and productive. "Strange," said Sir James at his club, "my man Khafiq would bugger a snake if it gave him a chance. But not with this one. Funny people, these ponces; but then my wrangler at Oxford always swore that old Socrates never put it in Plato's ruddy bum."

Between Sir James and Khafiq, the young prince had been well tended. He was guided through the British Museum and the directors' floor at Anglo; he lunched regularly at Wellington, in the company of ministers of the crown and industrialists who counted billions on their fingerends. Sir James took him to the Royal Garden Party and the Royal Enclosure at Ascot. The complaisance of the headmaster of Harrow was purchased by relocating the younger brother, who had done something extremely unpleasant in the masters' soup tureen, to a more forgiving school near Saffron Walden; the older prince was now free to spend nearly every weekend alone with Khafiq.

It was during one of those weekends that Suez boiled over. The two sat watching the dim images flickering on BBC. The prince, who was developing a fine public eloquence at Harrow but who spoke in few words in private, had looked at Khafiq.

"This is only the beginning. The Zionists won't stop now. The whole order of things will change. See those flames, Khafiq? That is oil burning."

When he came down from Harrow, Sir James had arranged for him to matriculate at Stanford. Sir James and Khafiq were by now the young man's fully accredited surrogate parents. It had been three years since he had been back to the Kingdom.

After Stanford he returned to London, to the London School of Economics, then a year at the Harvard Business School, a year and a half on Wall Street, in the money heart of the most powerful economic power on earth, and then, finally, back to the Kingdom. "Well, my dear Khafiq, we've done our best," said Sir James, as they watched the Comet jetliner climb the sky headed for Dumar where the prince was to begin his government service. Sir James was by now painfully afflicted with gout; he had hobbled toward his car, his arm around Khafiq's shoulders in an incongruous, affectionate gesture.

Thinking of those days, Khafiq had drifted off, absorbed in memories. Harrison saw it, so he remained silent until he was certain that the older man's attention had returned. Then he continued.

"I'm afraid the good old days are gone. Quite possibly for good, I'm afraid to say. I grew up in New York. I remember what it was, before the banks and the real estate types took it over. In those days lawyers wore dark suits instead of cowboy boots and blue jeans. We had metabolisms that could live without air conditioning. Our hair was cut regularly. You could play in the streets and in the park. The money belonged to the people, not to a bunch of politicians who borrowed against the people's credit until we were all busted paying taxes so that the city, and then the state, and then Washington could keep up with the monthly payments."

He felt his voice rising. "I'm sorry, Mr. Khafiq; I must sound like a revivalist preacher. You probably can guess that I'm not the greatest admirer going of our banks and politicians."

"Why, I should say we're of the same company, David. Our difficulties also seem to come from the same two sources: New York banks and Washington politicians. But what can we do about it?"

It was a question which Khafiq had pondered for a long time without coming close to a satisfactory answer. So he posed the question more to extend the logic of this conversation than for any other reason. When Harrison responded, it was with a bright, confident tone which made clear that this was a subject on which he too had done some considerable thinking. Khafiq saw he was clearly not content to slough the question off as purely rhetorical.

"I do think there's an answer, Mr. Khafiq. One that's very simple, in fact. I suppose a lot of those high and mighty thinkers whom I call chin-scratchers would find it preposterous. Would you be interested in hearing my thoughts on the matter?"

"Certainly." Khafiq expected no solution from Harrison. Global dilemmas weren't solved over iced tea in the Greek Isles. But no man was fonder of good conversation and the cut-and-thrust of ideas than Khafiq; it was certainly worth ten minutes.

"The way I look at it," Harrison began, "the Kingdom is really in the most extraordinary position any country has ever found itself in. The wealth we take as a given. Wealth is supposed to mean power. That has its ironies, though. Powerful though you are, it's a funny kind of power, at least by any conventional standards. It's fortuitous, largely an accident of geography, and it's exclusively economic. Power usually connotes the capacity to annihilate an enemy or at least win a war; it means bombs, troops, the Mafia. But you don't have any of that. Your power rests simply on the willingness of the Western world and the Japanese to continue to be good sports, for lack of a better phrase, so long as the price you ask for your oil can be diffracted in their economies and passed on to the common man. From what I hear, though, that patience may be running out."

"What do you hear?"

"Gossip, Mr. Khafiq, pure gossip. But from men who make a thing about knowing what's going on. The talk in Washington is that some kind of deal is being explored involving what the movies call a 'hired gun.' The name mentioned most often is India. They have a lot of men under arms; they're not far away from your oilfields, as these things go; they could certainly use the gas you're flaring."

Gossip or not, thought Khafiq, India had also been the name offered by the British prime minister.

"A little time's been bought, as I see it," Harrison continued. "Baxter tried to focus the animus of the American people on you and the others in OPEC, to get the people fired up, just in case some stringent action might be required. It was the smart thing to do, politically, given the condition of the country. Unfortunately for Baxter, one of those wonderful people he's got in the White House leaked his position paper to the *Los Angeles Times* and all hell broke loose in the Congress. He's had to pull his horns in. Only for a time, is my guess. Give him another year; let prices continue to go up and the feelings of the people will harden into a real hatred of OPEC, something much more dangerous than the current advanced state of annoyance. The stage will then be set for President Baxter to go to war, either through a surrogate like New Delhi or through the CIA. Your regime has enemies within the Kingdom itself, you know. After all, President Baxter understands politics even if it appears he doesn't understand anything else. You don't have to read very deep in American history, Mr. Khafiq, to come to recognize that the American people don't change presidents in the middle of a war."

Khafiq nodded. The idea of having to deal with President Baxter for another term was absolutely unpalatable to the rulers in Qu'nesh. The man had a kind of country cleverness; he traded like a camel dealer in the bazaar; after all, he had been some kind of a pig farmer. But the politics of the world wasn't suited to Baxter's style of horsetrading. His bluntness and clumsiness might in its way prove as dangerous as any of the diplomatic deceptions which journalists had alleged against earlier administrations.

"Well, that would certainly be unfortunate," Khafiq said. "I'm afraid we have lost whatever little confidence we may have had in President Baxter's ability to inspire or govern his own country, let alone negotiate with any sensitivity in any international matter in which we are concerned."

It was an opinion Harrison shared. He fancied himself a cosmopolitan sort, at home in the languages and mindsets of a half-dozen countries apart from his own. It gave him something of the perspective from which other nations stared in gaping amazement as one backwoods American President after another conducted the nation's foreign policy with the style and success of a Kansas tourist trying to bribe his way to the best table at Maxim's.

"That's not so surprising, Mr. Khafiq, given the normal paranoia of any middle-class American confronted with a language other than English. Of course, what other nation of 200 million people has entrusted substantive policy-making responsibility to foreigners? Our chief foreign policy officer is an Albanian; his predecessors were a German and a Pole. Do you suppose your King would assign such influence to a Kurd or Pakistani?"

It made Khafiq laugh. It really was incredible when he thought about it.

"I'm getting off the point," Harrison went on. "What I'm trying to say is that the Kingdom has what I believe to be a relatively short time, a year, perhaps a little more, to turn things in its favor. Reverse the tide which is building."

"Really, David, don't you think you're overstating matters a bit? Apart from London, Washington is our oldest and closest friend."

"Mr. Khafiq, hell hath no fury like an incumbent President seeking reelection and a population which is broke and cold. Especially since President Baxter seems to feel he has a divine mission to lead America to glory. Around the smart clubs in Washington, where the old money and old thinking soak up their martinis, he's known as 'Bound for Glory' Baxter. You know better than I what unshirted hell these religious types can raise if they get the right pulpit."

Indeed, indeed, thought Khafiq. One had only to look to Iran. Or to the King, for that matter.

"Anyway," Harrison said warmly, "I've got an idea whose time has come, I think. I've been nursing it for nearly five years, when you first raised the price of oil and the perfectly predictable way in which collective human nature behaves made it possible to see exactly how things would turn out down the line. There was just too much psychological momentum in my country, too many decades of total self-indulgence, to expect us to adjust to the new realities. To govern our appetites. We refused to taper off, so we created the inflation which has beat us over the head, and we act surprised."

Khafiq pursed his lips in agreement. He was thinking about the lost $20 billion in purchasing power, evaporated like water in a drainage ditch.

"It was also possible to see how your colleagues in OPEC might behave. Once a savage, always a savage; in about a dozen countries all that the money bought was a big, corrupt Downtown Saturday Night. It certainly turned out that way in Iran."

Khafiq rather liked the frankness of Harrison's remarks and he admired the younger man's choice of words. He paid closer attention.

"From then to now, Mr. Khafiq, things have run their logical course. But it's gone too far. The United States is tired; exhausted people become impatient if they don't get some sort of respite. When and if our temper finally is lost, Mr. Khafiq, your country will be the big loser.

"On the other hand, there's something the Kingdom *could* do which would turn the tables!"

Khafiq's eyes asked the unspoken question. Harrison smiled, raised a finger in a manner Khafiq found mildly but inoffensively schoolmasterish, and leaned closer. Almost casually, he said, "Why don't you *cut* the price of oil? Cut it substantially—back to, say, $10 a barrel!"

It was difficult to be offhand with a big, contrary idea like this, even though Harrison could dissemble casualness with the best. It was difficult for him to express serious ideas seriously; it went against his grain. Somehow, this time, prodded by something inside, rage perhaps, a breaking of patience, he got a strong, imperative undertone into his words, with a force that surprised him and riveted Khafiq's attention.

Years of playing for the highest stakes had educated Khafiq in composure under pressure. He had trained himself to sit calmly, steepling his fingers, while billions were placed at risk.

Now, the only sign of interest he gave was to sniff the air—tentatively—as if he could discern the scent of truth on the light afternoon breeze.

His mind ran quickly through the arithmetic. Having learned numbers on an abacus, he could get the zeros right in his head: if the posted price were reduced from $20 a barrel to $10, that would work out to over $100 million a day on the 11.5 million barrels a day that the Kingdom was currently producing. Nearly $35 billion a year in lost revenue! It was really quite unthinkable. Harrison could see him grimace at the thought.

He was quick to tune in to the other man's mental figuring. "In round numbers, that would work out to a reduction in revenue of something over $30 billion a year, allowing for downtime for rework on the wells. Let's stick that figure in the debit column. But look at the credits."

As objectively as if he were making a list of an ordinary Saturday's bachelor's errands, Harrison ticked off the points which underlay his thinking. One: It was reasonable to assume that such an action would materially strengthen the dollar; most, probably all, of the past depreciation of the dollar's value would be recovered. That was $20 billion to the Kingdom's account, using Khafiq's own number. Two: The Kingdom had been obliged to lend another $5 or $10 billion, also depending on whose numbers you used, to Third World countries which the earlier price increases had bankrupted. Those loans would start to look money-good. Three: The West supplied the Kingdom with 90 percent of the products and systems by which it was buying its way into the twentieth century. The prices which the Kingdom was being charged represented nothing more than a reexporting of the inflation which the high price of oil had laid on the heads of the consumerist industrial nations. No matter what the pundits said about the rate of inflation, that would probably jack up prices about 20 percent annually, which came to another $4 to $5 billion a year in the official budget for the Kingdom's recently announced Seven-Year Plan. Four: The Kingdom was obliged to hold the bulk of its foreign reserves in dollars and pounds, the specie of the two least disciplined economies of the industrial world. A strengthening dollar would attract the Hong Kong and Swiss speculators in droves, permitting the Kingdom to extricate itself from its dependence on the United States and England by selling into a burgeoning bull market in dollars and sterling.

"Novels are written about the possibility of your making a massive withdrawal from New York and London. It makes alluring fiction, but I wouldn't try it. I can imagine the reaction in Washington if you walked up to a teller's window at the Chase or the Certified or even the Fed and tried to withdraw $10 billion! They'd give you scrip or green stamps!"

Khafiq knew that Harrison had a point. From time to time, hot-headed young ministers in Qu'nesh, incensed at some U.S. policy or action, had angrily proposed a fanciful retaliation by pulling out the Kingdom's dollar holdings en masse. At one such session, Khafiq pointed out, too sarcastically perhaps, that such solutions more properly belonged in Scheherazade. They were stuck with the dollar; it was a matter of trying to find a solution within that quagmire.

As Harrison talked, the yacht turned gently on its anchor chain, a lulling motion disturbed only by the infrequent slaps of the wakes of speedboats racing up and down the narrow channel. Khafiq's face was hidden by his dark glasses and the sweeping brim of the ridiculous straw hat which Stavrapos had bought him in Mykonos. It sat atop Khafiq's delicate little head like an oversized bottlecap.

Although he seemed to Harrison to be drowsing, Khafiq was in fact doing some serious thinking. How foolish and hasty they had been to accept at face value the preachings of the free-market Elijahs who had assured them that higher oil prices would force a provident sanity on the energy consumers! They had pushed the price higher and higher, to the point where the money they got for their oil was trash and large pieces of the world were in shreds. Continue this way, he thought, and the Kingdom will be brought down. From within or without, what would it matter?

There was so little time left, as he saw things; there would be fewer opportunities to bring to heel the ravening corruption and disruption which it seemed they had unleashed. What this young man was proposing was outrageous, of course. It ran against all history, all experience. But as Khafiq thought it through, he perceived that it had one compelling aspect: it was absolutely unilateral. The Kingdom could play all the cards. It required no negotiation, agreement or treaty. So it was possible, and that fact alone made it worth looking into.

"All that is purely quantitative," Harrison was saying. "The sums are enormous and in themselves interesting for that reason. But from your point of view, the larger gains are less tangible, although no less measurable. To evaluate them, we have to go back to what you and I were discussing earlier: politics, psychology, and philosophy."

There was less passion but more conviction in Harrison's tone of voice now. "Take your own objectives," he said. "First, the security of the Kingdom and of the regime. Do something like this and you can write your own ticket. The American people will see to that. You will be the best friend this country of mine ever had. In return for $10 oil, the American people will let you resettle the Palestinians in downtown Tel Aviv—if that's what you ask. If you want a division of Marines in Qu'nesh to ensure the eternal prevalence of your royal family, you'll get them. The Shah could have done the same thing, but he was into his deity syndrome by then.

"I'm not being cynical, Mr. Khafiq. I'm just sick of the way things have turned out in my country. We run on confidence the way this yacht runs on oil. Confidence in the American popular mind is synonymous with money: money to buy television sets, gas for the Cadillac, steak on the table. I used to work on Wall Street; they had a saying down there: *Happiness can't buy money*. It was an impudent, cynical thing to say, and I hated the idea of it when I was younger, but I begin now to think it's true. As things stand, *you* control the money and, so, you control the happiness. Poor Jefferson, I think he'd be sad to see how far back up the track life and liberty have finished."

He paused as if for breath. Looking at Khafiq, he couldn't gauge whether his argument had carried any weight. But the older man remained calm, expectant. Poor Jefferson, Harrison repeated to himself; all he stipulated was the *pursuit* of happiness. Centuries of envy and ambition, of guaranteed wages with no relation to productivity, of bought-off electorates, had transformed what had been conceived simply as the right to *try* into the right to *have*.

"You know," he added as a scarcely considered afterthought, "the way things are, you could choose your own President. I know you don't like Baxter. He's a bit of a pious-mouthed fool with a lot of cheap panaceas and prescriptions and he's so busy being a Messiah that he forgets who elected him. If you were to get the word across that so-and-so, name your man, anyone, except I think they'd draw the line at Nixon, although maybe not; anyway, if you were to let it out that Mr. X was the man whose presence in the White House had caused you to reduce the price of oil, Mr. X would be the next President. He'd be a sure thing; what my friends who bet a lot call an overlay. Anyway, I'm sorry to have rambled on so. People tell me I've got to stop letting these big, unrealistic ideas engage me and work on more practical things. It's probably why they've all made so much more money than I have. End of sermon." He sat back and drained his glass of tea. He wished it were whisky; he needed calming down.

Khafiq smiled indulgently. "It's an interesting concept, David. You're a clever man and you are dealing with facts which, assembled in a vacuum, can be presented in a very rational, compelling way. I don't disagree with your view of your country. I never cease to be astonished at its waywardness and profligacy. But does it really seem possible to you that we would sacrifice so much to help you out of a problem of your own making?"

"You live in London, I believe, sir. They shoot a lot of birds there, as they do in my country. Rule number one in bird shooting is to aim at where the pheasant is going, not where he's been. If only we could manage as well as we shoot..."

"The world isn't like that, David." Khafiq interrupted, seeming a little impatient. "Governments are run by old men who have a limited future, haven't the patience to shoot at a bird which may fall beyond a horizon they may never see. They deal in present dangers only. Just suppose you might be correct in your analysis. What would our neighbors in OPEC do? Can you imagine the reaction of Colonel Qaddafi?"

"With all respect to the Colonel, I doubt he's a match for our Marines, even in these days of our national decline." Harrison's tone was sarcastic. There was nothing more to say, but he was glad to have had the chance, finally, to say what he had been thinking for a long time.

Khafiq rose. "It's still quite hot and I gather our dear host has organized another of his late evenings for us. But I've enjoyed our talk."

"So have I. Perhaps another time. There are so many things that could be added."

Khafiq nodded and disappeared into the cabin.

The afternoon sparkled on.

Harrison sat by himself for a while. If you had enough money, he thought, you really could buy anything. Jewels, jets, people. A country. Poor, tired, discouraged America. For sale. Since he was still tied to Wall Street, it also occurred to him that these Arabs were the only people who had the power to rig the stock market, the *whole* market with a peaceful gesture and a few words. Legitimately. Christ, he reflected, if you knew it was going to happen you could make a fortune.

The market was bursting to get moving. Even the contrarians, who swam against the tide, whatever the tide was, were jazzed up. Everyone was hot to go, on the brink of an investment orgasm: fundamentalists, Dow and wave theorists, futures gunners, chart wizards, the whole zoo! Even Barney had said to him a week before he left for Athens: "Dave, better get in. These meatheads in the banks are soiling their drawers wanting to buy stocks. It's gonna run."

On the flight over he'd read an interview with a famous investment deep thinker whose speculations had been so notoriously successful that the press had nicknamed him "the Wizard of Wichita." The Wizard had proclaimed that he was buying stocks. All well and good, Harrison had thought, but what it was going to take was a really big swing in the way the world looked. Like a cut in the price of oil. That would be *something;* that would do it; that would convince the oversymbolizing, oversimplifying American mind that a new day was at hand. Christ, the Dow would go to 3000. It was a lip-licking prospect. He was sure that Khafiq would be appreciative of this; he would bring it up, later.

He dwelt on it until his venal reveries were interrupted by the noise of the shopping party returning from Spetsai.

That evening Stavrapos had arranged for them all to dine with his English friends in their splendid new house. The Easter moon was full and very romantic. The host became drunk and aggressive and fulminated drearily against the Labour Party. Harrison played eye-games with his hostess. At the end of the evening, the *Zephiros*'s company, jangling with the nervous ebullience that characterized the end of cruises and honeymoons, tumbled into the tender. Harrison found himself putting his arm around Miss Pounonis as the launch swirled along toward the yacht. It was the retsina, but so what? They were happy. He was, as always, ready for the illusion of romance. It was nothing new. From time to time, he would let himself go with exorbitant feelings, and was blown about by operatic gusts of passion and vast, impulsive yearnings for this or that lady. This played hell with what he perceived to be his suitable persona: sardonic, witty, disengaged. The conflict invariably also played hell with the feelings of the women toward whom he directed his grand manner of loving. This wasn't quite on the grandest scale, but it wasn't bad.

Later, in her cabin, he made love to her fiercely, trying to obliterate the inevitability of their pending separation and the fondness he was feeling for her, emotions which even in his plunging exertions he recognized to be mostly a mirage born of open seas and skies and white, romantic islands. He rose above her so that they could both look down and see themselves hinging and unhinging. He saw her reach down between them, take him, and move him lower and then deeper into a different part of her. She gasped when he entered her this way, but she left her hand on him until what he felt was excruciating and he couldn't control himself.

When it was over, he lay next to her, gulping for air, his breath drowning out the plapping of the water against the hull. That was incredible, was his first thought. "I hope I didn't hurt you," he said.

He knew that she was smiling even if, in the dark, he couldn't see her. He *felt* her smile. "Oh, David, no. Of course not. After all, I *am* Greek."

The next afternoon, they parted company. Miss Pounonis had left immediately on disembarking. She had to be back at the National Museum, she said. She would see Harrison in New York when the Phidian Exhibition opened. She never did. She drowned off Lindos late that summer.

The Mercedes drove Khafiq, Mlle. duTronc, and Harrison to Athens Airport. Stavrapos, now an important Texas oil magnate, had gone on earlier to a meeting in Piraeus with Niarchos's commissaires.

At the point where the European and transatlantic passengers separated, Khafiq paused. He shook Harrison's hand. "I might wish to reach you. Do you have a card?" he asked. "I hope we shall see each other again. You have interesting ideas. I enjoyed our talk."

"Thank you. I hope to see you soon again as well."

Harrison watched Khafiq's small figure scampering into the crowd. When Khafiq was out of sight, through Customs, he turned and headed for the plane that would take him home.

8 "Reduce the price of oil to $10! My dear Khafiq, all that sun and those delirious Attic nights have softened your brain!" The Minister's laugh was not entirely sarcastic.

He was standing at an open window, looking out across the Quai President Wilson at the afternoon's activity on the paths which bordered Lake Geneva: children and their nursemaids; old men strolling arm in arm; drowsy readers on the benches. It was a brilliant day; from the sixth-floor balcony on the Hotel President, he thought, for an instant, that he could see all the way across the lake to the Vaud and the foothills of the Jura. The surface of the lake, lightly ruffled, was accented with the sails of small boats. It was early for sailing, thought the Minister. An unexpected gust, a capsize, and the water would be glacial, he thought; it was a chilling notion and he shivered briefly.

He turned back into the room. In the mirror over the sofa on which Khafiq sat, he looked at himself. Better. He looked thinner.

His meeting with the pinched-lipped men at the Caisse Suisse had run a full hour over its allocation. As at each of the last five such meetings, they had no good news to report. Young Monsieur Becker was the third generation of his family to have a hand in the management of the Kingdom's exterior investments. Like his ancestors, he was professionally leaden; he had been instructed by those forebears that humorlessness was a meaningful earnest of purposefulness and ability.

"Our results for the quarter have been disappointing," he'd said clinically, "despite the recent strength in the dollar. Efforts to effect substantial transfers into Deutschemarks and Yen were only moderately successful. Sterling has continued relatively favorable, so we maintained our position, but the economic situation in the UK remains uncertain."

The Swiss will never understand England, the Minister thought; in Switzerland, unemployment is corrected by deportation.

Uncertain. A banking euphemism for perilous.

"I am afraid, Your Excellency," Becker had concluded, "that only some major improvement in the dollar, virtually an upside calamity, if you will, will permit us to implement a material diversification of the accounts. As it stands, therefore, the general situation remains unchanged. The depreciation of the dollar in the foreign exchange market has produced a decline of approximately 22 percent, net, in the time-weighted value of the Kingdom's external holdings." Becker crossed his hands, palms down, piously. He radiated pity at the plight of those unlucky enough not to be Swiss, and therefore unable to translate 100 percent of their wealth into the holy franc. "If Martin Luther had been Swiss," Khafiq had once said, "the anthem of Protestant Christianity would be: *'Ein feste Burg ist unsere Geld.'*"

The Minister wasn't surprised. The last twenty-four hours had brought telexes from his deputies in New York, Hong Kong, and Sao Paulo which said about the same thing. Khafiq had carried similar miserable news from the City of London.

Twenty-two percent, more or less. It worked out to close to $30 billion in all the accounts around the world. A sum adequate to fund one full year of the Kingdom's admittedly ambitious development plan.

And that, thought the Minister, sitting bored in the honey-paneled room on the Rue de la Corraterie while Becker and his minions went over the portfolio item by item, isn't the half of it. The imported inflation was worse. Marked-up contracts and overpriced products. Agents and go-betweens swarming like ants on a corpse.

He often wondered to himself if other men who had brought great changes to the way things were regretted their inspirations. Would Marx have applauded Stalin? Would the Prophet, for that matter, have placed a benign, approving hand on the shoulder of the Shah? When he had come back to the Kingdom after his years in the West, years spent hearing Texas oilmen cursing the Kingdom for giving away its oil and forcing theirs to go underpriced, years watching Greek and Panamanian tanker owners risking $100,000 on the wheel at Monte Carlo, he had busied himself in the study of the financial statements of Anglo and its satellites. His analysis convinced him of the economic and moral injustice of the system as it stood. He had gone to the old King with the facts. It seemed a simple matter, then; there appeared to be plenty of room at the trough. "See what our sister states around the Gulf think," advised the King. Then, later, with a consensus of approval around the Gulf, "See if they also agree in Lagos and Caracas." Finally, "Go to Teheran and see what our brother the Shah thinks."

He had made the trips, presenting his case in cloistered, private discussions with emirs, generals, presidents, emperors. The ways of argument had been greased by the belligerence of Israel and its ally across the Atlantic. It reminded the Minister that Steinbeck's *Of Mice and Men,* which he had read and liked at Stanford, was a metaphor for Israel and America. America was like Lenny, a dim hulking presence in the shadows, while his petulant little friend picked fights.

Events brought matters to a head. He sensed properly that Watergate and Vietnam had caused the Americans' take-on-all-comers confidence to shatter like a glass dropped on a marble floor. Israel had become a side issue. The real crisis had emerged ten thousand miles away in Southeast Asia, in a part of the world as foreign to him as it was to the American boys whose bodies bloated in the sun at Da Nang, and in seedy Washington offices. The moment was propitious; it was an exceptional opportunity.

So, only six years earlier, although it seemed like a lifetime now to the Minister, they had raised the price of oil. And raised it again and again. And again. He had tried to argue against greed, but his ally, the old King, had been assassinated in the streets of Mecca by a deranged cousin. The money had drifted down like snowflakes, spreading through the ruling classes of the countries that set the price. His attempt to redress the wealth of nations had been perverted into a spendthrift's cornucopia. He tried to control the sudden, intoxicating effect of all this Western cash flooding into the Kingdom, and to a degree he succeeded. Although Qu'nesh got the lion's share of the OPEC windfall, there were only four million-odd people blessed by it. Beyond the Kingdom's borders, however, it was different. The flow of wealth was dammed at the palaces of the rulers. It bought airplanes, whores, extravagance, and corruption. To some, in the end, it brought revolution. Iran had fallen into the hands of priests and worse; the small states around the Gulf were awash in soft, vulnerable corruption. The Kingdom was isolated.

When he turned back into the room to address Khafiq, therefore, the Minister was skeptical—but interested in any idea which might work. The two men knew that they were no longer dealing with mere matters of quantities of money: inflation, exchange rates, development plans. Like it or not, it had come down to a matter of survival, life or death, of human character.

"So tell me this fantastic notion again, my dear old friend," he said. "You go on a cruise with that swindler Stavrapos, who has managed to bribe a major concession from our doddering old friend the Emir, and you meet a young American who convinces you that the answer to our predicament is to give away what amounts to $30 billion a year and to meddle definitively with the U.S. election next year? Is that correct?"

Khafiq drew on his cigarette evenly and said with some severity, "Those are some of the facts, Your Excellency."

Khafiq had spoken scoldingly to the Minister only once before, late one night at Annabel's in London, when the younger man had taken a fancy to a peach-cheeked young countess whose drunken, pugnacious husband was clearly ready to cause a nasty scene. Now he scolded him again: in the manner of an old, still-wise teacher whose star pupil, long having surpassed him in eminence and fame, had lost sight of his beginnings.

"I might remind you, Excellency, without seeming presumptuous, that good ideas, even great ideas, seldom come from old men like me. We hoard power and influence, which makes us unreceptive to change. Certainly *you* should know that better than I, much as you have dealt with the rest of the world. Besides, think of all those supposedly great and wise advisors we have consulted about our problems and plans. There is a point beyond which mere experience cannot stretch. We are at that point, I think. You know that, Excellency. I know you do." Khafiq's tone was factual and reproachful.

The Minister accepted Khafiq's mild admonishing. He could admit to himself that his role as the world's mover and shaker might have come to affect the intellectual flexibility of which he had always been most proud. He recalled that his reluctance to press the old King on the oil price had been largely overcome by Khafiq's enthusiasm and approval.

"It is always worth thinking about such things," he said. "But tell me, people in the West are always discovering great truths late at night, when fatigue and alcohol burn away their judgment. Who is this young man, anyway?"

"His name is David Harrison. He is something over forty years old. He has been an associate at the Verger firm and, later, at Blenheim Sécurities, which my sources tell me is an excellent small investment house in New York. He spent some years in Paris, with Mitchener, Suydam. As you know, we have dealt with them for nearly forty years. He is also well regarded in the City—and here in Geneva as well."

Khafiq's source in Geneva had been Marc-Antoine. In international finance, as matters increased in weight and importance, the circles in which critical decisions were taken became smaller, the number of useful men fewer. Khafiq often thought that the shape of the world's power was like an inverted cyclone: the winds were greatest at the narrowest point. In any event, Marc-Antoine operated very close to the vortex.

The evening before the Minister's arrival, Khafiq had invited Marc-Antoine to the Hotel President for a drink.

"And dinner too, I hope," Marc-Antoine had said; he was always anxious to flee his hillside villa and the icy company of Madame Marteau, who spent her evenings playing Couperin on the expensive harpsichord which he had given her as the price of silence. Besides, he had heard of a new girl at the Ba-Ta-Clan who deserved a closer inspection.

Khafiq had been waiting in the bar a good forty-five minutes when Marc-Antoine arrived, pleading the excuse of last minute telexes. Thank God for the telex machine, thought Khafiq. Not only indispensable for business, but so useful as a cover for adultery or lesser sins.

Marc-Antoine was barely seated, his drink ordered, when he excused himself and went across the room to a table where four men, Americans, had been noisily complaining about paying nine dollars for a shot of Scotch. Khafiq hadn't focused on them before, but as Marc-Antoine shook hands, he recognized the chairman of one of the largest American metal refining companies. Marc-Antoine chatted animatedly for a minute, then produced a worn leather address book; pencils and notepads came out around the table and scribbled busily and lasciviously while Marc-Antoine read telephone numbers from his address book. It was said that Mme. Blaise had opened a Geneva branch.

He had rejoined Khafiq. Knocking back a whisky, he looked around approvingly. "Excellent hotel, my friend: the only place in Geneva where you can get champagne and decent caviar at five in the morning." He launched into a reminiscence involving a strip-tease dancer and an ocelot.

Khafiq had framed his question carefully. He and Marc-Antoine had important private clients in common. They had collaborated on several not wholly irreproachable transactions together.

"My friend," he had asked, "I have a private client who needs some discreet work done in the States. He needs someone who can open the right doors and who is experienced and reliable, but who isn't connected with one of the big firms, where matters have a way of getting talked about and where he has existing relationships he does not wish to complicate. My own connections in New York are, alas, outdated; so I turn to you."

Marc-Antoine had responded quickly. "I have a friend in New York named Harrison. He should be perfect for the sort of thing you want. Assuming, of course, that it's *our* sort of deal."

His hasty answer had been helpful, permitting Khafiq to discard the laborious story he'd contrived in order to bring up Harrison's name. For his part, Marc-Antoine knew that transactions for Khafiq's clients invariably produced fat fees and commissions. If he could steer the business to Harrison, he could cream off a good half for himself.

"Tell me about him."

Marc-Antoine had recounted Harrison's credentials and history, chapter and verse. At the end, he had said, "But I must tell you this. My friend David, if you meet him, has a lot of ideas that run against the grain. On this side of the Atlantic we know, you and I, that the old ideas, like the Alps, survive even if the edges become less jagged. David hasn't accepted that—yet. Perhaps he never will. He handles himself well overseas, better than most Americans. He's cosmopolitan. His languages are passable. Technically he is a very good banker. But he has never fitted very well within what they call the Establishment. He knows them all, was raised among them, can work with them. He is as discreet as an American can be. Yet, in that world of self-made, or inherited, self-importance, I fear he's still a bit of a revolutionary. It seems to be a general failing of intelligent, educated Americans of a certain age. You know, he told me he voted for Goldwater *and* McGovern! I mean, can you imagine?"

Khafiq had been pleased to have his own impressions confirmed. Harrison and Marc-Antoine were obviously very good friends, in regular and close contact, he could see, but it was also clear that Marc-Antoine had no idea that Khafiq and Harrison had ever met, which meant that Harrison had said nothing of their encounter. Such discretion was critically important to Khafiq.

He told all of this to the Minister. He didn't feel it necessary to tell His Excellency that Marc-Antoine had later taken him off to the Ba-Ta-Clan after dinner and obliged him to sit through five hours of strip-tease. The night club was one of the great watering holes of international finance, along with the Kit-Kat Klub in Düsseldorf or New Jimmy's in Paris. The place was hot, noisy, vulgar, expensive, and filled with bankers of every shape and color. "My God," Marc-Antoine had exclaimed when he returned to their table, perspiring after a turn around the floor with a black dancer who had sequins glued interestingly to her pubic hair, "I've done a year's business tonight. I've given out so many business cards I'll bet I weigh ten pounds less than when we came in!"

The Minister was attentive to Khafiq's report on Harrison. None of this was news. It merely repeated the intelligence he'd gotten, in a circuitous way, from Benjamin Masters, the astute lawyer who watched over the Kingdom's interests in Washington. The cable relayed to him by the Consulate had read: SUBJECT WELL REGARDED/NOT MUCH LIKED BY LARGE BANKS/VERY ABLE AND CONSIDERED CREATIVE/SOME THINK DANGEROUSLY SO.

The Minister continued. "For the sake of discussion, then, let's accept that your idea has some sense to it. Political sense, principally. My dear Khafiq, we are talking not only about an enormous sum of money, but of other complex and sensitive issues. In our own country. Within the family. Among our immediate allies. In Islam. Not to mention what might happen if the Americans catch on to our intent to manipulate them."

"Let's defer the money question for the moment, Excellency. I think the political consequences are, if anything, less incendiary than if we let matters stand as they are."

Khafiq outlined his analysis. If it was to survive in its present form, and the al-Misaz family was to continue in power, the Kingdom needed the absolute protection of some great and reliable ally. There were only two possibilities, with the Shah gone: Russia or the Americans. Russia was out of the question. Marxism and the King's fervent Islam were anathema. So that left the Americans. But America was not about to install a full-fledged military presence in the Kingdom, which would inflame the Zionists, without an overwhelming incentive to do so. Old friendship would no longer suffice as a motivation, especially since that mutual high regard had been so drastically strained by the oil price increases, which had created a recession and which had sent the Americans off to find other friends with other sources, like Mexico; and to concentrate on their own coal lands and uranium deposits. The Kingdom's intransigence on the matter of Israel had exacerbated the situation. A great gesture was necessary to reconstitute that friendship, to create an unstoppable *public* impetus to embrace the Kingdom with all the might and resources of the United States.

"Cutting the oil price would be such a gesture," said Khafiq. "Everyone expects us to raise it further. Novels which predict $50 or $100 a barrel of oil and a world financial catastrophe sell millions of copies in America and Europe. You've read them yourself; I've seen you. They shape the public consciousness; half of America is still waiting for the crash of, 'Seventy-Nine."

"But what about our allies? The rest of OPEC? What about Libya? That madman is likely to bomb Qu'nesh at the very least, more likely to invade us!"

"Think for a minute, Excellency. What is proposed is that we not only cut the price, substantially, but that we make some reduction in output as well. Our friends can fill some of that gap, even if it means a second price tier for a time. We can use the cutbacks to put our wells in better order. And no one will touch us. If Qaddafi raises a finger he will find the U.S. Marines in Tripoli. I recall that they've been there before. What do we owe the rest of OPEC, anyway? For three years now you've argued and cajoled against pushing too hard. No one has listened. We are the ones who've paid the political price, not to mention the financial cost.

"And there's one nicety to which Harrison drew my attention. If we set the price at $10, say, that will put a politically acceptable but economically feasible lid on what can be charged for U.S. oil. Washington will like that. At that price, however, development of reserves alternative to ours and fuels alternative to oil will slow down. It is in our long-term interest to keep the Americans in our palm. And something must be done, something the Americans can't find the will to do, which is to stop the hemorrhage in the value of our dollar reserves. As we stand, we are caught in a circle which will bring disaster to us all."

The Minister admitted the logic of Khafiq's argument. Not that history in any way suggested that logic inevitably triumphed. But the risks did seem less than when Khafiq had first come to him with the idea. There was still something about the politics that bothered him.

"You know that I don't feel that we should trust President Baxter."

The Minister had met President Fulger Baxter a number of times. He was a short blocky man with pursed fat lips, and a pious, churchly expression; it was a face the Minister found unappealing and untrustworthy. The U.S. President resembled one of the pigs he raised in canal country Louisiana. The President's backwoods evangelism made him think in terms that were appallingly too simplistic, even if he claimed the authority of the Gospels. He'd been a successful small businessman who turned politician largely by accident; he had been elected to the White House by a bare plurality in an election in which the majority of a discouraged electorate hadn't bothered to vote.

"Nor do I," said Khafiq. "And that's the beauty of young Mr. Harrison's suggestion. If *we* carry it a step further. It does away with President Baxter!"

Indeed it did, thought the Minister, if all notions of ethical international polity went by the boards.

"I have studied American politics for a long time. As I told you, Harrison suggested that an announcement of a material price cut could determine the outcome of next year's presidential election. I agree. The mood of the American public seems desperate; Masters confirms this. What I think is that we can create an enormous psychological momentum in Baxter's favor and then jerk it up short. Give him the credit first for secretly negotiating our generous action; then blast him from office by appearing to retract, and laying on his head the blame for breaking faith with us. Create a political disaster for Baxter, Your Excellency, lose him the election at the eleventh hour!

"What we can do," Khafiq continued, "is to phrase our announcement of a price reduction in a fashion which implies that our decision has been influenced—no, *based*—on secret discussions and agreements with the Baxter administration. Such discussions and agreements will of course never have taken place. But from what you and I know of Baxter and of the probity of American politicians, especially with an election at stake, that will make no difference. It seems that nobody talks to each other in Washington anyway; look at their confusion on Iran! Baxter is in real political trouble now; it will probably be worse next year. But if Harrison is correct, and I would suggest he is, news like this will send the country dancing with optimism. The stock market will go up a thousand points. The dollar will recover. All thanks to us. The administration will jump to take the credit, which we will encourage by careful leaks to the U.S. press. The electorate will accept this. If we reduce the price of oil to $10 a barrel, say, six months before the election, President Baxter will become the overwhelming favorite for re-election. Over any other candidate.

"And of course," Khafiq continued, smiling, "who the Republicans nominate can be largely determined by us. This is my thought. With Baxter looking a sure winner, none of the major Republican possibilities, as of today, is going to try very hard to get a nomination which can only foretell crushing defeat and sure political death, in the national sense. Look at what happened to Goldwater and McGovern. Look at their histories; with the incumbent apparently certain of reelection, their parties, out of power, nominated fringe candidates with just enough organization and financing to seize the nomination, thanks to circumstances which discouraged more appealing or popular candidates. If we invest some political money artfully, which we can, through Masters, we'll get our own man nominated: someone good, someone we can trust. Like John Jordan."

Like John Jordan. The name had jumped immediately into Khafiq's mind. He had been Ambassador to the Kingdom and later in charge of the Middle Eastern desk at the CIA. It was thanks to Jordan that the al-Misaz family remained in the Royal Palace. When Langley had gotten word of a putative Libyan-financed coup in the Kingdom, and the White House and the State Department were trying to figure out which way to jump, Jordan had seen that the word had been passed back to Qu'nesh via Rome. A number of otherwise troublesome individuals had been sent swimming with the sharks in the Red Sea. Jordan had been put out to pasture for playing loose with the "Company's" rules. He was still very active in Republican politics, Khafiq knew. There were wings of the party that wanted him to run.

"Anyway," Khafiq finished, "a fortnight, possibly three weeks before the election, with Baxter sitting confidently in the White House and well ahead in the polls, we will *then* announce that because the administration has secretly *broken* its agreement with us, it is impossible to continue good-faith dealings. We will say we are therefore obliged to rescind the price cut, at least as far as the U.S. market is concerned, as of the following January. At the same time, our ambassadors and commercial people will start rumors to the effect that a reasonable settlement can be reached with the other party, whom we trust. They'll do this off the record, but effectively. The newspapers and networks will pick it up. The people will see their bird of paradise flying out the window, all because of Baxter. We *will* have our own President. And we will get from him whatever we want. Why should we busy ourselves buying American airplanes and American technology when we can buy America?"

The Minister asked Khafiq to go over it again.

Could they be sure of getting Jordan as the Republican candidate?

"Virtually sure," said Khafiq. "If the other candidates don't want it, and running becomes a matter of party loyalty and principle, it will come down to a combination of money and character. Jordan's character, as we know him, will oblige him to accept a call from his party. After that, it will require only money—and *that*, at least, we have in abundance."

The psychology of the plan agreed with his own recollections and observations of America. It was a system that needed good news as much as blood to keep it alive. Khafiq was probably right. His plan was probably practical. It was dishonorable, of course, but then what was so honorable in Baxter's handling of the dollar crisis? Or worse, in his dealings with Israel? It occurred to the Minister that the road down which you sold people could indeed be a two-way street.

Of course, there was the money. The price to the Kingdom.

"So let us say I agree with you so far," he said to Khafiq. "The political aspects are compelling. But I must come back to the cost. Thirty-three billion dollars a year. How can I justify that to Councillor Alrazi?"

"Excellency, I ask you, what is the value of absolute protection? For the Kingdom. For your family. For you. Ten billion a year, say? That brings the running cost down to $20 billion. We have lost close to that much in the declining value of our dollar reserves and the decline is accelerating. Fifteen percent this year! Twenty next? What is proposed should restore that, plus an additional $10 billion in potential appreciation of our exchange accounts, which would put us ahead of the game. Finally, don't you expect that the Americans will furnish and maintain for us gratis, or at a favorable price, unadjusted for our repriced dollars, a defense system for which we now propose to spend some $40 billion and which we haven't the slightest capacity to operate?"

Khafiq had said all he could. He had squeezed the plan dry before bringing it to the Minister. It was out of his hands now.

Once again, the Minister slept badly. The instinctive capacity of his mind to deal with great quantities and complications was pushed by his reflections and kept him awake. Several times he awoke and went to the window, looking out over the black lakescape. At length, when the stars in the sky were surrendering to dawn, and, like old troubles, were extinguished one by one, he fell asleep.

Khafiq was closing his suitcase the next morning when the phone rang in his suite. A limousine waited to take him to Cointrin for the flight back to London.

The Minister sounded exhausted.

"I've decided to take this idea to the King. He will make the decision."

9   Qu'nesh, the capital city of the Kingdom, had been laid out by an untalented but well-recommended English architect in the late 1930s, when the al-Misaz family had finally consolidated its power and driven its rivals into the desert to starve. The city had not grown much in the next forty years, except in moderate complexity. It was still a one-street town; the single boulevard along which it was organized began with the Royal Palace in the west and ended in the blocky stone pile of Her Majesty's Embassy. The boulevard, really a paved-over and widened caravan trail divided along its length by a row of struggling palms, was lined with various official buildings.

Two towers and a clump of lower buildings dominated the city, pulling together all the encircling sheds and arcades which were clustered around a spiderweb of radiating alleys and passages. One was the Marriott Oasis, formerly the Imperial Grosvenor Palms, which lodged the endless stream of commercial suppliants who spent their days hanging about the agencies and subministries looking for deals. The second, a minaret rising two hundred feet against the dry, pale sky, capped the Royal Mosque, the King's greatest pleasure and his single obsession. By royal command, every building in the city was painted white: the color of spiritual purity.

The Minister's parting words to Khafiq had only been partly accurate. While it was true that the King said the final yes and the final no, his decisions tended to be taken absently. The King's days were spent in continuous study of the Koran, in the company of his priests; he spent what time was left over planning grandiose additions to the mosque. The more ambitious imams tried to interleave their Koranic glosses and prayers with suggestions regarding politics and the economy, which they schemed to dominate, but to no purpose. The King's lack of interest in such matters was total. He was as much in the grip of his faith as a Sicilian grandmother.

So while the King alone had the authority to decree state policy, he had been more than content to leave the business of decision making to his uncle, Prince Alrazi, the First Councillor and *de facto* Prime Minister of the Kingdom.

The traceries of the al-Misaz genealogy were as complex as the carved screens of the Royal Mosque. The King had succeeded to the throne upon the assassination of Alrazi's older brother, thanks to the ambition of his mother and an astrologically auspicious birthdate. He often wished that Alrazi might somehow be King, especially when he had to wait on the tarmac at Dumar for one or another of the interminable processions of world eminences who insisted on coming to call. He would much rather have been back in his peaceful chambers in Qu'nesh, meditating on his Koran to the soft incantations of the chorus of imams. In addition to the psychosomatic pains of kingship, he suffered from a phlebitic swelling in his legs and was forced to stump about with a cane during his despised public appearances.

By contrast to his gentle fanatical nephew, Alrazi was an active, worldly man. He was the despair of the Kingdom-watchers in Washington and Moscow, whose conspiratorial view of life led them to search every line in his face and his speeches for a hint that he might be planning a takeover. It never occurred to them that a power-lover like Alrazi had no interest in becoming King. He had no need for the throne, as he had little need for any symbol.

Alrazi ruled the Kingdom without being subject to the inconveniences and scrutiny of the kingship. It was an arrangement which suited both him and his nephew. The price of his power was modest. Within the Kingdom, Alrazi comported himself with complete adherence to the King's overbearing religiosity. The *Washington Post* had described him as "fun-loving," which was journalese for a hearty preference for alcohol and sex. But if Alrazi loved his fun, and he did, he was scrupulous in paying it court strictly outside the Kingdom. The King was iron-willed only when it came to matters of Koranic law; his brief reign had been marked with horrendous penalties for sins against the Prophet's dictates: severed heads and hands; banishments; garrotings.

So if Alrazi kept a flashy English mistress in a villa at Cap-Ferrat, and was frequently carried drunk and thrashing from the Beaulieu casino to his bright gold Daimler, at home he remained cold sober, devout and paternal to his wives and children. He had no doubt that to do otherwise would have brought down on him the sanguinary vengeance of the King, whose customary placid temperament would turn bloodthirsty if the prayerbook decreed. A word from the Koran and the King would have put his own children to the executioner's sword.

Alrazi and the Minister liked each other. They were second cousins, linked through connections so obscure that blood kinship had nothing to do with their mutual esteem. Practical men of the world, they liked each other's company and enjoyed each other's point of view.

They met to discuss Khafiq's idea in Alrazi's apartments, which were behind the palace. Over coffee, the Minister went over the scheme. There was no one else present.

At length, he concluded, "If we handle it properly, we can eliminate Baxter, who is doubly dangerous because he is a moralizing fool, and this is no time for fools in high places, and also take care of certain other enemies in Washington."

"I'm sorry about your younger brother," said Alrazi when they finished. "But he tried fate once too often. A pretty girl, that one was; I can understand his passion. But our beloved King..."

He let it trail off. He knew it was a subject past discussing with the Minister. Etiquette had demanded some allusion to the matter. He picked up the main thread.

"Very audacious, this idea of yours. I think Khafiq has probably analyzed it correctly. He's a clever one, your friend Khafiq. We should make better use of him.

"Of course," he continued, "it's difficult for me to judge objectively. You know how I feel about the Americans. A childish, shortsighted, greedy people. Lovable but undependable. The politicians are worse. Baxter is a despicable opportunist. And there are worse in the Congress." Alrazi seemed to backtrack in his mind. "You did mention 'other enemies'? Do you think that such a plan might also eliminate Congressman Renssalaer?" There was a touch of eagerness in the question.

The Minister observed the dangerous hooding of Alrazi's eyes. Alrazi was a hater; he would carry a vendetta a thousand years beyond the grave.

Not that in this instance the hatred wasn't justified. The Minister knew the story well; he'd gotten it from Khafiq, who'd heard it all over London. The episode had occurred years ago at the Cranmont, a gambling club perched above Hanover Square. Alrazi, then just another Arab with a lot of money, had been playing backgammon. It was a *chouette,* one player contending at a time against three or four others. Alrazi had been with an idiotic Swedish air hostess whose enormous bland breasts had kept falling out of her dress. Alrazi was very drunk. The stakes had become monumental: a hundred pounds a point, with sixty-four points at risk in several games.

Among the men playing had been Sidney Renssalaer, a big, blond American boy who had made a fortune selling shipping insurance and who was reputed among London hostesses to own the largest penis in Christendom. Whenever Alrazi had bent to the board, moving his pieces clumsily with drink-thickened fingers, Renssalaer had given the girl the eye. Drunk as he was, Alrazi had been aware of her eye-blinking, wigglesome flirting. It made him reckless. In the last game, he had made a series of helplessly stupid moves; when it was over, he had lost £50,000 on the night. Renssalaer had asked for a check on the spot; then, looking across the table, he'd said to the girl, "How about a dance, sweetheart? I'll show you what a real man feels like."

As she moved around the table to twine her arm with Renssalaer's, Alrazi had made some moss-tongued protest. Renssalaer looked down at him. "Listen, wog," he had said, "why don't you just go back to your tent and fuck a camel?"

Alrazi hadn't forgotten. Renssalaer had gone back to New York. When, in the early sixties, politics became the hobby of rich young men with nothing to do, he'd run successfully for Congress. He became known as the champion of the Jews even though, in that fashion peculiar to American life, he spent his New York afternoons in clubs no Jew might ever

(115)

enter. Five months ago, when the Minister had picked up that morning's *Paris Herald,* the picture on the front page had shown President Baxter, flanked by thinly smiling Egyptians and Israelis, turning to hand the pen which had signed away the West Bank to a grinning Congressman Renssalaer. The Minister had made sure that Alrazi had gotten a copy; his years in the West had taught him that the sustenance of old hatreds was a fundamental political activity.

With this in mind, he said to Alrazi, "Oh, I think so." And let the matter rest.

After that, it was all downhill. Alrazi was a rare type for an Arab: he was a perfect pragmatist. He liked a rich, showy life, liked having the emissaries of countries in which he had once been so condescendingly treated come groveling now in search of cash handouts. It was a position worth protecting. The political aspects needed no elaboration.

"I'm also concerned about our two young cousins," Alrazi said. He referred to the al-Nouri twins, ambitious thirty-year-olds who commanded the Air Arm and the Royal Militia. Their mother was the King's sister. "Those two are being awfully quiet and their mother sees that they spend more time than is strictly desirable with His Majesty. She is an ambitious woman and has great dreams for her children. Those dreams most assuredly do not include us." He looked pointedly at the Minister.

"I think we are all agreed, dear Minister," he said, "that the last thing we want is a regiment of Sikhs in Dumar. I will speak to the King." That was all. Alrazi rose and gestured the Minister to the door.

As the Minister went down the steps to his car, he thought: How ironic, that the destiny of what, three hundred million people, more, perhaps, and their rulers, should be decided in minutes on the basis of a grudge.

Alrazi's audience with the King lasted two hours. The King was out of sorts. A famous historical prayer rug, said to have been used by the Prophet himself, was to have been purchased from the Chicago Museum of Folk Art. It would have been a crowning addition to the new mosque, along with the great shields from Hagia Sophia which the Turks in their constant bankruptcy had been obliged to sell. But some cultural agency in Washington had moved to block the export of the rug. Benjamin Masters was working on it at the State Department, but it would be a slow business.

The King was piqued. His listened with half an ear to Alrazi's summation. It occurred to him, vaguely, that pressure on the Americans might bring the rug to Qu'nesh in time for Ramadan. It seemed to make sense. "Do what you think best," he said impatiently to Alrazi. From outside, the evening caterwaulings of a muezzin broke the trembling late afternoon silence. The two men spread themselves on the cold marble floor.

The Minister had passed the afternoon in his darkened office in the subministry. He preferred to work in Qu'nesh; Dumar, the overbuilt commercial center on the coast, was noisy and distracting. As always, a flood of papers and reports awaited his review. He looked them over restlessly. From time to time he went to the window and looked down on the square, the old bazaar, which lay to the rear. Sad, awful memories engulfed him; his bustling aides, seeing him thus, left him undisturbed.

Alrazi telephoned him an hour after evening prayers and summoned him to his home. The two men spent three hours together. When the Minister returned, his aides remarked to each other on his excited, intent expression. He closed his office door behind him, picked up the telephone, and asked to be connected with London.

Harrison had spent a pleasant day in New York. There was nothing much on: a couple of small deals to think about, little more. His conversations with Khafiq had long since been tucked away in a reposeful corner of his mind. At eleven, the receptionist in the accommodation office he maintained on Madison Avenue put through a call from an old friend, Liz Bitsmer. "Darling," she began. Harrison knew what she wanted. These days, heterosexual extra men were as scarce as unicorns.

"Darling," she went on, "I know it's late, but can you possibly come to dinner this evening? I have someone very interesting that I think you'd like. Julienne Schlechter."

He had to hand it to Liz. She knew how to tickle his curiosity. Julienne Schlechter, formerly the Marquise de Cul, was a name to conjure with. The Marquise, as she styled herself, was a legend. She had made a second, rapid marriage with old Vilmos Schlechter, the octogenarian who controlled most of the supermarkets in West Germany. They'd discovered each other in Gstaad and married within a week. The wedding had been reluctantly attended by Schlechter's four stolid, cube-shaped stepchildren from Mainz. Julienne, so the smart gossips maintained, had taken one look at the implacable, disapproving heirs and set out to get what was theirs. Old Schlechter had been persuaded to change his will in her favor. Then she loaded her ancient husband on a Lufthansa flight for Buenos Aires and began a whirlwind, worldwide honeymoon. She knew what she was doing. Halfway between Sydney and Johannesburg, the old man's befatted heart stopped. As one bright young New Yorker put it over lunch at Mortimers: "Such a contemporary weapon, don't you think: she killed him with jet lag!"

The possibility was irresistible. He assured Liz Bitsmer that he would be there.

Harrison awoke to two distinct sensations.

Somewhere he could hear the telephone ringing. Lower down, there was a warm and pleasant feeling. He looked down and saw the marquise's head fastened to his groin like a limpet.

The digital clock said 3:24.

First things first, he said to himself, and reached for the receiver. Her bobbing head adjusted to his movement.

"Hello..."

"Mr. Harrison?" It was an overseas operator.

A second voice came on the line. "David? Good. Khafiq here. I'm sorry to bother you at this hour but there have been developments."

He tried to concentrate. The excitement in his groin was unendurable. It was an effort to keep his voice calm.

Khafiq continued. "You have a reservation on the Concorde at eleven today. To Paris. Air France. Come to the Plaza-Athénée. I'll see you there."

"All right," Harrison gasped. "Goodbye." He dropped the phone and let himself explode.

"'Oo was zat?" said the marquise, sliding up beside him. She licked her lips audibly in the dark.

"Just a man on business. I have to go abroad. At eleven.

We should get some rest." He looked at the clock: 3:32; May 20.

"Eleven? Oh, zen we have much time." She spoke like a vedette in a Lecocq operetta. Her hand went between his legs. His protests went for nothing.

10 The Air France people loaded Harrison with gifts: Concorde carryalls, lighters, a sweater. The crowd at the Concorde desk was small. The flights had thinned out after the opening weeks' sensation; no more special discounts for the flashy folk, who these days traveled, seeking shamefaced camouflage behind dark glasses now that they were using their own money, on the standby night flights to Gatwick and Brussels. He was at the airport early, as always. He once said to Barney, "You chase the plane down the runway; I get to the airport while it's being built." So he had a lot of time to hang around the boarding area, sizing up the other passengers. Like most men who spent a lot of time on airliners, he persisted in the fantasy that love would walk in and be assigned the seat next to him.

He got the next best thing. Just as the flight was called for boarding, a sweating black chauffeur panted up to the check-in desk with two briefcases and a fistful of tickets. "My man comin'," he puffed to the agent. Harrison, whose professional equipment included a fine-tuned memory for the secretaries, butlers, and chauffeurs of his clients, looked back down the hallway leading to the departure lounge. A knot of people was making its jerky way to the gate. In the middle, a tall, gray-haired man walked easily, pausing every few steps to scrawl on papers proffered by perspiring young men in three-piece suits.

As he approached the departure desk, he saw Harrison. "Hey, Dave, you on this flight?"

"No, but business is so bad I'm looking for a decent job as a skycap. Figured I'd start where the important folks are." Harrison could be fresh with Ezra Jenkins, who was an old friend and sometimes client.

"Well, on the offchance you're going to Paris, too, maybe we can sit together. I'll just arrange that." He said it to no one in particular, but two of his acolytes detached themselves

(**119**)

from the cluster and padded over to the boarding desk to take care of the matter.

Jenkins looked around the boarding area.

"Anyone interesting on this flight?"

"Not that I can see," said Harrison, "just the advertised collection of lawyers, accountants and civil servants on their usual, first-class rounds: busy screwing up this once wonderful world."

"As always." Jenkins mulled the point. "Wouldn't it be wonderful if all the business schools and law schools were shut down for the next ten years? Not to mention the government."

"Amen," Harrison said. He walked with Jenkins toward the plane.

When the Concorde was airborne and the digital readout on the front bulkhead settled at a steady Mach 2.3, the two men could converse.

Jenkins, it turned out, was on his way to Prague. He was a confident accountant from St. Louis who had parlayed a quick mind and decisive manner into the chairmanship of a fading manufacturer of light industrial valves. When Jenkins came on the scene, the old H. P. Bardley Valve Company, a ratty one-plant operation on the banks of the Merrimack, was creaking along at $45 million a year in sales and making profits which were, politely, negligible. In fourteen years, Jenkins's agility and opportunism, with the help of an army of bankers, investment bankers, lawyers, above all lawyers, had created Bardcom Inc., a conglomerate with 102 divisions doing $965 million a year in sales with profits after taxes approaching $80 million.

Among other things, Bardcom companies made aircraft stabilizers, sold china door to door, transported natural gas from St. Louis north to Columbus, made backhoes and road graders, and dressed fashionable women in $60 jeans. Jenkins ran the whole thing feudally out of a townhouse on Manhattan's East Side; the furnishings and appointments had caused "Aunt Betty" Garrison, New York's leading interior decorator, to gasp in admiration.

"Jesus, Ezra," Harrison had remarked when Bardcom had staged a grandiose champagne reception to open its new quarters, "I hope the stockholders don't ever get a look at this. You'll have a riot on your hands."

"Don't worry, Dave; I just follow Herman Hickman's motto when he was coaching Yale. Old Herman always said he'd have football teams just good enough to keep the alumni sullen but not mutinous. So do I with our stockholders." Jenkins had sipped confidently at his glass of Cristal champagne and reached for another caviar sandwich. Looking down, Harrison saw that there were glass rings on the marquetry writing desk for which Bardcom had paid £97,000 six months earlier at Mallett's in London.

Now, over the Atlantic, Harrison asked, "What takes you behind the iron curtain? In a way, I envy you, they say Prague's about the most beautiful city in Europe."

It turned out that a Bardcom division was in the final stages of making a sale of heavy mining equipment to the Czech national coal industry. The contract had gotten bogged down in technicalities and law talk; so Jenkins had decided, as he frequently did, to take it over himself. He liked going one-on-one in big deals. "No lawyers or yellow-pad people," he'd announce. "Just a closing."

"Shit," he sighed as he finished telling Harrison the story, "I got so goddamn many lawyers working for me I sometimes think I'm teaching law!"

Harrison turned the conversation to his own self-interest. "You get a chance to look at that stuff I sent you on the Mail Guild? That's something I really think you ought to move on. You could sell that stuff door-to-door, too."

The Mail Guild had been one of the high-flying stock stories in the Big Bull Market of the early 1970s. The intellectual cattle in Paul Stuart suits who ran the bank trust departments and the hedge funds had scrambled to the concept as if it were a saltlick. The Guild had been constructed from scratch by a hard-working husband-and-wife team who had decided that upwardly affluent America was ready to buy all sorts of expensive gewgaws by mail. They were right; in five years they were doing $150 million in sales: solid gold watches with dials designed by Salvador Dali; first editions of Erma Bombeck in hand-tooled $300 leather bindings. All the sorts of gear needed by newly, insecurely rich people who craved the visible reassurance of other people's taste, even other people's names and symbols, plastered, appliquéd, carved, or incised on everything they wore or carried.

It was a phenomenon totally alien to Harrison's taste, if not his commercial sense. But it worked. In ten years the Guild's sales were at $433 million. Profits chugged upward. The company's ticker symbol pulsed across the Stock Exchange tape like an America's Cup yacht tacking among dinghies.

It had gotten too big for the original founders to run by themselves. On the advice of their bankers, sharp-eyed financial experts were recruited from outside, professionally laconic men who ended every sentence with "Check," or "Got that?" Along with them came a squadron of financial public relations types, who waved their hands in the air and spoke in concepts.

No good thing goes on forever—not in the world of stocks and bonds. The business became elephantine; a constant flow of new products had to be developed, which put pressure on the founders. The Guild went heavily into debt. The sharp guys, who had been lured there by fat stock options, started playing games with the inventory accounting. But the momentum was now running the other way: not only the numbers, but the human factor. What had been a family place to work turned into a pressure cooker. Earnings sagged; a vengeful employee went tale-bearing to the Securities and Exchange Commission; the stock went straight south. Within a matter of months, the big institutional stockholders, without bothering to see whether there might still be a business back there behind the smoke, scrambled to get out. The stock sold down from 44 to 6.

Which was where it attracted Harrison's attention. The founders were gone, along with the sharp guys and the conceptualists. The Guild was being managed by experienced, diligent men installed by the lenders and the SEC. Sales seemed to be holding up. The company's credit experience with its subscribers appeared to be all right. People were continuing to order things and, more important, were continuing to pay for them.

The Street couldn't have cared less. The Guild was earning about 80 percent of what it had done at the top; *real earnings*, Harrison had written to Jenkins, not the pencilpoint fantasies of the sharp guys, and the stock languished at a small fraction of its former glory. Harrison wasn't surprised.

"These new people," he had been told by Clare Verger, "have no sense of value. And not much interest in it. It goes without saying that they have no idea what it is to run a business, what the general manager of a factory does with his day, for example. They can't live with their embarrassment if a pet idea goes down, even temporarily, so they never look at it again."

Harrison had analyzed the Guild up and down, talked to market makers, customers, competitors. The company was for real, he concluded. He put it down in a memorandum—in his usual succinct, literate way. He didn't go in for those six-hundred-page unread "studies" churned out by the big firms. He didn't necessarily think that his way was right; it was just that he couldn't stand bullshit. And bullshit with a Harvard M.B.A. was still bullshit.

"I read it, Dave," Jenkins was saying. "It's an interesting idea, but not for us."

"Ezra, think it over again. Don't miss this one. Remember Farmworthy." Farmworthy was a Harrison idea that finally got merged into a British grocery chain by a Wall Street house which advertised its capabilities with a lot of overdressed, overstylized photographs and oracular slogans of a phony Confucian sententiousness. Harrison had read one out loud to his friend Barney. The advertisement showed two lugubrious-looking, pinstriped men under the caption, HEADS THINK. *Heads think.*

Barney was equal to the occasion. "The runes of Wall Street," he had punned, "are the ruin of Wall Street."

Ezra Jenkins was talking over the whine of the Concorde. "I know all about Farmworthy, Dave. It was a good idea and this is probably a good, ingenious idea. But it's not for us, even though I've got as good a nose for business pussy as most. Let me tell you something. I'm fifty-nine years old. Last year I took down $450,000, in round numbers. I earned damn near another million in stock appreciation rights. I've got a board that loves me. But they're scared. Every time they turn around there's another lawyer with a subpoena. So we don't do anything now without experts. Let's say we take your idea to our investment bankers—say, to Bing Doolittle at Freiman. Shit, you've been in the business, you know what'll happen. They didn't think of it, so they'll piss all over it. *Not invented here!* They couldn't give a merry screw whether it's good for Bardcom; the fact is, *all* deals brought in by other guys are a bad thing, period, and especially if they come from you, who are not exactly the best-beloved citizen of the world at the big firms!"

True, thought Harrison.

"You see, Dave, why should I get out on a soapbox? Our goddamn stock isn't going anywhere. We have no *concept* which turns the Street on—except making money, which doesn't seem to interest them. I run the company for the goddamn government, anyway. You know what we spent last year filing forms for those sonsabitches in Washington? Fifteen million! That's dollars. That's the price of a new plant, of, say, two hundred new jobs in Appalachia. It's a marginal investment, though, so the $15 million which I'd spend on that plant after I've funded our high-return stuff, goes instead to a bunch of fucking GS-8s in Washington to subsidize their ability to make things tough for us!

"So why should I come in, at my age, and try to get us to take on some big unfriendly deal with a company like this one, that my directors are going to hear questionable things about, even bad things, at their club. You know how it is. Christ, we spend six months and $600,000 studying an acquisition, up, down, sideways, and we come to our board with it and one of those old farts announces he heard bad things about it from some guy he met on the train from Far Hills or at the Gorse and the whole goddamn deal goes out the window!"

Harrison recognized Jenkins's statement as a half, maybe even a quarter, truth. Ezra Jenkins *owned* his board. In addition to the $15,000 each of the board members were paid for nodding through a half-dozen meetings a year, half of the distinguished Bardcom directors made out very nicely working for the company on the side as attorneys, investment bankers, or consultants. Hell, thought Harrison, Ezra is still in the saddle, even after that payoff business in Malawi, which had created total moral outrage on the boards of two billion-dollar oil companies and sent a pair of million-dollar-a-year chief executives hustling to the phone to call the executive recruiters. But Jenkins had helped butter Harrison's bread, and so he said nothing further.

"You want to make some money off us?" Jenkins asked. "Do a deal with us? Find me something in energy. Shit, they've all got a hard-on to get in the energy business. Bring us a company that makes some gizmo you screw on an oil well and our guys'll fall all over themselves voting for it! And pay a hundred times earnings!

"Dave, you're a bright guy. Maybe the brightest I ever met. But you lone wolves are going out of business these days. Everyone's running scared, including me, I regret to say. It's a bitch to admit it. My people want to feel safe, first of all. They'll buy a terrible merger idea from a Mongoloid, if he's got a big investment banking name on his business card, rather than the greatest idea in the world from a guy like you, who's got nothing but brains.

"Christ," said Jenkins, "I had a kid in my office for an hour the other day from one of the big firms. It doesn't matter which. He was twenty-five years old. He didn't have an idea in his head, or ten cents' worth of experience, just wanted to show me a lot of ads and interviews, all with his picture in them. But he's the nephew of one of my directors. I've got fifteen thousand people working in this company, Dave; we operate ninety-seven facilities in this country and another twenty or so around the world. Our capital budget last year was 90 million bucks and that's low because of the chicken-shit economic situation. It takes up a twenty-five-hour day just to keep track and I have to spend two hours with an adolescent merger genius showing me his press clippings. No wonder I've grown to hate investment bankers!"

It was dark outside now. Jenkins had turned away to look out the window. His concentration had shifted to his mission in Prague. There was an hour yet to Paris. Harrison reached into his briefcase and took out his book. *The Way We Live Now.* Trollope understood what big-time business was all about: *"It was a part of the charm of all dealings with this great man that no ready money seemed ever to be necessary for anything. Great purchases were made and great trans-actions apparently completed without the signing even of a cheque."* Trollope would have been right at home in the swinging sixties, thought Harrison. Or now, when physical money, green, real money, seemed to have disappeared.

The Mach counter started to blink lower numbers. Harrison could feel the plane settle into its landing attitude. He read on. *"As for many years past we have exchanged paper instead of actual money for our commodities, so it now seemed that, under the new...regime, an exchange of words was to suffice."*

The plane landed, bumping him out of his absorption. They were in Paris.

There was a note from Khafiq waiting at the *reception* of the Plaza-Athénée. He would look for Harrison downstairs, in the Bar Anglais, at eleven. It was ten-thirty by Harrison's watch.

He was given a large, agreeable room overlooking the Avenue Montaigne. He didn't ordinarily stay at the Plaza, which was a hotel for ostentatious rich people. He preferred the Lancaster in the Rue Berri; it was a hotel for quiet rich people. He put his things away neatly. Harrison didn't like to live like a transient, even for a night or two.

When he walked into the bar, he saw that Khafiq was alone, perched on a large armchair in the rear of the room. Harrison sat down and the two men exchanged greetings.

Coffee and brandies, Harrison's with soda, were brought. Khafiq sipped his drink and looked at Harrison over his glass in a kind, fatherly way.

"It's very good of you to come, David, especially on such short notice. Something very important has come up. It needs the expertise and participation of someone like yourself. A major client. A great opportunity."

Twenty years ago, thought Harrison, I would have tried to sound crisp and would have rushed the questions: Who? What? When? How much? I must be getting *really* old. I've become a listener.

"The client wishes to meet you tomorrow. It is a name you would recognize; he has asked me not to disclose it just yet. I must ask that you keep your morning free. I will telephone you in your room tomorrow as soon as I know his plans."

He finished his coffee. Harrison stood up and shook Khafiq's hand. "It's still only late afternoon for me. I think I'll take a walk, maybe look in on some of my old haunts. I lived here for five years, you know."

Khafiq gave him a schoolmasterish look. "David, may I suggest that you make an early night of it? Tomorrow will come all too soon. Do you need something to sleep? I have something. Believe me, tomorrow will be the most important day of your life."

Khafiq had made his point. Harrison would have liked to look in at Castel's but God knows what trouble he might get into, he thought. Like a dutiful child, he followed Khafiq to the elevator. In his room, he took two Valiums. He hated pills, but they did the trick.

He was awake early. He called down for breakfast and the papers. *Oeufs brouillés,* scrambled eggs made perfectly, the way only the French knew. Flaky croissants. Steaming, rich coffee. It cost twenty-six dollars. The French papers were full of grave situations, public outcries, serious inquiries. Harrison was always beguiled by the stately, intellectualized language the French papers used to describe the public life of their nation. American newspapers, by contrast, spoke of a politics of personalities and events.

After the papers, he dressed and lazed around. He tried to give his book his attention, but he was impatient, his concentration fitful. Not even Trollope's tantalizing drone worked. For a time he looked down into the street, seeing the city come to life. While he watched, the iron shutters were rolled up on the elegant storefronts across the avenue; facades were hosed down; Citroëns and Simcas paused to discharge laughing, kiss-blowing shopgirls. The street began to fill. It was an energetic, beguiling spectacle.

At ten-forty there were two sharp raps on his door. When he went to it, he found Khafiq there.

"All ready, David? Good. Please come with me."

They climbed two flights of glass-enclosed stairs. At the top, Khafiq paused, blowing like a small dolphin.

"Tiring, no? Especially for an old man. But we shouldn't want elevator porters connecting us."

Harrison thought the statement peculiar as he followed the little man down the hall. They passed the open door of a waiter's pantry; the thug in there looked uncomfortable and disheveled in his bolero and apron. This hotel *is* declining, thought Harrison.

Khafiq stopped and knocked at a door at the end of the hall. It opened a crack, for verification, and then the unseen hand behind it drew it fully ajar. Harrison followed Khafiq in.

They found themselves in what was obviously the sitting room of an extensive, lavish apartment. It was furnished in good Louis XV pieces. A man was sitting in an elaborate *bergère* beside the fireless marble hearth. He rose as they entered.

"Your Excellency, may I present Mr. David Harrison."

Holy shit, thought Harrison. He knew the face from the papers. The Minister crossed the room and extended his hand. He didn't seem as tall as his pictures made him appear; he and Harrison seemed to be about the same size.

"How are you?" It was a firm, easy handshake. "Please take a seat." The Minister pointed to a small satin loveseat. "Would you like some coffee?"

Harrison heard someone come into the room behind him. He rose instinctively. Khafiq shot from his seat like a flushed quail.

"Good morning, Your Highness," the Minister said. "Our

guests have just arrived. You of course know our good friend Ali." Khafiq bowed. "And this is Mr. David Harrison."

"Good morning." It was Alrazi.

"Let us begin," he said.

Later, Harrison, talking to himself about that morning at the Plaza-Athénée, rerunning it like a football game film, found himself surprisingly imprecise about details. The fact of the event itself was so overwhelming that it pushed off specifics. "Of course," he would say to himself; there was no one else he could discuss it with, "I just couldn't believe it. So the details got lost. But the best part, goddamnit, was that I was there, *me,* with those men talking about that size deal. *Me,* not some big deal from Morgan, or the Certified. Me. Jesus, I wish I could describe it to old Barrow. He'd crap in his drawers with jealousy."

Alrazi had come right to the point. He addressed himself directly to Harrison.

"Mr. Harrison, what takes place in this room must never go beyond its walls. You will shortly understand why."

He paused while coffee was brought. The waiter who served it did so clumsily, thought Harrison; it was the same man whom he'd noticed in the serving pantry. His normal movements were impeded by the Mannlicher .380 in his armpit. The butt of the gun showed itself as he bent to hand Harrison his cup. Harrison felt cold all over, suddenly. This was no game.

When the waiter left, Alrazi resumed. Harrison found it difficult to focus his attention. He was in new, strange, and possibly dangerous territory. Ordinary people spend their lives light-years distant from great events, unless they are trapped in a war or an earthquake, and distant from truly powerful men, unless they fall under their command. In this respect, Harrison was no different. The power with which he was familiar was limited; the stakes definable; the risk acceptable. In the end, it had always come down to money. He had never presided over or been involved with any of those great, strangling decisions or actions with which these sorts of men dealt. Apart from books, he knew nothing of this level of life and had, really, no sense of how to deal with it. It made him uncomfortable. Nervous.

Scared.

He guessed that Alrazi and the Minister, even Khafiq, who were used to this sort of thing, could perceive his uneasiness. He hoped not. Unconfident and tentative as he felt, he nevertheless knew somewhere in the back of his consciousness that he wanted beyond all imagining to play a significant, hopefully professional, role in whatever was going to be proposed. So he stiffened himself and tried to look calm; calm and knowledgeable, he repeated silently; calm and knowledgeable.

Alrazi *had* sensed his discomfort, however, and was pleased. The man was not going to try to bluff his way through. He *ought* to be a bit nervous. It was only natural.

"Mr. Harrison, you have been strongly recommended by M. Khafiq to advise us on a major investment strategy we propose to implement. The Minister will describe it to you, and then you must give us your reaction."

Alrazi sat back. Harrison looked at him closely. Under his robes, he was a plump sort of man, with the kind of figure that even tailoring of genius could do little to improve. He had a bland face, thought Harrison, dominated by dark eyes which seemed fixed in a perpetual glare. Alrazi's face was a composite of incongruities: the features out of sorts with each other. The sheikh's eyes had a teary morning-after shine to them, Harrison saw. It figured. The word in Washington was that Alrazi was a major leaguer at elbow-bending.

The Minister, by contrast, struck Harrison as a real aristocrat, elegant in every aspect. That's a £600 Huntsman suit, Harrison thought. Alrazi appeared perhaps a generation away from the oasis and the tent life; the Minister seemed to have come from an entirely different culture.

"Mr. Harrison, it appears to us to be propitious at this time to consider placing a substantial incremental investment in U.S. common stocks." The Minister spoke a careful, faintly accented English; again a contrast with Alrazi, who had a staccato, overbearing diction. Alrazi had used his voice to emphasize his importance. The Minister's tone was by contrast instructive, assured.

"We have, as you probably know, several hundred million dollars in the American stock market. These investments are supervised, principally, by Certified Bank in New York, by Morgan Guaranty, and by a number of other American banks. We employ only banks to handle our investments, although results to date suggest that the wisdom of that policy seems to me to be open to question." The Minister smiled.

"Then, of course, additional commitments have been made from time to time by certain of our advisors in London, Geneva, and Singapore. At the last accounting, the total value

(129)

of our holdings in U.S. stocks and other equities, excluding money-market investments and Eurodollar participations, came to just under $590 million. Not a great sum.

"Recent events and certain anticipated developments have caused us to modify our view with respect to dollar investments, especially in common stocks." He saw that Harrison looked puzzled, but that was too bad; the Minister had agreed with Alrazi to be no more specific on the matter of motivation.

Harrison *was* puzzled. The fact was that he had for the time forgotten—perhaps put aside would be more accurate—his conversation with Khafiq. Harrison's flights of imagination so seldom had paid off that he assumed that the sole reason for Khafiq's summons was the good name for discreet professionalism that his Stavrapos involvement had disseminated. Developments? It was clear from the Minister's tone that all had been said on that matter that would be said. Maybe he could get something out of Khafiq later.

"So now," the Minister was saying, "it makes sense for us to expand, materially, our position in common stocks, for which we can foresee a significantly improved environment in the next year." God, thought Harrison, those words sound like one of those investment solons who pontificate in *Barron's*. He was right. Years of dealing with bankers and investment types had exposed the Minister to the contagion of their pompous, synthetic vocabulary. "I really have to wash my mind out," he had once said to Khafiq after a particularly lugubrious session with Leslie Merriman and a retinue of Certified trust officers. "Where do they learn to talk that way?" Harrison could have told him. It was called Business English, was taught in Business Schools, and had developed to confer a quality of intellectual and philosophical legitimacy on the otherwise simple, vulgar matter of buying and selling things.

"We want, therefore, to set in motion a buying program which will put a substantial amount of money in place over the next nine to twelve months."

A substantial amount of money?

"How much were you thinking of, Your Excellency?"

"Between $5 and $10 billion."

Ouch, thought Harrison! Five and 10 billion. *Billion.* It would be like starting the trust department at Bankers Trust from scratch.

"That *is* a great deal of money, sir." Harrison was buying a few seconds of mental computer time. The numbers started clicking away. Volume on the New York Stock Exchange was running at around 22 million a day. The average value of a share was, say, $30. Say $25, to be safe. That worked out to $550 million a day. Add another $50 million for the American Stock Exchange and over-the-counter trading. That would be low, but it was better to be safe. Now let's see; say you got going in July and had nine months, that would get you through next March; nine months at, say, twenty trading days a month, allowing for every Christian, Jewish, federal, state, and local holiday; the Stock Exchange took 'em all. That's 180 trading days. One hundred eighty times $600 million. Now the zeros got tough: $108 billion. Was that right? Yes, $108 billion. So you're talking, at $10 billion of new money, 10 percent of volume. Which is too much.

He looked across at the Minister. "Theoretically, sir, in nine months, you could put as much as $10 billion to work. But that would be 10 percent of the volume. Merrill Lynch today does perhaps 5 percent, so you're talking about, in effect, adding two Merrill Lynches to the market. That would attract a great deal of attention, which I suspect you wouldn't want. If you spread it over twelve months, say to next July, the figure comes down to around 7 percent. Lower, but still an attention-getter."

"July would be too late," Alrazi said. "The matter must be completed by the end of next March."

The Minister gave Alrazi a sharp, wrist-slapping look.

"We would certainly not wish to attract attention." He turned back to Harrison. "As a matter of fact, that is why we have asked you to consult with us. We must operate with the utmost discretion; with absolute secrecy, you understand? A great deal is at stake. Money obviously, but other things. We cannot entrust this to the normal channels. Your countrymen have a displeasing tendency to discuss other people's business. If this were to be brought to light, ever, the consequences would be grave for everyone concerned. Everyone."

Again, Harrison was perplexed. There were some political resonances in all this; there was something in the Minister's voice and choice of words that said to Harrison, You are being invited in as a coconspirator. Something was offbeat. He couldn't quite fix it. No wonder, really; Harrison had never in his life heard the flutter of danger's wings.

"What we want to know, Mr. Harrison, is whether you will undertake to manage the U.S. end of this affair for us. Khafiq will take care of the money transfers into the United States.

We have our own discreet machinery for that. But we would look to you for the supervision and selection of these new investments and to see, absolutely, that they are made in a manner which will create no attention or identification."

So here, just as Khafiq had suggested, was the biggest job of Harrison's life. Obviously he wanted it, but he would have to think it through to see if he *could* do it.

"Your Excellency, I must be candid with you. You are proposing what must be the greatest opportunity and greatest challenge for anyone in my line of work. Investments don't happen to be my specialty, in the sense of picking stocks, but the amount of money of which you speak is so great that it will have to be spread broadly across the market."

It certainly would. IBM was worth, what, $45 billion in the market, so we were talking 10 percent of the value of the biggest stock in the world.

"Precisely, Mr. Harrison. What is needed is not, in our opinion, a list of securities. What is needed is the imagination, the grandeur of conception, if you will, to devise a plan to meet such enormous, exacting objectives, objectives of both magnitude and timing. And the sense of detail to see that it is executed without flaw or misstep."

"You are most flattering, Your Excellency." Harrison was capable of a sort of literary courtliness when the situation demanded it. "May I have a fortnight to consider the matter? To consider, only, I want to emphasize, whether what you seek is feasible on the terms you have stipulated. It will take some study."

"That will be acceptable. Why don't you come back to Khafiq with your answer. You will be in London, then, Ali? In all events, you would be working on this with Khafiq."

The Minister looked first at Alrazi and then again at Khafiq before turning back to Harrison. "Very well, sir, we'll await your report." He stood up and put his hand out. "I've enjoyed meeting you."

He shook hands and dipped his head to Alrazi. The sheikh's farewell was brusque; before releasing Harrison's hand, he stared at him intently for an instant. It was a fierce, mistrustful look; later, Harrison would think that he found it physically threatening.

"I'll go with you downstairs, David," said Khafiq. He had said nothing since they had come into the suite. Nevertheless, Harrison felt that Khafiq had an influence on these men that needed no warrant of words.

At the door, the Minister took Harrison's hand again. They had exchanged no light conversation, no personal history, yet Harrison felt, and he thought the Minister felt, a real bond.

"Well, goodbye, Mr. Harrison. I don't know if we'll meet again. Mine is a peculiar life. It seems to have no dependable pattern." The door to the suite closed.

As they walked down the hall, Harrison said to Khafiq, "I don't suppose it would do much good to ask you about certain aspects of all of this?"

"Correct. But I will emphasize two things to you. First, this is not a matter of state. Second, the timing is absolutely critical. The amount of money invested is of less consequence than the requirement that it be invested by next March 31."

They separated at the elevator. Khafiq looked at his watch. "It's twelve-thirty. If I hurry I can make my booking on the three-forty-five flight to London. I'm going down to the country for the weekend. Call me when you are ready."

Khafiq was carried away by the elevator; Harrison pushed the "down" button. In his room he looked at his pocket diary. March 31 was no special date, just the Monday before Easter.

After Harrison and Khafiq had left, the Minister sat down and looked frankly at Alrazi.

"Are you content?" he asked. "This is a very dangerous idea, you know. If the King is apprised..." The sentence needed no conclusion.

He was not happy with the plan, not *entirely* happy, to be fair about it. He liked the prospects for himself, of course, if it all worked out. Khafiq was right. As he'd said at dinner the night before: "Face facts, Your Excellency. If left to his own devices, the King will yield to the imams and use his fortune to gild the streets of Mecca."

It was what had been on Alrazi's mind when he summoned the Minister to him after the meeting with the King.

"His Majesty has left the matter in our discretion," he reported. "I think we should do it. I am nervous about a number of things. There are murmurs in the bazaars of political agitation. We are unequipped to deal with terrorism and, in any case, the use of secret police never works for long. We need the Americans here. And we need them soon. So we will do what you have suggested, we will go ahead and try to buy them!"

The surprising two sides of Prince Alrazi, thought the Minister. Here was the sober, practical councillor of state. A cool mind informed with the good sense of history. And next week, or next month in Paris? There would be the tipsy, overweight oil sheikh throwing rubies at starlets in discotheques.

"I have considered the mechanics of the plan. And the timing. I think Easter would be an excellent, highly symbolic moment for us to announce the price cut. The great gift of Islam to the West on the greatest Christian holiday. A nice touch, don't you think? You will make the announcement. You are the voice of our oil policy."

The Minister looked at his agenda. "As it happens, I am scheduled to be in Honolulu next year during the week before Easter—which falls, let's see, on April sixth. There is an international Offshore Resources Conference; all the OPEC spokesmen will be there. I am scheduled to fly back on Easter Sunday."

"Excellent. Isn't the Friday before Easter a Christian holiday, too?"

"It is. Good Friday, they call it."

"That is perfect. They will be in a holiday mood with a long weekend. You will make the announcement Thursday night in Honolulu so as to reach the mainland on that Good Friday. America and the Christian world will go to their churches on Easter Sunday with something to rejoice in!"

"It's quite a long time off."

"I'm only following your first recommendation, dear cousin. That will be six months before the election. Enough time to build an enormous momentum. We want our benevolence to be fresh in that famously short American memory. And I have an idea about a way in which we might profitably employ what might be described as the waiting period."

The Minister looked curious. Alrazi was uncharacteristically intense and serious.

"What is the King's wealth, Minister?"

"As much as 7 billion—dollars, of course—perhaps as little as five. Property values are difficult to calculate exactly."

"And yours?"

"Mine?"

"Yes. And mine?"

"I don't really know. In my case, perhaps several tens of millions. In yours, perhaps several hundreds." Less now, the Minister thought. Alrazi had recently paid a Brazilian $43 million for a three-hundred-foot sailing yacht. Trifona of Milan was redecorating it; that would come to another $5 million.

"I have a very simple point of view," said Alrazi. "It is personally impossible to have too great a wealth, provided one gains it without violence or overt dishonesty. I also intend never to be poor again—even in a relative sense!" The statement didn't surprise the Minister. The westernization of Sheikh Alrazi had included reshaping his personal financial code into one fundamentally similar to that of the parvenu Maecenases of Europe and America.

"Now," he continued, "if our assumptions are correct, what we propose to do will produce a dramatic rise in the American stock market. Indeed. And a great deal of money will be made. Huge fortunes, perhaps." The Minister nodded.

"So," said Alrazi, "we are also going to make a large fortune, you and I and Khafiq. We will not have the chance again. After all, I don't think it has ever been given to such a small group to cause such a great effect on the price and value of securities and currency. Do you realize that with seven words—'We are reducing the price of oil'—you will mint many billions of value for the holders of stocks and bonds?"

"True. Of course, that is essentially the fortunate byproduct, what the Americans call a 'windfall,' of a major political and diplomatic thrust."

"Indeed. Now let me ask you, cousin, what do you think is to become of the King's fortune?"

"It will be passed to his family, to his sons and male descendants, as it was to him."

"Not so. I am close to the King, you know; but, regretfully, he listens to me only with one ear, and only on affairs which do not really interest him. What is his dream is to raise a holy city that will bring him everlasting credit and a blissful eternity in the bosom of Allah. Dear cousin, the priests have convinced him to turn his fortune over to them at his death. The pledge is inscribed in the Ledger of Allah in the mosque. I was obliged, sadly, to witness its being recorded. To change it will bring the curses of Allah on the King and will deny him access to paradise."

This was news to the Minister. Bad news. The King was frail and the phlebitic condition which ailed him was worryingly more obvious with each day.

"So, cousin, I believe that before anything happens to my dear nephew, we secure ourselves. I will not be poor ever again! Now, the King's privy funds are mingled with the reserves of the Kingdom, are they not?"

"Yes, we make no distinction of accounts when we deal

with our bankers in New York and elsewhere. The identity and holdings of each separate account are recorded here. In my ministry."

"Excellent. Well, what we are going to do is to borrow my nephew's wealth for a time. Interest-free. The Koran, after all, forbids the earning of interest." Alrazi smiled. "We will place this money in the American stock market. Before the election and before we rescind the price cut, we will sell out and return to the King what is his. The difference will be ours. An excellent plan, don't you think?"

Alrazi was grinning with satisfaction.

There was no point in moralizing. The Minister liked his job, which he held via Alrazi at the pleasure of the King. There were other claimants in the field. He would have to go along with Alrazi; and, since he must, why not profit by it?

"Excellent. Of course it is technically very difficult, perhaps impossible. One cannot just walk in and put down an order for several billion dollars' worth of common stock." The Minister wasn't sure of this. He seemed to recall Khafiq telling him that the Russians had bought up 20 percent of the American wheat harvest in one afternoon, using only the switchboard at a New York hotel.

"Technicalities," said Alrazi impatiently. "They can be dealt with. Involve your friend Khafiq in this. He'll come up with something. He always has."

Harrison went down to the Relais Plaza, the small restaurant on the Rue Marot side of the hotel where all the chic people, the *tout Paris*, gathered to make air-kisses and frantic social wigwags. He had a *Byrrh cassis* and watched the show. The place was packed with elegant, highly pitched men and women. The sweetish vermouth made him hungry and he ordered a *Croque-monsieur*, which he ate at the bar. The rest of the day was his own.

He spent a delicious afternoon by himself. He'd thought of visiting the Louvre, but that was like eating pistachios; you got started and couldn't stop and that was a full day's work. So he dawdled along the Faubourg and then along the Seine, poking into shops and stalls. At a fine, small gallery on the far side of the Seine there was an exciting show of Manet etchings. He bought a good signed state of *Le Guitarero* and chatted with the gallery's owner. He looked in on an old friend who ran an antiquarian bookstore in the Marais. From vitrines which had belonged to a Duc de Guise, he chose an Aldine *Petrarca* and a rare French translation of Boswell.

It was a little after five when he got back to the hotel. Two workmen were taking down a banner. Harrison didn't recognize it so he asked the concierge, who identified it as the flag of the Kingdom. "We just had their Prime Minister here," said the concierge. "Much commotion." He winked.

In his room, Harrison called Marguerite, an old girl of Blaise's with whom he had enjoyed a relationship "off the books." Now semiretired, she was kept in splendor in an apartment on the Avenue Foch by a Lebanese importer whose relentless parsimony often obliged him to be away from Paris conferring with his many bankers.

She was delighted to hear from Harrison. Yes, she was free for dinner. The Lebanese was in Frankfurt.

He picked her up at eight-thirty. He'd reserved a table at Chez l'Ami Louis, in the Rue de Vertbois. "It's like eating off the curb," Marc-Antoine had said, "but the *foie gras* is the best in Paris, the Beaujolais the best in France, and the *frites* the best in the world."

Harrison and Marguerite were gorging themselves in the nondescript restaurant when there was a slight break in the noise, a murmur around the room, and the Minister came in. He was splendidly turned out in blazer and flannels; on his arm was a tall girl whose hair was nearly white and whose eyes were an extraordinary violet.

No sign passed between the men as the Minister and his companion went by Harrison's table. Out of earshot, Marguerite said quietly to Harrison, "That's Meribel, one of Blaise's new stars. She's Danish. She gets three thousand francs an evening. They say she..." She whispered a description of excruciating indelicacy in Harrison's ear. He laughed. "I didn't think that was physically possible." His admiration for the Minister soared.

It was a splendid meal. As was his custom, the old man who owned the restaurant paid neither deference nor attention to his great and famous client of the evening. He cooked well for all, and was rude to all, without prejudice. People crossed Paris to be insulted by M. Magnin and to sample his *foie gras*.

Marguerite took Harrison back to the Avenue Foch. They were as good with each other as ever. "*Mort au Liban,*" he cried playfully, as she drew his head between her legs. Afterward, she cupped his face in her hands. "David, my darling,

(**137**)

you are a true international incident: a French tongue in an American mouth."

At dawn, she telephoned for a taxi. *"Je t'embrasse, David, je t'adore."* He kissed her. She was sleeping softly.

He packed and was at the airport by nine.

It wasn't until he had dozed through an hour after lifting off from Charles de Gaulle that his euphoria, which had been helped along by the residual kick of the prior evening's Beaujolais, evaporated sufficiently to let him start to try to sort things out. It was obvious that Khafiq was like family with the Minister. Their exchanges were marked with a familiarity as evidential as fingerprints. He had deduced that Khafiq had gotten Stavrapos out the hole with the Certified in the Galveston mess. Nobody, except the biggest biggies there were, could jerk the Certified around—so it was a good bet that the Minister, or through him maybe Alrazi, had put the arm on the Certified, probably on Merriman himself. Jesus, that would have been something to hear!

Now they wanted to stick ten big ones, very very big ones, in the market. Of course the market was down, way oversold, but still you didn't pop for ten billion on fundamentals or what the charts said. There weren't any fundamentals, anyway, and these people wrote the book on wizardry, so they weren't likely to buy charts and graphs. These were surething bettors, except on horses and falcons.

He hearkened back to his conversation with Khafiq on Stavrapos's yacht. No, what they'd discussed wasn't what happened in real life.

These were just good ideas and good ideas didn't turn the world around. There must be something else.

His exhaustion dropped the curtain on consciousness again. He dreamt he was in a vast courtyard, pointing an enormous gaping cannon at a crowd of tethered prisoners; Leslie Merriman and Arthur Mismer and Mac Lipton were in the front row, along with the President, Baxter, and a lot of newspaper-familiar faces he couldn't quite identify. He pulled the lanyard; the weapon fired a great spray of excrement which covered the prisoners with a reeking mess. Above the flatulent poundings of the cannon, he seemed to hear voices singing a clean, bright song. He fired again and again.

It was a great dream. He hated to see it mist away as he felt a hand on his shoulder, and the stewardess told him that they were beginning their descent into New York.

11 For ten days, Harrison immersed himself in the current literature on investments and the stock market. Mornings and afternoons were spent in the libraries of investment management firms where he had friends. Breakfasts and lunches were given over to meetings with those same friends, plumbing the techniques and attitudes of men who were paid to run the investment portfolios of unions, corporate pension accounts, old and new family wealth. Late one evening, at home, Harrison totted it up: nine business meals in one week had exposed him to the thinking of people who pushed nearly $20 billion around.

"What's this all about, Dave?" one friend had asked. "You don't fool with investments. You corporate finance guys work the markets differently. This isn't your line of country. Something going on I should know about?"

Harrison had demurred. "I'm just out of touch. All this theory has changed things. There're a lot of new buzzwords. My clients like to think I know what I'm talking about; I do too, for that matter. Nothing's going on right now so I thought I'd give myself a crash course."

He needed it. His only brush with the arcane world of money management had come as part of his early training at Verger. It wasn't Verger's main business, supervising portfolios, but the firm had rich clients who invested in private deals, and so it had taken on the rest of their investment action as a lucrative sideline.

In those primeval days, Harrison remembered, investment strategy consisted principally of sending research analysts out to interview companies. If the business prospects appeared good, the management honest and capable, the norms of worth, such as assets and profits, at least comparable to alternative possibilities, it was a simple matter of buying the stock and waiting for the market to reward early perceived virtue. The Aristotle, Thomas Aquinas, and Einstein of the business in those days was Benjamin Graham; he preached an investment gospel of looking at hard numbers, relating them to price, and deciding whether a share of ABC or XYZ represented fair value.

By today's standards, Harrison came to see, that was quill-pen thinking: the Wright Brothers compared to the Space

Shuttle. He was struck by the tremendous amount of gob-bledygook which had come into common usage. As he plowed through glossy stacks of *The Institutional Investor, Journal of Portfolio Management, Forbes,* and the like, fancy, abstruse terms filled the air like paper gliders in a schoolroom at recess. *Beta and Alpha*: measurements of the volatility of a given stock. *Indexing*: people being paid to invest portfolios in the popular stock averages. *Discrete regression. Heuristic determinism. Trading polyphonics.* His mind reeled.

"When I read this stuff," he said at breakfast one morning to Tom Hampton, who was a recognized investment expert, "I feel like I've been caught in a manure storm."

"Welcome to the club," said Hampton. "I can put the thing in perspective for you. First, we now have Uncle Sam in our pants twenty-four hours a day, with ERISA. That's the old 'prudent man' role bureaucratized. So, everyone who manages pension money has to run scared. Which opens the door to the computer gang. No one can accuse you of being imprudent if you throw your judgment out the window and simply do what a machine tells you to do. Second, these days the customer wants a lot of pseudoscientific bullshit for his dollar. He gives us fifty million bucks to invest and then spends another hundred grand hiring consultants to tell him how we're doing and more consultants to tell him how the first consultants are doing. And so on.

"Then there are the indexers. Their portfolios duplicate the Standard & Poor's stock average—so as not to be out-performed by the Standard & Poor's stock average—for which they get paid a nice, fat management fee. And there are the 'closet' indexers: guys who trick up what is basically an index fund with betas and alphas and pretend they're picking stocks; it's like putting a ten-dollar hooker in a Halston and saying she's a lady. And then we've got the MPT guys. *Modern Portfolio Theory.* You should see them in person. Which isn't hard; they spend about 360 days a year giving speeches.

"Finally, of course, we have the dart throwers, astrologists, and prayer-wheelers, but they've always been around."

By the time Harrison had finished his brief, unsentimental education in current investment thinking, the main lines of the solution he was after began to emerge.

He took as a given the Minister's assertion that the means existed to move the money into position. He guessed it would probably involve a kaleidoscopic passage through Europe, Asia, Canada, and the Caribbean into U.S. banks: probably twenty or so. From there, where he would take over, the money would have to keep moving. Large piles of idle liquidity attracted attention; the money mustn't sit too long in any place, *as cash.*

Velocity, he wrote in his notebook.

In its U.S. travels, the money would probably move through a second network of institutions, bank trading rooms, and computer hookups. It should all be as automatic and as inconspicuous as possible.

Automation, he wrote. And underneath: *No human hands.*

The investment was going to be aimed at a big market move to be brought about by a specific act. He thought he knew what it was. He wasn't going to have to buy stocks in particular; to buy the market in general was the objective.

Broadly diversified, he wrote. *Maybe 2000 issues?*

It had to be closely monitored. No orders so big as to attract attention. No accumulation in any one company of a size which would necessitate a filing with the SEC.

Control, he wrote. *No SEC. No regulatory.*

Last, it had to go undiscovered.

Camouflage, he wrote.

At last he came to conceive the armature on which he might hang the whole scheme. The best disguise, thought Harrison, would be total anonymity. An absolutely colorless, undifferentiated impersonality. The $5 billion, which he now felt to be the maximum which he could confidently and secretively put to work in the time he was to be given, must be made to fade into the market like a pickpocket in a crowd. The money must be broken down into small but manageable quanta, moving restlessly and continuously through a network of banks into a great range of stocks, never in outside trading lots. Each link in the bank network should control no more money than a good-sized institutional investment account would normally represent.

To help block it out, he did some quick figuring. He would need around a hundred accounts. Each account would hold between $20 and $75 million. These accounts would have to be fed instructions by a large number of telex inputs. Daily buying should not exceed 3 percent of volume: 80,000 to 1 million shares a day in all markets and exchanges.

It began to fall into place. On a page of his notebook he drew a schematic diagram, the felt-tip lines marking out the flows, indicating the connections and interchanges. The logistics were straightforward enough. The diagram looked like an electromechanical wiring plan. He knew when he looked at it that he had drawn a metaphor for the sort of unseen hand that would throw the switches and direct the traffic. The whole thing would have to be run by and through a computer.

He took up his notebook again, writing so rapidly that the lines often turned illegible; he didn't want to lose an idea while the fit was on him.

Khafiq would feed the money on order into certain U.S. banks. The machine would be programmed to give Harrison a continuous seven-day rolling estimate of his forward cash needs. Harrison would establish a hundred accounts at other U.S. banks, which would act as custodians and executants for the purchase and sale of securities. Cash transfers would be made on the bank wire, the communications system which linked the big money center banks with each other and their correspondents. Orders would be placed by Harrison, who would telex or telephone the orders as directed by a daily script prepared by the computer.

The computer was the key. Harrison knew next to nothing about the inner working of computer logic and programs. Naive in his conviction that machines were the servants of man, he simply assumed that a computer could be made to deliver what he wanted: a program which would orchestrate thousands of small investment "bits" over the allotted time. His crash course had given him an idea about where to buy such a program. He would commission a $700 million module, specifying an account distribution of 100 names and a position distribution of 2000 different issues. This was slightly less than 30 percent of the companies carried in the Standard & Poor's Compustat statistical service, which he could buy off the shelf.

He would find a way of scaling it up himself—or would simply run it through six or seven times.

One by one, he checked off the notes he had made. There were still things to be done, however, and the sheer size of the project was beyond one man's capacity to put it all in place, within the time they had given him. The calendar said May 25. He had almost ten months, beginning today.

He rechecked his original criteria. The computers and the telex machines would transfer the money, choose, direct, and allocate the stock purchases, and keep the records, all with the voiceless and faceless anonymity of machines talking to each other, just a reciprocal sparking of diodes and circuits.

But there were still some questions beyond his answering. And a tremendous workload. He thought for a moment. He would need help.

So he wrote *"People"* in a large hand across the bottom of the page. The next morning he telephoned Khafiq that he was ready to talk.

He was glad to be back in London, especially at a time when England was at its brightest. A month-long festival of lawns: Glyndebourne, Wimbledon, Ascot.

Harrison checked into his new favorite hotel: a red Victorian mishmash of turrets and foxhole corridors just off Sloane Street. The price was right and the clientele, mostly county families up to London for clothes and "the season," bearable. His old haunts in Mayfair had become uninhabitable: Claridges seemed to be reserved for the big spenders who chomped watercress sandwiches in the lobby and cursed the price of everything while a knee-britched quartet sawed away at Strauss waltzes in the background. The other great West End hotels resembled the slums of Baghdad.

It was a short walk to Khafiq's house. Like most American men, Harrison reveled in London. He liked the look of the buildings and the streets, liked what was in the shops, liked the loose bedroomy emanations of the women. He appreciated—without emulating—the flamboyant dressy anachronisms of the men. Overall, the food was a little shaky, but one sometimes ate well and from time to time splendidly. It was somehow a place where a glass of port and a fat cigar seemed in character for him. In New York he didn't smoke a dozen cigars a year or drink a single glass of port.

Khafiq's house was a pleasant surprise. The pale cream bowfront was about halfway along the Crescent, looking out on a small, fenced park. It was a quiet, shady enclave, well removed from the Knightsbridge arteries that bore the weight of the day's traffic back and forth to the West End or the City.

A white-jacketed butler opened the door. Harrison was ushered into a sunny sitting room opening on to a pleasant formal garden. It was a comfortable room. A Chippendale sideboard bore a tray of liquor bottles, siphons, and crystal that sparkled like lakewater. Three Delft pots of roses, yellow, peach, and salmon, accented the yellow fabric of the sofas. Harrison guessed that the furniture changed its skin with the seasons. The only heavy piece in the room, set back against the wall that received the least light and flanked by two *famille verte* K'ang-hsi dogs set on pearwood lamp bases, was a dark burgundy Edwardian chesterfield. The walls were the color of young limes. It was a room, Harrison felt, that would work as well and comfortably in the winter, with a fire burning in the hearth, as it did now in the June sunlight.

"David. Do you like my little house? I must show you the rest of it." Khafiq took his hand warmly. "How about some coffee? Was your flight agreeable? It's so uncivilizing, air travel."

"It's a marvelous room. Those are very fine." Harrison pointed to the rows of David Roberts watercolors, originals, he guessed, for the *Holy Land* series.

"Oh, those little things! Well, I bought them for the subjects, really. It's my small gesture by way of what the English call flag waving for my country. One must do something, after all, and my neighbors would complain if I pitched a tent in the Crescent and tethered a camel to the lamppost. They're having a bad enough time as it is with the Iraqis hanging their laundry on the Embassy balconies."

Harrison had to laugh.

"Well now," said Khafiq when the coffee had come, "what have you got for us? Will it work?"

"I think so. I've done a lot of research. However we go about it, we want to swim with the current. We must keep with the crowd. I've tried to come up with something that is reasonably straightforward. I've written it out. You'll have to bear with the typing. I did it myself." He reached into an old Hermes briefcase and took out a thin folio of typed pages.

"Tell me a little about it," said Khafiq.

Harrison recapitulated his work. Described the computer program which he expected to work up and the pretense under which he planned to have it written for him. He went over the basic arithmetic: 100 accounts; $50 million per average account; 2000 stocks in the portfolio; never more than 4.9 percent of the outstanding stock of any company.

"I'm going to buy a program to handle $750 million. It will be useful and will limit the purchase to 0.7 percent of the outstanding stock of any one company. That way I can run it through seven times to get up to $5 billion; not repeating it, but running it in reverse once, then around from the halfway point and so on, and still fall short of the SEC regulation that you have to show your hand with a 5 percent holding."

"It sounds interesting. And credible. I will review it."

"Is there anything else you might need to know?"

"Yes, there are. Two things. First, as automated as this may be, I cannot imagine that you intend to handle it entirely by yourself. You will doubtless be using some collaborators. May I ask whom you have in mind?"

It was a question Harrison had been expecting.

"I *will* need some assistance and, as a matter of fact, I'd planned to ask you for help there. I will need two people: one to help me open the accounts and place the orders and generally keep track of the details, and an expert at computers to work up the programs and the printouts and to cope with any technical problems and the machines. It is really best if you supply them. For me to hire anyone in a field that is new to me will cause talk. Besides, no matter what was said in Paris, this *does* seem to have political implications. Therefore, it's best that you put in your own people. I can work with damn near anyone who's competent. I do think it would be useful if the two you send haven't any obvious connections to one another. The more disparate, the better. A man and a woman perhaps. I need presentability, a decent level of general intelligence, and in one of them, specific expertise in computers."

"I quite understand," said Khafiq. "I will put the machinery in order. Assuming we go ahead, of course. Which I think we shall.

"Now," he added, "one final thing. What do you expect to be paid?"

Harrison had prepared for this. He might be mounting the largest single investment transaction in history. As a simple matter of professional standing, therefore, he felt entitled to the largest fee in history and he wanted to keep it for himself, and not simply dish it off to the Internal Revenue Service.

"Basically, I think a fair level of compensation, assuming the operation is successful, should be on the order of $100 million. Since, like any taxpayer, I resent working for the U.S. government, I would like this to be paid in a certain fashion.

"First, when you give the signal to go ahead, I would like $5 million to be available as a straight cash fee, paid into accounts I keep in New York, Geneva, and here. The last is really paying my tailors. Second, I own a small company in the U.S. which makes packaging machinery; I bought it six years ago with some friends and investors. They own a third of it; the rest is mine. When the operation is finished, you will cause it to be bought for $23 million, out of which I will realize $8 million after paying off some loans. Finally, when your investment program is completed, or should you advise me to stop, you will have deposited in Zurich and Geneva, in trust, a sum sufficient to provide an income to me or my heirs, *in perpetuity,* of $5 million a year tax-free. Concomitantly, it should be arranged so that I may borrow up to $75 million against that income stream and assign all or a part of it to repay the loan. The principal will remain with you or your nominee."

Khafiq smiled approvingly as he pocketed the notes he had jotted down. He liked ingenuity. "I will submit your fee to the client—along with this." He held up the sheets which Harrison had given him. "I have to go to Paris for several days. When I return I'll have the answer. Why don't you remain in London until my return? There are worse places to be than England in June, even if the poets prefer other months. We could dine here Sunday evening. If you take the Concorde Monday morning, you'll have a full day in New York."

Why not? thought Harrison. He nodded.

"Excellent. I'll put through a booking for you." Khafiq spoke into the telephone. "Is there anything else we can do for you?"

"I don't think so, really."

"Good. How about a drink before lunch, then?"

Harrison knew that Khafiq would bring a final answer back from Paris. As he walked back to his hotel, the day's Turf caught his attention at a newsstand. He bought a copy. On the front page was a photograph of Prince Alrazi. It had been taken at Longchamps. Over the Prince's shoulder, Harrison recognized the pompous, swollen face of the Aga Khan. The caption read: ARAB LEADERS TO CONTEST ON TURF. The sheikh was sending out Desert Prince in the Prix Malle on Saturday. Harrison wondered if Alrazi would be coming over to England the following week for Royal Ascot.

He had four days in London. Four free days. An exuberant prospect.

From the hotel, he called his friends, the Lyall-Marshes. Desdemona Lyall-Marsh answered. She was delighted to hear his voice; they were old friends. Desdemona and Billy Lyall-Marsh and Harrison had skied and shot together and explored most of the nightclubs in the Western world.

"David, you stinker! Why didn't you call earlier?"

"Hurry-up trip, Des, I couldn't. Look, why don't you and Billy dine with me this evening? Or whenever. I'm here till Sunday night."

"Oh, David, Billy's gone to Switzerland on business. One of those awful Arabs or something. He's not due back until Monday."

"Well, why don't you come, then? Can't have you sitting around like a golf widow."

"Oh, David, I would love to. The children are still at school; I've given the servants a holiday—you know how Billy insists on having them here every minute when he's at home—so this place is a positive mausoleum. I'm supposed to go to my sister Rosalind's for dinner, but I'll put her off. What time?"

"I'll be there at eight."

He wasn't at all displeased at the news of Billy Lyall-Marsh's absence. He'd always had a crush on Des, and Billy had gotten to be something of a bore. All antecedents and no brains, Billy worked at the Wellington Bank; in Khafiq's old department, as it happened, although Harrison didn't know that. When he wasn't being dreary about his rich Arab friends, Billy persisted in talking like Squire Allworthy, about shootin', huntin', fishin', and ridin'. And what a hot summer would do to the birds. He epitomized what a journalist had once said to Harrison: "The English upper class can talk passionately about two things only: other people's money and grouse."

Harrison wondered how Des put up with it.

He was outside the Lyall-Marshes's house in Chelsea promptly at eight. Desdemona came to the door and laughed. "You *will* be so punctual, David. Can't you be just a bit more English, at least when you're in London?"

She was a marvelous-looking woman. Even at thirty-six or -seven, which he knew her to be, she had a youthful high color overlaying clear pale skin. Her dark hair was in bangs, fashionable this year, but she didn't have a trendy appearance. She had large breasts on a slender frame; he found the juxtaposition very exciting.

"God, you look wonderful, Des!" He was the sort of man who complimented women with a natural, honest enthusiasm that they found very masculine.

He had booked a table at the Guinea. They ordered asparagus and steaks off the counter at the entrance and a bottle of Clos des Lambrays from the wine steward.

"How clever and divine of you to bring me here, David. I think I should scream if I see another bit of carrot and turnip artfully arranged by some all-the-rage Frenchman."

Over dinner they talked about trips they had taken, other friends, places to go. They exchanged news and gossip. The Burgundy was heavy and rich.

Over coffee, Harrison, looking at her through the cigar smoke, thought he detected an edge of sadness. "Something wrong, Des? You look a bit down."

She'd drunk enough to be open about her introspections. "Oh, it's Billy again, David. He's in Lausanne with that secretary of his. Making a perfect ass of himself in the Beau Rivage. My sister Portia's husband Jack saw them together at that frightfully expensive restaurant in Crissier. It's so humiliating."

Harrison knew the English and he knew Desdemona. The embarrassment was worse than the infidelity.

"Well, we can't have you moping about," he said. "A little dancing and bubbly will set you straight. Let's go over to Annabel's."

As they walked across Berkeley Square toward the club, she put her arm through his.

"Better?" he said.

"Yes." She cocked her head. "No nightingales about this evening."

At Annabel's they welcomed Harrison and bowed in homage to the Honorable Mrs. Lyall-Marsh. Louis gave them a good table. Across the aisle a table of Italians were noisily scooping truffle-sprinkled fettuccine into their mouths like Sicilian orphans.

They had a bottle of champagne. Danced. And had another. There were moments when they sat in silence.

It was nearly two in the morning when she let them into the house.

"I've got a half bottle of Pol Roger in the fridge. Why don't we finish it? It's been such a lovely evening."

The living room was painted pale cinnamon. Harrison looked approvingly at the good furniture, mostly Billy's, he knew. Over the mantel hung a three-quarter lifesize portrait, painted maybe a dozen years earlier, of Des's father, General St. Mostyn, resplendent in the plumes and cuirass of the Royal Horse Guards, with mustaches fierce as cannons. The general was posed surrounded by the five girls, who looked at him like adoring fawns. Olde Englande, thought Harrison, with love and wonder.

He was standing looking at the painting when she came back into the drawing room. Billy is in theory my friend, he thought. She passed next to him to get glasses from the bar. He stopped her and pushed her hair back from the sides of her face and kissed her, tentatively, on the corner of her mouth.

"No, David. Please. No, no, no, no, no." She didn't move away.

He kissed her again and this time she moved her head to cover his mouth with hers. He heard her fumbling to set down the bottle, then her arms came around him.

"Oh God, oh God," she said, not taking her mouth away. Then, "Upstairs, quickly."

They undressed without speaking. No nervous banter or haste, just two grownup people taking off their clothes to do something they wanted very much to do.

A sliver of moonlight fell across the bed. She was magnificent looking. Her breasts were royal. Her hand came across the sheets and took him and stroked flame into him. They drew together and then he was above her and in her, moving to bring her every pleasure that he could conceive of, and then she was round him, saying things he couldn't quite make out until, suddenly and unwished, it was over for a time.

She was gasping. "My God, David, it's been six months." And then, "Oh so good," and she kissed him and hugged him to her.

He thought they napped. Then she woke him. He wanted her again but she hushed him gently. "It's six o'clock. You must go, darling. Neighbors. I'll drive you to the hotel."

As they dressed, he thought he should say something. "I suppose in another century, I'd be horsewhipped."

"Billy's a shit," was all she said. Flat, factual.

"Will I see you again?"

"Of course, darling, I've already concocted some divine plans for us. While you slept. I'll ring you at the hotel."

She called at nine-thirty while he was dressing.

"Listen, my darling, I've arranged everything. You don't mind, I hope? We've been asked down to Hermione Wilston's for the weekend. She has a divine house near Brighton. And on the way we can go to Glyndebourne. *The Magic Flute*'s on for Friday. The tickets are like hen's teeth but there's this man at the BBC who's been trying to seduce me for three years now, so I rang him up and hinted...well, I'm having lunch with him at Mark's next week but I got us two good seats."

"You are shameless and depraved. In another century, *you'd* be horsewhipped!"

"Don't be so stuffy. I'll come round and pick you up before lunch. We can dawdle down. There's a decent inn at Crowborough, the other side of Tunbridge Wells. We can have a late lunch and change, and other things. Have you a dinner jacket? No? Well, paddle along to Moss Brothers before the Lebanese rent up everything for Ascot. Doesn't it sound fun? You'll like Hermione's. We can scamper along the halls after bedtime like *Upstairs, Downstairs*. Today, alas, my love, you can have one of those London men's days you Americans are always talking about. Tailors and gunsmiths and lunch at the club. I've got scads of errands to do and I simply *must* go to Rosalind's tonight."

Harrison chuckled. Old General Saint Mostyn had given each of his five daughters the name of a notable Shakespearean lady. He wondered how Titania, Goneril, Portia and Rosalind were. Des rang off.

He spent a busy day. He rented a black-tie outfit at Moss's. To play his part in the fantasy properly, he went to Lord's in the Burlington Arcade and bought a pair of appropriate pajamas: mauve silk with blue piping and embroidered frog closings. He bought some shirts and toured the Wallace Collection. The Velásquezes had been cleaned recently and were breathtaking. Lunch was with a friend at a merchant bank in the City.

"Not up to Hambro's standard, I'm afraid," said his host. "Nothing can compare with that *Turbot Reksten* they do there. Try the sole."

At about six o'clock he found himself in St. James's Street, with a modest load of parcels. A block ahead he saw the white pilasters and bulging windows of Bratt's. The oldest club in St. James's, with a rich anecdotal history of eccentricity and aristocratic misbehavior. The chair in which the late prime minister used to sit at twilight glowering at the traffic was still there, square in the middle of the big bow window.

Harrison went up the steps. He'd been a member a few years, but he didn't suppose he'd been in the place a dozen times. He gave his name apologetically to the porter and went into the bar.

Of course it was too much to expect that any day would be perfect.

It was an article of faith with Harrison that people should have the courtesy to remain in their proper context. Context was as basic an identifying feature as physiognomy. As Harrison had put it once, "If you come around a corner at the Bath and Tennis Club in Palm Beach and run into your Puerto Rican doorman from New York in an alligator shirt and puce linen pants, it's unlikely you'll have the immediate presence of mind to say, 'Hello, Jose' and shake his hand."

So when he came through the sitting room to the tiny bar at Bratt's and a face stuck itself in his announcing, "Well, hello, *Mr*. Harrison" in a grating New York accent, Harrison hadn't the slightest idea who it was.

Then he saw that it was Frank Castato and 50 percent of the pleasure went out of his day. Suddenly, he felt the unwelcome intrusion of all the old New York aggressions, bottled in concrete and aged to vintage hostility.

"Hello, Frank," he said, as civilly as possible, and asked and paid for a whisky.

"Wha'chew doing here, Dave?" said Castato. "You know Bimber, of course. He's working for us now. He's a member here." Harrison became aware of a large, palpitating shape behind Castato; it was making strange, snurfling noises. A damp, doughy hand reached for Harrison's.

"Nice to see you (snurfle)," said an adenoidal voice. "I say (snurfle), barman, don't slice that lemon peel too thin, for God's sake, you bloody fool! Got (snurfle) to keep an eye on these brutes," he asided to Harrison.

"Bimber's the Markiss of Sumpton," said Castato proudly.

Harrison made the connection. He'd heard of young Sumpton. John William Fortescue Saint George Landover, twelfth Marquess of Sumpton, known as "Bimber," first son of the Duke of Cirencester, heir to a line famous for its witlessness and ill manners. Young Sumpton was said to have trumped his unillustrious forebears on both counts. "He's also the biggest twit in England," a friend had said. "The stupidity and rudeness are hereditary, of course, but the twit work's all his own. I suppose you could call him a self-made man."

Castato and Sumpton made quite a pair, thought Harrison, noting that four or five other members were huddled in a corner, avoiding them like grouse seeking cover before the beaters.

It was going to be a fast drink, he thought, although he was goddamned if he was going to be driven easily out of his own club the way Frank Castato had driven him out of Wall Street out of pure disgust.

"It's a three-minute story," he'd told Barney the night he quit. "I left The Mitch. Time to go back to work. I've been at Blenheim five years. It's an OK place. Dinker Blenheim's a decent guy; he leaves me alone. We've got a nice little thing going: small underwritings; junk bonds; venture deals; special stuff for the *Fortune* '500.' Small, most of it, but not bad quality. And profitable, you better believe. But the firm's getting bigger and the last thing Dinker wants is to run a big firm himself and the next to last thing is to let any of his partners run it. Enter Frank Castato. Dinker brings him in from our accountants. Just here to dot the *i*s and cross the *t*s. Strictly administrative, Dinker tells us. But Frank the Accountant metamorphoses into Frank the Big Deal. He starts having breakfast at the Regency, hanging out with those real estate and political types. I start getting stuff to do for his friends. This morning, he called to ask would I use my Zurich connections to push a lease deal on some pizza franchises for Fat Ernie Goldheim? So, dear Barney, at eleven-fourteen a.m. precisely, Eastern Standard Time, I advised Frank the Fixer, in my most cultivated tone, that he could take that shit he's been sending my direction and shove it back up his ass. End of story."

Now here was Frank Castato grinning at him like a comic-book Jap, all glasses and teeth, in the bar at Bratt's. The late prime minister would have called for a shotgun.

"How's business, Frank?" Harrison asked with minute courtesy.

"Nothing but up, Davey. You shoulda stuck around and gotten rich too."

"Ah well, Frank, what do they say? Blessed are the poor..." He put down his glass and left. Behind him he heard Sumpton say, "I say, Frank, who was that beggar? (snurfle) Some kind of parson, heh, heh (snurfle, snurfle)."

It was the best weekend he had ever had. After lunch at the Cox'n Arms, he teased and kissed Des and touched her under her dress until she was breathless. *The Magic Flute* was wonderful and so was Glyndebourne. She'd brought a

(152)

picnic and they ate lobster and drank Piesporter on the lawn at sunset. The elegance of the dignified elderly men and women who promenaded in their worn evening clothes touched him. "There *will* always be an England," he said to Des, and kissed her hand.

At Hermione Wilston's it was as she had promised. It was a big, comfortable, informal house. The rest of the party was full of fun, amusing, and respecters of privacy. There was endless teasing of Hermione, who was a jolly, pink, fortyish lady with a mouse-colored little husband who did something about insurance. "I say, Hermione: I don't think *your* portrait of your rich American grandmother compares with the Wards's next door, or the Smythers's across the river." "I say, Hermione, is this the best caviar in the house? No Lafite earlier than '61?" And so on. It was a harmless, empty-headed society which he found congenial enough to suffer for a short weekend.

At night, when the house was quiet, Harrison would step out in his James Bellamy pajamas and sneak down the hall to Des's room. Under a puffy comforter, they made love and clung to each other, and said things that washed away their loneliness.

Sunday morning, with everyone else at church, they took a walk in the fields. It was a burning morning, hot for June, and the meadows and hedges blazed with color.

They walked along in silence, Harrison thinking hard, trying not quite successfully to convince himself that his feelings were legitimate, that this was not one of those relationships that start with a starburst: dinner, bed, and a week later a mildly guilty feeling that a starburst was all it amounted to.

"Do you think...?" he said. It needed no finishing.

"No David, really *no*. I've got the children and I'm used to Billy. He'll come back all guilty and I'll get six good months from him. Not in bed; don't worry, darling, that's over between Billy and me, I fear. It couldn't be like you, anyway. But, David, if you're near, or even far, and it can possibly be done, I'll come to you for a day, a week, an afternoon, whatever we can manage. Now smile, darling. It's a beautiful morning. Henry Green says such a nice thing in one of his books. I think it's in *Nothing*: 'Don't let our affair end in long country walks.' Or something like that. Isn't it sensible, though?"

He smiled. It was difficult to do. He felt as if his insides had been scooped out.

When she stopped the car in front of his hotel, he sat with her a moment before saying what he felt.

"You know what this has done to me, don't you? You've stripped off the shell. Someone's likely to come along and open me up like with a can opener." But what he said was more dramatic than what he felt.

She smiled with all the wisdom of a woman who is truly grownup and ruffled his hair. "Oh no, darling, don't worry. You'll be all right. Yes you will. Now hurry back." Her tenderness strung him out like a filament in the air.

He couldn't bear to watch her car out of sight. The stolid, ugly lobby was like a cold shower. In the creaky elevator, he looked at his watch. Khafiq was expecting him in an hour.

The butler led him into the drawing room. Although it was still vestigial daylight outside, the curtains had been drawn. The room was dimly lit. It was close and intimate.

Khafiq rose as he came in. He had been reading; a thick sheaf of publishers' galleys. He placed them on a knotted leather stool next to his chair and tucked his glasses in his breast pocket. "Ah. David. The memoirs of a recent Secretary of State," he gestured at the papers, "the recollections of an unexampled life. I suspect they will be widely read in your country, but I hope not entirely believed."

Drinks were brought. Harrison sat down expectantly. He was still thinking about Desdemona.

"Let's get our business over," Khafiq said. "Then we can enjoy our dinner. There's no need for suspense. The English practice with respect to transactions is to keep you waiting. The London Rothschilds specialize in it. Anyway, the client has accepted your plan."

He paused and Harrison felt a beating excitement which he forced to subside, taking long, long breaths, into an objective calm. Somewhere he had read that a killer's blood should run cold as the trigger finger started to tighten.

"Specifics first," said Khafiq. "All the money matters, as they affect you, we agree to. We know you use the Commerçante in Geneva; but Marc-Antoine, although a good mutual friend, is much given to nosing about. A great deal of money in your account might perplex him. I've taken the precaution therefore of opening a personal account for you at the Weisenhausesbank in Zurich. Here is the number."

The Bank of the Orphans, thought Harrison. A nice touch.

"The telex network you require will be set up tomorrow. A hundred and fifteen numbers. All you will have to do is telex any of them with your directions for cash transfers. It will get to me. If I'm away, my assistant, Mustaf, will clear it. Just for safety's sake, we might use a simple code, perhaps the name of the day previous; if you call on Tuesday, preface your remarks with the word 'Monday.'

"It takes four days to settle a stock transaction in New York. Obviously your plan contemplates this. Just for error's sake, give us five days. A week would be best. We wouldn't want to be wrestling with problems of clearinghouses, Federal Funds, and that sort of thing. Once the money is in your control, it will be up to you to direct it from there."

They went in to dinner. "I hear you like the food at the Guinea," Khafiq said, "so I've spared you the *cuisine nouvelle.*" They dined on duck, crackly outside and soft as an oyster inside, and watercress salad. Afterward, over good cigars and a Calvados older than Harrison's grandmother, Khafiq got down to cases.

"David, this is a project which involves more than money. I know you understand that. It could be dangerous; that I can't say for certain, but it could be. You know that. I am an old man, who has seen six governments burned beneath my feet. Life is no longer as important to me. But you are younger. Be careful."

Harrison sipped his Calvados.

"If your clients, our clients, are doing what I think they are, well, there's a chance of trouble. I understand that. But it's worth it. And not just for the money. Everyone will benefit."

Khafiq didn't respond, didn't nod.

At midnight precisely, the little man rose, drained his brandy, and showed Harrison to the door.

"Good luck, David. I'll look forward to hearing from you. You'll be hearing from friends of mine."

Back at the hotel, Harrison thought about telephoning Des. He didn't. A romance like this was like a ship's cruise, he thought; the emotional seal was ruptured at the first port or parting. "*Je t'embrasse,* darling," he said to the empty room, hoping his words would float to her across the London night sky and liking the poetry of the notion. Then, remembering Khafiq's last words, he opened his notebook and crossed out *People* with a firm, broad stroke.

12 It was a matter of record in the financial press that Axel Nyquist was *the* guru of advanced investment theory. He had started out as an assistant professor of calculus at San Francisco State. A flamboyant lecturer, whose chalk shattered and broke as it screeched across the blackboard trying to keep up with his dramatics, he was a popular teacher. And became even more so, when he left the abstrusenesses of Hardy and Ramanujan and started to talk about the stock market. He was in tune with the times. The students who ten years before might have crowded Sproul Plaza chanting for social democracy now flocked to Nyquist's lectures to find the key to professional success in the investment world. The old, seething antiwar crowds had evolved into constituencies of job seekers: nascent lawyers, doctors, stockbrokers.

He had started with a modest stock-market coup. He publicized the fact that a small legacy, a few hundred shares of an obscure Utah uranium mine, had, through one turn and another, and no fault of Nyquist's, which he didn't publicize, evolved into 5,000 shares of United Electric. Fifteen thousand dollars transmogrified in five years into $175,000 worth of UE. Evidence of genius.

Genius had to be packaged and marketed, however, and to Nyquist's credit he had taken a year's sabbatical with the fruits of his late aunt's benevolence and looked at the stock market. He had run three years of stock trading activity through the big Berkeley IBM 370/12 that no longer designed bombs; the results suggested a discernible pattern to the price action of stocks. He took his printouts and a typewritten memo to the Bank of America and convinced an ambitious young trust vice president to give it a try. The Nyquist model ended up the year 13 percent ahead of the Dow Jones Average, which was better than two out of the three dart-thrown portfolios the VP ran on the side, and, more important, better than 96 percent of the fully managed portfolios guided by the senior investment officers of the bank.

From there it was all downhill. Nyquist resigned from the

faculty at State and established *Modern Portfolio Logistics* (MPL) in a townhouse in Green Street, just off Nob Hill. As he built up business, lecturing around the country, psychologically subsidized by the Damoclean sword which Washington hung over the investment profession, the basements on Green Street filled with elaborate telecommunications equipment. Decks of printers and telephone-actuated processors interfaced with the banked computers in Palo Alto and Berkeley, which whirred through their offhours, massaging and manicuring MPL's statistics and pumping out investment formulas to New York and Chicago and Los Angeles, at first, and later to Hong Kong, Zurich, Riyadh, and a dozen other cities around the world.

It sold. Three years into the business, MPL was doing over $4 million a year in fees. As his business expanded, so did Nyquist. In size and pride. "Otto Eckstein may be a genius," Nyquist often declared, "but my numbers make real-time money." He bought the contents of a great London house and moved them in place to Green Street. He grew bushy sideburns and a walrus mustache, wore double-breasted suits in loud, raceday checks, slept with half the flying staff of Trans America Airlines, and sent $1,500 a week to his wife in Stinson Beach.

Nyquist's office was on the third floor. A double glass window commanded the Bay from the Golden Gate to Milpitas. On one wall hung the speaking trumpet through which Nelson had shouted his last command at Trafalgar. Fixed to the floor was the steering wheel from the *Andrea Doria*. Nyquist thought of himself as a navigator. A great captain. Often, late at night, with MPL closed down except for the humming electronics in the basement, he would stand at the wheel, Nelson's megaphone in hand, and shout investment commands to the foggy night sky.

The dominant piece of furniture in Nyquist's office was a huge, square Adam partners' desk. He had overbid Leslie Merriman for it at Christie's.

Looking across it as across rangeless spaces, he said, "Now, how can we help you, Mr. Axelson?" He turned his visitor's card in his hand, testing the quality of the raised print.

Harrison looked properly subdued, befitting an interview with a great man. He wasn't worried about the card. He'd ordered thirty dozen, each dozen with different names and titles, from an advertisement in the *Wall Street Journal*. He now rented six different post office boxes in New York.

"Mr. Nyquist, we represent a master trust which hopes to establish a diversified, risk-indented portfolio strategy for a group of large accounts. Mostly ERISA. Some Taft-Hartley, three large ESOTs, and the balance in executive pension series." Harrison had practiced the contemporary mode of speaking acronymically.

"I gather, then," said Nyquist, "that something like our STAB module would suit you?"

"STAB?"

"Yes, *S*ituation *T*ransaction *A*veraging *B*asis. Would you like to see the correlations?" Nyquist had been early to recognize that the creative coinage of buzzwords and professional argot had come to be as important in the investment business as in Washington. He reached for a folder of printouts hanging from a music stand that had once belonged to Brahms.

"Frankly, I don't think that would meet our requirements," said Harrison. "I'm sorry. I'm familiar with the program, but I didn't recognize its module designation." He felt quite proud of himself.

"No problem," said Nyquist kindly. "These days the number of new M.D.s gets pretty confusing. What order of magnitude are we talking about?"

"Well, our going-in increments add up to three-quarter K square."

"That is a very substantial GII, Mr. Axelson."

"It's a number of large accounts shifting transients."

"I see." Nyquist paused. "Would you like to stay for lunch, Mr. Axelson? I've got the finest Chinese cook in the Bay Area. Yon Choh. Used to work with Cecilia Ching at The Emperor."

"That would be very nice, Mr. Nyquist."

Nyquist spoke into an intercom artfully concealed in the base of an incense burner taken from the bedchamber of the Empress Dowager in Peking.

"You interest me, Mr. Axelson," Nyquist continued. "*A*bsolute *v*alue *w*ise—AVW, as we call it—you're reaching beyond our current on-shelf capability. How do you see this working out?"

Harrison pulled out the plan he had written out in New York and related to Khafiq. He had revised its language thoroughly. This was the part he had rehearsed for two weeks. He was reminded of Hamlet's instruction to the players: speak the gobbledygook trippingly.

"Well," he said, handing Nyquist the folder, "this is all in layman's language. I just don't have a handle yet on all the tangential percipients that go into a high-arc MPL-type matrix. Obviously, for these magnitude gradients we'll need a broadwash diversification—spectrumwise, that is. I've suggested a four-digit context. Since we'll be buying the universe, I think we can emphasize a heavier beta."

Harrison had culled this weird vocabulary from his reading, including transcripts of Nyquist's public speeches and writings and a number of private MPL reports which friends had shown him. He hoped it meant what he thought he wanted MPL to design: a computer program which would coordinate the investment of $750 million in a thousand or more issues, spread broadly across the market and industry categories and security types. The "beta" reference was MPL nomenclature for stocks that overreacted to the market, that rose fastest in up markets and collapsed helplessly in downturns. Since he and his clients were positive of a major upward turn, it made sense to favor the overreactors.

"Very interesting, net net net," said Nyquist. "Let's go down to lunch. Yon Choh should be ready now."

The lunch was delicious. Yon Choh cut chicken like a surgeon: DeBakey of the kitchen, thought Harrison. There was squid sliced transparent. Ginger salad. Pigeon packets in sweet oil. They drank beer. It was labeled Ah Ming. Harrison didn't know it.

"Langley gets it for us from Shanghai." Nyquist smiled confidentially. "We help the CIA run their funny money."

Harrison wasn't taken in by the jargon and the historical furniture and the important clients. There was something in Nyquist's eyes that seemed inconsistent with the gross, manufactured persona. This is all cover, Harrison thought. Something told him that Nyquist was smart and practical in back of all this crap.

Over gunpowder tea, Nyquist said, "I think we can do what you want. What's your deliverability capacity?"

"Three-seventy late series. Anything there. Burroughs A-12. CDC Magmas. Cray. Nothing fancy. Anything COBOL." Computer talk.

"OK. You'll want systemic quanta. Zero point seven PCs. Two K item base. Two hundred seventy days converse base. Seven hundred K squared GII. A hundred names."

Harrison hadn't the slightest idea what Nyquist was talking about. "Exactly," he said in self-defense. Then, remembering his lessons, "What about memory? Will you tape it? Or do we go floppy?"

"Whichever you like. Personally, we lean to floppy. Easier to massage."

It was like buying perfume in France, Harrison thought. Who cared how it smelled if the salesgirl was pretty?

Nyquist's hand slapped the lacquer table. "We'll do it! We've never done a scattershot before. It ducks a conservative beta/alpha quotient, which we don't like to see, but with this kind of GII, we've got to take a chance." He smiled benignly. "More tea?"

The time had come to get vulgar. "What would you charge for this?" he asked Nyquist.

"Depends. It's proprietary, of course. If we keep it, dollars two-fifty K plus rent; if you *buy* it, six-fifty."

"I think we'd like to keep it. The six-fifty is all right; it ballparks our clients."

"As you will. I've got an Indian downstairs, an *Indian* Indian, who tunes these things like a Stradivarius. Time-frame?"

"Yesterday."

"As usual. How about thirty days? Give us the Fourth of July. Say July 10?"

"You're the Einsteins. The sooner the better." Harrison folded his napkin.

"One second. We name these things around here. We're always working on a bunch of projects. Sometimes our clients call in instead of going through the computer and the girl on the board gets confused so we give each one its own name to make sure they interface properly."

Nyquist looked out the window. Sailboats whirled off Alcatraz. Coit Tower was a bright spoke against the sky.

"Got it," Nyquist said. "From now on, you're RAID. Random Access Investment Dynamics. RAID. Get it?"

After lunch, Nyquist took Harrison on a downstairs tour. In the basement, rows of gadgetry rose up the walls. A waist-high gallery of odd-looking devices ringed the room. Nyquist saw Harrison's curiosity. "Modems," he said. "Telephone interfaces with the black box." A buzzer sounded and a red light blinked. Nyquist brushed the attendant technician aside and placed a telephone receiver in the slots of the modem. A high squeal, nearly musical, filled the room; a printer started to clatter. Nyquist tore the sheet from the machine. A row of alphanumerics read: "6065/2/A R Beta Flintkote." Nyquist thumbed quickly through a sheaf of printouts on a lectern. He punched a series of numbers on a machine. The printer clattered again, briefly, then the lights went out, and the squealing stopped.

"What was all that about?" asked Harrison.

"I just told him to sell the sonuvabitch. Their earnings are off. My own money follows the fundamentals strictly."

As they went out, Harrison noticed four large cylinders against the wall. "What are those?" he asked.

"Propane. Yon Choh has to cook at an even 550 degrees. So I built him these special gas-fired cooking surfaces. You can taste the difference."

Nyquist showed Harrison to the street door. "Nice to see you, Mr. Axelson."

"I'll be back on the tenth to pick up the tapes. Tell me," Harrison asked; he thought it a fearfully stupid question, "how should I carry them?"

"Any suitcase, Mr. Axelson. They're tough." Then Nyquist added, "But don't check 'em. They might end up in Indianapolis."

The flight from San Francisco takes five hours, more or less. It took Harrison four days to get back to New York.

He started in Houston. At noon he presented himself at the trust desk of the City First Bank. A cheerful young lady led him to a seat next to her desk.

She looked at the card he'd given her. "Now, Mr. Geismar, how can we be of service?"

Harrison explained. The master trust he represented was the agent and payor for certain substantial accounts. It wished to open a custody account, agency name, for transactions that would be made. Clearinghouse funds would be available in the account prior to any transactions. He filled out the forms, giving one of his New York box numbers, and clipped his business card to it. Politely, he declined the young lady's offer of others of the bank's massive array of services.

He went downstairs and caught a cab to the airport. By the time he reached New York on Friday, after stopping in Shreveport, Jackson, Birmingham, Memphis, and other points north, he had thirty accounts. It was time to order new business cards.

13 Harrison had first operated independently out of a fancy office in the mid-fifties between Madison Avenue and Fifth Avenue. A girl he was seeing decorated it in grass-cloth walls and expensive reproductions of English country furniture; it rented for $2,500 a month. He employed two secretaries who glared at each other and drank at lunch. It was very pretentious and altogether too expensive. After two years he sent the secretaries packing and the furniture to the Saint Willoughby's church fair, taking a healthy tax deduction.

He didn't choose to work from his apartment, hating to contaminate his private space with traces of business, so he now made his office in one of a suite of rooms rented out by a young lawyer whose space had turned out to exceed his practice. There was a receptionist who took telephone messages and who could be prevailed upon to do reluctant, messy typing. It cost him $600 a month. His office held a wall of metal files and some beaten-up metal office furniture which he rented. Twice a week, a stenographer came in to take care of letters, bills, memos, and other paperwork which had to be neat. Once a month his bookkeeper came in and balanced things up. Harrison kept away from the office on those days. The bookkeeper was a ratty little man with a headful of dubious and promotional tax-avoidance schemes; he reminded Harrison of Frank Castato.

For such formal business meetings as he held, he used the Beaver, the Gorse, or the Squash and Quoit Club. The WASP clubs had a pompous, self-important character that he found revolting, but it seemed to impress his Denver or Spokane clients, expecially the Jewish ones.

When the buzzer on his phone sounded, Harrison was mulling over the long weekend days he'd just spent in East Hampton where Barney had rented a house. Despite Barney's active, obstreperous organizings, they had been four of the most boring days in the history of Western man, with nothing to do, apart from golf and tennis and the beach club gossip, but get sodden at an interminable round of cocktail parties. Not even Barney could make anything out of that social sow's ear. It was time, he thought, to get back to RAID. But the program wouldn't be ready in San Francisco for another week and he was waiting for the arrival of a new supply of business cards, so his bank account activity was suspended.

The buzzer on his desk rang again. It was the receptionist, Miss DiVitale. In an urgent, hushed voice, she said, "There's a man here to see you. Something about insurance." She dropped her voice an octave. "Mr. Harrison, he's *black*."

"Manners, please, Miss DiVitale," Harrison said. "Ask him to come in. Just show him the way without comment."

A *black* man. Harrison laughed. He understood the girl's anxiety. She was a nice Catholic girl from Queens who traveled over and back every day from Jackson Heights, where she lived under the duenna-like scrutiny of a bead-fondling maiden aunt. The subway rides made Miss DiVitale moist with fear of the black faces that crowded and jostled her, ready, she was sure, to steal her purse, cut her throat, or do horrible things to her with their giant, reptilian members.

"Good morning, good morning," said a luscious alto voice from the doorway. It came from a man a shade under six feet tall, with skin the color of freshly turned loam and finely cut features under a giant pair of Greta Garbo sunglasses. He had a slender figure, except for a high, plump behind, like a basketball player. He was dressed to kill. Soft, unstructured jacket of a nubbly cloth; khaki pants tied with a drawstring; tasseled, kilted loafers with pale crepe soles, a stringy tie dangling from a pale lavender shirt with tiny, rounded collars. Over his shoulder he carried a flight bag which appeared to be sewn from cloth of gold. It was quite an effect.

He came across the room with a bouncing, hippy gait that left no doubt in Harrison's mind as to what his visitor did with his evenings.

"Mr. Harrison? I'm from Chesham Insurance. You know our London office. They asked me to come and see you. Say, you may be needin' some of our coverage. My name's Rashad, Ichmon Rashad, but you can call me Ernie, seein' as I was born plain Ernest Cleveland Jones on the South Side of Chicago."

"David Harrison." They shook hands. Harrison, still not quite used to the unclosetting of America, was surprised at the firmness of the handshake.

"So you're from Chicago, then?"

"Yessir. I worked for the Prophet out there, Elijah Muhammad. Actually, I work for Herbert, his son. In the finance and EDP. We have a pretty big computer section. After all, the Prophet has millions and millions of dues-payin' subjects. Plus the money we get from your friends."

"My friends?"

"Yessir. All I know's that every month a million comes from Switzerland to the Freedom Bank. The Prophet uses the money to pay off his paras. You know, his muscle boys, the Leroy Brown types. The go-between he talks to is a Mr. K. S'posed to be a friend of yours. So when he asked the Prophet, and *he* ask Herbert, for a good, reliable computer soldier, he got attention and the best man. Which brings me here. What's the gig?"

Harrison wasn't surprised. He had guessed that Khafiq had a finger on every beating Moslem pulse; why should the Black Muslims be neglected?

He explained the RAID program. Ernie was to be his expert in setting up the RAID matrix to spit out a daily script of purchases and sales. Harrison had done all he could. Someone had to install the working touches and plug Nyquist's program into a functioning mechanism. He handed Ernie his primitive outline, the same one he'd given Nyquist. Ernie read through it.

"You got a good nose for this shit," he said to Harrison. "This is OK. It'll walk."

"Can you handle it?" Harrison asked.

"Mr. Harrison, you're like one of those people buys a million-dollar house in Beverly Hills. You know, up there near Sunset, on Canon or Beverly or Rodeo. Nice house. Better grounds. Great gardens when you first look. Everythin' from hibiscus to hydrangea. Except you got no idea how to make those gardens grow. You get this little Japanese gardener, the type talks to the flowers. That's the computer. 'Cept he speaks only Japanese and you don't. So you hire me. I speak the language so I talk to him and he talks to the flowers and everythin' grows and the house looks great; all because I speak the language. I can handle this. Computer language is like street talk to me."

He explained that he would run a printout of the RAID tapes which Harrison was to pick up, interface a timing program and relate them to cue-numbered banks through which orders would be directed, executed, and paid for, and then rewrite the whole thing into a small computer of their own. "Trouble is," he said, "order times are so long at HP and Wang, and DEC is impossible. Might take three months just to get goin' and *that,* from what you say, is impossible. We better use a service bureau. I'll write the action program and we'll just hire some computer time. Then each Monday and Friday I'll just sashay into the bureau and pick up the print-outs, script and inventory, and take 'em to you. Makes the most sense."

Harrison could see Ernie was a pro. "Where did you learn all this?" he asked.

"I played ball at Marquette, point guard, but I was too slow and a mite too little for the NBA, so I figured I'd best use some of my hoop scholarship money to learn me a trade. No pro ball for me; but no streets neither!

"Make any difference where I do this?" Ernie asked. Harrison shook his head.

"OK, I'm going to base in Boston. Company we used a lot in Oak Lawn has a branch there. They do good work and nobody knows me in Beantown. I can live in a hotel or get a cheap apartment. This gonna be a long job?"

"Maybe a year," Harrison said. "It depends."

Ernie whistled.

"Don't worry," said Harrison, "you can get back to Chicago most weekends. We'll work something out. But Ernie, re-member that this is a very tight deal. No pillow talk. Stay out of trouble."

His meaning was unmistakable. The black man lowered his dark glasses and looked evenly at Harrison.

"Mister David, I just happen to like boys. A natural pref-erence that I came with. I like the way they look and I like the way they feel. But I don't do chickenhawks and I don't do rough trade and I don't work men's rooms and I don't go to no leather joints lookin' for some stud to fistfuck or pee on me. Just straight and normal, that's me, except it's not ladies. Don't you worry about me none, Mister David. Ta-ta. I'll call you next week, to see if you're ready with those tapes."

Ernie went out the door, leaving Harrison gaping.

The next call came at home. Harrison had been sorting out the stacks of business cards he had diligently collected that day from his Manhattan post office boxes. There were forty-three dozen this time. He had them stacked neatly in rubber-banded piles on his campaign desk and was just work-ing out the logistics of his next trip in the *American Bank Directory* when the telephone rang.

"Mr. Harrison? This is Devon Linde. The Chesham Employment Bureau suggested I call you. About that opening in investment analysis."

It was a funny kind of voice, a mixture of contradictory accents: nasal, but broadening across the vowels, seeming overall flat and unlocalized, with a touch of finishing school. He thought it a voice that worked at being colorless.

"Yes," he said, "I've been expecting to hear from you. Are you in the city? What's your schedule?"

"Whatever suits you. I'm at Ninety-fifth Street. At a friend's. He's gone to Europe for the summer. I'm apartment sitting. My time is your time." She sounded tired, he thought, in the way a person does after a long flight: bags on the floor of an empty room in a strange city and a number to call.

"Why don't you catch up? Ring me in the morning and come by for a cup of coffee. I'm not far away." He gave her the address.

She called at eleven and was at his door twenty minutes later. The water on the stove hit the boil just as she rang, and he had barely time to look at her as he let her in and sprinted back through the apartment to the whistling kettle.

When he reappeared with the Chemex on a tray, she had seated herself on one of the leather chairs which flanked the main coffee table, the seat he normally took, and was looking around appraisingly, a cigarette in her hand. As he put the tray down, she rose and shook hands. Her hand seemed as large as his, but she was several inches shorter.

He poured her coffee, sat down across from her and looked her over. Appreciatively. She was a terrific-looking girl. Just right in every detail that counted with him, a girl who suited the complicated wishes of a complicated man. She had brown hair running to ash, combed away from her face in a pageboy; her features were sharp, composed, and cool; it struck him that smiling was something of an effort for her, a grin an impossibility. Her mouth was perhaps more defined among her features than he might have specified in his ideal woman, but she was clearly special. Her most compelling aspect was the frankness of her gaze. She looked at him with an objectivity that somehow drew him to her, that didn't make him feel like an insect on a pin or something the dog had done on the carpet. She was as organized as her clothes, which were plain and perfect and gave nothing away of her figure, he thought. Yet she was neither dry nor prim. Just terribly interesting.

(166)

She looked at him with frank green eyes. There was something in them that could have been ten years older than the thirty or so that he guessed her to be—a trace of fatigue, of seen-it-all sadness.

"It's nice to meet you," she said. "I understand you have an assignment for me."

Harrison pushed aside his instinct to investigate her personally.

"I'm working on a difficult investment problem. It's very complicated, very detailed. I asked my client for help. It can't be done alone. Hence, you."

"Tell me about it." Her voice remained as flat as it had seemed through the filter of the telephone connection. "You don't mind if I smoke?"

Cigarettes were Devon's talisman; she owed her life to them, as he would later learn.

She was thirty-one years old. She'd been brought up in Cincinnati in a rich suburb by a good, middle-class family. Her father was in insurance. Troublesomely ambitious, she'd pestered her parents to send her east to school to Ethel Walker, and then to Barnard, where what had been a tomboyish adolescent rebelliousness hardened into a deep and aggressive antisocial hostility. When she had reached the stage where she was ready to set crosses burning and buildings aflame, she'd hitched up with the local chapter of the Weathermen. It was 1968. She was then twenty. She had declared war on the world she came from.

One bright July Sunday, she'd gone downtown to the Village to help two friends prepare a big surprise for the Democratic Convention later that summer in Chicago. The work in the cellar of her friend's parents' townhouse on Twelfth Street was hot and tiresome. The owners of the house were away at the Cape. Devon left to go down to Greenwich Avenue to buy cigarettes. While she was gone, one of her coconspirators, a pimply boy with a universal grudge, had tried to force the fusewire into the glob of plastic explosive he'd collected the day before in Harlem. In his impatience, he'd failed to see that the wire was still loosely connected to the "A" cell on the workbench.

Devon was just getting her change when the explosive went off, pulverizing the townhouse and shaking the street so that dust hung in the air for two days afterward. Her own wallet, with her driver's license and student cards, had been incinerated except for her plastic student ID, which was spared. The firemen sifting the ruins found three hands, other blackened human scraps, and the card. Identification and an accurate body count were impossible. Besides, the police reckoned in those days that troublemakers got as good as they gave, so the follow-up investigation was cursory.

The explosion terminated Devon's recorded existence. Her parents were notified of her death, mourned briefly, and went about their concentric life, privately relieved to be no longer responsible, even by implication, for so rebellious and troublesome a child. When the drugstore shook with the rumbling in the air, Devon knew what it was. She took her change and her cigarettes and while the neighborhood crowded the ends of the street to watch and marvel at the pall of flame and black smoke which blotted out the pleasant weekend sun, she walked across to Sixth Avenue and dialed a number on a pay phone. Three days later, in the way that things went in those times, she had a new name and a passport, the first of what would be many.

He explained RAID to her. It took her three cigarettes for him to get through it. At the end, he showed her the stacks of business cards.

She laughed. "That I understand, at least. Names I'm used to. I've had a lot." Harrison thought her smile freshened the smoky air like the wind after a rainstorm. But good as he was with women, he couldn't quite figure her out.

"We must get you some business cards for a start," he said. "Do you have any favorite names? I get my pseudonyms out of Dickens, singles magazines, and the 1887 Harvard Classbook."

"You pick them. I'll use them"

He looked at his watch. "Let's go to lunch. We can talk there."

They walked down Park Avenue to the Cochon d'Argent. "I like this restaurant," he said. "I lived in Paris once, where people know how to eat, and this place reminds me of a real restaurant. A place where people eat food and talk. I stay away from the spots where the interior decorators and dress designers spend the meal blowing kisses to each other across my table and my veal."

She laughed. Harrison felt as if he had been knighted.

The restaurant was packed three deep at the small bar, but the owner liked the fact that Harrison never complained about waiting and understood the balancing act inherent in running a restaurant; he took them immediately to a good table.

She ordered a Kir; Harrison took a Contréxeville. He was feeling slightly liverish.

"Tell me about you," he asked.

"Not much to tell. I'm basically an anti-pig person. I learned about pigs as a child. At home where I could study them firsthand. Christmas Eve, my father and mother would sit over their bourbons and talk about niggers while the papers were usually full of photographs of black kids with nothing under the tree and nothing on the table. No food! There were Mummy and Pops at the trough, up to the eyeballs in Jack Daniel's, while children were starving in downtown Cincinnati. Pigs!"

Pigs, she went on, were defined as people who beat up on children, and other helpless people, when they could help if they only would.

"There are a lot of them. I'm flexible in who I admit to the category. The big banks are pigs, and the big unions, and the corporations, and the jet set. It's hard to differentiate sometimes; there are so many of them."

Over lunch he worked to draw out her story; he sensed that she would like to be able to tell it to someone she liked and felt she could be open with. So he warmed to the implied flattery of her confidences. He was frequently pleased to think that he had some special quality in his dealings with women that made them trust and confide in him. It was true that he was sympathetic and appreciative; the evidence of the bed was there. He pleased women, he thought; was gentle and thoughtful; his sardonic fits of temper blew over quickly.

Of course, what Devon told him over that first lunch was a highly selective, carefully edited version of her life that would have done as much credit to a novelist as to a biographer. Harrison, basking in the laving warmth of her green eyes and the intellectual intensity of that unmannered, unaccented voice, bought it whole. He couldn't have been expected to react otherwise. Cosmopolitan as he may have thought himself, she came out of a life in which deception and an indifference to human life and property were commonplace, whereas in Harrison's scheme of values, they were everything.

She told him a tale about dropping out of Barnard; about a year spent walking through Spain, plumbing the Castilian soul breathing El Greco and Cervantes; about six years of

(169)

various jobs from bartending in the Caribbean to banking in Charlotte; about the last two years in St. Louis working for a family foundation, tending investments, which gave her a grounding in dealing with banks and trusts—and computers.

Only the last part was substantively accurate; the earlier places and names were largely imaginary. What Devon didn't tell Harrison was that for the greatest part of her adult life, from the second when the house on Twelfth Street was atomized in the Manhattan air, she had been a kind of terrorist camp-follower. As a girl, she got it into her young mind that the way to cure the world's injustices was to blow up the offenders, that murder and mugging were the only midwives for the birth of social justice.

After the Greenwich Village explosion, the network which took care of such things got her into Mexico. She stayed there a year, learning Spanish, helping run money into Nicaragua. She went then to Italy, living for a time with a slovenly, boastful lieutenant in the Bregate Rosse, who smelled of garlic and anise and got her pregnant. The fetus and her fertility were scraped out in a crummy room off the Via Tunisia.

She left Milan and vanished for a time into the "anti-pig" network: PLO, Symbionese Liberation Army, Khmer Rouge, Baader-Meinhof. It took her twice around the world. There seemed to be enough money for airplane tickets, her passport worked, and she kept her nose and luggage free of dope. She was a courier, carrying high-sounding messages of brotherhood and reassurance, and sometimes a bit of money, between one collection of bloody-handed misfits and another; crossing from one pool of shadow to the next. She sat and watched while the gangs practiced their karate and knifework and blasted away at sandbags with their Uzis and Mannlichers and Smith and Wessons. She absorbed what there was to know about the theory of hand-to-hand killing. That was as far as it went. She had never practiced the violence she had learned.

She woke up one morning in a house in the Watts district. There were rags on the floor and shit and old food in the corners. She had $100 in her pocket. She got up, dressed, and walked out of the underground life forever.

After two years of odd jobs, and getting enough money together, her taste and handsomeness landed her a job as a design coordinator at Interglobal Hotels. She had become Devon Linde. It was a perfect matching of person and profes-

sion. Once a two-stop Iowa motel chain, Interglobal was opening a new hotel every six months. Its hotels shared a stan-
dardized, comfortless, pastel pretentiousness. A bedroom in
the Djarkarta Interglobal was identical to a bedroom at an
Interglobal in any of the bursting freeway cities in Nixon's
America. The Fiberglas halberds and pikestaffs that accou-
tered the walls and niches of Interglobal's "Olde Taverner's
Innes" were mass confected in a factory near Chattanooga,
numbered and dispatched around the world. Devon was one
of a dozen or so well mannered young ladies with clipboards
who pursued the stuff to its ultimate destination and saw
that it was nailed, glued, or stapled to its preassigned place.

The average assignment lasted six to eight weeks. In her
four years with Interglobal, she worked in twenty-six cities,
sometimes as part of a team, but generally alone. Unlike her
colleagues, who flirted outrageously and bedded down with
earnest Interglobal project managers with dreary wives back
in Des Moines, Devon kept in touch with her underground
avocation. But it was a hobby now, if helping to polish the
engines of revolution and destruction could ever be properly
called a hobby. At least that was what Habash told her in
Beirut; Vilas-Garza in Buenos Aires had said pretty much
the same thing, as had Oruzgarry one twilight over portside
coffee watching the lighted fishing fleet make a peaceful evening mooring in St. Jean de Luz.

They had been planning a bombing the following month
at the fiesta in Bilbao. It never occurred to Devon at the time
that her earnest detailing of the bloody horrors to come was
entirely at odds with the quiet scene, the port looking like
a violet mirror in the sunset, while the unexcited cries of the
fishermen floated across the water. Oruzgarry had sipped his
filtre and stubbed one Gitane after another into the ashtray.

When she was finished with her recitation of weights and
timings, he had exhaled a long, reflective streamer of smoke
which cut like a knife across the intensity of her scheme.

"The trouble with you, Linda," which was how he knew
her, "is that you really have no blood in this thing of ours.
For all your ideas, and all your sincerity and technique, there
is no land beneath you, no streets where you have walked
and cried over the graves of friends, no passion in your commitment. Your notion of hatred is merely an advanced form
of dislike. Intense, yes, but hardly murderous. What I feel is
to kill *them,* or *they* will kill me. Either way, there must
sooner or later be blood, passion, love!

"But don't be discouraged entirely," he added. "It's good to be impersonal to a point. Some people will be killed who have nothing to do with this—grocers, shopgirls, tourists. The press will call them innocent. You and I will be hard enough to know that they are merely unlucky!"

Ten days later, the Guardia Civil had cornered Oruzgarry in a Basque farmhouse just over the Spanish border, putting thirty-eight bullets into him. Devon had not known of his proper Hemingway death. By then, the roulette wheels of the Biarritz Interglobal were spinning profitably under a melange of fastidiously orchestrated plastic medievalia, and Devon was on her way to Tulsa on another job.

It really didn't matter where she found herself. She made and kept few local friends. Her memory was perfect and so she knew the names to look for and the numbers to call if she wanted to touch the underground nerves. Most of the time, she carried no more than introductions: coded, pompous revolutionary messages of an eighteenth-century formality. Even if she found herself in a new city, unconnected in the subversive sense, some antennae within her circled and beamed until she located the places where *they* congregated, like conger eels in the dark, rock-shelved eddies of a river.

She had no home base. Her father had died and her mother had moved to Arizona. She knew that, even if they were to meet in the street, her mother would never recognize the messy, muffiny adolescent in the spruce, restrained, bony young lady she was now. She kept in sporadic touch with the girls she'd worked with at Interglobal. They wrote each other chatty, vacuous letters which ended with drawings of little, smiling faces. Her relations with men were difficult. Although she preferred dangerous men with loud ideas, she'd learned her lesson in Milan and Watts. Now, it was enough just to talk with them, although there were times that their own loneliness and tension had gotten the better of the situation and she'd been bent gasping over a table while they ripped her underpants off and stuffed themselves into her.

Devon had made herself available sexually whenever there seemed to be a point of doing so; as long as she didn't have to pretend excitement or caring, what happened between her legs was of little interest to her so long as the ideologies of her intellectual alienation were served. Real pleasure had come only when she touched herself, and in the past, only on one or two occasions when fatigue or narcosis had burned away the insulation.

Of course, she told none of this to Harrison, who sat drinking his espresso, trying to make himself as good-looking as possible with the help of the mirror across the room.

"So, a couple of years ago," she said, "when I got tired of banks, and bankers particularly, and was trying to figure out what to do with my life, along came this job in St. Louis."

That much was true, more or less. The hotel trade had ultimately proved stifling. The sameness of the Interglobal designs overwhelmed the promising variety of peoples and cities. In the course of her last few assignments, she'd put it out among friends that a new challenge would be welcome. She had a reputation for discretion and reliability; just like me, he thought cheerfully, as she told him her story. An offer to join the Good Hope Foundation had been quickly accepted.

She worked there two years. In its early days, the Good Hope Foundation, which had been set up by old Phillip Hope to dispose of his petfood fortune, had a nice annual income, several hundred thousand dollars, which went mainly to local hospitals and schools. Old man Hope was foresighted, but he wasn't prescient, and he couldn't have predicted the fact that the fiscal policies of three administrations would make HopeyPups and HopeyKitties, a combination of soybeans and ground menhaden, a mainstay on the tables of the have-nots of post-boom America. The supermarket lines now regularly included old people and black people, fumbling apologetically for food stamps to pay for a dinner of catfood. The earnings of MEHOW Corp., which Hope Pet Foods had been renamed on the advice of a firm of New York consultants, for a fee which would have educated a generation of black children in East St. Louis, boomed ahead. By 1977, the Hope Foundation found itself with over $6 million a year to distribute.

It was at about this time that Devon joined the Foundation. The trustees were in over their heads. It was the usual board: a lawyer, a banker, two wimper-jawed Hope siblings, and the stockbroker husband of old Hope's granddaughter. When Devon arrived, the Foundation's director, a retired MEHOW vice president, had just been diagnosed with a melanoma. He was dead within five months.

Devon took over like a rich man's secretary at a funeral. She was old enough, and intelligent enough, to play her cards well. The stockbroker beamed gratefully as the Foundation doubled the rate of turnover of its portfolio, selling out its Hope shares, all through his firm, only weeks before a bent can of HopeyKitties yielded a botulism that wiped out six blocks of a Scottsdale retirement village. The Foundation's cash and the mechanics of its elaborately organized trust accounts were given to the banker. Devon squeezed her eyes shut and slept, in turn, with each of the Hope nephews; as they panted and stammered in her ear and spattered prematurely on her stomach, she took what comfort she could in reminding herself that the end justified the means.

"It's all so interesting," she wrote an old Interglobal colleague, "to be part of such a great cause." She didn't say what it was. "But *nothing*," she emphasized, "will be as exciting as our days building hospitality on the banks of the Orinoco." She drew two big, smily circles and signed "Grace," or "Jane." Devon liked writing letters; they gave her a feeling that she had some kind of a past.

In the first year after she took over, *de facto,* she contrived to arrange matters so that the fees and commissions paid by the Foundation salved the self-interest of the trustees and gave her room to operate. She began to direct a substantial share of the Foundation's subventions to organizations which, she knew, represented bland and legitimate counterfeits of the dark side of the moon.

People who had known her "when" became aware of her but never connected her with the moonchild who had once run with them. Personal difficulties intruded. Although she claimed an old, dying mother somewhere out West, and seldom went out, mixed little in St. Louis society, and never saw the ultimate beneficiaries of her generosity, jealous mutterings in the living rooms of Clayton and Saint Charles incited a Hope granddaughter to assert herself. Devon's position became uncomfortable. It was time for a change.

"So—and I'm always saying 'so,' like a character in a bad play—here I am," she said, turning to Harrison and hosing him down with a presence, eyes, bones, hands, that turned him inside out.

He turned his coffee cup in his hands.

"Well, you've certainly got the credentials." He felt like a fool, being so obvious. "We'll work well together. Let me fill you in."

She was turning him on. Trying to hide his reaction behind the explanation of RAID, he launched into a description of his plan to set it in motion. He didn't name the client. As he talked, he started to enthuse in the scheme.

"That's very straightforward, David," she said when he

(**174**)

had finished. "It sounds as if I'd better unpack for a long stay. Let's go back to your office and do a little map reading."

Walking back down Madison Avenue, they bought a dozen copies of the *Wall Street Journal.* In the office, while Harrison fetched an atlas, an *Official Airline Guide,* and the *American Bank Directory,* Devon clipped advertisements for card-printing offers. She found thirty.

It was close to seven o'clock when they finished. He would start in San Francisco on Tuesday, assuming the RAID tapes were ready as promised. She would work New York and Philadelphia and then head for Washington, Virginia, and the South. Then they would circle back, crossing but not meeting, until, in two weeks, they would between them have opened some ninety custody accounts.

Toward the end, when page after page of yellow paper had been filled with pseudonyms, bank names, flight numbers, and dates, she asked him, "I suppose it's out of place to ask what this is *really* all about? Nobody's really told me much."

It wasn't quite true. The telegram she'd received had instructed her to call a number in Detroit. The voice at the other end—a black voice, she guessed—had simply advised her that if she wasn't in New York in three weeks, a dossier and a trace would be promptly transmitted to the FBI.

"I'm afraid I can't say a great deal," said Harrison, "beyond that it's a very big investment project, for a large overseas client. As far as our part of it, it's all on the up-and-up. But it's so large that the client wants secrecy. He doesn't trust Wall Street. So it's just thee and me, and a guy I've got running the computer end. You'll meet him in a week or so. He's getting the mechanical part shaped up. You won't *believe* him."

At first Devon wanted to pursue all the details; but then she thought, why bother? After the Detroit call, what was the difference? She didn't want to end up in manacles like Patty Hearst.

"As you will," she said.

Harrison gathered up the papers. "I'll get these Xeroxed in the morning. Then we'll talk about getting the tickets."

Outside on the sidewalk, the late dusk had finally shifted to night. Madison Avenue was dotted with gesticulating, cab-seeking couples in dark clothes making their first move on a big evening.

"Would you like to grab a bite?"

"No thank you, David. Why don't we talk tomorrow?"

He put her in a cab. He wanted to walk, to cool down. It seemed to him that promise was always vanishing up a street in a stutter of tail-lights.

Devon was quartered in a small hotel off Fifth Avenue not far from the Metropolitan Museum. The evening paper was on the floor outside her door. The headline read: BAXTER TO ISRAEL/WHAT NEXT? Inside, she didn't turn on the lights. The room was lit well enough by the flares of the museum across the way; she went to the window and looked across Fifth Avenue. The fountains were bubbling, crowds were climbing and descending the broad steps.

She sat down on her bed, pulling pillows up to prop her against the headboard. She couldn't bother with the newspaper. She felt troubled. Abstractedly, she reached inside her dress, inside her bra, and touched the tip of her breast. Her other hand went down, pushing up her skirt, sliding under her pants; she stretched along the bed and watched the lights blink like a Mondrian on the shades until she forgot, or remembered, everything.

Harrison let himself into his apartment and flipped on the lights. A thick packet of mail and magazines was on the coffee table. He put down his briefcase and went to the bar, where he poured some Scotch over the tired spicules of ice which lingered in the bottom of the glass bucket.

He was too uneasy to choose a record. He punched a button and a classical music station came on. It was the end of the hourly news: "...said that a basic realignment of Middle Eastern relationships might be in order. Congress today..."

The phone rang. Harrison's life was measured in telephone calls and plane tickets.

It might be her.

"Hello?"

"Hey Mister David, where you been? I wanted to give you my new number." Harrison could hear disco music in the background. He wrote down the number. "You got a telex? Good. Now I been down to talk to the good folks at Digipoint. The service bureau; you remember? We got time on a machine when we need it. They usually charge by the bit, but you are so strong on this secrecy number, I signed up for flat time. OK? And they got a Wang kicking around, some customer deep-sixed, so I rented that, $3000 a month. We got a good setup here. And, Mister David, this ain't a bad town; say

(176)

hello to Henry. Met him tonight at the Waldorf Cafeteria, where the Harvard boys go. Hey, Henry, say hello to my fren', Mister David."

Harrison found himself on the line with a very drunk young man who was mumbling something about the need for the races to understand each other.

Ernie came back on the line.

"I know what you thinkin', Mister David, but don't you worry none. This is one reliable nigger. You call me when you got the stuff."

Ernie hung up. Welcome to the twentieth century, Harrison said to himself. He poured a little more Scotch in his glass and crossed to the sofa. Opening his mail, he guessed he might get to sleep sometime. He tried to make himself imagine Des now, in London. Would Billy be back? He tried to focus on her, to brighten and bring up the image of their weekend, tried to give it immediacy. He couldn't. Devon had taken over.

In bed, he consoled himself with the thought that sleeplessness was merely a matter of growing older. He kept thinking of Devon, but that didn't bring her any closer.

II

GREEN MONDAY

14 It was a day so clear that Harrison felt as if he could see a thousand miles from his window in the Huntington Hotel. The sky had a pale brightness that set off every edge and twist of the city like a Chinese carving. On a day like this, you had to envy the people who lived in San Francisco.

When he got to Green Street, he found Nyquist particularly expansive.

Two plastic-sheathed tape reels and a bright red folder sat on Nyquist's desk. Each displayed the MPL logo, a red dragon circled with ticker tape on which MPL was repeated. "These babies," Nyquist slapped the reels, "are the greatest thing we've ever done. There isn't a big bank or insurance company that wouldn't want them. They belong to you now; if you stop using them, or change your mind, give me a call. I'll buy them back at your cost plus interest." Harrison had earlier handed over a certified check for $650,000. Plus $30 cash. For the reel cases. "They don't give those things away," said Nyquist, pocketing the bills.

As Harrison rose to leave, Nyquist said, "Just a minute, I want you to meet our own Jascha Heifetz of binary." Nyquist pressed a buzzer and a slim, brown boy materialized.

"Mr. Axelson, meet Dalip Singh. He's the boy who stitched

RAID together. Dalip, this is Martin Axelson of Master Structural Trust Associates, our new client. Dalip is a Certified NIT: Neologismic Investment Theorist. Fill him in on the program, Dalip."

The Indian boy seemed nervous. "Well, sir, these programs spread your investment..." He had a shy, singsong voice.

"GII," interrupted Nyquist.

"...your GII across the 2900 large stocks—by large, we mean over $50 million of market value—on the Standard & Poor's Compustat tapes. You are probably aware of Compustat; it provides the basic data on every issue traded in size on any market in this country. In the end, we used 2345 issues. RAID programs the purchase of $700 million, in round figures, sir, of those issues in 115 account designations. The number of issues has been determined by their historical trading characteristics. You will never own more in total than seven-tenths of 1 percent of the voting stock of any investee company. On average, you will own 2.6 tenths."

"That's point zero zero two six VMV— Variable Market Value—any way you look at it," said Nyquist.

"Quite so, sir." The Indian was subdued. He struck Harrison as a delicate, feminine young man.

"It's a practical program, with good variability," Dalip added.

"OV, Optimum Variability," corrected Nyquist. Harrison hadn't said a word.

"As I have written it, you can time your investments as you please. The program will adjust itself. If you wish, for example, to invest the funds in six months or six days, it can be done by writing in variations. Everything is set out in the software package." Dalip pointed to the red folder.

"We call it OVOID," boomed Nyquist. "Optimal Velocity, Optimal Inflow Determinant." He gleamed in the glow of his own cleverness.

Dalip was excused. Harrison and Nyquist chatted briefly, of odds and ends, until Harrison looked at his watch. Eleven o'clock, and he had a noon flight to Seattle. It was July 14. By now, Devon would have covered Atlanta and Birmingham and should be on her way to New Orleans.

He begged off Nyquist's invitation to lunch. "Shredded Egg-Dogs and Icicle Radish Soup. Two of Yon Choh's specialties. Take a later plane." Nyquist made it sound tempting and sybaritic. He looked like Nero Wolfe in a vast, enfolding

(180)

mustard caftan. Around his neck was a porphyry evil eye on a chunky silver chain.

Duty called, however, and Harrison was in Seattle by mid-afternoon. He repeated his spiel to three different banks and caught the redeye back to New York. The stewardesses were plain and presumably horny, but though he left the lavatory door open, none joined him—which gave the lie to another of Barney's sexual boasts.

They landed at JFK just after seven. He called Ernie in Boston and was on the eight-thirty shuttle from LaGuardia.

He met Ernie in Brookline, in front of a dull cement-block slab just off Pond Avenue. "Digipoint Data Services, Inc." had been cut into the face of the building in foot-high letters.

"This is a good place for me to work out of," said Ernie. "Less crowded than out there on Route 128," referring to suburban Boston's miracle mile of high technology. Inside, he led Harrison through rows of rat-eyed Irish women squinting at cathode ray tubes. "How you, dear?" said Ernie, happily patting a beaming keypunch lady on the head. Everyone seemed to know him. And was pleased to see him.

He led Harrison into a cool, quiet room where banks of enormous tape drives switched nervously back and forth. Ernie spun the two RAID tapes effortlessly onto two unoccupied spindles. Harrison, who could barely screw in a light-bulb, watched while Ernie read through the material in the folder.

Ernie sat down at a console and tapped instructions onto a keyboard, the way Harrison had seen airline clerks do. The keyboard took a light stroke; it lacked the punchy, decisive character of a typewriter, and the pattern of Ernie's typing seemed oddly illogical. The instructions materialized on a CRT screen. Ernie checked them and tapped again. One of the tapes started to roll.

"I'm asking the program to show me a sample," said Ernie.

Next to the terminal, a high-speed Data Products printer tattatted rows of figures and alphabetical symbols, stuttering across the paper like a typewriter key, but a hundred times faster. Ernie watched the paper records fold out for a minute and tapped another button. The gunfire printing ceased. Ernie carefully separated the printed sheets from the machine and spread them on a table.

"See here," he said to Harrison, with the easy assurance of a good teacher addressing a child, "this is how the script will go. This '1A' designates a particular account. That sequence will run to '115A' for each of our bank custody accounts. You'll have to give me 115 account titles. I'll code them in. Then this next," Harrison read "600 KDE," "means account number one buys 600 shares of whatever KDE is."

"That's Walter Kidde & Company," said Harrison. "A conglomerate."

"Well, trade number one buys 600 Walter Kidde. Then this 'RPT' means to report in the price; you'll get that as confirmation from whomever does the order for you. That'll let us keep track of how much we're spending. Every trade will run that way. They'll report the dollars spent back to you; you'll report them to me and I'll plug 'em in here. Then this last '8500 K' means that this account, number one, will only spend $8.5 million; after that, it goes off the board. A dead man. No more trades. And so on through all 115 accounts. At the end of which you'll have spent $700 million. Any questions?"

Harrison nodded his understanding.

Ernie went back to the terminal and fingered more instructions, looking at the printout as he typed. The second tape began to back and fill.

"I'm just throwing in some sample prices. That first tape gives the orders. This one keeps the books." He pushed a key with a conclusive flourish. The printer began to rattle again.

"See here," Ernie said when he had the second set of printouts on the table, "this tells us that for this first set of orders, we've bought 600 KDE, spending $18,900 in account number 1, and that we now own zero point zero zero six percent of the outstanding stock. If the outstanding stock changes, a stock split or something, it will show up on the Standard & Poor's service. The people here will plug the new number into these tapes. I'll run spot checks back in the apartment on a little Radio Shack computer I've got at home. It should help keep us on top of things. Any questions?"

Harrison had one. "Ernie, we're playing a larger game. The $700 million is just a base number. Can you fix this deal by a factor of seven, so that we can run it again and again, seven times, starting in the middle sometimes, to confuse the bad guys, to get up to close to $5 billion?"

This was Harrison's big bet. He'd guessed that a supertechnician like Ernie, if handed a job, could deliver. It was more hope than knowledge. The book on computer language he had bought in the San Francisco airport had baffled him hopelessly beyond the title page. He felt like a sinner prostrate before a bishop. It was time for faith to take over.

"No problem. Take about a week, though, maybe ten days. That OK?"

Harrison found it interesting that Ernie didn't speak "black" when talking computerese. Every man has a different language for each object of his affections, he thought.

He did have one big problem. It had kept him awake on the flight from Seattle.

Remembering his early training days in the order room at Verger, Harrison figured it would take about three minutes to telephone or teletype an order. The way it looked, he and Devon would need more than a full day to handle the orders, both working full time, if they read the orders from a script. The exchanges were only open for eight hours. It wouldn't work. They had to spend about $25 million a day, for 180 trading days. If the average order size was, say, $20,000, they were talking 1200 orders a day: at three minutes per order, for two people, that came to 1800 minutes apiece: thirty hours. Plus report-backs. As he worked it through, the numbers got worse. He felt himself start to sweat. God wasn't making any forty-hour days. You could jack up the average order, but that risked attention.

The Indian boy who programmed RAID had been thinking in computer time, where machines spoke to each other in milliseconds. Dalip hadn't figured on the time used in picking up a telephone or typing on a telex, hadn't figured on the pleasantries, flirtation, and dirty jokes that were integral to transactions between people.

"Um, Ernie, there *seems* to be one other matter." Harrison never ducked his mistakes. Lacking the sanguine omniscience of the B-School boys, he had always believed that error and correction, even apology, being central to art, were acceptable in business. It was permitted to be wrong. Clare Verger had said, "You can tough out any kind of trouble, David, and get away with it. Except two: a bad heart and poor arithmetic."

He explained his fears.

"I thought that was going to come up. That's where Ma Bell comes in. These people here," Ernie took in the building with a sweeping gesture, "have an extra machine doing nothing back there. It's one reason I picked Digipoint. The machine's old but it's telecommunicative. I just need to add some gadgets to make it conversational. We can get them off the shelf. And I already took a lease-option on the machine: $3,000 a month plus the telephone hookup."

As Ernie explained it, the computer could be modified, through a series of electronic connections, to translate the daily script into a sonic code which would be fed into New England Bell's digital telecommunications interface with the rest of the Bell System. It would take less than ten minutes to transmit the orders, confirmations, and custody instructions to the RAID accounts. "This's an old machine," Ernie noted. "If we were state-of-the-art, it'd take ten seconds to process an order. And if we were on the leading edge, even faster; hell, Merrill Lynch can handle sixty orders *a second.* All we have to do is get 'em there!"

Riding back to Logan to catch the shuttle, Harrison felt very old. Maybe *old* wasn't quite the word, he thought: *antiquated? anachronistic? obsolete? Obsolete,* that was it. This had been Harrison's first close-up brush with the new technology, and a world in which children played with computers in grade school. Harrison didn't quite understand it, except he knew these machines could perform prodigies, and he wasn't sure he entirely approved. Of course, he did recognize that he was a words man, wandering around in a numbers world. Never really at home. At Verger he'd learned to do basic figuring on a slide rule. He bought a large, heavy Keuffel & Esser rule. It was ivory and teak and had the reassuring feel of furniture. Long series of calculations were cranked out of a clackety old Monroe desk calculator, a model which was now probably in the Smithsonian. He wondered if Keuffel & Esser were still in business.

Nowadays, the game belonged to Ernie and his sort. Computer scans checked your liver, managed your bank account, and sold your business. He didn't really fit, it seemed. "I can't do business unless I can look a man in the eye," was one of Dinker Blenheim's pet sayings. Well, today, where were the eyes to look into, Harrison wondered, unless you counted the blinking lights of the data processing consoles?

It added to his inbuilt sense of isolation. He thought of himself as an edge-type person, anyway, a notch off from the crowd, always a shade more the observer than the participant. An old girlfriend had gotten it right: "David, when you speak, you watch your own words in the air, like skywriting. I can see you doing it. You seem so far outside yourself. Stop watching for a moment; it's very disconcerting. Join the party!"

There was a thunderstorm over LaGuardia, so it was after

six when he let himself into his apartment. He was expecting to hear from Devon, but when he picked up the phone to call the answering service, the line was dead. He went down to the corner payphone and called the service number. A weary black voice told him the office closed at four; he could call in the morning. AT&T was now working the same hours as the federal government. Wasn't there another number to call? No, said the voice, in a tone which seemed to say also, "And go fuck yo'self, mah feets hurt!"

The air was heavy and darkening. He beat the first, heavy drops of the storm to the safety of his apartment and spent the evening with a bottle of Famous Grouse and three days of the *Times*.

Devon finally ran out of business cards in Phoenix. She was anxious to get back to New York. The trip had been a success, but she was tired of hotels. Well she might be, after a career of putting them together. She had opened thirty-three accounts in eighteen Sunbelt cities. It had been nearly three weeks since she had left New York. Tomorrow was August 2. She would be back in New York for the weekend. By her reckoning, they were within striking distance.

When she had talked to Harrison two days earlier, he had just come back from five days in the Midwest, making short, puddle-jumping hops between the industrial cities: Akron, Columbus, Terre Haute. It sounded like a traveling sales-man's itinerary. According to Harrison, they were at 113 accounts in sixty-eight banks.

"We have to be exact," he'd said, "but we can round up to 115 with a couple of the smaller banks around here. You might as well come back. Everything else looks all set."

What a trip, she thought, as she settled back and closed her eyes. If this is Tuesday, it must be Little Rock. Her clothes were disgusting, she felt. Nothing attention-getting, Harri-son had said. So no luggage to check; no luggage to get lost and be reported. No thick sheaf of tickets. Rereserve at every stop. Use all credit cards: Air Travel, Diners, American Express personal (gold), American Express corporate (green), Visa, Master Charge, Carte Blanche. Don't pile up the trip bills in one account. Thirty-eight banks visited. Five didn't have the right kind of telecommunications setup. Six bank vice presidents, one a woman, had tried to seduce her. She called Harrison from the airport.

He listened to her report, and invited her to dinner.

"David, thanks, but I'm filthy. I'm going to take about a ten-hour bath. Are we ready to go?"

"I think so. If you give me an hour or so, I can let you know for certain."

"Tomorrow will be fine. Will you need me this weekend? I'd like to catch some sun. I feel like one of those garden slugs. White and slimy."

"Go ahead. An old rule, and a good one, is never start anything big on a Friday. We can kick this off next week."

He called Ernie.

"How you doin', boss?" Ernie was into his much-fancied imitation of Jack Benny's Rochester.

"Just double-checking. Damnit, Ernie, I can smell the goddamn incense over the telephone."

"And that ain't all, Mr. Benny. You ought to see what I got here. Say hello to Gerhard. A sailor off the *Bremen*. Hey, Gerhard, say hello to Mr. Benny." A young German voice, complicated by a dope-thickened tongue, came on the line. Knowing Ernie was certainly a broadening experience, Harrison thought to himself, as he struggled with the remnants of his college German.

Ernie was back on. "Anything I can do for you, Mr. Benny?"

"As I said, before you turned me over to young Goebbels there, I'm just double-checking. You all set? Everything in place?"

"Just push a button and away we gooooooo..." Ernie had switched to Jackie Gleason. He was awfully good at voices, Harrison had to admit.

"OK. I think we might let it rip starting Tuesday. That's the seventh. We're running a little late and may have to push it a little somewhere along the line. Now for Christ's sake don't get lost or murdered between now and Tuesday. OK?"

"Yassuh, Mr. Benny." Rochester again. "Me and Gerhard are just twinklin' down to the Cape for a weekend of heavy pettin'. There's a wet jockey-shorts contest in Provincetown Saturday night that I was fixin' to win. Until I saw what Gerhard's got in his jeans. I didn't think they came that big in white!"

"It sounds riveting. Have a good time. I'll talk to you Monday." Harrison hung up.

He crossed his living room to the double-sized partners' desk which served as a catchall for his life. The green leather top was almost completely hidden by a carefully organized hodge-podge of papers and parcels: books from England still in brown paper; bills; invitations; postcards and letters from friends; a small stack of books still waiting to be sent for rebinding; sales and exhibition catalogues; pads; his passport. It was all very neat, though misleadingly so. Harrison arranged the papers in winnowed stacks. He unwrapped the books from England, curious works on colonial life which his bookseller persisted in sending him, and stuffed them up on a high shelf, next to the four copies of *Passages* which he had been given by four different women, each of whom had despairingly misinterpreted his self-containment as mid-life crisis. Then he rearranged them again. And so on, like a small boy chopping and pushing his liver around his plate to give the appearance of having eaten it.

He picked up a spiral pad on which he had been making extensive notes in columns. From a Fortnum and Mason cheese jar he took a felt-tip pen and started to work down through the columns. He didn't think he'd left anything out. Ernie's end was all set up. Of course, he was taking Ernie's word for *that,* but Ernie's real masters were heavily in debt to Harrison's client and he had no doubt of Ernie's loyalty and competence. They would have sent their best.

He and Devon had established 113 custody accounts around the country. According to Ernie, the way the RAID program was written, it would take pretty close to three weeks to activate to full speed. They could pick up the necessary two more over the next week or so.

Ernie had set the computer up to give them three pieces of paper a week. On Tuesdays, it would provide a forecasted cash requirement for all purchases for the next five trading days beginning with the following Wednesday week. The forecast included a 20 percent contingency factor to cover any issue that might run away from them. Harrison knew that in fishing with so wide a net he was sure to catch some aberrations: stocks which shot up on takeover news, for example.

On Fridays at noon, the machine would give the weekly position report. The printout would record the previous five days' purchases; the position in each stock, measured both in dollars, at cost and current value, and in percentage of voting capital; the status—our "open to buy," Harrison called it—of each account.

Harrison found its complexity alluring. "Jesus," he said

to Ernie, "this is incredible, what these goddamn machines can do."

"Shit, boss, this ain't nothin'. You should see what the big banks offer their big corporate customers in the way of cash management. Or the oil companies; hell, they sometimes handle 750,000 charge account slips *a day*. This baby ain't even sweatin' at our little game. We're just usin' the machine 'cause it counts quicker, and probably better, and talks faster."

Harrison, Devon, and Ernie would rotate the twice-weekly task of getting the printouts from Boston to New York. Harrison would report in to Khafiq—the name was never mentioned—each Saturday morning.

The pen checked off each of the entries. Harrison ran it through in his mind. It looked complete. Dotted and crossed.

From the dark mahogany notary's chest which he used as a bar, he poured some Famous Grouse over ice. A toast was in order, and he turned solemnly, glass raised, first north, toward Boston; then south and west, toward where he guessed Devon lived; and, finally, to the east, out across the Atlantic, across the world's wide waist, to London and beyond.

This made it all worthwhile, he thought, as he undressed for bed and set the alarm. He read himself to sleep from a new novel. It was the best thing—best *new* thing, rather—he had read in years. He was coming to the end of it. It made him sad. These days, good things were so scarce and over so quickly. Sleep caught up to him just as he finished the chapter: *"Thousands of feet above sea level, T. S. Garp cried in the airplane that was bringing him home to be famous in his violent country."*

The alarm went off at four a.m. He fumbled the light on and punched out the fourteen tones of an international call.

"Good morning, Mr. Khafiq."

"Good morning. Oh, David. Gracious, what time is it over there? Why are we always talking when it is the middle of the night for you?"

"We're ready to go, sir. We could start as early as Tuesday next. I know we're a little late, but I think we can make it up along the way."

"Very good. Our friends are a touch restive. What do you need from me?"

Harrison explained. They were going to use a dozen large money center banks as conduits. It would be up to Khafiq to orchestrate the movement of the funds into these banks, where Harrison, as guided by Ernie, had established a mechanism for making money transfers for the account of his fictional master trusts. Great piles of money would never be left heaped up in a way that would stimulate curiosity. Curiosity, not suspicion. Harrison knew that their greed made American bankers the least suspicious people in the world. But knowledge of large cash balances would send the bankers bothersomely trying to sell services.

"I have the first week's cash instructions. I'd like to telex them tomorrow to you."

"Why don't you come over yourself? It's not the season, but at least we can make sure we have everything straight."

So Harrison went to London for the weekend. It wasn't the first time. There were no diversions at this time of year. A surly young voice informed him that Mrs. Lyall-Marsh was in Corfu and that Mr. Lyall-Marsh had left that morning for Scotland.

He spent Saturday with Khafiq. He was glad he had come. The two men worked out a procedure that seemed safe and uncomplicated. They would start on Thursday. Khafiq would need the two extra days to pull his end of things together.

"Put the instructions on the telex. Geneva 83456. This week. When we confirm back to you we'll give you next week's telex destination. I think it is only prudent to move things around." Khafiq shook his hand and looked at him seriously. "Good luck."

He left on the early plane Sunday.

The taxi took him from JFK through summer-deserted streets and deposited him at his apartment just after two p.m. It was steaming; the sewery pores of the city were reeking.

Harrison got his keys, changed into a golf shirt and cotton pants, and went down to his office. One of the other rooms in the suite was occupied by a gold bug, who kept a telex machine on hand for his multiple dealings with Hong Kong, Johannesburg, and the Narodny Bank. Harrison had made a deal with him for the off-hours use of the machine on a pay-for-use basis until his own telex could be installed in a one-room office Harrison had leased on lower Park Avenue. As with his post office boxes, he was keeping things separate and anonymous.

He sat down at the teletypewriter and set up the punched-tape device which was used to precheck messages for accuracy. Using one finger, and referring frequently to the printed instructions tacked to the wall, it took him nearly forty minutes to tape his message. It had thirteen paragraphs. The first read: "Sunday Icon 3345/ B3 467/ M63 1573/CC48 1305." Reading from the left, it translated into instructions to send $3,345,000 to Merchants Bank in Dallas, which was "Icon." Harrison and Khafiq had agreed on thirteen major "entry" banks, each designated by a simple, clearly differentiated word. These were huge banks: Certified, Gotham, Merchants, and the like, which handled equally huge daily flows of money. Harrison wanted to stay lost in the crowd.

The next instruction block, set off by slash marks, advised Khafiq to instruct Merchants to forward $467,000 to the account of Guardian Pacific Advisors at the Lumbermans and Farmers Trust in Portland, Oregon. The balance would go to banks in Indianapolis and Jacksonville. The machine in Brookline would then take over. Harrison and Devon had used thirty-two institutional pseudonyms on the 113 accounts they'd opened. The institutional names were designated "A" through "FF," like theater seats. The accounts were lodged with sixty-eight different banks, numbered serially. There was no overlap between the "master" banks and the sixty-eight other, mainly good-sized regionals, where the actual buying and selling would be done.

The total money involved in the first week's activity would be approximately $68 million. He wanted to start slowly and build it up. But Dalip's program covered only $700 million. If he was going to be able to run it through seven times in the thirty to thirty-five weeks he figured he had, he would have to be running at pretty close to $120 million a week soon, and faster a bit later. He'd asked Ernie to set up OVOID on the basis of seven five-week cycles. OVOID! RAID! These goddamn acronyms were going to drive him nuts, he thought, as he checked the confirmation copy of the telex. It would be easier when he had Devon or Ernie to proofread with him. Of course, for a while, they'd have to use the telex at night or during the period before noon when the gold bug repaired to the Four Seasons to celebrate or bemoan that morning's London gold fixing. Weekends would be better. They'd have their own machine in three weeks. He'd talk to Ernie about rescheduling the cash-flow scan to Fridays. Then they could deal with everything at once.

The telex was signed off "Rude." He and Khafiq had agreed

to authenticate every transmission by including a word containing the letters "r" and "d" in the first two syllables.

He rethreaded the punched tape and transmitted the message. A minute after he was finished, the machine clacked back: "Confirmed. Red. 23 76543." A bell rang and the machine stopped. Harrison checked the printed list of the country codes: "23" was Kuwait. That would be next week.

He let himself out and strolled up Third Avenue. The city was as good as empty. His shirt was soon dark with perspiration; he could feel his hair curling in the wet heat.

Woody Allen's new movie was playing back of Bloomingdale's. There was no line for the four o'clock show. He figured it was worth the risk of pneumonia in the air conditioning and went in. He liked the picture. While the picture was built around a stock company of stylish neurotics with no visible means of apparently unlimited support, a lot of it was about people and the opening and closing shots, grainy cityscapes with Gershwin music coming up strong on the soundtrack, were a kind of gutsy anthem to New York which meshed exactly with Harrison's own feelings about the city. His home.

He ate a hamburger at Melon's and walked home. Unexpected free time was like a banquet to him. He straightened up his apartment and took three pounds of the Sunday *Times* to bed. He couldn't wait for the fun to start. He also wondered where Devon might be.

15

Monday, August 13. It was hot the length of the entire northeast coast, from Rehoboth Beach as far north as Portsmouth, New Hampshire. It was stifling even in the New England mountains. There was no hint of respite anywhere.

It was cool in the Digipoint offices in Brookline when Ernie got there at seven-thirty in the morning. The building was air conditioned to sixty-five degrees twenty-four hours a day. Four big Carrier units on the roof dedicated ninety horsepower and a lot of very expensive Boston Edison electricity to keep the interior at the prescribed temperature.

ERNIE'S CORNER, read the fancily hand-lettered sign outside the glass-partitioned stall, ten feet square, that housed his current dreamchild. The keypunch ladies had presented it to him, with wine and cheese and ceremony.

Waving an airy hello to the security officer, Ernie went

(191)

through the vestibule and made his way through the ranks of terminals to the cubicle. He set down the cassette player he was carrying and pushed the "play" actuator. *"Don't, don't be shy/Come and say hello,"* bounced loudly around the room. The Village People. Ernie syncopated as he sat down at the keyboard. The equipment had been considerably reconfigured since Harrison had last seen it. Head and shoulders twitching to the insistent bass of the music, Ernie activated the console. Like an airplane pilot, he flicked switches and pushed keys. The CRT before him glowed. Tape reels started to rotate. He picked up the receiver from a Touch-Tone phone next to him and placed it in the cradle of an instrument which sat next to the CRT; then he dialed an access code.

The computer sorted through the bits of magnetic information stored on the reel, dug what it wanted out of its memory, and bounced it like a pinball through a galaxy of micronfinitesimal connections until it emerged as a series of impulses, microscopic tones, which were fed through the telephone handset into the modem. Existing now as a pattern of minute electric impulses, the signal flew along the lines to the Bell switching center in Framingham, where they acquired a new existence as a wave fraction and soared into the air, finally being picked up by the microprocessors of a satellite then hanging fifty miles above Dayton, Ohio. The satellite cast it back to a ground station outside Tacoma, which gathered it in and flashed it to a microwave tower a quarter mile away. The tower in turn sent it winging across the countryside to a microwave disseminator in the far suburbs of Seattle, which gathered it and sped it along the telephone wires which ran pole to pole into the heart of Seattle. The switching station of Northwest Bell took over and directed the signal to the still-dark order room of the First Rainier Trust and Deposit Bank. The teleprinter there had been clattering away for almost an hour. It ticked off another line on the sheet which it was extruding.

Back in Brookline, Ernie pushed the "Check" key on his console. The CRT winked and then dit-dotted a line of alphanumerics across its face. He smiled; Seattle had confirmed. It was seventy seconds since the reels had first started to revolve.

He went outside to the payphone in the corridor and placed a collect call.

Harrison accepted the charges. He sounded tired. Not too much sleep, Ernie guessed.

"Hey boss," he said, exultant, "we got ignition!"

At five-thirty Seattle time, the first clerk came into the darkened order room and turned on the lights. He went around the room flipping the various switches which turned on the order room's electronics. He went to the teleprinter and scanned the sheets visually for any big orders that might require special handling. There was only one big order: 60,000 shares of General Public Utilities to be sold for a mutual fund in Honolulu. He punched out instructions which took that order out of the memory bank. The rest of the stuff looked normal. He punched another sequence. The order room memory interfaced with the bank's money control center, double-checking for accounts which might be cash-short.

The initial RAID order, for account 3 675B 087, Northern Diversifications, was for 900 Lockheed. Flashing like lightning, the money monitor computer confirmed $326,000 in 3 675B 087. Without pausing, it passed on to the next transaction.

The money had arrived in Seattle just after midnight Monday morning. The credit advice had been transmitted on the bank wire from Gotham Bank, which had received it on Friday, as part of a $4,500,000 transfer from Cumberland Street Trust in the Bahamas. The money had been wired to Nassau from Manila. In the course of its travels the deposit had changed currencies four times and stopped briefly in five cities, like an anxious jet-setter. Cumberland's instructions to Gotham were to break up the credit into a number of pieces, for deposit to various accounts with Gotham's correspondent bank. Gotham liked to chisel whatever "float" it could over the weekend and so, absent any instructions to the contrary, the Cumberland Trust credits were housed in the bank's automated funds transfer system, which was working twenty-four hours a day. The bank's impersonal machines had also handled another $2.2 million transfer from Singapore, also from Khafiq. This money greeted the Monday dawn in Des Moines.

Other banks had taken in and recirculated nearly $62 million in credits from Hong Kong, Luxembourg, Panama City, and elsewhere. New York, Philadelphia, Dallas, and Los Angeles moved the money to forty-three regional banks, to a total of eighty-six separate institutional accounts. Guardian Pacific Advisors, for example, was credited with deposits not only in Portland, but in Birmingham, Detroit, and Phoenix. Northern Diversifications was not only a valued new account of the Rainier in Seattle, but of the Downtown Trust in Cincinnati and the Bargemans National in Memphis.

The Seattle clerk's CRT showed only two accounts short. He cleared them off the system into the "refer to Officer" switchback. Quickly, he ran through the rest, punching out key combinations which directed the orders into various Seattle brokerage offices. When he came to the Lockheed order, he paused for an instant. This was a nice little order, with no keyline symbol indicating negotiated commissions. A nice trade for the broker. He owed a favor to the guy at First Northwest Securities who covered the bank's small business. The broker had come up with four good tickets to the Sonics' game last Tuesday. Why not? He tapped out the First Northwest code.

The First Northwest brokers got to work at 5:45. The clerks had come in minutes earlier and cleared the machines. When the man on the Rainier account sat down and uncapped his container of coffee, there was a torn-off strip from the teleprinter propped against his multibuttoned telephone console. "BY 900 LK MKT," it read. Checking the digital clock at the far end of the room, he wrote out the order, noting the time, 5:58, and initialing the order ticket, to which he stapled the printout strip, and stuck it in the conveyor belt which circulated among the brokers' stations.

At the end of the room, a flexible arm tipped the order tickets into a bin behind two teletype clerks. One of them reached back and grabbed the Lockheed ticket.

First Northwest did the bulk of its New York Stock Exchange business through three big New York firms. Stuck to the wall over the teletype machines was a memo from First Northwest's trading partner. The gist of it was that Shearson Loeb, Rhoades was not getting its share of First Northwest's floor trades and the firm was losing reciprocal business. The teletype clerk couldn't quarrel with the assertion. His direction of the orders which flowed through him was influenced by the cases of Jack Daniel's which the other two firms had kindly caused to be delivered to his house on a regular basis.

What the hell, he shrugged, orders are orders, and teletyped Shearson Loeb, Rhoades to buy 900 LK at the opening.

It was 9:00 in New York and the hive was humming in

the floor-wide trading room at 42 Wall Street. Twelve teletype operators, in two rows, gathered the orders from the
firm's fifty-three clearing accounts. It was a lucrative service
for out-of-town firms. Shearson processed their orders, balanced their account books, and kept their customer records.

The Lockheed order clacketed in on machine number 6,
halfway down the second row. The clerk tore it off and stuck
it on the red-rimmed track of the conveyor belt which circled
the huge room like a monorail. The red track carried the
order along to the six clerks who manned the consoles tying
the firm in to the trading posts and the firm's own brokers
on the floor.

The order passed by the first two clerks, who were busy
on the phone. The third snatched it off the conveyor. He gave
it a cursory look. Nine hundred LK. At the market. A nice
little order. Better than just being put on the screen. Something for Billy Johnson, who'd been bitching beerily last
night in Harry's Bar about not enough business, but who
wasn't a bad guy and had paid for five rounds. Besides, Billy
was good for a little cocaine now and then. He punched a
button.

A floor clerk came on. "Where the fuck is Billy?" asked
the order clerk. This time in the morning, he had time for
questions. Later on, when the market was open, the tickets
would come flying by like racehorses. When that happened,
the orders went down to the floor automatically.

"I'll get him for you. We'll be right back to you," said the
broker's clerk on the other end.

Billy Johnson was having his third shaky cup of coffee
upstairs in the Stock Exchange Luncheon Club when he was
paged. He felt like shit. He was fifty-two years old and had
been a member of the Stock Exchange for thirty years. His
collar was frayed and his old Rogers Peet suit didn't look so
good either. Not that it should. His wife was in Stonington
for the summer, in the beach house that she'd bought with
her money, and Johnson couldn't handle the sexual prosperity of summer nights on his own in New York. The evening
before had started at Harry's and that was about all he could
remember, until a couple of hours ago, when he woke up on
the floor of a strange living room in Bay Ridge. He hoped to
Christ his wife hadn't called the apartment.

He staggered to the phone and got his clerk. "What's up?"

"Loeb wants you."

"I'll be right down."

He made his way across the floor, shrugging into a tan cotton broker's coat with his membership badge pinned to it. His clerk looked at him reproachfully, pushed a button, and handed him the phone.

"Billy?"

"Yeah."

"Buy 900 LK at the opening. Not held."

"You got it. Thanks."

It was 9:58. Johnson was known on the floor as "the Pad Man," from a habit he had of flapping his pad against his forehead in the trading crowd while declaiming, "I could be very big in here." He wasn't a bad old guy, though, said the young traders, kind of a sympathetic drunk with a psychological hangover from the days when a seat on the Exchange was a license to print money.

At ten o'clock exactly the bell rang to open trading. Johnson had stationed himself at post seven, where Lockheed was traded. The post was ruled in imperial fashion by Ben Gardner, "the Old Trader," who was the specialist, the market-maker, in Lockheed and a dozen or so other stocks. He was a tall, well kept man in his late forties, with an unassailably superior bearing.

There were four other brokers jostling for Gardner's attention. Johnson edged in among them, pad flapping, exuding ninety-proof perspiration.

"How's Lockheed?" he asked. "I could be very big in here."

"Three hundred offered at a half," said the Old Trader. He checked his book trying to look casual. Everyone knew he'd eaten a ton of Lockheed the week before, when the stock had crumpled on a false rumor that the 1011 airliner had been grounded.

"Three-eighths bid for 900," said Johnson. Flap, flap.

"Sell you 500 at a half; 400 at five-eighths."

"Come on, Trader, cut the shit. I'll take 900 at a half."

"Nine hundred at a half. Done."

The two men noted the trade. Johnson made his frail way back to his post. "Bought 900 LK at 20½," he reported upstairs to the Loeb order room.

"Billy, that is some shitty execution," declared the order clerk. "You're gonna owe me a real summer snowfall for that one." He punched Johnson off and stuck the price information on the conveyor.

*   *   *

The order made its way back to Seattle and to Ernie the way it had come. It was 10:08 in Boston when it showed up on the printer in Brookline. Seattle's automatic printing, sorting, and mailing machines had already dispatched a written confirmation to a Newark post office box. From the time Billy Johnson had reported the trade, and it had been punched into the Loeb computer, no human hand or eye had participated in the recording of the transaction. It was all just numbers. RAID had spent $24,000 and change. By ten-fifteen, there were seven other confirmations on Ernie's printout. By lunch time, there would be twenty.

Satisfied that the program was working, Ernie left the machine on its own and got up to go down the hall for another cup of coffee.

Before that, he called Harrison again. "Boss, the baby's been baptized. Let's see if he grows up to be Pope."

Devon showed up at the office at a quarter to eleven. She had great color.

"Sorry, the Long Island Rail Road. The train broke down in the Hamptons. I had to take a cab from Sayville. With three transvestites. It's a hell of a fragrant way to begin a week!"

"No problem." Harrison thought she looked fantastic. Had she spent the weekend with someone? "That's the price of fun in the sun."

He tried to be offhand. "By the way, we kicked it off this morning."

"Great," she said. "Will you begrudge me a lunch hour? I'd like to get rid of this junk." She still had her duffel, with a tennis racquet sticking out of it. "And a shower. I smell like an aftershave factory." She was irritatingly indifferent to their shared great enterprise.

He was dying to take her to lunch. Exult a little. See where things led.

"Go ahead," he said. "Tomorrow's Tuesday, you know. Can you go to Boston? To pick up the cash list. We're full steam ahead on this thing now. All the way."

She thought he looked boyish and very, very sincere. Upbeat. This was no big deal to her. Naturally. What could be, after you'd seen your friends lying bleeding in the streets beaten to pulp by the pigs?

16 It took three weeks for them to get up to full speed.

Ernie had really scoped it out well, Harrison said. Forget the jiving, prancing, and disco talk; the black was a professional. Not that Ernie's personal style would ever have bothered Harrison. In business you worked with whomever they sent you. It didn't mean you had to take them dancing. Ernie's stuff was timely; there was no rushed, last-minute beating around to meet a deadline. It seemed to work perfectly.

Harrison was also awfully pleased with himself. After a lifetime spent in a profession which seemed to value process as much as result, his intellectual self-esteem, never inconsiderable, was gratified to see that all this computer paraphernalia could yet be enslaved to an idea which had an objective.

Harrison, Devon, and Ernie settled into an easy relationship built around RAID. A liturgy in which the sacraments were the routine business of collecting the weekly printout, telexing the instructions to Khafiq, and watching the totals and positions climb. Nine hundred shares of LK became 1900 shares, became 3500, became 6100, became 9700. And so across the board.

The city remained hot and smelly well into October. Harrison got restive. He was, he knew, working on the biggest job of his or anyone's lifetime, at least as measured by the insipid values of Wall Street, but even that didn't staunch his uneasiness. The day would come; that much he knew, but it seemed too distant to provide real comfort. He had planned it too well. The natural, elegant rightness of his inspiration, precise as the marquetry joinings of French furniture, had left him with nothing to do. There was no negotiation, no improvisation, no real excitement.

His initial enjoyment turned a bit sour around the edges as he came to realize the inescapable irony that as much as his intelligence had made the computer the servant of his ideas, so had the machine's capacity for flawless execution distanced him from his own project. He was bored. It was as dreary as those early years at Verger when he had spent tiresome nights plugging cash flows into a calculator. Either the work was supremely tedious, and he was involved in it to the last detail; or it was sublimely exciting, big and enterprising like this, and he was shut out because a computer could do it faster and errorlessly. It was a hell of a note, he thought, trying to suppress his innate impatience with thoughts of the consolations at the end of the road.

Khafiq seemed pleased. They spoke on the telephone every week or so. Harrison would summarize their position. It was going very well. The market was dragging along, dispiritedly celebrating rumors and false hopes, pinning a kind of dissipated jubilation on one day's news from Washington or Cairo; giving way the next day to an equally diffident gloom. Trading continued to churn at 20 to 25 million shares daily. The Dow Jones Average described a narrow, jagged shape.

On October 11, something over seven weeks from the day Ernie pushed the button for the first time, they entered the second RAID cycle. Ernie had been fiddling with the MPL software.

"This program's like a queen that needs bread," he told Harrison. "You get to start in at either end." He had figured it out. "All we doin' is shakin' dice. Don't matter whether we start rollin' at ten in the mornin' or ten at night. Sun time or moontime," he falsettoed. Harrison knew he was right and so, instead of starting with Lockheed, Ernie let the tapes run on for a while and began the second pass with 1400 Adobe Energy. It turned into a windfall within a fortnight when Adobe agreed to merge with North American Molymetal at a handsome premium. Adobe stockholders were offered a choice of cash, which would be immediately taxable, or Molymetal stock, which would not be. Harrison had prepared for this type of eventuality. He got on the phone to Ernie, who ran a position check on Adobe that evening. There were 7700 shares at a cost of $185,700. The Molymetal offer made them worth $259,000. The shares were held in three nominee names in four banks.

Harrison was going to make the swap for Molymetal shares. He wanted the RAID portfolio to be tax clean in the current year. Next year would be different. They would be out and gone between the next two April 15s. Plenty of time to compute and pay their taxes.

He consulted a notebook which contained the roster of account names and the post office boxes in New York, Newark, and Boston which collected their mail: proxy statements, interim reports, and other mailings, including, he noted disapprovingly, a rising flood of self-serving public policy bulletins and pronunciamenti from famous and important executives. There were thirty-two box numbers, eighteen in New York, six in Newark, eight in Boston. The Boston and New York boxes were cleared every day, the Newark drops every other. The stuff was discarded upon collection unless, like the Adobe proxy, there was something specific and important, which required action.

Ernie had informed him that the Adobe stock was held by Fidelity Participants, Jarndyce Associates, and Grubbe and Company. The first two had been assigned New York box numbers. Harrison made a note on his New York action sheet to keep an eye out for the Adobe proxy material which he or Devon would sign with their appropriate *nom d'investissement* and return to effectuate the exchange of shares.

Adobe was the most exciting event of the month. The trouble was that the work kept him close to New York; he couldn't take on other assignments. A few old clients turned up. He wrote a couple of cursory, inexpensive valuation letters, tailoring the numbers like a suit to fit preordained outcomes. A long, liquid evening at "21" and about a dozen bars was devoted to an effort to convince a client not to undertake an assuredly unsuccessful raid on another company. Satisfied that his companion had seen the path of corporate righteousness, Harrison went home to bed. The next morning his client arose, made a mighty growl like Goliath, and commenced an unfriendly tender offer which ended in his head being handed to him by Felix Rohatyn and the other smart people at Lazard.

There were other distractions.

Like "dates." The raked-over ashes of old flirtations. New encounters, matches made by well meaning friends, which touched on the ludicrous. The dyed blonde with the voice that could shuck clams whose siliconed breasts pointed at him like the guns of a battleship. He nicknamed her "Admiral Dewey." When he tried to inspect them closely, she pushed him away, saying, "They cost $3500 in Rio." He declined her offer of a compensating handjob and took her home. There was the liberated young person who bolted from his grasp because he had said, "I want to make love *to* you" instead of "*with*" you. She made a ludicrous figure, hopping to the door, trying to pull her tights back on and deliver a speech on the Equal Rights Amendment at the same time. There was a perfectly awful evening with a quintessential Jewish-American Princess; when he finally got her into bed, after a $200 dinner at Caravelle during which she alternated *quenelles* with Dentyne, she looked at his penis as if it was something on a laboratory slide, stuck her gum to the brass bedstead, and went down on him with the clinical enthusiasm of a biology student. After thirty fruitless minutes, they had both given it up as a bad job and she had retrieved her gum and made him dress and take her to Le Club to meet some equally awful friends. And there was the famous fabric designer who subjected him to three hours of her poetry while he struggled manfully with a collection of snaps and fasteners evidently designed at Fort Knox. "It was dreadful," he told Barney on the phone. "Her verse is of the 'Waves break/Gulls cry/My heart is lonely/I must die' school. All I ended up with was a death wish and a hard-on that a cat couldn't scratch!" It confirmed Barney's wisdom. Barney had orchestrated an obbligato of aphorisms to accompany his descent into the sere and pale of old age. One of his favorites was: "At my age, Dave, they not only gotta look good and screw good, they gotta talk good." Barney insisted on coming across as streetwise and delivering his pearls in Brooklynese, despite the fact that he had a Masters in Philosophy from Dartmouth. As with many of Barney's aphoristic strictures, the observance was customarily in the breach.

He found it depressing. He had been going on this way for far too long. The one girl he could really remember really loving had preferred to marry an older, more surely rich man and now measured out her life in Locust Valley dinner parties, and her nights spent ceiling-staring, trying to figure out how to keep the children away from the indefensible, drunken husband who snored raggedly beside her.

There had been others—interludes, when you came right down to it—some brief and flaringly passionate like Des Lyall-Marsh, others protracted over weeks and months which tailed off and vanished like smoke in the wind. Too many books and too romantic an imagination had given him sights set impossibly high. That was his fancy way of putting it. His real suspicion was that too much time alone in his private spaces and with his private resentments had crippled his capacity to open the door.

Door-opening. That *was* the right metaphor for what he was after. He had *heard* it once. Solti was conducting the Chicago Symphony in Bartók's *Bluebeard's Castle* in Carnegie Hall and when the fifth of Bluebeard's doors was opened, when the music revealed Bluebeard's kingdom whole and splendid, the air became aflame with a burst of brass and the hair stood up on his neck and his skin jumped.

He was opening no such doors these days, he admitted to himself. He had become a tactician of couch and bed, he thought, as he launched yet another pointless seduction. Expert in the frictions and sensitivities which turned on the erotic engine. As a lover, I am a statistical success, nothing more, he told the therapist he sporadically visited. A college stud twenty years out of date.

He remained deeply interested in Devon. But he felt it necessary to keep his distance. Wall Street had a dozen phrases advising against intraoffice entanglements. "Don't dip your pen in company ink," had been Clarence Verger's mild favorite. There were other, scruffier paraphrases from other, scruffier tongues.

Not that there was any encouragement for intimacy. Indeed, he complained to himself in lonely moments, she was altogether too professionally remote. Even at his age, Harrison liked to keep a bit of the playroom in things: a boyish, joky camaraderie. Devon appeared to want none of this. She arrived in the morning and left in the evening. Everything she did was brisk and effective. Sometimes heartlessly so, he thought when he was feeling sorry for himself. Two or three times a week they would have lunch: grab a sandwich or a salad. She no longer talked about herself or about what she did. In the late summer he had asked her, tentatively, to come up for a weekend at a cottage he rented on an estate in the Berkshires. He guessed she liked music, although he didn't really know, and he thought Tanglewood would appeal to her. "Bring a friend," he declared with a false magnanimity which he hoped would conceal his developing affections, but she had other plans.

She was absorbing. Always neat and stylish without modish little tricks. Her eyes were cool and her voice calm. She was there to do a job and she was doing it. He found her dispassionate objectivity professionally commendable and personally maddening.

For her part, Devon liked Harrison. Sooner than he, she recognized how much they shared a view of things. They disliked the way things were. They especially detested the self-concerned, shortsighted, morally illiterate generation that had brought the world to its clustered, polluted, angry state. They responded differently, of course. The ten years that separated them, ten years covering the tag ends of a depression and a world war, had legitimized violence and social insurrection for Devon and her contemporaries. Harrison took his unhappiness out in a sarcastic contentiousness which was in its way no less self-satisfied than the values of the men he mocked. Devon enjoyed his way with words. She told him so, and enjoyed watching him wiggle like a puppy at her approval. She had a gift, she knew, for focusing on men with a special destructive intensity, as if she were playing sunlight on a leaf through a magnifying glass, watching a small smoky pinpoint appear in the center, watching it spread until it consumed the whole.

"It's been a long time coming," he said. He quoted Eliot: *"So here I am, in the middle way, having had twenty years—/ Twenty years largely wasted..."* She picked up the thread: *"...Trying to learn to use words..."*

"I like that poem," she said. It was clear she knew it as well as he did.

"It's the greatest poem of our time," declared Harrison, his stentorian balloon soaring.

"*Your* time," said Devon. He felt like something in a museum.

By the first of November, it was apparent that New York had seen the last of the episodic Indian summers which marred the autumn. The days turned crisp, with a biting edge at first and last light. The city was its most attractive self. Lively, active, electric.

In Boston, RAID continued its inexorable pulse. On November 9, they reached a milestone.

It had been Devon's turn to go to Boston. She and Ernie had had an ebullient lunch at the Quincy Market. Like many defensive women, she found the company of gay men comfortable.

It was late afternoon when she got back to New York. Harrison was waiting for her at the office. Gold had closed that day in Zurich at $420 and the gold bug had stayed overlong at the Carlton House bar and staggered onto the early train to Pawling. Harrison looked through the printouts in a cursory way and raised his eyes to Devon.

"It's a big day today. We just went over a billion. It's also my birthday."

Rather than trek down to the other office, he sat down at the gold bug's telex and dispatched the Friday cash projection to a Luxembourg number. It took him fifteen minutes. She watched him with enjoyment; he was becoming very proficient, for a man who was clumsy in the age of elegant machinery.

When he had signed off and the bells and clatter of the machine had subsided, he looked at her with a smile.

"Friday...and all alone by the telephone. How about dinner? Come on, this time I won't take no! It's a very special day. Not every day that a couple of loose ends like you and me can smack our lips over our billion-dollar portfolio. You can bet our little pal up in Boston is celebrating. In his own unusual, anatomically specialized fashion, of course."

She laughed. "He is. I had lunch with him. There's a roller disco marathon at some big nightclub in Framingham."

"My God," said Harrison, "Framingham? I'll bet it's that big nightclub we used to go to from school. I heard Vaughn Monroe there once."

"Vaughn Monroe?"

"Just another relic in my private vitrine of antiquities. When the world was young. Don't give it a thought. How *about* dinner?"

Devon hesitated. The fact was that she was also bored and lonely. The Interglobal job had kept her moving, had a flux and discreteness that was distracting and liberating in itself. But in the last three months she had read enough books alone, gone to enough movies, stared at enough television for a lifetime.

She had made a few friends in New York. The odd connections through the old networks turned out to be dull couples in down vests and jeans who worked for IBM and worried about the rent and the crime rate. What little revolution was around seemed to be racial: Hispanics versus blacks; blacks versus everyone. Everyone else was too busy stealing or otherwise getting money to have time for social justice.

"All right," she said.

"I'll pick you up at eight. Where?" He still didn't know where she lived. He did have a phone number for her. Unlisted. Address unobtainable.

"I've got someone to see, and a couple of things to do. I'll meet you."

"As you will. Jack's. Over on West Fifty-third Street. Eight o'clock. I'll be lurking at the end of the bar."

Jack's had been a speakeasy once upon a time. Then it became a gathering place for the movers and shakers of corporate and political America. It was a comfortable masculine place, with large chairs and soft leather banquettes to handle its oversized clients. The walls were covered with the logos and emblems of the country's business and sporting elite. These were reproduced by Tiffany in sterling silver and enamel at Jack's expense and affixed to the wall with silver-headed nails. Space on Jack's wall was by invitation only, originally from the late Jack Berger himself, nowadays from his nephew, Max Thissel, who ran the place. Once in a while, some newly minted mogul would commit the unforgivable gaffe of appearing at Jack's with a Tiffany piece of his own commissioning. Max would put the emblem away in his desk drawer and graciously exile the offender for a time to the upstairs dining room usually reserved for clubwomen and out-of-town polyesters.

The downstairs dining room, where the action and eminence was, consisted of three large bays. A bar ran the length of the room. Harrison got there fifteen minutes early, by design. He shook hands with Max Thissel and with Tony and Fran, Thissel's young assistants. Jack's always had a kind of a family, homecoming exuberance about it. Harrison had been coming for twenty years, the first time, as with so many others, with Clare Verger. "Take care of this young man," Verger had said casually to Jack Berger as they were being seated. Berger hadn't forgotten; nor had Thissel, when he took over. The long memory of the owners was what made Jack's the classiest restaurant in the world.

Harrison settled among the regulars at the bar and ordered a Scotch. He was deep into his neighbor's tale of marital woe when Devon walked in.

Whatever it was she had had to do, it had included making herself into the most attractive woman in the world, Harrison thought. She wasn't beautiful in the pure sense, not movie-star perfect. Her nose was a shade too long, her mouth a trifle too firm. But she had presence and she was perfectly dressed. As she grew older, Devon wore her clothes the way she wore her independence, with an ease that concealed long and careful minutes of self-study. She was wearing something simple and looked like a million. It was dark gray, Harrison saw, and it moved with her and wasn't too long or too formal. *She* wore her clothes; the clothes didn't wear her.

Without thinking, he bent to kiss her cheek. Without thinking, she angled it to be kissed.

Tony showed them to a table.

"Drink?"

She asked for a vodka on the rocks. Stolichnaya. Lime. Harrison ordered another Scotch.

Harrison looked around. The landscape at Jack's was dotted with monuments to the way we live now. Harrison pointed them out to Devon like an Italian guide picking his way through the Forum.

Across the way sat a bald, craggily handsome man with a much older, gleaming, redheaded woman who could barely move her hands for the rings on them. They said nothing to each other; it was clear that no words had passed between them for some time—perhaps weeks, perhaps years.

"That's Smiling Fritz Donovan, leader of men. Head of GD Equities, the big machinery company. A real street fighter. Got his job on his rugged good looks and ambition; he makes Eichmann look like Captain Kangaroo. His path to the top is littered with the severed testicles of old friends and rivals who didn't realize until too late that Fritz sees business as a matter of life and death. A truly great industrial statesman. His company's stock price has been flat for the last five years, but Smiling Fritz's now the sixth-highest-paid executive in the world. The Street can't stand him. The guys in the banks who buy shares and make stocks go up think he's arrogant and a shade fancy. A lot of people think he's a fag. And not very smart. They won't touch his stocks with a thousand-foot pole, even if the earnings are OK. Which they have been. Fritz is too far away from the day-to-day business now to screw it up.

"But if you compare the price of GD with Commonwealth Machine, for example, you have to say that Smiling Fritz has cost his stockholders about $300 million in market value. For which he's paid three million six a year. He's made a bunch of big acquisitions, all through one business broker out in Detroit who, rumor hath it, owns an amusing set of photographs of our man getting it on with a couple of sailors. Of course, that was a long time ago, and in another country. The lady is Mrs. Smiling Fritz; she was Miss Indian River Grapefruit of '06 and the widow of Ted Glarner, the founder of Glarner Machine.

"When Ted Glarner died a dozen years ago, old wrinkle-pits married the Smiler, who was a small-time PR guy who was her 'walker,' and made him president of Glarner Machine. He changed the name to GD Equities, 'D' for 'Donovan,' and hired a bunch of B-School types and conceptualists; the company owns all sorts of crap now, some good, some bad, the bulk indifferent. Most people think Donovan's a fag. I think the only things they get off on together are his ambition and her jewelry. Or maybe the other way round.

"It's being bruited about that the Smiler has political ambitions. They'd look wonderful in the White House, don't you think? A handsome First Couple. Anyway, I keep an open one-way ticket to Geneva and an application for Swiss residency against the day he might get elected. Whenever I see him I have this nearly uncontrollable urge just to walk over and tip his soup over his head. I'd never do it of course; Max Thissel's too good a friend of mine.

"It's really thrilling," he continued sarcastically, "to be able to watch the New York business establishment at work and play."

Devon smiled. "Can I have another vodka? You're kind of a hater, aren't you?"

"Not really. Just an observer and a mild social critic."

Her nod said she didn't quite see him that way.

"Now over there," Harrison pointed to a table where an elegant, young-fortyish man was making conversation to a lady of ordinary if undeniable good looks, "is Dexter Dempster, New York's leading closet heterosexual."

"Closet heterosexual?"

"Sure. Husband has to go away on a business trip. What about the theater tickets? 'I've got it,' says the wife; 'I'll get Dexter to go with me.' 'Why not?' says the husband. To himself, he says this Dempster knows furniture and talks about books and pictures so he must be a fag. Q.E.D. The men in this town still think a ladies' man has got to have patent leather hair and a waxed mustache or be built like Arnold Schwarzenegger. So off goes the husband to Kansas City or Dubuque and off goes the wife to the theater with Dexter and nine times out of ten she ends up in the sack, if you will forgive my vulgarity, staring at the business end of the formidable Dempster organ. Which is supposed to be gigantic, although I must disclaim any personal knowledge of the subject. If Dexter ever gets married, God help these ladies. I wonder what he's doing out on a Friday, anyway? Dexter usually has to take the weekends off, to rest up, make time for spermatogenesis."

Devon broke up. She had a smile like sunrise and a laugh that was just right: not loud, not silvery, not giggly.

"How about some food? This place is famous for about ten

things and does them best when it's crowded, like tonight. The clams and the oysters are good, along with the smoked salmon, the chicken hash, the steaks. That sort of thing. Lay off the à la's and the fancy-sounding stuff."

She thought she'd have the smoked salmon and the chicken hash, a limestone lettuce salad on the side.

Harrison ordered Cherrystones. "Then I'll have my famous all-brown meal. Goujonettes of sole; French-fried zucchini on the side. Jack Berger's Brown Salad. The sight of it has been known to empty the restaurant." He ordered a half bottle of Sylvaner with the first course and a bottle of a light Bordeaux, Ch. Virgitti, for the main meal.

One of a tableful of men against the far wall waved to Harrison.

"Who's that?" Devon was enjoying herself.

"That's Rube Bowen, Reubén R. Bowen, who runs the Certified Bank while Merriman, the notional chief executive, runs around the world playing diplomat. Bowen's a good guy. Merriman's a jerk. He inherited the bank when his parents, who were a couple of anthropological nuts, got eaten by cannibals on an expedition to New Guinea. He's one of the grandchildren of old Moses Merriman who started the Certified and half of America. Anyway, Rube runs the bank day to day. The thin kid on his right is his assistant. I forget his name, but he's from Texas and is getting to be a real pain in the rear end. I don't know the others."

Devon liked her salmon and she liked the wine's sweet edge. She liked the attention that Harrison was getting, even with all these big shots around. And she liked best of all his easy, friendly manner with the people who were paid to wait on them.

There was a slight stir and Max Thissel, who had been talking to one of the men at Bowen's table, quickly disengaged and made his dapper way across the floor to the entrance.

Harrison speared a piece of fried sole and looked up.

"Ah, the men who rule our lives."

There were seven in the party which Thissel guided to a conspicuous table. Three couples and an extra man. The extra man was a blocky sort, about forty years old, with an open face under Comanche-black hair going to gray around the ears, and a suit that looked as though it had come from Sears, Roebuck. The ladies looked to be approximately half the ages of their escorts.

"Names and numbers, please."

"Well, the surly-looking man with the newly, naturally gray hair is our beloved senior senator, Fighting Bob O'Leary. He owns the governor, the Assembly, the five boroughs of this great city, and whatever isn't nailed down in Albany. He's been sounding presidential recently. Next to him is his girlfriend, the world's second richest orphan, after the Merriman brothers, but not a bad lady. I used to see her at parties. Then the guy with the head dancing around like a bobble doll and all the teeth is Michael Morgan, *né* Markowitz, the magazine king and Mr. Democratic Money in New York. *His* girlfriend is the daughter of the founder of Universal Communications, who is Mr. Big Broadcast. Morgan is known in the trade as Baby Broadcast. The fat guy with the blonde girl with the suspicious eyes is, I think, Duffield Marcus—Lord Jermyn now—who's a big deal in the Labour Party. The blonde is known to go in for pillow talk; since she's a journalism groupie who talks in bed, it means not much interesting or important is going to get said in front of her at that table this evening. Which is too bad."

"Really, David?" It was the first time Harrison could remember her using his first name. "Are you a gossip?" He ducked the question.

"You recognize the seventh guy, don't you? From the papers? That looks like Ferdimend, the famous Buster. The President's ADC? I think we're looking at a Democratic peace treaty shaping up, at least with the trouble this administration's in! Not the sort of thing those men want to read about in tomorrow's paper."

Max Thissel had gone to the door again. He shook hands with a sallow, slender man with frightened eyes and the newcomer and his wife, a short, marginally attractive woman whose looks were starting to desert her, were shown to a prize corner table.

"The fashion success story of the decade," said Harrison. "Born Jaime Something or Other in some barrio in San Juan, became Henry Markham somewhere along the way, and now he's licensing over $100 million a year in men's and ladies' clothes and luggage and you name it. What's interesting is that all his stuff is basically a knockoff of Brooks Brothers or Tripler or the kind of outdoor clothes you buy in the mail. He has a new line called 'Hank'; *'Gear for the established man,'* the ads say. The sort of stuff my old man used to wear on Martha's Vineyard in 1947, except this sells at Bloomingdale's to the Saturday Generation at about fifty times the price the Old Guard pays for the same stuff on Madison Avenue. The hot gossip is that he's going to start his own mail order business. He'll probably name it something pretentious and 'Olde Englishe' like 'Badminton House,' although if he matched it to his customer base he could call it 'L. L. Schmuck.'"

Devon put down her fork and covered her face. He'd caught her with a mouthful of wine.

"If you don't stop it," she sputtered, "I'm never going to make it to the coffee." Harrison was flying, showing off and enjoying it, and she loved it. In the midst of laughter, it struck her that the life she'd known had been perilously short on laughs.

After dinner, they walked slowly along Fifth Avenue. The night was sharply cool; the windows of the famous stores were as bright and curious as peacocks.

"A nightcap?" he asked.

"All right, but just a quiet drink. I've seen and heard about enough people for one evening, much as it makes me laugh to hear you talk about them, David."

"My place?"

"All right." His heart vaulted over the Plaza Hotel.

Afterward, much later, he would learn that she had made her mind up over dinner to try him. He amused her; he looked well and he talked well. He had nice manners. She was comfortable with him. It would do for a start. It was time to look for something stable. Let someone else blow up the palaces and sack the embassies. At least for the time being. She was lonely and nearly thirty-two years old and it seemed pointless to continue to chase after the old revolutionary excitements.

He let them into his living room. It looked wonderful to her. Bookish and secure. She enjoyed the special feeling that he really *lived* here with his mind and emotions and taste; that it was more than most men's apartments, much, much more; not merely a bedroom and a closet, a place to wash and sleep and hang clothes.

"I love this room."

"So do I. Drink?" He brought her a Calvados. "Now for a little night music."

A high, reedy, but compelling voice filled the room. *"The very thought of you/And I forget to do..."*

"Isn't this great? Al Bowlly. He was a singer with Ray

Noble's band in London in the twenties and thirties. Before both our times. Dance?" He extended his hand. She crossed the room.

They danced slowly, made a little awkward by the catchings of the carpet and by a sense of the need for this first time together. The extra sip of brandy had carried them to the phase where everything looked and felt wonderful; where separation must not happen, even though dawn was breaking.

"*I see your face in every flower...*" sang the phonograph. A saxophone caressed the singer's voice. Time turned back, vanished.

She drew her head back and looked at him. Smiling. "*Remarkable how effective cheap music is.*"

He picked up the scene from Noel Coward. "*You're looking damned beautiful in this moonlight, Amanda. Your skin is...*"

He never got to finish the line. She moved to him and kissed him with her mouth open; he felt her tongue pass with a flicker across his lips, calling up sensations which, because he had never felt them, he thought existed only in the imagination of writers. He tried to reciprocate, to give back something of the excitement. Drawing her down beside him on the sofa, he held her as if she were porcelain and kissed her what seemed like a thousand times, trying to summon up wellsprings of gentleness and affection that he could in his own turn communicate with his wordless, working lips.

She kissed him back. It was nice for her: comforting and comfortable. She liked that she could tell without reaching for him how totally, desperately he wanted her; could know how excited he was without having to reach and grasp him.

"Do you always make love with your clothes on?" she asked, rising to lead him to the bedroom.

Naked, she astonished him. She was not as thin as she had seemed with her clothes on. Her breasts were small but her nipples were large and dark. The thatch between her legs was thick and dawn-colored. She sighed when he touched her there, and when he kissed her breasts, she reached for him and he feared he would explode right there. They did nothing shameless or unconventional. When at last she pulled him above her and felt him slide into her, it was like making love for the first time, the first thrill of discovery and sensation still intact and tender, not yet a matter of unceasingly demonstrating technique or innovation.

(211)

She felt him move within her. His head was buried in her hair and he was saying something she couldn't quite make out. She was still in control.

Then, way back in the recesses of herself, back on the other side of the inner mounds and barricades she'd thrown up over the years to separate her from her feelings and her womanliness, Devon felt a stirring. Later, she would tell Harrison that it was like the starting up of a great machine, an earth auger drilling relentlessly through the hills, coming toward her, louder and closer, until its roaring filled her head, filled the room, filled everything. She heard it approaching, a great machine in the jungle, beyond the trees, tearing down the barrier between herself and herself. She tried to blot out the noise. "THIS . . . IS . . . NOT . . . GOING . . . TO . . . HAPPEN . . . TO . . . ME!" she said to herself wordlessly over and over but the roaring would not be silenced. "NOT. GOING. TO. HAPPEN." The world was filled with the roar, and she felt something *happening* within her, down there, then spreading and tingling every filament and fiber. "TO. HAPPEN." She couldn't any longer. She was strung out like a vapor arc, arched and burning. On the far side of everything she heard herself crying out, felt him around her and in her and everywhere, heard herself cry out and out and out, until she was nothing but skin and sensation and explosion.

When Harrison opened his eyes the next morning, Devon was standing at the foot of the bed, dressed. He looked sleepily at his watch.

"Now where are you going? It's nine o'clock, for God's sake. And it's Saturday."

She looked at him for a long moment, the longest of their lives. "I'm just going downtown to pack a bag. I'll be back in about an hour or so. You'd better clear some space for my things."

It was a statement, not a question, but he saw that it required an answer. He had one.

"An hour's too long. And pack a trunk."

17 Devon moved in. She kept her old apartment, however. Over Harrison's objections. He couldn't understand why she would ever need it. This was forever, this thing between them. They had been together three weeks. Of course, New York was the ideal setting for new love affairs. It distracted from the eventual, inevitable unfolding of the small aggravations and incompatibilities that must occur between two people who impetuously give each other their hearts.

She tried to reassure him. "It's just a bolt-hole, David. Some day you may not want me any more. When that happens, *if* it happens, I want a place where you can't chase me, where the doorbell won't ring in the middle of the night with you drunk and lonely on the steps. That's all. Let's not discuss it any further."

Apart from that, he felt that they were as nearly perfectly suited as he might ever have hoped. They drank the life of the city, day and night. They were coconspirators in love. His friends welcomed her—first purely because she came with him, then, gladly, for herself. Arm in arm, they conquered cocktail parties where fey young men named Kenn and Bobb passed trays of figs slathered in almond dust. They went to the opera and heard *Il Trovatore*. Architempo was singing Manrico; the famous tenor had never sounded in fuller, finer voice. "No wonder," Harrison whispered, "what you're hearing is the trumpet of relief. Another angry mother bought off; another season saved." Architempo's escapades with the little girls in the chorus were a legend in Lincoln Center's inner circles.

They walked in the Park on Sundays, dodging dogged, unhappy-looking joggers and aggressive cyclists. They went to the theater and the ballet. They looked at Rembrandt and Rauschenberg; ate Dim Sum and caviar. He kissed her on the steps of St. Patrick's and in the back rows of a dozen movie theaters.

"We match perfectly," he said to her. "I cook; you make the bed; we share the kissing and hugging chores equally."

She helped him recapture *his* New York, which he had thought completely lost in the oppressive vulgarity of the 1970s. In her company, certain old particularities reawoke in his memory and stimulated heartsprings: the lights on Park Avenue marking a path through the dusk like buoys; midnight piano in the Carlyle; dinner parties where no one drank too much and the talk was good. Piece by piece, like a jigsaw puzzle, she put back together the fragments of old happinesses. He was deeply grateful. At his age, memory was a larger part of the scheme of things; the future was less dependable. He said to her that she had restored him, like a painting in which the first colors had been brought up from under the concealments and discolorations of old varnish, not quite as good as new but a lot better than what had been seen in recent years.

He felt childlike and rejuvenated. *"Color and context/Milk and memory,"* he quoted to himself from James Merrill, chasing her through Saks at Christmastime as years before he had chased his governess.

RAID continued to grind away. He now thought of the computer as the fourth member of their partnership. Once in a while he would awake in a staring sweat, from a dream that some microscopic circuit had fizzled and everything was lost. He placed anxious calls to Ernie, who assured him that the circuitry was as certain and ageless as geology.

Their affair had no effect on their routine. Nothing was said to Ernie. If he had cottoned to it, he said nothing. Devon went to Boston most Fridays now. She went up early. She thought that Ernie—for all his clowning—was probably lonely for his old Chicago neighborhoods, for the Brothers. Ernie showed her how to operate the console.

"With this trainin'," he said, "you can get a job as a reservations clerk at any airline."

An old client asked Harrison to go to Dallas on a one-day job. He arranged to spend the night with a friend who'd moved down three years before. He declined his friend's offer of the company of a stewardess or a model for the evening.

"Too bad, Dave, you don't know what you're missing. This is the airhead capital of the Western world."

His friend met him at the airport.

"Where are your cowboy boots?" Harrison asked.

"I hate to tell you, Dave, but there isn't a pair in town. Neiman-Marcus buys them all up and sells them to New York stockbrokers." The last three words were said pejoratively.

His friend lived in an apartment building on a hill, the only hill, on the edges of downtown Dallas. His terrace looked west. It seemed to Harrison, who had spent twenty years looking fifty yards across the street into the private lives of people he never knew, to have a desirable, quiet spaciousness.

"People in New York are always talking about privacy," Ben remarked. "This *is* privacy."

He poured a drink. Famous Grouse.

Ben noticed Harrison's expression. "The Scotch? I get it

over on Oak Lawn." Ben put on a movie-western accent. "'Course we git a wagon train down here purt' near ever' other week, bringin' firewater and jerky and '66 Haut-Brion and a decent Brie."

They went out to dinner at a French restaurant where the food was surprisingly good. His friend's current girlfriend was a recent divorcee with blonde hair lacquered stiff, like a spun-sugar dessert, and the eyes of a starving fox. When she spoke, which was mercifully seldom, Harrison could swear his wine trembled at her sharp and nasal voice. After dinner, they dropped her off at the spreading North Dallas mansion which had been part of a tooth-grinding divorce settlement. Driving back, Harrison noticed the small red lights of safety alarms shining in the night like the wary eyes of forest animals; they seemed somehow symbolic of all those nervous rich people, peering insecurely out at the hostile, predatory world from the protective thickets of their money.

Over a nightcap, Ben finished his disquisition.

"There are a lot of things I miss about New York, Dave. Especially all those options: hundreds of movies, hundreds of restaurants, plays, concerts, stores. Too many options. Generally unused. But I'll tell you what I don't miss about New York. I don't miss being hated on the street by people I don't know. I don't miss being run down by some hopped-up messenger on a stolen ten-speed bike. And what I really don't miss is the fact that New York has turned into a place with nothing but one-way streets; not the physical streets, hell no, but the symbolic ones, that run between people. Here everything is still two-way. You do for me; I'll do for you. I'm tired of people crashing my party. I'm getting old; I can't handle all those strange, hostile faces in the street. I give up something, but I get something. End of sermon."

He drained his glass. Harrison thought he looked less happy than he sounded. Gasping for reassurance and justification like a fish dying on the beach.

Harrison cleaned up his business early and caught the three-twenty Braniff to LaGuardia. As he made his way to the back of the plane he saw the thin young man who had been at Bowen's table at Jack's the night he and Devon got started. The boy looked sad and prepossessed, not his usual aggressive self. A look of uncertain recognition passed between them, based more on clothes and haircuts than on names and faces.

They went over $2 billion five days before Christmas. Ernie flew down from Boston, a special treat, and he and Devon and Harrison went to Jack's for a commemorative binge. They spent an afternoon hour on the floor of the New York Stock Exchange. Barney fixed it up with his floor people and he personally came over from Pine Street to show them around.

It had been nearly a dozen years since Harrison had last gone down to the Floor. Then membership on the Exchange had guaranteed a nice six-figure income from fixed, unconscionable commissions. The members spent a good part of the day putting talcum powder on each other's shoes and pinning humorous notes on each other's backs. At that time every stock tip or investment idea seemed to work out, so what originality there was on the Street went into the creation and fabrication of an incessant supply of practical and other jokes. Following Barney across the floor, it occurred to Harrison that it had been a very long time since he'd heard a good joke creep uptown from Wall Street.

Barney's floor partner was a veteran.

"What happened to all the floor characters?" Harrison asked. "'Marry me' Buzzati; 'Twelvetoes' Todhunter; all those guys?"

"Shit, you remember *them?* Christ, most of them are gone! Working as Maître d's or bartenders uptown or selling real estate in Palm Beach. There're a few left. But they're a pretty scrubby lot. This isn't their kind of world. Isn't mine, for that matter! Hell, there isn't a decent bookmaker left on the floor. This place is a fucking morgue now. No fun." He was unaware of Devon's presence; his working vocabulary still hadn't acknowledged that women were now on the Floor, were almost as much a part of the scene as he was, a fact which never dented his locker-room point of view.

Harrison remembered when the Commission had forced the Street to chop its rates. He'd been having lunch with a friend who was a two-dollar floor broker with a nose for news. His friend had picked up the check.

"This one's mine, Dave. May be the last one I can afford for a long time. May Day tomorrow. The commissions come down. You've got to admire the Street. Only trillion-dollar business with no Washington lobby, so that Uncle Sam can force us to sell our services for less than it costs us to produce them."

The Dow Jones Average ended the year at below 850, up about 5 percent, but a loss in real terms adjusted for the inflation rate, which a variety of OPEC price increases had pushed to 13 percent. Winter came early and stayed cold. Cleveland and then Detroit ran out of fuel oil. The administration attempted to relieve the shortages by installing an interim increase in domestic energy prices, but the oil and gas producers smelled blood and new production was a matter of a trickle. A Louis Harris poll showed that 60 percent of the electorate disapproved of President Baxter's performance; only 22 percent indicated they might vote for him again.

In its issue of December 26, *Time* named the President and his Secretary, Isaac Nordlander, joint Men of the Year. *"In the more than two hundred years of the nation's existence,"* wrote the magazine's chief editorialist, *"there have been a number of personal calamities in the Executive Branch of the federal government. One thinks of the malfeasances of the Grant and Cleveland administrations; the manifest incompetences of the Hoover crowd; the non-entities Millard Fillmore and Chester A. Arthur; the make-believe despotism of the Nixonians. But nowhere in our recorded history does there appear to be an instance of such painful and costly and, to many minds, unnecessary disregard of the public weal as has been the case with the energy policies conceived and directed by Secretary Nordlander and approved by President Baxter. That it should have happened at all is astonishing. That it should be permitted to continue is incredible. And that it should all have been accomplished under the guise of intellectual and pragmatic good sense is beyond the capacity of this mind to grasp. It has been a singular performance, singularly awful, as devastating as a bomb. It deserves special recognition which we unhappily bestow in naming these two public servants Men of the Year."*

Harrison and Devon spent New Year's Eve alone. An evening for champagne and poetry. He made her listen to a recording which T. S. Eliot had made of *East Coker:* "...*The wave cry. The wind cry. The vast waters of the petrel and the porpoise...*" The old poet's voice was like parchment. *"In my end is my beginning."*

"The greatest poet of our time," he said.

"Of our time."

They spent the evening in each other's arms, saying everything that they had ever hoped they might someday be able to say to someone, making unembarrassed commitments and declarations, secure in the certainty that they were the only people in the world. And so midnight came and went, and, finally, they had exhausted every emotional and physical resource and had nothing special left for the first day of the New Year except a long, rounding sleep.

They went over $3 billion on a sleeting Tuesday in late January. By mid-March, by Ernie's count, they were at $4 billion and the goal was in sight.

18 "I'd stay the hell away from the Old Man if I were you," said the staff sergeant taking the shift as chief steward on Air Force One as it sped east after leaving Midland. "He's really hopping. Let him cool off." The young pool reporter went back to his seat.

In the rear cabin, Fulger Baxter, in his fourth year as President of the United States, drummed his fingers on the tabletop, almost spilling his glass of Diet Dr. Pepper, and glared out the window at the twilight deepening around the jetliner. Baxter's thoughts were of his Energy Secretary, Isaac Nordlander, and they were not kind thoughts.

He should have listened to his wife Ermabelle and his good friend Rebo Beauderon when all those highfalutin Washington advisors had urged him to appoint Nordlander as Secretary of the Department of Energy. Nordlander knew Washington, they told Baxter. Hadn't he been Deputy Secretary of Commerce? He can get things done. Nordlander is brilliant, they claimed. He has an intellect that can handle any situation, any task. Hadn't he written three books on management theory? Nordlander is a diplomat, they said. He knew the world. Hadn't he been ambassador to Argentina and the U.S. representative to the United Nations special session on Uganda?

He'd asked Beauderon to be Energy Secretary. Rebo was an old friend; they'd roughnecked together in the old days during summer vacations. It was during one of those vacations, when they were working offshore, in the Gulf, and based in Pass Christian, Mississippi, that Baxter had met and first courted Ermabelle Dally. Her daddy had been the fifth in a dynasty of Pass Christian toolpushers until one morning, when Ermabelle was still just a baby, the bull rope got loose on the floor of an offshore rig and tore off Dally's right leg. When he got out of the hospital, he sat up nights drawing plans until he had perfected the Dally clutch, which would keep the legs on drilling crews for the next thirty years. It turned into a nice business; when, after Ermabelle had graduated from Sophie B. Newcomb in New Orleans, he sold Dally Clutch to Baker Oil Tools for a nice block of stock, it made a nice dowry for Ermabelle and Fulger Baxter. Rebo had been best man.

Anyway, when he'd asked Rebo about taking the job, the Petrex chairman had turned him down. Later, when Nordlander was selected, Rebo said, "Well, Mr. President, they say he's smart as a goose in corn. I don't know the man but I got to say this. The first two Energy secretaries have been New York stockbrokers. Now you're fixin' to give us a business professor from UCLA. I know it would be a lot to tell those fancy advisors of yours that you're goin' to appoint someone who knows the oil and gas business. The way things are goin', they're likely to give the job to a dentist next, Mr. President." Beauderon was clearly ill at ease with the new, formal salutation for his old friend Fulger, already moving away.

Ermabelle had been equally direct. "Honey, you always said that you couldn't run drilling rigs with college boys. Well, isn't that what you're fixing to do if you appoint Nordlander?"

But there was a lot of pressure and confusion in those early, heady days in Washington and the glib professors had prevailed. Nordlander had taken his new mandate over with a vengeance. In the two and a half years since Baxter's inauguration, he'd built the Energy Department from its modest base into a spraddled, inefficient giant that employed more people and had a bigger budget than Shell and Exxon combined. The Secretary was completely inaccessible and dealt with the industry he regulated through layers of assistants, project executives, and other high-titled civil bureaucrats. He worked six-hour days and traveled extensively away from Washington, attending seminars.

It had been a mistake to hire him, thought the President, and now he couldn't get rid of him. Every time he'd start to, his aides would tell him that any concession to the oil and gas people, and the dismissal of Isaac Nordlander would be sure political death. In the early going, Nordlander had established a psychological hold on the President; he made Baxter feel intellectually ennobled, treated him as a peer, as it were, by his deference giving him an honorary Harvard degree.

Baxter had to admit that those fancy-talking Georgetown smartypants had figured the Nordlander deal right. Marvin Gottlieb had repeated to the President what a columnist had said over an M Street dining table: "Nordlander's just like a mynah bird, or something posing as a mynah bird, that Baxter paid $100 for in a bazaar. He's still waiting for him to talk, to do what he's supposed to do to make him worth $100. Baxter's damned if he's going to write off his C-note. Today he'd settle for a single word from his new pet; when he bought him he expected Demosthenes."

Postelection politics were as little fun to Baxter as the run in the sun which made him President had been a hoot. Of course, it had been kind of an accident.

After he and Rebo had graduated from Louisiana State with degrees in petroleum engineering, Rebo'd gone off to Houston to make his fortune and Baxter had gone back to Houma, in the bayou country, where he got a job as a junior land man with a little independent oil outfit that was just starting to spend some New York tax money wildcatting for deep stuff. The company didn't have much to pay its people with so it bonused them with pieces of the action. Baxter had lucked into a nice lease buy that made two good wells and was later unitized with some big Texaco production. He had already figured that the action was going to be offshore, so he traded his bonus money for the equity in a jackup rig; he got a contract with Shell in the Main Pass and the rig went and stayed out there. He had used some of Ermabelle's money to expand the business. Within six years, he owned two more rigs and a bunch of service boats. When one of his rigs went off lease for six months, he went partners with a broke geologist who had some leases offsetting Pan American in Timbalier Bay and some maps he'd bet his kids on. They made a nice well which they turned over to Tenneco for a fancy price.

By 1972, Baxter had wearied of the oil business. He was fifty-seven years old. Rigs he used to buy for $3 million now cost fifteen and he could see them going to thirty. He was a devout churchman who read his Bible every night, and there was a lot going on in the drilling business—payoffs, bribes, fast dealing—that he didn't like. He talked it over with Ermabelle until late one night and when he got to the office the next morning he made a call over to Houston. Three weeks later, Baxter Drilling became a subsidiary of Triangle Offshore Industries, and Baxter had $7 million of TOI preferred stock.

Back in Houma, he considered his future. He had a farm on which he raised pedigreed Danish and Berkshire hogs, but that was a hobby. He was still pondering his future when he got a form letter from the regional office of the Department of Agriculture advising him of a mass of complicated new hog-breeding regulations. He had calculated that the new policies would add five cents a pound to the cost of prime pork.

He had told Ermabelle what he planned to do and she laughingly went along with it. He drove into Houma to see about some signs.

Two days later, well before dawn, Baxter and his farrow boy had loaded the whole breeding herd—boars, sows, and shoats—into two trucks and drove the lot up Highway 1 to Baton Rouge.

When the Agriculture Department people had arrived at work that morning, they found the entrance blocked by a grunting, whistling herd of swine being tended by a hare-lipped boy with a stick. Two large hand-painted signs were propped against the wall on either side of the entrance. They read, WELCOME TO HOG HEAVEN, GOVERNMENT STYLE; LET'S PUT *ALL* THE PIGS IN GOVERNMENT.

He became an instant celebrity. The local CBS affiliate sent a crew over to film the scene and interview Baxter. He came over as a type the American people had loved since Lincoln: the articulate backwoodsman. A nice extra fillip came when a venturesome civil servant tried to rush the door and was nipped in the rear end by an angry Poland China boar. "Make it no mind," Baxter had said over national television, "jes' one hawg bitin' another."

Cronkite had used the material on the CBS news that evening. Affiliated stations across the nation were flooded with approving calls and letters.

The broadcast had caught the eye of the old man who ran Louisiana politics from the porch of his feed store down in Gonzales parish. They needed a lieutenant governor on the November ticket. It was a part-time job and a good toedip into the waters of politics, the old man had told Baxter. He was a canny, convincing salesman and he talked as hard at Ermabelle as at her husband.

Baxter had said yes. After that it became a blur. Five months after the election, the governor's helicopter had crashed in Vermilion Bayou and the Baxters had moved into the Governor's Mansion. Baxter tried to run things pretty much as he had at the drilling company, and to the same standards: efficient, careful, punctual. It worked sort of half-way, but halfway was better than any other elected official was doing in the United States, and so Baxter became a hero and a featured speaker at Good Government dinners and Citizens Independence League meetings from Jasper to Juneau. It was heady stuff. Fulger Baxter contracted a terminal case of Potomac Fever. He started to dream of the White House.

The media had jumped on the bandwagon. Months after his inauguration Baxter came to realize that the papers and the TV had remolded him completely to suit their own purposes. "Jes' like a handful of red clay," he said to Ermabelle. They had buried his successful business past and the fact that he was a college graduate. They praised only what they perceived to be his down-home, homiletic view of things. The brisk reporters and interviewers who flew down from Washington and New York never grasped the fact that in the South there is no such thing as "upperclass English," that Delta roughnecks and Rhodes Scholars from New Orleans make the same drawling, pithy, antigrammatical noises.

The alchemy of the press had thus created a Baxter who was a rough-handed, rednecked pig farmer, and whose literacy was limited to the Gospel. "Golly, honey," he complained to Ermabelle, "that hawg business was jes' a hobby. I mean, we wasn't doin' more than $50,000 a year. And only purebreds to sell at stock shows. These newspapers got me lookin' like I get up at six to do the slops."

On one score the press had made no mistake. Fulger Baxter was a full-time Christian. He had been raised in a God-fearing, church-going home. He found the Bible to be full of truth and useful wisdom, expressed as forcefully and beautifully as Shakespeare and the other important and esteemed writers he had studied. He kept the old King James version; it had, he felt, an elegance and eloquence fitting to its purpose. He laced his private conversations with allusions and quotations from Scripture, read a lesson each night before bed, and kept an open, charitable heart.

Fulger Baxter sincerely wanted to be a good Christian. He also sincerely wanted to be President of the United States. It was a calling.

He kept the lid on things in Baton Rouge. Around the nation he preached a farmhouse frugality and earthiness that his listeners found appealing, especially after the recent slimy doings in Washington. The times were right for the man, and he was the man for the times. A period when back-to-the-earth was magical, when Manhattan tax lawyers in $40 haircuts dressed like cowpokes, when *Women's Wear Daily* decreed Billings, Montana, to be the fashion capital of "Just Folks America."

The Baxter cause had prospered.

Buster had put it together.

Thurlow "Buster" Ferdimend was Baxter's alter ego, closest confidant, and best friend. Baxter hadn't really known anyone when he and Ermabelle had moved to Baton Rouge but he and Buster had picked up on each other within a few days. Buster was about ten years younger than Baxter. He was a thin, ambitious young lawyer from Dougie, a six-shack dirt and dust hamlet ten miles from Houma. He had put himself through school and had become a partner in a good Baton Rouge law firm that handled tax and lobbying work for a number of Texas oil and gas interests. After they became close, Baxter had prevailed on Rebo Beauderon to put some of Petrex's law business through Mayers and Ferdimend.

Buster talked easy, was as tough as a boar in rut, and, unlike most lawyers Baxter had known, conceived of his mission in life to be the attainment, rather than the frustration, of his clients' objectives. When it started to look like Fulger Baxter had some kind of a national political future, Buster Ferdimend set out to make it happen.

His coalition of pollsters, professors, and public relations pros had beat the bejesus out of the opposition in primaries in New Hampshire, Texas, and Iowa—and then New York, which cinched it. With half the delegates in hand, he swept to the nomination on the second ballot and in November edged a dreary Republican candidate who couldn't get out of his own way.

Then things had started to fall apart for Fulger Baxter.

First, on the advice of a Washington "insider" he took on to smooth the transition, he had tried to remake his image to suit what he took to be the style of a sophisticated, demanding capital. He went to an ex-musical comedy star who had made a nice profession out of coaching southern politicians in the public arts. She pounded the regionalisms out of his speech. When she was finished—it took three months—he had acquired a public speaking style so flat, unemotional, and mechanical that it seemed difficult to tell if he was alive.

Then, after his inauguration, he had found that he didn't have the same handle on things that he did in Baton Rouge, where the stakes and the favors were smaller. Congress was splintered into baronies of self-interest from which he could develop no consensus. In his first two years in office, Baxter's plans and programs were beaten to foam on the breakwaters of the House and Senate. His unmended fences proved as impregnable as granite walls. He had worse luck overseas. There was nothing in his past to equip him to deal with the subtleties and mindsets of Frenchmen and Arabs.

He was a man who came from a life in which handshakes closed even the biggest deals, but he now found himself confused and estranged by a world in which the traditional polities seemed to be dissolving. Overseas, whole embassies were kidnapped; senators and congressmen reneged wholesale after lengthy negotiations, repudiating their initials on memorandums of agreement. The President continued to reject the advice of his geopolitics-peddling advisors, but the old-fashioned ideology which had projected him into office was trembling. The shakier it got, however, the more sternly he clung to it, bolstered by Ermabelle, to whom moral compromise was a very small step short of adultery.

Through force of character and a cornucopia of promises, he had contrived a skeletal peace in the Middle East and in Southeast Asia. Instead of the rejoicing he expected, it seemed to set everyone on him. The traditional allies bridled and made angry, unfriendly noises and threats. Their reaction set fires in Washington. The President was used to the laconic dialectics of country horsetrading and he was astonished and irritated, then saddened, by the plants and leaks which sprouted on the front pages and compromised his efforts to effect a fair and lasting peace.

"Lord's sakes, Ermabelle," he had cried one evening in exasperation, "why can't people keep their mouths shut? Sometimes it seems to me that 90 percent of what's wrong with this country comes from people shootin' their mouths off without thinkin'. Or thinkin' too much." He was as distraught as she could recollect seeing him.

The Iranian situation failed to improve, oil supplies became tight, and all hell broke loose. The oil companies figured they had him by the short hairs and claimed they couldn't find any gasoline. They had a lot of good reasons for the crisis, and some bad ones too, but the American people weren't interested in excuses. Summer was coming, and they wanted gas. He caught hell in the Congress for missing the boat in Iran. By the time he could establish the fact that his Secretary of State had retooled the CIA situation estimate to suit his own politics of adventure, the *Washington Post* had the story first. At one desperate point, he had maneuvered things at the Federal Reserve Board so that drastic new policies were invoked, principally a tightening of credit which, in the case of small business, amounted to strangulation. The results were predictable: homebuilding halted and corner grocers and small job shops withered and died for lack of business and credit. Meanwhile, the Amalgamateds and Consolidateds and Uniteds went about their way, perhaps a shade less merry, but still amply funded by the big banks to pick up the more lucrative shards which littered the industrial vista.

Above all, he was galvanized by a conviction that he could somehow reach the nation, rally people on this energy thing. Brushing aside the always-sensible objections of Buster and Marvin Gottlieb, and duped by the sophistries produced by the unlikely combination of Energy Secretary Nordlander and a phalanx of advertising shamans dredged up by his press aide, he had thrown himself into an evangelical approach. The slogan writers, kit assemblers, and visual aids wizards helped him with a vengeance. Within three weeks from Nordlander's "go" signal, the "Save *A Gallon* for *God*" campaign, or "SAGG," was introduced to an incredulous nation by President Baxter in a televised fireside chat. It was probably this campaign that had carried Baxter past the mere derision of the people and the press to the knife-edge of contempt where he now so precariously balanced.

Fortunately, the SAGG business was short-lived. As throughout its great history, the country yielded a host of inventive types quick to seize on the profits inherent in any large-scale piece of public foolishness. Most of these operated around the edge of things, nicking off thousands, perhaps tens of thousands, of dollars; only a few had a true vision of the big time and, among these, foremost was the Reverend Dr. Gameliel Freep, like the President a born-again believer, but with a more steadfast congregation and more worldly appreciation of the benefits of sanctity.

Freep had perverted SAGG into GAGG, "Give A Gallon to God," and preached the revised version on a hundred-station TV ministry and at a series of stadium crusades and tent meetings in twenty-four large southeastern cities. While the good Reverend's evangelism bound a spell over arenas and tents brimming with country piety, his gowned minions prowled the parking lots, siphoning for the greater glory of God and the free market system. The million or so gallons thus obtained kept the Reverend's five carefully tax-articulated interstate truck stops pumping away all summer while the major company service stations sucked for fuel. In time, *60 Minutes* exposed the Reverend's scam and it and SAGG/GAGG had expired amidst faint mirth and little regret.

"Hell," Buster had said to the President, "you can dick around with the money supply or the reserve requirements all you want, but the basics aren't going to change until human nature does. These peacetime 'wars,' against poverty, energy consumption, you name it, are just so much talk to this nation of two hundred million thumb-suckers!"

Baxter had lost his important constituencies. Old friends like Rebo Beauderon, who were used to getting things done their way and expected the same of him, grew dismayed at the apparent floundering in Washington and went chasing off after new messiahs. The electorate at large, self-centered and fickle as ever, discarded its infatuation with frontier values and hummed the songs of other sirens. President Baxter found himself alone, except for Ermabelle, a few truly loyal personal assistants like Buster, and the comforts of Scripture. The papers showed him holding a confidence level of less than 25 percent. He could hear the movements of the political jackals in the underbrush.

He was a bad loser. No matter what the Gospel preached, Fulger Baxter didn't turn the other cheek. He was going to go down, if that's what it was to be, with the flags flying and the band playing.

Which was why that business with Nordlander this morning particularly infuriated him.

"Would you like a sandwich, sir, or something else to drink?" It was the steward at his elbow. Outside, it was dark now; Baxter guessed they were coming up on the Mississippi.

"No thank you, son." His fingers drummed away.

It had been a brutal winter. The gasoline had gotten really short by mid-August and what the refineries had been able to obtain went into building up fuel oil stocks and keeping the farms going. It had caught the automobile companies in the middle of their model introductions. America spent Labor Day at home, off the road, in no sort of a car-buying frame of mind.

They made it through somehow. Between the oil companies and the White House, a patched-together program was put over which sufficiently dispersed and diffused local shortages and local blame so that Congress got off the hook and the press was forestalled from completely politicizing the crisis. Of course, Baxter had been everyone's whipping boy, and had received the blame that might have been more justly apportioned.

A serious peace overture of the oil and gas people was clearly called for, a spacious diplomatic gesture no less attention-getting and symbolic than his sudden midnight flight to Cairo a year before.

It had taken all kinds of arm-twisting and calling in of due bills to arrange the speaking date in Midland. That was Herndon Dunstable country, the home base of the ex-senator, ex-everything big, who looked to be the Republicans' white knight, drawn from retirement to save the party and the nation. President Baxter had guessed that the Dunstable people had worked long hours trying to prevent his appearance. But Buster, bless him, had sat down in a closed room with Rebo Beauderon and a half-dozen other oil-patch big hitters and when he came out, President Baxter had been offered the opportunity to give the keynote address to the annual Groundhog Day get-together of the Oil Producers Association.

He ordered Nordlander to accompany him to Midland. He was sick and tired of hearing complaints about the Energy Secretary's condescending aloofness and inaccessibility. Nordlander complained. He showed the President an organization chart and a long computer printout which, he asserted, held the keys to the energy problem. The President wasn't impressed.

"Tell you what, Isaac," he said, "you take that out to California and show it to some Chicano who's got no work 'cause he can't get gas for his pickup. If he'll agree that you got the solution right there in them pages, why, I guess I'll have to go along with you."

If the Secretary was loftily displeased, the President couldn't have cared less.

"Now, Isaac," he said emphatically. "We're goin' out to

Midland, you and me. That's oil country and that's Dunstable country. We are both goin' to make a very good impression, we are. You in particular are goin' to come over real sympathetic to what those good folks are goin' to be sayin'."

It was a good place to get started, Midland: the capital city of the independent oil men, fierce and entrepreneurial, who thought that finding oil and selling it and finding more oil was the whole point of life. Houston was a big company town, now, filled with business-school clones in gray and blue suits and executives who spent their working days in meetings. Dallas was a business center; oil and gas was just one of a dozen money games down on Elm Street. Baxter anticipated a tough-minded, tooth-and-claw audience in Midland, but, with the good Lord's help, he was going to give as good as he got.

The President's 707 and the Secretary's Gulfstream had arrived within minutes of each other at Midland Regional Airport. The President and Buster had gotten into one Cadillac; the Secretary's party into another. They were accompanied by the officers of the OPA.

Nordlander had tried to appear interested. Inside, he was mad as a snake. He'd had to leave an extremely interesting program on macrogeosynergies at the Aspen Institute to come and mingle with these hicks. And, to make it worse, it was a political trip. Secretary Nordlander was above common politics and commerce.

On the road in from the airport, Nordlander's curiosity was engaged. It was his first visit to the oil country. In several fields beside the road, he noted tall, beam-like devices which seesawed majestically in a manner which reminded him of nothing so much as exaggerated versions of those glass-bodied novelties which drank bobbingly from a water glass.

Finally, he pointed to one and asked, "That's quite an interesting machine over there. Some sort of irrigation gadget, no doubt? What is it exactly?"

To the young man's credit, Nordlander's special assistant tried to cut the dialogue off at the pass, but their official host was too quick and canny to let this priceless chance go by.

Turning around in the front seat of the Cadillac, he threw a big, helpful grin at Nordlander. "Why, Mr. Energy Secretary, that there's an oil well!"

When they arrived at the Petroleum Club, it took Nordlander's guide about thirty seconds to pass it on. Within fifteen minutes, it seemed as if all Midland, and probably

Odessa too, was in on the gaffe. The President heard about it from Buster. There was nothing to do but go on.

With his audience thus warmed up, Baxter's speech was not a success.

"Hell, Buster, I'da done better jes' goin' out there an' stickin' my thumb up my butt for laughs," he said as they climbed the steps to the airplane.

It had been a long day. At one point in the course of his speech, the President had even thought he'd caught sight of the tall, courtly form of ex-Senator Dunstable in the back of the meeting room. He couldn't be sure. Afterward, exchanging perfunctory handshakes with the OPA officers, Baxter searched the crowd for Dunstable but the big man wasn't there. Doubtless, he was back at his ranch, gloating.

His political coffin was getting nailed up pretty good, the President thought to himself. Young Senator Monohan was coming on strong. That damn Nordlander. Baxter pressed the button set in the bulkhead. When the steward appeared, the President thought he'd have a little toddy.

It had been one of those days when there were few occasions for happiness anywhere. The stock market had declined another six-odd points, finishing the day at 889.67. A Merlin commuter plane had come in short of the runway at Santa Fe, killing all eighteen people aboard. The deputy mayor of Philadelphia had been indicted in a kickback scheme. The usual bad news. No bright spots.

It was a gray, unpleasant March day in Dallas, adding to the sadness of the occasion for which the small group had gathered in one of the side chapels of the University Park Presbyterian Church. They had come to bury Nellie Camran. It was hard to imagine life in the Park Cities without Nellie. For thirty-five years she had presided over the junior circulation desk at the Free Library, shaping the reading tastes of nearly three generations of Dallas's best and brightest boys and girls. Thirty years a widow, ever since the day that the Judy Keet number one well had caught fire over at Placedo, incinerating everyone within fifty yards of the drilling floor, including a cementing crew from OWSCO. Mackenzie "Big Buck" Camran had been the boss of that crew. His death had left his thirty-three-year-old wife with $25,000 in company insurance, $5,000 in the Park Cities Bank, and the small house, free and clear, on Rosedale Avenue. It also left her with three children: Little Buck, Margaret, and the baby,

(229)

Alex, named after his maternal grandfather. Nellie's innate Presbyterian modesty had prevailed over her husband's wish to give their youngest one of those glamorous football-type names like Lance or Donnie Joe.

Somehow, Nellie had managed to bring all three children up right. Little Buck and Margaret were popular in school and went to Southern Methodist on scholarships. Buck played shortstop on the baseball team and was a big man at SAE. Margaret had gone Pi Phi, studied the piano, and given a recital in Selecman Hall on the eve of graduation.

Life had turned out well since SMU for Buck and Margaret, thought the women in the congregation, looking at the three red-blond heads of the Camran children in the front pew as the minister eulogized Nellie. Buck was the general manager of the Dallas office of the big New York stockbroker firm of Cantwell & Co. He had a fancy corner office in the OWSCO place downtown and was well spoken of by the important men at the corner table in the Dallas Club who parceled out the power in the city. His wife, Ann, a cheerful Kappa from the University of Texas, presided over the nice stone house in University Park, and kept their four children doing the right things. Buck coached junior soccer and Ann worked hard in the Junior League. The Park Cities were heaven, of course, but Ann anticipated the day, now probably not too far distant, when they could move to a bigger house in north Dallas, maybe on Seneca or Strait Lane, and the girls could go to Hockaday and be presented at Idlewild. Maybe even join Creek Dip, the *summum bonum* of Dallas club life.

If the men in the congregation knew that Buck begged off the family table every other Wednesday or so on some business excuse and had a few drinks with the boys at Arthur's, or the Stoneleigh, and ended up the evening at the Coinage Club out on the Loop chasing after some desperate thirty-five-year-old secretary, why, that was just Buck's own business.

Of course, Margaret was married to that big orthopedic surgeon down in Houston. He'd have to have been a star to lure a native girl, and a Pi Phi at that, away from the Panglossian perfection of Highland Park to the bumptious, more sumptuary delights of River Oaks, the Houston subdivision, where one-acre lots changed hands for sums which would have rebuilt "Niggertown," as the adjacent residential area was described over margaritas at the club. Her husband was said to be right up there alongside Doctors Cooley and DeBakey when it came to deciding where the medical money in Houston was to be spent.

Alex Camran was the exception. He'd been a few days short of his third birthday when his father died, which made him thirty-two now. Maybe it was not having a daddy, but Alex never quite fit in Dallas. He didn't cause any problems. No fights or tantrums or anything like that. No problems with cars; of course, the Camrans hadn't been able to afford one of their own, other than the one Nellie drove to work, until Buck had put his summer earnings from the job at a 7-11 down on a 1950 DeSoto. Alex wasn't a problem child at school or at home. He made good grades and ate everything Nellie put on the table without gaining a pound. He read a lot and was always quoting from some fantasy book or other, in a manner that made it clear to his listeners that he found Dallas vulgar and boring compared to Camelot and Oz and Paris and a lot of other fancy places. After a while, young Alex came to be known as "Clouds" Camran, because that's where his head was. Since he wasn't a troublemaker, nobody paid him much mind; they all liked Nellie and the other two kids were outgoing and a real part of things.

Alex had a couple of other qualities which didn't go down so well. He was competitive, in an individual way only, since he refused to play in any of the junior team leagues his mother and older brother tried to talk him into joining. And he was curious; downright nosy, most folks said. His own family would have agreed with this estimate. Buck and Margaret were always complaining about him going through their things. His teachers said he went after a problem like a bloodhound: what, who, when, where? It was as if he just couldn't stand not knowing what was going on.

Apart from reading, he had a natural aptitude for golf, which he attributed to his Scots heritage, and he hung around the Dallas Country Club, caddying and picking up pointers, until he could cruise it around in the low seventies. The SMU coach had wanted him for the team and let him play along with them. But when he was sixteen, he got beaten in the fourth round of the Dallas City Championship by a fat and fortyish man from Creek Dip who could putt the eyes out of a salamander. Alex shook hands on sixteen and threw his clubs in the pond fronting the green. Watching him stomp off, his vanquisher rumbled to the caddy, "That l'il flatbelly could play this game, if he could only handle that temper."

It would be five years before the fire of that defeat would be banked in Alex and he would pick up a club again. Since he was Scotch, he was thrifty; so, the evening of his defeat, he snuck back on the golf course in his bathing suit and sneakers and fished around in the pond, among the watersnakes and snapping turtles, until he found his clubs.

He had stayed so apart from the mainstream of University Park life that it came as no surprise when one day he just left for good. Not really, of course. He won a scholarship to Andover, then to Yale, and finally to Wharton and, for all intents and purposes, he was gone from Dallas, period. He came back to see his kinfolks at Christmas; when the cancer started to waste his mother, he would appear regularly. Eventually, he moved into a motel across Harry Hines from Parkland Hospital and held his mother's hand the whole awful final vigil; they waited for death together.

The Certified Bank had given him a leave of absence. He was doing well. Assistant vice president handling special assignments for Reuben Bowen, the bank's president. He was proud that it wasn't valet's work like that creep Mismer did for Leslie Merriman, the chairman of the Certified. Three or four more good years and he'd make vice president. Certified wasn't like Gotham Bank, with its gaggle of under-thirty wonder boy executive VPs.

Alex had been a beanpole as a boy and he had grown into a tall, slanty young man with narrow, confident features. From his clothes to his voice, he had "gone New York"; so his few old Dallas friends and classmates claimed. To their irritation, he cheerfully accepted the indictment. Cheerfully now, but it had once been otherwise: there were better things to have been than a first-year student from Dallas in a New England school when the news arrived that "they" had murdered President Kennedy in Dealey Plaza. Dallas was the sort of place "they" lived. All through that terrible, weeping weekend in front of the television, with classes and activities suspended, the school under a pall, Alex felt and was made to feel as if he had pulled the trigger himself. It was going to take him as long as Dallas itself to recover. Maybe forever. He didn't want to be dubbed with "them." Every day he blessed the bank because it had taken him away from Texas and closer, he thought, to that dreamland which had been painted in the books of his childhood.

Perceiving himself clever, sophisticated, newly useful with a menu and a winelist, Alex presented himself very much a man of the world. "A real New York smartass," was the way his brother Buck put it. Standing in the church next to Buck's son Boober, Alex thought that, with his mother's death, it would be a cold day in hell before he would see "Big D" again. New York was where it was, where he belonged.

After the burial across from Northpark, Buck's wife took the grandchildren back to their house. It was time for Buck, Margaret, and Alex to be alone. They stood for a while beside their mother's grave while a chill-edged Blue Norther blew across the flat land. This was goodbye.

In the car, Buck said over his shoulder, "Well, with Momma gone I 'spect we won't be getting together much now. Margaret's got her own life in Houston and New York's got you, Ally. I got to get back to the office by two. But how about for old times' sake we go get some barbecue at Peggy's? That's the one thing about Dallas you both still like."

Peggy's Beef Bar was a University Park landmark. Peggy dished out the best beef and sausage links, onion rings, French fries, cole slaw, and fried fruit pies, sluiced down by custom with Dr. Pepper. Alex ordered the full deal; pigout time in the land of cotton, he said to himself.

"So what's new, Bucky?" he asked through a mouthful of beef. "Business good?"

"Just fine. Better than that. I am right now just going and blowing. You know that bank out in El Paso, the Rio Trust? The one that really got me started in the institutional business?"

Alex did. He added a little red sauce to his sausage, speared a slice on his fork with a garnishment of slaw and munched away, nodding.

"The guy out there handles the corporate orders is a friend of mine. Even though he was a Delta at Baylor. Well, he's been doing his Dallas business through me and a couple of other guys; Bobby Joe Youngs, you know, SAE at Texas, he's a Rauscher now, and another fellow over at Paine Webber. I think he was a Kappa at Tech. Old Bobby Joe got himself hit by a Mexican in a pickup and he's been in a coma for seven weeks, and the Paine Webber guy moved out to Lake Cherokee and opened a bass fishing lodge—that was a couple of months ago—so I just been walking through the tall cotton for the last six weeks. I mean *writing tickets!* Good ones—and no discount on the commissions!"

Alex stuffed fingersful of deep-fried onion rings in his mouth.

"And the best part," Buck added, "is that not only am I getting all the business from El Paso, but *they're* doing ten times the volume they've ever done. I have cut me a *real* fat hog, Ally." He was boasting; he never did mind laying it on his smartass little brother, his smartass little *New York* brother who thought that everything worth a damn was up North.

"How come, Bucky? Some pecan zillionaire out there been checking out Ann's drawers?" Alex crunched into a fried pie.

"Hell no." Buck didn't have much fun in him. "All my friend knows is they're doing a lot of custody and execution business for a huge new master trust back east somewhere. Not Certified neither, little brother!" Buck liked to stick the needle in. "These guys never talk to anyone. Stuff just comes in on the wire. All over the map. New York, American, NASDAQ. Beatrice Foods. Caesars World. Walter Kidde. Sunlite Oil. Nice orders, three, four, five hundred; did 900 Ashland Oil yesterday. Ol' Bobby Joe's gonna kill himself if he ever wakes up!"

Alex's competitive fuse was lit. It was all right for Buck to do OK; he was family. But another bank, in El Paso yet, doing custody stuff for a big master trust that wasn't a Certified master trust. That was to think about. Hell, master trusts, the profitable monitoring and bookkeeping and data banking of huge corporate investment pools were the Certified's specialty! If this one was throwing its custodial diversification as far out as El Paso, it must be a big bastard indeed! He pushed away the remaining half of his fried pie. His appetite was ruined by the thought of a bank other than Certified doing some big business. It was bad enough being number two behind the goddamn B of A.

In his office the next morning, Alex looked down Park Avenue and, having mused on the details of Buck's boasting, dialed a number in the Pension Services Department.

"Dugan? Alex Camran here, in Mr. Bowen's office. He's asked me to check up on a couple of things. Part of the repositioning study. That's right. No, the CEO has delegated it to this office. Anyway, we're trying to track recent CMT activity. Any big new developments at Certified Master Trust? Nothing, huh? What do you hear across the street? Oh yeah? All quiet. You hear anything underground: B of A? First Chicago? Security Pacific? Good. Well, keep us posted."

He put down the phone and sat looking at his watch as if

he was taking his pulse. Ninety-seven seconds later, his secretary buzzed. Mismer was on the phone.

"Yes, Arthur. No, Rube heard a rumor that Gotham picked off a big master trust. Nine hundred million. Scuttlebutt says it's Petrex. No, Art, we're not trying to butt in on your bailiwick."

That ought to fix them, Alex thought. His combative fantasizing saw Bowen and himself pitted against Merriman and Mismer, knights and squires bumping shields and lances in a metaphorical sunwashed meadow. Of course he'd made it up about Bowen hearing anything. The secretarial grapevine had told him that Merriman and his valet were giving an evening of fancy food at Le Grenouille, to a bunch of Korean shipbuilders. This ought to curdle their *sauce moutarde*. A small consolation for the lousy loan commitments Merriman was likely to make.

The next item on his daysheet was to check on the status of the Petrex loan. As he reached for the phone, the mental filecard with Buck's news slid into the back of his memory.

Two weeks later, Harrison and Devon were sitting in the office twiddling their thumbs when the phone rang. Devon picked it up.

"It's Ernie." Ernie came on in his Rochester voice. He sounded troubled. "Boss, I think I've pulled a booboo. A biggie!"

Harrison broke into a soaking sweat. It was an affliction he hated. "What's the problem?"

"Well, boss, I think I miscounted. I just ran a spotcheck. Don't hold me to it, but we may be a billion short!"

"Ernie, are you crazy? Are you sure?" Rivers of perspiration ran down the sides of his face as always happened when he was nervous. "Jesus Christ, Ernie! Listen, check it over. How soon can you do it?" His goddamn suit felt glued to him with sweat.

Ernie's voice changed tone and dialect. He was back to being Rochester again.

"Saints preserve us, Mr. Benny. And happy April Fool's Day!" His guffaws filled the receiver.

Harrison was barely halfway through his string of maledictions when he looked across the room at Devon. Her face was in her hands; she was shaking with laughter. He put down the phone.

"And fuck you too!" He crossed the room and kissed her.

And more. When Miss DiVitale peeked in to say goodnight and saw what was taking place on the office carpet, she nearly fainted.

19 Press headquarters for the Offshore Resources Conference were housed in the old Royal Hawaiian Hotel. It was not a popular billeting. The reporters hated having to struggle back to Kalakaua Avenue, through the heavy Waikiki tourist traffic, to the flashier, more comfortable Ilikai where the main sessions were held.

The presence at the ORC of both the Minister and the U.S. Energy Secretary had caused the media to dispatch some of their pretty big hitters. The Chivas Regal crowd. They sat in the bar, dripping wisdom like baptismal water on the heads of younger reporters who slavishly carried back bulletins from the Ilikai, and bitching at the shabby furniture and the general lack of action at the Royal Hawaiian.

A few didn't mind. Bix Berger, number three on the NBC news ladder and widely rumored to be in line to replace John Chancellor, had brought his girlfriend along and left bed and the beach only long enough to do a nightly one-minute "no news" wrapup. Mostly, the press drank and tried to outmaneuver swarms of Japanese businessmen for the better-looking whores. It was a losing proposition.

The session dragged on, so it wasn't until nearly six o'clock on Thursday, April 3, that Sir Montague Bath, deputy chairman of English Oil and the Conference's presiding officer, finally called for adjournment. The late adjournment was the last straw. The reporters would have to sit around and wait for the midnight commercial flights to the mainland, blowing half the next day's holiday. It was all right for these corporate bigshots, whose limousines were now moving out of the Ilikai driveway to their Grummans and JetStars parked out at the airport. But the poor working stiffs would have to blow a good piece of the holiday weekend, the *long* holiday weekend.

This all suited the Minister's design perfectly. Nordlander, the American Energy Secretary, had left earlier in the afternoon on his Air Force jet. The Minister and Nordlander had made no contact, except for the usual hypocritically cordial photograph sessions. The Minister disliked Nordlander intensely. The American was one of those intellectuals who seemed to have no intelligence whatsoever. A gray, crewcut man with a practiced, distinguished manner, who sucked interminably on coughdrops, Nordlander liked to fondle a pocket-watch and offer pompous nostrums for the world's problems. The Minister thought that President Baxter kept Nordlander in the Cabinet only because of his lofty demeanor. Certainly the President paid little attention to Nordlander these days; Benjamin Masters had reported on the Midland fiasco from Washington. Masters was usually accurate, thought the Minister; he had good, deep sources and was worth every cent of the $250,000 yearly the Kingdom paid him to keep an eye on things. He wished he might have been able to brief Masters on the forthcoming announcement, but he was certain nevertheless that the Washington lawyer would improvise to handle the uproar in the Kingdom's best interests.

At seven o'clock, with the flotilla of official and private aircraft mostly departed for other parts of the world, the Minister judged that the time was right. He had his secretary get through to the Conference's press officer, who was making last-minute travel arrangements for his surly charges.

"His Excellency would like to call a brief press conference. There will be an opportunity for questions, and he may wish to make a short, important statement. His Excellency is aware that there is a holiday in the United States tomorrow and that many of the press corps have made plans to leave on flights departing later this evening. His Excellency does not expect the press meeting to end later than nine. It will begin promptly at eight-fifteen in the Kamehameha Room of the Royal Hawaiian Hotel."

The press officer managed to corner all but a half-dozen of the remaining reporters and broadcasting people. The few holdouts lurked in the bar, sucking on Scorpions and speculating derisively as to the point of the hastily called session.

"I'm so tired of these fucking OPEC announcements," said one UPI bigshot. "Today, we hear from this guy, who probably wants to say how useful this shindig has been, but that the official price of crude is going to $30. Tomorrow, the Venezuelans will take it to $35. Then the Nigerians. And the Iraqis. Thank God for small blessings, though; can you imagine what we'd be paying if the French had the oil?"

There were roughly a hundred in the audience when the Minister entered the function room. There was only one television camera set up, by the local ABC affiliate which happened to have a crew on the premises.

The Minister was pleased. Before leaving Dumar for the Conference, he had met at length with Prince Alrazi. They had decided to schedule the press conference on the spur of the moment, as it were. It would be best if the Minister's counterparts in the world of high energy affairs were somewhere in the air or asleep and out of immediate touch when the news broke.

He walked briskly behind a table on which a cluster of microphones and a couple of cassette recorders had been placed. The red light on the TV camera went on, although it was transmitting only to the videorecorder that its operator had activated.

"Good evening. I thought this might represent an opportunity for an informal meeting. Are there any questions on the business just concluded?"

Tired and impatient, journalistic courtesy obliged them to ask the formula questions he'd expected.

Yes, the Conference had provided a forum, a most helpful forum, for an exchange of ideas. No, the situation in world oil prices continued troublesome. Yes, it was hoped that the U.S. administration's newest announced conservation program, and other measures proposed elsewhere in the Western industrial world, might effectively reduce inflationary demand.

The Minister was one of those men who was good at meetings. He had a sense of the pulse and pace of things, an instinct for the mood and involvement of the other participants. There was a pause in the questioning, which he read as a signal of the exhaustion and depletion of the attention and interest of his audience.

Time to wake them up, he thought, taking a folded sheet of paper from his robes.

"I have a brief announcement to read. Since it may be of interest to you, copies will be distributed when I have finished. There may be time for one or two questions." The crowd of reporters showed no particular interest.

"His Royal Majesty, our King, sends greetings to our brother nations of the world." He read the announcement very precisely.

"For some time, we have been concerned at the rate of inflation which had been generated within the industrial nations of Europe, Asia, and America. We have also been

(238)

concerned with the tendency of our fellow producing states, with whom we have publicly disagreed from time to time, to intensify this state of affairs by continuing to increase the price of crude oil, even though this is to a great extent justified by the rising prices of the goods and services which we buy in the world. We continue to be concerned with the failure of the United States to reduce its rate of consumption of imported energy."

"For Christ's sake," said *KSOP-TV* to the *Sacramento Bee,* "can you believe this? A lecture on economics."

"We are also concerned with the political alienation which these conditions and circumstances have brought about. The recent negotiations between Egypt and Israel, initiated by Washington, are of gravest moment and threaten the political and ideological equilibrium of the Middle East."

"Shit," whispered *Newsweek* to the *MacNeil/Lehrer Report,* "here comes more blackmail. Five bucks says it's a 10 percent jackup in the crude price."

The Minister continued to read deliberately.

"These problems must ultimately threaten the internal stability of every nation in the free world. Statesmanship of the highest order will be required to bring about solutions . . ."

"You're on," said *MacNeil/Lehrer.* "I know these guys. 'Statesmanship' with these cats means 'grin and bear it.' At least 14 percent!"

". . . which will be effective in both the political and the economic sense.

"For some months now, at very high levels, we have been pursuing discussions with certain of our oldest allies—in particular, at the *highest* level in Washington—with regard to matters of mutual diplomatic, military; and economic advantage. The imagination and goodwill displayed at these secret meetings by the Baxter administration's representatives have been impressive."

By now, thought the Minister, Alrazi would have briefed the Kingdom's embassies in London, Bonn, Tokyo, Paris, and Washington, as well as the UN office in New York. Masters, too, would undoubtedly have been contacted. The machinery would be in place.

He raised his voice a fraction.

"We now believe that it is possible to foresee these negotiations with the United States leading to certain arrangements which will secure the stability and peace which we desire.

"Accordingly, we are pleased to announce modifications of our existing arrangements with respect to the production and pricing of crude oil. We wish to emphasize that these actions have been determined unilaterally by His Majesty and by the Prime Minister, Prince Alrazi al-Mutr Adaf, and do not represent consensual agreement with our fellow producing states."

He looked around the room. He had his audience off-balance. Pens were coming out; he noted that the TV cameraman had edged closer.

"Effective May 1, therefore," he paused for effect, "the posted price of crude oil F.O.B. Dumar will be reduced to $10 a barrel."

"Am I fuckin' crazy," hissed *Oil & Gas Journal* to *The Philadelphia Inquirer.* "Did he say $10 a barrel? Ten? Ten!"

Half the audience was suddenly on its feet, confused and noisy. The Minister was pleased to see that his bodyguards were standing against the doors which led to the hall and telephones.

"Ladies and gentlemen, please!" The press officer took over the microphones. "Please. There is more. Most of you have missed your deadlines, anyway. Please be seated for just a minute more! Let His Excellency complete his statement. Please."

The news crowd was buzzing. This was the scoop of the century!

"You have to admire the SOB," said the *New York Times.* "He's managed it perfectly. We'll be scooped by the *Post.* Abe is going to chew the carpet when he hears about it." The managing editor of the *Times* was well known for his view that his paper should govern the events it reported, and not vice versa. "The motto of this paper ought to be, 'All the news that is fit to *happen,*'" he often declared fervently to the pressroom.

They took their seats slowly, muttering and clucking.

"Concurrent with this, we will be decreasing the level of oil which we will make available for shipment to 9.5 million barrels daily.

"This step is taken in friendship, trust, and the confidence that a continuation of the discussions to date will produce the state of peace toward which we all aspire."

The Minister concluded. "This statement is signed by His Majesty, and is dated, Qu'nesh, April 3, by the Christian calendar."

He signaled his secreatry to distribute the copies of the announcement, which had been Xeroxed only hours before at the Ilikai. His bodyguards moved away from the door.

A forest of hands grew in the room. The experienced reporters recognized that the few minutes necessary to fill in the story wouldn't cost them a newsbreak. The wire service people scrambled for the door. As did the reporters from west coast papers and the *New York Post* and the rest of the eastern afternoon papers. They could be on the streets with an extra.

"Your Excellency." The Minister recognized the energy editor of the *Washington Post,* the paper's OPEC expert. "Your Excellency, in your announcement you alluded to 'discussions,' I believe that was your word. Can you amplify on that?"

"Unfortunately not, Mr. Dinwiddie. The matters being considered are highly sensitive, of course. It would be premature to make any statement beyond what His Majesty has chosen to say."

The correspondent looked disappointed.

The Minister hung out a carrot. "I think I can assure you, sir, that the productive secret discussions have been held, as I suggested, at the *very* highest level, so that matters may perhaps move forward now to an early, mutually beneficial conclusion."

"Your Excellency, if you are still in the midst of conversations, why have you taken this action now?" The *New Orleans Times-Picayune,* President Baxter's hometown paper.

"We are confident of the good faith of the men with whom we are dealing. So much so that, in view of the intense and disturbing deterioration of political and financial factors in recent months, His Majesty has determined that action at this time would be appropriate."

The Minister said that he would entertain one more question.

"Your Excellency." The *Wall Street Journal.* "You are accompanying this material price reduction, nearly 50 percent, by a 17 percent cutback in daily production, to 9.5 million barrels daily. Would you care to expand on your thinking on this?"

"Mr. Boswell, we are willing to accept the fact that the rapid and dramatic increases since 1973 in the price of oil have contributed to global inflation. We have seen it ourselves in the cost of the products and services we purchase from the oil-consuming nations. We also believe that some material reduction in the consumption of imported fuel by the United States must be effected. With all the goodwill in the world, political and other considerations have prevented your administration from either meaningfully shrinking demand or increasing supply by stimulating domestic production in a fashion and at a price which the Congress might find politically palatable. His Majesty believes that our new policy will mandate a modest reduction in supply while offering an acceptable pricing framework within which to consider various alternatives to the stimulation of new production.

"I might also add, Mr. Boswell, that it must be recognized that we are at present supplying something less than 25 percent of your country's daily consumption of imported petroleum. Our brethren in OPEC, who have in many cases larger populations than ours and who have undertaken important military, industrial, and social programs predicated on a continuation of existing price levels, may thus be able to maintain a pricing policy which will generate revenues sufficient to continue those programs. As inflation abates, as we hope and believe it shall, the balance of world pricing may adjust lower to approach our postings."

It was a commanding, literate presentation. Two hours later, when the CBS man finally got through to his sleepy superior in Martha's Vineyard, he would say, "Walter, it was the greatest goddamn performance I've ever seen. It made John Connally look like something on *Hee-Haw*."

As the crowd rose—it was time now to break for the telephones—the Minister raised his hand and added, "One last word. Tonight is the eve of the greatest period of devotion in the Christian calendar. His Majesty has also asked me to send the good wishes of Islam to our Christian friends in America and Europe."

It was a nice closing touch which he and Alrazi had concocted. He knew it would not go unnoticed in Tel Aviv. And New Delhi.

The reporters rushed for the door. Trotting along beside another colleague from the *Washington Post,* Frank Dinwiddie asked, "Did you see anyone from the administration here tonight?"

"Oh, hell no. The only guy besides Nordlander was the OPEC liaison officer, and I know he left on the Carbolite jet. He told me there was nothing open commercial except coach.

Hell, Frank, you know those Washington people won't ride in the back of the bus."

Every payphone in the hotel lobby was taken, Dinwiddie could see; he was sure the direct-dial lines from the hotel would be clogged. Reporters were screaming into the lobby telephones, making up leads as they went.

He ran out on to Kilia Road. A hundred yards up the street he found a bank of pay telephones. As his coin rattled in the slot, he thought for a minute. The night air was sweet and breezeless. The Easter moon hung in the sky like a travel poster. Patriot or reporter Dinwiddie asked himself. What the hell, he thought, one time, just one time, even if the managing editor did kill him. He dialed the number of the White House.

Thus it was that the greatest, most consequential event since Watergate was brought to the ear of the President on a station call to the White House switchboard from a payphone on a Honolulu sidewalk.

The Minister was pleased; but he was hardly prepared for the scene in the Ilikai lobby and outside when he came downstairs to leave for the airport. The news had spread. The lobby was packed with cheering people, some holding up small children, clapping and waving at him. His bodyguards had to push a path through the crowd for him. As he passed, they pelted him with flowers: roses, narcissus, gardenias.

As he paused at the door of the Lincoln, a little girl was propelled out of the crowd which now stretched up Ala Moana Street three deep. She was carrying a bunch of orchids. She handed them to him with a small, shy curtsy. "Thank you," she said in a tiny, bashful voice.

He took the flowers and climbed into the car. The crowd shouted and blew kisses.

It was the same at the airport. Finally, airborne, he relaxed. The Royal Concorde turned westward over the ocean toward Guam and the Kingdom.

It had worked out as they had planned. Despite the very careful inclusion of the words "military" and "political" in the announcement, all that the American reporters had asked about was money.

Not that money was entirely absent from his own thinking. He felt very prosperous. The day before he had departed Dumar for Honolulu, Khafiq had telephoned. The American, Harrison, had gotten over $4.8 billion into the market. Naturally, Alrazi had fumed when he heard the $5 billion objective hadn't been reached. Still, the Minister found it a comfortable prospect. He settled back and called for coffee.

There had been no late night volume in the history of the Hawaiian Telephone Company comparable to that of April 3–4. Supervisors had been called in to the handsome Victorian building on Bishop Street but their fiddling with the switching codes and traffic routing had done no good.

Frank Dinwiddie had been lucky. Within seconds after being connected to Washington, the circuits from Oahu were completely jammed. Anticipating this, he had asked the voice on the other end to relay the bare outlines of the story to his editor.

At two-thirty in the morning, a single window was still lit upstairs in the White House.

"So now, with little more than half a year to run until the inescapable quadrennial elections which the wisdom of its Founding Fathers has decreed, the United States is perhaps in the most parlous political condition in recent memory. The administration of President Baxter, so promising in its early pragmatic approach to problems not of its making, has over the last three and a half years lost both its control of events and its credibility with its constituency. It is to a weary government, then, that a weary nation turns for leadership. What President Baxter should do, he cannot; what he must do, it would seem he will not." The editorial was bylined by the former British ambassador.

"Aw, bullroar," said Fulger Baxter, dropping the current issue of the *Economist* on his nighttable. "Goddamn Englishmen. *They* ought to come over and try to run things." And this goosehead knows about Washington, too. He was talking to himself. Damn paper'd made him so mad he wasn't going to be able to read Scripture with a Christian heart. He tried to calm himself. Ermabelle had told him to keep his blood pressure down. He gave himself a one-phrase sermon about a soft answer. It went down badly.

The bedside clock read two thirty-six a.m. Shoot, he never used to sleep this bad in Baton Rouge.

He reached for the light. Not that he'd sleep, but he had to try. Wordlessly, he repeated the Lord's Prayer to himself. He had his hand on the lightcord when the red buzzer on his bedside console sounded.

"Mr. President, something's come up you have to know about." It was Marvin Gottlieb, one of Baxter's two special assistants. He was a bright Brooklyn lawyer who had been recruited during the President's successful New York primary campaign.

Gottlieb outlined the story as Dinwiddie had given it to him over the telephone. The President suddenly felt warm all over.

"Marvin, we've got to get together on this right now. I'll be downstairs in twenty minutes. Where's Buster?"

"I'll try to find him, sir." Gottlieb's tone of voice said unmistakably that he'd tried already. Buster was undoubtedly pursuing his fondness for Wild Turkey and good-looking ladies over in Georgetown. Buster was a newly minted bachelor who ventured out late and often and seldom slept in his messy apartment off Dupont Circle.

"Call over and get him out of wherever he is," said Baxter. "Now, let's see. Better get the Secretary of State. No, don't. But I guess we have to get Nordlander in, seein' as it's an energy matter. Anyone else you can think of?"

"Well, there is one thing, Mr. President. I got this news from Frank Dinwiddie at the *Post*. He called me first; I don't even think he's talked to his paper. And I doubt he can get through now. It's bedlam out there. I had the Pentagon contact Hickam Field and Pearl, but they don't know anything. I told them to get their feelers out."

"Who've we got out there, anyway? Wasn't Nordlander sayin' somethin' about goin' to Hawaii?"

"Well sir, he *was* out there. But he left after the formal program." There was a pause. "The fact is, sir, I'm afraid there's no one from the executive branch on the scene. I talked to Nordlander's Special Assistant. It seems that Deputy Secretary Falk was told to stay over, just to keep an open ear, but I had Hickam Field send a courier around to his hotel and he was told that Falk got out of there right after Nordlander. On a company plane." Gottlieb said this with relish. Like most of the people on the President's immediate staff, he had neither affection nor respect for the Energy Secretary and his arrogant, expensive subordinates.

"Are you sayin' that we have nobody out there? Nobody! We got this big honcho from a country we buy $25 billion worth of oil from a year sittin' out there in Honolulu, which, unless I am incorrect, *is* a state of the union, and our man is off fartin' around in some oil company plane?"

"That's the way it appears, sir."

There was a dangerous silence on the President's end.

"When Mr. Falk turns up," he said calmly after a moment, "I b'lieve I'd like to visit with him. I'll visit with Nordlander after our meeting. Anything else?"

"Well, sir, as I was saying, Dinwiddie called *me* before his own paper. I think we owe it to him to give the *Post* what he gave us. Hickam's putting a copy of the announcement on the telecopier. It should be coming in downstairs anytime now. We could also send that over to them."

"I'll take care of the *Post*, Marvin. I'll see you in the office."

After hanging up on Gottlieb, the President thought for a minute. What was it that Gottlieb had said about "secret meetings"? Was somebody trying an end run? He'd have their ass. Darn it, he wished Ermabelle were here but she was down with her mother in Pass Christian. There was a lot of figurin' to be done, and she was the best and most reliable when it came to that. He punched the button for the White House operator. "Get Miz Baxter for me, honey."

The phone buzzed back within a minute. His wife.

"Listen, honey, I think you better hurry on home. How's Momma? Good. Well, tell you what, I'll send a plane for you tomorrow. Fine." He explained what he thought had happened. From her voice, he could tell she was as pleased and excited as he was.

He put on his half glasses and read a list of a half-dozen phone numbers which was taped to the console; the list was in his own writing.

He dialed on his private line.

A sleepy voice answered. Baxter put some honeysuckle in his tone.

"Evenin', Sally darlin'. How you? Wonderful. Ben there?"

That was one thing Fulger Baxter really liked about his job. No matter what the hour or the weather, the sound of his voice produced instant respect and instant wakefulness.

The news was also borne into the heart of the oil company over the telephone.

The sprawling ranchhouse on the edge of Packer Lake, an hour's drive from Midland, was dark and sleeping at two in the morning. As was the normal practice, all the telephones had been silenced except the hotline in the large guest bedroom occupied by ex-Senator Dunstable's two personal aides.

That phone had rung twenty minutes before. Now, after

a brief conversation, one of the two men in the room was sitting on the edge of his bed in his underwear looking cross and anxious.

"I suppose *I* have to tell him. You're senior and you're overseas and defense, and *this* is national and energy," he said to his colleague.

"Wrong," said the other man. *"This* is the election. *Was* the election, to be absolutely correct." That silenced them both for a while. Not three weeks earlier they had gloated and stomped in celebration. As *The New Republic* had said:

After two years of sulking in his tent like Achilles, after leaving the Democratic Party and declaring himself an Independent, the hour of vindication is at hand for Herndon Dunstable. His organized, expensive yet nevertheless impressive write-in plurality in the New Hampshire Republican primary has perfectly positioned him to command a draft by the party at its convention this summer, a draft he will surely accept, since it offers a candidacy this November against an incumbent president who seems mortally weakened by his own ineptitude and the force of circumstances.

"Well, never leave undone..." said the younger man finally. He wrapped a terrycloth robe around himself and padded down the dark hall to where Herndon Dunstable, ex-senator, ex-Deputy Secretary of Defense for Air, ex-senior partner of Burbank, Scuggins, Gresham, and Dunstable, the biggest law firm in Midland, and now the front-running prospect for the Republican presidential nomination, slept among rose-winged dreams of his inauguration.

The young aide knocked on Dunstable's door. Elizabeth Dunstable had her own suite at the other end of the house, so he had no need for elaborate caution. There was no answer so he opened the door and turned on the light. "Senator..."

Herndon Dunstable awoke like a disturbed rattler. His hand flew under his pillow and reappeared with a large, glinting revolver. "Jus' you hold it right there, boy." It was all reflexive; Dunstable wasn't yet fully awake.

The aide waited until the ex-senator got a grip on consciousness.

"Uh, Senator, there've been some developments. Colonel Grew just called. You remember, he was with you at the DOD. He's chief air officer at Hickam. Well, he just called from Honolulu. He thought you better know." He recited the news in a flat, factual way.

Dunstable got out of bed. He liked to think on his feet. He was a big man, a perfect picture politician. With his hands he brushed his hair back in gray, wavy wings over his ears. Bright blue eyes squinted over a mouth like an east Texas snapping turtle.

"Bull*shi-it!*" he said. Then he brightened. "Ted, who do we know over there in the Kingdom? What'll it cost to get them to change their minds?" It was a foolish thought and Dunstable and the young man knew it.

"That cussed Baxter," he said next. "Suppose he put the old voodoo on me? They say those Cajuns have strange powers."

Ted felt sorry for the Old Man he worshipped. Damnit, just two nights before, five hundred fat cats had crowded the ballroom of a River Oaks mansion in Houston and signed up for $498,000 in campaign pledges. That was batting a thousand. Now Dunstable's dream lay broken like a hammered piggybank.

Whatever the weather, the ex-senator was tough and practical.

"So, boys," he said, "life is life. Back to the drawing board. After all, I'll only be sixty-six the next time around. No point in going out there and getting whomped by Fulger Baxter's new prosperity. I'll bet he's got those Madison Avenue hippies writing copy already. The important thing is not to lose control of the party. We got to find us a horse: proud and good-looking, but slow and gentle enough for us to ride. Go get Joe Bob and a bottle of bourbon whiskey and let's us get to work."

He shrugged into a bathrobe and went off to tell his wife that it would be another four years before she'd get to redecorate the White House.

Allied Petrex maintained a dove-shooting lodge some seven hundred miles southeast of the Dunstable ranch, near McAllen, just across the Rio Grande from Mexico. The place was kept for the use of Petrex's directors, executives, and honored customers and guests. Rebo Beauderon had taken a small group down there for a little early shooting.

The Petrex chairman was installed in cabin three. He was being vigorously fellated by a thirteen-year-old Mexican prostitute from Reynosa when his telephone rang.

(248)

It was his executive vice president for marketing. "Hey, Rebo, guess what?" He sounded excited. Beauderon pushed the child's head away and got down to business.

"Boomer just called from Hawaii." Boomer was the chairman of Kaanipali Mortgage and Title and a director of Petrex. Beauderon had put him on the Petrex board when it looked as if there might be something geologically interesting on the island of Maui.

"Rebo, you ain't goin' to believe this! The fuckin' Kingdom just cut the price of crude! No shit! Ten dollars a barrel, startin' the first of next year. Yeh, the Minister hisself! He made the announcement personally. Fred just saw it on TV. You know he never sleeps. No doubt about it. I checked it on the radio. No, nothing from Washington yet. I called Selser, you know, number two at the API; no, hell, number one's over in the Middle East somewhere. Anyway, Selser says it's true. He heard it on TV too. He checked and says the Washington papers have got the story now. Ten dollars a barrel! Rebo—how about that!"

"Hot-doodley-doo," shouted Beauderon. He started making plans, speaking rapidly into the telephone.

While he talked, he gestured the little girl away. "Take a hundred dollars, *cientos,*" he said in Spanish, pointing to his pants with his hand over the receiver. *"Vamos,* honey." He was feeling munificent, very imperial. She crept out the door. Her uncle was waiting in a pickup truck outside; but she had two sisters and a cousin working in three other cabins so she curled up on the truckbed to catch a nap.

Rebo had a thought. "How many Arabs we got working for us?" he asked.

"I don't know. Two, three hundred, maybe."

"Listen," said Rebo Beauderon. "Give them all a 30 percent raise.

"From now on," he added grandly, "in this company, niggers is niggers and Messicans is Messicans, but Arabs is *folks!*"

20 Harrison and Devon had invited Barney to spend the Easter weekend with them in Lenox. Barney had brought a girl with him, a big red-headed blossom who successfully peddled a combination of municipal bonds and a behind as sublimely rounded as the Berkshire foothills. Barney's wife was deep into self-realization programs and had gone off to a three-day interreligious EST session at Grossinger's, which Barney considered sufficient to abrogate his customarily strict territorial limitation on adultery.

They had all driven up Thursday evening, stopping at the Red Lion Inn in Stockbridge for dinner. Afterward, safely in the cottage, with a fire to cut the chill, they'd stayed up until three, drinking red wine and sampling some new miracles that Barney's unlicensed pharmacist had provided. They had laughed a lot; Barney had never been funnier, especially with a complicated story involving himself, a Knoxville housewife, a yardman, and two dogs.

"Too much, Barney," Devon had giggled. Harrison in his haze had leaned over to kiss her. Relaxed, she seemed radiant. She hugged him back.

The next morning, Good Friday, Harrison got up early with a buzzing head and went into Lenox for the morning papers and the rudiments of breakfast. The early *Boston Globe* and the city edition of the *New York Times* had nothing much to offer: street violence in Kuala Lumpur; conflict on the Boston City Council over a bond issue; Mayor Koch attacking Con Edison on a rate application. The market had closed for the long weekend at 848 on the Dow, down 1.68 on 24 million shares. Magic Johnson had led the Lakers to an easy win in the NBA playoffs. Jim Rice had hit two out for the Red Sox in an exhibition game in Sarasota. A famous actor had died.

Barney and the redhead didn't appear until eleven. Devon was still asleep. Harrison made an omelet. He had Mozart's G Minor Quintet on the stereo, music suitable for a morning like this; the sun was bright on the early buds on the tree-branches.

At a quarter to twelve Devon came downstairs. She looked great.

"Barney, what is that stuff you gave me last night? No hangover—and I must have drunk a gallon of the Beaujolais." Barney grinned.

She didn't want any breakfast, so Harrison proposed a walk before lunch.

They took a leisurely forty-minute meander down the hill and across the meadows of Tanglewood. The empty shed where the orchestra would play in the summer was skull-white in the sun.

"You've got to come back here this July, Barney," Harrison said. "We'll bring some wine and a picnic and lie out here on the lawn and get stoned to Debussy. Nothing finer."

When they got back to the house, the phone was ringing. Harrison ran ahead to get it. It was for Barney.

"Sorry, Dave. I left my number on the answering machine in case Melissa decided to run off with Werner Erhard." Barney took the phone.

His face narrowed, then broke into a beam. "No shit." He shouted the words. "Sure. I'll be there. Yeh, between ten and eleven."

He hung up.

"You're not going to believe this. The Arabs have cut, *cut*, the price of crude. Apparently it came over the tube early this morning. It's in the early editions of the *Post* and all over the radio and TV!"

He looked at Harrison. Harrison's expression didn't change.

He went over to the stereo and switched to FM. A little fiddling with the tuner and he homed in on a news broadcast.

"...major change in the economic circumstances in the world. President Baxter has been conferring with his cabinet all day. He is expected to make a statement shortly. Reaction in all Western capitals is jubilant. Let's go to our correspondent in Paris."

Another voice took over, static-blurred. "The scene here outside the Elysée Palace is pandemonium. The news reached President Giscard at 8:32 this morning, as he was meeting with his deputies to discuss a further devaluation of the franc. France buys nearly 40 percent of its crude oil from the Kingdom. It is estimated that this action may place the French balance of payments in the positive column. The president has already telephoned President Baxter to congratulate him on the greatest feat of statesmanship since Talleyrand rearranged Europe after Waterloo."

A moment later: "Here, outside Buckingham Palace, the crowds are as turbulent as they were when Winston Churchill stood at the King's right hand on V-E Day. They are waiting for Her Majesty to come out to them. We understand from a well placed palace source that she has spoken on the telephone to President Baxter and has congratulated him on the greatest act of diplomacy since Lord Castlereagh redrew the map of Europe at the Congress of Vienna."

And later: "Herr Chancellor Schmidt has issued the following communiqué: 'Not since Metternich altered the European balance of power in 1815 has a Western statesman accomplished so extraordinary a feat of personal persuasion as has President Baxter. Our thanks and congratulations go out to him.' Chancellor Schmidt is personally meeting with representatives of the major German banks and of German industry to assess the situation."

And so it went. Tokyo. Canberra. Ottawa. In Rome, the Pope was on the balcony of his apartment; there were a quarter of a million people in St. Peter's Square.

In Dallas a mob had borne the Kingdom's consul in triumph the entire length of Turtle Creek Boulevard.

Barney looked at Harrison. "Dave, I've got to get back to New York. Monday's going to be a riot. That was my clerk. Our chairman's already had fifteen calls, *big* calls, from big clients. Shit, the president of the fucking Equitable called him personally at eight this morning with an order."

Barney went upstairs. When he came back, he had a small black box, about the size of a pocket calculator, in his hand. He punched out a number on the phone, listened for an instant, then held his black box to the receiver and pressed another button. Harrison heard a distant, high signal. Barney had a pencil and a pad with him. He listened, scribbling as fast as he could make his hand move.

When he hung up he looked disbelievingly at his pad.

"Holy shit, I've got orders for 500,000 shares here—and the tape on my answering machine ran out. Every one a market order. Listen to these. A hundred thousand IBM. That's six fucking million dollars. Fifty thousand Exxon. Ninety thousand GM. Fifty thousand Superior Oil. *Seven million* bucks for that one alone! Jesus, give me a drink!"

For a man who had nearly $5 billion invested in the Market, Harrison thought himself splendidly composed. "I've got a bottle of champagne in the refrigerator. It sounds to me as if a celebration is in order. Then we'll have lunch."

Devon said nothing, but she squeezed his hand as he passed her to go into the kitchen.

Barney took him aside by the refrigerator. "Listen, Dave, how can I get to New York? There's a lifetime in commissions for me, even at negotiated rates—and I'll promise you they won't be negotiating, they want stock! You and Devon have got a nice weekend coming up, but I've got to get back. Is there a bus, a plane I can charter? Christ, after Monday, I can retire."

"When do you have to be at the office?"

"The game plan seems to be that we'll batch all the orders tonight and meet downtown Sunday morning to sort it out. The clerks are coming in today to put the stuff in the computer. Thank God for those fucking machines!"

Amen, thought Harrison.

"OK, Barney, why don't we do it this way? Relax. Call your clerk. He can get a key from your doorman and change the answer-phone tape, and refer calls to the office. You've got a big machine there, don't you?"

Barney thought for a moment. Ten years of slow machines had diluted his drive. He believed that Harrison would rather take a romantic walk in the country than make a million dollars; but this was *his*, Barney's million dollars in commissions. He took another gulp of champagne. On a light breakfast it got back to the night before and made his head whirl.

"We'll drive down tomorrow after lunch," Harrison reassured him.

The big redhead looked lasciviously at Barney. She had done a lot of municipal bond business on her back; now, with a tigerish instinctive sense of self-preservation, she sensed that the old bond world had just died. Time to get into a new end of the securities game.

"C'mon Barney, David's right. Let's enjoy the day. We'll hit the road tomorrow. Early." She crossed to Barney and put her arms around his neck. "C'mon, sweetheart."

"Oh shit, I'm an easy lay. Let's go find some caviar. And some more champagne." Barney laughed.

Later, Devon and Harrison agreed that the promise of prosperity became Barney as a lover. The little cottage positively shook. Judging from the noise, the redhead showed a healthy level of enthusiasm for her new commitment to equities.

Like Barney, the Old Trader had also felt the heat of new business.

Having been recently separated, he was a target for all the divorced ladies in East Hampton: women with three children, not enough money, and messy, rented houses on the beach. Thursday night he'd set off on a round of Easter cocktail parties with his lawyer's imprecations to be circumspect ringing in his ears. The Old Trader loved his money. His lawyer wanted him to keep it.

"Keep your nose clean, Ben," his attorney had told him

after reviewing the fifteenth draft of the separation agreement. "Fool around and she'll cut your nuts off."

When the phone rang, he thought that it was the alarm clock and that it was time to go to work. He reached for it, remembering slowly that it was a holiday.

Drunk as he'd been the night before, he thought he'd made it home clean. He unstuck his eyebrows and saw the sun in the viridian branches outside the dormer window of the house he'd won in the early negotiations with his estranged wife. The birds in the oak tree were making more noise than the goddamn Philharmonic. He could vaguely hear the rabble-some sound of his two teenage boys having breakfast downstairs.

The ringing stopped. Someone elsewhere in the house had answered.

"Hi, honey," said a voice next to him. He walked his hand across the sheets. Skin there. Mature skin, his fingering told him. Quite old skin, really.

"Hey, Dad," said another voice from the bedroom door.

"Don't come in," he croaked, "I'm sick."

"It's your partner on the phone, Dad," said his son from around the corner ell. "He says he has to talk to you. Big night, huh, Dad?"

"OK, OK. You and Jock go over to the club, huh. I'll see you there. OK? Maybe we'll play tennis later, OK?" He could barely make his voice work. What in Christ had he drunk?

He picked up the telephone, dropping it twice before he finally maneuvered it to his ear.

"Hey, Ben, how you doing? Beautiful day, huh?" His partner's cheery voice was like a scalpel. The sonuvabitch had probably jogged ten miles already. Christ, he hated joggers.

"Figured you haven't heard the news yet. We get the papers in Cedarhurst early."

Fuck you, thought the Old Trader. Fuck you and your socially ambitious wife and your awful, smart kids and your mortgage and your gourmet cooking and all the rest of your goddamn stupid upwardly mobile life.

"What news, Irving?"

"Don't you watch *Today?*"

Thank Christ, thought the Trader. He was afraid they were going to pay him a surprise visit. Want to go to Maidstone. He started. There was a veiny, blotched hand in his crotch. It wasn't his own.

(254)

"No, Irving, it's a holiday. It's Good Friday. No, I *haven't* seen *Today*."

"Well rise and shine, then, Trader. The millennium is here. The Arabs chopped the price of oil to ten bucks a barrel. You can guess what that means. I already had a call from Merrill. They've got 20,000 Lockheed to buy and we've got nothing on the book."

"Cut that out," the Trader whispered, removing the invading hand. He waved his own hand in the air, to chase the cobwebs.

"So what should I do, Irving? Call Burbank? Ask Lockheed to print up some new stock?"

"No shit, Trader, this is serious. You better get your ass in here early tomorrow. We're going to have a riot on Monday. I've been on the phone since six-thirty. Paine Webber's called in all their back office; Hutton too. Merrill Lynch is on red alert. The Governors of the Exchange are supposed to be meeting tonight. I've got our people coming in at nine tomorrow. I had a call from Western Union. The telex is jammed. Probably out of paper."

The hand was back; the Trader felt things happening to himself down there. It didn't feel too bad.

"Look, Irving, there's nothing we can do except wait and try to match it up. I sense your urgency, goddamn it! Get the clerks in to pair it up. Overtime. I'll be there Sunday morning, for sure. Shit, today and tomorrow it'll just be running in circles." The hand in his groin was insistent.

"As you will, Trader. They say they're gonna open the Floor Monday come hell or high water. See you Sunday. Hey, Trader, you know something? We're gonna get rich again!"

The Trader hung up. He turned to the woman in his bed. Looking at her, he thought, Christ, when you got old, it happened awfully quickly. The hot sun beat through the window. The house was quiet. He closed his eyes, trying to shut out the sight of his bedmate, and shifted on the bed. There was a remote possibility he could hump himself out of his hangover.

On the way back to New York, Harrison and his party pulled into the Old Drovers Inn for lunch. He'd called ahead, but there was still a wait. They sat and had a drink in the bar. A television set was running. Harrison recognized the severe, professorial features of the Energy Secretary.

The moderator was talking.

"Mr. Secretary, the announcement in Hawaii appears to have caught the entire world by surprise, but I must say you seem very calm. Would you care to comment?"

Nordlander's lips pursed around the ever-present cough-drop.

"Well, Larry, obviously this administration has been working for a long time to find an equitable resolution to the problems posed by the energy situation. I'm afraid that's all I can say now."

"Bullshit," said Barney. He asked the waitress to change the channel.

On ABC, Howard K. Smith was interrogating the Secretary of State.

"Mr. Secretary, in this moment of national elation, some people are asking: 'What is the price of this new accommodation?' I understand Mr. Begin has personally telephoned the White House for reassurance?"

The Secretary tried to appear knowledgeable in his heavy Slavic way, but could not comment in detail.

President Baxter sat on the edge of a daybed in his wife's sitting room in the White House, holding Ermabelle's hand while they watched the news shows on the five-screen television. A stack of praiseful cablegrams lay on the floor.

She turned and gave him a hug.

"You old silly, why didn't you tell me you were up to this? Momma will be so proud."

In forty years of marriage, Fulger Baxter had never lied to his wife, not even the tiniest, whitest distortion.

He hesitated for an instant. "Well, love, there's just some things that're man's work."

Early in the afternoon Buster Ferdimend showed him a snap poll taken that morning in downtown Philadelphia. He was running 60 for/30 against/10 undecided. Three weeks ago, in the same districts, he'd run 38/55/7. He hugged her back and switched all five screens to CBS. The Jazz were ahead by 10 at halftime. He'd get to the bottom of this later.

The electronics technicians arrived at the Stock Exchange at five-thirty on Saturday afternoon. With the mayor's co-operation, Broadway and Wall and Broad streets had been closed off to permit the ten big tractor-trailers to close in on the Exchange building.

The president of the Exchange was there to meet them,

along with the president of the American Stock Exchange and the chief paid officer of the Securities Industry Association, which ran the over-the-counter market.

They huddled on the steps.

"What are you guessing for volume?" asked the Bunker Ramo man.

"I just don't know. We've talked to the member firms. Maybe 90 million shares. Maybe more. Another 20 million from these gentlemen of the American Stock Exchange. Is that right?" The other two nodded. They had notes and EDP estimates, but they meant nothing.

"Well, we'll try to fix it up. We can't do anything with the display on the Floor, of course. At that volume level the printout will be subliminal. But we may be able to work out something to give real-time reporting upstairs." He signaled the trailers to move in closer.

They dropped Barney and the redhead off at her apartment shortly after eight o'clock on Saturday night.

"I think I'll check the battlefield from here," said Barney. "Melissa tells me that Erhard has made $50 million out of this shit of his. He's probably been on the phone to his broker since Friday, so Melissa may be home."

He paused outside the car.

"Dave, you and Devon ought really to go downtown Monday. It's going to be a kick! I'll leave a couple of passes to the VIP Gallery at the Exchange in your name. It'll be the shits."

Saint Willoughby's dominated upper Madison Avenue in much the way the Chartres ruled its own plains and meadows. It was the richest church in the richest Episcopal diocese in the world, a white-collar temple of Capitalism. From the pulpit, the Reverend Jessica Knowlton, rector of Saint Willoughby's sensed that her audience was restless. The Easter congregation was larger than usual; all the last rows on the sides were filled. After the processional, with the choir singing Byrd's "Third Introit" more note-perfect than at King's College, she had watched approvingly from the altar as Leslie Merriman and the other ushers had rolled up the white carpet separating the rows of lily-edged pews.

Originally, she had planned to preach on II Philippians 14: *"Do all things without murmurings and disputings."* She knew her flock, however, and had perceived that the weekend's news would require a more apposite text.

(257)

"Today's lesson is from X Ecclesiastes 19: 'Money answereth all things.'" Looking down, she could see rows of open hymnbooks, behind which the male parishioners seemed to be intently active with pencils and pocket calculators, while their wives beamed up at her. Such a nice young girl to be a vicar, their faces said.

After the service, she stood on the steps. Almost the first out were the Chauncey DeFords. He had a chin like a late Hapsburg and a mind to match. Communion at Saint Willoughby's was the weekly highpoint of his life. He normally stopped to shrug and twitch and make small talk. This Sunday, Easter Sunday, he squeezed her hand briefly and trotted rapidly down the steps and made for a payphone on the corner. She saw that he had a piece of paper in his left hand; it looked like the torn-out page of a hymnal.

Devon and Harrison were walking arm-in-arm up Madison Avenue. They paused at a red light; across the street, Saint Willoughby's was emptying. There were three pay telephones on the opposite corner.

"What do you think that means?" asked Devon, pointing.

At each telephone was a small line of men. They looked like replicas of each other: undersized hard brown fedoras perched on fish-featured heads; gray flannel suits with the pants ending three inches above polished brown oxfords; club neckties.

"Gracious," said Harrison, who had been a Sunday-school pupil at Saint Willoughby's, "God must have dished out a tip."

"Let's eavesdrop."

She altered their route of march to pass close to the nearest phonestand. A man with a chin that lapped like waves down his front was talking in the loud voice of the semideaf.

"Bobby, listen, I *can* get a loan on Isabelle's silver. Buy me 500 Mobil tomorrow at the opening. *Please.*"

The Jazz won the second playoff game. Baxter was happy. Ermabelle went off to sign some letters. He sat in her sitting room absentmindedly watching a movie star shoot a kudu with a machine gun, when the phone buzzed. Gottlieb.

"Mr. President, the Secretary of State would like to see you. He's downstairs. Should I send him up?"

The President went back to his own sitting room.

The Secretary of State entered the room with the uneasiness of an immigrant looking for a job.

Along with Nordlander, Drzlag was the most visible figure of Baxter's cabinet. The Secretary of State was a small, chirpy man of obscure Serbian origins, with staccato, anxious, boastful movements and bright blond hair which flicked up from his round forehead in cheerful little sprouts. He bounced around the Washington cocktail circuit, ubiquitous and sprightly, chased jealously by the Energy Secretary, a tall clumsy Baltic type who seemed never to put a foot, political, social, or physical, right. The irreverent editor of a recondite Washington journal, noting the endless, fruitless competition between the two, had nicknamed them "Sylvester" and "Tweety" after the frustrated cartoon cat and the tiny elusive bird.

The President disliked Drzlag intensely—almost as much as he had come to dislike Washington itself. Known euphonically to the press as "Dishrag," the Secretary had been foisted on Baxter by his fellow CUNY professors; they had masterminded the New York primary for Baxter and he owed them one, which turned out to be Drzlag. Drzlag liked to bomb small nations. "Well, honey," Ermabelle had said, "be kind to the poor man. His people ain't never won a war."

"What's up, Tweety?" the President asked.

He knew that Drzlag hated the nickname, but he *did* look like the cartoon canary. Besides, he thought, who gave a diddle?

The Secretary flinched. "Mr. President," he said in his pinched, precise diction, "we've had a communiqué from Tel Aviv. In view of the Kingdom's announcement, the Knesset would like assurance that nothing has changed in terms of the longer term relations between us."

"Tweety," said the President, patiently, "don't be a pussy. Have you seen these polls? You anxious to go back to teaching the Treaty of Versailles to them nigger sophomores for $18,000 a year? We're goin' to be flexible for a while. You tell those good folks in Israel that we're watchin' and waitin'. Give 'em an evasive answer. Tell 'em to chase the hog and when his tail is straight, to give us another call."

At four o'clock on Monday, when the bell finally rang to end trading, the stock report display overlooking the Floor was still three hours late. Network news crews were stationed upstairs in the executive offices of the big brokerage firms.

At four-fifteen, CBS, which wouldn't hesitate to extrapolate the hour of the Second Coming from its computers, went on the air with a Merrill Lynch projection that volume had approximated 105 million shares. Over at Dow Jones, ABC countered with an inside projection that the Stock Average was up over 68 points. Desperate for ratings, NBC produced Irving Dorweiser, the investment guru of public broadcasting, who opined that the market was in an upward mode.

None of this mattered to the men on the Exchange.

In his two-and-a-half decades on the Floor, the Old Trader had acquired a reputation for a distinctive waggishness as great as his renown for piecing together complicated trades to his own grossly remunerative advantage. Certainly today had served the latter cause in spades; he calculated that he had turned a profit on the day of close to $600,000.

A celebration was in order. From his pocket he produced an Arab headdress and a pair of black plastic spectacle frames attached to an enormous, hooked false nose, which he now put on. Then he reached into each of his jacket pockets, where he had stored $200 in dollar bills, the fruit of his weekend backgammon and golf. He drew his hands out, and threw them upward, releasing the bills, straightening his arms until they extended high and prophetlike toward the ceiling of the vast trading room. As the bills fluttered about the trading post, he cried sonorously, mimicking the wail of a muezzin, "Praise be to Allah. His day has come!"

He jigged and danced in a circle. Then made a mock salaam on the floor. It was infectious. People came running across the Floor and surrounded him, hopping and prostrating themselves in rhythm with his prancing.

"Hallelujah!" A tornado of bills whirled around his head. "God be praised," he declaimed, dancing and bouncing. "Salaam, salaam, salaam! The Great Day ain't coming—it's *here.*" The crowd surrounding him threw more bills: ones, fives, fifties; they fluttered around him like a green penumbra. Everyone was around him now: other specialists; squad boys; even governors of the Exchange.

There was no stopping him now, with this audience.

"The Day of Salvation! The Great Green God of Money is risen! The Great Day! Money Day! Green Monday!" He sent his last handful of bills winging, but they were lost in the maelstrom of currency which swirled about the Floor. The crowd screamed its support.

First here and then there and then everywhere, the great

room filled with the skittery green glidings of a linesquall of bills. The chant was picked up. "Green Monday! Green Monday! Green Monday!" The Floor shook to the clapping of a thousand traders and clerks. "Green Monday! Green Monday!"

And the old Floor characters, the Pad Man, Dirty Bill, Twitches, who had thought they'd never see a day like this again in their lives, hopped and danced and cackled until it rang around the room like an oratorio: "Green Monday! Green Monday! Green Monday!"

III

PARADISE

21   And so the curtain rose on a time of general blessedness. Even the weather improved. Spring ended on cue and by Memorial Day the mornings bore a pleasant hint of lazy hot days to come.

The world at large staggered about in a condition of euphoric confusion. The opinion makers and the historians and pundits could cite endless acts of hostile aggression in analyzing the Kingdom's action. None could adduce an instance of what seemed absolutely benevolent aggression. Treaties of peace, declarations of war, mobilizations, riots, insurrections, and plots were suspended throughout the world like particles in water. Mankind was so confused by its great good luck that it sat on its hands and waited and basked in the light of the bright new day.

In the United States, the stock market was the immediate and evident beneficiary. Lines formed outside brokerage offices at sunrise. Prices and volume ascended riotously. On the Friday before the Memorial Day weekend anxious investors, not wishing to miss out on whatever good news the long holiday might bring, made the market bat .300 for the first time: the Dow Jones was up 150 on the day and trading volume shaded 150 million shares. The ticker tape was eight hours late. Brokers and their clerks worked into the weekend with glad hearts. The world was lullabied by the siren song of Wall Street.

Everything looked better, even though the bond market was a disaster. The big traders were delirious as common stock prices rose and swept away their heroic bond losses. Short-term Treasury yields declined in a month from 11% to 6%. There were soft spots. The price of gold declined to $200 and change, since the only buyers were jewelers and industrial users. The money market funds faced a liquidity crisis. Everyone wanted to convert back to paper. To stocks. In London, Sotheby's and Christie's announced the extension of their traditional summer sales into August to handle the onrush of pictures and furniture sent in for auction. A fine Cézanne still life made barely $500,000; the seller was willing to forgo a reserve in order to get cash to follow up on a tip on Ford.

As he had told Khafiq he would, Harrison kept RAID on the sidelines during those first few weeks of mainland euphoria. "We'll be able to get out twice as fast as we got in," he told Devon. "With this kind of volume, we could be finished in eight or nine weeks." Ernie fiddled RAID into a "sell" mode. Harrison decided he would pull the trigger when the Dow hit 1300. It was then 1135. He told Ernie to take a week off and took Devon to London to see the glories of an early English summer.

They dined with Khafiq in his garden. Khafiq was as resplendent as his table, on which a de Lamerie wine cistern reflected the hazy crimson of roses in the late-staying dusk.

"That's a wonderful piece," said Devon, touching the wine cooler.

"Isn't it, though?" beamed Khafiq. "I got it only last week—off that silly young ass Bimber Sumpton. His father's become a tax exile in Monte and the little fool's selling all the silver at Cholmondeley to buy shares. It seems young Sumpton's on to a good thing, prancing around on the cusp of the dukedom and peddling stocks to all his socially ambitious American friends. He tells me he's had a 'can't miss' tip on IBM. Fortunately, I've got all the IBM I need," Khafiq concluded.

Indeed you do, thought Harrison; 2,680,000 shares. IBM had closed the night before at $90. That worked out to $240,000,000. It was their largest position. Next came Kodak and Exxon. When Harrison had recognized this, he cursed himself in a halfway fashion; here he was running the greatest single investment operation in the world and he ended up doing just what the banks did.

"I hope young Bimber gets some more tips," Khafiq was saying. "He's got a couple of Restoration epergnes that would suit my dining table very well."

The time had come for them to start selling. When New York cabbies and the young British aristocracy started betting on stocks instead of baseball and horses, Harrison recognized that the pigs at the trough were in a feeding frenzy.

He looked at his dining companions. If Devon and Khafiq were in touch with each other, it wasn't apparent. Certainly Harrison didn't give the possibility thought. In the way of normal men leading straightforward lives in which danger was confined to the highway, he was unaware of the dark possibility of subterfuge; that was a matter for spy novels; he would never conceive of it as flesh and blood.

There was other interesting news in London. Desdemona Lyall-Marsh had left her husband for a much younger man, a Peruvian grandee who did something in the City. It was a year exactly since that weekend in the country. To Harrison, it seemed more like an episode from another incarnation.

He had planned to stay ten days. Devon was enjoying herself. She seemed to like his "man's London." One afternoon, however, they dropped in on Hamper and Knight, a Bond Street bookselling firm which had been formed by two of Harrison's old friends from Heywood Hill. Harrison helped himself to a stack of choice items they had put aside for him. As the parcel was being wrapped, John Hamper drew him aside, away from Devon's earshot; obviously he was about to retail a choice and indelicate tale of highest level depravity, quite possibly reaching into Downing Street itself. "I say," he hissed into Harrison's ear, "what do you think about Control Data? My broker thinks it's going to 100!"

It was definitely time to go back. Harrison booked on the first flight the next morning. He could call Ernie on arrival. It was time to leave the party.

"Can you imagine," he said to Devon over lunch at Wilton's, "John Hamper wanting to talk about stocks when he's just turned up the only known copy of the first edition of *The Wind in the Willows* in its original dust jacket. The world has gone mad!"

It occurred to him only in passing, as he dipped his forkful of plaice in the lemon butter, that it was all his fault.

In Washington, President Baxter moved quickly to consolidate his unexpected good fortune. A $10 ceiling on domestic oil was a price he could live with politically; it was a price the oil companies could manage to live with financially. The energy market was in a state of benign chaos. The average spot price for sweet crude was close to $15 a barrel, but the American people were convinced they were paying $10. When Mike Wallace attempted to prove otherwise, 27 million viewers switched channels. The dollar strengthened dramatically; hordes of happy travelers headed for Europe to take advantage of the forty-cent Swiss franc.

Dazzled by his fresh new halo, Baxter ignored Secretary Nordlander's urging for a full-dress study and moved quickly to implement immediate decontrol of oil and gas prices. Working quickly and efficiently in the rabbit warrens of Capitol Hill, Buster Ferdimend and Marvin Gottlieb got a decontrol bill out of Congress by mid-June, burying the objections and short-lived presidential prospects of young Senator Monohan.

The President remained puzzled by the cause of his windfall. Puzzled and isolated. Rumors to his advantage kept surfacing around the world. They strengthened his image as a statesman, an image which fit him like a borrowed suit, and his political grip. The *Paris Herald* had been tipped, source undisclosed, to the possibility of a mutual defense agreement with the Kingdom. This brought a top-level delegation of militant rabbis and big shots from the United Jewish Appeal and the Federation of Jewish Philanthropies screaming to the White House. The Jewish leaders of Wall Street declined to attend. Baxter ducked the meeting.

In San Francisco, someone in the retinue of the Arts Minister, on hand to open the big Islamic Exposition, let it out that the Kingdom was considering canceling its telecommunications deal with the Swedes and giving it instead to Western Electric. The angry contingent from Stockholm was advised unconsolingly in Dumar not to believe everything they read in the papers; in Washington, Fulger Baxter graciously accepted the homage of the president of AT&T and the Baxter Reelection Committee was pleased to bank a $100,000 campaign contribution from the Telecommunications Workers of America.

President Baxter enjoyed his dream world. To dig to the

bottom of things might produce a dangerous hole in the ground. Everything looked swell. He was pecan pie happy. Best to keep it this way. He made sure to include a nice bread-and-butter note when he sent the head of the National Arts Endowment off to Qu'nesh in Air Force One to deliver that fancy piece of carpet to the King.

Alrazi was also delighted with the way things were working out. Like the President, he thought it best to keep his secrets. Only the Minister, Khafiq, and he were in on the whole scheme. When Benjamin Masters flew in from Washington pleading for information and instructions, Alrazi pleaded ignorance. Assuming an expression of unconfident speculation, he advised Masters: "Well, Benjamin, as you know, His Majesty is increasingly keeping his own counsel and developing new avenues and new advisors. Obviously, his decision is based on issues within his purview and that of his advisors. We *are* a large family, you know."

He couldn't have orchestrated it more effectively. Ten days later, David Broder's lead in the *Washington Post* read: *"High-level sources have confirmed a growing rift between the family branches who dominate the decision-making process in Qu'nesh."* U.S. *News* carried a cover montage of Alrazi, an oil well, the King's two nephews, and the caption: THE OLD ORDER CHANGETH?

It suited Alrazi perfectly. The King never read anything but the Koran and, besides, he was preoccupied these days crooning over his new prayer rug. The two ambitious nephews had been sent off for six months to Kaiserslautern to observe the NATO war games.

Alrazi was content. He summoned his secretary and asked him to call France and have them ready the villa at Cap-Ferrat. Oh yes, and please have London advise Mrs. Fotheringill that his plane would be arriving in Nice on the evening of Thursday fortnight.

Ambassador John Jordan had retired to a contemplative life of mastiff breeding and memoir writing in Northern Virginia. Pasture wasn't half as bad a place to be as he'd expected. While he missed the sense of the world's pulse beating against his fingertips, he decidedly did not miss the petty jealousy of official Washington which had pursued him like a small, nasty dog through the corridors of power, finally hounding him from public life. His calendar, once broken down into minuscule fragments of time and space, now comprised a stretch of quiet, even days with his wife Margaret. An amiable, routine existence which reminded him of an animated Currier and Ives chromo: a fire in the grate; the dogs asleep beside his chair; Margaret knitting; a pipe, slippers, and Mark Twain to chuckle and nod over. A life of private and useful decency, out of sync perhaps with this hasty century, these rustling times, but a fair way to finish up at sixty-three, after forty years devoted to God and country.

Not that he didn't keep in touch. Every Thursday he drove across the Key Bridge and out Foxhall Road to a friend's house where he and a crew of other old-timers from State, CIA, and the press met for lunch. Twelve weeks a year he gave to his public persona: lectures and visitancies, which added comfortably to his pension and the income from his and Margaret's trust funds, and to Republican fund raisers around the country. He was a clever, articulate speaker who could enunciate basic principles in a manner which avoided simplicism yet could still be enthusiastically grasped by the least lettered audience. Forty years around the world had given him a storehouse of anecdotes. He could bring out the faithful and make the party cash register ring. He had built a deep foundation of loyalty within the party.

He and Margaret had just come in from a leisurely late afternoon stroll with the dogs and he was popping a can of beer when the phone rang. The voice on the other end boomed as if it didn't need the Bell system to bridge the distance.

"John? Herndon Dunstable here. Sure good to hear your voice again. Oh fine, fine. Listen. Me and a couple of my boys'd like to come up and visit with you. Got an idea. You bet. Wednesday? No, I think it's better if we come out to your place. Say about four, four-thirty. We'll be wheels up out of Midland 'bout ten. Say four-thirty. No, hell, we'll get a car. See you then, John. Love to Margaret."

Margaret Jordan came into the kitchen as her husband put down the phone.

"Guess who that was? Twenty guesses. Fifty. Give up? That was none other than the almighty Herndon Dunstable. He's coming up here Wednesday. Wants to see me."

"What on earth do you suppose he wants? He *is* such a vulgar man. So noisy."

"Probably wants to talk about a cabinet job. Some sort of

advisorship. After all, he can be the candidate, if he wants it. He *did* win New Hampshire. And as an Independent available for a draft. And even though he stayed out of Pennsylvania last month, the boy who won the primary just wants to be a favorite son troublemaker at the convention. Unfortunately, darling, even Dunstable hasn't got a chance in November. This oil price business has locked it up for Baxter. Funny, as well as I know those people in the Kingdom, I never would have guessed they'd have done anything to help Fulger Baxter. They don't like him and don't trust him. He must have really pulled some rabbits out that idiotic-looking Stetson of his."

He took a sip of the beer. It was frosty. The weather was starting to get summertime sticky. He put his arm around his wife as they went out on the porch. There was a faint low haze on the hills.

"Oh well," he said, "it can't hurt to hear old Herndon out. If you don't think you can bear the noise, why not drive over to Richmond to see your brother?"

Life was not ecstatic everywhere in the world, however. In Foggy Bottom the atmosphere in the office of the Secretary of State was morbid. In the first place, there had been a renaissance on the Situation Room bulletin board of those awful Serbian jokes that had scarred Drzlag's early months as Secretary.

More important, Secretary Drzlag had been obliged to suspend "Operation Curry," the planned invasion of the Kingdom which he had secretly been negotiating with his opposite number in New Delhi. The Indians were furious and were threatening to complain to the President. Drzlag had never informed the President of his "Curry" caper. He wanted to present Baxter with a *fait accompli* that would make his predecessor's unauthorized incursion into Cambodia look like peanuts. Now Drzlag was scrambling to cover his tracks. "Excrement!" he swore to himself in Croatian. If he'd been able to swing "Curry," it would have been good for a million-dollar book deal and a lifetime network contract.

He was still cursing when he climbed into his limousine to go to the White House. He had to talk to the President about this Libyan business which the CIA had surfaced only an hour before.

The big Alfa-Romeo made its way slowly along the crowded

Tripoli waterfront. As it turned away from the port, to climb into the hills toward the Presidential Palace, the Italian ambassador saw with no surprise that there was considerable activity down at the military docks. A number of large hovercraft had evidently moved into position early that afternoon and were loading what looked like military stores.

The ambassador was in an excellent mood. He'd had a fine nap after a marvelous *capellini alle quattro formaggi* prepared by the chef he'd stolen from the Ristorante Al Cantunzein in Bologna. The morning mail had brought a letter from his banker in Lugano—like most wealthy Italians, he had moved his money to Switzerland—informing him that his inheritance from his father, who had been Mussolini's Minister of Petroleum, had increased by 40 percent in the last month. Mainly, however, he was positively relishing the message which the Quirinal had directed him to deliver to Colonel Qaddafi.

A uniformed aide led the ambassador down muraled halls, chipped souvenirs of the final Roman Empire, and announced him.

Qaddafi came around the desk and shook his hand. The ambassador bowed deeply and stylishly. He observed that the Colonel was dressed for battle: revolver on his hip; parachute boots; a helmet lay on a sidetable. A street Arab dressed up like General Patton.

"Excellency, I have just finished decoding a message from the Foreign Ministry. They have instructed me to deliver it verbatim and to assure you that Rome is acting without prejudice as a conduit between two of our great friends and allies, Libya and the United States, who unfortunately do not maintain cordial diplomatic relations.

"President Baxter sends his greetings. He begs to inform Colonel Qaddafi that United States intelligence sources, including satellite transmissions, have detected concentrations of military and transport matériel and apparatus in Tripoli port and at Bizerte. Documents and orders of battle which have been acquired suggest that possible overt military action may be contemplated against a Persian Gulf state. This has been corroborated by covert intelligence in Dumar and Qu'nesh. Names and locations have been furnished to Royal Intelligence in Dumar and the President believes any incipient revolutionary or insurrectionist elements have been effectively dispersed.

"The President knows that Colonel Qaddafi shares the

wish of the United States to maintain peace and stability in the Middle East. He believes that it would be in the best interest of all concerned, lest the intention of Libyan maneuvers now under way be widely misinterpreted, that these operations be terminated and that military elements massing in Tripoli and Benghazi be stood down.

"The President wishes to advise, with a sense of deep mutual respect, that the departure of any naval or air transport units from the staging areas will be regarded gravely by the United States. He wishes to advise you that he has placed two wings of F-5 tactical fighter-bombers on standby alert. These will commence the immediate destruction of Tripoli on his orders. Only advanced conventional armaments will be employed. As this will necessitate the establishment of an interim Libyan government, he intends to furnish former Emperor Bokassa I, now in exile in the Ivory Coast, sufficient military advisory personnel and matériel to occupy and to maintain provisional order in your country until normal political conditions are restored. President Baxter sends his compliments."

The ambassador finished reading. He extracted an envelope with an elaborate wax seal from his pocket.

"A copy for you, Excellency. Is there any reply?"

Qaddafi said nothing. The ambassador thought he detected a trace of foam at the corner of the president's mouth. He bowed deeply and retired from the Colonel's presence. As he passed from the anteroom, a growl and then a yelp of pain came from the Colonel's office. Aides rushed in. In his rage, the president of Libya had bitten his desk and broken off two of the teeth which were his greatest pride.

President Baxter flew to Houston to speak to the annual convention of the American Medical Association. As he came down the steps of Air Force One, parked among the flock of corporate jets like a mother hen among its chicks, a roar went up. Even Buster was taken aback. "Godawmighty, Mr. President, there must be 20,000 people out there." Ermabelle squeezed his arm. They were shouting and waving, calling his name and beating the air with the Texas flag. The University of Houston marching band was blaring *Hail to the Chief*. Batons twinkled in the sky while the crowd screamed and waved. At the foot of the ladder stood the governor, beaming, and behind him, ten-gallon hat in hand, stood Herndon Dunstable.

The Gulf Freeway had been closed for the presidential motorcade and so the first ten miles were traveled quickly, in relative calm. But when they turned off through downtown Houston and out Westheimer toward the Galleria, where Baxter would be lunching, before going on to the Convention Center for his speech, the streets were lined three deep. It would later be estimated that over a million people had massed along the route; Houstonians, mostly, but thousands of country folk too, who had come up to town just as nearly two thousand years earlier, other such people had thronged the cities of Galilee to see another redeemer. The comparison was not lost on the President as he soaked up the adulation.

On television, the correspondent for a major network described it as "a great evangelical tent meeting dedicated to Mammon." He was sharply rebuked by the chairman of the network, whose tax-avoidance drilling program had just tripled in value.

The roaring, loving mob filled Fulger Baxter with an overpowering sense of pride, so much that in his excitement he quite overlooked the mystery of it all.

That same morning, Ernie tapped out the message which reversed RAID. The actual sales transaction took place in the huge CDC computers which Merrill Lynch was now using to match orders on a twenty-four-hour basis. At 10:03:15 the Rainier Bank confirmed the sale of 900 Lockheed at 37¼, the shares bought almost exactly nine months before at 20½. A minute later the cash proceeds from the sale were rippling through the insomniac wires of the world financial network on their way to Macao.

Ernie telephoned the details to Harrison in New York.

"Nice normal pregnancy, boss. Baby's almost twice the size it was when conceived."

22 The view from the seventeenth tee was breathtaking. Even Alex Camran, who was, as usual, impatient with his deserts, had to agree. After a terrifying hundred yards of sand, thorny scrub, and hedge, the raw land became an emerald fairway which ran down to the edge of a white-beached bay, the first of a series of sapphire cuts which stretched east along the Peconic bluffs to the horizon.

"I think it's the most wonderful vista in golf," said one of the men in the foursome. "Better for my dough than the eighth and ninth at Pebble Beach."

"I believe you're up, sir," said Camran.

The fat man waddled between the tee markers and with some difficulty got his peg into the ground. He was an old friend of Rube Bowen's, an ex-Certified officer who had retired to the bucolic life of an Ohio country banker. He fussed about the ball for a minute, making stiff uncertain waggles, until with a painful whoomphing expulsion of breath he managed to hurl the club around the orb of his belly. The toe of the driver caught a reasonable fraction of the ball and sent it softly into the air in a banking climb until, like a shot bird, it fell from its apogee and plopped softly onto the fairway, well to the right of the trouble and about a hundred and fifty yards from the tee.

"Nice shot, partner," said Camran. Both cheeks on this one, he thought, setting his feet. Par in for a nice little seventy-five. He took a swing so long and lazy that it seemed to last a full minute. The ball busted off the face of the club, appeared to hang in the afternoon sunlight for about twelve hours, and finally stopped rolling two hundred sixty yards from where Camran stood holding the pose of his follow-through. Just a little bump wedge to the green, he preened.

There were eight foursomes in Reuben Bowen's annual outing at the Hamptonian Golf Links. The "Fly In," they called it at the bank. The business jets had started arriving early that morning in a mighty display of corporate peer group pressure. Everyone brought his Number One airplane. Rebo Beauderon, whom the Certified president was personally courting back to the bank after the falling out with Merriman, had shown up in a DC-9 that had been tastefully redecorated in chintz by Marco Buasso. There were five Gulfstream IIs, a bunch of smaller stuff, and, trumping everyone's symbolic ace, the chairman of World American Airlines had contrived the use for the two-day outing of the prototype Boeing 767 of which his airline had just ordered fifteen copies—to the tune of $3 billion.

At lunch, everyone agreed it was just like the old days. Fat, rich, and good. Beauderon licked the last of the mustard mayonnaise from his lips and surveyed the table over a small hill of lobster carcasses. "Rube, old buddy," he shouted at Bowen, "I'm as happy as a pig in shit!"

Alex Camran was not happy at the outcry. If he was

Bowen's assistant, he was also the only working two-hand-icap golfer in the national division, which had placed him in jeopardy for the dreaded "gofer" assignment. Most of the other young officers at Certified would have jumped at the task. You got to mingle with the heavy hitters, give top management your opinions as to the bank's shortcomings, and generally attract career-shaping notice. That was the theory.

Camran didn't see it that way.

"Let me tell you what it's about. The 'gofer' sleeps in the same motel with the pilots; works out the pairings; plays golf with the worst golfers in the group and fills in at bridge; passes out the golf balls with the bank logo; arranges for the taxis; and otherwise does about a hundred things which make him out to be 'help.' And I don't like to be 'help.'" He pronounced it "hep."

Dinner was mortifying. Alex had to get on his feet and announce the next day's pairings and that afternoon's results and divvy up the day money. Just like some clerk. After dinner, though, Rebo Beauderon had come over to Camran and thrown his arm heavily across the younger man's shoulders. Beauderon was pretty drunk, Alex could see, but with the Petrex business on the line, politeness required at least the appearance of attentiveness.

"Say, boy," Beauderon's voice was like a muffled drum, "is my ears lyin' to me or did I catch a little Texas harmony in that voice of yourn?"

Inwardly shamed, Alex admitted he'd been born in Dallas. He tried to phrase it to suggest it was some sort of accident, not to be held against him.

"Well boy, I get your point. Dallas ain't Houston, but then *nothin'* is. You got to come down and see my towers! I'm goin' tell old Rube to send you down for a couple of weeks. Get to know my people. Tell you sumpin'," Beauderon became hushedly conspiratorial, "we find it tough to get anything done with these chickenshit New York smartasses. We're down there to do business, not sit around wtih our peters in our hands. Y'all come on down. We Texas boys can do some good together."

Rebo shambled off to find Bowen. Alex's face wore the expression of a man sentenced to Devil's Island.

He needed a drink. He wasn't about to buy the idea that a Texas accent might be more useful and valuable than his cherished Wharton M.B.A.

His partner of the afternoon was at the bar. He was a

jolly, calm man, unembarrassed by his fat stomach and his lousy golf. He was talking with another man whom Alex knew to be the head of the Lumbermans bank out in Portland. Both former Certified bankers for whom the New York pace had gotten too intense and competitive and who had seized on the opportunity to swim among smaller fish. Old friends and colleagues of Bowen.

Camran joined them.

"Well, Alex," said the Ohio banker, "you certainly play a wonderful game of golf. This young man," he turned to the Portland banker, "can hit a golf ball about ten miles. What'd you have today, Alex, seventy-four, was it?"

Camran found this kind of admiration embarrassing. Nodding his head and mumbling, he tried to deflect the conversation.

"How's business these days? This oil thing must have made an enormous difference out your way. I know our people tell us they're starting to see some good loan demand from industry."

"Hell, Alex, it's been good across the board. Sam'll tell you the same thing about Oregon. Loan demand's good, sure. And the service business has been great, even before this. We've been getting some heavy master trust business farmed out to us. It's about time some of that got out of New York, with all due respect. Sam here's had the same thing. Good business. Pays fast and pays well."

"What sort of master trust business?" A bell was ringing somewhere in Camran's mind.

"Oh, small stuff by your standards. Five, maybe 10 million for a bank our size. Custody and bookkeeping. Fast in, fast out. Everything on the wire, but we get a nice fee and a little overnight money to play with."

"Same with us." It was the Portland banker. "Hell, we've got an account in common. What's it called, Jim? Guardian something or other. We've handled pretty close to $20 million for them. Just as Jim says. Good, fast pay and a little float to work with. Of course, we're just seeing bits and pieces. My guess is this Guardian deal could run a few hundred million around the country. Anyway, I learned years ago, when you've got a good customer who likes his privacy, *you* leave him alone and *he* won't leave you."

Back in his motel room on the Montauk highway, Alex sulked in the dark. He was trying to make the connection.

Lord, if there were hundred-million-dollar MTs around and Certified wasn't getting its share, that was unendurable! This conversation with the two bankers had reminded him of something. What? He pushed his mind around, lifting its corners, looking under its cushions. Just before sleep he got it. It seemed at the time disappointingly trivial after all the effort he'd made to dredge it up. Buck. His brother. Dallas. Momma's funeral. Bucky'd said something about master trusts, something about El Paso. He was still turning it in his mind when he drifted off.

Monday morning, Alex Camran waited until Bowen had cleared his desk. They both had come in at seven-thirty. There wouldn't be any serious telephoning until nine although the overseas boys, Merriman's and Mismer's crowd, would have been burning up the wires. The staff group meeting was at ten.

He stuck his head in Bowen's office. "That was a nice party, sir."

"It sure was, Al, and mostly thanks to you. Great job on the arrangements. And you sure made a hit with Rebo Beauderon. How about that old fart, anyway? Making a hole-in-one on four? Shit, he normally couldn't hit a cow in the ass with a peck of salt! Anyway, he wants you to get involved on the Petrex account. It may just be we can undo all the screwing up of those assholes on fifty-two!"

"Well sir, I think that would be interesting. Something has come up which I think we ought to look into." He explained about the master trusts, big business going away from the Certified.

Bowen listened patiently. He was a very straightforward, some might say uncomplicated, man for whom banking meant *lending* to companies, *domestic companies,* with numbers you could read and assets you could get your arms around. It meant knowing the customer and keeping him satisifed. He had little interest in retail banking: cash machines and scenic checkbooks and Visa cards. He thought trusts and investments a bigger pain in the rear than they were worth. He thought "full-service banking" was a silly, expensive slogan cooked up by some advertising man with wool in his head.

After Alex had finished outlining what he thought might be done, Bowen reflected for a minute. In spite of his potential for silly-assed citifying, young Camran was a smart kid with a good, organized mind. Rube Bowan was a people person: an orchestrator and motivator. You had to give good young people a bit of their head.

"I'll tell you what, Al. I think you've got an interesting project there. Has to be handled very carefully. There are a lot of sensitive toes over there in T&I, especially after that piece in *Forbes* about how lousy a job they've done. So if it's going to be productive, it's got to be done just right. Which means you've got to do it yourself. Now, right at the moment, item number one on *our* agenda, yours and mine, is to get this Petrex thing stitched up. Old Rebo got pretty drunk down there at the Hamptonian and told me in deep, dark confidence that with this new oil price he's going to add a hundred thousand barrels of refining capacity at Bogalusa. At $6500 a daily barrel, that's $650 million! I know the Pru will give him $300 to $350 million and old Rebo'll poor-boy the equity down to $150 million, which means there's probably a $250 million revolver in there for the banks. And that's a loan I want, and a loan we are going to get! Or die trying! Those assholes upstairs let Gotham crash our party on Petrex, but only for one dance. Old Rebo's not happy with those junior geniuses on Fifty-sixth Street. He'll come to Certified. He's asked for you, Al, and I want you to go. We've got some fences in Houston that need mending. You can look after those while you're there. Although you don't like to admit it, you speak Texas, and that's the native tongue in the energy game. I told Rebo you'd be in his office at nine tomorrow. When you get back, there'll be plenty of time for this master trust study. I'll see you after the Fourth. And take your golf sticks. You talk pretty good with them too!"

Alex shrugged and went to call the bank's travel coordinator. As intriguing as the trust thing was to his natural snoopiness, he smelled a vice presidency on this Petrex deal. He made himself repeat: "There are worse places than Houston. There are worse places than Houston. There are worse..."

John and Margaret Jordan had discussed Dunstable's proposal through the night.

The ex-senator had been at his formidable, wheedling best. Always blunt, which grated on Jordan's fastidiously off-handed polish, Dunstable had come right to the point.

"The party's in trouble, John. This oil thing's going to make Baxter virtually impossible to beat. *Virtually* impossible. But John, if I'm the candidate, it will be a disaster and

(277)

Baxter will be *absolutely* impossible to beat in November. You know those Arabs still remember that speech .. mine at Omaha. I wish I hadn't made it, but there it is."

Two years earlier, just after he had quit the Democratic party and turned Independent, Dunstable had lit a fire under a National Farm Bureau convention with a characteristic thunder-and-lightning, ground-stomping speech. As he'd wound up, he'd gotten carried away with an exhortation for the administration to put the Marines in Dumar. Appropriate as it might have been then, in that screaming, smoky barn of an auditorium, the remark had returned to twist Dunstable's tail. Only three days before his call to Jordan, when the ex-senator and his aides, having chosen their quarry, were refining their strategy, the weekly summary from the London clipping bureau which Dunstable paid to keep an eye on Europe, had included a note from the *Nouvel Observateur* to the effect that "one heard" that the Kingdom's pricing decision had in part been influenced by the commanding role ex-Senator Dunstable was increasingly assuming in the U.S. presidential outlook. It was not a prospect which pleased the Kingdom. The Kingdom's commercial attaché, in Paris to discuss a joint venture, had rehearsed his lines to perfection. Alrazi had been very pleased.

"John, if I run, it may well spell the end of the two-party system. And yet I've been too effective for my own good. I look to go into the first ballot with 487 votes in hand if I accept the draft. I *own* those delegates. If I pull out—and that's what I'm thinking of doing in order not to be the man that presides over the death of the Republican Party—we'll be in Detroit until the next century trying to get a candidate. Which is why I've come to see you. Those Arabs trust you, John. Have you seen this?"

He handed Jordan a clipping. It was from *The Dynast,* a much esteemed British journal of political commentary and opinion. The paper had been on the verge of extinction when one of Dunstable's clients, anxious for the approbation of the intellectual community and an honorary degree or two for the wall of his den, had ridden to its financial rescue. Jordan put on his half glasses and read:

"Although the obvious if unknown role of President Baxter in reversing the spiral of rising energy prices remains to be delineated fully, it is clear that he must now be seen as the overwhelming favorite in November's election. So much so that this paper, among others, holds legitimate and grave appre-

hensions with respect to the future of the two-party system which has been so integral to the American nation's historical greatness. It remains for the Republican Party, in the jaws of what must seem certain defeat, to acquit itself honorably and to keep faith with its distant past greatness. This must perforce manifest itself in the nomination of a candidate incontrovertibly identified with the highest political and personal values. Such a man will be difficult to find in the ranks of the party as it stands today even though one hears mentioned at the most influential level the possibility of overtures to Ambassador John Jordan, honorably retired after forty years of dedicated and distinguished service to his country, especially in sensitive Middle Eastern postings. At sixty-three, Ambassador Jordan is surely young enough to lead a party which has recently contemplated handing the laurels of leadership to a septuagenarian former band leader or an opportunist of no proven political persuasion. In addition, he has enjoyed long and cordial relations with the world's benefactors in Qu'nesh. President Baxter appears assured of a second term. He has richly earned it, as he has assuredly earned the thanks of all civilization. It would be an imposing performance, though, and in earnest of its high ideals and values, if the Republican Party, in defeat, should fly its finest flag, the banner of Hamilton, Lincoln, and Willkie."

Dunstable watched Jordan closely as he read the clipping. The ex-senator had written most of it under a pseudonym, although it had been properly Anglicized by one of his aides who had been a Rhodes Scholar. His friend, the owner of *The Dynast,* had been only too glad to cause its publication. If only all of Herndon Dunstable's due bills could be discharged so cheaply!

Jordan finished and handed the clipping over to Margaret, who had been sitting quietly beside him.

"That's very flattering. Of course I haven't heard anything from 'L' Street, but then I guess party headquarters is wherever *you* are these days, Herndon."

Dunstable moved for the kill.

"John, I'm asking you, for myself, for the Party, for the Country, will you consider the nomination? If you will, I'll step aside and endorse you. I'll put all my resources at your disposal, all my staff, all my money! I'll keep in the background. John, Margaret, we need to do this. For us and for America!" A lachrymose film misted over Dunstable's shrewd little eyes.

"I understand, Herndon. I will think it over. Obviously Margaret and I must discuss it, you know. We've gotten pretty used to the lazy life. There's a few others I'll want to consult. How long do I have?"

"Will ten days do? The convention's in August."

"I'll let you know in a week, then."

"Fine. Just call me in Midland."

The Dunstable Falcon was airborne by seven o'clock. What with the time difference, they'd be back in Midland for a late chicken-fried steak at the Petroleum Club. Herndon Dunstable settled back with a glass of Wild Turkey and Pepsi and said, matter of factly, "We've got the sonuvabitch."

He grinned at his two assistants. "These eastern gentlemen are all the same. You kill them with honor and principle and all that bullshit! They ain't never met a payroll or got their hands dirty or seen blood. They're still tryin' to figure out why all them high ideals just got us our balls blown off in Vietnam. But they keep tryin'. Tell you one thing, you want a first-class loser, give me those Ivy Leaguers every time. They're *trained* to go down in style. Shit!" He took a big swallow of his drink. "Tell you one more thing, I could see it in Jordan's face; he and his buddies'll figure this'll give him control of the party. Politics to those boys is jes' one big Yale-Harvard game. More handshakin' than football!

"Well, son, as my daddy told me, you don't have to see the hole to get your pecker in, but you sure 'nough got to smell it, and, boys, I'm smellin' *hole!*" Dunstable took a deep, satisfied pull on his drink.

Margaret had filled the coffeepot for the third time when her husband made up his mind. He had talked the idea over with his gang out on Foxhall Road. He had flown up to New York and lunched at the Century with Lucius Barrow. They all agreed that the odds on victory were impossibly long, but miracles *did* happen, and of course it was a heaven-sent opportunity to recapture the party from those parvenus and adventurers. Give it a try, they urged him.

Finally, he and Margaret, alone, had worried it to death, like terriers.

"I suppose this is what we are trained for, dear," he said finally. "It's what makes us different from *them,* from the Herndon Dunstables and the Fulger Baxters. We've been in this country a long time. It's in our bones and our breeding. It's *our* country."

Our country, he thought. It was time to restore some of the solid idealistic values which were still taught in the old schools and which meant as little as Sanskrit to these bohoes like Dunstable. The country had taken too many body blows: Dealey Plaza; King; Bobby; Vietnam; OPEC. It was time for a bright new crusade to stitch up the bleeding fragments.

"I really think I must do it, dear."

"I suppose you do."

"I think I should call Dunstable."

"Heavens, John, it's four in the morning." She smiled. "It's rude to telephone anyone after ten or before nine-thirty."

He chuckled. Being a gentleman, educated and courteous to the point of a certain moral opacity, it never occurred to him that he was being set up.

Devon woke up when she heard Harrison laugh out loud. He was standing by the bed, naked as always, looking at the front page of the *Times*.

"What's so funny!" She reached out and gently pulled him to her.

"Look at this. Dunstable's pulled out of the Republican race. He's endorsed John Jordan. You know, the Arab expert. Old school tie. *Very* old school tie."

Devon didn't think he seemed very surprised. She felt him thicken and firm in her grasp. He dropped the paper and, like a wrestler reversing, got his head between her legs. In the last second, before his tongue sent her off like a rocket, she thought that everything they did now was shameless. But no less fun and every time a first time.

23 In late July, Alrazi summoned Khafiq to the south of France. The Prince felt it was timely to review the progress Harrison had made so far.

Khafiq's flight was delayed, successively, by industrial actions involving baggage handlers at Heathrow and air controllers in France, the latter a sort a prevacation nosethumbing at the public convenience, and so it was after ten o'clock when he arrived in Nice.

Alrazi's driver led Khafiq to the dull gold Daimler which

was solicitously tended by three gendarmes. He bore a message. The Prince and his party had already gone on to the tables at Beaulieu for the evening. Knowing Khafiq's distaste for casino gambling, Alrazi suggested that he go directly to the villa at Saint-Jean-Cap-Ferrat. Supper would be waiting. They would see each other later that evening, or, at worst, the next day. The serious discussions could follow lunch.

Khafiq had an omelet, half a liter of wine, and went to his room to read, tired by the aggravation of the long, unnecessary hours getting there. He dozed off, until he awoke to a bumping commotion in the hall; he opened his door a crack, as discreetly as possible. A strange procession made its lurching way down the half-lit corridor. The Valkyrie figure of Mrs. Fotheringill, grand and menacing, with a bosomful of rubies that went badly with her highly colored auburn looks, led the way; behind, stumbling and muttering in the supporting grasp of his butler and driver, came Prince Alrazi. Every few shambling steps he would reach into the pocket of his dinner jacket for a handful of ten-thousand-franc notes and strew them about him like petals. Bringing up the rear was a young manservant dutifully collecting the Prince's scattered largesse on a large vermeil salver. "Now Ally, dear, only a few more steps," Khafiq could hear Mrs. Fotheringill saying. She sounded soothingly maternal, a surprising quality in a lady Khafiq knew to be monstrously adept with leather and petroleum jelly.

He closed the door.

His room looked across the pool to the odd little trapezoidal harbor. The moon danced on the water, sending opalescent gleamings off the hulls of the small yachts and fishing boats moored below the modern silhouette of the Hotel Voile d'Or. There was a movement and a slight noise from the pool. Two figures emerged from the water. One, newly slender from what must have been a very rigorous diet, Khafiq recognized as the Minister. The other was a girl whose blonde hair was paler even than the moonlight. The couple moved to a mat in the half shadow of the poolside cabana. Khafiq saw the girl's hand move under the Minister's bathing trunks. He was an old man and his preferences were elsewhere, but he felt stirrings. Reluctantly, he turned away and went back to bed.

Alrazi's party assembled for lunch the next day on the dining terrace above the swimming pool. After a light lunch of prawns, Salade Niçoise, and a biting little Provençal white wine, Alrazi sent the woman away to shop or nap, leaving the three men alone at the table.

"Well, my dear Khafiq, how goes our project?"

Khafiq had brought the computer summaries in his suitcase. As he had instructed, Harrison had delivered a sealed envelope to a room at the Regency Hotel in New York, from which the information had made its way to London.

Khafiq spoke from memory. After an early reconnaissance of Saint-Jean-Cap-Ferrat that morning, he had closeted himself with a pot of tea and Harrison's figures.

"As of the close of business last Friday, the Dow Jones Average stood at approximately 1390. As you will recall, it was approximately 845 on August 13 of last year, when we made our first investment. Prior to the events of last April, we had committed $4,400,000,000 in round figures to the U.S. markets. As per your instructions, I have also invested an additional 480 million sterling in London, using an extrapolation of the investment matrix devised by our American colleagues.

"To return to the United States, we began to liquidate our portfolio on June 21. Because of the much higher volume of daily trading today, nearly 50 million shares on average against something over 20 million when we commenced, we have been able in slightly under eight weeks to make a substantial withdrawal of our commitments. As of last Friday, we have made sales netting, after commissions, $3,201,000,000. This represents around 40 percent of our portfolio—$1,750,000,000 at cost. Our remaining positions have a current market value of $5,148,000,000—against a cost of $2,600,000,000. If we were to liquidate as of last Friday, the operation would show an overall profit, before adjusting for last commissions, of $3,999,000,000."

Alrazi grinned salaciously. Four billion dollars! More than enough for a thousand lifetimes at Beaulieu, a hundred million chances on the black.

"Of course," Khafiq concluded, "things are moving more slowly in London. One must be more cautious there. The English still have a nose for the unusual. The American computers have, thankfully, no sense of smell."

"When would you expect to be concluded?" It was the Minister.

"Certainly no later than the second week in October. In London, perhaps a week later. But *no* later. It that acceptable?"

"I should think so. The OPEC Ministers' Plenary in Vienna is due to end on the twenty-sixth. A Thursday. I would expect to make our announcement on Friday. The American elections are November 4. That will give our exciting bit of news almost a fortnight to percolate in the political consciousness of the Americans."

The talk turned to politics. Alrazi described with relish the net of rumor and allusion which he had cast over the guileless peoples of the West. "They really are the most manipulatable people. Entirely blinded by self-interest which has, I suppose, habituated them to the falsehoods and deceptions of a generation of politicians. I am now devoting some time to the matter of Congressman Renssalaer." The Kingdom's commercial attaché in New York had advised oil companies who supplied the gasoline and fuel oil dealers serving Renssalaer's district that an allocated surcharge might be invoked in view of the congressman's continually vocal Zionist statements. It could add 15 percent to 20 percent to the energy costs borne by Renssalaer's constituents. All informal or off the record, of course, but it seemed to be having its effect. The residents of the hundred or so blocks represented by Renssalaer were going to receive a brief notification of these facts with their monthly rent bills. The oil companies had been only too pleased to underwrite the modest cost of this supplemental mailing. The *Village Voice* had reported that Renssalaer was in trouble.

"Of course," Alrazi concluded, "I think we must admit to ourselves that the presidential business has worked out better than we might ever have expected. It would have been too much to count on Dunstable's taking himself out of the race so early and in so precipitate a fashion, but it has happened. Masters tells me that Jordan looks a sure thing on either the first or second ballot. I am sure that when he is elected he will do something for Dunstable. He will have to. Frankly, it doesn't much concern me. I've quite forgotten that unfortunate speech, although I'm equally certain Senator Dunstable has not. After all, one can easily understand that things will be said excitably under certain circumstances that should not be; look at that animal Arafat! We can manage with Dunstable. For one thing, we know he can be bought. Masters tells me there's no doubt in Washington that he took a payment from Bergarzak. I've instructed Masters, incidentally, to guide $500,000 to the Jordan campaign now. Of course, there'll also be another $30 million available for television time the week before the election."

"I must say, dear Khafiq," said the Minister, "your young friend in New York has certainly been correct in his estimate of things. I assume he can be trusted to see this through and then to keep his silence. Or should we consider alternatives?"

Khafiq was startled. That was unlike the Minister. Of course, he didn't know that Alrazi had framed the question earlier and requested the Minister to ask it.

"Oh I should think so. You know, of course, that I receive regular reports from the young woman we have on station there?"

"Indeed. Well, we shall see." Khafiq had felt it unnecessary to report that Devon was living with Harrison; Khafiq's servant had reported the unslept bed in Harrison's room during their June visit. Alrazi knew, however. The Embassy was maintaining a regular, intermittent surveillance. If the trigger would have to be pulled, Alrazi would pull it.

Alrazi concluded matters by reporting with great amusement that the King's twin nephews were hating their summer in Kaiserslautern. He had made sure that they received plenty of postcards from their cousins scattered in the watering spots of Europe from Deauville to Ischia. Of course, at the moment, the boys were off on tank maneuvers in the Black Forest.

Khafiq was pleased to find the Prince in so jubilant a frame of mind. The Minister looked well. Everything was going swimmingly.

Dinner was a grand affair. Mrs. Fotheringill had invited the aging British writer whose villa lay just down the road to bring his houseparty to dine. Over a grand meal, whose outer movements were golden Beluga caviar and a raspberry-mango soufflé, the actor proved as charming and amusing as on stage or in the pages of his recently published memoirs.

"I say," he declared, swirling his glass of Charmes Chambertin '66, "wars have been fought over lesser grape than this. I remember Sir Alexander Korda..."

He had brought his daughter and son-in-law along. The girl was subdued by the raucous attention clamoring of her father and her husband. The young man, a jolly, beefy sort, talked animatedly of the great fortune he was making on Wall Street in the new golden era. Khafiq found his happy confidence a very pleasant antidote to the heavy, soporific meal.

It wasn't until they were drinking the last of the Château d'Yquem that he noticed the busboy. He was probably the same young man who had trailed Alrazi the night before sweeping up banknotes. The boy was Tunisian, Khafiq guessed; he had black eyes and a head off a Phoenician coin, skin like basalt. Very handsome.

After dinner, the crowd set off for another turn at Beaulieu. Khafiq sauntered to the library. The villa had been built by the Hungarian mistress of a great Kansas industrialist; the library was ranged with elaborate, unread sets of the great English writers. Khafiq was the most passionate of Anglophiles. Whig England stood at the apex of his inner universe, the fairest, brightest constellation in all his personal galaxy of mind, memory, and taste. It was an infinity removed from his shoeless childhood in the dirt streets and camel tracks of Qu'nesh.

His mind was forever wandering to that sure-gaited life of country and city, of elegant levees and elm-bordered walks, of the great men of that Augustan age. David Cecil in *Melbourne* had called them "the most agreeable society England has ever known."

At random, he took down a volume of Horace Walpole's letters. It was a fine early edition which had been bound sometime in the mid-nineteenth century, he guessed. Twelve decades of standing unread had left the leather fresh and shiny. Opening it at random, he found himself in 1773; Walpole was writing to Sir Horace Mann:

"What is England now?—A sink of Indian wealth, filled by Nabobs and emptied by Maccaronis! A senate sold and despised! A country overrun by horse races! A gaming, robbing, wrangling, railing nation, without principles, genius, character or allies; the overgrown shadow of what it was!"

No less resentfully than any peer of the realm, Khafiq thought of the laundry hanging on the Adam balconies of Wilton Place and the robed figures squatting and defecating in Marks & Spencer. How odd and awful it was to have come so far only to be back where one started.

He was settled and reading when there was a rapping at his door. The young busboy came in. He was wearing a white flax wrapper that accented the pale olive of his skin. Approaching the bed, he smiled and drew his robe aside. He had genitals the size of a carthorse. As the boy bent over him,

Khafiq closed his eyes and thought that Mrs. Fotheringill was indeed an observant and considerate hostess, and that, with all due respect to Laurence Sterne, there *were* some things they ordered better in France.

If there was anything that could be said about Alex Camran's obsessive curiosity, it was that it was as constant as the dawn. He had returned from Houston victorious, having recaptured the Petrex business, and had promptly held Reuben Bowen to his promise about the master trust study.

Since he had brought home Rebo Beauderon's written agreement on the agency for the Bogalusa credit, Bowen had to indulge him.

"Take a month, Alex. But that's about all. You're going to have better things to do. I'm sending your name upstairs for a vice-presidency."

Camran started by pulling together what little he knew. He wanted to get specifics on what seemed to be going on so that he could get Certified into the field with a competitive program. It was just a matter of business. Eat the other dog before he eats you.

Like many business school graduates, Alex Camran was a functional illiterate. Apart from the codified, self-serving pragmatism imprinted by the business schools on their people, he had little sense of reality. Besides a Texas patrimony of exotic similes, he had no small talk, no interests except his career, and little grace apart from his golf swing. His early reading was flown away, long gone. Four years of economics at Yale plus the business course at Wharton had funneled his view of life through a tiny, clear monocle and cleansed his mind and memory of all that imaginative childhood fantasy as if it had been scrubbed away with a wire brush.

Aside from *Forbes, Fortune,* and the like, his only reading now was detective stories. The literature of nosiness. They were cheap and discardable; the only permanence they held for Alex Camran was in his reinforced conviction that life was best perceived in terms of a series of purely sinister motions and actions to be found out and conquered.

He started with clues and guesswork concerning this big business which should rightfully go, as should *all* business, to the Certified Bank. "Guardian" something. That was the only name he had. Size? Probably a few hundred million. Worth chasing. Bits and pieces scattered all over. Everything on the wire.

Like an English detective questioning the suspects in the drawing room, he decided to start with the Certified's ninety correspondent banks. They certainly represented a reasonable cross-section of the universe of American banking.

He devised a questionnaire to go out over Bowen's signature. It was very general. The other banks, no matter how close or amorphously dependent their relationship to Certified, were not going to give him specific names and numbers on new, lucrative business. The questionnaire was innocuous enough, following a prefatory note to the effect that Certified was reviewing its master trust activities with a view toward updating and improving its service to its customers and correspondent banks. What was then requested, on a no-name basis, was information regarding new master trust account activity, as manager, agent, or custodian, within the last twelve months; approximate amount of new master trust activity; and questions involving procedures: confirmation timings; cash management; other details significant only in the aggregate.

After four weeks, he had what seemed to be a representative sampling. Sixty-one banks had replied. Of those, thirty-nine indicated that they had been handling significant new master trust business. Thirty-six were doing custody business only, among them Bowen's friends' banks in Ohio and Oregon. None showed any cash management function, which meant that cash was moving in and out at an extremely fast rate. The average order seemed to be between 1000 and 5000 shares. Issue distribution was surprisingly broad. Camran counted nearly 2000 different stocks.

As a gauge of transaction value, Camran had set up a multiple choice to check off: "under $5 million; $5–10 million; $10–20 million" and so on to "in excess of $100 million." There were only two in the last category. He added these up, taking a middle range in each category. When he was finished, he refused to believe the sum of his calculator. He redid the addition, checking and rechecking the glowing red digits. There was no question about it. Unless something had gotten screwed up in the circuits of his Hewlett-Packard, the reporting banks had handled $860 million of new master trust activity! All of it custody business, which meant that some huge unseen hand was guiding the whole shooting match. *That* was the customer he wanted to get for Certified. He needed to know more.

As he sat in his office, trying to put the honking of Park

Avenue out of his mind, it didn't occur to him that his questionnaire had asked nothing about trend and direction. Were the accounts buying or selling? What was the pattern? Later, of course, he would see the importance of those questions.

What was it his old professor of accounting had said? "In this country, when you need something, look to the Club." The Club: the old-boy network of Wharton M.B.A.s who watched out for each other, saw that the class rolls were maintained at full employment, and buried the traces of failure, God forbid. The Harvards watched out for the Harvards; the Stanfords for the Stanfords and even, God help them, the Amos Tuck boys from Dartmouth, although it was Camran's impression that most of the Tuck graduates ended up as plant managers in New England mill towns.

He took down the latest Wharton directory and went through the index, looking for a classmate or acquaintance who might help him out. Late in the Bs he found him: Benjamin Bolster, IV, now a first vice president with the Bargemens National in Memphis. He got his Wharton classbook from the shelf and thumbed to Bolster's photograph. He remembered him now. A nice-looking, red-headed guy, lot of freckles; they'd been in the same analysis unit in old Ferberman's course in Statistical Policy of Corporations. Came from Nashville or Knoxville. One of those places. As he prepared to close the book, he saw a picture immediately below Bolster. Beth Sue Brinning. He remembered poor old Beth Sue, the class pig but an arithmetical genius; she could add, subtract, multiply, or divide a legal sheet of figures in her head. But really a dog. He wondered what had happened to her. He seemed to recall she was working up the street at Gotham. She was from San Antonio; he recollected seeing her at a couple of Young Texan functions he'd been dragged to when he first came to New York.

He placed a call to Memphis on the WATS line. Mr. Bolster was out of the city but would surely return Mr. Camran's call in the morning. Could anyone else help him? No? Well, he could expect to hear from Mr. Bolster first thing.

He spent the rest of the afternoon trying in vain to track down "Guardian" this or that in various money-market directories. The boys in T&I whom he queried knew five "Guardians" but none of them fit. He went home that evening irritated and frustrated.

Benjamin Bolster was on the line at nine-fourteen the next morning. Sure he remembered Alex. How was everything in the big city? Master trusts? Well, he was in commercial lending so it was out of his area but he'd check with the Trust people and get back to Alex.

He got back by midafternoon. Yes, they were handling some big new business. It had started coming in toward the middle of last year. Obviously, it was fiduciary stuff so he couldn't name names. He knew Alex'd understand. The funds came in through a half-dozen big money-center banks and went out the same way, although the names changed. On volume, this was one of Bargemens biggest accounts, even though they just did executions and acted as nominee. No, unfortunately, the officer who'd opened the account had been on that DC-10 that bought it at O'Hare. Glad to be of help; hey, when he came to New York he'd give Alex a whistle and they could hoist a few. "Do that," said Alex, without enthusiasm.

Alex Camran knew no more, really, than when he started. He figured he had only a week left on the project. Bowen was getting impatient. Before he'd left to go fishing in Idaho, he'd said that he wanted Alex back on the job by early August. Leave this foolishness to those computer types over at Certified Center.

Bolster had said something about big money-center banks. Gotham was the biggest, next to Certified. He knew a bunch of people at Gotham. After all, the two banks were in bed on a hundred deals, although they would have cut each other's throat in a second. None of the people Alex knew at Gotham would be right for what he wanted to find out. He kept a Gotham internal directory on his window ledge. Flipping through it idly, in search of serendipitous inspiration, he read, "Internal Control and Audit Group: B.S. Brinning (*Ms.*), Vice President and Manager, Special Programs." On a hunch, he dialed the number next to her name. She was out, but would he call back after lunch.

His call caught Beth Sue Brinning at precisely the right moment in her career. She had decided that noon that she hated the Gotham Bank, which was a dangerous thing for a bank, since her capacious brain had gathered and stored up a vast amount of prospectively harmful information. Unlike most institutions, the bank seemed to encourage romance among its young people. Gotham-bankers were always marrying each other. Some Sundays the social pages of the *Times* seemed to include little besides the engagements and marriages of bright and scrubbed young people from the Gotham Bank.

Unfortunately, this hadn't worked out for Beth Sue. She was a fat girl, despite diets that would have starved a fakir, with damp, stringy hair and moist, bovine eyes. She wore expensive clothes—after all, she was making $57,000 a year—but they hitched and wrinkled around her. In the summer her large, rippled thighs got mottled and itchy and required copious saltings of bath powder to maintain even the meagerest comfort.

She had been in a stall in the ladies' room just before lunch powdering away determinedly, when she overheard a small, snippy voice say, "Did you hear that Harry Maxton is going to marry a girl over in Fiduciary Products?"

"No, when did that happen? I thought he'd been seeing Beth Sue Brinning."

"Who, B.S.? No, seriously. I mean, he told my boyfriend that B.S. could cook and all that, and she's got this great group rental out on Fire Island which is good in the summer, but..." the voice dropped to an obscene, conniving whisper for a minute and then rose again, "...smells so awful that he'd put a clothespin on his nose if it wasn't so awkward. Physically, I mean."

The door closed. She sat there as red and uncomfortable in her mind as in her swollen, rash-ridden body. Finally, large silent tears dripped down, making small craters in the powder on her thighs. The emotion soon settled. When Alex Camran called after lunch, her feelings had congealed into a vengeful hatred of the bank, whose laissez-faire policies concerning office romance she blamed, rightly or wrongly, for her humiliation.

Alex met her for lunch the next day at Marco's, on neutral ground between the Certified and the Gotham. He had used the ruse of wanting to discuss an idea he had for their Wharton reunion. She was even less prepossessing than he remembered. This didn't bother him. His mother had been the only woman who'd interested him emotionally. He didn't pay much attention to sex. At Andover and Yale, you could just spit on your hands and get yourself off if the urge or the old hangover hots got you all riled up. In New York the girls were so fast it wasn't a problem; every week or so he'd go down to the bar on the corner for a few beers and pick up some secretary and bring her back to his apartment. It was mechanical, to be sure, but so exclusively in love was Alex with himself and his career that it never occurred to him to handle it differently.

He didn't have to be very sensitive to discover the extent and sharpness of Beth Sue's unhappiness. She wasn't going to quit the Gotham. For a day, no more, she'd thought about going back to San Antonio, but she knew she couldn't compete with all those Braniff stewardesses for the men down there. The business opportunities would be small and boring. The money at Gotham was good and she liked her work there. Her unit had the free run of the bank, an open warrant to search and probe. The more she thought about it, the more she came to see that she didn't really *hate* the Gotham, it was just that this business had burned away whatever claim it might have on her absolute loyalty and discretion.

As might be expected of two people who were interested and solaced only by their occupations, Beth Sue and Alex empathized with each other, a circumstance compounded by their Texas roots, although neither would have readily admitted it. Of course Alex had a goal in view, which tended to sharpen his perception of whatever it was in Beth Sue that he might turn to his advantage. She was obviously lonely, and resentful of something, although he didn't then know what. So he recognized by the time the espresso was brought that, like it or not, he would be able to screw his way to the bottom of whatever she might know.

Yes, she did happen to be free for dinner that night. And he began the seduction of Beth Sue Brinning.

He was careful to be oblique in his approach. Night after night, for the first ten days, he lay wretchedly in her tumultuously perspiring embrace, slipping and sliding on top of her, counting silently to a hundred, to a thousand, until they had brought each other to orgasm and to sleep. She was, to his surprise, very direct and undemanding. She simply wanted sexual respect; the acclamation of his body; the accolade of his excitement. There were no handholdings or soupy gazes in tearoom corners. For his part, he didn't vulgarize or alienate whatever it was between them by asking pointed, factual questions. He worked the threads of his interest offhandedly into the fabric of their companionship. Finally, he felt he was able to ask casually, "Do you get involved in this master trust field? We hear there are a couple of big new ones around but that they're doing their business away from New York. It'd be interesting to see what the experience has been over at your place." He left it at that.

She was still huffing wetly from their exertions of the minutes just past, panting heavings on the edge of sleep. He wasn't even sure that she'd heard his question.

The group rental she shared was a stilted four-room shack just off the beach in Davis Park. There were two bedrooms which were occupied by two other girls and Beth Sue. By agreement, the arrangement was that one of the principals could bring a date to the house every third weekend; unless one of the three was away, which would allow privacy for two couples, the two dateless girls would occupy the downstairs bedroom, staring through Friday and Saturday night at a ceiling which seemed to amplify the cheerful groanings and thumpings from the upstairs waterbed.

Beth Sue's rotation fell on the first weekend in August and she had brought Alex. They had been glad to get out of New York. The city had been made uninhabitable by a hot spell and the crushing inflow of frontmen for the Democratic Convention which was to begin in nine days. Leslie Merriman had committed the entire resources of the Certified to an orgy of sycophancy: receptions; cocktail parties; breakfast and lunch briefings for key delegates; the whole round to culminate in a private supper party which, so Mismer superciliously advised his colleagues, might be attended by President Baxter himself. The only fly in the ointment was the intelligence that the Gotham Bank had cornered the services of every prostitute within a hundred miles of Manhattan and was having a greater success through their efforts than were Merriman and his political heavies.

After dinner Friday night, Beth Sue's housemates excused themselves early and went off to bed. Beth Sue and Alex sat on beanbag chairs in the main room, looking at the distant blackness of the ocean and watching the candle in the chianti bottle gutter down. They were both a little woozy with red wine.

"Do you remember you asked me something about master trusts a week or so ago?" She asked it matter of factly. "Well, I did a little checking. We haven't been doing anything *per se* new, other than what might be normal. But we have handled something over $80 million in business coming in and out, some from foreign banks and mostly U.S., which might be what you've heard about since it looks like pieces of one account. It's all on the wire, goes in and out the same day, all to other banks, seventy-three, to be exact, and all for custody accounts; at least that's what it appears to do, the wire directions all have CIDs—*Custody Interface Designations.*"

"How can you pinpoint the number of banks? You must have two hundred banks you work with on some basis like this."

"That's true. Except this group has one funny thing in common. They all seem to run as a herd. We started sending them money sometime in the summer of last year. Sometimes $5 million a week, sometimes more; I think the biggest was $20 million over Christmas and New Year's. Anyway, we sent them just a shade under $790 million. We got a few dribs and drabs coming back on the sell side, maybe $15 million, as if it was just for show. Then, around Easter, everything stopped; there were just no transactions for a while. Eight to ten weeks. Everyone else was doing business as usual except this group of accounts for which, as nearly as we can make out, we've handled nearly 250,000 separate transfers in an eight-month period! Then zero! And now, it's all coming back through us, nearly $500 million—$487 million, to be exact— and again nearly a quarter-million transactions!"

A half-million transactions, Camran thought. Mind-boggling in another era, but today just a few minutes' hard work for one of the big IBM processors that the banks used.

"You know something else," Beth Sue was clearly pleased with herself, "I checked with a friend of mine at First Puritan and Pilgrims in Boston. She looked into it, after I told her what to look for, and they've run about $450 million in and out the same way."

"Is she going to talk about what you asked her?" Alex was anxious to preserve his competitive advantage.

"Good heavens, no. I know too much about her. I'll tell you one thing, Alex, I don't know how much you know about computers..."

"Not much, really."

"Well, if all this action is part of a single program, it's being run by a computer. It's not that complicated really, it's just that it's so darn *big.*"

He took her to bed gratefully. In thanks, he summoned up a patient rigidity which brought her to six vast, grunting completions before she subsided into sleep. Downstairs, the thrashing and moaning had driven the other two girls past

the last barrier of self-control and into each other's embrace
where they now slept exuding unfamiliar, delightful tastes
and odors with which they would have to deal guiltily in the
morning.

Alex lay awake through most of the night. At first light,
he went out to the beach to think things over. The sun was
rising with a glare that argued a burning Saturday. He
walked west along the beach for a mile or two, trying to
formulate his conclusion to Bowen that there was at least a
billion dollars of business out there that Certified wasn't in
on.

He sat down on the sand. There wasn't a breath; the ocean,
flat as plate glass, gleamed gray and bronze in the sunrise.

"Hi, fellow, got a match?" said a cool and languid voice
behind him. Alex turned where he sat, startled. A naked male
member dangled eight inches from his face.

His Dallas upbringing got the better of his hard-bought
New York poise. This was the sort of thing that Momma said
happened out on Cedar Springs. Try as he might, there were
some things a Texas boy just couldn't take about New York.
He jumped to his feet and ran back up the beach until he
stopped, nearly retching from breathlessness, in front of the
general store. The owner was just unbundling the morning
papers. Alex charged a *Times* to Beth Sue's house account
and walked the last hundred yards to the shack. The front
page of the *Times* headlined that the Republican Party, con-
vening in Detroit, had nominated Ambassador Jordan.

24   "The fix is in," announced A.P. Peech to the rest of
the press gallery. Below, on the Cobo Hall stage, John Jordan,
with his wife and grown children and grandchildren, along
with Senator Maxness of North Dakota, and his wife and five
small children, were waving to the delegates. All around the
hall banners and placards proclaimed the candidate's "Three
Js" slogan: "Jordan/Judgment/Justice."

"Do you know what Dunstable said about Jordan's slogan
privately?" Peech continued.

"I understand he told a small group at the Gorse, you
know, that club in New York where the elephants go to die,
that he agreed with the 'Three Js' except that it ought to
stand for 'Jews, Jerks, and Jigaboos' because that's what we

were going to get if ever Jordan and the rest of his liberal
crowd gets in. Which I don't think is going to happen."

"You going to byline that, Pits?" asked the reporter from
the *Chicago Tribune*.

Alfred Pitney Peech, "Pits" to his colleagues and competitors in the press corps, was the chief political reporter for
ENS, Enterprise News Services, the third of the big wire
services. He was the only reporter whose stuff was so good
that it was regularly carried, under his byline, on the front
page of the *New York Times* and the *Washington Post*.

He was as good as there was. He outwrote, outsourced,
and outmaneuvered his competitors with an aggressive pa-
nache that ate them up. "That SOB wasn't born of woman-
kind," groused the bar crowd at the Algonquin and Duke
Zeibert's, "he was invented by a coalition of John Peter Zen-
ger, Joe Pulitzer, and old man Hearst." A legend. It was
rumored that Peech had in fact been "Deep Throat," feeding
Woodward and Bernstein the goods in order to protect a
source of his own inside the Nixon family. He was said to
have heard the missing eighteen minutes. He was credited
with having legitimized the candidacy of Fulger Baxter, after
picking up on a stringer's report that cowtown primary voters
in the prairie states were really buying Baxter's pig routine.
The jealousy of his professional cohorts couldn't prevent ENS
from paying Peech $150,000 a year, couldn't prevent the
Times and the *Post* and three hundred other papers from
frontpaging his bylined articles, and couldn't keep him from
stealing the journalistic scene in any major campaign. About
all they could do was intrigue against him successfully at
Pulitzer Prize time. He didn't care.

Peech threw himself body and soul into presidential politics. Which was why, although he was the highest-paid reporter in the game, ENS reckoned they had a bargain in
Peech. Sure he got $150,000 a year, but that was a hell of
a lot less than they would have to pay the three or four people
who'd be required to cover a campaign if something happened
to him. He had to rest between campaigns like a tenor between *Tristans*. He had spent the three years since the Baxter
campaign reviving himself in Rome, the city of his heart,
where, apart from covering the fall of Idi Amin, he contented
himself with producing elegantly wrought weekly trifles on
pasta and Manzoni and scribbling fitfully on his pet project:
a detailed, physiologically descriptive Washington *roman à
clef,* which would be published in two volumes. The first

volume would be a $10.95 potboiler. The second would be an index and would sell separately for $100 a copy.

Not even Peech's prose could make the Jordan nomination exciting. The Dunstable professionals had moved about the floor like thuggee assassins, knocking off the favorite sons and bringing the convention into line. There was no need for Peech to scramble around, digging and scratching for a news-break. So he sat seignorially in the Cobo Hall press gallery, composing his lead with a gold Cartier pen, half listening to the eloquent admonitions of candidate Jordan and pretending not to notice the close attention his neighbors were paying to the flashing eyes and regal poitrine of the lady who had accompanied him to Detroit.

"What do you mean, 'fix'?" The guy from the *Tribune* pressed the point.

"Look," said Peech patiently, "on the one hand we have Herndon Dunstable, who, to paraphrase Andrew Marvell on King Charles, nothing does that common isn't, or mean, opting out of a foreordained defeat for the good of the party. On the other hand, we have Jordan; nice but not exactly heavy, who Dunstable cajoles into becoming the candidate, to lay his head on the chopping block which those Arabs seem to have so nicely polished up for Dunstable's silver, flowing locks. Now Dunstable, noblest Roman of them all, playing out of Midland, Texas, is to be seen as Mr. Generosity himself. 'Take my funds,' says Dunstable. 'Take my media experts, my frontmen, my writers.' Dunstable's bought the convention for the next trip round. And in the process he's probably knocked off, for the last time, all those poor sweet lambs from Cambridge and the Union Club who still think this is the party of Hamilton and Lincoln.

"Dunstable doesn't mind waiting four years for a sure thing. Damn it, if he had the money, I'd say that he paid the Arabs to pull this number with the oil price, but even old Herndon's friends aren't that rich, including if you throw in that quarter million they said he took from the Iranians. All this noble altruism. It makes me want to puke!"

Peech's leader the next morning wasn't quite so direct.

"Last night, in the subdued delirium following his expected, early nomination Friday evening and the confirmation early yesterday of Senator Jonathan Maxness (R–N.D.) as the vice-presidential candidate, Ambassador John Jordan declared for a new politics of ethics and decency. To many observers, this appears to be a nothing-lost ideological gesture

(297)

in the face of the seemingly unassailable strength which the worldwide economic recovery, prompted by the reduction in the world oil prices, has produced for President Baxter. Nevertheless, Ambassador Jordan's apparent conviction and enthusiasm carried the hearts of the party faithful assembled here in this splendid new convention hall, claimed by many to symbolize the spiritual and economic rebirth of 'smokestack America.'

"As he stood surrounded by his applauding family and by equally demonstrative party leaders, including, most prominently, former Senator Herndon Dunstable (Ind–Tex.), himself the frontrunner until weeks ago, Jordan professed a full heart and untroubled mind as he took the first step on perhaps the steepest uphill road faced by any presidential candidate within memory.

"Not that the convention closes the Republican book on all matters of interest. Senator Dunstable's dramatic withdrawal from the race virtually on the eve of the convention and with close to five hundred committed delegates strikes some observers as a highly ambiguous act of political self-sacrifice. A visitor who queried party chairman Preston Wood as to whether it was Ambassador Jordan or Senator Dunstable who was in fact making the greater political sacrifice, received in reply only the statement that, clearly, all good men had come to the aid of the party."

While readers across the country were devouring this, Peech cased his Olivetti and took himself and his lady to Cape Cod, to wait out the two weeks until the Democratic Convention, which promised to be equally uninteresting.

Camran laid his enormous suppositions and his modest store of hard facts before Reuben Bowen. Admittedly, it was a part of the banking business that the Certified's president found uncongenial. But billions in prospective business, what must be the largest unified investment program in existence, even though Bowen and Camran knew of it only inferentially, nevertheless called for attention. Highest level attention.

"You see, Rube," it was first names now, since Camran had brought the bacon home from Houston, "what I've been able to trace looks like three-something billion." Camran thought only in amounts, as did Bowen. Banker's perspective. Thrust and direction were beside the point. In or out, it was all the same.

Bowen was impressed. "What next?" he asked. "Nobody's

going to name names. God knows how you got the dope you have on the Gotham, but still, no names. I mean Guardian something; not much to go on, is it, if we're trying to locate the customer?"

Camran had one thought. "I've done some checking. Money this big scattered this way without a phone call, not *one,* according to my source at Gotham, is working for a computer. That seems for sure. And our own people over at T&I—and a couple of sources of my own—say that for a computer to do this job, it has to be working from a specialized program. A kind that only one of three or four outfits, all on the west coast, where they go in for this sort of thing, could put together. Doesn't that make sense?"

"If you say so, Alex. Of course, I don't know shit from shinola about investments and the market, but then neither does anyone else around here, especially those assholes over in T&I. What's your plan?" Bowen was getting restless with the lack of specificity.

"My thinking is that we find out which of these three outfits has done work like this on a huge scale, if any of them has. And if one has, we buy it."

"The program?"

"Sure, if we can. But we'll probably have to buy the business."

"Well that sure as shit won't be anything new around this loony bin. You know what I mean, Alex. They love to buy things up on fifty-two. It's that 'diversified financial services' crap. Then I have to straighten them out. Your idea'll be right up their alley. It'll go nicely with that mail order bond scheme that got us fined by the comptroller; and that planning research outfit that couldn't plan shit through a goose and ended up selling one client's trade secrets to another. And the credit card company. I think it's the third time we've owned it. And the *Certified Library of Finance.* And that export-finance outfit those friends of Merriman stole blind in Oubangui. A little really expensive computer wizardry'll go nicely with all of them!"

Camran knew he was trying Bowen's patience. "The thought, Rube, would be to drop the matter in the chairman's lap. You won't have to get involved. But, really, this sounds very big. This could be that pool of *Fortune* '500' pension accounts there's been a rumor about."

There had been no such rumor and there was probably no such pool, but Camran was bright enough to recognize the need to lace the conversation with a little plausibility. And Reuben Bowen positively turned neon at mention of the *Fortune* "500."

Camran pressed his argument. "Why don't you put it to the chairman, suggest, I mean, that he get involved in this personally? You know how he likes to talk *'billions'!*"

"Rolls off his tongue like lies in Washington. You're right, Alex, I agree we should chase this thing a little further. Hell, the point of this business is our relationships with the big boys, guys like Rebo Beauderon. If this thing is as big as you guess, Gotham could cuddle up to some of our big customers through this chickenshit pension thing. Christ, they'll have corporate loan types all over these accounts like lice on a tick-hound."

Bowen made him run through it again, taking cursory notes on a yellow pad. Both men recognized that they were dealing in suspicions, diffuse whiffs and scentings of a matter which seemed of little real interest in itself, of consequence only because it was business somebody *else* was getting. That was the point—and the rub.

"Good morning, Miss Merit. It's Mr. Bowen. Is the chairman in? Might he have a few moments?"

After an instant of barely perceptible sounds on the other end, Camran saw Bowen suffuse with exasperation. He couldn't quite control the rising vexation in his voice.

"No, Miss Merit, I don't wish to speak to Mr. Mismer. When I need my suit pressed, or my shoes shined, I'll call Mr. Mismer. I would like to speak with the chairman. Yes, I know. But I'm sure the nice gentlemen from Burundi will spare him a moment to speak with the president of this bank. About business. Miss Merit, that's B-U-S-I-..."

Bowen muffled the receiver and smiled at Camran with a knowing helplessness.

"Do you suppose this is the way all banks work? After all, our competitors don't seem to do much better. Yes, Miss Merit?" he returned to the phone. "Hello, Leslie? Good morning, sir. Yes, I heard. Oh I'm sure it's a very exciting possibility. Seventy-three million, you say? And secured by the coffee crop? Closing in Bujumbura—and Secretary Drzlag has promised to send someone? Leslie, that's very exciting news, congratulations are most assuredly in order. Of course, we'll have to send someone quite high up. Oh, of course, no, I know you can't make it; no, *I'm* not going to the Grove this year. But Leslie, why not send Arthur? Mismer. That's right.

He speaks real good French and they say early September is the best time of year in Bujumbura. Good, good. Leslie, the reason I called was, *my* assistant, Alex Camran, may be on to something that Gotham is up to. Yes, it sounds very big. Alex guesses it might involve *billions*."

He gave megalithic weight to the last word.

"If we could just have a few minutes of your time. Fine, fine, we'll just stick our heads in after lunch, say, two-fifteen. Of course. I understand, we'll be well out of your hair by then. Yes, I'll confirm it with Miss Merit."

Bowen replaced the receiver. "Can you believe that? Anyway, $73 million of loan exposure is a small price for the thought of Arthur Mismer and his acne loose in the streets of Burundi."

Bowen and Camran spent thirty-eight minutes with Leslie Merriman. Merriman lost interest in the details practically from the first minute. Mismer hovered in the background, a spiky, distracting presence fluttering a sheaf of appointment slips. Mr. Merriman was due to greet the Wogo of Kazir at Fraunces Tavern at three-fifteen; Mr. Merriman was due at the Council of Foreign Relations at six-twenty-five to introduce Sir Pomfret Gulb; Mr. Merriman was due here, was due there. "Always to introduce. Never to close," muttered Bowen.

Bowen summarized Camran's suspicions and conclusions. "What it looks like, Leslie," he wound up, "is as if there is around $5 billion, maybe more, of new pension business in the market, and we haven't gotten any. Now what we recommend..."

"Excuse me, Mr. Merriman." Mismer. "Jean-Giorgio will be here in fifteen minutes to do your styling."

The chairman of Certified had recently listened to a friend and gone to New York's most fashionable haircutter. Blown dry and sprayed, his hair pressed over the tops of his ears like peculiar varnished muffs. Bowen thought he looked like a perfect fool.

He chose to overlook Mismer's interruption.

"If you don't mind, Arthur," he said gently, and then, to Merriman, with a gravity that Camran, as well as he had come to know Rube Bowen, found new and startling, "The thing is, Leslie, we understand that Gotham got the jump on us because they have been working on the Q.T. with a couple of west coast research firms—in the interest of *synergism* and *multifacetism.*" The neologisms stalked off his tongue like pachyderms carrying a thousand pounds of ivory.

Merriman looked up sharply, a trace of interest in his expression. "Are you suggesting, Reuben, that we may be in the position of being *outconceptualized* by Gotham Bank?"

"So it seems."

"Gracious. That won't do. Well, what do you and young Mr. Carm——, *Camran,* here propose to do about it?"

Bowen explained. Merriman listened; at his signal, Mismer reluctantly took notes. If Camran had been any sort of a student of history, if his recent reading had gone beyond Peter Drucker and Conan Doyle, he would have perceived what was taking place was a ritual as constructed and precise as a *levee* at Versailles: an authentic litany of deference and procedure. Suppliants, scribe, and Merriman sitting Solomonic. He learned more watching Bowen handle Merriman for those six minutes than anything he had been taught at Wharton. About the way to success, that is.

When Bowen had finished, Merriman pursed his preacher's lips, a pause for effect rather than reflection, and then rendered judgment.

"Obviously, Reuben, this could develop into a very troublesome competitive disadvantage. Goodness, imagine basing investment policy on computers instead of on prudence and seasoned judgment. Just the sort of thing, however, that those people over at Gotham are likely to do; they're probably working on an advertising campaign right now. Arthur, how does my schedule look?"

Mismer produced a morocco ledger.

"Well, sir, you take off for the Grove day after tomorrow, after the prayer breakfast for Ayatollah Muza and then, an hour later, the ribbon-cutting at the Iranian Emigrants Bahamas Bank. You're due to remain at the Grove for two weeks. Camp Roundelay. *He'll* be there, of course. Then back on the thirteenth. A long weekend at Broken Point, after which we're due to fly to Kabul." Mismer sounded like a nurse in a home for the aged.

"Suppose I left Roundelay a day early? On the twelfth. I suppose I could stop in San Francisco for a morning. Arthur, call that man—what's his name, Reuben, oh yes, Nyquist— Arthur, call Mr. Nyquist and tell him I'll be there at ten-fifteen on the thirteenth." Leslie Merriman did not make appointments; he advised of his forthcoming presence.

"Since Alex here is familiar with all of this, Leslie," said Bowen, "it might be a good idea if he went along."

"To the Grove?" said Merriman, horrified.

"Of course not, but to see Nyquist. Alex is one of our best young men. I think you'd find him helpful." There was a shade of mischief in Bowen's voice. Mismer looked as if something unpleasant had occurred in his trousers.

Merriman and Mismer exchanged a glance. Five years of groveling and letter-perfect protocol arrangements paid off.

"Oh, I don't think that will be necessary, Reuben. After all, these will be entirely preliminary discussions. Nothing definitive. We wouldn't want to overwhelm Mr. Nyquist with personnel. We'll certainly brief you immediately on our return. Arthur will take most complete notes."

The phone buzzed on Merriman's desk. Mismer answered it. "Yes, Miss Merit. Just one more minute. Why don't you show him where to plug in his blowdryer?" Mismer closed Merriman's appointment book. The interview was over.

Riding down from fifty-two on the private elevator, Bowen said, "Well, Alex, I gave it the old school try. I saw you looking at all those pictures of Merriman and his big deal friends. Watch out, the disease is catching!"

He was right. Alex had let his eyes wander to the wall of photographs of Merriman with Schmidt, with LBJ, with the Pope: in each of them, as precisely placed as a pawn in a chess gambit, was Arthur Mismer. He had envied Mismer— to have been present at such meetings.

Later, Bowen called him into his office.

"One piece of advice, Alex. You're smart and you're doing a good job. But don't chuck away your Texas birthright and your common sense. You didn't have a daddy to grow up with. A father's a good thing, especially when he can tell you who he is and how he got that way, and who *his* daddy was, and what's good and what's bad about where he came from; what's worth keeping and what you flush. You can be successful and country both. It's a great advantage. Let me tell you a story.

"Years ago I caught three touchdown passes for Tech against the Bear in the Sugar Bowl. On graduation, the grateful alumni gave me a trip to Europe. On the boat there was a tour of snotty young girls from one of those fancy schools in Virginia. I started hanging around them, just flirting and lying a little. They were all talking about Rembrandt and Venice and once, when I tried to say something, the prettiest and snottiest one said to me, 'Anyone with an accent like yours can't have an IQ of over 80.' Well, I just bided my time and before we got to Genoa I had her gobbling my pecker behind the lifeboats. As Coach Dodd said, 'It don't matter if you can talk like a stage actor; diction ain't quality; country ain't crude. They only pay off on touchdowns, not talk!' Coach was right, as he usually was. Plain food's messy to cook and messy to eat, and a lot of people like it, but a plate of good barbeque tastes better than licking another man's butt. And you can lick it standing up."

Just before quitting time, it occurred to Camran that Bowen always spoke in the same soft Georgia drawl, merely adjusting his vocabulary to the occasion. It bore pondering.

There was a distant, rumbling threat of thunderstorms and the evening's program at Tanglewood featured contemporary Slavic music, so Devon and Harrison had no regrets at having given up this Friday to dine with their landlords at Windfair. Besides, the cottage had no television and Harrison thought that it might be amusing to watch President Baxter's acceptance speech after what he was sure would be an early dinner at the big house.

At seven, dressed in the bright formality of Eastern summers, they walked up the hill and across the broad spill of the lawn. It was still daylight; the heat was scarcely damped. Devon reached for his hand, bringing him to a stop.

"It's still quite beautiful, isn't it?"

Windfair crowned the rise, a tall brick block fronted on this side by a columned portico which looked across the valley to Egremont notch. Most of its original ramblings had long since been amputated by inflation, lopped and truncated by twenty years of rising costs and shrinking trust funds.

"It's really kind of a metaphor for old money," he said. "Much diminished but still pretty adequate."

Their hosts waited on the portico. A drinks table had been set out, covered in a lace throw. To his surprise, Harrison saw that a bottle of champagne was cooling in a cut-crystal bucket that belonged in the Corning Museum.

"We're so pleased you could join us," said their hostess. Her serene, fine face, its wrinkles like the craquelure of a well kept old painting, was framed by waves of hair whose mysterious blue tint seemed to Harrison to register something of the early twilight glow beginning to edge the distantly buzzing hilltops.

"Some champagne?" Their host was splendid, there was

no other word, in a vaguely yellowed white linen suit that might well have sat down to dine with Henry James. He carried himself with a painful and cautious elegance. A combination of old bones and old manners, thought Harrison.

"We've called dinner for seven-forty-five. A bit earlier than we usually eat in Louisburg Square, but Grace and I thought you would rather enjoy watching the convention on the television. The President will be making his acceptance speech. Quite a man, Baxter." There was something in his tone of voice that promoted Baxter right up there with the Cabots and Lowells.

Dinner was a sweltering business. The dining room was as close as a coffin; the eight candles burning in the silver branches sucked the oxygen out of the air. The old couple's conversation was cheerful and optimistic.

"A good time to be alive, don't you think?" said their host, raising his glass in a deeply meant toast. The wine caught the light and shimmered like rubies. "The Dow went through 1650 today. I heard it on the radio."

He noticed Harrison trying to wipe his sweating forehead as unnoticeably as possible.

"Yes, it *is* hot in here. Grace and I were just saying, before you arrived, that we're going to look into having Windfair air conditioned. Now that the price of fuel seems to be what it should be."

And the value of your trust funds just about doubled, thought Harrison. Ernie had phoned in just before they had left New York. Less than $800 million to go. Close to $9 billion withdrawn. At the rate the market was going, volume averaging 70 million shares a day, never below 60 million even on the doggiest days of summer with half the country on vacation, they would be out and gone easily by Labor Day.

"And Frederick has suggested we might rebuild the conservatory. We used to have the most wonderful musical evenings before the war. All the first-desk players from Symphony. Koussevitzky himself used to get drunk and play the piano all night." The elderly woman's smile was as triumphant and brilliant as the candlelight on the silver.

Prosperity as a tourniquet, Harrison reflected, staunching the hemorrhage of Copleys and Revere bowls sent to the auction rooms to pay for fuel oil and gardeners and new drainpipes.

After dinner, they carried their wineglasses into the study. Old brown photographs of children in sailor suits were studded among the bookshelves. Their host fiddled uncertainly with the aging Philco television set until finally a shaky image appeared: people in white plastic boaters prancing and cavorting, waving banners and placards, making broad masklike grimaces into the camera, the air of Madison Square Garden filled with streamers and confetti. Watching it, Harrison was reminded of that Monday on the Stock Exchange five months before, when the Floor had erupted with the pent-up, hysterical exuberance of a revival meeting.

The voice of the commentator cut over the crowd noise. "...awaiting the arrival of the President and his family and the Vice President and..." The rest of his sentence was gulped up by a roar and the camera cut to the stage.

Baxter appeared by the rostrum, his wife behind him holding tightly to his hand; then Vice President Reilly and his wife.

"Look at Mrs. Baxter," whispered Devon. "You can bring a lady to Halston but you can't change her beehive."

The four figures stood on the stage, arms around each other, waving with their free hands, waiting for the mob to spend itself. Behind them a small group of insiders and family collected. Buster Ferdimend, keeping emotionally just beyond the perimeter of the delegates' excitement, seeming to study each face in the rabble. A hawklike woman carrying a Bible whom Harrison recognized as the President's sister. The Vice President's hairy children.

At length the convention floor settled down, bursting to its feet only to cheer the introduction of the President.

As Baxter spoke, Harrison let his eyes and attention wander. Politics bored him. The general excitement of the event, conveyed only by the quivering screen, was enough; it would only be trivialized by the rhetoric he expected from Baxter. He would have to have a close look around this library, he thought. Probably a real trove. He knew that Windfair's big rooms had sheltered generations of great New England figures, from Santayana and William James and Berenson to Updike and Rawls. The world as it was made to be, he thought contentedly. His head dropped in a winey, happy half doze.

A sharp elbow from Devon made him shake his head.

Baxter was still speaking. The President had modulated his flat public style to a professionally intense and compressed intonation.

"Evangelical zinger coming up," he said to Devon out of the side of his mouth.

"...take what God and generations of great Americans have taught us," Baxter was saying, "and shape it into a slogan for this campaign, for this era, for all the great immortal future of this Republic. Partners in Prosperity! Partners in Morality!"

The President's picture slipped away from him. Prosperity. Morality. The words suggested something. Was it some kind of *déjà vu,* Harrison wondered at first. No! Not this room or these people arranged this way, not these books or this confident face talking at him from a television screen. He squeezed his eyes shut, flicking about in memory like one of Ernie's tapes, slip-slapping back and forward, clockwise, counterclockwise until the right particle of recollection was located.

Often, driving, when another car would shoot unexpectedly out of nowhere, Harrison would be jolted to a sudden adrenal alertness. It happened now. He recalled as from nowhere the yacht rocking easily in the Spetsai channel. His conversation with Khafiq. "Point the finger at *that* man. Pick your own President." Was that what he'd said? Yet somehow he felt that the man on the screen was *not* that man. The feeling was troublesome.

But Harrison was awake and shaking within his skin. Not visibly, he hoped. Spetsai. Paris. The Minister. The big hitters. Alrazi's insistence on timing. The price cut in oil. The election. It was *all* his architecture. He felt immensely proud; he could barely stay seated, appear restrained, yet there was still something bothering him, something about Baxter. *Not* the man. Then the feeling passed.

His host crossed to the television and turned it off. The image of the shouting crowd, still celebrating like a drunk trying to make a party last, faded. Glasses were passed, and a decanter. Harrison took his almost unconsciously.

"A toast," said the old man, "to the President. To the nation."

And to me, thought Harrison. I created this, reflecting on Baxter's speech. He had never been so happy, no man ever had. The possession of real power, the ability by action or idea to cause great changes, especially like this, gave a man a fulfillment beyond the ecstasies of love or the laughter of children. At that moment, he possessed that power, possessed that happiness. He could do nothing more now than to watch events unfold.

Their host took leave of them at the terrace steps. The sky

was brilliant. They had never heard the thundersquall which had washed it clean.

"Remarkable man, Baxter," said the old gentleman. "I'm going to vote for him. First time for a Democrat since I made the mistake with Roosevelt in '32. Of course I feel sorry for poor John Jordan. I fear he'll be squashed like a bug. He's a good man. I know his people. His father and uncle used to dine at the Somerset." He looked to Harrison for approval.

They walked down the lawn, Harrison on air. Halfway down the slope, beyond the sight of Windfair, Harrison took Devon and kissed her and then, under a wide sky filled with trailing lights, God's and man's, made love to her, slipping and curling in the wet grass, trying to bring her into the orbit of his private celebration.

Of course, on that night it was impossible to expect that he would ask himself certain obvious questions. As a professional, it seemed logical that his clients should wish to share in the benefits they had conferred on the rest of the world. That they might limit their gains by selling now—well, $5 billion profit was a lot of money. As they said on the Street: Bulls get something, and bears get something, but pigs get *nothing*.

25 The unseasonable morning fog spoiled the final dawn of what had been an utterly delectable fortnight at the Bohemian Grove. As he completed his meticulous toilet, Leslie Merriman tried to force his vision through the brumous yellow half light to the foot of California Street, where his money had underwritten the erection of a city within a city—Merriman Pier: shops, bars, apartment houses; ten thousand affluent inhabitants, mostly single, mostly young. Seeing it was hopeless. The fog had misted within a few feet of the windows of his tower suite. How glorious it would be, he thought, to be able to peer triumphantly down Nob Hill to the wonderful new monument to old money which bore his name.

He adjusted the needlework suspenders which Miss Merit had wrought with the Certified logo, gave them a fast, confident snap, and brushed into place the artfully bouncy waves of gray hair.

As good a Grove as he could remember. No doubt about it. Simply not one nonentity. Not that this was unexpected in an election year. Of course, as far as he knew—and who could care, really?—a lot of the smaller fry in the other camps had spent their evenings with prostitutes at the Russian River motels, leaving Camp Roundelay to men who counted. In a way too bad, he reflected, that the press couldn't be there—to see what grand fellows truly important men could be. Imagine, the Low Jinks, normally dominated by those Los Angeles film types from Camp Hapoville, really taken over, this year, by all his old Hasty Pudding friends!

Naturally, it was difficult to overlook that unfortunate episode at Ramapos Camp. The Minister of Roads of the Bundesrepublik had been discovered in the redwoods "spreading the buns," as Merriman's informant put it, of a sturdy young waiter. It was common gossip in the Grove that the temporary help wasn't above supplementing its wages. Not that something like this could happen at Roundelay, thank goodness. Their fine waiters and busboys were all members of the Stanford football team.

And *he* had gotten a wee bit tiddly last Tuesday night. It was difficult not to overrelax sitting on a redwood bench, eating charcoaled ribs, between the chairman of Amalgamated and the Attorney General. Listening to fine, significant talks by the Austrian ambassador and the president of Imperial Manganese. It was all too easy to signal for another mild gin and tonic from the bar laid out under the lapping branches.

And *then,* what a moment! He would guard it forever in his memory. "When nature calls, heh, heh," he'd said jocularly to the group at large, and made his way out into the trees. Of course he *was* a little shaky, standing there under a full California moon, playing his stream against a sequoia as large as Saint Willoughby's steeple. It was grand fun, pissing his initials on the base of the great trunk. Until he became aware of another figure, sharing the tree perhaps a yard to his left. Startled, he had wavered, sprinkling his neighbor's shoes.

"Plizz, vot is dis? Do you mind?" He recognized the effulgent baritone immediately. It was *him.* In the moonlight, the features became clear: the plump face with the hair receding like rice terraces from the broad forehead.

"Plizz," said the shadowy figure, reaching for a joke to rescue the situation, "as I once said in Paris, 'Pee is at hand,' but this is too much." The figure chuckled ponderously; his jokemaking had the subtlety and nimbleness of a water buffalo.

Merriman had been overcome to be in *the* presence. But his manners hadn't deserted him, he would be pleased to say later.

"Excuse me, sir." He took a handkerchief from his pocket and, without even bothering to zip himself, knelt in the moonlight and wiped the droplets from the other man's shoes. It made him proud to be a Republican.

As he rose, the shadowy figure said, "May I plizz have the handkerchief? My publishing contract forbids the distribution of unauthorized souvenirs." Another heavy chuckle.

Merriman handed it over. Safely zipped, he tottered along the boardwalk back to the welcoming campfire. He felt feverish with the reflected fire of greatness.

The memory made him feel warm again as he went downstairs to deal with this tiresome business of Rube Bowen's.

Alex Camran was waiting for Merriman in the lobby. He had made the trip to San Francisco after all. Arthur Mismer had been summoned to Wisquisset by his mother, the resident all-seasons gorgon of coastline society. The latitude varied with the season. He was needed to help with the seating at the annual Wisquisset Witching Ball. When he protested the press of business, an urgent mission for Certified, Mother had simply picked up the telephone and dialed Leslie Merriman's private number. The Certified's chairman was no match for Proserpine Mismer. He remembered being exiled from Wisquisset in 1947 for crossing his legs at a formal dinner. So, while Alex Camran waited downstairs in the Stanford Court, Arthur Mismer was already three hours deep into the difficult business of deciding whether to put Mr. Looby, who bred Labrador Retrievers, at the same table with Mrs. Rune, who was rumored to be in love with one of them.

Neither man spoke for the first three blocks of the short ride from the hotel to Green Street. Merriman was frankly uncomfortable without Mismer and his omnipresent clutch of schedules and agendas. His personality had come to be an extension of the elaborate protocol which governed his private and public existence. With a script he was letter-perfect; without one, he was a man of small conversation and less charm.

Alex had come to understand this. When enough of a decent interval, two red lights, had elapsed, he turned to Merriman and handed him a single sheet of paper, filled for half its surface with double-spaced typing.

"Being as you've had other things on your mind, sir, I thought a short recap on this meeting as well as some background on MPL and Nyquist would prove helpful."

Merriman's greatest professional asset was that on a subject like this he was a phenomenally quick study. If the rehearsal papers were in order, he absorbed names, vagaries, and objectives like Olivier studying Shakespeare. Presidents of the United States might fumble through briefing books and mispronounce names at the summit of negotiations. Not Leslie Merriman.

Camran's outline was succinct and pointed. He had prevailed on Miss Merit, who mothered properly obsequious young men at the Certified with the same dedication with which she guarded the chairman's time, to give him a copy of an obsolete Mismer protocol. Camran had produced an excellent facsimile. Pretending not to look, but in fact watching closely, Camran saw Merriman's features relax as he digested material which had been carefully served up in a familiar fashion; he seemed as comfortable as if at his favorite corner table at Diego's.

When the limousine drew up in front of the MPL townhouse, Merriman was prepared.

Nyquist himself came to the door to meet them. A visit from Leslie Merriman was the greatest thing that had happened to MPL in its short existence. It called for conservatism. Nyquist was thus vastly elegant in a gray-flannel lounge suit which six Chinese, working from a Savile Row model "borrowed" from the valet at the Pacific Union Club, had labored through the weekend to produce. He wore a white shirt and a Guards tie. Only the dragon buckles on his black moccasins hinted at his customary flamboyance.

"Please come in, Mr. Merriman," he boomed. "You do this house honor. Wong, take our guests' things.

"Before we go upstairs, let me show you around." Leading the way, Nyquist led Merriman and Camran on the same tour on which, almost a year earlier exactly, he had taken David Harrison. On the surface, Harrison would have seen little change. With the exception of the big propane tanks, there was simply more of everything. MPL's business continued to explode. A favorable press, Nyquist's talent for acceptably eccentric publicity, and an investment market which paid happily and exorbitantly for obfuscating jargon and statistics, continued to enrich MPL beyond its founder's improbable early dreams.

"Honestly," Nyquist said to Merriman, pointing pridefully to the military hoard of electronic gear, "if we keep this up, we're going to burst one day."

Upstairs in Nyquist's splendid office, undiminished even by the fog which blotted out the accustomed panorama of the Bay, the men settled around a lacquer tea table. Nyquist knew you didn't big-time the Leslie Merrimans of the world from behind a huge desk. He called for tea.

When it was brought, and Nyquist had poured for his guests, he turned the talk to business. In making the appointment, Miss Merit had been emphatic that Mr. Merriman's Gulfstream was due to depart at one o'clock precisely.

"Well, sir," he sounded like Sydney Greenstreet, thought Camran, "again, it's an honor to entertain you. I trust you had a good Grove?"

He tried slyly to suggest a common level of experience, although he and Merriman knew that, except as a one-shot speaker perhaps, Nyquist would never be included as a celebrant in the redwood rituals.

"Very good, thank you, Mr. Nyquist. Many interesting sessions and, naturally, a group of absolutely grand fellows. Of course at Roundelay we are rather used to that." Camran recognized the name; Camp Roundelay was to the Bohemian Grove what the Pacific Union Club was to San Francisco. He mentally added another item to his inventory of ambitions.

"Now, to business," said Merriman. The skirmishing was over; the cannon could be heard being dragged rumbling to the front. "Some of our fellows, our people, have expressed an interest in adding to our stock of investment media. Something between a full alpha-beta orientation, as I believe you call it, and a comprehensive alpha master program. I believe you call it 'CAMP'?"

Both Nyquist and Camran were astonished, the former more so because he had come to accept that anyone over forty-five—Nyquist was then a lying thirty-nine—would be completely ill at ease with the usages of contemporary investment technology. Camran had heard tales of the chairman's prowess at this sort of badinage. But it was still startling.

"To revert to my pedestrian language, Mr. Nyquist, we are interested in acquiring for our own customers, *certain* customers and preferably on an exclusive basis, a program which can automatically direct the investment of large sums, shall I say billions, into a broad list of stocks, perhaps several thousand. We think that one of our major competitors may already be in or close to the market with such a system, perhaps designed by one of the Los Angeles firms."

It was designed to provoke a rise. It didn't. Nyquist kept well paid moles inside Comidas Partners and Pico Associates, his two chief rivals, who worked within five floors of each other in Century City. If it had been necessary to infiltrate their computer banks, he would have done so. It wasn't. They were still doing the same old thing and, with the one exception at MPL a year ago, there wasn't anything particularly new among the three of them, even if the argot had gotten more elaborate.

"Really, Mr. Merriman. I must say *that* would surprise me. I am fully conversant with what is being done by the three or four of us who straddle the leading edge of investment semiotics. To the best of my knowledge, the only meaningful work in broad-spectrum matrix units has been done right here. And *that* was a custom job. Not, to the best of my belief, for anyone you might logically consider a competitor." He hoped it would satisfy Merriman.

Camran broke in, despite a children-should-be-seen look from his chairman. "Could you describe the job so at least we might get a feel for whether it's the sort of thing we're after?"

"I'm afraid not. The work we do is, after all, highly confidential." He smiled at Merriman, one adult to another, confirming the sanctity of professional confidences.

But Nyquist also wanted the Certified's business. He went on. "I can tell you this. The work we did seemed to incorporate the sort of modulae you've specified: generally, to be sure. Specific quanta would have to be grossed up. Unfortunately, the program we did *is* proprietary, tantamount to copyright for our client. What I can do is to try to contact my client and obtain a release. Otherwise, we're looking at months to come up with something that won't transgress copyright. The schemata's cut-and-dried enough, but you know how long it will take to build in sufficient variants to satisfy my lawyers that there's been no infringement."

Merriman accepted that. Accepting at face value the great wide world of twentieth-century marvels, he assumed that only electrical failure or a posse of lawyers could bring the inexorable diligence of a computer to a halt. There seemed no point in pursuing the matter further. Obviously, this ridiculous man would do what he could; he clearly was anxious to have a major account with the Certified.

Merriman saw an opportunity to make his escape. A covert glance at his wristwatch suggested that they could be airborne nearly an hour ahead of schedule. Perhaps make Wisquisset for goodnight cocoa.

"So be it, Mr. Nyquist. Why don't you see your client and see if he'd be amenable to making some kind of arrangement. And, Mr. Nyquist, in your discretion of course, don't overlook the fact that the Certified is always in the market for *acquisitions*."

The magic word, the hook. Camran could see Nyquist turn on. Like anyone vaguely connected with Wall Street at the time, he fancied a dream role as a merger broker: getting his picture in the papers and journals, talking shrewd and tough like Felix and Steve and Bob. Merriman's suggestion opened broad and tempting vistas.

"I'll get right on it, sir." Nyquist's ambition had completely surfaced; it subdued his self-confidence. He could see himself pictured with Merriman on a flying Mideast visit, advising sheikhs and kings. Having his photograph taken. "I'll be back to you as soon as I can."

In the car to the airport, Merriman remarked that he found Nyquist a very peculiar sort. That was all he said until, somewhere over southern Illinois, he smiled at Camran and remarked, "You handled yourself very nicely out there, Alex."

The fact that he had, to his recollection, said two complete sentences to Merriman and Nyquist, and only two, did not in the least blight Alex Camran's admiring recognition of his own capability. There were all sorts of routes to the top. In his ambition's house were many mansions. And the doors certainly opened for Merriman.

Back in San Francisco, Nyquist had his own complications to sort out. He had implied an intimate client relationship, but the fact was that, apart from two meetings a year ago, he had nothing to go on. At the time he thought that he was grossly overcharging that fellow Axman—was that his name?—for a program which handled great batches of data in a fast, efficient manner. Quite simple, really. Which was the problem now. He knew the goddamn Certified spent money like water for conceptual gimmicks which had selling pizazz. He should have seen at the time that Axelrod's commission was that sort of thing. If he had, he would never have signed that last sheet in the folder which accompanied the tape reels he'd handed over so jovially to that fellow Edelson—what the hell *was* his name? The page simply described the elements of the RAID program, and its little brother OVOID, and acknowledged the transfer of all proprietary rights to the fellow's firm.

"Tina!" He buzzed his secretary. "About a year ago. August last year. We did some work for a man who came in over the transom. Axton, Ackleman, something like that. You'll remember: he came in and picked up the stuff himself. Right, right. Well, check the files. See what the name of his outfit is."

Tina was back to him in five minutes. She had the contract. August 4. It was with a Master Structural Trust Associates. New York City post office box. New York phone number. The man's name was Martin Axelson.

He punched the buttons impatiently. "I'm sorry, your call cannot go through as dialed. Please..." The metallic monotone with which Ma Bell addresses her impatient, erring children. Nyquist stabbed at the buttons again. Same result. He buzzed Tina. "Check this number with New York information." She was back in a minute. They had a Master Structural Trust Associates in the directory. The number was unlisted. Their number couldn't be checked. Goddamn it, thought Nyquist, this is the sort of thing they go in for in Beverly Hills. He felt helpless. Over the intercom he dictated a letter to Axelson which she finished quickly. Scribbling his signature, he reflected that it was a hell of a note to have to *write* letters to do business. Hadn't microelectronics and telecommunications sent all that to limbo? Writing was for lawyers and novelists. Outside his window the fog drew closer, pattering into the city. Not that Nyquist had heard of Carl Sandburg.

His letter came back in ten days: "Addressee Moved—No Forwarding Address." By that time, what with the rush and pace of Axel Nyquist's busy life, the matter had receded somewhat in importance in the MPL scale of things. The reappearance of the letter stirred the matter up again. Thinking of what a contract with Certified could mean in dollars and publicity, he grew choleric and kicked the desk as hard as he could. Neither the old British walnut nor the soft Italian shoe leather were meant for kicking. Within half an hour his toe was as swollen and red as abalone meat. Shamefacedly, he had to lean on Wong to help him to the car and to drive him to the clinic to have the toe set.

The Jordan campaign was going as badly as expected. John Jordan had to admit that Dunstable had delivered what he had promised. His tireless people were out in front, setting up the meetings in the eight big cities in which the August "precampaign" was to be run. They were as effective and suave as Byzantine diplomatists in dealing with logistics. Young and endlessly cheerful, they radiated what Jordan found to be a kind of bleak synthetic quality. Perfect by the numbers. But the evidence was in the small crowds: less than 10,000 in Chicago; 5300 in Birmingham; 8500 in Madison Square Garden; and, ignominiously, less than 21,000 in the Astrodome, when Dunstable himself keynoted the appearance of the Republican candidate.

There seemed to be no shortage of money. True, at Dunstable's suggestion, they had gone slow in preparing a heavy television lineup for the fall campaign. The money would be there if needed, Jordan had been assured. Not by Dunstable—who never seemed to talk figures. Jordan assumed it to be a specific reticence engendered by that Iranian business a few years back. Dunstable had been accused of engineering the prepaid political asylum of the then head of SAVAK, the Iranian Gestapo, for an astronomical sum. Although Bergarzak, the gentleman in question, was safely in Palm Springs, the assertions against Dunstable had gone unconfirmed. Surprisingly, no less to Jordan than to the man who had been instructed to carry the message, the assurance came through his old friend Benjamin Masters, the Washington attorney who represented several of the candidate's former client states from the old CIA days.

Masters had driven out to Jordan's house, now picketed by bodyguards, expressly to convey the good regards of certain of *his* largest clients. The two men were sharing a long bourbon as the sun turned to haze over the distant mountains.

Masters had come quickly to the point. "You've got a lot of awfully good friends in the Kingdom, John. It seems that no one's forgotten your hand in that business back in '75. You know I do a lot of work for them now, special interest stuff, Capitol Hill and the Pentagon, that sort of thing. You'd probably be doing it yourself if you and Margaret hadn't had the good luck and good sense to come out here. My God, it's beautiful here. I can see why those weekly lunches of yours are enough of the District for you. Until this, of course, the campaign, which you *had* to make. It's going to be tough for you, God knows, and you're sure as hell the better man than this clown and his merry crew of rednecks, but you and I know he's riding a hell of a horse. Anyway, I'm not here to analyze politics, let's leave that to Joe Kraft. What I *am* here to say is that certain of my clients, old friends of yours, John, have advised me, hell, let's be frank, John, have instructed me to tell you that if, at any time, in this campaign, you decide you could use some money, you'll have it. On the up and up. As much as you need."

John Jordan was properly appreciative. But he was also from conservative, prudent New England stock.

"Ben, that's awfully kind of your friends—*our* friends— and I know you'll tell them so for me. Obviously, this conversation can't leave this porch. You're not carrying one of those little recorders that seem to have become *de rigueur* in the District since the *Kaiserszeit?*"

Laughingly, and truthfully, Masters said he was not.

"Well, then," continued Jordan, "I'll keep their very generous offer in mind. It does sort of balance the books, after what they've done for Baxter. He must have made some pretty spectacular promises, though. Nobody in Foggy Bottom seems to know a darn thing. My people say that Drzlag is going crazy trying to find out what's up, but Baxter just fobs him off."

"It's worse than that, John. I'll tell you something I heard from someone who is very big at Langley *and* the White House. You won't believe it, but the backstairs gossip at 1600 Pennsylvania is that even Ermabelle Baxter doesn't know what the hell the story is!"

"Good heavens! That *is* extraordinary. I don't believe it for a minute, of course. If it's true and Ermabelle doesn't know, I'd almost have to say that Baxter doesn't either. You see what I mean?"

"I'd agree, John. If that were possible. Anyway, that's my scoop for the day. Good luck in Cleveland on Tuesday. Don't wear yourself out."

"Don't worry, Ben. This election is lost but it pays to keep slugging. After all, this party can stand the loss of an election; but the country can't stand the loss of this party."

The absence of hard news made it a weird summer for everyone who had a stake in the politics which had been so traumatically reshaped by the Kingdom's action. The protagonists were simply unavailable to the press. Alrazi and the Minister were incommunicado. The King had taken himself into the desert to prepare for Ramadan. He would be joined there by the rest of the government. So much for the visible figures in the Kingdom.

President Baxter, firmly convinced that ignorance was in fact bliss, and seeing the evidence of bliss everywhere, stayed distant. He was vague and amorphous with Drzlag and Buster. The polls argued for the status quo. He kept the latest polls in his pocket. The *Chicago Tribune* showed him with 75 percent of the vote as Labor Day approached.

Prosperity had its discontents, of course. Like the Capitol's one-time innermost insiders who now stood, like Secretary Drzlag, foaming and agape with vexation at their minuscule role in things. Worse still, this had become known to the press. The *New York Times* had abruptly canceled a *Sunday Magazine* cover article on Drzlag. Queried by the State Department press officer, the *Times'* Sunday editor had elected to observe curtly that the magazine's cover stories were by policy limited to personalities and matters of significant public interest and consequence. Since neither criteria now seemed to apply to Secretary of State Drzlag, the article had been tabled.

The meddlesome, pugnacious little nations of the world were obliged to shut up. In Tel Aviv, the prime minister was quietly advised by the British ambassador: "Moshemin, be calm. Say nothing." The Ambassador used the nickname by which he had first known the Prime Minister. "The feeling of the Americans toward the Kingdom is such that any aggressive noises by you would probably result in your abandonment by Washington. The public would not stand for any other policy. Baxter wouldn't risk it politically anyway. And, dear Moshemin, though we have been friends for thirty years, I can tell you I would advise my country to do the same." H.M. ambassador was feeling assertive. A cable that morning had advised that his bid to repurchase the family seat in Sussex had been accepted by the Genoese tanning magnate to whom he had been obliged to sell it three years earlier. The Italian was returning home, now that the general financial improvement had produced a stable, tough right-centrist government in Rome. There had been no public outcry, in Italy or in the world, at the summary execution in the Piazza del Duomo of the cell of Milanese terrorists who had been captured in March. The example appeared to have been set. There seemed to be no terrorists active. Anywhere. Even the PLO was quiet.

The oil companies were not entirely happy. The President's action in decontrolling all domestic oil had temporarily spoiled their long-range plan to drive the independents out of business. Nevertheless, as the heads of the nine big companies agreed at their underground parley in Jamaica, they had most likely missed a bullet. If Baxter's political situation had been desperate, he probably would have blown the whistle on their secret deal last summer with Nordlander to force conservation on the American people by drumming up a gasoline shortage. They were still in business; given the clumsiness with which they handled their politics and their public relations, it was a wonder. They crossed themselves, sipped reflectively on their rum punches, and got down to the serious business of figuring out how to put the blocks to the independents. It would have been eye-opening to anyone who thought that the oil industry was a vast amalgam of common interests. All they had in common was oil.

So it went, around the world. The gambling handle at the famous casinos of Europe was higher than ever: the English and French were back in action, along with the Americans, and the Arabs had never left. The most expensive resorts were more crowded than ever. Even the small, bankrupt countries saw the merest glint of hope on the horizon. Their prayers of thanks were echoed by grateful sighs in banking offices across the world from Cheapside to Pine Street and the Ginza.

26 The Dow was at 1724 when Harrison called Khafiq to advise him that they would be closed out by mid-September.

"I'm glad you called, David," said the perfumed accent, faint over the distance. "I'm leaving tomorrow night for Capri for a fortnight. It's the best season, really. Why don't you join me for ten days or so? I can book you rooms at the Quisisana; I have some influence there. Bring your friend."

Harrison always thought that phrase odd. Devon was

really Khafiq's employee. He had no way of knowing that Devon had turned up in Khafiq's order of things as naturally and uninvolvedly as a rented car presented itself at a strange airport on Harrison's arrival. It was simply a matter of making a phone call and having an account, although the numbers were all unlisted and the existence of the accounts unknown.

It was a very tempting offer. Like any man of soul, Harrison's heart, like Peech's, like Goethe's, lay somewhere between the Boot and the Alps. Often late at night, he would hold Devon and croon exaggeratedly: *"Kennst di des Lend/ Wo die Zitronen bluehn?"* Italy was Harrison's Mecca.

"I'll call you back. Tomorrow morning, no later," he promised. He finished reciting the week's activity. The instructive telex had gone out earlier. They were down to less than $350 million and Ernie was pacing himself.

When he finished, Khafiq added. "My dear David, with so little time left, and so little money really, what harm to take a short vacation? I can promise you that the clients are very pleased, very pleased indeed. Why not just shut down for a fortnight or so? Spend ten days with me in Capri? Then you can go on to Venice? I'll phone the Cipriani? In any case, the transaction will be completed by early October at the latest. Nothing will have changed by then." He was very convincing. And the customer was right, thought Harrison. Always.

Devon was excited. She had wanted for a long time to see Italy straight up, not as a fugitive, not through sewer gratings and the slitted air vents of hidden attics. She could go safely now, she knew. Stopping by a foreign newsdealer's in Madison Avenue one afternoon a few weeks back to pick up a copy of *Apollo* for Harrison, a stark cover on *Paris-Match* caught her eye. Under the caption JUSTICE ÉFFICACE À MILAN was a photograph of a dozen bodies stacked like cordwood under the massive dignity of the Cathedral. An arm protruded from the pile; it wore a bracelet which Devon could recognize even through the deforming grain of the photograph. It belonged to her former, now late, lover from the *Bregate Rosse.* With his death, she now ceased to have any existence in that part of the world other than as the shadowiest of memories.

"Let's do go, David. I do want to see Khafiq again. He's such a special little man." She was very persuasive. "Besides, I want to make love to you under a Mediterranean moon.

Let's do go. I want to do *this* to you with a tenor singing in the lemon tree outside the window." If her imagery was a trifle offbeat, the way in which she touched him and what it did, gathering his nerve ends into a single screaming fiber on his outermost point, was not.

"All right," he said, already near breathlessness with excitement, "I'll confirm it in the morning. But now you've got to finish what you've started." He got no argument. Her clothes were already puddled around her ankles. After so many times, so much time, he could still not get over the way she looked naked. He could see she was as excited as he was, then he could feel it, touch it, taste it. He remained in her for what seemed like hours, it was a new ability, bringing her off again and again, until neither could stand it further and they fell apart.

Devon had gone off to buy film and Harrison was standing in the TWA terminal, ticking off the last-minute checklist. Ernie had shut down RAID. He was delighted to be able to take a few weeks off, to get back with the Brothers and the old South Side connections. There was a big do set for Labor Day. Harrison had gone to Boston and picked up the tapes. They were locked in the air-conditioned closet in his apartment with his good wine.

They would regroup in three weeks. The first Monday after Labor Day. There was $480 million of market value left to run out. The Dow looked like making 1800 by Labor Day, better than doubling since Easter! Because RAID had bought the big stocks, into which the institutions and the public had jumped with both feet after Green Monday, it had actually done a little better than the market. The public was now chasing speculations; nothing really rank yet but the signs were there. If they cashed in tomorrow, Harrison figured, they would have taken out a little better than $9.5 billion. In round numbers, a cozy profit of slightly better than $5 billion. He had earned his fee. The biggest commission ever paid on a single market deal. Most of it was already safely and anonymously lodged in seven banks around the world. None in the Commerçante, of course. But when this was all wrapped up, he'd throw a little their way, a few mil, just to give Marc-Antoine something to think about.

"Mr. Axelson?" said a voice at his shoulder. He didn't look up. "Axelson?" The repetition interrupted his thinking. A hand fell heavily on his shoulder and he turned to stare, curious, then surprised, into the huge, triumphant features of Axel Nyquist.

Nyquist was a blinding spectacle. His bulk was accentuated by a red and buff plaid suit with six-inch checks. He was leaning on a silver-tipped knobkerrie. Behind him a young TWA stewardess stood simpering, trying to balance her wheeled suitcase with Nyquist's enormous buckled briefcase.

"Goddamnit, Axelson, you're a hard man to find." Harrison caught on. Until this moment, "Axelson" had long since disappeared in some city incinerator along with forty other pseudonyms. *He* was "Axelson"!

"How are you, Nyquist," he said, hoping that Devon had been enticed into the duty-free shop. "Long time."

"You bet. I've tried you everywhere. What's wrong with your phone? And your mail comes back addressee unknown. Jesus! I mean, this isn't Switzerland!"

Harrison pleaded the hopelessness of the phone company and the post office. Excuses so redolent of possible truth that Nyquist couldn't argue. The great gift of an inefficient government to its constituents: Excuses.

"What's the cane for, Axel?" Harrison asked, confident in his new/old identity.

Nyquist lied. "Gout. That damn Yon Choh discovered a colonial British cookbook. He does everything in port now. Delicious, but I've got a big toe the size of Singapore." Like all promoters, Nyquist slid easily into the trappings of his stage presence.

"Listen," the big man said, brushing aside Harrison's solicitousness. Over his shoulder the stewardess teetered and set the briefcase down with a toppling thump. "Easy, dear," Nyquist exclaimed, "there's six grams of the best coke in there and six boxes of amyl." He grinned at Harrison, men of the world sharing expensive naughtiness. Harrison grinned back; ten years with Barney convoying personal pharmacies through airports had inured him to the confidences of the high life.

"Listen," Nyquist picked up the thread, "you know that program we did for you a year ago? RAID? OVOID?" He turned away to scold the stewardess who was trying to make the case sit upright. Over Nyquist's head, Harrison saw Devon coming out of the tunnel. He flashed a high sign with his eyebrows which she caught, thank God, and turned back into the main terminal.

Nyquist resumed. "Listen, on that program? I don't know how you're coming, but you've really got something there. You still using it?" He didn't wait for an answer. "Maybe yes, maybe no. Don't be coy. I'll lay it on the table. We've got a very big client, very big," he salivated on the adjective, "who wants something just like it. I'll offer you a million for the right to use it, still exclusive to you except for this client. Christ, this market'll stand two of you working at the same time. I'll level with you, Axelson, this could be make or break for us. How about it?"

Never answer anything for at least twenty-four hours. That had been Clare Verger's advice to Harrison years ago.

"Axel, I can't say. I'll have to talk to my associates." Harrison meant it. He liked the idea of fathering a best-seller but his responsibility was to Khafiq.

"How soon?"

"When I get back from this trip. Say three weeks."

"Where're you going, anyway?"

"Really, Axel. I'm going west. Where you just came from, I guess, and a little beyond." He tried to put allusive resonances of the Far East in his words.

"I get it. Hong Kong. I always figured as much. That or the Gotham Bank. You're too old school to deal with the Mafia and the only other guys with that kind of money, the Arabs, buy nothing but Treasuries."

"Alex, don't guess. I'll take it up with the client. I'll call you yes or no when I get back. Middle of September. OK?"

Nyquist accepted the fact. "Don't let me down now. There could be a hell of a lot more in this for you." He was as suggestive as if proposing an assignation.

"Let me help you." Harrison picked up Nyquist's enormous briefcase and the stewardess' overnight bag. He followed Nyquist's stumping path to the curbside. A limousine the size of a battleship awaited. Harrison saw them into the car.

"Don't forget now. This could be very big. For us both." Nyquist pulled the door shut. Through the half-open window he said, "Jesus, what a break for me running into you after this trouble. Makes a man think about the dynamics of chance and will. Von Neumann needs retooling." He took a calculator from his pocket.

Von Neumann occupied Nyquist for about twenty-five yards. Harrison, watching the car out of sight, saw Nyquist's head move suddenly, smotheringly across the rear window to the stewardess.

Inside, Devon was toe-tapping. "Who was that?"

"Just a guy I used to know on the Street. He sells insurance now."

If she thought differently, she said nothing.

After landing early in the morning at Ciampino Airport, they slept through lunch. That afternoon, they walked down the Spanish Steps to the Via Condotti. Rome itself had gone to the beaches for August but the stores were open. Devon loaded up, like a child with a blank Christmas check. Harrison gave her an hour and a half, then forced her into a cab for a late afternoon coffee in the Piazza Navona. Sant'Agnese and the Bernini fountain glorified the very fact of their being alive and together and the noise of children and barkers in the square provided a spirited, happy counterpoint to the fatigue of the day's walking.

"Some time we'll come back here for a month. Do a week of the Renaissance, a week of the Baroque, a week of Saint Peter, and a week of the Caesars."

"Sounds very organized. Do I have to sleep with the tour guide?"

"You better believe it." Excited, he paid the bill and rushed her back to the Eden.

He had alerted friends that they were coming. After a drink at the Hassler, they went over to a taverna in Trastevere, across the Tiber, where a low arbor overhung a garden. The stars sparkled among the vines. His friends flirted outrageously with Devon and she reciprocated playfully. The white wine made Harrison jealous—in spite of himself—but that mood soon passed. It was the last night out for serious Roman businessmen; the tables were filled with attractive men and their mistresses. Everyone was happy. The cautious intensity of year-long affairs needed the welcome relief of a three weeks' separation. Soon a guitarist appeared and everyone sang. Old Roman songs: *'Barcarolla Romana'*; *'Campagnola Bella'*; the singer sounded like Claudio Villa. Harrison's head was swimming and he joined in loudly, trying to conceal his flats and sharps with sheer enthusiasm and volume. No one minded.

After dinner, they drank Armenian brandy on a balcony overlooking the Forum. The old ruins were patched with shadow and light like a Piranesi print. The Campidoglio blazed in the distance, across a field of domes and towers. Harrison, quite drunk now, recited the opening lines of the *Commedia*. Then his few remembered fragments of Ariosto. Then Leopardi: *"Sempre caro me fu quest'ermo colle..."* His audience of three ignored his thick-mouthed stumblings and applauded; they were all in love with Italy. It occurred to him that there were about fifty thousand things he wanted to say to Devon but something had got between his brain and his tongue.

He wrenched her out of bed early the next morning, fed her rolls and *caffelatte,* and dragged her squeaking across Rome to San Luigi dei Francesi to commune with Caravaggio. "Apart from the Sistine, merely the greatest thing in Rome," he declaimed. As they left he put another hundred-lira coin in the paybox, just to keep the fantastic paintings lit and alive for another five minutes.

Khafiq was waiting for them on the pier when the Naples-Capri hydrofoil docked. With a series of monosyllables and small gestures, he organized their baggage and led them to the taxi which carried them up the hill into town.

"I thought I'd best meet you," he said. "Your rooms are ready at the Quisisana, but in order to accommodate you there has been a bit of unpleasantness with a guest who wished to stay on but whose room I've appropriated."

They ambled through the town, bustling with its six o'clock parade of the world's most conscientious shoppers.

As they walked onto the Quisisana terrace, Harrison was given an opportunity to meditate on the few odd kindnesses of coincident fortune. Presiding over a pile of luggage and a small, aggressively shrewish wife was Frank Castato, screaming expletives at a serenely indifferent concierge, who bowed at Khafiq's approach. Castato stopped when he saw Harrison and redirected his bile.

"You better not unpack your fucking bags, Dave!" Khafiq and Devon passed unnoticed into the hotel lobby, followed by the attentive desk clerk.

"These fucking guineas," Castato continued, "better watch their goddamn step! Reservations don't mean a goddamn thing!" He waved a slip of paper in the air. "We should've bombed these fuckers flat in '42!" When Castato was three years old, Harrison reflected. He noted with approval that the Campari drinkers on the terrace paid Castato no mind.

Ugly Americans were no longer a subject for general resentment, merely curiosities.

Harrison usually had no time for Castato, but this opportunity was precious.

Castato was wearing pale mauve Henry Markham jeans; his navy golf shirt had a polo pony embroidered on it; his belt closed with a large brass *H*. The cross-fittings of his shiny white loafers featured intertwined *G*s. He stood quivering with rage beside an enormous mound of brown luggage covered with *L*s and *V*s.

Harrison looked him up and down carefully. "You going to a costume party, Frank?"

"Whaddaya talking about?"

"I'm sorry. I was simply trying to guess why you're dressed up like a letterhead."

Castato started to say something, but Harrison cut him off.

"Sorry about all of this, Frank, but I need a bath and a change. I'm sure they'll come up with something. If not, the late mail barge to Naples isn't too bad and I'm sure you can find something there. The toilet won't be too far down the hall. Anyway, it sure as hell beats West Hampton."

He smiled generously and stepped lightly into the cool lobby. Castato had only time to aim one "You smartass fuck!" at his back before his wife resumed her whining antiphony. It was going to be a long winter on Mother Cabrini Drive, Harrison thought.

They spent a long week in the sun, one lazy, overfed day following another, eating pasta at Luigi's in the shadow of the Faraglioni, the tall rocks which columned the entrance to a small cove. In the afternoon they shopped, buying shoes at Canfora and small jewelry at La Campanina. Evenings were given to late dinners, after a six o'clock nap, and a quiet midnight espresso in the square. Khafiq vanished right after dinner, so Harrison and Devon found plenty to talk about. For distraction the evening sideshow in the Piazza, principally gangling young men with whistling hips, filled the silences.

"My God, this is pleasant," he said to her one night. "Do you realize it's a week to Labor Day? I don't think we miss all those cocktail parties in Lenox."

She didn't.

The next day they were stretched out, the three of them, on mats on the rocks near Luigi's.

"Really quite a bearable world," said Khafiq. Neither muscled nor bony nor fat, his small porcelain body, now lightly tanned under a slick oil coating, was clothed in what looked like a tiny diaper. "It's nice to have the world in some sort of peace."

Harrison agreed. The sun was beating through the screen of his white wine contentment. "You know," he said, "we may even have another career."

Devon, pleading heat, arose and went down to the water.

"Just before getting on the airplance," Harrison continued, "I ran into Axel Nyquist at TWA in New York. You'll recall he's the man whose firm designed our investment program. He'd like to buy it back. From the way he talked, he's got an important potential customer, some bank probably, that wants the same sort of thing we've been doing. Offered me a million. I said I'd talk to my associates. He's guessing they're Chinese. Anyway, what do you think? We're almost finished, after all."

"Let me think about it." Khafiq turned on his stomach and dozed off on the hot stones.

It was two in the morning when Khafiq got back to the Quisisana. He had been too preoccupied to enjoy what had promised to be a most amusing evening. Eventually, he had settled with the two young sailors and the old fortune teller with the dog. Full rate, although the contracted excitements had not been required.

A waiter brought a last espresso. He loaded it with sugar to the thickness of syrup and pondered the state of play. At length, he concluded that he was faced with a momentary technical difficulty, not worth troubling Qu'nesh with. In any event, Alrazi was in Deauville and in a filthy temper, Khafiq guessed, knowing that he had to go back shortly for Ramadan. To make matters worse, the Prince's horses had consistently run behind animals belonging to a group of English Jews. Out of sorts, Prince Alrazi tended to overreact, to clear all decks, blow everyone out of the water. He, Khafiq, was a man of parts. More levelheaded. It could be handled. He finished his coffee and went to bed.

Khafiq was up early the next day. After a light breakfast, he strolled up the hill to the Postal Telegraph office, which had a direct overseas line. From a purse which hung from his wrist he paid the toll in full, in cash, and went into a booth.

The phone rang three times in an apartment in Damascus. When it was answered, Khafiq identified himself in a special way and then talked without interruption for ten minutes. When he hung up, satisfied, he sat in the booth for a minute before walking back down to the hotel. He was on his third cup of morning coffee and immersed in the *Paris Herald* when Harrison and Devon appeared, ready for another day in the sun.

IV

OSMAN

27 Dalip Singh lay on top of the sheets, staring through the dark in the bedroom of his small Berkeley apartment, glorying, gloating, and trying to keep his hands off the slender figure sleeping noiselessly at his side. Love—call it that or whatever you will—had been a long time coming, he thought. For twelve years, since he'd first come to Berkeley to do graduate work in advanced calculus at the university, he'd searched for romance. Friday and Saturday nights, sometimes Thursdays too, saw him driving his snappy red Datsun 280Z back across the Bay Bridge into the bright promise of San Francisco.

But until tonight, no luck. The shiny-toothed optimism that had seen him through all the years of lonely, unachieving nights had started to wear thin. He was tired of working the circuit: the tough bars and the no-holds-barred places on Polk Street; the singles action out on Union and Sacramento streets; the daylight pursuit and side-eyed glances on the jogging paths of the Marina and the Presidio; long nights sitting in the Etoile listening to Peter Mintun play the old, sad songs in the midst of cheerfully flirtatious couples; even Trader Vic's, where the bartender had looked him over like kitchen help on a night out and intimidated him into leaving.

All dressed up, and tricked out with the sparkling appurtenances which his $60,000 in salary and bonuses from MPL bought him, Dalip still retained the dark, anxious aura of his native Madras. There was no getting away from the Indian-ness of his looks, which seemed to deflect prospects as much as the comic singsong of his English, so precise and self-parodying. So his few "successes" had been casual affairs with a basic dirtiness, bought and transitory, that no amount of alcohol or drugs could disguise. Persons of lower class, Dalip would think, without a jot of understanding of him or his work or his culture. Dirty little grapplings before dawn.

Not tonight, however, and praise Allah for it!

He had been later than usual getting away from work. Nyquist had kept him overlong. Dalip was Nyquist's principal assistant. Their relationship was part father-son, part master-slave, as it had been from the first day Dalip had gone to work as a grader for Nyquist who was then still teaching at State.

"Something very big may be coming our way, Dalip. The biggest yet. You know who was here the other day?"

Dalip knew, but the tone of the question demanded the pretense of ignorance.

"No, sir."

"Merriman. Leslie Merriman, no less, that's who. By God, Dalip, we may be on to the Certified business. Twenty-three billion they've got under management!" The thought had so excited Nyquist that he catapulted from his chair and paced before his picture window, hands behind him, gazing across the Bay, like Nelson in that last dawn off the Spanish coast.

"I finally tracked down that Axelson fellow. The man who we built—you built, really, Dalip—the RAID program for. You know, he scarcely recognized me. Me!" Nyquist was wearing a velvet suit piped in electric pink. He looked like a barge at Henley.

"Anyway," Nyquist had continued, "he promised to get back to me about licensing the program. Of course we'll have to rename it for Certified, Dalip. I've been doing some thinking on that. What do you think of CRAB? 'Certified Regressive Analysis Base!' Better, don't you feel, than 'Analysis Program,' which was my first thought?" Nyquist chuckled hugely.

"I think it's most excellent. Really, sir." Nyquist's verbal cleverness was a genuine miracle to Dalip.

He had promised Nyquist to get to work on blocking out

the modifications necessary to accommodate RAID to the dimensions likely to be required by Certified. It never occurred to Dalip's exponentially methodical intellect to run the thing repetitively. No, to build the cathedral necessitated first to tear down the church, he thought as he went off to the files in search of the RAID material. He became absorbed in it and in his pondering of the twists and possibilities. When he looked up from his scratch pad, it was seven-thirty, he saw with surprise and then vexation, for it meant that he had missed the Thursday happy hour at Perry's Grill, territory which Dalip ardently still believed, in spite of all the aridity of his experience, to hold the romantic riches of Golconda.

Too late to go all the way to Berkeley and back again, he had thought as he paused on the steps. Outside, his mood took on something of the pleasant calm of the evening. He nodded agreeably to the man shutting the doors of the Pac Tel van.

"Everything all right?" The modems had been acting up, something about the circuits, he supposed. Lukins, who usually took care of the mechanical end of things, was still on vacation, and so Dalip was in charge of the circuit room until Tuesday. Business would be slow over the Labor Day weekend, anyway, he supposed. Not that he had any plans. Dalip never had any plans. He guessed he would work on RAID; at home, since Nyquist had declared MPL headquarters in quarantine for the weekend. Dalip imagined correctly that there was to be a lady on the premises.

Anyway, this modem business was a bit of a nuisance, but he could understand the irritation of MPL's customers, who paid $50,000 to $100,000 to converse freely with MPL's basement computer room, to have their interfaces fizzing and spitting out meaningless numbers because something had gone on the fritz at the telephone company.

The Pac Tel repairman had nodded. "All clear now, sir." He tugged at the peak of his cap. An immigrant like me, thought Dalip, who detected an accent which was not immediately identifiable. Then, magnanimously, he said, "Well, good; very well done, indeed. Good. Well, good evening."

Ed's, or the Midnight Moon, was the choice he had pondered as he pulled the 280Z away from the curb and headed east. He would try Ed's; it was close enough to the outer limits of Noe Valley to attract a well dressed, spending singles crowd, but "Castro Street" enough to have character. It was the kind of place where Dalip could legitimately believe that his high salary might give him an edge.

He had trouble parking his car, which was evidence that Ed's was having a big night. The place was packed and he had trouble squeezing up to the bar. As he reached through the press for his glass of white wine, an accidental movement by the man on his left caused his arm to jerk, spilling a few drops on the arm of his right-hand neighbor.

"I'm sorry. So sorry. Please, oh excuse me." When he was flustered or insecure, Dalip couldn't get his words organized.

"It's all right." The responding voice was soft. Again, an accent he couldn't identify. "No harm done."

Dalip had looked into dark eyes. Nice, modish clothes. Skin like espresso. His insides flipped. He felt himself want. Very badly.

"Please, may I give you a drink? Wine should be for the inside so it has been for the outside." It was a bad joke to begin with; his linguistic confusion made it worse. "Please," he continued, hoping he didn't sound desperate, "they have here an excellent Chenin Blanc which I most highly recommend."

"That would be nice." The eyes kept smiling, doing miracles for Dalip's poise. And then another miracle, a table cleared.

"May we sit down? Together?"

Smiling eyes assented.

At the table, more wine was drunk; confidences and discoveries flowed. Mutual loneliness was bartered. Dalip's new friend turned out to be an exchange student from Conakry, who had attended Stanford and was now studying nursing at Cal General and living uncomfortably with three other students in a billet development outside Orinda. Happiest of accidents, this was no more than fifteen minutes' drive from Dalip's apartment.

Drinks had led them to dinner at a good Italian place below Russian Hill. The headwaiter greeted Dalip with impressive warmth. It was nearly midnight when they finished coffee.

"May I drive you home," Dalip asked tentatively. "The buses and BART are now most dangerous, quite really so."

His friend had smiled and nodded, letting a hand rest absently and briefly on Dalip's cashmere sleeve.

The Bay Bridge was strung like pearls across the night. The world sang. His new friend had marveled at the Datsun which Dalip kept polished like lapidary enamel. He drove *strongly*, if that was possible. Neither spoke for the width of the crossing. It was as if the little car was pumped full of a heavy, overwhelming perfume.

Dalip swung off the bridge and turned up into the hills which ridged the cup of the bay.

"May I please offer a nightcap? I have some very excellent brandy. A gift from my superior, who is a man of great and good taste."

"Why not? It's been such a lovely evening. I still don't know why I was in the bar. A friend had said she'd meet me if she could. But she didn't and yet I feel so very, very lucky."

The voice spoke to Dalip as a downright invitation. He became excited.

He had led the way upstairs to his apartment and flicked on the lights.

"Be comfortable," he said. "I'll get ice and glasses." He was aquiver. When he returned, his friend was looking at a reproduction of a Rajput painting of a tiger hunt.

"This is very interesting."

"Yes, from the English period." Dalip's eyes had locked on the appreciative gaze from across the room. He moved across the room, reaching out his arms, having them filled, having his mouth filled with heat, fingers at his belt, touching him *there* and encircling him until he was as hard as he had ever been, harder than he had ever made himself. It was almost beyond control. He touched back, feeling hair, moisture, pulsation. Clothes fell to the floor. Stumbling, desperate haste into the bedroom, a moment's preparation, then friction, wildness, angles: the painful geometry of coupling. Touching each other, reaching around, stroking, then bang!

The recollection made him jumpy with excitement. He touched the shoulder of the sleeping figure; reflexively, a dark, fine hand went out to stroke him, brought him onto a pinnacle of excitement and sent him, Dalip the All-Conqueror, reeling through his private, flaming spaces. It was a matter of seconds. Dalip screamed and then collapsed flat, hyperventilating, breathless in love. "Wonderful. So good. Yes. So wonderful." He heaved with passion.

"Ssssh..." A gentle calming finger touched his lips. Dalip thought he could taste himself. The voice was sincerely, supremely maternal.

"Sleep now, dear. I'll be here. Sleep."

It was Ernie.

The street was unlit and, at this hour, empty, so Colonel Osman was able to discharge his task in his customary matter-of-fact way. He was a professional man, as much so as an optometrist or an attorney; he did nothing wasteful, made no movement which was not precise, economical, architectural.

Crouching at the curb, beside the 280Z, he kneaded the claylike substance into short, plump rolls about two inches long. There was enough for just four such rolls; the rest of the slab which Osman had brought from Chicago had been deployed earlier on a bigger job. It was a new matériel, the latest thing, more powerful and workable than the stuff the Irish and the Mossad were using, and eminently more stable. Expensive stuff; there were only ten slabs in existence; it had cost a half-million Deutschemarks to purchase the unauthorized exit of five of these from the closely watched experimental laboratory of the Hoechst plant outside Duisburg. Five slabs: one had gone to London; one to Paris; one to Bangkok; and two to Baghdad. It was one of the latter that had been flown in the diplomatic pouch to Chicago—to rendezvous with Colonel Osman, himself just arrived from Damascus.

Osman was well traveled. He was given to making painstaking estimates of the trivia of his life: once he had calculated that the ink used in the entry stamps in his four passports would aggregate nearly half a kilo. This was his first visit to America in over a decade.

Osman didn't go in for gadgetry: no tooth darts, grenades made up like shaving canisters, cars which flew. Good stuff for the movies, but unreliable in the strange hotel rooms or dark roads where he got most of his work done. He wasn't a mass bomber, trying to pinpoint the blowoff of kilotons of TNT to vaporize a passing car. He killed chosen individuals, one at a time and alone; he didn't scatter his stock of death. Besides, working as he did, hundreds, thousands of miles from Damascus, he couldn't possibly cope with the paraphernalia his PLO associates insisted on lugging around to their latest mass outrage.

He could shoot, if necessary, but—better—he knew exactly how and where to hit a man and send him down the short road to eternity. He liked to work against other professionals; head to head, those encounters tended to be as meticulously ordered as a quadrille, and he was simply a better dancer. Of course, he took on any assignment. A wife and three daughters buried in Lebanon, charred by Israeli flame-throwers, had cemented his purpose. A small store of technical knowledge, six languages, five passports and an American Express card were all he needed to get on with the job.

He always worked alone, figuring that his own wits would stand him best if not responsible for the conduct and safety of anyone else. He didn't care where the battlefield was pitched: Wardour Street; the Row of a Thousand Knives; the Unterdenlinden. He wanted only first-class tools and a schedule with a margin of flexibility. None of the headline-grabbing stuff, all noise and altogether too risky. Osman was a careful man. He intended to meet the Prophet shod, smiling, and at peace, in the heat of his beloved desert.

He finished shaping the explosive. From his pocket he took four standard circular half-volt camera batteries. Each had a hair-fine copper filament soldered to its surface; the last sixteenth-inch of the filament was shielded with plastic winding. One by one, he pinched the middles of the explosive sausages flat and then, with his thumbs, very, very gently and carefully, pressed the batteries into the rolls. Taking a bottle of clear nail polish from his jacket pocket, he coated the joining of plastic and battery case, leaving the filament tips loose and clean.

Using a penlight, he examined each battery for the numerals 1 to 4 which he had scratched on their surfaces earlier. Placing number one carefully on the paving, he felt under the right front fender of the Datsun, reaching around to the back of the tire, to the groove which signaled the meeting of rubber and rim. He left his finger there to mark the spot and, with his right hand, took out a tube of special epoxy cement. From his finger down, he squeezed what he judged to be a half-inch worm along the tire rim. He gave it thirty seconds to set, then picked up the explosive and pressed it gently into the hardening epoxy. It was fixed hard. Osman smiled; you could hang a Rolls-Royce from a quarter-inch blob of this stuff.

Slab number two went into the same place on the right rear tire. He loosened the hood at the rear and placed number three on top of the engine serial number. The last slab went behind the spare tire in the trunk. He relocked the doors and silently pushed the hood closed. It had taken forty-five minutes; only twice had he been obliged to flatten himself into the night as a car passed. Dalip's street was not much visited.

It was too poor to steal from, an artists' colony, and therefore too peaceful to patrol.

The job finished, Osman walked down the hill to the rented car he'd left parked at the bottom of the street. No one would notice a middle-aged man walking briskly to his automobile even at this time of night; these hills and cul-de-sacs were filled with doctors, mostly foreigners, likely to be called out at all hours. His car displayed a set of "M.D." plates purloined at Oakland Airport. He made a U-turn and drove back to an all-night self-serve filling station he'd noted during his survey of the neighborhood. He parked on the far side of the self-service island, which screened the view of the drowsy attendant in his fortress. He pumped a tankful of gas and, while the meter ticked, changed the license plates back.

Stopping about three-quarters of the way back across the Bay Bridge, with no car within a quarter mile of him, he threw the borrowed plates, wrapped in a set of Pac Tel overalls, over the side of the bridge. He headed down 101 to the San Francisco Airport and the Airport Hilton. The hotel was noted for its hot-sheet business and no one noticed or cared at the sight of his car pulling up in front of his room at nearly five in the morning.

It had been a long day. He was thankful that he could sleep at least eight hours.

When Dalip awoke, Ernie offered him steaming tea with papadums. Ernie was dressed. Dalip's digital clock said eight-thirteen.

"What are your weekend plans?" Ernie asked. He knew the answer. The dossier the Brothers had handed over on Dalip was complete. Ernie wondered where they'd bought it. Mafia, he guessed. The Prophet and the dons did a little back-scratching from time to time, he knew.

"Shit," Ernie's control in Chicago had said, "we can get the skinny on any well placed faggot in this country. Our friens' started this before the closet door opened, 'case they ever had to make a move. Show a man a picture of him suckin' another man's dick and he be pretty ready to help you any way you want. Why do you think ol' J. Edgar let Mr. James E. Ray get away so far so fast?"

"'Course, you be careful now," his control had added. "I'm thinkin' 'bout *you* personally. Don't forget, in San Francisco it's OK to shoot gay boys. Don't turn your back on anyone with a square jaw and a bellyfull of junk food." A deep, rumbling laugh.

"Well then," Ernie continued to Dalip, "you are just going to have to join us. Friends of mine have a little house near Pescadero; you know, just north of Santa Cruz, on the Coast Highway. I'm driving over from San Jose; we've got a class there, a visit to a hospital. I was going to be odd man out this weekend, but this way will be just perfect. We can match up. What do you say?"

As he expected, Dalip would have broken a stone wall with his head to accept.

"Wonderful. You can just drive down there tonight. Tell you what; I'll wait for you at the Marlin Inn near Pescadero. When do you think you'll be there? It's about two hours, two and a half at most, straight down the Coast Highway. In no traffic. We won't get there until ten-thirty or so. If you leave here around nine, you'll miss the traffic—it is Labor Day, after all—and we should meet up just perfectly."

Dalip agreed. He thought that a late departure would also give him a chance to pick up a few presents for his new friend—new *lover*, he reminded himself—whom he knew only as Jacquin.

"I should be getting along." Ernie/Jacquin interrupted Dalip's dreamy speculations.

Dalip shrugged into trousers and shirt. He drove Ernie to the beginning of a long, pocked driveway which let up a hill to a cluster of concrete buildings.

"Just drop me here," Ernie said, "we don't want people talking."

He got out of the car and started up the hill, then, after pausing to watch the Datsun out of sight, walked back down and around the bend to a bus stop where he joined a knot of old colored women waiting to cross the bay for another day's dogwork.

In forty minutes, he was back in his room at the Fairmont. He dialed a San Mateo number and spoke briefly with the sleepy voice on the other end. Then he hung up and went into the bathroom. He looked at himself contemptuously in the mirror and got into the shower, where he scrubbed and rinsed himself until his dark skin flushed, trying to eliminate all physical traces of the Indian boy. The recollection of their lovemaking made him sick.

*   *   *

By six, Dalip was so anxious to leave that he felt sick. The house was beginning to fill up with early orders of Yon Choh's cooking; Nyquist was evidently planning a festive weekend. Dalip's mind was filled with his new lover. It was hard to concentrate. He drummed his fingers on the cover of the RAID folder, unable to get started. Then, just after six, all hell broke loose in the computer room with a hot-line request from a $100,000 client in Singapore. MPL was deserted. The rest of the senior staff had headed out early to get the jump on the holiday traffic. Except for Yon Choh, now immersed in his chopping and stirring, Dalip was alone on the business floors of MPL. Nyquist was secreted upstairs, taking his early pleasures with the slim blonde girl who had arrived with her flight bag in midafternoon.

Singapore had a complicated question involving the alpha/beta of Intel, portfolio seasonality, and the right mix of aggregate equities. Dalip fiddled up the answers, got the registers tracked back to square, and finally satisfied the client. Singapore signed off.

It was eight-thirty by the time Dalip trekked back to his apartment, carefully assembled his weekend kit, and started off for Pescadero. He had been lucky enough to steal a few minutes at lunchtime on Union Street: to pick up a good Brie from nice Mr. Innes at the Cheese Place, a couple of bottles of red wine, and a dynamite satin shirt for Jacquin. The shirt salesman at Gogo's Gaiety had eyed Dalip lasciviously. After so long a famine, Dalip thought, now an embarrassment of riches! For the first time in his life he felt he had a future.

The RAID folder was in his suitcase, locked safely in the trunk. He knew, guiltily, that Nyquist would have raised the roof if he knew that class one material had left the premises. That was the rule. But Dalip knew that he could get a headstart on the modifications working with the plug-in Texas Instruments minicomputer sitting on the back seat. MPL had a dozen of these, which it issued to its senior staff for on-site jobs the way a newspaper issued cameras.

He drove across the bridge through San Francisco, cutting around Golden Gate Park onto the Skyline Drive toward the highway which ran along the coast as far as Monterey Bay. It was dark now, the 280Z whirred along smartly, and there was virtually no traffic. Dalip let himself relax. He turned his mind to the RAID business, wandering among the parameters of the Certified job. With half his mind on the road, he turned into Route 1 South at nine-fifteen.

Osman was three hundred yards behind him, driving a heavy, clunky, rented Continental. On the seat beside him, numbered 1 to 4, the Day-Glo numerals legible in the dim dashboard light, were four small transmitters, about the size of cigarette packs. Each emitted a single impulse; each impulse was different.

Osman had been covering Dalip since early afternoon. He had waited in Ernie's room in the Fairmont until Ernie called from his watching post to say that Dalip had come back from lunch and was inside MPL. Osman had driven along Green Street and double-parked just ahead of the Avis car from which Ernie was watching MPL. The two men had switched cars. No one took any notice. It was a quiet residential neighborhood, sparsely populated, especially at this time of day and on the eve of the holiday.

Osman noted with interest that the house on the far side of MPL was vacant; a realtor's sign was nailed to the porch. Shortly after four o'clock, a couple with two young children and a Border Collie who stared at Osman suspiciously, in the way of the breed, packed up a Volvo station wagon and drove away, emptying MPL's nearest neighboring house.

Osman was glad they had gone. His business was generally with equals, where subtle differences of degree in training or alertness decided the outcome. He was no terrorist who blew innocent folk into oblivion to prove some twisted point. The people he terminated died for specific reasons. The difficulty, although it had its advantages, of dealing with amateurs, as now, was the confrontation with unsuspiciousness, innocence, a total lack of acceptance right up to the final second when the ultimate undeserved shadow swept over them. Amateurs tended to perish unreliably. This job, however, looked to be easy.

He had driven over the route three times in the last week. He knew it cold and had chosen his battleground carefully. He had alternatives in mind, if something unexpected happened.

Nothing did. The trip went as smoothly as he had anticipated. By the time the two-car convoy had gotten thirty miles south of San Francisco on Route 1, they were about the only cars on the road. Ahead, Dalip's mind vacillated between the erotic and the mathematical; he was oblivious to the persistent headlights gleaming abstractly in the mirror. The highway became hilly as it drew closer to the coast. Cliffs

(339)

dropped sharply to pebbled beaches punctuated with rocky outcroppings and escarpments. The curves became sharper.

Osman had picked out a stretch about two miles south of Moss Beach, just before the highway swept along the curve of Half Moon Bay. The road took an elongated S-curve along the cliffs, not ten yards from the edge, which was marked by a spindly guard rail; Osman had gotten out and tested it, happy in its fragility. Coming out of the last curve, the road ran downhill for nearly half a mile; any oncoming car would disclose itself by its lights from at least a mile away.

Dalip turned into the stretch at ten-fifty-eight. He slowed as his lights picked out the signs warning of the curve. He was down to around 40 mph.

Osman followed, slightly narrowing the gap. As always at such times, his world seemed to slide into cinematic slow motion. There were no lights in his mirror; he could see nothing coming up ahead. He drew within fifty yards of Dalip's car and, double-checking the numerals, pressed the buttons on transmitters number one and two.

Dalip was two-thirds of the way through the first turn when the impulses detonated the small charges attached to his cliffside tires. He barely heard the report as the walls of the tires blew out and the car dropped sharply on its right rims, skewing and screeching with a clatter of sparks toward the guardrail. Its gouging skid slowed the Datsun to less than 10 mph as it approached the side of the road.

Despite the fancy car, Osman had correctly gauged Dalip to be as poor a driver as he looked. Ahead, Dalip was fighting the wheel, trying to turn away from the skid. Osman closed on him.

Dalip saw the lights grow and then fill his mirror. It sank in on him what was happening and he started to scream. At such low speeds, the contact between the two cars was gentle. Osman got his right front bumper against the left rear wheel of the Datsun and pushed it through the guardrail and off the cliff. The little sportscar was no match for the weight of the Lincoln. The 280Z's front wheels cleared the cliff edge; the Datsun hung for an instant, until one final acceleration by Osman nudged it over and it began its tumbling, scarring slide down the rockface.

Osman's front wheels were within eight feet of the cliffs. He braked joltingly and reversed. Then he pressed the 3 and 4 buttons. Halfway down the cliff, the Datsun exploded, scattering tendrils of flame for a hundred yards on either side.

Dalip, his luggage, and everything that wasn't hard steel were incinerated; the car was reduced to a fiery skeleton that tumbled the last yards into the ocean and came to rest, half under water, clothed in steam and trickles of flame.

It had all taken less than a minute. Osman drove serenely on. Minutes later, a car came barreling from the north, its driver pushing to make up time. In his haste, he never noticed the gap in the guardrail and the steam rising from the ocean. By the time he would have caught Osman, the Lincoln had turned off on Route 92 and had headed back to San Mateo. The police weren't summoned until daylight. Dalip was beyond identification.

Ernie was fidgety and pissed off. Here he was, stuck in this dump, nothing to do, no action. Shit, he'd done his job. He couldn't see why he couldn't head back to Chicago, have a hot weekend with the Brothers, and jet on to Boston. The boss'd be back in a week.

But he had his orders.

"You be there until the man say you through," he had been instructed in Chicago.

"Who is this guy?" Ernie had asked.

"Don't know myself," said the control, "but the Prophet all excited and asked for you special. And you is just to sit and when the man say 'jump' you be jumpin' and when he say 'go' you be goin'. Those are the orders; come through from the Mosque itself."

So Ernie sat late in this jerky room at the Airport Hilton. It was at the far end of the wing nearest the highway. When Osman had taken it, he had stressed the need for extreme privacy, exchanging leers with the desk clerk. Ernie had been there for nearly two hours. He had followed his instructions: checked out of the Fairmont, watched MPL, switched cars with Osman, and driven Osman's car to the Avis lot at the airport. There had been a room key on the seat of the car. Ernie had taken the shuttle bus to the Hilton and walked to the room and let himself in.

What a pain in the ass, he thought, clicking the TV from channel to channel.

There was a sharp double knock at the door. Ernie checked the peephole and unchained the door.

"Man," he said, "where you been?" He turned back into the room.

The door closed behind him and then Osman was on him

(341)

like a panther. He hit Ernie as hard as he could under the left ear with the edge of his hand. The black man went down, all but unconscious. Osman eased him to the floor and dropped on his throat with his full weight, crushing Ernie's larynx with his knee. The small sounds of the struggle were obscured by the television.

Ernie's fight for life was weak and reflexive. Gurgling death came on swiftly. As his life swam out beyond his eyes, into the mist that was filling his head, Ernie thought that Harrison must have something to do with this but, hey, the Boss was a good man, almost a Brother. . . . And then he was gone.

Osman rose and went about his business. He went through Ernie's pockets and his two bags and removed anything that looked remotely personal or identifiable. Turning off the lights in the room, he checked the parking area; all quiet, except for late drunken laughter down toward the pool. He unlatched the trunk of the Lincoln and lugged Ernie's body out of the room and wrestled it into the car. He put Ernie's bags beside the body and shut the trunk.

He drove the car into the long-term parking lot, taking a ticket from the automatic gate. He would mail that back to Hertz later—much later. He walked through the parking lot to the nearest main terminal building and hailed a taxi, which he instructed to drop him off on Market Street, which was still alive and jumping at one in the morning. He walked a few blocks toward Union Square and then caught another cab to the Huntington Hotel. In his room, he thought he could use an hour's nap, so he set the alarm for four-thirty. Just to wake up briefly to check on the final phase.

Actually, the sirens awakened him moments before the alarm went off.

At four-thirty exactly, by the Rolex movement which Osman had used as a timing device, the "C" cell battery sent a three-quarter volt charge along the length of the wire embedded in the two-kilo slab of explosive which Osman had taped to the rear of the propane tanks in the MPL basement. On its own, the explosive would have done the job properly; it went off with the force of a pair of thousand-pound bombs, and the chemists at Hoechst had compounded a fine incendiary additive. But when coupled with the exploding propane, it created a hundred-foot-high column of white heat, which blew out the walls and floors of the house, and in its ten-second life demolished and charred to cinders and melted metal everything that had been MPL and next to it.

It was an unfair ending for the inhabitants of the house. Before the fireball burst through the floor of the bedroom and cremated him and his bedmate, Axel Nyquist had smoked a goodnight joint and contemplated the glories of his existence. To his surprise, he had been able to discharge himself stertorously no less than three times into the willing young lady who now slept exhausted by his side. On Monday, a team from *People* was arriving to celebrate the Nyquist lifestyle with camera and tape recorder. And if the Certified thing worked out...

Now, all was ashes. Standing at his tenth-floor window, Osman watched the whooping fire engines race up California Street. Sirens had broken out all over the city; he thought he could detect a vague glow in the sky over Pacific Heights.

He judged the operation to be a success. He had been certain of the pyrotechnics. He knew his tools and used them as skillfully as any man in the world. But the human side had also worked out satisfactorily.

He was gone, shadowy and traceless, early the next day. On the plane, he allowed himself a slight smile. In all respects, a successful operation. It was a cardinal tenet of Osman's canon of professional standards to leave no wounded and take no prisoners.

The vaporization of MPL occurred at one-fifteen in the afternoon, Venice time. Devon had wanted to go to Harry's Bar again. She couldn't believe that liver could be so good. The launch from the Cipriani deposited them a short walk from the restaurant, but first they took a turn through the Piazzetta, where Harrison indulged his daily, uncontrollable urge to inspect the bookstands which sat beside the Doge's Palace.

"You know, David," she said, "this'll be the tenth guide to Venice you've bought since we've been here. And you *brought* three with you."

"Do not be a bore," he instructed her sternly.

During the hour it took four San Francisco fire companies to put out the blaze and start the search for the few charcoaled bones and reeking fragments that remained of Nyquist and his friend, Harrison and Devon drank two Bellinis, the mixture of Asti Spumante and fresh peach juice making them hungry. They ate plates of *carpaccio,* beef sliced thin as writing paper with a mustard sauce that Harrison said was worth murdering for. Devon ate her liver and Harrison wolfed a *risotto* cooked in cuttlefish ink. They drank a bottle of Pinot Grigio.

The team from the emergency office had just concluded its inspection of the ruins when Harrison paid the check after coffee.

They blinked in the sunlight.

"What next, my love," she asked, hoping for the answer he gave.

"Well, I think we should go back to our hotel, which is the greatest hotel on God's green earth, and go up to our little room, and I will kiss you *there*," he pointed naughtily, "for about a lifetime. And then we'll take a swim and wave with gay familiarity to the poolside crowd, who will envy us our youth and good looks and the things they suspect we do to each other in the privacy of our room. And then we will take the launch back to the city and I will lead you to the church of San Salvador by the Rialto and show you an *Annunciation* which is arguably the greatest painting ever done by Titian, who is unarguably the greatest painter this fabulous city has produced. And then we will buy some more things we don't need: books for me; shoes, probably, for you. And then I will take you back to Harry's where they have the greatest sandwiches in the world and I will drown you in more Bellinis and after that, my darling, it is up to you."

All she could do in the launch was look at him and shape *I love you* silently with her lips. Which was all he wanted to do in return.

They went to Torcello and Murano on Monday. It was late when they returned and the concierge was all apologies. A terrible confusion attended. The *Paris Herald* had not arrived and now would not. A most lamentable episode, but there it was.

"No problem," said Harrison. Nothing happens over Labor Day, anyway, he thought. It's the most desperately boring holiday: typically American—to celebrate the end of summer, as if that was something to celebrate. Venice took one out of time, anyway. They might drive over to Padua tomorrow. See the Giottos. So he never saw the squib reporting the death of Axel Nyquist. Of Ernie, decomposing in the trunk of a rented car in an airport parking lot, there was, of course, no mention.

28 Alex Camran did not miss the note on Nyquist.

In his anteroom office in Merriman's suite at Certified, he was making his morning run-through of the papers, beginning with the *Wall Street Journal*. He was working for Merriman now, on a temporary basis. Arthur Mismer had eaten a bad clam at the Wisquisset August Beachbake and was still tucked in bed at his mother's, groaning less at the pain in his troubled stomach than at the certain knowledge that someone else must now be guarding at Merriman's office gate. Since young Camran was the only junior officer at the bank that Merriman had seen in five years on a remotely personal basis, it was natural that Camran had been summoned to fill in when news of Mismer's ill-timed indisposition had reached the chairman.

Alex jumped at the chance. Bowen was off somewhere in Botswana, "improving his leopard for Rowland Ward," whatever that meant, and Camran had been around the bank long enough now, especially with his recent experience, to respect the role of luck—his good and other people's bad—in shaping a career.

Item number one in his daily routine was to scan the financial pages for items momentous enough to elicit those notes of congratulation or sympathy which Leslie Merriman regarded as a cornerstone of customer relationships. As Miss Merit had put it: "After all, Alex, think of it, a personal note from the chairman. It's enough to add light to a sunny day or to chase away the clouds when death occurs." She sounded like an advertisement for a funeral parlor.

It was just a squib at the bottom of the front-page news summary. *"Died,"* it said, *"Axel Nyquist, 39, founder of Modern Portfolio Logistics Inc. and a leading investment technician."* He scrambled for the *Times*. The obit there was more complete. It recited the facts. A late night explosion and fire. Nyquist's remains had been identified through dental charts. The article itemized Nyquist's life and career. *"A spokesman for the San Francisco Fire Department,"* concluded the notice, *"identified the cause as the accidental explosion, probably resulting from electrical failure, of propane gas tanks in the basement of the MPL building."* There followed bylined superscriptions by the *Times'* financial and cooking editors,

(345)

embellishing the wire service accounts with additional details concerning Nyquist's accomplishments in the stock market and at the dining table.

Unnerved, Camran had his secretary send a messenger to Times Square for a copy of the *San Francisco Chronicle*. The local story was fuller and included photographs. The quoted interview with the fire chief offered nothing new. A feedback from the overloaded electronics in the building's basement had somehow sent a spark into the propane tanks, causing the explosion. Prompt action by the Fire Department had limited the damage to neighboring buildings. The interview ended with a panegyric on the dangers of inadequate wiring and the storage of volatile gases.

It excited Camran's sense of the sinister. Could there be some connection with his and Merriman's visit? After an instant's hesitation, he accepted the likelihood of the Gotham's commissioning a gangland hit to forestall a major competitive move by the Certified, and so he began, hastily, to assemble a dossier to set before Merriman. His head was alive and jumping with notions of button men and wiretaps. Vast conspiracies. He toyed briefly with the idea of putting the bank's San Francisco representative on the scent right away. But there was of course the possibility, remote as it seemed to his inflamed imagination, that the facts were as related, that it *had* been an accident. To stir up a fuss without Merriman's approval would be risky to his career at the bank. The chairman liked things orderly and unincendiary. Best to wait.

Merriman appeared just after eleven o'clock. The airstrip at Wisquisset had been fogged in. Although it would have been quicker to travel by land, no car was readily available, at least not with a decent chauffeur, the train was filthy—and, in the bargain, Merriman had promised a ride in the Gulfstream to the local rector.

Nerves itching, Camran waited until Merriman reviewed the morning's priority business with Miss Merit. When she gave him the high sign, he entered the chairman's office and proffered the sheaf of newsclippings.

"Something really unusual has happened, sir. Look at these. Axel Nyquist—you remember, the man we saw in San Francisco three weeks ago? He's been killed in an explosion. Sir, it smells funny. Look at these."

Merriman read through the clippings. Half glasses tipping his nose, he punctuated his reading with small, snorting ex-

(346)

clamations of "Goodness gracious," or "How sad." His interest gave Camran hope.

Merriman finished reading and laid the papers carefully on his desk.

"I really think, sir..." Alex began, but Merriman's upraised hand cut him off.

"Miss Merit," said the chairman, "to Mrs. Nyquist, wife or mother, find out which or both, send a number three condolence. Make the proper adjustments in the salutation. Flowers, of course. Grade two. If there's a charity, send $1,000. And another $1,000 to the San Francisco Fire Prevention League."

Merriman turned back to Camran. "I'm sorry, Alex, you were saying?"

"Well sir, this sure looks real strange." In his excitement, Alex heard himself slipping back into Texas grammar. He corrected himself. "I mean, we call on Nyquist" ("Old Nyquist," he'd started to say), "and he lets on that he's been doing the sort of thing we're interested in, and then all of a sudden he's gone. Blown up! I mean, it does sound awful queer." He couldn't help his anxious vernacular.

"In what way?" Death was either a distant, ceremonious business to Leslie Merriman, a matter of war and statistical slaughter and humanitarian high commissions, or, closer to home, the celebrations of the great and near great, Merrimans included, which meant pallbearing among canyons of lilies, the White House in the front pew, and eloquent obsequies which elegantly cloaked the meanness of death and dying.

"To me, I mean, it looks odd, really, but after all, Nyquist *did* imply that he had a big customer, to *us,* and well you know, sir, with wiretapping and all that, maybe somebody didn't want us to know something, and so they stuck a bomb in his basement. I mean, sir, it all sounds farfetched, but..." He couldn't find the words. This context was all wrong for notions of murder and bombs. The Certified was rumored to have connived at the destruction of kings and dictators, at wars which obliterated governments so that the happy new rulers might pay off or roll over loans which had looked shaky. But to organize the death of a fat computer expert... Alex knew he was becoming farfetched, no matter how strong his instincts.

In the back of his mind he was betting on the wiretap syndrome. He knew that Merriman had read an article in which the head of Gotham's foreign exchange department had boasted of having his offices swept weekly for "bugs." The Certified was now swept twice daily. It cost $4 million a year, but it reinforced the sense of the bank's senior officers respecting their own importance.

"Alex," Merriman sounded impatient, "what are you proposing?"

"Well, sir, I thought we might ask San Francisco to talk to someone out there—police, fire, maybe the mayor—just to fill them in and maybe follow up. Do some checking. Just see,"

"Alex." Merriman's voice was wanting to be kind. "If we ask those questions, it'll get in the papers. San Francisco's a small town, although a lovely one. How would we look, for us stirring up trouble? The man *did* have those gas tanks in his basement, you'll recall. We're trying to get a good foothold in San Francisco. For the bank, of course, irrespective of the fact that I have some personal investments out there. That city's had enough trouble, that zebra killer and those ghastly homosexuals, without us suggesting that mad bombers are now roving the streets. And... you wouldn't know this, of course, but the honorary chief of the Fire Department out there is a campmate of mine at Roundelay. His report must reflect the truth. No, no, I really don't think so."

Camran could see the issue was closed.

Merriman wanted to seal the matter. "Besides, Alex, look at it this way. Nyquist's gone. He can't work for us, to be sure. But then, he can't work for anyone else either. Not us; not Gotham. And, after all, my Board would hardly approve the acquisition of a business that's been blown up. Please consider the matter closed."

The chairman signaled for Miss Merit. As she came in, he looked at Camran kindly. "I stopped to see Arthur Mismer this morning. He's not doing well at all. His mother thinks she may have to take him to Florida for a rest. The World Bank meets next month in Washington. I'm going to make you my permanent assistant. Miss Merit will fill you in on the World Bank. It's going to be awfully busy. Many important people will be there and we must show our best foot. I'd like you to handle the details. Reuben can spare you, assuming he ever gets back from shooting those monkeys or whatever it is he does in Africa. If we play our cards right, we might get a slice of the Witteveen Fund to manage. Of course, with Arthur unavailable to show you my ropes, you'll have to cram pretty hard. Miss Merit, have you got the preliminary agenda?"

Whatever thoughts Alex Camran might have had about San Francisco, insistent as they were, drowned in the prospects of conquering Washington at the right hand of Leslie Merriman. And after Washington, why not the world?

"I can't find Ernie anywhere," said Devon over the phone from Boston. "Nobody here's seen him since, what, three weeks ago."

Harrison was surprised—and then again wasn't. Although he hated himself for it, he thought immediately of an old joke he'd been told one drunken night years ago by a Georgia lumberman.

"Know why they don't give niggers coffee breaks? Costs too much for job retraining."

It wasn't fair and it wasn't funny and Harrison had tried to make a small-mouthed laugh of a size sufficient to placate his cracker clients. Yet he had to admit to himself that he wasn't surprised. You took 'em as they came, sure, but twenty years of black maids putting his sheets in the china cupboard and his cigars in the dishwasher had inured him to the undependable. He liked Ernie, and Ernie was good, good tethered to his job, but maybe it was like on the old plantations. Every day brand new. He didn't know what to think. Hated all those old prejudices welling up to explain things.

Against his inclinations, he forced a justification.

"He probably got our dates wrong. We *did* stay an extra day. Where are the tapes?"

"Back in my hotel, locked in the suitcase. Listen, my love, I know enough about this to run them out. Ernie showed me a lot of things. You want me to start? He'll probably turn up tomorrow." Devon sounded uncertain.

"I don't know. Let me think. Go back to your hotel. I'll call you in an hour."

He tried Khafiq in London. No answer. Tried the Quisisana. No, Signor Khafiq had left several days ago. No forwarding address.

Out of places to call, he paced around the apartment. It had all been so smooth. He had a drink, then another. Finally, with what seemed to him the piercing, insightful wisdom of alcohol, he called Devon in Boston, trying to disguise the slur in his voice.

When she answered, he said, "Look, go plug it in tomorrow. You know what you're doing? No, I'm not being hard. No, I'm not drunk. We'll close it up. Pack our tents," if you'll excuse the expression, he wanted to say, "and leave what's left kicking around."

Devon didn't agree. She could finish it all, she claimed. Harrison knew that she probably could.

"Listen, my darling, my angel, my own," he rhapsodized, "I *know* you can do it. But if Ernie doesn't come back, your beautiful face will stick in the minds of those good New England ladies too long. Time for us to leave this party. The dance may be over."

Devon complained, but she agreed. They blew kisses to each other over the telephone. Hanging up, he sat down heavily. The Dow stood at 1793; volume on the New York Stock Exchange was running 64 million shares a day, on an average. He tried to read the stock tables, sipping another drink, but he had no eye for figures.

In Boston, Devon felt uneasy about Ernie's absence. For the first time, the blissful surface of the last months was disturbed by the prickling alertness to danger which her years on the run had bred in her.

The President had made up his mind to fire both Nordlander and Drzlag after the election and to break up the oil companies. The Indian prime minister had made a state visit to Washington at the end of the summer. Baxter had spent three hours with him, alone, in the Oval Office. It had been a very expensive three hours for the nation. He'd left Drzlag waiting angrily on call in Foggy Bottom. When he'd made a deal, he had Drzlag secretly driven in a circuitous route, under a rug in the back of an anonymous station wagon, through Virginia and back through Chevy Chase to the side basement of the White House. Then the three men had gone out to meet the press. Drzlag's briefing had been a matter of seconds. The President had simply handed him his press release on the Indian agreement and a Xerox copy of current faculty pay scales at obscure midwestern universities. The working press, mainly concerned with the details of the subsidized wheat deal with India, had been content to note in passing the Secretary of State's enthusiastic noddings as the President detailed the terms of the agreement. Intent on their notes, few had caught the fiery, hating glance which the Indian prime minister had cast in the specific direction of the Secretary of State.

Jordan called a meeting at his house in Virginia. The campaign was going badly and promised to go worse, now that President Baxter had announced his intention of going out into the land to seek a total mandate.

The tone of the session was colored by the false optimism of dedicated men facing certain disaster. The only honestly positive note was struck by Benjamin Masters, still accepted as a certified Republican despite his known Middle Eastern connections, who urged the preparation of a series of television pilots. They might not be used, said Masters, especially if the election looked like a lock for Baxter, but it would be useful to have them on the shelf. Just in case. The Dunstable representative at the meeting had squealed with outrage. This sort of thing should be approved by his boss, he complained, and Dunstable was out of pocket, presiding over a Santa Gertrudis sale in Tomball.

"Listen," he said altogether too brashly, "the boss has made this party work since he came over from the other side. But you folks throw good money away like this, money he's raised, and he might just jump back."

"That's a nasty little threat, young man," said Benjamin Masters. "So I'll tell you what I'll do. I'll personally guarantee the cost."

"You realize you're talking big dollars, maybe $700,000?" said Jordan's media consultant.

"I do." The group accepted it. Masters was thick with the Arabs, they knew. The association had probably made him rich as Croesus. They went back to business. They would shoot the pilots in New York in two weeks. Have them on the shelf by October 1.

Armed with Miss Merit's A, B, C, and D lists, Camran flew down to Washington to set the wheels in motion for Certified's performance at the upcoming joint conclave of the IMF and the World Bank. The biennial meetings in Washington were a high spot on the calender of every financial leader in the world: ministers of state; bankers; traders; the world's money elite; and every financial gypsy with a deal in his pocket and enough money to get to Washington to try to promote it.

Orchestrating Merriman's three days in Washington would be his first big job for Merriman. Bowen, he knew, would only come down for the big dinner the Certified gave at the Sulgrave Club. Gossip at the bank said that there had been quite a scene, once, between Merriman and Bowen when the chairman had tried to force Bowen's attendance at the whole run of cocktail parties, receptions, and breakfasts. Bowen had won and now he stayed in New York and ran the bank while Merriman wowed 'em on the D.C. cocktail circuit. Now, of course, he was sore as hell at Merriman for pirating Alex away.

This wasn't the sort of banking he'd been taught at Wharton or by Bowen, but Camran thoroughly enjoyed his work in Washington. He checked Merriman's rented house in Georgetown, made sure it was properly staffed and outfitted. He discussed the menu and the winelist with the chief steward at the Sulgrave, who found him surprisingly knowledgeable. Never before, in thirty years, had he ever met a Texan who could get his mouth around French pronunciation. Camran visited legations and economic outposts, setting up a roster of engagements for Merriman with the overseas financial bigwigs who would be staying on Embassy Row.

"I must say, Mr. Camran," said a grinning subminister in the Gabon Embassy, "you people at Certified are certainly more diligent at this than certain of your competitors, who shall be nameless. You can be sure when we want to borrow more money we'll come to you first. And that won't be too far distant." The dashikied figure leaned confidentially across the desk. "You might be giving some thought to the fact that our great President is planning an expansion, a *material* expansion, of the Gabonese navy. Needless to say, we intend to borrow the entire cost. We should perhaps mention that to Mr. Merriman when he is here."

As he made his way around Washington, taking care of Leslie Merriman's diplomatic light housekeeping, Alex found himself enjoying the attentive respect of the men on whom he called in his leader's behalf. Not that reflected glory could be quite the same as having it for himself, on his own account. That would come, he thought, that would come. There were already some considerable satisfactions in the jealousy which his appointment as Merriman's Cerberus had generated in the bank. And God knows old Beth Sue had slobbered all over him, but he couldn't see taking her along to the Merrimans' to meet the kind of people he was now meeting there. He just phased her out, leaving her phone calls unreturned until they stopped coming; whatever slight guilt he might have felt was staunched by asserting to himself that he'd given her a pretty good run and a pretty good summer.

Alight with flame of secondhand distinction, he mopped up his Washington business, finishing with a small protocol arrangement at the Treasury Department. That task concluded, he found himself standing at noon in the lobby of the Treasury Building, trying to decide what else he might do, when his eye was caught by a line *"R.F. Grimes—International Transfers"* on the building directory. Camran remembered Grimes. They'd started at Certified together; Grimes had come down from Harvard, an intense, late-working MBA who'd gotten sidetracked into throwing his evenings away working for a Baxter election offshoot in Brooklyn Heights and which had eventually yielded a summons to Washington. Thinking that Grimes might enjoy having news of the bank, including a rundown on his own new prestige, Alex asked the guard in the lobby to call upstairs.

Grimes was delighted to hear from Camran. Could he stay for lunch? Yes? Great. Three minutes later Grimes was in the lobby, pumping Alex's hand enthusiastically and leading him off to lunch.

Over lunch at the Palm, Grimes enthused over political life and life in Washington in general.

"Christ, Alex, I look out of my window right at the goddamn White House. We go over and meet with the President all the time. The Pres's a good guy but you can't believe some of the assholes he's got on his staff and in the cabinet. This guy Drzlag is just fucking unreal. His staff calls him the Mad Bomber. The scuttlebutt across the street is that when the Arabs cut the price of oil last spring Drzlag was on the brink of launching an unauthorized invasion of the Kingdom, by the Indians, no less! The only two guys who are really close to Baxter are Ferdimend and Gottlieb, and they are very *good* guys and very very *very* smart."

Grimes's talk turned to other Washington marvels.

"Alex, there's more pussy out there than you can eat. I know you didn't chase it much, at least not at the bank, but here, damnit, there's so much it just gets fed to you."

It turned out that Grimes was first assistant to the deputy secretary, charged with the money watch, monitoring the big movements of currency across borders and around the world.

"Up until last spring, Christ, we just about shit in our pants every morning. The Arabs were running down their deposits and their treasuries and everyone thought there'd be a run on the Chase and the B of A. Now we haven't got a goddamn thing to do. Gold is selling for peanuts; a buck'll buy you three Swiss francs, fifty or six French, or four Deutschemarks, if that's your pleasure. And a gallon and a tenth of gas! Who'da thunk it?

"But it sure is boring," Grimes added. "After November, when the old man's got his mandate, either there will be some real fun and games or I'm going to cut and run. Think the bank'd take me back? Anybody who's ever been a janitor in Washington can get a hundred grand on Wall Street, but that's real asshole country compared to this power trip. I'd go apeshit listening to those guys down there talking about themselves. What're you doing now, anyway? What brings you here?"

Camran told him. Grimes was clearly pleased at the news of Mismer's indisposition.

"I hope it's a hemorrhoid the size of a grapefruit," he said brightly. "What else do you know? Anything he'd be interested in?"

It occurred to Camran that the whole business with the master trust and Guardian whatever, all those country banks and MPL, seemed to fall in Grimes's bailiwick. He took it from the top and related it as he saw it. Grimes listened, more indulgently than intently.

"Hell, Bob," said Alex, "before the old man yanked me upstairs, while I was still frontlining for Rube Bowen, I saw something really big." He outlined his efforts at tracing the elusive master trust, emphasizing that neither Leslie Merriman nor Rube Bowen felt it was worth chasing further.

"Interesting," said Grimes when he finished. "Of course, I think we can skip the spy story stuff. There aren't any James Bonds left in the money racket. But that's a lot of dough you're talking about. And you didn't get any of it at the Certified? Boy, I'll bet that really pisses Merriman off! Anyway, it's something to think about. I'll take a quick peek and, if anything pops up, I'll let you know. In the meantime, save me a seat at the bank if things get dull here."

Grimes saw Alex into a taxi and went whistling off down Connecticut Avenue.

In the White House, Baxter had finally figured how to stick it to the major oil companies. The polls showed him that he was going to carry Congress on Election Day, maybe with an eighty- to hundred-seat majority in the House and probably as many as sixty-two senators. His people were out on the hustings, systematically working over the candidates who were on Gottlieb's list as being in the pockets of the majors. The word was out in the precincts and districts that, in the last month before Election Day, the President was going out into the country again, this time selectively, to run specifically *against* any candidate, no matter of what party, who was on the "energy hit list" known to have been drawn up by Marvin Gottlieb. The word had had the desired effect. No less than thirty-six incumbents, congressmen and senators, more than half of them from the President's party, had been jettisoned at the district and state level, replaced by candidates more likely to deserve White House approval and benefactions. And the first thing on his list would be to appoint public directors to the boards of the majors. "We're getting the business from the oil companies, Buster," he said to Ferdimend, "and the only way we're gonna find out how they do what they do is to get inside the sonsabitches and break 'em up."

Gottlieb was also sitting in the Oval Office across from the President.

"Marvin, I want you to build an anti-trust case, if they don't cooperate. It pains me to do this, as much as I believe in the free enterprise system, but this has got to stop."

What the President meant was that, in spite of decontrol, in spite of a $10 to $13 crude price across the board except for some anomalies in the Rotterdam spot market, in spite of a relatively modest increase so far in consumption, in spite of incentives, the majors were still crying poor and there were still some gasoline lines and a hundred tankers flat down to the waves queued up along every coast and outside every port.

"I knew it was mistake not to veto that oil and gas bill last year. You know, Marvin, I figured this Arab deal would paper it over, get the majors back diggin' holes. Lord, the independents are shut down; the tax boys and accountants saw to that. So we have got to do somethin', and I want to do it startin' right after the election, like on Wednesday."

Gottlieb nodded. "I'll start with the Congress. I think we know whose payroll which congressman is on and who's conspiring with whom. Then I guess you'll want a draft bill. Are you thinking of nationalization as a final resort, Mr. President?"

"Marvin, I'm thinkin' of anything that'll get things fixed

(355)

right. Or this country is goin' to go broke. Those people out there are spendin' money like sailors on leave. And when the new model cars get out, that gasoline usage is goin' to go no which way but up!"

Gottlieb knew what the President meant. He'd heard that General Motors was starting to work on a twelve-cylinder engine to power the biggest Cadillac ever. It looked like a good bet to the marketing men in Detroit. The demand was going to be there.

"Anything else, Mr. President? I'll get right on this."

"Good, Marvin. I sure appreciate it. Oh, and I don't believe we should bother Secretary Nordlander with this. Not quite yet. Now leave Buster alone here for a minute, would you?"

Baxter motioned Ferdimend closer to his desk. "Buster, I want you to go do a little nosin' around. I'm startin' to get itchy. It's been six months now since those boys cut the price of crude and we haven't heard a darn thing from them Arabs. Not that we've busted our backs tryin', either. No news is the bestest news of all, the colored folks say. But this is too much no news. Somebody around here's made some kind of a deal somewhere, no question of that in my mind. We got what, five weeks, six, to the election? Well, let's just us find out what's goin' on. Maybe it's someone in the administration. Maybe not. A bank? An insurance company? One of the oil companies? Now's the time to know about it."

Buster looked thoughtfully out the window. It was a beautiful autumn afternoon. Nice for a walk.

"Well, sir, I believe I'll just mosey on down to the State Department. Got to start somewhere."

Harrison finally caught up with Khafiq over the telephone in London.

They were down to $168 million. He mentioned that one of his people appeared to have skipped out.

Khafiq was apologetic. "My goodness, David, did I forget to tell you? Of course, you were in Venice and I went off to the Turkish coast on a cruise, and it just must have slipped my mind. Anyway, after you left Capri, just after, in fact, I received a call from my friends in Chicago. It seems they needed the services of your young man. Something overseas, I believe. In any event, not knowing your exact whereabouts as you were driving to Venice, as I recall, I agreed to release him. Really, they were most generous in the first instance to have made him available for so long. In addition, I seem to remember your nice young friend telling me that she understood the system. I must have just assumed with our present level so low, she could complete the task."

It sounded very plausible to Harrison.

It didn't to Devon when he repeated his conversation with Khafiq. The old pricklings edged back. You didn't leave a covert operation, of any kind, unfinished. It was a matter of commitment and training. Something didn't make sense.

Anyway, Harrison went on, Khafiq wanted to wrap it up. Run it out for ten more days. Two weeks at most. No more. After that, shut it down.

Everything went swimmingly for Alex Camran at the IMF until the night of the Certified dinner at the Sulgrave. He piloted Merriman effortlessly and punctually through his labyrinth of appointments. They were going to get the first look at the Gabon financing: $300 million term loan to buy three militarily outfitted cruise ships which were being converted in Rouen.

The reception before dinner went well. Merriman and Bowen shook hands with each of the guests. The room blazed with power; to Alex, the air seemed to quiver with the immanence of great men.

Then there was some kind of noisy disturbance at the front table, where arriving guests exchanged their invitations for place cards. Camran bustled over to see what was going on.

At the front table was a very drunk man with a large black woman wearing a dress of blindingly fluorescent yellow silk. The man was Rebo Beauderon.

"What y'all mean, she got to have an invitation? I'm tellin' you, her husband's comin' in a while. He got the invitation cards in his pocket. He just had to get a few things signed up with some of my boys."

Before Alex could intervene, Beauderon saw him.

"Hey, Alex," he shouted, "old buddy, how about helpin' me out? One good ol' boy to another. We Texans got to stick together. Can you get this old dumbass here," he pointed to the gray-haired club servant who was in charge of the desk, "to get it through his fat head that this here's no ordinary boogie," Beauderon pointed to his companion, "this here's the wife of the Energy Minister of Olabungi!"

The room whirled. Camran saw Merriman standing frozen, a look of absolute distaste pinching his mouth, his hand locked with that of the Tanzanian ambassador, who appeared to have been poleaxed. Camran had a flashing vision of Mismer recapturing his desk in Merriman's anteroom. Somehow he made peace, guided Beauderon and his bemused guest, who spoke no English and smiled flashing, uncomprehending gold, into the room. The crowd noise resumed and the party went on. It was a great success.

He didn't find it funny when, after dinner, Bowen dragged him into a corner and said it had been the funniest goddamn thing he'd ever seen.

As a matter of fact, he found it so upsetting that he forgot to call his friend Bob Grimes at the Treasury Department to see if anything had turned up.

29 Bob Grimes was a very diligent young man. If his conversation was a little flip, he took his work with missionary seriousness. His job was to monitor money flows and, if there was something going on below the threshold of his department's scrutiny in that area, he would surface it.

So a few days after his lunch with Camran, he made a date with an opposite number in the office of the Comptroller of the Currency. He explained what he was after. The man from the comptroller's office looked at him askance. Jesus, did he realize what a job that would be? And what the hell, they were only talking a few billion dollars: peanuts. Grimes was obdurate. The directive from the Secretary had been to put a trace on anything over a billion and that directive had not been remanded, even though conditions were a hell of a lot different than a year ago. He wanted this information, and he wanted it *yesterday*, no later. If the comptroller wanted to speak with the Secretary, that would be fine.

"Goddamnit, Bob, take it easy. I mean, what kind of questions am I going to ask? This is private dough, obviously. The banks report directly to you on the official balances, agency deposits, and that sort of stuff. Christ, I don't know where to begin."

Grimes was patient. "Look," he said, "there are only three things about big money on the move. It either comes in or it goes out. That's one. Two, it has to get parked while it's here: T-bills; CDs; whatever. Three, someone's got to be telling that computer what to tell the banks. Now look what we've got. We know that the money has been coming in and out, shuttling from the moneycenter banks to the regionals for custody accounts. We have one name: Guardian something. Who opened these accounts? Who at the bank signed off on them? What was bought in these accounts? How big were they? Come on, Jack, do a little original thinking."

The comptroller's man agreed to check out the five hundred largest banks. It would take a little time—not in the comptroller's office, understand, but in the banks themselves—to dig up the answers. Maybe a week. Next Wednesday or Thursday at the latest. That would be October 10, say. Yes, he'd promise to light a fire under the banks' asses.

Grimes thanked him warmly and went back to his office. Might as well wait and see. It all sounded pretty farfetched, and how about that computer stuff, spies, and assassins? Hell, it never hurt to be thorough. He picked up the phone and dialed a friend over in the FBI.

Devon phoned from Boston on Tuesday night.

"It's all over, David. We did the last trade an hour ago."

"Finished? I can't believe it. October 7, a date that will live in infamy. Financial infamy, that is. Just for sentiment's sake, what was it?"

"What?"

"The last trade."

"It was 900 shares of Sunlite Oil at $45 even. We're out, David. Zero balances everywhere. We did that Sunlite through the Tecumseh Bank in Annapolis; that's where that cute vice president tried to get me drunk at dinner and go to his beachhouse at Rehoboth."

"Angel, you're making me erect with jealousy. If you get my meaning. Come on home. Don't hang around saying goodbye. Are we all paid up at the service bureau? Good. Oh, you might drop the tapes in the Charles River on your way to Logan."

Hanging up, he took the running total from his desk and added in the day's total. It called for an appreciative whistle. They'd started with $4,350,000,000. Everything in, dividends, gains, the odd losses, they had sold out for $9,867,000,000. The greatest turn in history.

It called for a drink. He poured a Grouse and toasted himself in the mirror. By God, he was shaking; he had to put the glass down as the recognition swept over him that it was over. Clean as a whistle, just as he had expected. Trailless. Just a string of empty accounts and untenanted post office boxes piling up corporate reports and bank statements. He went round the apartment gathering up the artifacts of his adventure: notebooks, worksheets, records. His fireplace worked; he burnt the lot, saving only the single sheet, unheaded, on which he'd carried the running total for the last fourteen months.

Devon walked in just after seven.

"You are the most beautiful woman in the world, and we are both very, very rich and the job is ended so it is now appropriate for me to ask for your hand."

"I thought you'd never ask. As Barney would say, Harrison, you got a deal."

They got wonderfully drunk and he quoted long, silly passages of erotic poetry. "From *This is my Beloved*," he said, "in my day the Bhagavad-Gita of prep school masturbation." Later he passed out.

"Congratulations, David. Yes, the client will be very pleased. I'll convey the news to him. As a matter of fact, he's in Paris. The Arc de Triomphe is this weekend, you understand. Of course. Perhaps we could take a trip together early next month; it's a wonderful time for the Loire and the Burgundy country. Excellent, we can talk further then. It will be a great pleasure to see you. Yes, and my best regards to your friend. What? Oh, David, that is wonderful news indeed. My congratulations to you both. And our trip to Burgundy will serve two purposes. 'Til November then. Goodbye."

Khafiq replaced the telephone in its cradle. They were really a fine young couple; might Allah bless them, unanointed though they were. Everything was in place. The King's funds returned to their proper homes. Alrazi's, the Minister's, and his own new billions deployed in a hundred discreet new locations around the world. They had each chipped in to make up the $125 million trust fund for Harrison at the Weisenhausesbank. Khafiq had arranged for Harrison to have a call on a loan of $75 million. The sale of the flexible-packaging company to a German shell would close in Winston-Salem in three weeks' time. That was strictly a matter for the lawyers now.

It was all as neatly knotted up as the precise little bows on his small, gleaming shoes. He thought he would go around to Bond Street. A modest celebration was in order and he had always wanted to own a Rembrandt. He buzzed his secretary.

"Have the car brought, please. And then ring round to Agnews. Tell Mr. Julian that I'll be there in half an hour."

It was a perfect day outside. Khafiq thought that the special brightness of the English fall was better than ever today. He might just acquire a nice Turner water color to go with his Rembrandt.

Grimes finally heard from the comptroller's man after lunch on Friday. He wanted to come over to the Treasury Building.

"No time like the present," said Grimes.

"Well, Bob," he was told, "you were sure as hell right. We ran a new account profile trace. From what we can see, there were probably about a hundred banks involved. Fewer account names than that; we've only turned up sixty so far, mostly with Newark or New York P.O. boxes. The whole thing worked out to several billions. We figure maybe three-four billion coming in and might be as much as nine going out."

"Going out? Nine billion?"

"Yeah. *Gone* out, actually, for all we can tell. Lot of standard interbank transfers, so much every day, pretty regularly over the last twelve-thirteen months, all of it runs out overseas, Switzerland, HK, some London, and everywhere else. Beyond the two-mile limit, my authority runs into a brick wall. I can get *our* banks to talk, but once that dough's gone into the sunset, I'm no help."

"Why, *gone?*"

"Well, that's the funny thing. At one point these accounts were holding maybe $8 *billion* plus; as of last Tuesday, my record date, they were down to $7 *million*. There were only three accounts not in zero balance although no accounts had been closed."

"What was it in? T-bills? Certificates? Long governments? Agencies? Triple As?"

"That's funny, too. You're not going to believe this. The whole thing seems to have been in equities. Mostly common stocks, with a few hundred million in preferreds and convertible bonds. And all over the lot; the list looks to me like maybe a couple of thousand issues, all the way from Kodak and the Telephone down to some pretty junky little oil companies. Of course, in this market, these guys made out like bandits. How'd you like to double on four bil? Shit!"

"What else? Anything on who or when?"

"It's all in here." The comptroller's man extended a manila folder. "But if you want to play detective, I don't think we've got the answer. Half the banks don't remember the account. It was all order room stuff. Computer talk. No service. No personal stuff. And I'll bet my ass you won't find diddlesquat in those post office boxes. Anyway, it's all yours. Good luck on it. It looks to me as though no harm's been done. Not even a boat-rocker. Have fun." He waved jauntily and left Grimes's office.

Grimes went through the folder carefully. The comptroller's man was right. There was very little to go on, except that the numbers were so big and there was something disturbing—"unusual" was the better word—about the pattern. It needed higher level eyes than his, that was for sure. He telephoned the Secretary himself; his own boss, the deputy, was in Nairobi.

The Secretary was fond of Grimes and took his call.

"Yes, Bob?"

"Sir, something's come up which I think you should know about. Can you give me a half hour? Tomorrow morning? At your house? Yes sir, I'll be there at ten sharp. Have a good evening, sir."

Then, to wrap up a few loose ends, he telephoned his contact at the FBI. In his excitement, it didn't occur to him to call Camran. This was government business now.

The Secretary lived in a big, ivied brick house in Chevy Chase. It was the closest thing his wife had been able to find to the mansion in which she'd gloried in San Marino during the years in which her husband had built Command Parts into a billion-dollar company. He was a former professor of philosophy with a taste for logic and first-things-first; failure to get tenure at Ann Arbor had led him to invest a small inheritance in a modestly profitable forging shop in Columbus. Ten years later, his practical bent had so transformed and built upon the one-building job shop that it was the largest manufacturer of industrial components in the country.

He was the most admired member of the Baxter administration. He kept his own company and counsel, took long contemplative walks with his wife along the Canal, and left his business at the office. He avoided Duke's and the Rive Gauche. At night, instead of company reports, he read Sophocles and Racine. When Command's sales passed the billion-dollar mark, he fell into a "what next" *accidie* from which he was rescued by the invitation to join Baxter's cabinet.

As much as he despised Washington, although he liked the physical look of the place, he persisted in an optimism about the possibilities of the power he held. Open-minded, he encouraged a free discourse within the Treasury Department. His accessibility soothed the bruises his bright young men acquired bouncing off the granite obduracy and opacity of the civil servants with whom they had to wrestle.

Grimes pulled his three-year-old Colt into the driveway at five to ten. He had been here a number of times. It was one of the finest houses in a town of fine homes. As he was ushered through the hall to the Secretary's study, he saw that the rooms were still filled with fresh flowers and that, somehow, the setting was as cheerful in the morning as he knew it to be impressive in the evening.

The Secretary put down his cigar and book when Grimes entered. He had been reading *Andromaque*.

"How are you, Robert?"

Grimes thought he looked a thousand years older than when they'd all first come to Washington. He guessed it was in the nature of the job and made a mental jotting to take a closer look in his own mirror that evening.

"Tell me about this problem of yours," the Secretary said. As always, no messing around with preliminaries.

Grimes told him. He finished up with the information his FBI friend had given him.

"The San Francisco office of the Bureau talked to a few of the people who worked at MPL, sir, before it blew up. They didn't have much to say. Apparently, this man Nyquist ran the place like a CIA drop: the clients didn't see each other and the staff was kept out of sight. There was some intimation that MPL was working on a big program; it was handled by one of the house computer wizards, an Indian named," Grimes checked his notes, "Dalip Singh. Which dovetails with what our friends at Certified tell me. They're the ones that picked up on this, actually went to see Nyquist about buying the program; Merriman himself went, sir; you know how paranoid they are about the Gotham Bank. I gather they thought that Nyquist had come up with something hot for the Gotham and they wanted to buy it away.

"Anyway, sir, this Singh has disappeared. He may have been in the house when it blew up. There was a lot of propane in the basement; this Nyquist was some kind of a Chinese cooking nut and had fancy special stoves; when the propane went up, everything was turned to cinders. The San Francisco Fire Department thinks they've found fragments of two people in the ruins; they've got Nyquist's teeth so of course they know he was there, but that's about it. I've summarized the whole thing here." He handed the Secretary a two-page summary. It was the way things were done.

When he had read it, the Secretary blew a fragrant ring of Maduro smoke into the air.

"I assume the Bureau's looked into these post office boxes?"

"Yes sir. Stuffed with stockholder communications, reports, and that sort of thing. Any dividends were directed to the agency accounts. Which are now, incidentally, 100 percent dry. Judging by the dates on the postmarks, no one's been near those boxes for over a month. The Post Office is starting to bitch about the overflow. The Bureau's got them on stakeout but, personally, I think it will be a cold day in hell before someone turns up to gather the stuff. Hell, they don't own anything any more."

"Except damn near $10 billion cash," said the Secretary. He exhaled another long plume of smoke.

"Let's take it from the top," he said next. "Make some rational guesses. This has got to be a private deal. Now who has $5 billion they can run into this country? Taipei is one. Qu'nesh, of course. And I can think of a couple of people in Florida. Them I can do something about. The others are out of any jurisdiction I've got a handle on. But we can at least reduce the field."

He went to his desk and dialed a number.

"Hugo? Good. Look, I need a quick favor." He detailed his request.

Turning back to Grimes after hanging up, he said, "The director promises the Bureau will give us one answer no later than Monday. As for the others, frankly all I can suggest is that we do a little brainstorming, much as I loathe the phrase, on Monday. My office. Two p.m. Just you and me and the deputies. Get your boss back from Kenya. I'd make it earlier on Monday, but I've got a very important lunch. Meanwhile, total silence. I'll see you Monday. Thanks for coming."

The FBI Learjet settled into Miami International Airport just after ten o'clock on Sunday morning. It was hotter than hell, and mid-October too, thought the assistant director, as he climbed into the unmarked Bureau car.

They drove across the causeway onto Key Biscayne and into the driveway of the Key Biscayne Hotel. The assistant director told his driver to wait and walked quickly through the hotel lobby out past the pool and on to the pitch-and-putt golf course. He paused, searching out his quarry. There they were, two middle-aged men in undershirts and workpants thrashing awkwardly. They looked up from their putts as he approached.

"Morning, Vito. Giuseppe."

"Sam." The older one spoke. "What's a nice Irish boy like you doing out of church on a Sunday morning?" He smiled like a python.

"Got an absolution. You have a minute to talk?"

"For you, Sam, always. *Possiam' finir' più tarde, Bepp'.*"

They led the assistant director to a crummy two-bedroom cabana close to the beach. It was littered and messy. A fat woman in a black dress sat knitting on a rocker in the screened-in loggia.

"Scusi, Momma." She got up and left the porch.

"Have a seat, Sam. Coffee? Maybe a glass anise? Wine?"

"No thanks, Beppe. This shouldn't take long."

"So Sam, what's on your mind? We're flattered, Beppe and me, to have such an important visitor in our little vacation home. Right, Bepp'?" A nod.

"Vito, have you guys been in the stock market in a big way in the last year?"

"No, Sam, but I wish we had been. Coulda made a killin'. Not the usual sort, of course." The man smiled.

"Cut the shit, Vito, and lay it on me straight. Don't forget. We've still got those tapes we made in Yonkers two years ago. That was very indiscreet of you. I think some of your friends in Vegas would find them interesting. Now, we just thought you might be having fun with some of that Colombian money. From the dope racket, Vito."

"Sam, Sam, Sam, we don't do dope." He looked at his brother, then back at the FBI man. *"Cosa diceva la Mamma,* Sam, what would Mamma say?"

"I hope you're not shitting me, Vito."

"I'm not shittin' you, Sam. You ask a question. The answer is no. *Lo giuro.* On the heads of my grandchildren. Right, Bepp'?" The other man nodded again.

"Vito, I'll buy it. If you're giving me the business, just

(365)

remember, it's tough to play golf in concrete shoes. *Comprende?*"

"Sam, Sam, Sam, would I lie to you? You ain't some fuckin' senator with oil-money shit in his pants. I'm tellin' you how it is. Right, Bepp'?" A third nod.

They swapped pleasantries for ten minutes. Then the assistant director took his leave. At a payphone in the hotel lobby, he called Washington. When the director came on the line, he said simply, "Not here."

Walking to the car, he thought it was a hell of a note to fly two thousand miles for six minutes of conversation with a couple of Guineas and a two-word report.

With the October religious holidays imminent, the Minister was back in Qu'nesh. He and Alrazi met daily, refining the wording of the announcement he would make at the OPEC meeting in Geneva. They had fixed on Wednesday, October 22, when the Conference would be on its second day, to make the statement. It was less than ten days off.

Alrazi was in a jubilant mood. His stallion Tristesse had run third in the Arc, beating all six of the Aga Khan's entries. He had rejected a syndication bid of 60 million francs for the horse. It had been made in the paddock, just after the race, by the hefty Kansan who was the world's largest breeder. After all, Alrazi thought, with a personal fortune of some $4 billion scattered around the world, who needed the money? And Mrs. Fotheringill had been delighted with the egg-sized diamond Van Cleef had dredged up from its Paris vaults.

At length, they agreed on the wording:

"The Kingdom is most reluctant to announce," the Minister would say, *"that the U.S. Government has for its own reasons decided to renege on or abrogate certain matters of firmest understanding it was believed to have reached with the Kingdom earlier this year. These understandings, which the Kingdom regarded as critical to its earlier decision to reduce materially the wellhead posted price of crude oil, have for some reason been wilfully terminated privately by President Baxter, presumably with the knowledge and consent of the Democratic leaders of the U.S. Congress. Accordingly, the Kingdom has no alternative, reluctantly, but to take certain actions in its own interest. Beginning next January 1, but effective earlier, the price of crude oil will revert to $27 a barrel and shipments to the United States will be curtailed to 500,000 barrels a day. In order not to penalize its European and other allies, this*

price increase will apply to only 50 percent of crude shipments to the EEC and the Third World.

"The King deeply regrets this action. Pending the outcome of the U.S. presidential election on November 4, the King will withhold final decision. The decision with respect to a price change will therefore not become final until November 5 and will not go into effect until January 1."

Then, Alrazi and the Minister agreed, the Minister would let float, on the storm of questions that would surely follow the announcement, the notion that the election of Ambassador Jordan, long a friend of and trusted in the Kingdom, might cause the Kingdom to reconsider its decision.

It seemed foolproof. Masters would be ready in Washington with $30 million to buy prime television time for the commercials now stacked and waiting in a Manhattan advertising agency.

Wait and see, Harrison kept repeating to himself. He was becoming very nervous. He tried to busy himself resuscitating old deals and business connections, but there weren't many out there now. With a prospective income of $15 million a year, it was ridiculously obvious that he didn't need the money, so obvious that he found it embarrassing even to admit it to himself. He hated the obvious! Anyway, most of his clients, who had sought his advice in the tough days, when financing needed to be creative, were banging out bond and stock issues into a public market which gobbled up anything that was offered like a rooster after grain. The merger business was dead. "Why buy when you can build much cheaper?" was the motto in executive suites. The prime rate was at 6 percent.

He had three dates to look forward to. Election Day. It would be interesting to see what happened. November 6, when he and Devon planned to be married. And sometime right after that, the trip to Burgundy with Khafiq.

So he spent his days in long lunches with his lady and his afternoons looking at apartments, galleries, shops: all the normal business of the Manhattan idle, whom he had so long despised. He tried to draw a comforting measure of distraction from what he had so long prided himself to be: an unfathomable well of "important" cultural and intellectual interests. He remained fidgety, could listen to music with no more than half an ear, read with no more than half a mind. His inability to rediscover his old solaces led to his confronting himself with the possibility that he was an intellectual phony. If true, and his uneasiness made him doubt that it wasn't, it became an obsessively inadmissible notion.

Increasingly crotchety, he wanted it *all* to be over, the pattern to resolve itself one way or the other. His instinct, so shadowy and tangential that it resisted analysis, was telling him that maybe he should do something, jump in some direction. But how could he? He had the uneasy feeling that the game part was over, that his "fix the bastards" rhetoric had always been more a matter of mischief than ideology. Now the game may have switched to something serious, something deadly. What the hell *had* happened to Ernie?

Then, one day in his dentist's office, he had picked up a recent issue of *The Bulletin of the Portfolio Managers,* which his earlier research had identified as particularly abstruse and pretentious. He had leafed about halfway through it when a title caught his attention: *"MPL Post-Nyquist: Whither? Whither?"* Post-Nyquist? The text began, *"With the sudden, tragic passing of Axel Nyquist, and the demolition of MPL's elegant San Francisco headquarters, the question of succession at this vanguard firm..."* The print blurred and he suddenly felt as if all his nerve ends had jumped to the surface of his skin. Nyquist dead? Demolition?

It was all he could do to get through Dr. McGinnity's ministrations. The dentist prattled about what he was going to do with his *next* million.

"Nothing too fancy, Mr. Harrison, just a bit of triple-hedging with a medium-rich trace beta. Me, I leave the fast lane to the hotshots, the surgeons and suchlike."

McGinnity's Celtic gabble summoned up a vision of Nyquist in his office, revived memories of their two meetings on the Coast and that other time at JFK. Harrison needed to find out more.

He fled the dentist's chair, finally, and McGinnity's importunings about March soybeans, and flew uptown in a taxi, making for the Society Library. He pulled the two most recent months of *The New York Times* and riffled through the obituary pages until he found the article which had transfixed Alex Camran a few weeks earlier. As he read it over and over, the wintry thought came to him that he might have somehow had something to do with this, accident or not. Hell, it had to have been an accident; he remembered those big gas cylinders and all that wiring. Sure, said something in his mind then, he would swear it wasn't himself, sure—and what about Ernie?

When Ernie had vanished, Harrison had been quick to listen to his genes. What could you expect, he'd said to himself, the guy was a spade and was a fag, not exactly preferred ingredients in any recipe for dependability. But Nyquist *and* Ernie, that was too much, he thought, and shamefully too, knowing that Ernie hadn't probably just minced off in pursuit of some twitching rear end.

And so he began to wonder what exactly was he involved in? What the hell was going on? When he got home, he thought about calling London, but then some second sense told him just to keep his mouth shut. Which is what he resolved to do, not even to talk to Devon.

Then it broke on him that all along he had thought of this whole business as a sort of gigantic game, just as he had tried to make games out of all the important interludes and occasions of his life: boards and pieces to be neatly boxed away at the end of amusing afternoons and evenings. Well, this wasn't a game, he recognized, no way, nor for that matter had been so much else in his life.

As the days passed, his misgivings and apprehensions rose in his mind like monsters from a swampbed. Fueled by his innate tendency to self-dissection, he began to worry at himself. He analyzed his career. He came to see that all those deals he'd cooked up, like this one, went far beyond all that easy crap about market symmetry and synergy. He came to see that those facile merger formulas he cooked up on a pocket calculator embraced and probably annulled the dreams and opportunities of people as real and specific as himself. Christ, he reflected ruefully, I'm no better than Drzlag or those other miserable jerks in Washington, merrily scissoring and pasting the bright map of the world as if there would be no scorched flesh, no rib-thin orphans, no starvation. And then he began to be afraid.

Devon noticed. One Sunday afternoon in Avery Fisher Hall, when an old and legendary pianist had subdued the audience with absolutely incandescent musicmaking, she took him to task at intermission.

"Darling, what *is* the matter? I don't think you heard a note."

It was the first time in their life together that she had ever sounded helpless in dealing with him. He made an impatient, diffident gesture with his shoulders. He couldn't tell her anything. His mind spun with pictures of Baxter and Jordan; the morning newspapers, reporting their campaign speeches, were a fresh reminder of what was going on, what he thought he knew. He couldn't tell Devon. There was too much at stake; it was too improbable to share.

Finally, the crowding images and ideas anesthetized his prickling concern. There were simply too many particularities and problems. He was entirely solipsistic now. Ignorant of the rush of events actually happening outside him, naive despite his inferences and recollections, it occurred to him that "danger" might now be an operative word in the vocabulary of this adventure.

Since he knew absolutely nothing of fear, for the terms of his life had provided no opportunity to confront it other than in odd schoolboy scuffles and near-misses in cars, he was hopeless to deal with this brand-new emotion. Again, therefore, he was attentive to his genes and reached for the whiskey bottle.

He saw himself becoming feckless, watched the tattering away of his confident, humorous enthusiasm for life—which he knew to be his most attractive and essential characteristic. It seemed another lifetime, another century, since he and Devon had stood looking triumphantly down on the Stock Exchange on Green Monday. His absorption with his real and extrapolated problems made him distracted and impenetrable. Only at night could Devon reach him, when he would thrash about in the grip of a nightmare, making thin, frightened moans, until her cool reassurances would settle the monsters for another few hours.

Buster's odyssey through the chanceries of Washington in search of the truth had brought him to the Treasury Department. He had a long lunch with the Secretary. At the end of it, he felt the same way he had at State, at Commerce, and at the Pentagon. He met a lot of clever and ambitious people who were as usual up to a lot of self-serving mischief, he was sure, but his antennae, in which, like most country people, he trusted absolutely, fed him back zero with respect to the Kingdom. There was nothing going on here. He was sure of that. No plots or secret deals. He was running out of real estate.

"Buster," said the Secretary over Sanka, "you never get a chance to see what goes on around here, the Old Man keeps you so damn busy. If you've got an hour, come on down with me. I've got a meeting downstairs in fifteen minutes. There's an interesting problem on the docket. I doubt that it's really important, but it will give you a chance to have a look at some of the people I've brought in here. How about it?"

Why not? Buster thought. The President was in Jacksonville and Gottlieb was minding the store. So he followed the Secretary into the elevator and into the fourth-floor meeting room.

The Secretary asked Grimes to outline the situation. Buster listened with half an ear. He'd hardly ever owned a share of stock. His father had lost the farm to the Goldman, Sachs Trading Company in 1935, and that had been enough for Buster.

"...and so, the accounts in question have sold out 100 percent in the last six months," Grimes wound up.

From the head of the table, the Secretary looked around at his five deputies.

"Any thoughts?" he asked.

Only infants and idiots have the requisite innocence to express strong opinions in the company of recognized experts and deep thinkers. The Deputy Secretary for Financial Markets was in this sense an idiot. A generous contribution to the Baxter campaign had given him a due bill. He was a marginally intelligent Bostonian broker who knew that money talked best and so he pushed his way into the Treasury, leaving his partners in the State Street brokerage rejoicing at the fact of his retirement from the firm. The Secretary had surrounded him with able assistants, so that the damage he could do was negligible, but nothing could stop him from thrusting his ideas into any discussion.

"Pretty stupid," he said now. "Selling out, I mean. Good Christ! This market's still got another thousand points left in it. The only thing that would stop it from breaking 2800 on the Dow would be if the damned Arabs raised the price of oil back up again! And that ain't bloody likely!

"Hell, no one in his right mind would bail out here!" The Deputy Secretary was insistent, almost indignant; his lumbering mind clicked only on matters of stocks and bonds, on paper profits seized or slipped.

"I think you've made your point," said the Secretary impatiently. To his high-minded, cosmic view of things the goings-on of the stock market were inconsequential sandbox stuff. He looked around the table; the Deputy subsided in his chair. "Any other ideas?"

None of the others around the table had anything to offer, nor commented on the Deputy Secretary's assertion. They were narrow-focused, crisp young men, the newest breed, who counted existence in abstract quantities. The Secretary had burned into them the notion that matters of economy and finance were nicely calculable and above such irrational mechanics as politics and emotion. Anyway, the amount in question was trifling, a mere nine billions at most, small change. So no one around the great oaken conference table stirred in their rich leather chairs at the Deputy's reaction to Grimes's report.

Except Buster.

He would later tell the President, "I felt like I was all of a sudden wearing an electric suit." The air and the other presences seemed pumped out of the room, as on a prairie the instant before a twister rises over the horizon like a cobra. Buster felt himself suspended in that kind of non-atmosphere, in which the only sensation of which he was aware was a tingling at the roots of his nerves, a feeling he'd had before.

Buster's antennae suddenly vibrated, with a force he had known only twice before in his life. He felt his Indian-straight black hair stand on end, a flush and rush under his skin, an apprehension so intense that it touched on elation. Memory burst in.

When Buster was ten years old, he'd cut across a marshy field on his way home from school. Perhaps it had been an infinitesimal shiver in the grass beside the path, he would never know, but something tingled down his spine from his cortex and, without sensing why, he jumped backward just as the open-fanged mouth and half the length of a three-foot coral snake shot out of a clump of mudfern and gnashed a weedpatch just where his ankle would have been.

Then, when he was twenty-seven, Buster had awakened suddenly in the middle of the night in a bed where he shouldn't have been, in a house that wasn't his. The same tingle. He recognized it as a danger signal. He dressed without waking the sleeping woman and let himself out the back door. He was hidden in the shadow of the spreading oak on the lawn, well out of the moonlight, when the dusty pickup had coasted in, lights and engine off, and the man of the house and his two half-retarded nephews had gotten out, eyes glittering with moonshine whisky, knotted hands clutching axe handles.

Now, for only the third time, the old cortical quiver returned. Buster had once read how the undersea world would freeze, all life and activity sucked out as if by a vacuum, when a great white shark would appear. His world was frozen now, his old instincts alerted, the same instincts that brought the spiders down from the cypresses when a real toadstomper was starting to blow up out over the Gulf of Mexico, out of sight but as present in the air as if the roofs were already coming off the houses.

"Say that again," he asked the Deputy Secretary.

"Well, Mr. Ferdimend," said the other man, preening in the spotlight, "in a market like this, where they're throwing money at stocks with both hands, you just don't sell out unless you're real drunk or unless you know something. And what is there to know?"

Buster looked over the man's head. A notice tacked to the bulletin board reminded that Election Day, November 4, was a Federal Holiday.

"I see," was all Buster said. He contained himself, but he thought he knew why the Arabs hadn't gotten in touch.

He waited out the meeting. The rest of the group pressed over the deputy's observation and pushed for more substantive ideas. There were none.

Ermabelle and Fulger Baxter were finishing a late lunch when the speakerphone at the President's place beeped.

"Mr. Ferdimend's on his way up, sir."

Buster burst into the room. He looked as if he had seen a ghost.

"Fulger, we got trouble! We got to talk!"

It was the first time since his inauguration that Baxter could recall Buster, normally so punctilious in his observance of the dignity of the office, calling him by his Christian name.

It was more than Ermabelle could stand. Placing her half-eaten tuna sandwich on her plate, she looked at Buster severely.

"Lord's sakes, Buster, where are your manners?"

30 The President didn't like what Buster had to tell him, but he did, finally, go along with his assistant's conclusions.

Ferdimend recounted the meeting at Treasury, returning emphatically twice to the deputy secretary's offhand remark.

"'Course, he wouldn't recognize the truth if it up and bit him in the fanny," Buster noted, "but it appears to me that this dumb sumbitch may just have hit on somethin'." He added that his initial reaction had been reinforced by a couple of calls he'd made after leaving the Treasury.

As Buster traced the story, it seemed to the President that Buster's argument was awfully logical.

"There hasn't been anything to worry about in the campaign, Mr. President. Not until now, that is. But, anyway, I've had this boy planted over on Jordan's staff. Just bein' careful. Nothin' special to look for, but I do like to keep my hand on things. Anyway, I talked to him a little while ago. Seems that they had a meetin' over the weekend. You're really whippin' Jordan's butt in the polls; Gallup's goin' to show you 72 percent next Tuesday, or so Pep tells us; so, anyway, they're all sittin' around cryin' and someone gets the bright idea to make a bunch of TV commercials costin' $700,000, or some such figure like that, to have ready, just in case."

"In case of what, Buster?"

"That's the thing. My boy says they're just gonna film 'em and have 'em around, like a shotgun sittin' in the closet."

"For $700,000?"

"Good thinkin', Mr. President. 'Parently the Dunstable representative—Jordan's no more runnin' this election for the Republicans than I am—screamed like a stuck hog. You know Dunstable's worse'n we are about pissin' away money. And, what do you know, Ben Masters stepped up with a personal guarantee—$700,000 worth! And you know whose money he's speakin' for?"

"Refresh me."

"Mr. President, Benjamin Masters gets $250,000 a year to keep a handle on things for our friends in the Kingdom. But he ain't quite rich yet. I had our man in the IRS take a peek at Masters's records. He's doin' good, all right, but no way can he come up with $700,000 in hard cash."

"OK, Buster, I can see your thinkin'. Let's say that Qu'nesh is payin' for these commercials through Masters. So what and for what? Anyway, those Arabs love that damn Jordan. He's always treated 'em like folks, to begin with, and we all know 'bout that Libyan business. This could be just a little kiss-your-butt-and-go-away present, couldn't it?" Baxter didn't sound convinced.

"I don't think so. It's just one more knot on the log. Like

(374)

I told you, the Treasury hears about a few billion dollars which came to visit last fall, stayed a while, and has been leavin' over the last few months. Nothin' in a size to get really hot about; shoot, it probably don't even come to $10 billion."

As Buster said it, the President remembered when the two of them didn't have fifty dollars between them. Now they threw "billions" around as easy as chaw money.

"Except the thing is," said Buster, "this is all stock market money. Pretty smart money, too. Got in right, way back last year when prices were down; probably wasn't more than $4, $5 billion then. Now it's cashed out, but way too early. Or so it looks to the experts. 'Cept *now* I don't think it is too early!"

Buster's pretty emphatic, thought President Baxter. He's smelling something. The President had an evangelical faith in Buster's sense of smell.

"What I think, Mr. President, is this. Those Arabs have been bitchin' about the dollar for six years now. They have been bitchin' about this Israel peace treaty. They're scared shitless that they are goin' to wake up one bright mornin' to find the Marines sittin' on them oilfields, along with some Russians and Japs and Europeans, and their oil bein' sold *by* us *to* us for $4 a barrel. Tarnation, everybody in Washington knows that the State Department tried to work a deal with the Indians to invade the Kingdom. Anyway, these Arabs must have just about been lettin' go in their skivvies what with one thing or another.

"So somehow they get the idea they can buy some time and, if they can buy time, why not buy the election? I promise you, Mr. President, there's nobody in State or Treasury or the Pentagon who knows one damn thing about any secret deal with Qu'nesh. Hell, they've all got each other's wires tapped and what they're not coverin', the Russians *are* and *we're* all over *them* like a baby on a warm tit. They all think you and I did a deal with the Kingdom, and I don't speak for you, but I know *I* didn't, and I know you didn't; Marvin's Jewish, so he couldn't. I don't believe Miz Ermabelle did it on her lonesome, much as you let her have her head. So I just got to think that after you run out the possible candidates, endin' with the four of us, you got to conclude that their announcement about secret deals, and all them other press leaks, was just so much hogwash! Mr. President, good as it felt, there's no secret understandin' with the Kingdom.

And we've been like tethered sheep sittin' here chompin' away while the wolf's sneakin' up in the bushes. 'Cause that's what they've been doin'."

The President felt the chilly truthful ring of Buster's surmise right down his spine. To buy time to think, he asked Buster to run through it slowly.

"The way it looks to me," finished Buster, "they kinda looked like they was handin' us the election and now they're just goin' to jerk it away. I been doin' some figurin' on my calendar. The election's on the fourth of November. Today's the fourteenth of October, so we're talkin' about three weeks to Election Day. But we got less time than that. I called over to Langley and talked to the OPEC desk officer. The OPEC meetin's in Vienna on the twenty-fourth, -fifth, and -sixth. Their Oil Minister will be there starting the twenty-third to represent the Kingdom. Just like he was last spring in Honolulu at that big offshore foofaw. And what the prickles on the back of my neck are sayin' to me is that on Prickday night, say, maybe Saturday, but over the weekend, 'cause that seems to be when they like to work, just when this country's fartin' around feelin' fat and happy, the Minister'll call a press conference, just like he did in Honolulu, and he's goin' to put that official oil price right back up to $25, maybe $30, and he's gonna say just like he did in Honolulu, except this time it'll be the other way round, that they sure are sad to have to do this to all their good ol' friends in the U.S. of A., but it seems that *you*, Mr. President, broke your secret deal, and there it is."

And there he was, thought Baxter. Shoot, if that happened, him and Ermabelle and Buster could swear until they were blue as seawater that none of it was true. But try telling that to a vast, greedy people who were well into the greatest binge of spending and speculating in half a century. Hostages to their own self-indulgence. The President's disclaimer wouldn't buy ten votes.

"And Mr. President, just one more thing. I believe we can expect a few well chosen words favorable to the candidacy of Ambassador Jordan, to the effect that if he was to be elected, well, the Kingdom just might reconsider the rescission. And then I think you can expect to see those Jordan TV commercials come flyin' off the shelf like Lake Charles pintails."

"You think Jordan's in cahoots with them on this, Buster?"

"Lord awmighty no, sir. Jordan's like us, or like we have

been. He's as clean as fresh tar. This is one smartass deal, Mr. President; you got to admire those folks. Look at what happens. You get knocked off; I'll bet that half the Israeli lobby in the Congress gets blown out; even old Dunstable, smart as he is, ain't goin' nowhere 'cause if Jordan gets elected, that finishes old Herndon as the Republican leader. Damn, it looks like Bess Dunstable's never goin' to get to repaper the East Room!"

The President found himself nodding almost metronomically in time with the flow of Buster's alarming hypotheses. When Ferdimend appeared to have finished, he had a question.

"Buster, what do you make of this stock exchange business that tipped you in the first place? What's all that about?"

"Hard to say. Looks like some of those boys got wind of what was up and may have decided to take a little flyer on a sure thing."

"Buster, you don't 'get wind' of somethin' like this. That particular breeze just don't blow."

"If we're thinkin' the same thing, Mr. President, and I b'lieve we are, then it means that the top guys are in it. Although Langley tells me it ain't likely it's the King hisself, which is funny, 'cause Treasury says it has to be his money!"

Actually, what Buster had gathered from his meeting at the CIA was that *if* any large investment dollars had originated from the Kingdom and was in stocks, it was likely to be the King's own private fortune. The Treasury itself handled the dollar portion of the state funds.

"How come, Buster?"

"Well, Treasury just says there ain't another individual over there with the kind of money we're talkin' about. They figure maybe $6 billion's involved. But Langley says, and you got to excuse me here, sir, that the King's some kind of a religious nut. A born-again Moslem. Now that he's through havin' children, all he does is pray and read the Book and what money he spends goes into that big church of his. I hear it's a right nice church, but it ain't about to cost $9 billion. Not even with things like the prayer rug."

The President smiled. A week after they knew that Air Force One had delivered the Chicago prayer rug safely to Qu'nesh, the Kingdom's ambassador had rung up the White House for an appointment. His mission was brief. He presented President Baxter with a check made out to the New

Orleans children's clinic, which was his and Ermabelle's pet charity. The check was for $25 million.

"So it's the King's money," said the President, thinking aloud more than framing a thought, "but it ain't the King. But it's somebody way high up. The Minister, obviously, he does all the talkin'."

"Maybe yes, maybe no," said Buster, "talkin' and the money may run separate. The CIA boys—our guy, that is—says if you're talkin' money in the Kingdom, you start with the Prime Minister."

"Alrazi?" The President had met the Crown Prince at a fruitless energy summit three years earlier. The two men hadn't particularly liked each other.

"Alrazi. Seems he's got all the need for money a man'd ever have: gambles millions like grains of sand and likes to chase booger and give 'em fancy cars and big diamonds. But he ain't got real money, at least by his standards. I couldn't follow it all, but our people explained it has somethin' to do with his birthline not bein' auspicious enough. And he's in a position to move a whole lot of the King's money around."

"What I can't quite figure, also, Buster, is how this whole thing got goin' without anybody here pickin' it up. What's the matter with the Treasury, anyhow? I thought they was supposed to be watchin' these Arabs' movements."

"Hell, I think they just got fat, dumb, and happy like us. This ain't such a hot deal sum of money anyway, not these days. And *we* ain't been worryin' much about our Arab problem too much, Mr. President, we got to face *that*. You and me been asleep since last Easter. But to get back to your question, what the Secretary of the Treasury told me as a backgrounder was that all these big money transfers travel today by wire and satellite, and if you break 'em down into a whole lot of little pieces, and scatter 'em around, comin' and goin', in all directions, ain't nobody goin' to pick it up, unless by accident or if they got 'em tagged like alligators. Hell, the way I heard it from the Secretary, this whole deal got discovered just 'cause some kid in New York got jealous 'cause his bank wasn't gettin' some business."

"Yeh, but how'd it get off the ground? I mean, you still got to go to a bank to open an account?"

"Mr. President, when was you in a bank the last time? This ain't like Louisiana in the old days when bankers looked you up and down and made up their minds if you was their kind of people. Nowadays, you just talk to a clerk and get a number and a card and as long as you don't want to borrow money or steal some, only thing in the bank that *knows* you is some itty-bitty piece of magnetic tape. Hell, this whole deal was run by a computer, the Treasury thinks."

Ferdimend paused for a minute. The President's watch ticked like thunderclaps. They had twelve days. Maybe as few as ten.

"Well," Baxter said, "any leads? I mean, bad as it is these days, Buster, where there's a computer, there's got to be some people. Somewhere? Don't they?" Buster thought that his old friend Baxter sounded a touch plaintive. He could sympathize. This modern world was a bitch to get used to.

"No time, no point, Mr. President. I started to activate the FBI—the Treasury's had them to do a little checkin', but only to eliminate one suspect out of about five—and then I got to thinkin'. If we start askin' too many small questions, folks become right curious. Newspapers get to hear about it. We got to settle this thing privately at the top. I don't want Pits Peech askin' on the front page of the *Post* why we got the FBI lookin' into Wall Street and I sure as hell don't want a lot of banks talkin' to each other about the White House takin' a big, hot interest in Arab money. 'Cause the Arabs'll hear about it and just move quicker. We got maybe ten days to find the key and make a deal."

Buster thought also, but did not say, that somewhere out there was some smart sumbitch who'd cooked this thing up. That's the guy he'd like to get his hands on. He'd skin his unpatriotic ass like a coon at Christmas!

His vindictive reverie was interrupted by the President.

"Buster, I got to do some thinkin'. Alone. I'm goin' upstairs for a bit. Don't you get out of pocket. And for goodness' sake, if you run into Ermabelle, don't say nothin'; I ain't goin' to."

The President got up. In Buster's eyes, he had aged twenty years in the two hours since he'd first looked up from his tuna sandwich.

For a long time Fulger Baxter, alone, searched in his Bible hoping for an answer. The fulminations of the Prophets proved as useless to him as the comforting moderations of the Evangelists. He needed tactics and weapons. He wasn't much of a philosopher, he thought, although he prided himself on the supremely moralistic character of his thinking. But he fancied himself a hell of a bar fighter. The Baxter administration had been characterized by one confrontation after another, with eruptive events and situations which longer sighted men had spoken of and anticipated. Baxter and his closest colleagues had no sense of history. Baxter had once delivered a Lincoln's Birthday speech without mentioning the sixteenth President. On the advice of the Secretary of Agriculture, he had talked about thrift and soybeans.

"They seem deaf," Peech had written, *"to the resonances of history, the long reverberating lines that bind actions to consequences. It is impossible to telegraph a punch to this administration; no one is ever available to sign for the message."*

On the other hand, they didn't do too badly in the close corners of crisis. Instinct and fast dealing and confrontation were the stuff of back-country success and respect. These were Baxter's and Buster's native arts. They left such deep thinking as the administration required to the Nordlanders and the Drzlags.

It was natural, therefore, that, after a little initial confusion, after the shock of surprise and the recognition of the audacious magnitude of what seemed to be taking place, Baxter's mind, settled down by Scripture like a child rocked by its mother, would start to sort things out.

If he could, he wanted to make a deal with Qu'nesh. That was for damn sure. And fast. He could give them what he thought *they* wanted. But so could Jordan—as soon as he was inaugurated. And on what they knew, Jordan was the Kingdom's man. They *liked* him. Military action was out as far as Baxter was concerned. Congress had recessed for the last weeks of the campaign and, even if he got them back tomorrow, it would take them six months to agree on the composition of committees to consider the question and another year to recruit staff. If he was going to interdict what he was deepeningly certain was going on, he would have to do it by trading.

He pressed the private buzzer for Ferdimend.

"Buster, we got to see what kind of leverage we got. Have our guy at the CIA set up a run-through of the Black File on the Kingdom. Here. In my office. And have him pull it hisself. Give him one of those superpasses. We'll do it right here, in three hours. And nobody but you, me, and him. And no names given. I mean that, Buster, tell him that clear, no matter what they say out there. Three hours. Eight sharp. I'll fix us some sandwiches after. No, Ermabelle left an hour ago. Her Momma's doin' poorly so I told Ermabelle to stay in Pass

Christian till the old lady feels better. She's ninety-six. You know, Buster, I jus' started feelin' ninety-six myself. 'Bout lunchtime." He chuckled, but it was hard.

When the lights snapped back on, the President stretched and blinked and looked at his aide. The screen which the man from the CIA was rolling up into its stand had stayed flickeringly alight for scarcely fifteen minutes.

The President was disappointed in the CIA trove. "Shoot, Buster, if that's all we got to work with, we ain't lookin' too good. I probably got more than that *personally* on them boys."

They settled over their sandwiches, having dismissed the CIA man. Actually, they could have done a lot worse. The President and Buster were a crafty pair. As they riffled through the pages which footnoted the slides and films that they'd been shown, ideas came to mind. It began to seem that there *was* enough to work with.

At length, an idea arose in the President's mind. He plotted it for Buster. Buster added a few of his own embellishments.

"Ain't a whole lot to trade with," the President said.

"No sir." Buster was flat and undeferential.

"Best we got, though. And at least it's something."

"B'lieve so."

They looked at each other, faintly disappointed in their common brainchild; like it or not, they were playing with a stripped deck.

The President had held back his own zinger until last. He dropped it on Buster.

"'Course, neither you or me is goin' to handle this personally. Not in the beginning. Too tricky. Besides, when you need to get a deal made that may be the biggest ever, it makes sense to get me the best deal-maker around. Now," he gestured Ferdimend closer, "let me tell you what you got to do to get us in high gear."

After he finished, Buster's eyes were wider, but he was smiling. "Fulger," he said, "you ain't lost a step. Think he'll do it?"

"Bet my butt on it. Listen..."

Hearing the President out, Buster Ferdimend reflected that this was the way he liked the action. High, wide, handsome, and let 'er roll. Buster played around only with women and power. His dream, the one that he woke from fresh and plump-chested, was of action, of sitting down to a Las Vegas poker shootout, just him and Slim, and the Sailor and C.A., a fast game of "hold 'em" with $150,000 on the table and only one winner. What Baxter was talking about had some of the essence of Buster's dream.

"Now go find him," ordered the President. "We need him at Camp David tomorrow night. We'll get him up here. You make the arrangements. And, Buster, if he frets, tell him it's a major security matter, tell him it's *humongous*! And, for the good Lord's sake, use a tight phone."

Baxter left to take care of his end of things, after carefully locking the CIA material in the safe in the bathroom which adjoined his study. It was concealed by a highly detailed Wyeth painting of an enormous Cochin boar he had once owned. It reminded him of more private times, when life was simpler and more fun.

Upstairs, he asked the operator for a certain number overseas. "And scramble it," he added. While he waited for the call to be completed, he wondered why it was he was stretching so far, why he just didn't let things slip. Let Jordan get the job, however he got it, Arabs or no Arabs. There were a lot worse things than going home with Ermabelle. Buy some more hogs. Have some fun.

Except that he didn't want Jordan to be President. *He* ought to be President. It was best that way for the country. There was nothing imperial and very little that was self-centered in his thinking on this point as he saw it. Jordan was a fine man, but he was an easterner, and he didn't understand power and the shift in the country's values. Easterners were good at influence, at the "why don't yous?" of life; easterners made great consciences. They were intellectually decorative. But easterners didn't know how to say "Hey, boy, go do that. Right now!" And get it done. This country couldn't be swayed. It had to be told. It needed to take orders, and that was something Fulger Baxter knew it was his mission to give. It was something they understood in the South and the West. Trouble was, the minds of the voters were still elsewhere—although they seemed to be swaying.

The operator came back on the line. "Your call is ready, Mr. President."

In search of a safe phone, Buster got two rolls of dimes and five quarters from the White House cashbox and headed west. He parked his Buick outside the Watergate and went downstairs into the arcade where he knew there was a bank of pay telephones. Working from a penciled list of numbers, he started dialing. On his eighth call, already out $4.30, he got his man.

The Minister was furious, but what could he do? It would mean a detour of nearly ten thousand miles, a whole day lost to flying time plus, another two days of meetings; no more, he had exacted that promise from his caller.

"A matter of extreme urgency has come to our attention," President Baxter himself had said over the scrambler phone, "which may involve the military security of the Kingdom, and most certainly your regime." The President seemed to intimate a plot; internal or external, the Minister could not infer. The United States was anxious to be helpful; this seemed a matter graver in all respects than the earlier affair which had involved Ambassador Jordan. It was too bad, the President said, that current political considerations made it difficult for Jordan to take a hand, although he would of course be briefed at the appropriate time.

Even though he was the senior government official in Qu'nesh, the Minister had pointed out that this was properly the sphere of the Prime Minister and the Minister of the Militia. The latter was unfortunately away, Alrazi having arranged for a month's tour for him on a Russian missile frigate in the Barents Sea; he was not due back in Murmansk for another ten days. The Prime Minister was unavailable. He was with the King in the desert for meditation. It was impossible, unthinkable, to reach him, although he would return late on Sunday. That would be the nineteenth.

The President was understanding but firm. Matters were absolutely urgent. A joint effort undertaken immediately might forestall the problem. It was that serious. The Minister couldn't quite read him. Was he hinting something about Moscow? Or New Delhi?

At length, the Minister agreed. He would arrive late on the afternoon of October 18. He calculated he could be back in Qu'nesh by morning prayers on the twenty-first. That would give him two days to confer further with Alrazi and to consider any late developments that might break on the eve of his departure for Vienna.

After hanging up, he was struck by the fact that the President's voice seemed to have lost its rich coloration. He'd met Baxter once a long time earlier, when Baxter was still governor of Louisiana, and the Minister, then barely anointed, was making a tour of the oilfields. He remembered the governor's accent as being striking and curious then, to a degree which would have carried across space. Had he been speaking with an impostor?

He toyed with the idea of getting on to the Embassy in Washington to do some probing. Instead, he called Khafiq in London.

"You'll never believe this, old friend," he said, "but I've just rung off from none other than the President of the United States. Baxter himself. So he said. Yes. Something about a military problem; my guess is that it's got to do with our friend in Tripoli. But maybe Moscow. No, just over and back, and then to Vienna. Oh, Ali, do you know the most peculiar thing? I met Baxter years ago in the South and could hardly understand him, he had such a thick accent. Talking to him just now, he sounded note-perfect, like Omar Sharif."

He heard Khafiq laugh on the other end. "My dear friend, you've not heard? Baxter takes voice lessons from a retired *soubrette* in Washington. It's really quite marvelous, don't you think? The President of the United States taking lessons to speak English? In the event, do keep me posted. Perhaps Washington will prove interesting. And Vienna should be spectacular. An extraordinary week for one man."

Replacing the receiver, Khafiq thought for a minute. This was all very curious. He asked his secretary to put him through to Damascus. It took a long time, which Khafiq used to think further through the probabilities. At length, Syria was on the line. Khafiq spoke in old Aramaic, asking that Colonel Osman hold himself available for the next fortnight. He agreed to see that $250,000 would be placed on deposit, in equal shares, in the Lombardshandel in Basel and the Pyongyang Bank in Seoul.

Next he called New York.

The phone rang just after midnight and woke Harrison first. Devon made uprooted, muttered noises and shuffled her pillows around.

"How are you, David?" Kahfiq's usual greeting.

It had been a strange, uncentered telephone call, thought Harrison afterward, even though at the time he had been three-quarters asleep and barely conscious. Khafiq had seemed just to want to chat. What were his plans? He might come up next weekend. How did the election look? Through his haze, Harrison surmised that it might just be loneliness.

When he hung up after ten minutes, and slid back next to Devon, into the halo of her warmth, she said, half muffled by the pillow over her head, "Wha' he want?" Harrison was drifting back to sleep. "Noth'. Prob'ly lonely."

"Poor little man. Poor *this* l'il man." He felt her hand enclose him with silken fingers, then guiding him, fitting him to her. Then, later, they both sank back into that deep, dreaming, muscle-aching sleep which is reserved for those who make love in the small hours of the morning; Khafiq's telephone call was forgotten.

The three men sat in the main room of the elaborate lodge, drinking whisky and scrutinizing their new surroundings.

"This is the best room in the house," said the eldest of the three. "Except of course where the President himself stays, which is in the lodge over past that pine grove right west of here."

"As it should be, sir," said one of the younger men smartly.

"I've been here a bunch of times before, of course," said the older man, "but never have stayed here until now. Quite something."

"What do you guess this's all about?" asked the other younger man.

"Who knows? I just do know that when the President calls, you get the feet moving. It can't hurt. Especially when the trip's paid for."

The White House 727 had picked them up and been airborne at eight-fifty-seven. It was usually three hours to Andrews Air Force Base, but headwinds had cut them back, and it wasn't until nearly two o'clock Eastern Time that they set down. Buster had been waiting with the helicopter on the far edge of the field. Thirty-six minutes later, they were on top of Catoctin Mountain and installed in Pinecone Lodge. The President will arrive in an hour or so, Buster said. Just make yourselves comfortable.

There was a knock at the door.

With surprising agility, the older man jumped from his chair, brushed past his younger companions, and opened the lodge door. He had a big smile for the figure who stood there alone, wearing a sweater and old pants which contrasted strikingly with the cowboy elegance of the man who received him.

(385)

"Evening, Mr. President." He put out his hand.

"Evenin' yourself, Herndon." The President shook Dunstable's hand and moved into the room.

"You comfortable enough here, Herndon? Good?" He shook hands with the younger men, looked around, and settled in an armchair, gesturing Dunstable to one catty-corner. The ex-senator's assistants hovered nearby. They were clever young men and they had done yeoman work for their boss right down the line. Unswervingly, adoringly loyal, they were wreathed in an ill-concealed, gloating anticipation of finding out whatever it was that had obliged President Baxter to ask their peerless leader to come to his aid.

Baxter smiled at them piercingly.

"Herndon, you and me's got some serious business to visit about. Why don't these young men just run on down to the rec hall for a Dr. Pepper and a corn dog? They got a TV down there and a pool table and all sorts of them electric games. Dinner's at seven over in my cabin, and they can just mosey straight on over. The Service'll point the way."

The assistants went out, sullenly.

"Nice boys," said Baxter. "My skinny tells me that one of them knows all there is to know about the Arabs."

"Yes sir, he sure does. I got him from Dumbarton Oaks. M.B.A. and a Ph.D. from Harvard. Strong."

"Well, that's wonderful, Herndon. That may come in handy. Now, let me get down to cases."

He looked at Dunstable evenly and appraisingly.

"Herndon, somethin's come up which looks to put you and me on the same side of the table. Before I tell you what it is, and what I want you to do for me, I'm goin' to tell you what my deal is if you say yes."

"You tryin' to buy me, Mr. President?" Dunstable looked only halfway aggrieved; there was still a trace of a smile at the joinings of that menacing mouth.

"Let's just say I'm thinkin' about it. Now just sit still there for a minute and hear what I got to say."

When he finished, Dunstable sat quite still for a very long minute. Then he said, "That sure would cut the odds down, Mr. President. I like odds as short as that, especially for somethin' I want that bad."

"That's the way I see it, Herndon."

Dunstable thought a bit more, rubbing the wattles under his jawline, smoothing down wings of hair, cracking his big hands together. The President said nothing. Just looked at him closely, smiling.

Finally, Dunstable's features became settled in decision.

"Mr. President, I believe I'll go with it. 'Course I got to see what my part is. But if it's realistic and I think I can sell it to Bess, I got to jump."

"No tellin' Bess, Herndon, not this time. I'll tell *you* somethin'. Ermabelle don't even know 'bout this little deal. If she does, she's just guessin'."

"Well, that does say somethin'. Mr. President, I'm your man."

Baxter reached out and he and Dunstable shook hands. It was a deal, a handshake between southern gentlemen, as castiron as if it had been contracted and vetted and signed off in New York by fifty lawyers.

"It'll be good to have you on board," said the President. "Now let me tell you what's on my mind." It took him an hour. He left nothing out, distinguishing judiciously between fact and speculation, the only disproportion in his account being perhaps an overemphasis on the structural consequences, for both political parties, of a surprise Jordan victory. The point was not lost on Dunstable.

"I see what you got to have, Mr. President," said Dunstable. "But how can I get it for us? Why me?"

"Herndon, you're the best arm-twister in the whole lower forty-eight, and this is gonna be some hellacious job of arm-twistin'. I'll tell you what I suggest and then, after dinner, you and your boys can look over the stuff. It's locked in that closet over there. Here's the key. I'll get the Secret Service to set up the screen for the movin' pictures. You'll know everything I do: all the CIA dope; what the Treasury's found out; the whole shootin' match. Now let me give you my idea about the metes and bounds." He talked for another hour.

After dinner, the President went back to Washington. Dunstable and his aides watched the helicopter blink off beyond the treeline. They went back to their lodge and started to work through the files of photographs and reports. The film was run off three times. They talked and brainstormed, Dunstable bending the data right and left to shape it into some kind of efficient negotiating lever, to force the pieces into some sort of cohesive picture that made sense, that might work.

Finally, before midnight, the aide who was an Arabist had what Dunstable thought was a hell of a good idea. It took them another hour to work up a rough script. It could be worked over and refined and rehearsed in the morning. The audience would be arriving in forty-eight hours.

Before going to bed, the three men had a nightcap and watched the late news on an independent station. One clip showed John Jordan speaking from the stage of the Grand Ole Opry. There appeared to be less than a thousand people in the hall.

31 Like a giant mechanical egret, the Concorde skimmed over the marshy pineflats on the perimeter of the airfield and settled on the runway, its white surface taking on some of the rose of early twilight. Through the open cockpit door, the Minister could overhear the crackle of the tower's instructions. The jetliner turned off on an arterial taxiway and made its majestic way to a spot on the distant edge of the airbase where two Sikorsky helicopters and a small group of men waited.

Watching the plane approach, the President turned to Buster and remarked, "That sure is one good-lookin' machine. Think we'll ever have the money to own one of our own?" He was only halfway facetious.

The engines whined down and the oval door in the Concorde's fuselage opened. The Minister came down the ladder. Sharp as a tack, thought Buster; tailored within an inch of his life in a dark gray suit. There was no honor guard on hand, which the Minister took as confirmation that President Baxter really did have something important to discuss, substantive enough to keep their meeting entirely off the record.

He shook hands with the President. "How are you, sir?"

"It's real good of you to come, Mr. Minister. I think you'll find the trip to have been worthwhile. May I introduce my associates? This is Mr. Ferdimend, I don't believe you've met; Mr. Ferdimend's my special assistant and counselor. And of course this is former Senator Dunstable, who has agreed to work on the matter I contacted you about. It's big enough so that we feel a bipartisan approach is justified."

The Minister shook hands with the other men. Dunstable. How extraordinary that he should be here. The Minister found it suspicious. There was no such thing as "bipartisan" in an American election year. He'd like to get Masters's view

(388)

on all of this, but he knew the lawyer was already on his way to Rotterdam and Vienna. Both Alrazi and the Minister had felt it would be a good idea to have Masters on the spot at the OPEC sessions to get firsthand instructions on the political orchestrations which were planned to follow the price rescission.

Dunstable was a larger man than he remembered. The Minister thought he looked twice as "presidential" as Fulger Baxter. He was tough and unprincipled, the Minister knew; he found the prospect of having to deal with Dunstable on any protracted basis very unsettling. Hopefully, he might be there simply as an observer. Somehow the Minister doubted it.

He followed the President to the lead helicopter, along with Ferdimend and Dunstable. His aides and baggage were dispersed in the second.

"Beautiful evenin' for flyin'," the President said. He had to strain to make himself heard over the popping of the rotors.

The Minister nodded. Below them the hills were wreathed in haze; the dying sun had changed the colors of the landscape to smears of blue and purple.

"I thought we could have our meetin's at Camp David," the President said. "I don't believe you've visited there. I think you'll find it comfortable. It isn't as noisy as Washington. We can finish our business and get you back to Andrews right on schedule, just like I promised."

The Minister smiled. He felt Dunstable eyeing him with an intensity he found threatening. He tried to keep his expression bland and confident. It wasn't easy.

The rest of the short flight was nothing but small talk. Shortly after seven, they set down at the helipad. The President led the Minister along the path which led to Pinecone Lodge; Dunstable and his aides had vacated it earlier in the day.

"This is where Sadat stayed," the President remarked, deliberately untactful. "I trust you'll find it comfortable. We're used to gettin' a lot done up here, as you know. I hope you'll find our time together to be as productive as we believe it'll be."

He showed the Minister around Pinecone. It was a minor masterpiece of rustic bad taste. "You'll surely want to rest, so I thought we'd have just a little early dinner. It's almost tomorrow mornin' for you now, anyway."

The Minister found himself irritated by Baxter's folksy

delay in getting down to the purpose of this so imperatively, urgently summoned meeting.

"I'm not really tired, Mr. President," he said. "Your invitation to come here stressed the immediacy of the matter. Shouldn't we get to the business at hand?"

"It's not somethin' that can't wait dinner," the President answered. "Why don't you just freshen up and then stroll on down the path, first right, to my lodge? Your people'll be looked after. For dinner, it's just you'n me. I've asked Senator Dunstable to look in afterward.

"There's just one other thing. We're security-conscious up here. Got to be. All outgoin' communications funnel through the telecenter down the trail. The phones in the lodges just connect with each other. So if you want to visit with your people on the other side, just dial the center and they'll fix you up with a scrambler, Satcom, anything you need.

"Dinner'll be at eight sharp," the President concluded. He left the Minister alone. Alone in his cabin, pondering, he could hear small forest noises.

The Minister was edgy. He found the President's offhandedly covert words menacing, like the glow of distant lightning beyond the clouds. He wished he hadn't come here, that he had waited for Prince Alrazi to reappear from the desert to deal with this. He knew that there had been more than a little vanity in his acceptance of the President's invitation, and there *had* been mention of extreme urgency. Which had counted more in his decision to come here, he couldn't really say, if he was absolutely candid with himself.

He was out of his depth among older men like Baxter and Dunstable: exigent, political beings with enormous experience. By comparison, his own world was limited. No matter how it appeared, the OPEC pricing decisions, with which he was so closely and famously identified, were still money decisions made in hotel ballrooms. Decisions which the indulgent nature of Western commercial ethics had permitted so far to stand. But these men waged war and coped with recession and insurrection as a matter of course, and sensed and shaped the will of 100 million voters.

In this isolated camp high in these strange hills, the Minister felt himself to be a prisoner. He would have to proceed very carefully and make his escape as quickly and gracefully as possible. Intimidated, he began to wonder if the leverage *was* still on his side of the table.

* * *

Over a presupper bourbon in Laurel Lodge, Baxter looked at Dunstable.

"This boy ain't very old to be such a big shot, Herndon."

"Forty-six, Mr. President."

"That young? Well, that might be helpful to us, though. Depends how tough he is. Think you can scare the piss out of him?"

"Mr. President, I am sure as shootin' goin' to try."

The Minister and President Baxter dined alone. Baxter made careful, unproductive small talk which sorely tried the younger man's patience. He talked about the American economy, the election, the rebirth of moral values which was a principal aspect of his campaign. Not one word did he utter which suggested to the Minister anything of the crisis proportioned emergency which had led the President of the United States to make a personal call to Qu'nesh. It was very irritating.

During dessert, a uniformed attaché entered the dining room and handed a slip of paper to Baxter. He looked at it and signaled to the Minister.

"Call for you, sir. Jones here'll show you the phone."

It was his chief pilot calling from Andrews. A routine maintenance check had turned up some trouble in one of the outboard engines. It was very curious. In any event, a team was on its way from Toulouse, but there would be no way to depart Andrews for at least thirty-six hours. The pilot had wished to advise His Excellency in case His Excellency might be planning an earlier departure. The Minister's spirits dropped as he hung up.

Returning to the dining room, he found that they had been joined by ex-Senator Dunstable. Coffee had been brought. It was a disgusting syrup.

If Baxter noticed the Minister's grimace as he put his cup down, he made nothing of it.

"Hope you like the coffee," he said cheerfully, "we've tried to get it just the way you people like it. Added extra grounds and all. 'Course since sugar's bad for you, we used Sweet n' Low. I'm sorry we couldn't give you sheep's eyes or some of your other traditional food, but my mess crew just won't cook 'em. Says it's bad luck. Anyway, make no mind of that. Herndon, what do you say we get down to cases?" Dunstable nodded.

"Well, sir," began President Baxter, "there seem to be some

things goin' on that as far as we can make out have a whole lot to do with the security and stability of both our great nations. Now we all know how beneficial for just about everybody your rational decision about the oil price has been. And we are in your debt for it. And we'd like to be *everlastin'ly* in your debt. And hope we can be. If things'll work out.

"But Minister, you folks got us right confused. Way back in April, when you announced the price cut, you talked about some kind of deal you'd made over here. Well, I got to admit you had me foozled. First, I figured that either the Secretary of State or the Energy Secretary'd been up to his old tricks. Neither of 'em thinks very much of me, Minister, so they spend a lot of time tryin' to run things their own way. You probably got the same problem with some folks in your shop.

"Anyway, I figured that sooner or later y'all'd come round to hand us your want list and we'd work somethin' out. I figured you'd want to see things settle, get your edge, and let it harden and then let us see your shoppin' list. Tarnation, I even got my Secretary of Defense—him and my man at Treasury are the only two worth a damn of the whole sadass pack—anyway, I've had the DOD work out an arms and assistance package which'd keep you people invulnerable for another hundred years. Just wanted to have it on the shelf waitin' in case you asked. And at a real good sweetheart price, too. Less than $6 billion over four years.

"So we got all these good feelin's and big plans and good vibrations, but nobody comes visitin' from your side. Which is mighty odd. 'Course everybody gets busy, with the election and all, and generally jumpin' for joy, so exactly how odd it is don't get noticed until maybe later than it should have been. And meantime, just through an accident, Senator Dunstable here learns about somethin' which he follows up on and then, bein' a great American, comes to see me personally about. And that's why we asked you to take the time to visit with us."

As the President spoke, the Minister had been doing some fast thinking. This wasn't like facing down some unlettered Nigerian general about an extra ten cents a barrel. Rustic he might be, thought the Minister, but Baxter *is* the President of the United States.

When Baxter finished, he had his answer ready.

"Obviously, Mr. President, I can't follow all your allusions. I can say this. I am strictly my country's chief appointed official for matters of energy and external finance. This may be the first time that I have been involved or have involved myself in the larger matters of our nation's external relations. These are properly the sphere of activity of the King and the Prime Minister. With whom they parley and to what informal agreements they may come is something of which I am not informed, at least not in the process and frequently not after the fact. I am here because you, sir, intimated great urgency on a matter concerning the security of the Kingdom and our ruler and his principal minister are unavailable. For reasons which you, Mr. President, as a deeply religious man, must respect."

The President looked over at Dunstable and then back at the Minister. Lord, he thought, it sure is tough to negotiate when everybody's lying. This boy's got a regular Santa's bag of hypocrisy.

"Mr. Minister, I obviously can't quarrel with your description of the way you people run your show. I will say that ain't exactly how it's been described to us by folks who're s'posed to know. But there we are. So let me switch gears for a bit and then I'll get back to what we were talkin' about."

For ten minutes or so, the President expounded on the glorious new condition of the world. Inflation had been damped. The dollar was back to being the unshakable foundation stone of world markets. The Third World looked to be crawling toward solvency. As far as the United States itself was concerned, the billions that had been budgeted to develop other energy sources were now being profitably redeployed in a more productive fashion: planning and funding the establishment of three huge new bureaucracies to administer a spectrum of social benefits which the President planned to unveil in his Inaugural Address.

"Funny thing is, though," said Baxter, "I got this won't-go-away feelin' that I just might not get to the Capitol steps to make that speech. Which just ain't the right thing to have happen, Mr. Minister.

"Look at it this way," the President continued. There was not an atom of pleading in his voice or his face. Fulger Baxter was a tablet carrier; he viewed his opinions, received or personal, as the truth, and that was that.

"Now I know you folks don't like me and, Lord knows, I can see what your reasons might be. You think I play too much ball with the Jews. Hell, Minister, in this country you got to get along with 'em. Just like you get along with the coloreds. They ain't a whole lot of them but they make a terrible great noise. Tarnation, the Jewish own all the newspapers and TV stations. And about half the Congress. And for the last few years, you Arabs ain't exactly curried much favor with the votin' public, until last Easter, that is. 'Course the way things are now, *you* could run for President, Minister, and you'd get elected. Assumin' you'd want to. Which I guess you don't.

"But I *do*! We got to get the good old values back. Get ahold of our traditional virtues. Thrift. Honor. Minister, it's so critical right now to elect an administration that can lead the country in the path of righteousness that I'd spend billions or lie, cheat, or steal if it would assure this great land four more years of our good Christian leadership.

"But we're suspicionin' now that maybe you folks don't share our enthusiasm. And you can do everything about it and, unless we see eye to eye, I can't do diddleysquat, if you'll excuse an old southern expression. If you was to do anything in Vienna next week that might upset the voters, and we—I mean me—was to get blamed for it, I don't think I'd get fifty votes in the whole country.

"Which'd be a sad day not only for me and Ermabelle, that's Miz Baxter, but, many of us reckon, for the country generally. One of those who comes out the same way is ex-Senator Dunstable here; and, bein' the great American he is, he's crossed party lines to take a stand for what's right.

"We ain't exactly sure what you got in mind, but we're sure you got *somethin'* planned. Old hounds like Herndon and me; hell, we can smell a coon in a cypress tree clear across the Mississippi Delta! So we'd like to see if maybe we can get you to change your mind."

The Minister smiled with intentional condescension.

"I'm afraid you're barking up the wrong tree, sir, if you'll forgive an extension of your metaphor. Whatever may happen at the OPEC sessions next week will only be normal for such a meeting at such a time. I anticipate nothing dramatic. As for your other suspicions, it is hardly my place to comment on them and, as a matter of national policy, it is not for me to discuss the position of the United States with respect to Israel."

Why you little brownassed pissant, thought the President. But he stayed calm. The Minister continued.

"What I fail to perceive, sir, with all respect, is any specific military threat to the Kingdom. That is what, frankly, has brought me here at a time which was otherwise most inconvenient. Unless, of course, the threat comes from you. I seem to recall a proposal to that effect from Senator Dunstable a few years ago." The Minister smiled snidely. He was in control, feeling his oats.

"Well, Mr. Minister, that obviously isn't true. As a matter of fact, in the last six months, we pulled the fangs on a couple of snakes who wanted to get into your nest and eat the eggs. We don't go around threatenin' folks. 'Sides, we got a Constitution. No matter what, the President can't on his lonesome just up and start a nice little war. The last one that tried that is sellin' used cars in Los Angeles. No sir, you can rest your mind on that."

Baxter continued, "What we *do* think is that there are goin' to be a few problems within the regime, but that would be strictly inside stuff. Which is why I asked ex-Senator Dunstable to join us. He's got a much fuller picture of the whole deal. Right, Herndon?"

Dunstable nodded. The President looked at his watch and stood up.

"I got to be gettin' back to the White House. It's gettin' real late for you, Mr. Minister, so why don't you visit with ex-Senator Dunstable in the mornin'? It'll give you a chance to look carefully at what he's turned up. Anyway, you ain't goin' anywhere until those Frenchmen fix that airplane of yours."

He shook hands with the Minister and Dunstable. As he left the room, the Minister agreed to meet Dunstable in the morning. Walking back to Pinecone, he wondered at his earlier apprehensions. There was nothing to worry about, so long as he stayed firm.

Overnight, it turned very cold. The Minister dressed and ate a full and hearty breakfast. He liked English and American breakfasts. The mess sergeant who waited on him placed a note at his elbow. Would he join Senator Dunstable for a briefing over at Aspen Lodge at ten o'clock? Confident and refreshed with sleep, the Minister sent along his compliments and his acceptance.

He took a stroll after breakfast. The camp was deserted except for its two visitors, their modest retinues, and the permanent staff. The Minister could see his breath in the air. The pines along the walkways seemed frosted. As he strolled along, alone in the outdoors, he sensed some invisible, overwatching presence. He felt comfortable with the situation.

Strong. It would really be quite pleasant, he mused, if he had some attractive female companionship; it was really a very romantic place, Camp David. No wonder it had cast its spell over Sadat, who was normally so sensible and clearsighted a man.

When he presented himself at Aspen, Dunstable was waiting on the steps of the lodge. The big man did not look as if he had slept well, if at all, thought the Minister. Dunstable ushered the Minister into the living room. There were two young men sitting on one of the sofas, who rose as the Minister entered; Dunstable introduced them as his assistants.

"Both of these fine young men are very familiar with your part of the world," said Dunstable. "Ted here has a Ph.D. from Columbia in Arabic Studies. Joe Bob was with Anglo in the Persian Gulf until three years ago, when he joined my permanent staff." He looked at the assistants, then back to the Minister. "Well, gentlemen, shall we get started?

"Your Excellency," said Dunstable, "as the President indicated last night, a few weeks ago a banker close to me brought to my attention the likelihood that a large sum of overseas dollars had cycled through our capital system over the last year. We believe it may have been as much as $5 billion goin' in."

"Going in?" The Minister radiated a healthy, open curiosity.

"Well, yes, sir, because it seems to have come out as a whole lot more, thanks to the stock market. We estimate quite possibly as much as $9 billion!"

"My word," said the Minister mildly, "that's a great deal of money."

"That's the interestin' thing, Your Excellency, it *is* a lot, but then it isn't really."

"What do you mean by that, Senator Dunstable?"

"Well, sir, it's all a matter of scale. It's not a large enough sum to suggest a major shiftin' of dollar balances by a state or major corporation. So it's almost certainly individual money, which limits the number of possibilities. Anyway, it's not the amount that's got us concerned. It's the timin'."

"The timing?" Again the bland, innocent response.

Looking at him, Dunstable thought that he was going to enjoy pushing this cityslick smartass as hard as he could.

"Yes sir, who'sever runnin' this money was just letter-perfect. At least on the buyin' end. Might even say he must have known somethin'. All this money kept pourin' into the market right up to the week before you made your announcement in Honolulu. That was about a thousand points ago on the Dow Jones Industrial Average, you'll recall. But even that doesn't bother us. After all, we welcome investors to our markets. And a $5 billion profit is a resoundin' testimonial for our great American system."

He eyed the Minister, who said nothing.

"What bothers us is that for some time now these accounts have been sellin' out. Investors take profits when they get 'em, but this just doesn't make sense. All our smart people tell me that this is the first stage of the biggest fat bull market in all of recorded history. The banks that run my blind trust have been tellin' me to raise all the cash I can to buy stocks. I been sellin' my cattle, my oil royalty, my real estate, everything 'cept my ranch. It's the same for a whole bunch of my buddies down in Houston.

"So we have to ask ourselves why would some big investor, the biggest anyone here has ever seen in one gulp, who knows enough to buy the whole market just at the right time, start gettin' out now? Does he know somethin' maybe we should know, that's the question the President and his people and I have been askin' ourselves. And we've pretty much concluded that the answer is yes. And we've also kind of decided that one of the people who can probably give us the right answer has just got to be you, Mr. Minister."

Dunstable's tone remained level. His eyes, bright blue questioning poignards, fixed themselves on the other man's face. Dunstable watched the Minister carefully. He looked younger than Dunstable had expected, and a little weak around the edges. Dunstable was a connoisseur of other men's weaknesses. I'm gonna eat you for breakfast, boy, he thought, I'm gonna make a hatband out of your pecker.

The Minister had some difficulty in holding his own voice even while he sorted out his options. What recourse did these people have? he wondered. In any case, the cure was predicated upon the disease, and he intended to give them no clues about *that*.

In as contemptuous a tone as he could muster, he said to Dunstable, "That is an amazing statement, Senator. I really don't understand your drift. If you can perhaps be a little more clear with me, perhaps I might be helpful to you, although as it sounds, I very much doubt it. I might also add, sir, without intending to complicate matters, that there are implications in your position which I, personally, find offensive."

Dunstable smiled. The first discernible rise. No more than a slight wrinkling of the surface, but to the experienced fisherman evidence enough of the presence of a very big trout. Dunstable had been measuring men and exploiting their weaknesses for forty years. His instincts were honed. He sensed conclusively that the Minister knew what he was talking about. Of course, bringing the fish to the fly might be another matter.

"Well, sir, let me be as explicit as I possibly can. There aren't but a very few investors in the world that can lay hands on $4 or $5 billion cash to put in the stock market. Not at least as far as our Treasury people and the fifty biggest banks and Central Intelligence Agency know. There're two Chinamen, a Brazilian, a couple of Italian fellows down south. And then there's your King. A very rich man, the King. Our fellows guess he's worth eight-nine billion, includin' real estate. And most of it in cash. The King's a pretty religious fellow, they tell me. Kind of like President Baxter. Reads Holy Writ a lot, like the President does; 'course the books're different. Sticks to the Gospel. What the Koran says, the King does. A very devout man."

Dunstable's drift seemed ominous, thought the Minister. Like the first tickling particles of a sandstorm. The ex-senator went on.

"The way we see it now, somebody got the King to sink most of his personal capital in the stock market, knowin' that there would surely be the biggest rally you ever saw come the announcement that you people were reducin' your wellhead price. Except that also doesn't make complete sense."

"Senator, I really can't follow you now. This is all too absurd!"

"Just hear me out, sir." Dunstable raised an impatient hand. "Our folks tell me the King doesn't much care what happens to his money, or his oil for that matter, just as long as he piles enough up to buy everything he wants for that fancy church of his. We know he's got no real interest in politics and not much in money, and yet it would appear that he's personally playing the biggest politics and the biggest money these gray hairs have ever heard of. And that includes forty years in Texas! So it all just don't track."

"Mr. Dunstable," the Minister forced himself to suppress his discomfort. He hoped his voice sounded as firm and conclusive as he was trying to make it.

"I have come a very long way at the request of your President—on what I am now certain has been a false premise. On my arrival, I was informed that I was to deal with you, sir, a man who no earlier than five years ago was advocating military action against my country. Normally, I would have departed on the instant, but the King's aircraft has become disabled under circumstances which are, to say the least, mysterious. In any event, I am now secluded in this place, which is more renowned for its isolation than any other distinction. I am obliged to listen to a litany of accusations suggesting the participation of my country and my King in wildly notional financial adventures. Yours is a prosperous country, Mr. Dunstable. Solely because of a decision taken by us. I would think we would have deserved better at your hands than this. I can see no point in continuing this conversation along these lines."

Dunstable seemed unimpressed. "Well, sir," he said, "no point in gettin' all worked up. Let's break for lunch. Afterward, we've got some real interestin' stuff to show you."

The Minister was relieved. But at lunch he could manage no more than a glass of tea.

Once a year in Qu'nesh was plenty, thought Harry. Of course he was dealing with the same drop who'd got him into that sideshow a year or so ago, and that made things easier. The CIA contact was different this time, though; this young man was bearded and bone-tired, having flown through the night from Andrews to Athens in the instructor's seat of a Phantom, and then on Air Hellas into Dumar. He was damn near too tired to talk when Harry showed up in his hotel room.

"Here's the stuff," he said wearily, handing over an oblong parcel. "It's all in there. A six-year-old could make it work. You got your glad rags?"

Harry nodded. He was pleased that this was simple. Of course, most of the new stuff was: the years of fiddling in the dark with wires and batteries and exposure meters seemed happily behind him, thanks to the burgeoning cottage industry which manufactured new hardware for covert operations.

"It's all set," he answered. "The drop's back in town. Everything'll be in place tomorrow night." He got up and left.

The CIA man lay back wearily on his pillow. He could use a drink but they didn't serve booze in this country. Looking at his watch, he reflected that he could catch three, maybe four, hours of sleep before heading back. He hoped his wife and children assumed he was still in the mountains, where it was impossible to call home.

When the Minister returned to Aspen Lodge after his unsatisfying lunch, he was not at all reassured to see that a projection screen and film and slide projectors had been set up.

Dunstable was infuriatingly expansive. "Eat well, sir? By golly, we sure did. Surprises me how these Yankees can make good barbeque! Well, sir, make yourself comfortable and we can start the entertainment."

The Minister started to protest but Dunstable was firm. "Just sit back and enjoy yourself. This here's very interestin' stuff. It won't take too long and then you can be on your way, if that's your pleasure."

"Really, Senator, I can't..." The Minister's objections dissolved before Dunstable's aggressive presence. He felt like a schoolboy.

"Now what we're goin' to do," said Dunstable, satisfied that his guest was going to sit still, "is what our school kids in this country call 'Show and Tell.' I think you'll get the spirit as we go along."

He signaled for the lights to be extinguished. "OK, boys, let 'er roll." In the midst of his distress, the Minister couldn't help but draw back from his own concerns to admire Dunstable's command of the scene. No wonder Masters had reported the ex-senator to be the most electrifying figure on the American political stage.

The slide machine flickered forth its beam. On the screen flashed a Kodachrome of the Royal Mosque, towering above the huddled profile of Qu'nesh. The picture had obviously been taken on a brilliant day. The sight of the city produced a distinctly sentimental feeling in the Minister. He wanted to be home, away from these darkly forested hills and blue mountain haze.

To his right, the young Columbia Arabist launched into a disquisition: "...building commenced seven years ago at the express command of his Royal, Most Holy Highness. The minaret is the tallest in Islam, standing nearly 200 feet above the Qu'nesh wadi. Planned by a consortium of U.S. and European-trained Moslem architects who are still at work on the site. Reputed to have cost $377 million to date, including several tons of gold." Actually, the Minister knew, the figure was now close to 5 tons. The King's purchases had combined marginally with the speculators to push the price of gold pre-Honolulu to well over $700. In the declining market since then, the royal bullionists had made very advantageous purchases.

It was very exasperating, the Minister thought, to be forced to sit through a tourist lecture on his own country. The young man continued: "The interior of the mosque has been decorated at great expense," slides of details now followed one another, "and has incorporated such treasures as the original prayer shields from Hagia Sophia in Istanbul and the Amram Prayer Rug, until recently the centerpiece of the Chicago Museum of Folk Art..." Folk art! the Minister thought resentfully, "...with the consummation of the pending purchase of the Sword of Suleiman, the Royal Mosque will represent a treasury of the history and traditions of Islam second perhaps, and only *perhaps,* to the Great Mosque in the Kaaba at Mecca. In terms of the specific articles of the Moslem faith to be stored and displayed there, the Royal Mosque will be to Islam what the Vatican Reliquary is to Christendom." He sat down.

"Pretty stylish buildin'," said Dunstable jovially. "The King must really have his heart in it to spend all that money. And bringin' in all that stuff from other countries. Now that's impressive. We sure got nothin' like that in Texas, although the Petrex Tower in Houston's real grand. Well, boys, let's keep the show movin' along."

This time it was the motion picture projector that blinked. From a speaker, the soundtrack gave forth an orotund, official voice: "This is the Fort Johnson Explosives Test Facility." The screen showed a flat, scrub-covered meadow. "The subject is Hoechst New Model Explosive-Batch Three." The camera telescoped to a tabletop on which rested a slab of what the Minister took to be a dull, rust-colored clay or soft Plasticine. "Weight of the sample used in this test: nine ounces, approximately 250 grams." The camera cut back to three bunker-like structures placed in the middle of the scrubby field. "Targets for the test: two concrete emplacements, twelve-inch concrete filled with fifteen-pound sandbags. Destructive tolerance: three tons TNT." The camera, obviously from a considerable distance, zoomed in on the buildings. The Minister could see that sand had been shoveled around their lower flanks. They looked like enormous tortoises built from concrete, perdurable as granite. Suddenly, as the Minister watched, the screen filled with a light as brilliant as a magnesium flare, the speakers gave a thumping roar, blurred by the inadequacy of their bass response, the image of the bunkers was lost in blowing, choking vortices of dust and fragments of matter, blasted randomly through the air. Then silence on the loudspeakers, except for a telltale clunk as an odd bit of rubble banged to earth near the monitors. When the dust settled, the Minister saw that the middle of the field, where the emplacements had been, was now scarred by two wide, shallow craters staring sightlessly upward into the sunny sky.

"How about that," enthused Dunstable. "Now that is really somethin'. Have you seen that before, Mr. Minister? I tell you, you just can't keep them Germans down. Tell our guest about that stuff, Joe Bob."

The young man stood up, notes in hand, like a junior executive addressing a board meeting.

"This explosive matériel was developed in two batches of 90 ounces each—that's 2600 grams—by the Experimentisches Laborität August Hoechst, which is a division of Hoechst Chimiefabriken GmbH. The laboratory is located in a suburb of Duisburg, not far from Düsseldorf. The matériel was fabricated into ten slabs of 18 ounces apiece. Five of these disappeared from the laboratory in May of last year; the balance had been transferred earlier that day to the West German Defense Forces.

"The batch that was illegally removed from the laboratories was dispersed almost immediately by the man who arranged for its removal. A single slab was purchased in Paris by one of our agents. We are fairly certain two other slabs are in the hands of one or more Middle Eastern terrorist organizations. The operation was financed with funds originating either in Damascus or Baghdad, although the money was probably paid through Switzerland or Korea. The financiers probably thought they were buying the entire batch of explosive, and were outraged to discover they hadn't, judging by the very unpleasant death of the insider at Hoechst who arranged the theft. The whereabouts of the other two slabs remains unknown.

"The test we have just witnessed was made at Fort Johnson nine weeks ago. We obtained the film from Army Ordnance through Langley. As noted, the test involved approximately one half the matériel on hand. Ordnance won't hand over their spectroscopic analysis of the compound, but these things are fairly easy to replicate once the chemical tricks are understood. My guess is that this one is based on a series of hydrocarbon polymers; electrically activated, of course. That explosion on the test grounds was probably actuated by a penlight battery operating a single-signal transmitter."

He returned to his seat. Dunstable was suitably grave. "Thank you, Joe Bob, for a very lucid presentation." He might have been overseeing a meeting to discuss the marketing of a new brand of breakfast cereal. He turned to the Minister. "Any questions, sir, or shall we continue with our program?" There was a shade of sarcasm there, the Minister thought. He could make some obvious connections between what he had seen, but it would be better to see all the cards played.

"No, Senator. Pray continue. I must say I find this as confusing as you find it fascinating. But if it gives you pleasure..."

"Good, good," Dunstable rubbed his hands together. "Ted, do you want to pick it up from here?"

The young man went to the slide projector. On the screen flashed a brightly colored photograph of a group of men in front of the building which the Minister had already seen at length that afternoon. He recognized the photograph. It had been taken by the *National Geographic* on the steps of the Royal Mosque, then unfinished, as part of a long, praiseful article on modern Islam.

"Pictured here are the King and the supreme religious rulers of the Kingdom, the Council of Imams, the nine priests who administer the internal laws of the country, where no distinction is made between civil and religious jurisdiction. Behind them stands the Royal Mosque, still some stages from completion, which is planned to celebrate the renewal of Islam and the dominant role of the Kingdom in that process." The young man was reading the caption from the magazine.

"Got any mug shots there, Ted?" asked Dunstable.

The aide quickly ran off nine head shots, giving a name to each: "Imam Bakr el-Tas, Imam Ali Mounir..." and so on. The Minister knew each one of those ascetic, fanatical faces. He had looked into each of those nine unforgiving pairs of eyes on that awful morning when he had gone to the King and the Council on his knees, head bared and unshod, to plead for his brother's life. They had looked back at him as indifferently as if he had been a goat in the market square. The law was the law, the chief priest had said sternly; Allah made no exceptions.

(403)

The lights went on.

"Now, Mr. Minister," said the ex-senator in a voice so candidly threatening and tough that the Minister found it surprising, even from Dunstable, "let's talk business. Don't interrupt me, please, until I get through. There'll be plenty of time for questions.

"First, the President and me believe that you are plannin' somethin', probably at the OPEC meetin' next week, which you think will make a difference in the election. Like raisin' the price of crude and blamin' the administration. Two, somebody over there got greedy and just plain mixed politics and money, which let me tell you from experience is a bad idea, and decided to make a killin' on the market turn. Now, you don't have to say anything and I don't expect you will, but on our side of the table we're just goin' to regard those as matters of fact.

"Which leads me to three and four. Both of which have somethin' to do with what I've been showin' you here.

"Number three: the other nine ounces of that explosive you saw, which can blow the bejesus out of anything on God's Green Earth, was planted last night in that fancy mosque of yours; it's armed and ready to go. And we got a man on the scene who's got nothin' to do but push a button and the whole mosque'll go straight up in the sky. That pretty tower'll snap like a matchstick. They tell me that the explosive develops a temperature of about a thousand degrees Fahrenheit. That gold'll sure look pretty all melted down. Kinda like that gloppy jewelry my wife Bess buys in the Galleria when we visit Houston.

"'Course just blowin' up a buildin' got no purpose unless it proves a point. Which is Number Four. If the mosque goes up, the King's going to hear on *the* best authority that it's a punishment from Allah, brought on his head because some of his friends and relatives got a mite too clever and played games with *his* money, collectin' interest and all. The King's likely to get pretty angry, what with his mosque in little bitty pieces, and his rugs and shields and God knows what else in ashes and every Moslem in the world screamin' at him for gettin' their sacred relics burnt up.

"C'mon now, son," said Dunstable, in a wheedling, fatherly manner the Minister despised, "we all know what happened on the far side of the desert, when those other folks started messing with the mosque at Mecca. Couldn't have been much different than the moving picture show we'll be watching;

(404)

more private, of course, although I wouldn't think that'd make it feel any better when that sword hits."

The Minister watched Dunstable carefully. He wasn't lying about the explosive in the Royal Mosque, that seemed certain. It was a desperate act, but Baxter and Dunstable were desperate men. Yet he doubted they'd pull the trigger unless they were certain it would somehow change the course of events which would be unleashed at Vienna next week. And there they were stonewalled. They could never get directly to the King. Thanks be to Allah, he was totally screened by his priests. Alrazi was the only secular personage who spoke directly with the King.

"Mr. Dunstable," he said carefully, "this is getting out of hand. You are now threatening the destruction of a religious monument which is sacred to millions, hundred of millions, of devout Moslems. It is too ridiculous. If you do press the button, as you say you may, it will only bring the obloquy of mankind upon your head. You have perhaps also insinuated some of your magical explosive in the Royal Orphanage and the hospitals?"

"Mr. Minister, you and I ain't lookin' at this different. I know that the King has got to be made to believe it's a just visitation from Allah if he's goin' to want to chop some heads. And that's my hole card. You saw those pictures of the Council of Imams, or whatever they are. Nine good men and true; I'll leave it up to you, Mr. Minister, to guess which one of them's been workin' for us for five years, since your King came to the throne! I'll tell you this, the man came to us. He didn't want the Russians in Qu'nesh and he didn't want them Iranian Ayatollahs there neither. Just wanted the Kingdom to get along peacefully and for the mosque to get built and maybe over a period of time get the King to make sense about the oil business. We don't ask a whole lot of him, just to keep us ginned on anything he hears that can do us some good sometime."

What Dunstable suggested was inconceivable. One of the imams was an American agent? Impossible. The Minister called Dunstable's bluff.

"Senator, I don't believe you. You can't force this on me."

Dunstable glared at him. "Don't play poker with me, boy! A pissant'll pull a freight car if I tell him to!" He raised a finger.

The lights came down and the film projector whirred.

"This here's a silent picture," said Dunstable viciously, "but I believe you'll be able to grasp the plot."

The image on the screen bucked and jerked like a bad home movie, until the hand that held the camera steadied. His insides seizing up in growing horror, the Minister became aware of what he was watching. He knew now why they had wanted *him*. It was hideously familiar, an unendurable replay of events and feelings it had taken him a year to put far enough behind him so that he no longer woke sweating and shaking in the night, every night. The film had the awful, unreal clarity of a nightmare. It focused on his brother's terrified face, the black eyes flushed with fearful, pleading tears; panned along his body, pausing crudely and cruelly on the urine stain which darkened the boy's groin. When, at last, the sword had done its flashing work, the camera lingered with a perverse attentiveness on the youthful head, its features frozen in the terrified rictus of a horrible death. It closed on the severed neck, on the last thickening drops of blood fading into the dirt of the square. Then it panned around, finally coming to rest on a shadowed window; as if in an old, blotched mirror, the Minister could dimly make himself out. At last the film sprocketed to its conclusion, but by then the Minister was past caring or control.

"Where did you get that?" he gasped. His eyes were full of tears. He shifted in his seat, trying to make himself more comfortable, frighteningly embarrassed at the incontinence which had overtaken him. His voice was a grating whisper, choked almost below the threshold of audibility.

"You figure it out, boy," said Dunstable. There was not the merest edge of pity. "That execution was tighter'n a deep well in West Texas. That was the deal you made with the priests. No one was to be there except them. There was supposed to be a dozen only, admitted by special pass. If you was to count the passes, you'd find there was thirteen. Now, each one of them passes had to be signed by a member of the Council of Imams. That was your arrangement with the Council, if you'll recall."

The Minister recalled. It was just as Dunstable claimed. He nodded weakly, sighing agreement.

"And," Dunstable added, "how do you think we got that explosive in the mosque? Got it past the guards?"

It was all deadly clear to the Minister.

"Now, sir, we can fix all this up," Dunstable was suddenly softer, almost paternal. "No need for that film to be a preview of coming attractions for you or anyone else. We can just make us a deal. If you're willing. Would you like some time to think it over?"

The Minister would. He wanted to think, to cleanse himself. He made a wobbly, gingerly exit.

Dunstable smiled at his aides. He looked benignly confident. "Say, Joe Bob, that's some home movie. Think it got the point across?"

The young aide had been standing by the chair vacated by the Minister. He touched the seat perfunctorily and smiled back. "I have to think so, Senator. Looks like the poor bastard's peed in his pants!"

Five minutes later, the phone rang. One of the aides answered it and listened for a second. "Go ahead," he said, "but let us know when he's through talking. Hell no, give him a tight line if that's what he wants. This'll be a personal call." He hung up and looked at Dunstable. "He's asked for a scrambler phone. He wants to talk to Qu'nesh. To the Prime Minister."

Dunstable grinned. Big fish, indeed. Just what he expected. He asked Ted to get him the White House. When the connection was made, he took the receiver. "Fulger," he said, "looks like we have a deal." Hanging up, he looked at his aides in turn. "Well, boys, a good day's work. What do we all say to a little bourbon whisky?" They settled down to wait.

It took a while for the Minister to reach Prince Alrazi. The Prime Minister, exhausted by the rigors, physical and moral, of a fortnight's isolation in the desert, had departed Qu'nesh for London within hours of the royal caravan's return to the capital. The Minister was not surprised. The formidable ministrations of Mrs. Fotheringill were generally necessary to return Alrazi to his accustomed spirited form after any extended period of good behavior required by religion or matters of state.

It was three in the morning in London by the time he got through. By then he was in a state of near panic. Alrazi calmed him down. The Prince was, in his way, as tough a customer as Dunstable. Thankfully, he was sober, if a trifle breathless, when he came on the line. The Minister spoke openly. Whatever his misgivings about Dunstable, he was certain of the ex-senator's assurances respecting the secure nature of his connection.

When he had finished reciting the events of the last two

days, he paused, expecting a fusillade of anger from the other end. Alrazi was surprisingly unemotional and philosophical. His reaction revealed his priorities.

"Well, dear cousin, what will be will be. Let's be realistic. Don't sound so discouraged. Come to an understanding with them. You can be certain the Americans couldn't care less about the money. Oh, Dunstable may want money; he has that sort of character. If he indicates something in this area, throw him a few million. He's a powerful man, but nowhere as rich as he'd like to be. The politics is all they really care about. So guarantee them no interference in the election. Business as usual next week in Vienna. What it all works out to, dear cousin, is: If they let us keep the money, we'll let them keep the Presidency. It will all come down to the same thing. We'll make it up to Jordan one way or another."

The Minister ran through some thoughts on the way he planned to handle it. Concluding, he asked, "Is there anything else?" There were: details which Alrazi described as "lagniappe." Just before going off the line, Alrazi made a curious, clinical sounding statement: "Don't worry about the loose ends. I'll take care of those myself. I'll see you in Qu'nesh week after next. Enjoy yourself in Vienna." That was all. Altogether too matter of fact, thought the Minister.

He set the phone down and walked around the room, organizing his thoughts. At length, when he felt entirely composed, he rang Aspen Lodge. A voice he recognized as belonging to the young man named Ted answered. The Minister asked for Dunstable. When the senator picked up the phone, he said, "Senator Dunstable, I've spoken with certain people. I would like to get under way early in the morning. If I might perhaps share a few minutes with you, I think any misunderstandings which have come up between our two countries might be most expeditiously resolved. Have you time to talk?"

The ex-senator's voice boomed over the line as heartily as if he was greeting guests across a stack of smoking ribs at his Midland ranch. "Mr. Minister, you know where we are. Just stroll on over and we can visit a bit. As long as you want. Look forward to seein' you."

The stars were ringed with frost as the Minister walked to Aspen Lodge, rehearsing the precise words he wanted to use. As before, Dunstable was waiting on the porch, his breath making streamers in the cold air. When the Minister came up the steps, he took his hand warmly. "Cold out there. Come settle yourself. I've got a nice fire goin'. So's we can talk man to man, I've let my young men go to bed early. They've had a tirin' day. Kids these days seem to wear out faster than us old folks. Now, sir, what's on your mind?"

The Minister looked at him firmly. "There have been some very serious allegations made here today, Senator. Sufficiently serious to cause me to look into them at the highest level. Which I have done in the last three hours. As a result, I can give you the solemn oath of my government and myself that nothing is intended which will conceivably affect the forthcoming election in your country. In any way. You can be assured that our role in the OPEC meeting beginning Thursday will be essentially placatory; our pricing action of last April has created some consternation among our colleagues in the producing states. Fortunately, the reduction in output by us has affected the allocations of the free market sufficiently favorably to offset any significant economic disruption. In fact, it would appear to be more than counterbalanced by the improvement in the value of the dollar and sterling and the more beneficial realignment of world currency and trade relationships which seems to have ensued." The Minister thought he sounded like an editorial.

"Of course," he concluded, "we expect now that the discussions with the Baxter administration which preceded our announcement of last April can be brought to their logical, fruitful conclusion as soon after the election as possible." He was pleased with the way it had come out. It would record harmlessly. He was certain that a battery of machines was whirring away, taking down every word.

Dunstable gave a grin as broad as the Permian Basin. "Sir, I'm sure glad to hear you say that. And I believe I can speak for the President. He will be pleased to hear it. You can count on us. As a matter of fact, in the time since we were last together in this room, we've been doin' a little further checkin', me and my boys. The way we see it, there just isn't enough in this stock market business to make a fuss over. I believe we may have gotten a bit ahead of ourselves in takin' an emergency view. The way things are goin' in the world, a few bitty billions don't make a bunch of difference. Of course, it would be better if we could wipe the whole thing off the tax collector's books, eliminate all the computer records the banks give the tax folks, but that might take some doin'." He laughed promiscuously. "But it can be done."

The Minister looked at him with an easy scorn, and reached into his pocket for a gold Bulgari pen and a small notebook. This kind of business he did in his sleep. Tearing out a leaf, he wrote eight digits on it and extended it to Dunstable; his eyebrows asked the question.

"I believe that'll do real nicely," said Dunstable. He reached for the Minister's pen and wrote the name of a Bahamas bank under the figures.

The Minister looked at it carelessly and remarked, "It'll be there the Wednesday after the election.

"Now, Senator," he asked, "have we additional business?" Dunstable shook his head. "Well, in that case," said the Minister, "there *is* one more thing." He related Alrazi's last request, seeing Dunstable's eyes widen momentarily, then settle back to their usual snakelike glitter. The senator nodded vigorously.

"Well, sir, we'll just do that and any other cleanin' up that's properly ours." It struck the Minister that Dunstable's words almost precisely duplicated Alrazi's unsettling final phrase.

Dunstable walked him to the steps. He put his left arm across the Minister's shoulders and pumped his right hand with the other.

"Mr. Minister, it has been a pleasure to deal with you." The Minister broke off the handshake and went down the steps and on to the walkway that led back to Pinecone. Behind him, Dunstable's percussive farewell echoed through the night, shivering the pine needles.

"You all come back and see us now, hear?"

At just that moment, from London, Alrazi was winding up the second of two calls. He had first called Khafiq. The old man had argued initially, but then accepted, resignedly and regretfully, what the Prince instructed. The second call was to Brussels; they would take it from there via Dublin.

32 Harrison could see that his intransigent fretfulness was really beginning to wear on Devon, but like most men who see themselves in difficulty with a woman, temporarily or otherwise, he didn't seem able to do much about it. He felt himself slipping into the sort of assertive selfishness he deplored in his friends' children. Devon would tell him how childish he was, but then she would kiss him, make him feel like a man, and that would settle things for a few hours, a day, a week. Anyway, he guessed—guessed and hoped—in another ten days the whole business would be settled; peace would come with resolution.

He had taken to waking up uneasily and going through the days feeling disconnected from his own life, as if with a hangover which felt closer to last night's drunkenness than to the supposed half health of the morning. Of course, he *was* drinking more. Devon had remarked on it; at first patiently, because she was habituated to angry men who depended on booze or drugs for courage or soothing. Harrison only half listened. Day after day, it was harder and harder to know if he was alive in the real world or simply stumbling around in some alienating dream.

She became more insistent. "David, don't drink so much and stop pacing. It's all very dramatic and not very effective."

The booze was necessary, he claimed; it was ambrosia, he declaimed, misquoting Pope's translation of Homer: *"And with sweet ambrosial dews, He restores his freshness, and his form renews."*

He was afraid it sounded as pretentious and hollow to her as it did to him.

In fact, she did find it quite trying. It was David at his worst, hiding his feelings, his regrets, with play-acting.

Finally, one evening, when his pacings and window starings and extra Scotches were just too much, Devon allowed that she was going away for a few days. She had friends on Nantucket, a writer and his wife. The wet air and the cold autumn beaches would do her good.

"It'll only be for three days, David. You've become difficult to be around. I'll meet you in Lenox Saturday morning. A few days alone will do you good. You're obviously dying to go out and tie one on. Get Barney; he'll be good therapy for you."

She left in the morning. The island air was as fresh and renewing as she had expected. Her friends were comfortable and solicitous. Her first night on the island was a miracle of rejuvenation. Snorts of fabulous cocaine. Tickety-tack sentimental music on the record player. A warm fire inside playing against the immanence of the bitter winter beach. Her host reading from his book in progress. But she missed Harrison terribly. They had been so closely involved for so long; apartness wasn't the way to solve things, she thought. When she called him in New York a day later, his voice croaked like the frog prince and she guessed that Barney had done a proper job of it. Thank God for other men, she thought. "I'll see you Saturday," she said, "day after tomorrow," and blew him a kiss. The connection from the island was so full of static and hisses that she couldn't be blamed for not hearing the clicking that might have told her there was someone else plugged into the line.

Khafiq had spent the better part of the afternoon in Mayfair, as he generally did when he was either exhilarated or despondent. He needed the sight of beautiful things to plane the peaks and hollows of his moods. In various shops, he asked for things to be sent on approval to Chesham Crescent. At a dealer in Albermarle Street, however, he found a brilliant piece of majolica, a dish depicting *Hercules Cleansing the Augean Stables*, which he wanted to have with him immediately. Its rich blues and browns would meld splendidly with the fall clothing of his sitting room. It was a very comforting piece.

With the parcel under his arm, he left the shop and, crossing Piccadilly, walked down St. James's. As he walked, he cast an ironic eye on the clubs across the way: Bratt's, Brooks's, and the others. Places he would never enter as a member. Even his old friend Sir James, for all their closeness and community of purpose, had never taken him for a drink at Bratt's. And yet, he reflected, no man has done as much as I to see that things could still be affordably unchanging, that the peers of the realm and the great men of the City might still convene for an early whisky in insulated comfort. Until Saturday, he thought.

It was a pleasant afternoon, early overcoat weather. He thought he might take an extended stroll, perhaps down and through Green Park; at Buckingham Palace he was sure to find a cab to carry him back to Knightsbridge. It would be pleasant to be out of the hustle of the West End; a touch of nature on this brisk day might do him good. He still felt passingly depressed. He had been fond of the young people, had in fact looked forward to their trip to France together.

Ah well, he thought as he came down the steps onto the curb of the Mall, it is best to be philosophical. The game is worth the candle. It was such a pleasant day that Khafiq decided to walk all the way. He turned up Constitution Hill, skirted Hyde Park corner and paused at Grosvenor Place.

The boy who peered at Khafiq's small figure through the windscreen of the trailing lorry had no philosophy and less prospects. His only talents were for cruelty and violence, in which he had with time acquired a crude expertise. The man who supplied such young men for hire had scouted him at the soccer riots in Tottenham Court Road, stomping and laying about with the savagery of the truly hopeless.

He was kept caged like a pit dog in a bed-sitting room near Bethnal Green. Saturday was his day off. First the soccer match and then if 'Spurs had won and he'd avoided arrest, a riotous evening of broken glass and broken heads and one lager after another until he came to the end of his week's money. Now he had the prospect of a big Saturday. Jobs like this paid a nice bonus, enough to pay for brandy.

The youth watched the dapper, short man get halfway across the pedestrian zebra, about two hundred yards away, then mashed down the accelerator with his heavy Vibram-soled boot. The lorry screeched forward. It was up to forty miles and hour when it hit Khafiq, crushing his spine and ribs and bursting his spleen. His parcel went spiraling through the air, bounced, and was pulverized as the lorry sped down Grosvenor Place, veered past Apsley House, and lost itself in the traffic on Knightsbridge.

A crowd gathered around the broken body. It was perhaps just as well that Khafiq was dead. His heart would have broken in the knowledge that the beautiful plate, which had survived centuries of war and looting, should have been destroyed on his account in an instant's loutish work.

"Piece of cake," said Harry. "Here's the stuff." He handed over the oblong parcel. "The old guy never knew what hit him."

A smooth operation, he thought to himself. The gardens behind the mosque had been tranquil in the early evening; the old Imam, Harry's drop, had appeared on schedule, and had returned the explosive. There had been no time for small talk. The two men had shaken hands, activating the hypodermic device concealed in Harry's palm like a jokeshop hand-buzzer. It worked as it was supposed to. Scuttling through the shadows, Harry thought, well, he was an old geezer anyway and a heart attack would seem natural.

"Just let me stick this in my bag here and we'll have us a little Jack Daniels." The contact bent to his suitcase. When he straightened, his right hand held a small .22 automatic with a silencer. He took just one shot, through Harry's left eye. The young man had been on the small-arms team at Texas A. & M., and *this* was a piece of cake for him.

There would be no trouble about the body, he knew; his boss in Washington would have seen to that. The boss would be mighty pleased. He snapped his bag shut and left the room. It was a matter of ten minutes to the Qu'nesh airport. The chartered Cessna was waiting.

The little plane was halfway over the desert to Dumar when the bag exploded. Harry had been careless and had set the timing device five minutes earlier than instructed; it wasn't easy, working hurriedly in the dark of an alleyway, and at his age his eyes weren't what they once were.

Five miles above, the pilot of an airliner called his passengers' attention to what he took to be the dramatic flaring of gas from an oil well. He could hardly have known that what he had spotted was the tying up of loose ends, as Prince Alrazi called it.

Harrison moseyed north on Route 22, taking his time. Dawdling this way enjoying the scenery—it was leaf time—he checked his mirror only cursorily, in the manner of law-abiding men keeping a loose eye cocked for the police. It wasn't to be expected that he would have taken special note of the rented Aspen with New York plates that had been following him since Amenia. At this time of year, there were hundreds making the trek to catch the weekend glories of the New England foliage.

As always, Osman had scouted his ground carefully. The call from London had rushed him from Damascus to London to Boston within the space of a day. He'd rented a car and driven to Pittsfield, using a map that the consular official who met his plane at Logan had given him. "The man's as regular as clockwork," the official reported. "We trailed him last weekend. The girl's away; she'll be returning Saturday. She called him last night. She'll be there tomorrow. You can pick him up on Route 22 about here between three and three-thirty." He jabbed at a spot on the road map north of a town called Amenia. "We'll let you know when he leaves the city. And anything else that happens. *Salaam*. May Allah be with you."

Osman followed the directions. By the time he reached the Lenox/Lee exit on the Massachusetts Turnpike it was too dark to reconnoiter effectively. He drove past, at one point noting the white wooden gates which he knew to give on the grounds of Tanglewood; a few minutes later, he passed high brick gates; slowing, he could make out the dim shape of the bronze plaque which read "Windfair." He continued on into Pittsfield and checked into a motel.

The next morning, Friday, he was outside the gates of Windfair; he waited in his car during the hour it took for the cleaning woman who set the cottage in order to arrive and leave. He had several hours now, he knew, until the caretaker at Windfair would make his ritual Friday afternoon visit to the cottage to prepare a fire. The briefing from New York had been complete.

Turning into Windfair, after making sure the road was empty, he checked the battleground. He wasn't entirely satisfied. The road which ran past the gates of Windfair was a narrow two-lane blacktop, closely bordered by low stone walls. Depending on whether one went through Lenox first, Windfair could be approached from east or west. In daylight, that meant that he would have to pick up the quarry out on the main road; to stake out the place would attract notice, which was unthinkable to Osman. The total surprise which invisibility gave him was his most lethal weapon.

He pulled up behind the cottage; the driveway ended in a small garage. He made short work of the lock on the back door. It opened into a small kitchen. Refrigerator, stove, usual accouterments; a door which he guessed led directly to the garage. It was locked.

From the kitchen, a hallway ran past a small bed-sitting room and a dining room to the living room, which was dominated by a stone-ledged brick fireplace. The hearth was flanked by two picture windows which looked out over the hills. It was a comfortable room, inexpensively furnished with faded, stuffed chairs and sofas; there were half-filled bookshelves, records, and a stereo, and a bureau in a corner serving as a bar. Upstairs, there were three bedrooms and two bathrooms.

The upstairs didn't concern him; after he dealt with Harrison, he would wait for the girl downstairs.

He let himself out the back door. The floor plan was printed in his mind. Driving back the way he had come, he found a place off the driveway he liked. The trees backed off. He could leave his car here during stage one; afterward, he would bring it around the cottage.

Satisfied with his reconnaissance, he spent several hours driving around the area, familiarizing himself with the roads in and out of the area. At one, he turned back down Route 7 for his rendezvous. Driving well within limits, it took him just over an hour to reach Amenia. At two o'clock, on plan, he dialed a number in New York City. "He left twenty-five minutes ago from Sixty-fourth Street. He's driving a bright green Camaro, license ZHN 568. There have been no other calls. We're discontinuing surveillance now. May Allah keep you well and grant you a safe journey home."

It was just getting dark enough to make distinguishing the license plates of passing cars difficult when Harrison turned up at Amenia. Osman pulled out three cars behind and followed.

Ahead, Harrison was speculating that if they followed the same scenario as at Honolulu, it would be in the wee hours Sunday morning before the news would be on the radio. He would have to make sure to stay awake. The conference in Vienna had been pushed back two days at the request of the Venezuelans, who were dealing with food riots in Caracas. The reports from Vienna had so far been largely circumstantial: who wore or ate what. There had been a handsome photograph of the Minister attending the opera. *Salome,* the papers had related. Harrison thought that was one of history's nice little ironies; his imagination summoned up the image of Fulger Baxter's head on a silver dish.

It was just after five when he turned off Route 22 for Lenox.

Devon had missed Harrison terribly. She was in a strange position. She had been sent to him under duress; she knew enough of threats to evaluate the menace in the call which had lifted her out of St. Louis and sent her to New York to work for this man with whom she had fallen so terribly in love. But that was all she *knew.*

Oh, there were things bothering her about the situation, events, and tonalities of events that jarred certain instincts which her years on the run had bred. She didn't like the way Ernie just up and pulled out. The news of the MPL disaster, had seemed even more ominous. David was on a high worse than pills, a kind of cranky, fractious frazzle.

But all she had were tinglings. The job itself seemed straightforward enough; only its size, no more, struck her as justifying the covertness which was so clearly basic to the computer rhythms which first Ernie, then she, had superintended. Job or no job, though, her woman's instinct told her to be watchful.

(416)

So Nantucket was a respite for thirty-six hours—no more. Her friends were kind, helpfully leaving her alone to organize and recompose herself and walk on the cold, empty beach. The husband's new book, read aloud after dinner the first night, was enormously, restfully amusing.

But she awoke Friday morning knowing that she had to be with David. After all, they had been together so constantly for so long. His aura had become a shelter for her. Had they become a composite? she wondered. Making love, which they did long and often, she felt herself locked to him, as if he expanded within her, sent out grappling tendrils which rendered them inseparable and pulled them inside each other's skin. The thought of him inside her made her squirm; for an instant she considered doing herself, but then thought, I can wait until tonight, and got on the phone to Air New England. She knew her host and hostess would understand.

For once, Air New England lived up to its advertisements and was permitted by the weather to meet its schedule, more or less. By one, the mist which had kept Nantucket Airport below minimums burned off and, by three o'clock, Devon was headed toward the Massachusetts Turnpike in a rented car.

It had occurred to her, but for no more than seconds, to call Harrison in New York and tell him she would be coming this evening. No, she thought, the surprise of her turning up might shock him back to sense.

Harrison bore right on the Tanglewood road. It was dark. As well as he knew the road, he still slowed to take the turns cautiously. Behind him, Osman kept his distance.

When he saw Harrison swing left through the gates of Windfair, Osman continued on past for several hundred yards before making a U-turn. He doused his lights down to the parking bulbs, turned through the gates, and crept up the hill. The trees lining the driveway creaked in the wind. Keeping his distance, he saw Harrison's taillights brighten as he drew to a stop beside the cottage. Osman extinguished his lights completely.

Turning in, he left the car down the driveway, in the place he had chosen earlier, and made his way slowly up the hill, silent on the grass, keeping in the shadow of the maples. All his senses seemed intensified by his compressed excitement; the wind crashed in the trees; although the moon was half hidden behind high, skidding clouds, it seemed as bright as the sun. Moving behind the house, he confirmed that the garage door was closed and locked. As he made his way back around the house, he saw lights go on in the front rooms. Calm, lightly balanced, expectant, he went to the front door.

Normally he would have taken the car to the garage, but Harrison was damned if he was going to eat alone at home tonight. He was out of sorts with Devon for leaving him alone. Even through the miasma of self-absorption which had been gathering around him as this particular weekend approached, her absence was acute and he couldn't duck the strong particularity of their relationship.

Letting himself in, he felt the warmth of the cottage and saw that a fire had been laid in the living room. He lit it. The flaming wood sounded friendly by comparison with the hobgoblin screeching and whistling outside. He blessed Yunkerman, the caretaker, for taking the time to build the fire.

He stretched. Christ, he was tired; Barney and he had really done a number for the second night in a row. He would have a couple of drinks, get a book, and drive over to the Red Lion Inn in Stockbridge for dinner. It would be crowded with leaf watchers, but he knew the people there and was sure they could make a place for him.

The doorbell rang.

Thinking it could only be Yunkerman coming for his money, although he generally came Saturday, Harrison went to the door.

The widening lighted sliver of the opening door disclosed Harrison's head. Osman moved to the light, forcing the door with his left hand, and launched a chopping, wicked blow with his right. Somehow Harrison got his head out of the way. Osman's hand split on the doorframe, leaving a quarter-inch dent in the shingle and causing him to grunt with pain as he drove in on Harrison, who cried out with fear at this horror coming at him out of the squalling night.

Feeling the other man's fingers scrabbling at his throat, seeking purchase in the sockets of his larynx, Harrison fought back. He breached and shook like a netted seal, thrashed, tried to kick the other man in the groin, which was the sum of his comic-book knowledge of hand-to-hand fighting. For a brief moment, he thought he was doing all right; he tried to use his size, tried to set himself. But he was an amateur, and this finally gave Osman the decisive advantage. Harrison tried to neutralize him, hug him into a hesitation long enough to allow for pleading, but Osman made small balancing movements and adjustments, used Harrison's own weight against him, and, patiently, got him turned around. He made a vise of his forearms and, bracing himself against Harrison's back, drew his head slowly back. Whether Harrison died of fear, strangulation, or a broken neck didn't much matter to Osman; he had plenty of time to finish the job.

All Harrison could hear was Osman's terrible, harsh panting as the pressure closed on his throat; the sound seemed to fill the room. He knew that this was all due to Ernie somehow, to Nyquist, that this was vengeance. Weakening, losing breath and composure, he began to pray with the little energy that remained to him. The world was running away from him.

Devon was just letting herself into the kitchen from the garage when the doorbell rang. She had been locked in the garage for twenty minutes. The bulb was burned out. Wanting to make her surprise complete, she'd bolted the garage door in place; wrestling it open once was enough, it moved so rustily on its slide.

In the dark, she had felt for the key which was supposed to be hanging on a nail near the kitchen door. It wasn't there. Goddamn Yunkerman, she swore wordlessly as she started to go through her catchall by the light of the dashboard. She had another key, she knew she did; she had seen it that morning; or so she thought. It was ten minutes before she finally found it down among the shreds of Kleenex and emery boards in an inner pocket of the bag.

That's strange, she thought, hearing the doorbell as she stepped into the kitchen. Then she heard the front door slam, heard thuds and exclamations and a choked cry of fright that sounded like David, and she knew that something was terribly, terribly wrong.

Afterward, she would recognize that the instincts and reflexes she had been husbanding all these years had simply taken over before she was even conscious of them. She would wonder whether she might have done as she did if she had stopped to think.

She grabbed a chef's knife from a block on the counter and trotted down the hall, feet balled to keep her silent.

The living room glimmered in firelight. She took it in at once.

Osman had Harrison up against the wall, face toward the fire, and was bending him back, arms around his neck, against the inexorable fulcrum of his knee.

Something Oruzgarry had showed her during knife practice behind the salting sheds at Saint-Jean-de-Luz came into Devon's mind. Osman never saw her. His concentration was on his work. She crossed the room in three quick steps and jammed the knife with all her strength into Osman's neck where it joined his right shoulder. "Just like killing a bull," Oruzgarry had instructed, "sink the blade in the middle of where the blood flows."

The carbon steel blade sliced Osman's carotid artery. His blood jetted out in great, spattering gouts, staining her hair, getting into her eyes and mouth. Speckled with blood, she watched Osman slide lifeless down Harrison's back, shrinking gently to the floor, a drained island in a scarlet pond.

For a minute, Harrison remained retching, face to the wall. He was sick with fear and relief; his vomit mixed with Osman's blood. His pants were wet.

When he turned from the wall and saw Devon, then Osman, he was beyond speech. Blood and death were strangers to David Harrison's world. He knew about kitchen cuts and the small, gallant wounds of the playing field, and that was all. A decade before he had bent to kiss his father's dead cheek, which was as near as he had come to a death in the same room.

His mouth was making strained, inarticulate noises. It didn't matter to Devon. She knew what he was trying to say to her. She also suspected that, just as she now knew, he understood about Ernie and Nyquist and God knows how many others there might be before something like this got finished.

Then she was back to business. "We must deal with this now, David. We can talk later."

She was in command.

"Tell me what to do," he said.

She got paper towels from the kitchen and they cleaned up the mess as best they could and threw the towels in the fire. The dark floor had had a hundred coats of varnish; Osman left no mark.

The corpse's pockets yielded nothing. Devon knew that men like this traveled light and anonymously.

"Let's put him in my car." She stuffed a towel in the gash and removed Osman's jacket, wrapping it tightly about the body's head and shoulders. "We don't want him dripping on our kitchen floor."

They lugged him into the garage and got him into the trunk of Devon's car. Devon told Harrison to get hold of himself and to clean up while she went to look for Osman's car.

"It's halfway down the driveway," she said. "We'll deal with all that after dinner. Now I think we better have a drink."

He was astonished and a bit aghast at her self-possession. At the kitchen table she watched him closely while he dragged at his Scotch until he seemed relatively collected.

"David, I don't know what this is all about. Not exactly. But there are always more where this one came from, although I am sure this one worked alone. We have got to protect ourselves. I want you to sit down tonight, *now,* and put down everything you know about this. All the names: Khafiq, Ernie, Nyquist, anyone else. *Everything.* Then you are going to put your little history somewhere absolutely safe, where only you can get at it. And for God's sake, David, never tell me where you've put it. That's a promise. They like to work the woman over first, these kinds of people."

Harrison thought of the knife in Osman's neck and the blood in her eyes and hair, now miraculously washed away, and shook his head.

"I'll do it right now," he said, "before all this sinks in on me and I'm too drunk to write. And I've got to change my goddamn pants."

It took him forty-five minutes to get it down on the old Royal typewriter he dragged from the closet. He gave it to her to read. When she finished, all she said was "No wonder," as she handed him back his folded typescript. He knew a place to put it; much as he wanted to tell her, he took her at her word, and kept it to himself.

After midnight, they set out, Harrison following in Osman's rented car, until she stopped at one of the stone bridges which cross the Housatonic, narrow at that point.

"Quickly!" She had the trunk open.

They manhandled the body over the stone abutment and heard it splash below. The river was running higher than usual, swollen by a rainy autumn.

They left Osman's car in the Red Lion parking lot.

When they got home, she straightened a few things, then,

"Bed, I think. We're having lunch with Pat and Jim tomorrow in Stockbridge and *that's* always fun."

In bed, he reached for her. The energy which sprang from fear ran through him like electricity. He managed an insane patience in his lovemaking: calm, capable, fierce, extending it to the point of cruelty, reclaiming himself. She came until the hand that pressed her up to him was soaking, until, finally, when he felt as if he would shatter, he let himself go. Unintelligible with exhaustion, all he could say was, "Jesus, I love you" over and over again until he slept like a baby in her mothering arms.

The next morning, he was so entirely dislocated that he failed to appreciate the report in the lower center column of the *Times* that the OPEC conference in Vienna had adjourned without incident or excitement. There was a photograph of the Minister waving from the steps of his Concorde; he was smiling broadly.

It also didn't occur to Harrison, although he was normally sensitive to this sort of thing, that it was sad that Osman, a man of small dreams whose only great hope was to die in his hot and fragrant homeland, should finish as an unmarked corpse in a strange, freezing river, drifting down with the other debris of winter to a dark, unwelcoming sea.

On Monday, after Harrison assured her that the letter was safely stowed, Devon telephoned a number in Detroit. She wanted them to be aware of the existence of the letter.

"Pass it on," she said, hanging up, cutting off the sputter of threats on the other end.

33 Onscreen, the Great Correspondent removed his half glasses and laid them on the desk before him. The clock behind his head, one of a row which showed the various time zones of the world, read 8:45 Eastern Standard Time. Looking squarely into the camera, he intoned: "Our computers here at CBS Election Central have now confirmed an overwhelming victory for President Fulger Baxter and his running mate, Vice President Andrew Reilly. Using sampling techniques perfected at the Stanford Research Institute since President Baxter's narrow victory four years ago, our projection is that President Baxter will capture all 537 electoral votes in the fifty states. This is the earliest confirmation of an election result since this network first introduced computerized electoral forecasting some twenty years ago. Of course, it is, expectedly, the greatest victory in presidential history.

"The polls are still open across the nation for a few minutes in the East yet and for several hours in the Far West and in Hawaii. Nevertheless, our sampling of early returns in selected key districts confirms a massive triumph for the President in an election which as recently as months ago seemed hopelessly beyond his reach. I am told that if the present trend continues through the night, the Baxter-Reilly ticket will receive something over *73 percent*," he laid a biblical stress on the figure, "of the popular vote. Nowhere in the annals of this nation's history can a plurality of equal magnitude be found."

The camera drew back from the commentator; he took off his headset and stickpin microphone. He was on his way to the earliest Election Night dinner in his lifetime. He might amble over to Jack's; there was nothing left as far as CBS was concerned but to tot up the final count.

Harrison had knocked off five Scotches before settling in front of the set to watch what he had come to accept as the inevitable. The episode in Lenox told him that something had gone monstrously wrong. The alcohol and an exhaustion inside himself that he couldn't shake made him woozy. All he could do was look blankly at the set. He watched as CBS ran through the races for the House and Senate. The network's analysts had isolated a group of congressional candidates which had been designated as "Baxter Specials," men and women for whom the President had personally and intensively campaigned with the specific objective of unseating approximately fifty members of Congress whom he described as "improperly critical or recalcitrant." By ten o'clock, when Harrison's living room had started to whirl, most of those races were over. Not surprisingly, all but one of "Baxter's BSers," as the group was irreverently known around CBS— out of the chairman's earshot—had won. Individually and collectively, it was a dreary group, given to emulating the President's hortatory moralizing and his down-home ethics. "This Congress is going to look like the First Baptist Church in Peckerwood Junction," Pits Peech remarked, off-camera. On camera, garnishing the events of the day with the phil-

(423)

osophical icing for which CBS paid him $50,000 on a one-shot deal, he was suitably orotund.

"The President will go into his second term with more arrows in his quiver than have been vouchsafed any Chief Executive in memory. He will control absolute majorities in both House and Senate. His people will chair crucial committees. He bathes in the adulation of the American people and of the entire Free World to which, with an initiative which still remains as mysterious as it appears to have been invincible, he has restored political and fiscal equilibrium. These are powerful tools. It now remains to be seen whether President Baxter, whose mental and executive capacities many, including this correspondent, have been wont to malign, can wield them in such a fashion as to reshape this mighty and diverse nation into the moral, peaceful, and thrifty Utopia which he admits to be his vision. The effort will begin in January. For now, and for CBS, goodnight."

Alone, Harrison watched Jordan's concession speech.

Watching Jordan reminded him of childhood newsreels of Franklin Roosevelt. The man seemed *solid*; the old Mitch catchword jumped into his mind. There was something in that voice and intonation, that old school flattening and pursing of the vowels, which came across with patrician, headmasterish authority which was immeasurably comforting but different from a man like Merriman. Jordan had proffered an umbrella of moral quality and ancient values under which the country might take shelter. Of course, the man had never had a snowball's chance of winning the election. Harrison knew that money was made riding winners, yet he found himself wanting, for an instant so intense that it was almost painful, that Jordan might somehow have brought it off. Hell, he thought, his own clients had bought the thing for Baxter. But somewhere inside he felt this terrible wanting, for himself and the whole gobbling, tricked-up country, to be able to crawl into the shelter of Jordan's values and be saved.

The only significant political figure to escape the Baxter avalanche was Congressman Renssalaer. Baxter had run at him hard, twice touring the littered sidewalks of the lower Manhattan district, shaking hands with tenement dwellers and small shopkeepers. But Renssalaer's Jewish constituents felt the stirring of ancient malefactions; they would have endured privations far worse than the loss of light and heat to continue their champion in office. The district's *rebbe* personally pleaded Renssalaer's cause in *shul*. On Election Day, over 95 percent of the district's Jewish voters had turned out; the able wheeled the halt and infirm to the polling places. The *Daily News* would later report that all but three Jewish votes had gone to the incumbent. Renssalaer survived with a four-hundred-vote plurality over the beetling young goon whose wealthy father had bought the conservative Republican candidacy for him in an effort to get him out of the family business.

Politics bored Devon, so she had gone to a movie with a friend. When she let herself in just after eleven, she found the lights on in the living room and Harrison snoring lightly on the sofa. The television was still on; CBS was rerunning *Mr. Smith Goes to Washington*. She turned it off and tried to budge Harrison. He was too heavy. She eased his shoes off. Sadly, she saw that he looked as miserable in sleep as he now did through the waking hours. "Oh my love, my love," she said softly, "what have you done to yourself?" She kissed him and turned off the lights.

When it was all totaled, 68 million Americans had gone to the polls; nearly 50 million had voted the Baxter-Reilly ticket. John Jordan went back to the blue Virginia hills. He had done no better than he had expected, yet in his heart he felt as if he had been paid a cruel and awful insult by the electorate, especially the voters of his own party who had crossed over. No fewer Republicans than usual had gone to the polls. But nearly 30 percent of those who voted had pulled the lever or checked the box for Baxter-Reilly. "Adlai was right," he told his wife, "it *does* hurt too much to laugh."

"Cheer up," she said, "look at the sunset." She was secretly glad. She loved her husband and she loved this house and once again she had them both.

The weeks following the election provided two other personal tragedies.

No one in the Federal Aviation Administration could later figure out how Congressman Renssalaer, an accomplished pilot flying a twin Cessna loaded with advanced avionics, had strayed into restricted airspace. He was headed for the Caribbean for a post-election vacation. His normal route would have carried him over water only briefly, abeam Cape Lookout, before turning back inland toward Charleston.

There was cloud and mist all the way to 30,000 feet, which was beyond the Cessna's upper limit, but perfect for the air force test. Renssalaer was flying on instruments; before setting them, he'd carefully noted the red-lined "Restricted Airspace" designation on the latest Jeppesen map of the area. He'd been careful to write up his coordinates and headings to give the space a wide berth. His instruments must have betrayed him. Certainly the air force people weren't to blame. The secret Cottonmouth II experimental missile, undulating through the cloud cover like a snake in search of a bird's nest, had impacted Renssalaer's aircraft well inside the test area. It was surprising that Renssalaer hadn't picked up the all-channels warning that was being broadcast at ten-second intervals over a hundred-mile radius. The FAA concluded that the plane's electrical system must have gone blooey from atmospheric static. The file was closed.

In his district, women keened in the streets and whole neighborhoods sat Shiva, orthodox Jews mourning a congressman who had spent his weekends sailing and playing tennis at clubs no one of their faith could ever enter. In Qu'nesh, there was no mourning. When the news was communicated to Prince Alrazi, he smiled. As far as he was concerned, enough of the loose ends were snipped. The whole matter could be considered neatly at an end. He so advised the Minister.

In early December, the President sent Andrew Reilly to New Guinea on a goodwill visit. The young Vice President comported himself in the exuberant, athletic fashion for which he was admired, climbing palms, kayaking down infested, infected rivers, feasting in jungle clearings with local headhunters, and generally promoting a spirit of hearty avuncular interest in New Guinea's affairs and customs. In the course of his exertions, he sustained the run of bruises, minor cuts, and upset stomachs which was normal in this kind of work.

It was only after Reilly returned to Washington that he began to exhibit the early symptoms of what would later be diagnosed as a complicated, hitherto unknown variant of dengue fever. It was assumed he had picked it up in Papua, at a feast with the mudmen of the Mapuga tribe. At first mild, the dizziness and muscular weakness intensified until the

Vice President was sent home by his doctor to recuperate. The sickness worsened. When his pulse rate slowed alarmingly, it was decided to check him into Walter Reed, where the tropical disease specialists could work him over. Neither they, huddled around his bedside, nor his family, nor indeed anyone else outside the White House suspected that the virus which had lodged itself so malevolently in his bloodstream had in fact been implanted there before he had left Washington, had in fact traveled no further than down Wisconsin Avenue from a vault at the National Institutes of Health in Bethesda, had in fact swum in the same solution, in the same syringe, as the cholera serum.

Winter was with them now for a good long spell, John Jordan had observed to his wife over dinner. With a fire crackling happily in the grate, the study was warm and pleasant. Jordan had wheeled the television in from the living room. It was time to turn to winter garments, winter configurations. He had a glass of excellent brandy and one of the last of the real Cuban cigars, a pre-Castro of about 1958, that Jack Kennedy had given him when they'd worked on the photo evaluations during the missile crisis. He would rather have had these cigars than a gross of the signed, silver-framed photographs his former colleagues coveted so desperately and displayed so pompously.

"This is a damn good movie," he said to Margaret. They were watching a rerun of *The Thirty-Nine Steps*; Robert Donat had just recoiled after noticing his host's missing finger when a voiceover declared: "We are going now to the White House, for a special message from the President of the United States." The black-and-white image was replaced by the presidential seal in color, then by the face of President Baxter; he was wearing the pronouncedly grim expression which skeptical viewers had come to identify with his "significant" public addresses.

"My goodness, what now?" Margaret asked. "Haven't we had enough excitement for one year?"

"My fellow Americans..." the President began, clasping his hands. He really *is* the most lugubrious speaker, thought Jordan, and he gestures as if he were wearing a tin suit. "...to you tonight with very sad news. I have today received, with the greatest regret, the resignation, for reasons of health, of Vice President Andrew Reilly, my friend, associate, colleague in the great task of government, and most recently running mate in our great Democratic victory.

"Vice President Reilly is seriously ill with a disease contracted in the service of his country, during a visit of state to West Irian. His doctors have concluded that his cure and convalescence will be extended and that during this period he will be unable to carry out the great duties of his office. He has sent me this letter..."

Baxter read Reilly's note of resignation. It was short and to the point. The President held it up and the cameras closed on it; it was barely possible to make out the Vice President's weakened, spidery signature, the shaky handwriting of an old man, not the vigorous boy who had waved from the White House balcony on Election Night. Jordan guessed that Reilly's wife had guided his hand to sign the note. The poor devil must be deathly ill, he thought, half listening to the platitudes the President was heaping on the character and record of his departed colleague. At one point, the cameras panned away from the President; it was a very distinguished audience: the Chief Justice, the Speaker of the House, all the nabobs. Jordan began to feel that something else was in the air.

The President's tone took on an affirming lilt which drew Jordan's attention back to the screen and to Baxter's words. "...not only a time for regret at the departure from public life, even for a brief while, of this young and distinguished public servant, but a time for rededication, and thanks, that a country so great as this can so easily fill the place of those lately fallen..." Jordan shuddered at the pompous gracelessness of Baxter's words. The President went on to describe the qualities he would expect of a Vice President: loyalty above all, a team player; experience; toughness of mind; piety, a churchgoer; diplomacy. It was the usual, predictable catalogue of civic and private virtues.

"I am pleased to be able to say that a great public servant who possesses those qualities in full measure has agreed to permit me to submit his name for the advice and consent of the Congress next January to become Vice President of the United States of America. He has been a loyal Democrat for many years. When, some years ago, our party alienated itself from its traditional moorings in the soil and in the South, he took himself out of the muck of ideological squabbling and held himself apart from the party, which was a tragedy. Until recently, those of us who have cherished the dream of a reconstructed Democratic Party, a dream which now seems within our grasp, feared that he might yield to the overtures of the other party, which had all but placed its destiny in his hands if he so wished. As an honorable man, concerned with his nation and above mere politics, he acceded, but his roots were ever with *us,* with the ideals of Jefferson and Jackson and FDR. He has over thirty years of experience in public life as a member of the executive branch of government and as a member of the U.S. Senate..."

"Margaret, you won't believe this," breathed Jordan, "but I think he's talking about Herndon Dunstable."

"...as well as a distinguished, productive private citizen. I will miss having Andy Reilly at my side, but I know that he would be as pleased as you will be, fellow Americans, to know that the office in which he served with such dedication will now be filled by Herndon P. Dunstable, Independent of Texas, and an old and admired friend."

Jordan was speechless. As Herndon Dunstable, grasping both the President's hands with his own, moved stage center from the wing of the East Room and then raised his hands for quiet, Jordan flipped off the television. He went straight to the bar.

As Margaret Jordan told her bridge group a few weeks later, she didn't think John Jordan had been drunk since his freshman year at Yale. But he had finished a quarter of a bottle of brandy and then started in on the Virginia Gentleman. When he finally came reeling to bed, he smelled so awful and snored so loudly that she had been forced to sleep on the daybed in her sewing room.

Vice President Reilly's was not the only resignation tendered in the United States at that time. The managing editor of Enterprise News Services found a letter from Pits Peech on his desk on the morning following Baxter's naming of Dunstable.

"...A reporter is only as good as his understanding of his beat," the letter read. *"It is clear to me now, as it has been for some months, that I no longer have the slightest understanding of what is going on in the political life of this country. Perhaps I spent too much time in Rome, although I remain amazed that a genial, brief indulgence in 'Abbachio alla Romana' and the music of Frescobaldi should have so completely wrecked my perspective on my own country.*

"Please accept my resignation from ENS. Either we are

*entering a period of absolute corruption in our public life, a
predictable historical outgrowth of Watergate, or I am living
in a dream world. I am unwilling to continue to ponder either
of those in the public print. I have some money and it is my
intention to marry and retire to a mountain in Vermont...."*

Is everybody going fucking crazy? the editor asked himself.
He hadn't slept while trying to get together a story on the
Reilly-Dunstable business. He fumbled in his desk drawer.
He knew goddamn well there was a pint of Chivas in there
somewhere.

It seemed to Harrison that everyone he had met in this
affair was vanishing one by one: like distant stars expiring
on the outer edges of a dying constellation. First Ernie; then
Nyquist; then Khafiq. He had called London after the election
only to be told by Khafiq's secretary that the master had been
killed in an automobile accident just a week previous. Accident? Sure. God alone knew how many others there might
have been or attempted. Not counting Devon and himself.
And that man they'd put in the river, whoever in hell he was.

What *had* he become now? he wondered. A year ago he
was a clever man in early middle age, fresh out of boyhood
with a lot of bright ideas. He hearkened back to the first long
conversation with Khafiq. The sparkling Aegean and the hot,
buzzing afternoon seemed a hundred eternities in the past.
He recalled vaguely that they had talked at one point in
terms of debits and credits. Well, what did it work out to
now?

Credits? Well, there was all that money in Switzerland.
And Devon, of course, but he felt he was wearing her down
with his moping. Would she stick it out with him? Debits?
He was an accomplice to one murder; the near victim of an
assassination; indirectly responsible, probably, for other
deaths. Worse still, it had all turned out exactly opposite to
the way he had expected. The crooks and fools were in solider
than ever. Which meant that he had in a way betrayed his
country, if—as he most surely had done—helping to perpet-
uate the very monsters he had sought to extinguish was a
betrayal. Not that he'd be tried or convicted for it; the country
was fat and happy. The payment of the check had only been
postponed; nothing had really changed. So much for deep
thinking; so much for crusades.

It was ironical, he thought. Here he'd been bitching for
years that the country was being brought to its knees by a

mélange of muddy-headed establishment types and boorish, sly country boys. So he'd cooked up and sold this idea, it had seemed, to some people who felt the same way but were in a position to do something about it. And look where we were. The dopes and the crooks were in bed together. The Merrimans of the world had been bailed out. And some guy had come out of the darkness and tried to murder him, and God knows there was probably another one out there who wouldn't miss.

There was absolutely nothing he could do about it except to try to save himself and Devon. The icy finality of that recognition sobered him up, that, and the knowledge that he didn't have a clue as to what he could do—except pray.

He stood by the window. The first snow that had fallen last week was about gone. The street was empty. He had put the Schubert *Nocturne* on the record player; it had a wrenching, desperate sort of beauty that suited his mood. Ironic, he thought; this used to be my prize seduction music; now it suits as a dirge.

As he looked out the window, night thoughts, memories and misgivings seemed to beat against the pane like bats fleeing a storm. He couldn't believe Devon could sleep so soundly, but then she had always been unbelievably calm, calm about Ernie's vanishing, calm about mopping up after killing that man.

Was he a Jonah, Harrison wondered, peering at his reflection. Into his head swam lines from Cummings: "And how do you like your blue-eyed boy Mr. Death?" And from Don Marquis: "I'm as full of death as a drugstore." What in God's name had he gotten them all into. Khafiq, a friend, dead. Ernie. Probably. Nyquist. Yes. He must be next. He considered jerking the window open and launching himself out into the night. Instead, wanting to live, to take his best shot, he went to the bar and made a big Scotch. The first sip sent a blade of heartburn bisecting his chest. Puffing like an old man, he sank into the sofa, scared of his heartbeat, hearing the record change.

He tried to fix on the music. The whisky was swelling his mind.

"And solitaire's the only game in town/And every road that takes him takes him down/While life goes on around him everywhere,/He's playing solitaire."

He listened to the song with a mind as unsteady as his feet and then rose and crossed to the machine, playing the song again, and again and again, ten times, until he was worn out. When he finally got to bed, Devon was serenely asleep, breathing softly, with an arm extended, hugging a pillow where he should have been.

Time now to grow up, David, he continued to himself as he undressed. If he got out of this, he'd hang up the Captain America suit and stop trying to save the world. These big ideas were wonderful things, until they got loose and caused sorrow and destruction. He was no longer a little boy in a Scotch cap playing by the pond in Central Park on Sunday mornings. He would push his boat off, send it skimming over the surface until the winds got it and the wavelets, and it was no longer his but completely beyond his control; he would burst into tears, watching it bumping and tangling with other boats, until at last it nosed up against the stone sides of the pond and he could run around the rim of the pond on anxious short legs and pluck it from the water. But in this kind of thing, in this grownup world, there was no running around the pond to retrieve a toy and the bumpings brought death and disappearance. Actions had consequences that lurked over the horizon like thunder; it was better not to act, better to leave the tree branches calm and unshaken.

In that instant, he recognized that childhood was flown forever. Nothing was just games any longer; no, that wasn't it, quite. It was that making a game of everything was not only behind him now, like toys and tears, it was *beyond* his reach. How much had he lost? What did Housman say: *"It is the land/Of Lost Content/I see it shining plain/The happy highways where I went/And cannot come again."*

The realization of his role as a shaper, a stimulus, in the great scheme of things had been exciting—once. Now he had done it and had seen what could happen. It was time to hide, if he could ever get out of this business. He opened the bedroom window to let in the December air; he always slept best in the cold. Of course, it was hard to sleep, knowing that *they* might yet be out there in the dark.

As the air hit his skin, he remembered a remark made by his old philosophy professor at Princeton:

"Considering how much time we're obliged to spend alone with our thoughts, isn't it a pity they're not better company for us?"

Lying down, he felt sleepy. He was starting to calm down. Why not, there wasn't anything else to do.

34   Margaret Jordan had gone to her brother's investiture as Bishop of Virginia. Jordan had begged off; he had no stomach for the prospective genteel condolences and sympathies of Richmond's Episcopal gentry. He remained annoyed with himself at the difficulty he was having in extinguishing the inner rancor he felt at the extent of the beating he had taken in the election.

At least the country seemed settled. In spite of what Jordan saw as awful deficiencies in taste and style, Baxter had done some good. His flying trip to Qu'nesh over Thanksgiving had brought back agreement on the basic terms of a long-term mutual security and energy pact with the Kingdom. Conspicuously, both Secretary Drzlag and Secretary Nordlander had been left in Washington. The rumor on Foxhall Street was that "Tweety" and "Sylvester" would not be included in the new cabinet. Jordan was pleased with the news; it was time to get the civilian warriors out of government. Laymen should militate for peace only, he thought; let the generals judge the wisdom of war.

The hours were empty without Margaret. He tinkered away the morning, thumbing through the *Post* and the *Star*, airing the dogs, and trying fitfully to wade through the latest exposé of the Agency.

At noon he walked down the long drive to collect the mail. Along with the usual batch of bills and flyers, there was a small parcel addressed to him in a firm round script which he guessed belonged to a woman. He didn't recognize the handwriting; he weighed the package thoughtfully as he walked back up the driveway, the dogs prancing beside him in the crisp air. The sky was graying over; it looked like snow.

In his study he slit the package open with a small dagger that his friends in Qu'nesh had given him years before. It reminded him that he ought to give Ben Masters a call one of these days, have lunch with him. By God, that was a noble thing Masters had done, putting up the money for those television pilots which still sat unshown in a New York advertising agency.

The package contained a tape cassette and a note written in the same aggressive woman's hand which had addressed

(**433**)

the envelope. The note read: *"Dear Ambassador Jordan: Please listen to this and then call the number below any afternoon between six and six-fifteen."* He didn't recognize the number, although the 202 area code told him it was somewhere in the District.

It took him a while to figure how to work the tape part of the elaborate stereo player he'd given Margaret as a retirement present to them both. At length, between the pidgin Japanese instructions he searched out in his desk and his own common sense, he got the knobs and buttons properly organized.

The tape hissed for a moment, then a woman's voice—southern, Jordan thought, and vaguely familiar—said: *"This tape is labeled WH/OO"*—Jordan guessed that meant "White House/Oval Office" in bureaucratese—*"Observation Series X/ Sequence Two dash Nine...date unavailable."* There was more hissing; then the recording began in what was surely the middle of a conversation.

"...did it go? Does he understand the difficulty we might have in granting asylum under those circumstances? It isn't easy, what with all those goddamn students here and everything..."

Jordan stepped quickly to the machine and pressed the "pause" button. The words were difficult to make out, blurred by the distortions in the recording, but he knew that voice as well as he knew his own. He had listened to it for thirty years, beginning with the hectoring of witnesses at the House investigations of homosexuals in the Commerce Department. Listened to it grow in weight and deepen slightly as it aged. But it had never lost that mouthy false earnestness, that mechanical, strained awkwardness of expression which Jordan had always attributed to a synaptic conflict between calculation and cruelty. My God, he thought, as he restarted the tape player.

Another voice cut in. "Well, Mr. President, I believe he appreciates our problem. I told him that getting him in, well, that would be about as difficult as it could be. There's a whole lot of folks here think that letting him stay here, assuming it all falls apart, would be about the same as giving asylum to Adolf Hitler..."

Again, Jordan stopped the machine. He recognized that succulent, easy voice, too. He'd heard it right here in his study eight and a half months ago, telling him he ought to be President. Good heavens, Herndon, he thought, pressing the button again.

There was a pause. The only sound was the susurrus of the recorder, and Jordan guessed that the conversationalists had moved out of microphone range. Then an indistinct murmur overrode the tape static and the first voice was heard again, getting louder as the speaker moved back toward the recording source.

"...not as difficult as bringing in Hitler himself, Herndon..."

The volume increased and there was a familiar unoiled squeaking; the famous presidential swivel chair, Jordan thought.

"...more like asylum for Eichmann or that spade in Uganda, heh, humph." The speaker chuckled in a heavy orotund way that showed how uncomfortable any level of wit or laughter was for him. What sense of humor the man had, Jordan thought, was essentially restricted to gloating.

"Anyway," the voice continued, "how about our allegiance to the top man? He's the one that's our ally. He's the one that stands alone against the international Communist conspiracy. He's the one who's really spent some money over here. Why I remember telling..."

The voices moved out of range again.

Jordan sat there feeling each second's silence to be a gulf encompassing a lifetime.

"...nothing to worry about." It was the second voice—Dunstable's—speaking with his old easy confidence. "He's in real good shape. Talked to the folks over at the CIA. Politics are good. Owns the army. Only trouble he's got is with some diddleysquat priest in Iraq, and he ain't much. Hell, I was there a while ago for that celebration; you never saw such goings-on; the Shah's got their peckers in his pocket. But this old boy, hell, he's burnt just too many butts. He's got to get out..." The voices faded again.

"...but he says he'd be prepared to be right generous if we can get him in." It was Dunstable's voice that had reappeared.

"How generous?" Jordan let the tape roll. Dunstable's voice again: "...million for you, a half for me, say a half spread around Foggy Bottom..." The voice faded again. There were ten seconds of silence, then the first voice said, "I see. Well, certainly something like that deserves consideration. What do they say in Foggy Bottom?"

"I visited with the man in charge. We can get it done, if

we get the papers in order now, especially if you include that bit about 'loyal allies' in your talk next week to shut the goddamn liberals up, I can take care of the other details for you and me both."

"Well, damn it, these people have been good friends of ours. Can you keep it away from the media? Those shits would kill me on something like this. Why can't they realize that you can't make an omelet without breaking eggs?"

"Don't you worry your head a minute, Mr. President," the voice was suave, confident. "And I'll run it through the Certified so it just looks like a l'il old real estate commission."

"Do it the way you think best...." The voices faded away. Then the same female voice that had introduced the dialogue came back on. "This has been WH/OO Series X/Elision Sequence Two dash Nine. As of..." Jordan checked his wall calendar; the date was three days ago. "This tape was in the sealed vault of the White House sergeant at arms..." Then more hissing.

Jordan sat transfixed. The tape ran out its full length before he rewound it and played it again without a break. And then again. While he listened, something jiggled in his memory until he caught it. There had been a picture in the *Star*'s Sunday supplement not three weeks earlier of Bergarzak, the former head of the Iranian secret police, playing golf in California. He remembered noting the caption at the time: *"Evil has its own reward/Nasser Bergarzak, Iran's answer to Heinrich Himmler, tees off in a Palm Springs golf resort where the cheapest house costs $750,000. Playing with him are Rosmer Beauderon, chairman of Allied Petrex, and two bodyguards. Bergarzak has been a resident of Palm Springs for the last four years, since his dramatic flight from Teheran."* Over Bergarzak's head the *Star* had stamped, in red, *"Why is this man laughing?"* As Jordan remembered, the *Doonesbury* cartoon strip had worked over the humor in the fact that while the Shah and his family were packing clods of Iranian soil to accompany them in exile, Bergarzak was addressing the Palm Springs Chamber of Commerce on the subject of economic laissez-faire. He had been granted asylum over three years before the Ayatollah returned from Paris.

It was the longest afternoon of Jordan's life. He guessed he looked at his watch a hundred times. He snapped at the dogs. A long meandering walk through the hills, the tape in his pocket, ate up a couple of hours. Finally, after a shaky cup of tea, it was six o'clock.

He dialed the number. The voice that answered was the same as on the tape.

"This is John Jordan. I was told to call this number."

"Oh yes, Mr. Jordan, how are you? This is Ermabelle Baxter. Just a second, the President's right here."

Fulger Baxter came on. "Evenin', John. I wanted to thank you for your nice letter. I'll get around to writin' you soon enough, but things've been real hectic around here. You listen to that stuff on that tape, John?"

"Yes sir, I have."

"Well, it don't take no hard figurin' to know what it could mean to the political ambitions of persons unknown if that got in the hands of the *New York Times*. We're just lucky *we* found it. Buster traded it from the State Department in return for some cute pictures, real cute and unusual, that our people got of some funny goin's-on in the men's room of the Fairfax. It sure beats me what goes on in this town!" the President added parenthetically, "I didn't even dare show the goshdarn things to Miz Baxter.

"Now, John," Baxter continued, a new intensity in his voice, "I want you to listen real careful."

"Yes sir."

"Dunstable don't get a passkey to this place until January. When he does, you can bet on it he'll come lookin' for that tape. He knows it's around. He'll find it too, and it'll just vanish. We put the original back in the vault. After all, it's private property. What you've got is a copy, the only copy. Ermabelle made the copy you've got on that fancy equipment those nice folks in New York gave us for listenin' to music. She understands all that stuff. I tell you, John, you got to get up early to keep up with these Sophie Newcomb girls." Jordan thought he could hear Ermabelle Baxter giggling in the background.

"Anyway, John, I took Dunstable in here for plenty of real good reasons. You got to believe me on that. He took the bait, 'cause he wants my job in the worst way. When he gets here next month, Gadawmighty, he'll own the town in a month or two. Already got his due bills out on half the bureaus. You and me, we're just two decent boys tryin' to do good the best way we can, even if we do come from different sides of the swamp. Herndon's different. He's got the biggest ego and the mightiest ambition I ever saw.

"Now, John, it just ain't a good idea for a man like that to be President of these United States. Which, in the ordinary course of things, he will be. I can't run again, hell, knowin' Herndon, I might not even make it to the end of my term. Wouldn't surprise me at all if in a year or so there ain't some old boy out there with a rifle and a scope. That's the chance I got to take. A man takes this job, he's got to show hisself to the people. You get me?"

"Yes sir." Jordan felt a sort of sad admiration for the President. He was glad he wasn't the man in the White House.

"John, I tricked old Herndon into gettin' where he is now. Don't ask why, but I did because it was best. I always try to do what's best. He don't realize what's happened yet; he probably never will; vanity and ambition are a powerful pair of blinders. I ain't goin' to comment how he foofawed you. But he sure did. So here's your chance to get even. If that's your motive, although personally I don't think so. Hell, John, people like you *are* this country. Your people were writin' their names on the Declaration of Independence when my great-great-great-great grandpappy was scratchin' dirt for General Oglethorpe. But we both got somethin' to contribute.

"One other thing. John. Old Herndon ain't exactly unknown to the oil companies. I got this program goin' to break their backs and if he was to take over, the fox would not only be in with the chickens, he'd be in charge!

"John, you take that little thing I sent you and put it in the safest place you know. And when the time comes, you use it. We got a sayin' back home: *'The chickens ain't safe till the fox's tail is nailed to the wall.'* You're a fox-huntin' man. Have we got a deal?"

Jordan hesitated, only because there was a lot he thought he wanted to say to this man whom he and his friends on Foxhall Road had so often mocked for his farmhouse ways. But he couldn't find the words.

"Yes, Mr. President." Then a question bubbled up that he had to ask. "Can I ask you, sir, why you picked me?"

"Hell, John, *folks* got to stick together. There's nothin' in the Constitution that says the President can't be a patriot too. Well, Ermabelle joins me in sayin' Merry Christmas to you and Miz Jordan. You'll understand if we don't talk again for a while?"

"I understand, Mr. President. Merry Christmas to you both. And God bless you, sir."

The line went dead.

Jordan sat silently for a while, mulling the President's instructions. The safest place. He toyed with the notion of hiding the tape in a buried pumpkin somewhere on the farm; there was a precedent for that. No no no, he said, impatient with himself for not being brighter and then he knew exactly where he should go. Looking at his watch, he guessed he had enough time to catch the last shuttle out of National Airport. He left a note for Margaret saying he had to go to Isis.

Isis was the third-oldest but by agreement most prestigious of the senior societies at Yale, which each year welcomed into their mysterious, windowless tombs, delegations of fifteen apiece of the college's brightest and noblest souls. No one except the members knew what went on inside, although there was a great deal of speculation, mainly pornographic. Whatever had happened, Isis was plainly important to its members; so important, to all men of Yale of a certain age, that Jordan knew that Margaret would accept his excuse of a sudden summons to New Haven without quiver or question.

By midnight he was in New Haven. It had taken him a while to find the right keys in a shoebox tucked back in a closet, but he'd caught the flight. He parked his car on Chapel Street. Yale was on Christmas vacation and the streets were quiet. He walked under the arch of the art gallery and up the steps of the neighboring building which loomed windowless like an Egyptian mausoleum. In the dark, he could still visualize the eye of Ra which was carved on the lintel. He rang the bell impatiently until a shutter opened in the door and a sleepy Negro voice asked what his business was.

"I'm 'Imhotep,' 1936," said Jordan.

"Oh yes sir, please," and the tomblike doors swung open.

"Good evening, Booker, I've got to go down to the Memorabilia Room. Can you turn on the lights?"

"Oh yes sir, Ambassador. Sorry; I mean, Mr. Imhotep, sir. Would you be wanting to stay here? The sanctuary's closed this time of year, I'm afraid, but I can make you up a couch in the Hypostyle and fix you a sandwich."

"No thanks, Booker. I've just got a little business down in the Memorabilia Room."

"Very good, sir. Will we be seeing you at Pyramid Island this year? 'Course, you was pretty busy this last summer. We all voted for you; the young gentlemens thought it would be nice to have a fourth Pres'dent up there on the wall." He pointed at three portraits hung high above the floor.

"Thank you, Booker. I'll try to get there—to Pyramid, I mean. Now I'll just get this done. It's been a very long day."

He went down the lighted stone steps to the great vault which had been installed in 1893 when the new temple was built. The first of his keys opened it; inside, he pulled the chain on the bare single bulb and searched the shelved walls until he found the inset metal box marked "1936" in raised pewter letters. In the box which the second key opened, there were three envelopes; once there had been a dozen, but most of his classmates were now no more than memories and names cut into the limestone walls of the refectory upstairs. He placed the manila envelope containing the tape in the box. On the outside he had written: *"In the event of my death, please deliver to Managing Editor, care of Enterprise News Service."* Inside, he had enclosed a handwritten, signed note outlining the circumstances of the tape's arrival in his hands. God willing, he would be alive to collect it when the time came. If not, well, it was the best he could do. The box was always opened on the death of a member of a delegation.

The steward let him out. They exchanged goodnights and Christmas wishes. Jordan pressed a five-dollar bill on him. There was no need to caution Booker about secrecy. That was the point of Isis. As he headed back to his car, he touched the sphinx-shaped pin which he always wore on his undershirt. Thank heavens, he thought, *some* things abide.

When he got back to Virginia, after spending the night in a motel near Westport, Margaret was on the lawn with the dogs. "I read your note about New Haven," she teased, "but, John, after all these years, you can't fool me. You've a girl in Georgetown, haven't you?" She hugged him. She was sure he was home for good.

The phone rang in Harrison's apartment early in the morning. Devon disentangled herself from Harrison and answered it. "Of course," Harrison heard her say, "eight o'clock? We'll be there."

She fended off Harrison's gropings and informed him, "That was the Kingdom's Embassy in Washington. The Minister's asked us for dinner. I've accepted, of course. Let's take an early shuttle; I'd like to see that El Greco show at the National Gallery."

When they presented themselves at the modern building

on Massachusetts Avenue, they were ushered into a sitting room, all white and Plexiglas and Italian modishness. It was out of kilter with the Islamic traceries in the walls. The Minister joined them after a short wait. He shook Harrison's hand quickly and lingered over Devon's. His admiration was so obvious that it made Harrison jealous.

"If you don't mind," he said, "I've booked a table at Jean-Pierre for dinner. The food here really isn't very good, our last cook deserted us for the Brazilian Embassy, and, as you can understand, there's not a drop of wine in the place."

When they were settled in the restaurant, and Jean Michel had seen to it that they were given a meal which would have choked the elder Dumas, the Minister relaxed. He was in great form; Devon seemed transfixed. It made Harrison quite jealous.

"I think we'll get this mutual-security treaty signed in good order," the Minister remarked. "I've been dealing with your extraordinary Mr. Ferdimend. He's an extremely practical man."

Over the pigeon, the Minister said: "I had a semi-state visit today, from the great Leslie Merriman. Our gossip is that he's on the short list for Secretary of Commerce. Merriman becomes more pompous every time I see him. He's been down here negotiating some sort of credit, he told me, for the Maldive Islands. Can you imagine?

"Merriman brought his assistant, a very ambitious young man I should say. I'd watch out for that one. More of this Haut-Brion?"

The big wine was making Harrison cheery. He recalled seeing an announcement in the *Times* that Merriman's assistant, his name was something like Cameron, was engaged to Merriman's daughter. He would be Maria Merriman Stanhope della Vittoria's third husband; the girl wasn't yet twenty-five. No, he told the Minister, he didn't think he'd met Merriman recently or that their paths had crossed. The Minister thought that was a good thing.

Over coffee, the Minister looked keenly at Harrison and said, "I expect you were as saddened as I about our good friend Khafiq. I like to think, however, that he must have died knowing how good a cause it was that he had served. The world is at peace. We are all rich. Life has a positive quality for once. Times like these are worth anything, even if the cost seems high or sad. And things so seldom turn out exactly as we intend. It's time to leave well enough alone.

(441)

What does the English poet say about us? That we pack our tents and softly steal away? Well, that time has come. We can all rest." He smiled serenely.

His eyes had never left Harrison's face. With a surge, Harrison realized that the Minister was telling him that he and Devon were safe. He saw from the Minister's sidewise confirming look at Devon that this business was, at last, all over. He was rich, and safe. The last counted most.

Harrison tried to pick up the check but the Minister wouldn't have it. Outside, on the sidewalk, the Minister kissed Devon's hand and took Harrison's in farewell. Repeating what he had said—was it a millennium ago?—in Paris, the Minister looked at Harrison. "Goodbye, David, Ms. Linde. Mine is a strange life. I don't know when we'll meet again."

Outside, he climbed into his Rolls. As the taillights twinkled up K Street, Devon said, "What a splendid man!" In his relief, Harrison was, for once, not jealous, although he sought to pretend that he was.

The parking attendant got them a cab. There was no rush, so Harrison told the driver to take a scenic route back to the hotel.

It was a bare, clear night, bone-cold, with scant early dustings of a coming snowfall. The moon seemed to be filtered through gauze. They held hands in the taxi. Devon squeezed close to Harrison and laid her head on his shoulder. He stared out the window, trying without much success to make himself look morose and pensive in spite of his inner relief. At length she said, "David, stop acting! The bad part is over now. I love you." She tried to draw him to her.

The cab radio was tuned to a country music station, from which came the unmistakable voice of Willie Nelson: *"Power is, and power does, and power slips away/It's so easy to abuse,/Who'da thought them Ayrabs woulda bought the U.S.A./Just to give it to the Jews?"* It was too much for Harrison's invented gravity. "Shee-it," he exclaimed in his best west Texas imitation, bent to Devon and kissed her. The fit was off him. "I guess we can start thinking about life again." They filled the cab with laughter.

Their passage took them by the White House, ablaze and garlanded for Christmas, then past the Washington Monument and around by the Lincoln Memorial. Across the Potomac, the Custis mansion glowed moon-yellow above the dancing flame that marked John Kennedy's grave. They followed the course of the river until, finally, they were back under the dome of the Capitol, and the other great arks of the city, imperious pale colossi floating in the night, as luminous and imperishable as the Republic itself.

Dallas-New York-Tryall
1978–1979

Afterword: Many people helped with *Green Monday.* My partners, Charles E. Selecman and Dan C. McQueen, showed inordinate patience in putting up with an activity which was far from our principal focus. To Charlie, as to James R. Sowell, Elizabeth Ferguson, Jenny Ferguson, Henry D. Lindsley, Patricia Patterson, Boyd R. King and Jack and Winnie Carter, I am indebted for much guidance in the subtleties and details of Texas life and lore. Betsey Brown did the same for Washington, and much more. As did Helen S. Morris in the Berkshires and elsewhere. Whatever is insightful about investment banking is largely due to my late father, Joseph A. Thomas, and to my late mentors, Harold J. Szold and Edgar B. Kapp, all three of whom have, alas, left us much poorer than when they were alive. Jean-Francois Malle has been my cicerone in European money matters, as have Herbert P. Patterson, Donald M. Roberts and Donald Glickman in a number of aspects of commercial banking. Fred R. Sullivan and Orin H. Atkins have taught me much about corporate life, and are due more thanks than words can convey. My knowledge of the working of the New York Stock Exchange comes from over thirty years of friendship with John F. Horn and L. Stoddard Horn, and I have benefitted from the wisdom, wit and insight of William H. Young.

Jane V. Marshall and Margaret Anderson deciphered the manuscript and gave invaluable help in ways beyond counting.

Without the generous advice of Joan Hitzig, the book, quite simply, could not have been written.

ABOUT THE AUTHOR

Michael M. Thomas has taught art history at
Yale, served on the curatorial staff of the Metropolitan Museum of Art, and has been a partner and executive officer of two major investment banking firms, as well as a director of
various business corporations. A native of Manhattan, he spends his time there or in Dallas,
where he is an independent financial consul-
tant and a director and officer of a private man-
ufacturing concern, and where most of *Green
Monday*, his first novel, was written.

NEW FROM FAWCETT CREST

☐ **THE NINJA**   24367   **$3.50**
by Eric Van Lustbader

☐ **GREEN MONDAY**   24400   **$3.50**
by Michael M. Thomas

☐ **VIDA**   24409   **$2.95**
by Marge Piercy

☐ **EMILY**   24410   **$1.95**
by Jilly Cooper

☐ **CALIFORNIA AND OTHER STATES OF GRACE**   24411   **$2.50**
by Phyllis Theroux

☐ **THE SHADOWED SPRING**   24412   **$2.50**
by Carola Salisbury

☐ **REFLEX ACTION**   24414   **$2.50**
by Christopher Fitzsimons

☐ **HOT TYPE**   24415   **$2.25**
by Marjorie Lipsyte

☐ **NIGHT OF MASKS**   24416   **$2.25**
by Andre Norton

Buy them at your local bookstore or use this handy coupon for ordering.

COLUMBIA BOOK SERVICE
32275 Mally Road, P.O. Box FB, Madison Heights, MI 48071

Please send me the books I have checked above. Orders for less than 5 books must include 75¢ for the first book and 25¢ for each additional book to cover postage and handling. Orders for 5 books or more postage is FREE. Send check or money order only.

Cost $_____   Name _____

Sales tax*_____   Address _____

Postage _____   City _____

Total $_____   State _____ Zip _____

*The government requires us to collect sales tax in all states except AK, DE, MT, NH and OR.

This offer expires 1 March 82   8175

CURRENT CREST BESTSELLERS

☐ THE NINJA
   by Eric Van Lustbader   24367 $3.50

☐ SHOCKTRAUMA
   by Jon Franklin & Alan Doelp   24387 $2.95

☐ KANE & ABEL
   Jeffrey Archer   24376 $3.75

☐ PRIVATE SECTOR
   Jeff Millar   24368 $2.95

☐ DONAHUE *Phil Donahue & Co.*   24358 $2.95

☐ DOMINO *Phyllis A. Whitney*   24350 $2.75

☐ TO CATCH A KING
   Harry Patterson   24323 $2.95

☐ AUNT ERMA'S COPE BOOK
   Erma Bombeck   24334 $2.75

☐ THE GLOW *Brooks Stanwood*   24333 $2.75

☐ RESTORING THE AMERICAN DREAM
   Robert J. Ringer   24314 $2.95

☐ THE LAST ENCHANTMENT
   Mary Stewart   24207 $2.95

☐ CENTENNIAL *James A. Michener*   23494 $2.95

☐ THE COUP *John Updike*   24259 $2.95

☐ THURSDAY THE RABBI WALKED OUT
   Harry Kemelman   24070 $2.25

☐ IN MY FATHER'S COURT
   Isaac Bashevis Singer   24074 $2.50

☐ A WALK ACROSS AMERICA
   Peter Jenkins   24277 $2.75

☐ WANDERINGS *Chaim Potok*   24270 $3.95

Buy them at your local bookstore or use this handy coupon for ordering.

COLUMBIA BOOK SERVICE
32275 Mally Road, P.O. Box FB, Madison Heights, MI 48071

Please send me the books I have checked above. Orders for less than 5 books must include 75¢ for the first book and 25¢ for each additional book to cover postage and handling. Orders for 5 books or more postage is FREE. Send check or money order only.

Cost $_____   Name _____

Sales tax*_____   Address _____

Postage _____   City _____

Total $_____   State _____ Zip _____

The government requires us to collect sales tax in all states except AK, DE, MT, NH and OR.

This offer expires 1 March 82   8177

CLASSIC BESTSELLERS
from FAWCETT BOOKS